CHUNG KUO

BOOK EIGHT

"Give me a flower on a tall stem, and three dark flames, for I will go to the wedding, and be the wedding guest at the marriage of the living dark."

—D. H. Lawrence,
Bavarian Gentians

By the same author:

in the CHUNG KUO series

Book One: THE MIDDLE KINGDOM

Book Two: THE BROKEN WHEEL

Book Three: THE WHITE MOUNTAIN

Book Four: THE STONE WITHIN

Book Five: BENEATH THE TREE OF HEAVEN

Book Six: WHITE MOON, RED DRAGON

Book Seven: DAYS OF BITTER STRENGTH

and

TRILLION YEAR SPREE:
THE HISTORY OF SCIENCE FICTION
(with Brian Aldiss)

and

MYST, THE BOOK OF ATRUS
(with Rand and Robyn Miller)

MYST, THE BOOK OF TI'ANA
(with Rand Miller)

CHUNG KUO

BY DAVID WINGROVE

BOOK EIGHT:

THE MARRIAGE OF THE LIVING DARK

DOUBLEDAY CANADA LIMITED

Published in paperback 1999 in Canada by Doubleday Canada Limited

First published in Great Britain by Hodder and Stoughton
A Division of Hodder Headline PLC

Canadian Cataloguing in Publication Data

Wingrove, David
The marriage of the living dark

(Chung kuo; bk. 8)
ISBN 0-385-25736-8

1. Title. II. Series: wingrove, David. Chung kuo; bk. 8.

PR6073.I545M37 1999 823′.914 C98-930089-7

Cover illustration by Tim White
Cover design by Heather Hodgins
Typeset by Hewer Text Compositions Services
Printed and bound in Canada

Published in Canada by
Doubleday Canada Limited
105 Bond Street
Toronto, Ontario
M5B 1Y3

TRAN 10 9 8 7 6 5 4 3 2 1

For Brian Griffin

For all the long hours of work you've put in. For all the commentaries, and encouragement, and most of all for making me think hard about what I was writing. This one's for you, with heartfelt thanks.

PS: Look what we began, all those years ago in the letter columns of *Vector*!

CONTENTS

CONTENTS

MAJOR CHARACTERS

Ascher, Emily – Trained as an economist, she was once a member of the *Ping Tiao* revolutionary party. After their demise, she fled to North America where, under the alias of Mary Jennings, she got a job with the giant ImmVac corporation, working for Old Man Lever and his son, Michael, whom she finally married. When America fell she fled with Michael to Europe, but tiring of that high-level social world she went back down the levels and became a terrorist again. It was while undertaking a terrorist mission that she was attacked and badly wounded. Lin Shang, a simple "mender", found her there and nursed her back to health. She stayed with him for almost two decades, until his death, finally returning to her husband, Michael, during the great plague. Now, once again, she is a rebel, fighting DeVore from her mountain fastness.

DeVore, Howard – A one-time Major in the T'ang's Security forces, he has become the leading figure in the struggle against the Seven. A highly intelligent and coldly logical man, he is the puppet master behind the scenes as the great War of the Two Directions takes a new turn. Defeated first on Chung Kuo and then on Mars, he fled outward, to the tenth planet, Pluto, and its twin, Charon. From there he launched a new, massive attack on Chung Kuo, which was only defeated at great cost to Li Yuan and his allies. After a dozen years away, he returned with an army of his genetic creations – his Neumann – throwing out the old T'ang. But his success was only partial, and six years on the war he began is not yet over.

Ebert, Hans – Son of Klaus Ebert and heir to the vast GenSyn Corporation, he was promoted to General in Li Yuan's Security forces, and was admired and trusted by his superiors. Secretly, however, he was allied to DeVore, and was subsequently implicated in the murder of his father. Having fled Chung Kuo, he was declared a traitor in his absence. After suffering exile, he found himself again, among the lost African tribe, the Osu, in the desert sands of Mars, where he became their spiritual leader, the "Walker in the Darkness". Returning to Chung Kuo, he played a major part in helping Li Yuan defeat DeVore and was pardoned. Blind, he now lives with Kim Ward and the other colonists on Ganymede, part of the great space fleet that is on its way to distant Eridani.

Karr, Gregor – one-time Marshal of the European Security forces, he was recruited by General Tolonen from the Net. In his youth he was a "blood" – a to-the-death combat fighter. A huge man physically, he is also one of Li Yuan's "most-trusted men". As a respected pillar of society and the father of four growing daughters he rose beyond all early expectations and became a pivotal figure in the politics of City Europe, but when offered the role of Emperor, he demurred, instead joining Kim Ward and the others on the journey to Eridani.

Li Yuan – T'ang of Europe and one of the Seven, as second son of Li Shai Tung, he inherited after the deaths of his brother and father. Considered old before his time, he none the less has a passionate side to his nature, as demonstrated in his brief marriage to his brother's wife, the beautiful Fei Yen. His subsequent remarriage ended in tragedy when his three wives were assassinated. Despite his subsequent marriage to Pei K'ung, his real concern was for his son, Kuei Jen, until, that was, he met and married the fox-like Hsung Lung hsin – Dragon Heart – whose debauched nature infected his judgement. After the downfall of his City, he fled to America, where he now lives in exile.

Shepherd, Ben – Great-great-grandson of City Earth's architect, Shepherd was brought up in the Domain, an idyllic valley in the south-west of England, where he pursued his artistic calling, developing a new art form, the "Shell": a machine which mimics the experience of life. In his middle years, however, he became far more involved in politics and against all expectations became Li Yuan's closest advisor. But with Li Yuan's defeat at the hands of DeVore, he withdrew from politics and began once again to pursue his ideal of a perfect artform.

Ward, Kim – Born in the Clay, that dark wasteland beneath the great City's foundations, Kim has survived various personal crises to become Chung Kuo's leading experimental scientist. Hired by the massive SimFic Corporation as a commodity-slave on a seven-year contract, he finally achieved his ambition of marrying the Marshal's daughter. As head of NorTek Europe, he was one of City Europe's richest and most powerful men, but his falling out with Li Yuan turned his face away from the internal struggles of Chung Kuo. In an audacious gamble, Kim built a great spacegoing fleet and, using four of Jupiter's moons, sent out four separate expeditions to the nearest stars, hoping to set up new colony worlds out there.

* * *

OTHER CHARACTERS

Ai Lin – Sampsa Ward's girlfriend and twin to Lu Yi
Aidan – orphan, trained fighter
Alan – duty officer to Mark Egan
Amenon – rebel morph

Anders – rebel soldier
Armstrong, John – General of the American Western Armies
Ascher, Emily – real name of Emily Lin
Baker, Jed – colonist on Ganymede
Benoit – orphan, trained fighter
Bernadini, Charles – Senior Technician on the North American Immortality Project
Brevitt – Sergeant in North American Security
Chalker, Alan – Colonel; Head of Internal Security, North America
Chang – Li Yuan's body servant
Cho – a rebel
Christian – orphan, trained fighter
Chuang Kuan Ts'ai – "Coffin-filler", adopted daughter of Cho Yao
Chung – Master of *wei chi*
Coover, Dan – King of California
DeVore, Howard – himself
Dogo – Osu warrior; one of the "eight"; one-time lover of Catherine Shepherd & father of Dogu
Douglas – military aide to Mark Egan
Dublanc, Eduard – Core Leader in Eden
Echewa, Aluko – Head man of the Osu and one of the "eight"
Ebert, Pauli – bastard son of Hans Ebert and Golden Heart, and Head of the GenSyn Corporation
Efulefu – "Worthless Man"; chosen name of Hans Ebert among the Osu
Egan, Josiah – Head of NorTek America and grandfather of Mark Egan
Egan, Mark – grandson of Old Man Egan
Egan, May Ji – daughter of Mark Egan and Li Kuei Jen
Egan, Samuel – elder son of Mark Egan and Li Kuei Jen
Egan, Yuan – younger son of Mark Egan and Li Kuei Jen
Emtu – a morphed copy of Emily Ascher
Fei Yen – see Yin Fei Yen
Haavikko, Axel – Colonel in Security
Hannah – anglicised name of Shang Han-A
Hannem – new generation morph/Neumann copy
Harding, James – Chancellor, North America
Heather – member of the Cult of the Well and the Spire
Hiuden – one of DeVore's morphs
Ho Jen – a rebel
Horacek, Josef – son of Vilem and Bara Horacek; Marshal of DeVore's youth forces in City Europe
Horton, Feng – "Meltdown"; Leader of the North American "Sons"
Hun – a rebel
Ishida, Ikuro – Japanese asteroid miner
Ishida, Shukaku – eighth brother of Ikuro Ishida
Ishida, Tomoka – third brother of Ikuro Ishida

Jeffers – pilot, working for Feng Horton
Jem – member of the Cult of the Well and the Spire
Jerud – one of Devore's morphs
Ji – surgeon on Ganymede
Johann – orphan, trained fighter
Ju Dun – orphan, trained fighter
Jurgen – a rebel
Kao Chen – ex-Major in Security; plantation worker
Kao Jyan – eldest son of Kao Chen
Karr, Beth – youngest daughter of Gregor and Marie Karr
Karr, Gregor – Marshal of Security, City Europe
Karr, Hannah – daughter of Gregor and Marie Karr
Karr, Lily – daughter of Gregor and Marie Karr
Karr, Marie – wife of Gregor Karr
Karr, May – eldest daughter of Gregor and Marie Karr
Lanier – Major in Security, Fortress San Angelo
Leon – orphan, trained fighter
Lever, Michael – Head of the ImmVac pharmaceutical corporation and husband of Emily Ascher
Levitch – Steward to Chancellor Harding
Li Kuei Jen – son of Li Yuan and heir to City Europe
Li Yuan – T'ang of City Europe
Lin Chao – eldest adopted son of Lin Shang and Emily Ascher
Lin Chia – adopted son of Lin Shang and Emily Ascher
Lin, Emily – partner of Lin Shang; real name Emily Ascher
Lin Han Ye – adopted son of Lin Shang and Emily Ascher
Lin Lao – adopted son of Lin Shang and Emily Ascher
Lin Pei – adopted son of Lin Shang and Emily Ascher
Lin Sung – adopted son of Lin Shang and Emily Ascher
Lin Teng – adopted son of Lin Shang and Emily Ascher
Lu Yi – Tom Shepherd's girlfriend and twin to Ai Lin
Mark – adjutant to DeVore
Masso – village leader in the Swiss Wilds
Mo Teng – a rebel
Mussida, Daniel – orphan, trained fighter
Neville, Jack – Head of SimFic
Novacek, Sasha – daughter of Catherine Shepherd
Novacek, Sergey – sculptor; first husband of Catherine Shepherd and father of Sasha Novacek
Nza – "Tiny bird", an Osu, adopted by Hans Ebert, and one of the "eight"
Raditz – Second-in-Command at Camp Eickel
Raeto – boy "boss" in Camp Eickel
Richards – Advocate for Old Man Egan
Robbie – orphan, friend of Daniel
Rogers, Cal – Governor of Fortress San Angelo

Russ – go-between; friend of Horton
Scaf – Clayman helper of Ben Shepherd
Schutz – Commandant, Camp Eickel
Shand, Gill – Personal Assistant to Kim Ward
Shang Han-A – daughter of the late Shang Mu and historian of Chung Kuo
Shepherd, Ben – "shell artist" and Chief Advisor to Li Yuan
Shepherd, Catherine – wife of Ben Shepherd
Shepherd, Dogu – illegitimate son of Catherine Shepherd and Dogu, the Osu warrior
Shepherd, Meg – sister of Ben Shepherd
Shepherd, Tom – mute son of Ben and Meg Shepherd
Siri – a rebel
Slaven – orphan, trained fighter
Stewart – leading businessman in City Boston; brother-in-law of Warner
Tanner – businessman from Fortress San Angelo
Tom – boy at Camp Eickel; friend of Daniel Mussida
Tsou Tsai Hei – "Walker in the Darkness"; one of Hans Ebert's given names
Tuan Ti Fo – Master of *wei chi* and sage
Tybor – one of DeVore's new morphs, his *Inheritors*
Wang Ti – wife of Kao Chen
Ward, Jelka – wife of Kim Ward; daughter of Knut Tolonen
Ward, Kim – Clayborn scientist; owner of the NorTek Corporation of Europe
Ward, Sampsa – son of Jelka and Kim Ward
Warner – leading businessman in City Boston; brother-in-law of Stewart
Wiley, Dan – assistant to Bernadini on the Immortality Project
Wu Ye – surgeon working for the rebels
Yang Chung – trivee actor; hero in *Moving The Mountain*
Yin Fei Yen – "Flying Swallow"; Minor Family Princess and divorced wife of Li Yuan
Yin Han Ch'in – son of Li Yuan and Yin Fei Yen.
York – Captain in European Security; assistant to Core Leader Dublanc
Yueh Ho – a rebel
Zelic – Captain in North American Security force

* * *

THE DEAD

Adler – General in Security, City Europe
Althaus, Kurt – General in Security, North America
An Hsi – Minor Family prince and fifth son of An Sheng
An Liang-chou – Minor Family prince
An Mo Shan – Minor Family prince and third son of An Sheng
An Sheng – head of the An Family (one of the Twenty-Nine Minor Families)
Anderson, Leonid – Director of the Recruitment Project

Anna – helper to Mary Lever
Anne – *Yu* assassin
Ashman – henchman of Pasek
Barrett – GenSyn "sport"; brothel-keeper in the Clay
Barrow, Chao – Secretary of the House at Weimar
Barycz, Jiri – scientist on the Wiring Project
Bates – leading figure in the Federation of Free Men, Mars
Beinlich – ex-Security lieutenant, working for Van Pasenow
Bell – Colonel in charge of Security, Bremen spaceport
Bercott, Andrei – Representative at Weimar
Berdichev, Soren – head of SimFic and later leader of the Dispersionist faction
Berdichev, Ylva – wife of Soren Berdichev
Berrenson – Company Head
Bess – helper to Mary Lever
Blaskic – henchman of Pasek
Blofeld – agent of special security forces
Blonegek – "Greasy"; Clayman civilised by Ben Shepherd
Brock – security guard in the Domain
Brookes, Thomas – Port Captain, Tien Men K'ou, Mars
Bujold – General in Security, City Europe
Calder, Alan – Mashhad-born terrorist
Calder, Eva – sister of Alan Calder and maid to Warlord Hu
Cao Chang – Financial Strategist to Stefan Lehmann
Carl – security guard at Karr's mansion
Chang Hong – Minister of Production, City Europe
Chang Li – Senior Surgeon at the San Chang
Chang Te Li – "Old Chang", *Wu*, or Diviner
Chao Chung – Senior Warden of Edingen Prison
Chao Ta-nien – "Slow Chao", Red Pole to the Iron Fist Triad
Chen So – Clerk of the Inner Chambers at Tongjiang
Ch'en Li – associate of Governor Schenck
Cheng Lu – Lehmann's ambassador to Fu Chiang's court
Cheng Nai shan – assistant to Ming Ai
Cherkassky, Stefan – ex-Security assassin and friend of DeVore
Chi Hu Wei – T'ang of the Australias; father of Chi Hsing
Chih Huang Hui – second wife of Shang Mu and stepmother of Shang Han-A
Ch'in Shih Huang Ti – the first emperor of China; ruled 221–210 BC
Cho Hsiang – Hong Cao's subordinate
Cho Yao – *Lu Nan Jen* or "Oven Man"
Chou – third-year schoolboy at the Seventh District School
Chou Te-hsing – Head of the Black Hand terrorists
Chu Heng – "kwai", or hired knife; a hireling of DeVore's
Chu Po – lover of Pei K'ung
Chu Shi-ch'e – *Pi-shu chien*, or Inspector of the Imperial Library at Tongjiang
Chu Te – Commissioner for Mainz

Chuang Ko – private secretary to Tsu Ma
Chuang Tzu – ancient Han sage and Taoist philosopher from the 6th Century BC
Chun Wu-chi – head of the Chun family (one of the Twenty-Nine Minor Families)
Chung – "Ice Man" Chung, Big Boss of the Iron Fist triad
Chung Hsin – "Loyalty"; bondservant to Li Shai Tung
Clarac, Armand – Director of the "New Hope" Project
Coates – security guard in the Domain
Cook – duty guard in the Domain
Cornwell, James – Director of the AutoMek Corporation
Costas – friend of Alan Calder
Crefter – "Strong"; Clayman civilised by Ben Shepherd
Cui – Steward of Marshal Tolonen's household
Curval, Andrew – Head of Research, NorTek Europe
Cutler, Richard – leader of the "America" movement
Dawes, Richard – Security Captain reporting to I Ye
Dawson – associate of Governor Schenck
Deio – Clayborn friend of Kim Ward from "Rehabilitation"
Deng Liang – Minor Family Prince; fifth son of Deng Shang; Dispersionist
Dieter, Wilhelm – Black Hand cell-leader
Donna – Yu assassin
Douglas, John – Company Head; Dispersionist
Dublanc, Matthew – son of Core Leader Dublanc
Duchek, Albert – Administrator of Lodz
Ebert, Berta – wife of Klaus Ebert; mother of Hans Ebert
Ebert, Klaus – head of the GenSyn Corporation; father of Hans Ebert
Ebert, Lutz – half-brother of Klaus Ebert
Ecker, Michael – Company Head; Dispersionist
Edmonds – Security Captain
Edsel – agent of special security forces
Eduard – guard in Marshal Karr's employ
Egan – head of NorTek
Ellis, Michael – assistant to Director Spatz on the Wiring Project
Endacott – associate of Governor Schenck
Endfors, Pietr – friend of Knut Tolonen and father of Jenny, Tolonen's wife
Erkki – guard to Jelka Tolonen
Eva – friend of Mary Lever
Eyre – henchman of Pasek
Fairbank, John – head of AmLab
Fan – fifth brother to the *I Lung*
Fan Sheng-chih – neighbour of Emily Ascher and Lin Shang
Farren – General; Commander of City Europe's Second Banner
Fen Cho-hsien – Chancellor of North America
Fen Chun – First Secretary to Heng Yu
Feng Chung – Big Boss of the Kuei Chuan (Black Dog) Triad
Feng Lu-ma – lensman

Feng Shang-pao – "General Feng"; Big Boss of the 14K Triad
Fest, Edgar – Captain in Security
Fox – Company Head
Franke, Rutger – Vice-President of SimFic; Dispersionist
Fu Chiang – "The Priest", Big Boss of the Red Flower Triad of North Africa
Fu Ti Chang – third wife of Li Yuan
Fung – *Wu*, or Diviner to Yin Fei Yen
Gesell, Bent – leader of the Ping Tiao – "Leveller" – terrorist movement
Golden Heart – concubine to Hans Ebert and mother of Pauli Ebert
Grant – henchman of Pasek
Green, Clive – Head of RadMed
Griffin, James B. – last president of the American Empire
Haavikko, Vesa – sister of Axel Haavikko
Haller – Security operative
Hama – Osu wife of Hans Ebert
Hammond, Joel – Senior Technician on the Wiring Project
Hamsun, Torve – Captain of the *Luoyang*
Harris, Joseph – young host at the *Chao Hao T'ai*, the "Directory"
Hart, Alex – Representative at Weimar, Dispersionist and ally of Stefan Lehmann
Hart – General in Security, City Europe
Hastings, Thomas – physicist; Dispersionist
Hei Fong – merchant
Henderson, Daniel – pro tem Governor of Mars
Heng Chi-po – Li Shai Tung's Minister of Transportation
Heng Yu – Chancellor of City Europe
Henssa, Eero – Captain of the Guard aboard the floating palace Yangjing
Herrick – illegal transplant specialist
Ho – "Madam Ho", owner of a brothel in Hattersheim *Hsien*
Ho Chang – merchant friend of Lin Shang and Emily Ascher, and one-time landlord to them
Ho Chin – "Three-Finger Ho"; Big Boss of the Yellow Banners Triad
Ho Ko – "Harmonious Song"; sing-song girl on the flower boats
Ho Tse-tsu – Third Secretary to Su Ping
Hoffmann – Major in Security
Holzman, Daniel – palace guard
Hong Cao – middleman for Pietr Lehmann
Hooper – senior engineer aboard DeVore's craft
Horacek, Bara – mother of Josef Horacek
Horacek, Vilem – father of Josef Horacek
Hou Ti – T'ang of South America; father of Hou Tung-po
Hou Tung-po – T'ang of South America
Hsiang K'ai Fan – Minor Family prince
Hsiang Lu Yeh – Minor Family Prince
Hsiang Shao-erh – head of the Hsiang family (one of the Twenty-Nine Minor Families)

Hsiang Wang – Minor Family prince
Hsueh Chi – Big Boss of the Thousand Spears Triad of Southern Africa
Hsueh Nan – Warlord of Southern Africa and brother of Hsueh Chi
Hsun Chu-lo – Minor Family Princess and first daughter of Hsun Teh
Hsun Lung hsin – "Dragon Heart"; Minor Family Princess and second daughter of Hsun Teh
Hsun Teh – Head of the Hsun Family (one of the Twenty-Nine Minor Families)
Hu Feng-lo – second son of Warlord Hu
Hu Wang-chih – Warlord of the Mashhad Region
Hua Shang – lieutenant to Wong Yi-sun
Huang Peng – Steward at the Ebert Mansion
Hui Tsin – "Red Pole" (426, or Executioner) to the United Bamboo Triad
Hung Mien-lo – Chancellor of Africa
Hwa – Master "blood", or hand-to-hand fighter, below the Net
Hwa Kuei – Chief Steward of the Bedchamber to Tsu Ma
I Lung – "First Dragon", the head of the "Thousand Eyes", the Ministry
I Ye – Colonel, Chief of Security in the San Chang
Ishida, Kano – eldest brother of Ikuro Ishida
Jackson – freelance go-between, employed by Fairbank
James – friend of Alan Calder
Jeng Lo – Security Pilot, Rift Veteran
Ji Wang – First Minister to Warlord Hu
Jia Shu – Steward in Li Yuan's palace
Jill – principal helper to Mary Lever
Joan – *Yu* assassin
Johnson, Daniel – personal assistant to Michael Lever
Judd – boy in the tunnels
Jung – madman
Jung Wang – the madman's wife
Kan – *Wei*, or Security Captain of Kuang Hua *Hsien*
Kan Jiang – Martian settler and poet
K'ang A-yin – gang boss of the Tu Sun tong
K'ang Yeh-su – nephew of K'ang A-yin
Kao Jyan – assassin; friend of Kao Chen
Kavanagh – Representative at Weimar and Leader of the House
Kemp, Johannes – director of ImmVac
Kennedy, Jean – wife of Joseph Kennedy
Kennedy, Joseph – head of the New Republican and Evolutionist Party and Representative at Weimar
Kennedy, Robert – elder son of Joseph Kennedy
Kennedy, William – younger son of Joseph Kennedy
Kennedy, William – great-great-grandfather of Joseph Kennedy
Krenek, Henryk – Senior Representative of the Martian Colonies
Krenek, Irina – wife of Henryk Krenek
Krenek, Josef – Company Head

Krenek, Maria – wife of Josef Krenek
Kriz – senior *Yu* operative
Kubinyi – lieutenant to DeVore
Kung Chia – *Wei*, or Captain of Security of Weisenau *Hsien*
Kung Wen-fa – Senior Advocate from Mars
K'ung Fu Tzu – Confucius (551–479 BC)
Kustow, Bryn – American; friend of Michael Lever
Kygek – "Fat"; Clayman civilised by Ben Shepherd
Lai Shi – second wife of Li Yuan
Lai Wu – secretary to Cheng Nai shan
Lao Jen – Junior Minister to Lwo Kang
Lao Kang – Chancellor of West Asia
Lasker – Captain, Decontamination, Ansbach *Hsien*
Lauther – Security Captain at Edingen Prison
Lehmann, Pietr – Under-Secretary of the House of Representatives and first leader of the Dispersionist faction; father of Stefan Lehmann
Lehmann, Stefan – "The White T'ang"; Big Boss of the European Triads and one-time ally of DeVore
Lever, Charles – head of the giant ImmVac Corporation of North America; father of Michael Lever
Lever, Margaret – wife of Charles Lever and mother of Michael Lever
Li Chin – "Li the Lidless"; Big Boss of the Wo Shih Wo Triad
Li Ch'ing – T'ang of Europe; grandfather of Li Yuan
Li Han Ch'in – first son of Li Shai Tung and once heir to City Europe; brother of Li Yuan
Li Hang Ch'i – T'ang of Europe; great-great-grandfather of Li Yuan
Li Ho-nien – servant at the Ebert Mansion
Li Kou-lung – T'ang of Europe; great-grandfather of Li Yuan
Li Pai Shung – nephew of Li Chin; heir to the Wo Shih Wo Triad
Li Pei K'ung – fifth wife of Li Yuan
Li Shai Tung – T'ang of Europe; father of Li Yuan
Lin Ji – youngest adopted son of Lin Shang and Emily Ascher
Lin Pan – Uncle Pan; adopted uncle of Lin Shang
Lin Shang – Mender Lin, partner to Emily Ascher
Lin Yuan – first wife of Li Shai Tung; mother of Li Han Ch'in and Li Yuan
Ling – "Old Mother Ling", worker on the Kosaya Gora Plantation
Ling Hen – henchman for Herrick
Liu Chang – brothel keeper/pimp
Liu Tong – lieutenant to Li Chin
Liu Yeh – First Steward to Tung Wei
Lo Chang – Steward at the Ebert Mansion
Lo Han – tong boss
Lo Wen – Master of *wu shu* and tutor to Li Kuei Jen
Lu – Surgeon at Tongjiang
Lu Ming-shao – "Whiskers Lu"; Big Boss of the Kuei Chuan Triad

Lu Song – terrorist leader from Krasnovodsk
Luke – Clayborn friend of Kim Ward from "Rehabilitation"
Lwo Kang – Li Shai Tung's Minister of the Edict
Ma Ching – servant at the Ebert Mansion
Maitland, Idris – mother of Stefan Lehmann
Man Hsi – tong boss
Mao Kuang-li – Fourth Secretary to Su Ping
Mao Liang – Minor Family Princess and member of the *Ping Tiao* "Council of Five"
Mao Tse Tung – first Ko Ming emperor (ruled AD 1948–1976)
Mao Tun – Warlord
Matloff – middleman for Michael Lever
Matyas – Clayborn boy in Recruitment Project
Melfi, Alexandra – wife of Amos Shepherd and real mother of the Shepherd boys
Meng K'ai – friend and adviser to Governor Schenck
Meng Te – lieutenant to Lu Ming-shao
Meng Yi – Warlord of Ashkabhad
Mien Shan – first wife of Li Yuan; mother of Li Kuei Jen
Milne, Michael – private investigator
Ming Ai – Personal Secretary to Pei K'ung
Ming Huang – sixth T'ang emperor (ruled AD 713–755)
Mo Nan-ling – "The Little Emperor"; Big Boss of the Nine Emperors Triad of Central Africa
Mo Yu – security lieutenant in the Domain
Moore, John – Company Head; Dispersionist
Morel – The Myghtern, "King Under The City"
Mu Chua – Madame of the House of the Ninth Ecstasy
Mu Li – "Iron Mu", Boss of the Big Circle Triad
Nan Fa-hsien – Master of the Inner Chambers and eldest son of Nan Ho, promoted to Chancellor of City Europe
Nan Ho – Chancellor of City Europe
Nan Tsing – first wife of Nan Ho
Needham – Captain of *Shen T'se* elite security squad
Nolen, William – Public Relations Executive; Dispersionist
Pao En-fu – Master of the Inner Chambers to Wu Shih
Parr, Charles – Company Head; Dispersionist
Pavel – young man on Plantation
Peck – lieutenant to K'ang A-yin (a *ying tzu*, or "shadow")
Pei K'ung – fifth wife to Li Yuan and daughter of Pei Ro-hen
Pei Ro-hen – Head of the Pei Family (one of the Twenty-Nine Minor Families) and father of Pei K'ung
Peng – Madam Peng; matchmaker
Peng – servant to Su Chun
Peskova – Lieutenant of guards on the Plantations
Peter – fruit-stall holder

Peters – cell-leader in the Black Hand terrorists
Ponow – gaoler in the Myghtern's town
Ravachol – the "second prototype"; an android created by Kim Ward
Reiss, Horst – Chief Executive of SimFic
Rheinhardt, Helmut – General of Security, City Europe
Ross, Alexander – Company Head; Dispersionist
Ross, James – private investigator
Ruddock – minor official, employed by Lehmann
Rutherford, Andreas – friend and adviser to Governor Schenck
Sanders – Captain of Security at Helmstadt Armoury
Schenck, Hung-li – Governor of Mars Colony
Schwarz – lieutenant to DeVore
Seymour – Major in Security, North America
Shang – "Old Shang"; Master to Kao Chen when he was child
Shang Ch'iu – son of Shang Mu and half-brother of Shang Han-A
Shang Chu – great-grandfather of Shang Han-A
Shang Mu – Junior Minister in the "Thousand Eyes", the Ministry
Shang Wen Shao – grandfather of Han-A
Shen Lu Chua – computer expert and member of the *Ping Tiao* "Council of Five"
Sheng Min-chung – "One-Eyed Sheng"; Big Boss of the Iron Fists Triad of East Africa
Shepherd, Amos – great-great-great-grandfather (and genetic "father") of Ben Shepherd
Shepherd, Augustus – "brother" of Ben Shepherd, b. 2106, d. 2122
Shepherd, Hal – father (and genetic "brother") of Ben Shepherd
Shepherd, Robert – great-grandfather (and genetic "brother") of Ben Shepherd
Shih Chi-o – servant at the Ebert Mansion
Shu San – Junior Minister to Lwo Kang
Siang – Jelka Tolonen's martial arts instructor
Si Wu Ya – "Silk Raven", wife of Supervisor Sung
Song Wei – sweeper
Soucek, Jiri – lieutenant to Stefan Lehmann
Spatz, Gustav – Director of the Wiring Project
Spence, Leena – "Immortal", and one-time lover of Charles Lever
Ssu Lu Shan – official of the Ministry
Steen – captain of shuttle craft
Steiger – Director of the Shen Chang Fang of Milan
Steiner – Manager at ImmVac's Alexandria facility
Stock – boy in the tunnels
Stocken – lieutenant in Hu Wang-chih's household guard
Su Chun – tong boss and twin brother of Su Ping
Su Ping – *Hsien L'ing*, or District Magistrate of Weisenau *Hsien*, and twin brother of Su Chun
Su Yen – youngest half-brother of Su Ping and Su Chun
Sun Li Hua – Wang Hsien's Master of the Inner Chambers

Sung – Supervisor on Plantation
Tak – the Myghtern's lieutenant
Tan Sui – White Paper Fan of the Red Flower Triad of North Africa
Tan Wei – Chief Eunuch at Tsu Ma's palace in Astrakhan
Tanner, Charles – General in Security, City Europe
Tarrant – Company Head
Teng Fu – plantation guard
Tewl – "Darkness"; Chief of the raft-people
Thorn – security operative
Tie Ning – young prostitute on lantern boats
Ting Ju-ch'ang – Warlord of Tunis
Todlich – giant morph
Tolonen, Hanna – aunt of Knut Tolonen
Tolonen, Helga – wife of Jon Tolonen; aunt of Jelka Tolonen
Tolonen, Jenny – wife of Knut Tolonen, and daughter of Pietr Endfors
Tolonen, Jon – brother of Marshal Knut Tolonen
Tolonen, Knut – Marshal of Security, Acting Head of the GenSyn Corporation; father of Jelka Tolonen
Tong Chu – assassin and "kwai" (hired knife)
Tsao Ch'un – tyrannical founder of Chung Kuo
Ts'ao Wu – cell-leader in the Black Hand terrorists
Tsu Kung-chih – nephew of Tsu Ma
Tsu Ma – T'ang of West Asia; son of Tsu Tiao
Tsu Tiao – T'ang of West Asia; father of Tsu Ma
Tsu Tao Chu – nephew of Tsu Ma
Tsui Ku – *Tai Shih lung* or Court Astrologer in the San Chang
Tu Ch'en-shih – friend and advisor to Governor Schenck
Tu Fang – *liumang* ("punk") and triad runner
Tu Fu Wei – private secretary to Tsu Ma
Tu Mai – security guard in the Domain
Tuan Wen-ch'ang – see Wen Ch'ang
Tung Cai – low-level rioter
Tung Chung-shu – MedFac's senior arts reviewer
Tung Po-jen – club owner in Bockenheim *Hsien*
Tung Wei – merchant in Weisenau *Hsien*
Tynan, Edward – above businessman and Representative at Weimar; Dispersionist
Vesa – *Yu* assassin
Vierheller, Jane – Black Hand member
Virtanen, Per – Major in Li Yuan's Security forces
Visak – lieutenant to Lu Ming-shao
Von Pasenow – ex-Security Major
Wang – *Hsien L'ing*, or District Magistrate of Kuang Hua *Hsien*
Wang – Steward at Astrakhan Palace
Wang Chang Ye – first son of Wang Hsien
Wang Hsien – T'ang of Africa; father of Wang Sau-leyan

Wang Lieh Tsu – second son of Wang Hsien
Wang Sau-leyan – T'ang of Africa
Wang Ta-hung – third son of Wang Hsien; elder brother of Wang Sau-leyan
Wang Tu – leader of the Martian Radical Alliance
Ward, Mileja – infant daughter of Jelka and Kim Ward
Wei Chan Yin – T'ang of East Asia
Wei Feng – T'ang of East Asia; father of Wei Chan Yin and Wei Tseng-li
Wei Hsi Wang – second brother of Wei Chan Yin and heir to City East Asia
Wei Tseng-li – T'ang of East Asia; younger brother of Wei Chan Yin
Wei Yu – First Steward to Michael Lever
Weis, Anton – banker; Dispersionist
Wells – Captain in Security, North America
Wen – "Big Wen", butcher in Weisenau marketplace
Wen – "Old Wen", boatman for the flower-boats
Wen – Steward in the San Chang
Wen Ch'ang – assistant to Kim Ward; also known as Tuan Wen-ch'ang
Wen Ti – "First Ancestor" of City Earth/Chung Kuo, otherwise known as Liu Heng; ruled China 180-157 BC
Wiegand, Max – lieutenant to DeVore
Wiley – Captain in Security, Edingen Prison
Will – Clayborn friend of Kim Ward from "Rehabilitation"
Wilson, Stephen – Captain in Security under Kao Chen
Wong Yi-sun – "Fat Wong"; Big Boss of the United Bamboo Triad
Wu Shih – T'ang of North America
Wu Wei-kou – first wife of Wu Shih
Wyatt, Edmund – Company head; Dispersionist
Yang – "Old Yang"; Deck Magistrate, employee of Lehmann
Yang Chih-wen – "The Bear", Big Boss of the Golden Ox Triad of West Africa
Yang Lai – Junior Minister to Lwo Kang
Yang Shao-fu – Minister of Health, City Europe
Yang Wei – "Old Yang"; hardware store–owner
Ye – Senior Steward at Tongjiang
Yi Ching – Colonel of Internal Security to Tsu Ma at Astrakhan
Yi Shan-ch'i – Minor Family prince
Yin Chan – Minor Family prince and second son of Yin Tsu
Yin Shu – Junior Minister in the "Thousand Eyes", The Ministry
Yin Tsu – head of the Yin Family (one of the Twenty-Nine Minor Families) and father of Fei Yen
Ying Chai – assistant to Sun Li Hua
Ying Fu – assistant to Sun Li Hua
Yu I – proprietor of the Blue Pagoda tea-house
Yue Chun – "Red Pole" (426, or Executioner) to the Wo Shih Wo Triad
Yun – Third Cook on the Imperial Barge
Yun – lieutenant to Shen Lu Chua
Yun Yueh-hui – "Dead Man Yun"; Big Boss of the Red Gang Triad

Yung Chen – eunuch from the women's quarters in Tsu Ma's palace at Astrakhan
Ywe Hao – "Fine Moon"; female *Yu* terrorist
Ywe Kai-chang – father to Ywe Hao

Of Gifts and Stones

OF GIFTS AND STONES

Where did it all begin? When was the first step taken on that downward path that led to Armageddon? Perhaps it was on that fateful June day in 2043 when President James B. Griffin, last of the sixty-presidents of the United States of America, was assassinated while attending a baseball game at Chicago's Comiskey Park.

The collapse of the 69 States of the American Empire that followed and the subsequent disintegration of the allied Western economies brought a decade of chaos. What had begun as "The Pacific Century" was quickly renamed "The Century of Blood" – a period in which the only stability was to be found within the borders of China. It was from there – from the great landlocked province of Sichuan – that a young Han named Tsao Ch'un emerged.

Tsao Ch'un had a simple – some say brutal – cast of mind. He wanted to create an Utopia, a rigidly stable society that would last ten thousand years. But the price was high. In 2062 Japan, China's chief rival in the East, was the first victim of Tsao Ch'un's idiosyncratic approach to *realpolitik* when, without warning – following Japanese complaints about Chinese incursions in Korea – the Han leader bombed Honshu, concentrating his nuclear devices on the major population centres of Tokyo and Kyoto. When the dust cleared, three great Han armies swept the smaller islands of Kyushu and Shikoku, killing every Japanese they found, while the rest of Japan was blockaded by sea and air. Over the next twenty years they would do the same with the islands of Honshu and Hokkaido, turning the "islands of the gods" into a wasteland while the crumbling Western nation states looked away.

The eradication of Japan taught Tsao Ch'un many lessons. In future he sought "not to destroy but to exclude" – though his definition of "exclusion" often made it a synonym for destruction. As he built his great City – huge, mile-high spider-like machines moving slowly outward from Pei Ch'ing, secreting vast, tomb-white hexagonal living sections, three hundred levels high and a kilometre to a side – so he peopled it, choosing carefully who was to live within its walls. As the City grew, so his servants went out among the indigenous populations he had conquered, searching among them for those who were free from physical disability, political dissidence or religious bigotry. And where he encountered organised opposition, he enlisted the aid of groups sympathetic to his aims to carry out his policies. In Southern Africa and North America, in Europe and the People's Democracy of Russia, huge movements grew up, supporting Tsao Ch'un and welcoming his "stability" after decades of chaos and suffering, only too pleased to share in his crusade of intolerance – this "Policy of Purity".

Only the Middle East proved problematic. There, a great Jihad was launched against the Han – Moslems and Jews casting off centuries of enmity to fight against a common threat. Tsao Ch'un answered them as he had answered Japan. The Middle East and large parts of the Indian subcontinent were reduced to a radioactive wilderness. But it was in Africa that his policies were most nakedly displayed. There, the native peoples were moved on before the encroaching City and, like cattle, they starved or died from exhaustion, driven on by the brutal Han armies. Following historical precedent, City Africa was re-seeded with Han settlers.

In terms of human suffering, Tsao Ch'un's pacification of the globe was unprecedented. Contemporary estimates put the cost in human lives at well over three billion. But Tsao Ch'un was not content merely to eradicate all opposition, he wanted to destroy all knowledge of the Western-dominated past. Like the First Emperor, Ch'in Shih Huang Ti, twenty-four centuries before, he decided to rewrite the history books. Tsao Ch'un had his officials collect all books, all tapes, all recordings, allowing nothing that was not Han to enter his great City. Most of what they collected was simply burned, but not all. Some was adapted.

One group of Tsao Ch'un's advisers – a group of Scholar-Politicians who termed themselves "The Thousand Eyes" – persuaded their Master that it would not be enough simply to create a gap. That, they knew, would attract curiosity. What they proposed was more subtle and, in the long term, far more persuasive. With Tsao Ch'un's blessing they set about reconstructing the history of the world, placing China at the centre of everything – back in its rightful place, as they saw it. It was a lie, of course, yet a lie to which everyone subscribed . . . on pain of death.

But the lie was complex and powerful, and people soon forgot. New generations arose who knew nothing of the real past and to whom the whispers and rumours seemed mere fantasy in the face of the solid reality they saw all about them. The media fed them the illusion daily, until the illusion became, even for those who worked in the Ministry responsible, quite *real* and the documents they dealt with, some strange aberration – a mass hallucination, almost a disease that had struck the Western peoples of the great Han Empire in its latter years. The officials at the Ministry even coined a term for it – "racial compensation" – laughing among themselves whenever they came across some clearly fantastic reference in an old book about quaint religious practices or races of black – think of it, *black*! – people.

Tsao Ch'un killed the old world. He buried it deep beneath his glacial City. But eventually his brutality and tyranny proved too much even for those who had helped him carry out his scheme. In 2087 his Council of Seven Ministers rose up against him, using North European mercenaries, and overthrew him, setting up a new government. They divided the world – Chung Kuo – among themselves, each calling himself T'ang, "King". But the new government was far stronger than the old, for the Seven made it so that no single one of them could act on any major issue without the consensus of his fellow T'ang. Adopting the morality of New Confucianism they set about consolidating a "peace of ten thousand years". The keystone of this peace was the Edict of Technological Control, which regulated and, in effect, prevented change. Change had been the disease of the old, Western-dominated world. Change had brought its rapid and total collapse. But Change was alien to the Han. They would do away with Change for all time. Their borders were secured, the world was theirs – why should they not have peace and stability until the end of time? But the population grew and grew, filling the vast City and, buried deep in the collective psyche of the European races, something began to stir – some long-buried memory of rapid evolutionary growth. Change was needed. Change was wanted. But the Seven were against Change.

For more than a century they succeeded and their great world-spanning City thrived. If a man worked hard, he could climb the levels into a world of space and luxury; if he failed in business or committed a crime he would be demoted – down toward the crowded, stinking Lowers. Each man knew his place in the great scheme of things and obeyed the dictats of the Seven. Yet the pressures placed upon the system were great and as the population climbed toward the forty billion mark something had to give.

It began with the assassination of Li Shai Tung's Minister, Lwo Kang, in 2196, the poor man blown into the next world along with his Junior Ministers while basking in the Imperial solarium. The Seven – the great Lords and rulers of Chung Kuo – hit back at once, arresting Edmund Wyatt, one of the leading figures of the Dispersionist faction responsible for the Minister's death. But it was not to end there. Within days of the public execution of Wyatt in 2198, the Dispersionists – a coalition of high-powered merchants and politicians – struck another deadly blow, killing Li Han Ch'in, son of the T'ang, Li Shai Tung, and heir to City Europe, on the day of his wedding to the beautiful Fei Yen.

It might have ended there, with the decision of the Seven to take no action in reprisal for Prince Han's death – to adopt a policy of peaceful non-action, *wuwei* – but for one man such a course of action could not be borne. Taking matters into his own hands, Li Shai Tung's General, Knut Tolonen, marched into the House of Representatives in Weimar and killed the leader of the Dispersionists, Under Secretary Lehmann. It was an act almost guaranteed to tumble Chung Kuo into a bloody civil war unless the anger of the Dispersionists could be assuaged and concessions made.

Concessions were made, an uneasy peace maintained, but the divisions between rulers and ruled remained, their conflicting desires – the Seven for Stasis, the Dispersionists for Change – unresolved. Amongst those concessions the Seven had permitted the Dispersionists to build a starship, *The New Hope*. As the ship approached readiness, the Dispersionists pushed things even further at Weimar, impeaching the *tai* – the Representatives of the Seven in the House – and effectively declaring their independence. In response the Seven destroyed *The New Hope*. War was declared.

The five year "War-that-Wasn't-a-War" left the Dispersionists broken, their leaders dead, their Companies confiscated. The great push for Change had been crushed and peace returned to Chung Kuo. But the war had woken older, far stronger currents of dissent. In the depths of the City new movements began to arise, seeking not merely to change the system, but to revolutionise it altogether. One of these factions, the *Ping Tiao*, or "Levellers", wanted to pull down the great City of three hundred levels and destroy the Empire of the Han.

Among the ruling council of the *Ping Tiao* was a young *Hung Mao*, or "European" woman, Emily Ascher. Driven by a desire for social justice, Emily orchestrated a campaign of attacks on corrupt officials designed to destabilise City Europe. But her fellows on the council were not satisfied with such piecemeal and "unambitious" methods and when the new Dispersionist leader, DeVore, offered them an alliance, they grabbed it against her advice.

Once a Major in Li Shai Tung's Security service, Howard DeVore was instrumental in both the assassination of Li Han Ch'in and the "War" that followed. Based on Mars, he sent in autonomous copies of himself to do his bidding, using any means possible to destroy the Seven and their City. The House of Representatives, the Dispersionists, the *Ping Tiao* – each in turn was used then discarded by him, cynically and without thought for the harm done to individuals. Aided by a network of young Security officers he had recruited over the years, he fought a savage guerrilla war against his former Masters, his only aim, it seemed, a wholly nihilistic one.

Yet the Seven were not helpless in the face of such assaults. Tolonen, promoted to Marshal of the Council of Generals, recruited a giant of a man, Gregor Karr, a "blood" or to-the-death fighter from the lowest levels of the City, the "Net", to act as his foil against DeVore and the Dispersionists. Karr was joined by another low-level fighter named Kao Chen – one of the two assassins responsible for the attack on the Imperial solarium that had begun the struggle.

For a time the status quo was maintained, but three of the most senior T'ang died during the War with the Dispersionists, leaving the Council of Seven weaker and more inexperienced than they'd been in all the long years of their rule. When Wang Sau-leyan, the youngest son of Wang Hsien, ruler of City Africa, became T'ang after his father's suspect death, things looked ominous, particularly as the young man seemed to delight in creating turmoil among the Seven. But Li Yuan, inheriting from his father, formed effective alliances with his fellow T'ang, Wu Shih of North America, Tsu Ma of West Asia and Wei Feng of East Asia to block Wang in Council, out-voting him four to three.

Even so, as Chung Kuo's population continued to grow, further concessions had to be made. The great Edict of Technological Control – the means by which the Seven had kept change at bay for more than a century – was to be relaxed, the House of Representatives at Weimar reopened, in return for guarantees of population controls.

For the first time in fifty years the Seven began to tackle the problems of their world, facing up to the necessity for limited change, but was it too late? Were the great tides of unrest unleashed by earlier wars about to overwhelm them?

It certainly seemed so. And when DeVore managed to persuade Li Yuan's newly-appointed General, Hans Ebert, to secretly ally with him, the writing seemed on the wall.

Hans Ebert had it all; handsome, strong, intelligent, he was heir to the genetics and pharmaceuticals Company, GenSyn – Chung Kuo's largest manufacturing concern – but he was also a vain, amoral young man, a cold-blooded "hero" with the secret ambition of deposing the Seven and becoming "King of the World", an ambition DeVore assiduously fed. While Ebert turned a blind eye, DeVore began to construct a chain of fortresses in the Alpine wilderness at the heart of City Europe, preparing for the day when he might bring it all crashing down. But that was not to be. Karr and Kao Chen, aided by a young lieutenant, Haavikko, uncovered the plot and revealed it to Marshal Tolonen, whose own daughter, Jelka, was betrothed to Hans Ebert. Tolonen, childhood companion of Ebert's father, Klaus, went straight to his lifelong friend and told him of his son's betrayal, allowing him twenty-four hours to deal with the matter personally.

Hans, meanwhile had been instructed by Li Yuan to destroy the network of fortresses. His hands tied, he did so, then returned to face his father. Klaus would have killed his only son, but Hans' goat-like helper – a creation of his father's genetic laboratories – killed the old man. Hans fled the planet and was condemned to death in his absence.

Li Yuan, it would seem, was saved. Yet the seed of destruction had been sown elsewhere, in the infatuation of his cousin Tsu Ma for Li Yuan's beautiful wife, Fei Yen. Their brief, clandestine affair was ended by Tsu Ma, but not before the damage was done. Fei Yen fell pregnant. Li Yuan was at first delighted, but then, when Fei Yen defied him and, late in her pregnancy, went riding, he destroyed her horses. She left him, returning to her father's house. There, alone with him, she told him that the child she was carrying was not his. Devastated, he returned home and, after his father's death, divorced Fei Yen, thus preventing her son – born two days after his coronation – from inheriting. The rift, it seemed, was final. He married again that day, taking three wives' determined to put the past behind him.

But time casts long shadows. Just as the brutal pattern of the tyrant Tsao Ch'un's thinking was imprinted in the restrictive levels of his great world-spanning City, so the blight of those twin betrayals – by his wife and by his most trusted man, his General, Hans Ebert – was imprinted deep in Li Yuan's psyche. A darkness settled within the young T'ang, leading him to pursue new and quite radical solutions to his City's problems – solutions like the Wiring Project.

As civil unrest proliferated and control gradually slipped from the Seven, as the lower levels of their great Cities slowly fell into the hands of the Triads and the false Messiahs, so the temptation to control the civilisation by other means grew. For Li Yuan there had long been only one solution. All of his citizens would be "wired" – a controlling device placed in every adult's head so they might be tracked and, if necessary, destroyed. It was a vile solution, but no viler, perhaps, than the alternative – to see the great Cities melt away and the rule of the Seven at an end.

As if to emphasise that necessity, new opposition groups sprang up one after another – the violently terrorist *Yu*, the North American-based Sons of Benjamin

Franklin, the Black Hand, and many more, each wishing to destroy what was and replace it with their own vision of what a society should be. The demand for Change became a mad scramble for power. Yet still the Seven maintained control . . . of a kind.

In the Summer of 2208, Wu Shih, T'ang of North America, decided to draw the dragon's teeth, arresting the Sons and incarcerating them, refusing to give them up to their powerful fathers until a guarantee of good behaviour was signed and sealed. He got his way, but in doing so sealed his own fate, for it was now only a matter of time before his City would fall. In seeking to stem the Revolution, he had merely fed its flames. When the Sons emerged from their fifteen-month imprisonment they had been hardened by the experience. Under the leadership of Joseph Kennedy, the latest scion in that long and prestigious line, they formed the New Republican Party, determined to bring about a political sea-change and to wrest power from the hands of the Seven.

Within the Seven the internecine fighting had worsened, and when the T'ang of Africa, Wang Sau-leyan, attacked Li Yuan's floating palace and killed his wives, war between them seemed inevitable. But lack of proof and fear of even greater chaos stayed Li Yuan's hand. The Seven were divided as never before, yet still the Cities stood. Even so, the experience had once again scarred Li Yuan deeply and served to throw him ever closer to his fellow T'ang, Wu Shih and Tsu Ma. Between the three of them, perhaps, they might yet rule strongly and wisely. The unthinkable – the destruction of the age-old rule of Seven and its replacement by a strong triumvirate – was now openly discussed.

But Li Yuan's greater schemes had once again to be set aside in the face of trouble in his own City. The death of DeVore's earthbound copy – pursued and finally killed by the giant Karr – left a power vacuum in the lower levels, a vacuum soon to be filled by one of DeVore's erstwhile allies, the albino Stefan Lehmann.

Lehmann, estranged son of the one-time Dispersionist leader, fled to the icy Alpine wastes after the fall of DeVore's fortresses. It was from there he returned in the spring of 2209, hardened by the experience, and set about making a name for himself in the lowers of City Europe, infiltrating the cut-throat world of criminal activity and ruthlessly climbing the ranks of the Triad brotherhoods until, in a massive campaign in the summer of 2209, he defeated the combined forces of the five great Triad lords and became the White T'ang, Li Min – "Brave Carp" – sole ruler of the European underworld.

At that single instant Li Yuan might have acted to crush Lehmann, for the albino's power was weak after his efforts. But Li Yuan – emotionally shattered by the death of his wives and the depth of division that had been revealed among the Seven – failed to take advantage of the situation. Li Min, the "Brave Carp", survived and began to consolidate his dark and brutal empire in the lowest levels of Li Yuan's City.

On Mars the real DeVore, learning from the failures of his first "embassy" to Chung Kuo, was planning a new assault upon the Seven – preparing a new range of genetic copies, subtler and more deadly than the last. Even there, among the nineteen cities of the Martian Plains, unrest had reached fever pitch and needed only a single incident to trigger violent revolution. Yet when it came, it was from an unexpected direction.

Hans Ebert, much changed after his great fall from power, had found himself on Mars, in DeVore's employ as a humble sweeper in one of his huge genetic factories. Wearing a prosthetic mask to conceal his features, Ebert had slowly refashioned himself, motivated by a deep aversion for the creature he had once been. However, pushed beyond his limits, he killed a man, placing himself once more in DeVore's power. Fastening on the opportunity, DeVore planned to use him in a scheme to destroy Marshal Tolonen emotionally by kidnapping Tolonen's daughter, Jelka – on Mars on her way back to Chung Kuo – and marrying her to Ebert. But Ebert refused to take part in DeVore's schemes and, aided by a lost race of Africans, the Osu – descendants of the early settlers of Mars – he helped release Jelka even as the cities of Mars burned.

As the cities of the Martian Plain had fallen, so too might those of Earth – of Chung Kuo, the great Han Empire, for there too it needed but a single incident to trigger violent change. And of the seven great Cities of Chung Kuo, the most powerful – North America – was also the most vulnerable. Rumours of a lost American Empire – thrown over by the Han – were rife, and old and young alike had begun to clamour for a return to past glories. Wu Shih, T'ang of North America, saw this and, much concerned, strove to control the leaders of the new movements – particularly Joseph Kennedy, who seemed to embody the spirit of the age. But for all his power, Wu Shih did not have it all his own way.

One of those facing him in North America, and standing in stark contrast, was Emily Ascher. Smuggled out of City Europe when the *Ping Tiao* movement disintegrated and given a new identity – as Mary Jennings – she met one of the Sons, Michael Lever, and became his wife. That marriage made her rich beyond all dreams, yet riches of themselves meant nothing to her. She was still driven by a vision of Change, and now began to pursue it by other means, playing Conscience to the great North American City and taking on the role of "Elder Sister", determined to alleviate the suffering in the lower levels of her adopted City. Ranged against her, however, were other forces with different agendas: the Old Men – Michael Lever's father Charles foremost among them – with their insane pursuit of Immortality; Wu Shih with his desire for stability at any cost; and Joseph Kennedy, whose crusading zeal had been effectively neutered by Wu Shih. All in all, it was a recipe for disaster, and disaster eventually overtook them in the winter of 2212 – though not from any of these sources.

Wu Shih might have survived Emily's "Elder Sister" campaign; he might even have survived Joseph Kennedy's on-air suicide; but when one of the orbital factories – its systems' refurbishments long overdue – fell from the sky into the midst of his City, he could not ride out the political storm that followed. Wu Shih died, attacked in his own Imperial craft, while his great City burned.

Many got out – Michael and Emily among them – but billions perished when North America fell, and the dark shadow of that fall etched itself deep in the minds of those that remained. Tsao Ch'un's dream of stability – of an utopia that would last ten thousand years – once so solid and unchallengeable, was coming to an end.

For some time, the actions of the young T'ang of Africa, Wang Sau-leyan had created divisions among the Seven, particularly in Council, where all important decisions were made. In the autumn of 2213, however, division tipped over into open warfare. Wang's direct assault on his fellow rulers at one of their ceremonial gatherings – an attempt that almost succeeded, with two of his cousins killed and another badly wounded – brought a swift reprisal. Li Yuan's dream of a ruling triumvirate finally came about – though in darker circumstances than he envisaged – when he, Tsu Ma and Wei Tseng-li, the new T'ang of East Asia, sent their armies into Africa to destroy Wang Sau-leyan's power.

The death of the odious Wang closed one chapter of Chung Kuo's history, yet it could not stem the headlong tide of Change. In the seventeen years since Li Shai Tung's Minister, Lwo Kang, had been assassinated in the Imperial solarium, all respect for the Seven had drained away. Li Yuan sought to reverse this tendency by giving the people greater representation in government and – in the war against Wang Sau-leyan – by creating peoples' armies, but it was not enough. The great House of Representatives at Weimar spoke only for those with money and power and then only on a limited range of matters, for real power remained firmly in the hands of the Seven. And all the while, a number of other factors – the corruption of officials, the constant nepotism, the vast disparity in wealth between those at the top of the City (First Level) and those in the Lowers, the ever-increasing population – only served to stoke the great engine of popular discontent.

To be honest, these were not problems which had begun with the City – such things were millennia-old long before the first mile-high segment of Tsao Ch'un's world-spanning megalopolis was eased onto its supporting pillars – but conditions within the City exacerbated them, and while the rich continued to prosper, the poor grew daily poorer and more hungry. Something had to give.

Indeed, something *would* give. Yet, behind the struggle for power – that age-old battle between the haves and have-nots – was another, far greater struggle for the imagination, and for the very *soul* of Mankind: the "War of the Two Directions", a war that would ultimately centre upon a pair of individuals who, in their work and lives, would embody entirely different approaches to existence.

Those two were Ben Shepherd and Kim Ward, the former the most talented artist of his time, the latter the most gifted scientist. Growing up during these years of dramatic change, their work came to represent a level of creative life which, for more than a century, had been harshly suppressed by the Seven. The world into which they were born was culturally sterile: its science was at a standstill, filling in gaps in old research and perfecting machines developed centuries before; its art even worse, having returned to principles more than 1500 years old. Its scientists were technicians, its artists artisans. Coming into this climate of creative atrophy – a climate carefully nurtured by the Edict and the "Rules of Art" – Ben and Kim could not help but be revolutionary.

Ben Shepherd, the great-great grandson of the City's architect, was born in the Domain, an unspoilt valley in England's West Country. There, in those idyllic surroundings, was nurtured his fascination with mimicry, darkness and "the other side" which was to culminate eventually in his development of a wholly new art form, the Shell. Over the years he would shamelessly draw upon his own life – the death by cancer of his father, the lost love of a young woman named Catherine, and his complex sexual relationship with his sister, Meg – weaving these elements together to create a powerful tale.

Kim Ward, on the other hand, was a product of the Clay, that dark land beneath the City's foundations. Rescued from that savage hell, he spent the formative years of his early youth in State institutions, surviving that brutal regime through an astonishing quickness of mind and a matching physical agility. His innate talents recognised by Berdichev, Head of the great SimFic Corporation and a leading Dispersionist, Kim was bought and then, almost as casually, discarded when Kim's darker side – rooted in his experiences in the Clay – emerged after one particularly provocative incident when he badly hurt another boy.

Fortunately Berdichev was not the only one to recognise Kim's unique intellectual talents and he found an unexpected benefactor in Li Yuan, who, when Ward emerged from a long period of character reconstruction, gave him both his freedom and the wherewithal to begin his own Company in North America. But that was not to be. The Old Men, seeing in Kim the means of achieving their dream of Immortality, deliberately set about destroying his business venture, hoping to force his hand. But Ward would not serve them.

Kim had other dreams, among them that of marrying the Marshal's beautiful daughter, Jelka. But Tolonen would not permit the match and sent his daughter away on a tour of the colony planets. Kim, devastated, swore to wait until she came of age and signed a seven year contract as a Commodity slave with the SimFic Corporation in a deal that would make him fantastically rich. And while he waited he would pursue his other dream – his vision of a great Web, first glimpsed in the dark wilderness of the Clay.

Shepherd and Ward, Shell and Web – the two were antithetical, representing in many ways those very things over which Li Yuan and DeVore had fought for so long – the "Two Directions" facing Mankind.

Ben's Shell was the image of inwardness, a body-sized sensory-deprivation unit designed to replace objective reality with a subjective experience that was more powerful than real life. Unlike reality, however, its very perfection was as seductive and consequently as addictive as the most lethal drug, its perfection a form of death by separation – a withdrawal from the world.

The Web, on the other hand, was the very symbol of outwardness, a vision of an all-connecting light: quite literally so, for Kim's Web was conceived as a means of linking the very stars themselves.

The safety of the past or the uncertainty of the future? Inwardness or outwardness? Connection or Separation? These choices, like the perpetual Yin and Yang of the ancient Tao itself, would determine Chung Kuo's future. Yet the shadows cast by past events would also play their part.

Back in the summer of 2203, Li Shai Tung called together his relatives, his advisors and his closest friends, to celebrate the betrothal of his son, Li Yuan, to the Princess Fei Yen. But while outwardly he smiled and laughed, secretly the old

T'ang had misgivings about the match. Fei Yen had been his murdered elder son's wife and, though the marriage had never been consummated, it felt wrong – an affront against tradition – to let his younger son, now heir, step into his dead brother's shoes so blatantly.

That same day, his son received two special gifts. The first was from Li Shai Tung's arch-enemy, DeVore. It was a *wei chi* set, a hardwood board and two wooden pots of rounded stones. Such a gift was not unusual, yet whereas in a normal *wei chi* set there would be one hundred and eighty-one black stones and one hundred and eighty white, DeVore had sent three hundred and sixty-one white stones. Stones carved from human bone.

Symbolically the board was Chung Kuo, the stones its people. And white . . . white was traditionally the Han colour of death. DeVore was telling Li Shai Tung that he would fill the world with death.

But there was a second gift, this time from the Marshal's daughter, Jelka. Her betrothal present to Li Yuan was a set of miniature carved figures: eight tiny warriors – the eight heroes of Chinese legend, their faces blacked to represent their honour.

Shocked by the symbolic message of the first gift, Li Shai Tung was delighted by the second. A bad omen had been overturned. There would be death, certainly, yet there would also be heroes to fight against its final triumph.

Yes. It was written. When the board was filled with white, then, finally, would the eight black heroes come.

And so it transpired. When DeVore finally returned, at the head of a vast army of copy selves, it was Hans Ebert and the Osu – eight black heroes – who faced him and, aided by the Machine, a benign Artificial Intelligence, defeated the great arch-enemy. The mile-high city was destroyed, the rule of the Seven effectively ended. Li Yuan, for once totally indebted to his servants and allies, was forced to promise to build a new world. In the years that followed, what remained of that great City of Ice was torn down and a new environment, more humane than the old, a veritable "China on the Rhine", was built in its place, based ironically on Ben Shepherd's best-selling fiction *The Familiar*.

Indeed, that new experiment in living might have worked – might even have brought a new flowering of humanity – had not Li Yuan, tired and wishing to absolve himself of responsibility, handed over the reins of government to his fifth wife Pei K'ung.

Pei K'ung proved a capable and efficient ruler, and if any one person could be said to have held the Empire together in those first ten years, then it was Pei K'ung. But what had once been political virtues – her stubbornness, her ruthlessness, her desire to succeed at any cost – eventually became liabilities. Slowly she replaced her husband's officials with her own, surrounding herself with lickspittles such as I Ye, her Head of Security; Ming Ai, the eunuch, her Private Secretary and shadow Chancellor, and the odious Chu Po, her lover and confidant. With such half-men running things, court life once again became a spider's web of deceit.

In short, Pei K'ung became a monster. Worse, she came to despise her husband

and consider him a weak man, incapable of action. And so it seemed when Ben Shepherd came to visit the San Chang – the Three Palaces Li Yuan had had built at Mannheim after the war – Li Yuan was encouraged by Ben to become involved once more. Between them, they hatched a plan to discredit Pei K'ung and seize the reins of power again.

And what better way than to finally give Pei K'ung what she wanted – permission to try to unify the world once again; to bring back the ancient certainties of a single world state: Chung Kuo. But though Li Yuan signed Pei K'ung's edict levying taxes on the common people – taxes that would finance that great war of reunification – it was his hidden purpose to lose the ensuing war and then to abdicate in favour of his son, Li Kuei Jen, thus wiping the slate clean and giving his son and his new wife the chance to start anew.

Such was the plan. A formal alliance was made with the North Americans, who would provide troops and weaponry. Marshal Karr was sent east to Mashhad to meet with Hu Wang-chih, a West Asian Warlord, to form a secret alliance against his fellow Warlords. Everything, it seemed, was in place. And then Li Yuan fell in love, a hopeless infatuation with his son's bride's sister – a fifteen-year-old Minor Family princess named Hsu Lung hsin, "Dragon Heart". Bewitched by her, Li Yuan defied common sense and pursued her, willing to wreck his plans simply to have her. In the midst of everything, he divorced Pei K'ung and married Dragon Heart.

Yet even as Li Yuan emotionally self-destructed, the situation disintegrated about him. Warlord Hu was assassinated, and Li Yuan's Second Banner Army – sent in to pacify the region – was destroyed by the new Warlord, Li Yuan's own cast-off son, Han Ch'in. Faced with a war on two fronts – against his son and his ex-wife, Li Yuan made a deal with Han Ch'in, then sent Karr to deal with Pei K'ung. But arriving at Pei K'ung's citadel, Karr found that Pei K'ung's generals had slit the old Empress's throat.

There was peace. But it was peace at a high price, for the bonds that once tied Li Yuan's servants to him had finally broken. His son, Kuei Jen, hurt badly by his father's new marriage, fled to exile in North America, while Ben Shepherd, having lost all patience with Li Yuan, returned to his Domain. Most tragically of all, Kim Ward, who had done so much to try to make the new society work, finally turned his back on Chung Kuo, returning to his base on Ganymede, from where he began to build a great fleet of starships; his aim, to colonise the stars.

In the years that followed, things slowly deteriorated as Li Yuan indulged his new wife's whims and fancies. In the face of food shortages and riots, Li Yuan began to wire his population. Marshal Karr, appalled by this development and realising he could do more outside of government than as a servant of the T'ang, resigned his commission. Even Li Yuan's staunchest supporter, his Chancellor Heng Yu, was riven with indecision. Things came to a head, finally, when an outbreak of plague – a strain of an ancient GenSyn drug, Golden Dreams – ravaged Chung Kuo.

The ensuing devastation was great. Nearly ninety per cent of the population were killed, the survivors bearing the mark of the plague in their thin and wasted forms, and in the gold of their eyes.

Among those survivors was Li Yuan. Reunited with both his sons, and with his wizened first wife, Fei Yen, he fled his shattered Empire for North America, even as DeVore returned at the head of a force of thirty thousand morphs.

And so things are. Out in the orbit of Jupiter, Kim Ward has launched four great fleets – each accompanied by one of the gas giant's moons – to sail to the stars, while back on Earth a new phase of the long war has begun, with Emily Ascher once more cast into the role of terrorist, using the old Dispersionist bases in the Swiss Wilds to fight a new enemy, her erstwhile ally and admirer, Howard DeVore, now ruler of a depleted City Europe.

PROLOGUE – SPRING 2240

THE FATHER OF LIES

Why was I so frightened in my dream that I awoke? Did not a child carrying a mirror come to me?

"O Zarathustra," the child said to me, "look at yourself in the mirror!"

But when I looked into the mirror I cried out and my heart was shaken: for I did not see myself, I saw the sneer and grimace of a devil.

– Friedrich Nietzsche, *Thus Spoke Zarathustra.* 1885

THE FATHER OF LIES

The bee climbed the outside of the flower's bell, lifting and dropping in the air, its jointed legs grasping the rim, the flower swaying beneath its weight, its delicate, translucent wings half-raised in balance.

Ben watched. Close by, only inches from his face, the flower gaped, blood red above the rich, dark green of its leaves. Its scent was sweet, intoxicating. It had drawn him as inexorably as the bee. His hand, outstretched to touch, had paused and now rested near the flower's base, almost cupping the petals.

Leaf shadow fell across his hand, moving gently with the wind's movement through the branches of the tree above, forming a gauze upon the fair, hairless skin.

He glanced up, hearing music. A haunting Dowland melody. Lute and voice. Sighing, he looked back. The lawn was damp. Moisture had soaked through the thin material of his trousers. He watched the bee pull itself up onto the flower's rim, then tilt forward, down into the dark red mouth.

Encased, the insect's body seemed suddenly huge, the perspective of the bell abruptly changed, grown vast and yet filled by that presence at its heart. The insect moved, its antennae searching frantically, erratically, like a blind man in a strange house, yet at the centre of that great furred body there was a perfect stillness.

And the colours. Ben shivered, drinking in the colours. The richly golden "fur" of the bee – a yellow-gold slashed through with black, the same blackness that was at the flower's heart. Intensities of red and gold and black. *Primal.* And all about him in the garden, innumerable, overpowering shades of green. Colours enough within the green to frame another spectrum.

How the universe once was. Vivid. A sensory explosion.

Ben stood, the memory stored, and as he looked about him he was aware suddenly of the underlying silence, of that perfect realm of nothingness that underpinned the Cosmos.

A blank sheet. His eternal starting point.

In the morning light the garden seemed renewed. Long beds of flowers bordered the gentle slope of the lawn, alive with flaming tips of perse, cerise and cadmium; colours he loved for their precise shadings, for the way they varied from the primaries. Gazing at them, he felt a profound satisfaction, his eyes tracing their gradual ascent until he found he was staring at the vine-hung back wall of the old thatched cottage.

The music changed. From the dark interior of the house came the beautiful opening strains of the Seventh Symphony, the second movement – the *Allegretto*. Smiling, he went inside.

"Coffee?"

Ben turned, looking across the shadowed length of the dining room, past the silent, standing shapes of the dark oak table and tall-backed wooden chairs, to where Meg stood in the doorway to the kitchen. Smiling, she drew a strand of her long, dark hair behind her ear, and in his mind he saw his mother standing there, the gesture, like the outward form of both women, identical.

"Yes," he said softly. "I'd like that."

Ben watched her turn and vanish into the kitchen, then went across and sat in the armchair by the latticed window. His workbook lay where he had left it earlier, on the floor beside the chair. He reached down and set it in his lap.

It was no ordinary book. This was a big, square, leatherbound book, its large white pages filled with all manner of colourful symbols and strange, shorthand notations, as if it had been written by some ancient alchemist or archimage. Underlying the whiteness of the paper was a faint, grid-like structure, while at the top right-hand corner of each page was a number, drawn in bright vermilion ink.

Built into the arm of the chair in which Ben sat was what at first glance looked like a painter's palette. It held Ben's pens – special pens which he had made himself. Taking one, he paused, staring fiercely into the air, as if fixing one of the dust motes that drifted in the beam of sunlight from the nearby open window, then began to write.

For a time he worked, conscious of some vague, not-to-be-articulated shape to the thing on the page before him. Page *S.627b: 67–80*. That red ink notation in the top corner of the page provided the context in which he worked; a precise reference on a much larger and more complex grid, most of which he held within his head.

Returning to the room, Meg set down the coffee on the low table next to Ben, then took a chair across from him, watching her brother work.

After a time he put the pens away, closed up the palette and looked up at her. He was still handsome. Clean shaven, his hair neatly trimmed, he seemed far younger than he actually was. And no youth-enhancing drugs kept him that way. In fact, he scorned their use, preferring the lines of approaching age to the smoothness of the jaded-young. Rumours abounded of some secret potion, but Ben Shepherd was young by nature.

"Your coffee . . ." she said.

He stared at it a moment, observing its surface, the way the light fell on the dull, coated liquid, then looked up at her again, smiling, his eyes, which seemed forever full of seeing, studying her features as one might study a familiar landscape.

"Has Catherine called?"

Meg shook her head. Ben's wife was rarely here these days, and even when she was, it was never a comfortable arrangement. But that was scarcely Catherine's fault. She was what Ben had made her. If she chose to spend her days elsewhere, that was as much Ben's fault for neglecting her as hers for finally abandoning the relationship.

Catherine had loved him, almost as much as she herself loved him, but in the end her patience had worn thin. So it was. And yet she herself remained. Until death. His sister-wife.

Ben was watching her now; waiting for her to ask him. Finally she succumbed.

"How's it going?"

"Poorly," he said, his eyes not moving from her face; gauging her, all the while appraising her. This – this unnatural watchfulness of his, this intensity of vision – was what disconcerted most people. She was quite used to it; after all, she had endured close on fifty years of being watched by him. She had nothing to hide. But others feared to meet his gaze. Some tried to brazen it out, but most of them simply wilted before that fixed and iron stare. It seemed to them that such an excess of seeing was not simply unnatural but, in a way, *super*-natural. To encompass so much; to see so coldly and so clearly – *through to the bone*, as Ben so often said.

And in a sense they were right. It *was* unnatural.

"What's wrong?" she asked. "I thought things were going well."

"It's something in the story itself," he said, and for the briefest moment his eyes seemed to look inward; then they resumed their fierce, acquisitive gaze. "Something that no clever games with surfaces and textures can eradicate. A basic design fault, you might say."

At that he laughed, but at the same time his right fist was clenched, and she, almost as watchful of him as he was of her, noted that and read its meaning.

He looked down at the workbook in his lap and shook his head. "I mean to give it up."

"*Ben*?" Meg almost stood, she was so surprised. She leaned forward, staring at him. "But you *can't*. You've spent so long on it! You can't just discard it because of some momentary sense of disaffection! Persevere. Ride *out* the storm. You'll feel different in a month."

But even as she said it, she saw that her words were having no effect. He had decided. In those few moments, tinkering with his notes – in the length of time it took a cup of coffee to grow cold – he had decided to abandon eight years' work. It was all there in his face; the determination to make a break with it. To start something new.

Meg sat back, sighing deeply. Mad. Her brother was mad.

"I suppose I realised it earlier," Ben said, his fist slowly unclenching; something relaxing in him even as he spoke, "when I was out in the garden. But I didn't understand it. Not until a moment ago."

"Understand what?"

"That I was on the outside. Small, insignificant. And what I was doing was small and insignificant, too. I had to get *inside*. Into that dark intensity at the heart of things. Over the rim, so to speak."

"But I thought that was what you were doing."

"No," he said, the boyish smile returning. But for once Meg found she couldn't follow him. Just what exactly did he *mean* when he said he had to get "inside"?

"But eight years, Ben. All of that careful, painstaking work . . . *wasted*."

He shook his head. "No. Not wasted, Meg. Think of all the things I've learned. All of those tricks and techniques I discovered along the way. Things no one else can do. I can use all of that. Refine it. Focus it all on something *real*, something meaningful."

And Death? she wanted to ask. *Isn't Death meaningful? Or was that merely rhetoric*?

"What will SimFic say?" she asked, changing tack, trying to bring the discussion back from its metaphysical heights and onto firmer, more practical ground. "Oughtn't they to be in on any decision you make about the work? After all, they paid you enough for it."

He smiled. "I've already thought of that. I'll give them HeadStims. Three of them. I can cut them pretty quickly, from the basic background material. They can get one of their boys to run basic plots over the top. There's a big market for them now, especially in America."

He paused and, for the briefest moment, looked away. It was a strangely revealing gesture. Then he looked back at her, defying her to gainsay him.

"In fact," he continued, "they'll probably be more pleased than if I'd given them a completed shell. They could have the first of them six months from now."

"And Jack Neville?"

"Jack will go along with whatever I want."

"Maybe. But he'll be disappointed. You said . . ."

"It doesn't *matter* what I said," Ben said, a slight irritation creeping into his voice. "As long as he makes a profit on the deal."

"But I thought you said . . ."

"*Meg*!"

She looked down, stung by the reprimand. It was so unlike him.

For a long time after that she sat there quietly, running it through her mind. It all seemed much too quick, much too neat to satisfy her, yet she could see that something *had* happened in the garden earlier; something that had crystallised his thoughts. But she knew that the real genesis of that moment lay several days back, when he had begun to re-read his workbooks. Moreover, she suspected that it was not so much to do with the meaning or direction of the work as with something else. Yet to ask Ben would be to break another of their unspoken rules. For a time she hesitated, then, her voice soft, almost apologetic, she asked:

"Were you *afraid*, Ben? Was *that* it? Afraid that you couldn't match *The Familiar*?"

Ben didn't look away. His eyes held her own. Nor did he flinch at her question, yet his stare became fixed and fierce, as though tormented. Finally, it was she who looked away.

My God, he was *afraid* . . .

Afraid. Ben, who had never been afraid of a single thing in his life. Afraid of failing? Afraid, what? . . . of being merely human?

And how long had he felt like this? Since the reading? Or before? Was that why he had failed to heed her advice? Had the crisis come long ago, and she had missed it?

It was quiet where they sat. There was only the sound of the grandfather clock in the shadowed hallway. Then, unexpectedly, he got up and walked over to the window. Standing there, looking out through the open casement, he began to talk.

"It's all quite simple, really. The challenge I set myself was to try to create something better, more powerful than *The Familiar*. But how could I do that? *The Familiar* was perfect. I see that now. I said all I had to say in that, showed all I had to show. To go *forward* from that . . ."

He paused, shaking his head, then.

"I fled into complexity. Into the realm of intricacy and fine detail. I thought that somehow the answer might lie there. But I was wrong. Worse, I thought I could nail Death. Pin him down and copy him. I thought that maybe that way I could finally out-do myself, by landing the biggest fish of all. But I couldn't. I was only fooling myself. It was all semantics and sophistry. And when I came to understand that, I had to take a step back and reassess what I was doing. That's when the fear first came."

"But Ben . . ."

"No. Hear me out, Meg. If I don't say this . . ."

Ben looked down. For the first time in his life he had been humbled by something; for the first time he was in awe of something bigger than himself. And when he met her eyes again it was a different Ben Shepherd looking out at her.

"You were right, you see," he said quietly. "I *was* afraid. But it wasn't just that. The fear . . . well, I can live with that. What's much more difficult to live with is the possibility that I'm *wrong*. That *The Familiar* isn't my final word on things. That I really *can* improve on what I did. But not with this. *That's* why I have to throw this other thing off. *That's* why I have to start anew."

"I see," she said softly. "But what will you do? Where will you start to look?"

"I have no idea."

"And you're sure that this other thing . . ."

"Is a dead end?" he finished for her, a slight smile at the corner of his mouth because of the pun. "Yes. Quite sure."

She shivered, as if cold, then, stepping closer, held him to her tightly, feeling the faint tremor in him.

"You understand then?" he asked softly, whispering the words into her ear.

"No," she answered. "But if it's what you want to do."

* * *

Two days later Catherine returned.

Ben was out in the upper garden, digging out the left-hand flower bed ready for replanting. Hearing voices inside the house, he set the spade down, then turned and wiped his brow. Guests were rare enough at Landscott these days, but when this one stepped out from the back door into the late afternoon sunlight, even Ben was surprised at so rare – so *unexpected* – a visitor.

"*DeVore*?"

The man came toward him. A small, neat-looking man with swept-back dark hair and an air of self-confidence that only acute megalomania brings. Coming closer, DeVore offered his hand in greeting.

"Ben? May I call you Ben?"

Ben moved his head back the tiniest bit. *Might* he? He looked past DeVore, to see Catherine, standing, smiling in the doorway, her long red hair let down. It was easily three months since he had last seen her. He looked back at DeVore, then took his hand, surprised to find it warm, the grip pleasant, friendly almost.

"And what should I call you?" he asked, meeting DeVore's eyes. Brown eyes, he noted. *Warm* eyes. Again that surprised him, for this man was, Ben reminded himself, a killer. Perhaps the most ruthless and effective killer mankind had ever bred, plagues and natural disasters notwithstanding.

"Call me Ishmael," DeVore answered, and then laughed. "No. Howard will be fine. You don't mind me being here, then?"

"Why should I?"

"Some people object to my company."

"They've told you that?"

"Not to my face."

"But you think I might."

"You have a reputation for plain-speaking."

"And you for subterfuge."

"And masks, neh?"

For the briefest moment Ben almost succumbed to the man's charm; almost smiled; but something made him wary of becoming too close, too intimate with this one. One did not, of choice, drink hemlock.

"And what mask do you wear today, Howard DeVore?"

"The mask of Reasonable Man. You wish me to discard it?"

"And wear your own face?"

DeVore looked past Ben briefly, his eyes taking in the beauty of the valley; then they locked with Ben's again, their intensity matching Ben's own. "I have a use for you, Ben Shepherd. And as circumstances seem to favour the opportunity . . ."

"Circumstances?"

DeVore gestured toward the now-empty doorway. "Your sister spoke to your wife only last evening. She in turn spoke to me. It seemed – how shall I put it? – too good an opportunity to miss."

Ben gave a short laugh, astonished. "You want to *hire* me?"

DeVore's smile was pleasant, almost boyish. "I hadn't thought of it in quite those terms, but I guess that's what it amounts to. I've been meaning to come and see you for a long time now."

"But you've been busy."

The smile broadened. "One or two little things, yes."

"Tell me," Ben said, his eyes taking in the full figure of DeVore in a manner which, in another, would have been quite rude, "Why should I want to talk to you?"

"Because we are both interesting men. We live in a world of half-men and dullards. Such men as we are rarities. We should take every opportunity to talk."

"And what would you have us talk of?"

DeVore laughed, showing small, white perfect teeth. "Of shoes and ships and sealing wax, and cabbages and kings."

Ben nodded, staring all the while at the man who stood before him; comparing what he saw with other images in his head – images from across four decades. From what he saw this man had barely aged a day in all that time. Which was impossible. He frowned, then asked what was at the forefront of his mind. "Forgive me for asking, but how old *are* you?"

"To be honest with you, I forget. I've witnessed so many changes, done so many things." He shrugged, then. "A thousand years? Two thousand?"

"Impossible."

"Yes," DeVore said, as if it did not concern him whether Ben believed him or not. "Could we go inside, perhaps? I'd like to see where you work."

"Of course."

As they ducked inside, beneath the low lintel and into the shadows of the wood-panelled hallway, DeVore looked to Ben.

"Your wife is an interesting woman, Ben. I can see why you chose her."

Ben glanced at him. "You've slept with her?"

DeVore smiled faintly. "Certainly. But only out of curiosity."

"Curiosity?"

"Oh, don't get me wrong, Ben. She's a lovely woman, but my tastes are rather *special*."

So Ben had heard. In fact, he had bought one of DeVore's devices – a saddle, decorated with an obscene variation on the *T'ai Ch'i* – fascinated by the mentality that could obtain its pleasure only through another's pain.

Ben turned, his hand resting on the rail at the foot of the twisting steps, studying DeVore's profile, surprised to find himself standing beside the man. It was not, after all, every day that one met and talked to a living myth such as DeVore – even if that myth were synonymous with death and pain and suffering on an unprecedented scale. So soft he seemed. So vulnerable. How could so limited a being have achieved so much ill?

"Are you really you?" he asked.

"Yes," DeVore answered. "Oh, there are copies of me, certainly. Why, one of them sits, even now, in my office in Munich, signing papers and giving its instructions, but the real me is here."

Ben stared a moment longer, then, with the tiniest nod, began to climb the wooden stairs, DeVore following just behind.

"How go your campaigns?"

DeVore glanced up at him. "There is no need to be polite. You know as well as I how bad things are. The blockade is having its effect."

"And is that why you're here?"

"Why don't we talk of such things later. Right now I'd like to find out a few things about you."

"Such as?"

"Such as why you chose to abandon Li Yuan."

They had come to the hallway at the top of the steps. On the wall behind Ben was the portrait Catherine had done of him at college, almost thirty years before; an impressionistic piece of vivid reds and greens and black.

Ben paused a moment, his left hand resting loosely on the wooden post at the top of the stairs.

"I guess I grew tired of it."

"Of *it* or him?"

"Of both."

"And yet the game amused you?"

"For a time."

"Have you ever thought of doing it again?"

"Are you asking me to be *your* advisor?"

"If you want the job."

"But that's not why you came?"

"No."

Ben looked away, for once genuinely intrigued. "I'd have thought that you were the last person who would need advice."

"So you might think. But I have much to occupy my time, and there are few I can trust."

"And you think you could trust me?"

DeVore met his eyes and nodded. "I think the arrangement could be quite amusing, don't you? Two great illusionists, working together to mould a world."

"And if I don't want that?"

DeVore shrugged, again as if it were of no great consequence. "It's very beautiful here," he said after a moment, his eyes looking out through the landing window to the slope and the bay beyond. "I can understand why you prefer to stay here."

"Rather than out there in the world, you mean?"

DeVore turned, studying him. "You could have been a great man, Ben Shepherd. A truly great man. A king, or an emperor. Nothing was beyond you. You had the intelligence, the strength, the *will* for it. Instead you chose to be an artist. Why was that?"

"Kings die."

"And so do artists."

"But not their art."

"You think so?" For the first time there was a slight ironic edge to DeVore's voice. "Art is like bones. Both rot, *eventually*."

"Some bones remain in the ground."

DeVore shrugged. "So you think your art is somehow greater than the world of men?"

"Why should it bother *you* what I think?"

"Because, in my way, I am an artist too. Only my canvas is far greater than yours. You see, you have chosen to copy the world. Oh, yours is an ingenious and wonderful copy, certainly, but it's still a copy, whereas my canvas is the world itself, yea and the flowers and the beasts in the fields. Moreover, my ultimate aim is not to copy but to mould. To *transform*. You've seen my creatures?"

Ben nodded.

"I take it, then, that you're not impressed."

When Ben did not answer, DeVore gave a soft laugh, then walked across and placed his hand against the handle of the door to Ben's study. He looked round at Ben. "May I?"

"Certainly."

Ben followed him inside, trying to see it new – as DeVore was seeing it at that moment.

Little had changed in almost thirty-five years. The blinds were drawn over the facing window. A low wooden table dominated the centre of the room. On it was a small comset, its simple design out-of-date long before Ben had been born. Bookcases rested against three of the walls, their shelves stacked tight with old clothbound books and other bric-a-brac. In the space above them were a number of sketches and diagrams. It was to one of these – one of four hanging on the left-hand wall – that DeVore seemed drawn.

"Is this supposed to be Ward?"

"Yes." Ben came and stood beside DeVore. The sketch was one he'd done six years before: a pen and ink study of Kim Ward as a spider, four thick, sticky threads stretching out over his right shoulder as he strained to pull four moons along behind him. The surfaces of those tiny moons were cratered and pitted in the finest detail.

"I take it you don't like our Clayborn friend."

"Does it matter now?"

"I guess not."

DeVore moved on, looking at the next of the four sketches. "And this?"

"Is Death."

DeVore raised an eyebrow. "Why do you draw Death with a horse's skull?"

"It's how I see him."

"Ah . . ." DeVore turned, looking about him, nodding slowly as he took it all in. "I'm surprised it's all so . . . cluttered. So . . . low-tech."

"My work-room's down below."

"Can I see that?"

Ben hesitated. This sudden interest was strange. "What do you want? I mean . . . what do you *really* want from me?"

"I want a shell."

Ben laughed. "What good would that be to you?"

"You want to know?"

"Yes."

"Then let me explain. What I'm offering is a deal. You want to tape death, Ben Shepherd. Well then, I'll give you death, a thousand times over."

"And in return?"

"In return, I want you to make me something so powerful, so seductive and beautiful that whoever experiences it will be trapped. I don't know quite what it ought to be – a vision of God, perhaps, of pure love and beauty, of bliss and magnificence, perhaps – but whatever it is, I want it to be so . . . *addictive* that not even the most pure and strong-willed man could escape its sticky threads."

Ben whistled. "You ask a great deal."

"Do I?" DeVore faced Ben, his whole expression set suddenly in a fixed, attentive stare that was inhuman. "Are you saying that you can't do it?"

"Oh, I could do it, certainly. But what would be the point?"

DeVore smiled. "Come . . . I think you know the point. Such a work would be a weapon, neh? Perhaps the greatest weapon ever devised."

"Against the Americans?"

"They are always looking for distractions, so I've heard."

"But what if they ban it?"

"Then we'll smuggle it in. Word of it will spread. People will want it more than they've ever wanted anything. And in time . . ."

"A plague," Ben said. "You're talking about using my art as if it were a plague."

DeVore laughed. "Am I?" Then, relenting. "Do I offend you, Ben Shepherd?"

Ben considered a moment, then shook his head. "It's . . . *interesting*."

"There! I *knew* you'd find it so!"

"I didn't say I'd do it."

"No, but you'll consider it, neh?"

"Yes."

"Good." DeVore held his shoulder briefly, then turned, facing the door. "Well . . . I think we've neglected the women too long, don't you think?"

But Ben, to whom the thought of neglect was wholly alien, merely shrugged; his mind following a different course. "Is it true?"

"True?"

"What Hans Ebert said to me once. About you having been on Mars, in a strange, invisible ship."

"Yes, that was true."

"And what other wonders have you?"

DeVore smiled broadly. "Plenty. But you must come and see them, Ben. Simply talking about them doesn't do them credit. You ought to *experience* them."

Ben smiled; a cold, calculating smile that DeVore saw and recognised, as in a mirror. "Maybe I will," he said. "Maybe I will."

* * *

Meg set the large blue earthenware bowl down on the table among the other bowls, then slipped off the oven gloves and set them aside.

"Mmmm . . ." DeVore said from the far end of the table, "that smells delicious. What is it?"

"It's Ben's favourite," Meg answered, looking to where Ben sat, facing Catherine across the table. "Rabbit stew with dumplings."

"It sounds wonderful," DeVore said, his dark eyes sparkling at his hostess.

"Oh, it is," Catherine said, reaching across to lay her hand over DeVore's. "There's nothing in the city can touch Meg's cooking. She has a genius for it."

"Then I am honoured, Miss Shepherd."

"You're welcome," Meg said, a slight awkwardness to her manner as she lifted off the lids and began to ladle first stew and then carrots and potatoes into the deep bowls by her elbow. "But I cannot honestly accept your praise. The rabbit was as he was made. We merely caught him. And the spices are mixed to my mother's recipe. I but carry out her instructions."

"Very modest," DeVore said, his eyes seeming to drink in Shepherd's sister, "but I know there is a kind of magic in good cookery. And if Catherine praises it . . ."

Catherine had put on weight, Meg noticed. Not much, but enough to make her seem more solid, less cat-like than she'd once appeared. As the years went by her natural beauty was being slowly swallowed up by a kind of matronly quality. Ben had commented upon it more than once – on one occasion even to her face. But just now Ben was silent, as he had been this past hour.

Meg lifted the first bowl and handed it across to Catherine to pass on to their chief guest.

"Thank you." DeVore unfurled his napkin and placed it on his lap, then looked about him, waiting until the others had received their bowls.

When all were ready, Ben gave a little nod and they all began to eat.

"Oh, yes," DeVore said after a moment, looking across at Meg with a beaming smile. "This is indeed a delight. That taste!"

"We forget," Ben said. "Once the whole world was as fresh as the taste of a young rabbit."

DeVore nodded. "That's true. But things pass. New things must have their time, don't you think?"

Ben shrugged and looked down, content, it seemed, to eat his stew and dumplings. Catherine, conscious of the awkward lull, leaned forward, determined to fill it with talk.

"I was in Dortmund last week, at the Klaiser Gallery. They've an exhibition of the new art. It's wonderful, Ben. Such vivid colours! Such life!"

"I've seen it," Ben said without looking up.

"Ben's not a fan of the new," Meg said, looking to her chief guest.

"Maybe so," DeVore said, reaching across to break a hunk of bread from the nearby loaf. "And yet he's single-handedly revolutionised art. I saw a preview of the exhibition Catherine's talking about and must say that, personally, I found it . . . *regressive*"

"That surprises me," Ben said, looking across at him.

"Surprises you?"

"Yes. I thought you of all people would be an admirer. All that brutality. All that vigorous expression of sheer will."

DeVore laughed. "You mistake me, Ben. I admire power, certainly, but not the posturings of power. No," he went on, offering an apologetic smile to Catherine. "I hate to disagree with you, Catty, but I found the work shallow, lacking in real understanding. They were . . . how might I put this? . . . *propagandist* in intention."

Meg looked down. Catty, eh? She almost smiled, but reminded herself just who this was calling her best friend pet names. It was rather like finding oneself suddenly related to Genghis Khan.

Raising her eyes, she studied DeVore, letting the flow of talk drift past her. She had noticed earlier how nice and neat his hands were, the nails perfectly manicured, the skin well scrubbed. In the same manner, his whole form had a pleasing neatness about it, his face a handsome cast, that lulled one into a false assumption.

The devil is a handsome man . . .

As if conscious of her sudden attention, DeVore looked across the table and smiled at Meg.

"Would it be rude of me, Miss Shepherd, if I were to ask for a second helping?"

"Not at all," she said, rising quickly to her feet and going round the table.

As she stood there, ladling stew into his bowl, she could sense his eyes on her and felt a flush come to her neck.

"That perfume you're wearing?" he asked, his voice low and intimate. "Is it something you made yourself?"

Meg forced herself to meet his eyes and smile. "It was my mother's."

"Ah . . ."

She handed him the bowl, then went back to her place, but she was no longer comfortable. In those few instants it was as if he had violated her. As if the query about the perfume – harmless in itself – masked some other question.

"I saw Sergey the other day," Catherine said, reaching out to take her wine glass, oblivious of what had transpired.

"Yes?" Ben said, with marked disinterest. "And how is he?"

"He's well," Catherine answered. "Sasha's staying with him. He's been teaching her sculpture."

Meg tensed, but the explosion she'd feared did not come. Ben dipped his bread into the stew and popped it in his mouth, as if the news were nothing special and all of the long enmity that had existed between Catherine's first husband and himself was as nothing.

"Well?" Catherine asked after a moment. "Don't you mind?"

Ben looked at her, finishing a mouthful, then answered. "Why should I? She's a grown girl. She can make her own decisions. You do."

Catherine looked down. "You don't care, then?"

Ben laughed, but said nothing.

"I'll clear the plates," Meg said, getting up as the silence descended once again. "Unless anyone wants more?"

DeVore smiled across at her, as if he alone had been addressed. "Thank you, Miss Shepherd, but no." He put his hands flat on his stomach, like the archetypal fat burgher in one of the historical soaps that were so fashionable these days. "It's sorely tempting, but I must leave some space for pudding, mustn't I?"

And as she stacked the plates beside the sink, then turned to face the oven, Meg found herself wondering just what it was in nature that could make a monster seem so *human*.

For she had no doubts now. Tonight they supped with the devil. And the devil had the appearance of a healthy appetite.

Meg slipped on the oven gloves, then took the apple pie from the top shelf, pushing the door closed with her knee. Straightening up, she found herself looking out through the open flap of the garden door, and saw the full moon shining brilliantly in the blue-black night, like a staring eye, watching her. And into her head came the two questions that had been hovering there at the back of her consciousness ever since the meal had begun.

What are you up to, Ben? And what precisely does he want from you?

She shivered, cold suddenly, and frightened for her brother. Then, forcing herself to smile, to play the perfect hostess, she turned and took the pie through.

* * *

Meg stood beside her brother, his arm about her waist, as DeVore's craft came down in the upper meadow, its lights making her shield her eyes and look away to one side. They had already said their farewells, and it only remained for them to watch as the two dark figures climbed the ramp, briefly silhouetted against that intense white glare.

"Like the dead," Ben murmured, as if he'd read her mind.

"Yes," she said. "I'd hoped she might stay."

The figures waved. They waved back. The hatch hissed shut. The roar of the engines grew once more, gusting warm air across to them.

The craft slowly rose, then accelerated away to the east. As its noise receded, Ben turned to her and smiled.

"I'm glad she didn't."

She looked back at him, trying to read him through his eyes. "Are you?"

He nodded. "Come on. Let's go to bed."

"There's the washing up . . ."

"Leave it," he said, taking her arms and lifting her from her feet. "Now. Before I change my mind."

* * *

Meg lay there on her side, the darkness wrapped like a shawl about her. Ben's lovemaking had been unusually violent, as if he had been trying to breach some hidden barrier deep within himself. Now he lay there silently beside her, his naked body sheened in perspiration as he stared up at the shadowed ceiling.

Through the open window she could see right across the valley. The surface of the bay shimmered in the moonlight, a great sheet of stippled light that contrasted starkly with the darkly wooded slope beyond. In that early hour it all seemed so peaceful, so *eternal*, yet for once its tranquillity failed to lull her. She could not sleep while Ben was troubled.

"What is it?" she asked quietly, turning and laying a hand on his wrist where it lay beside her naked hip.

"It's nothing."

"Nothing?"

"Yes, now go to sleep."

But she knew now she was right. "What has he asked you to do?"

Ben turned his head, staring at her. "You don't like him, do you?"
"No. Do you?"
"I don't *dis*like him. He's a charming, intelligent man."
"And well-mannered and attentive and . . . a devil."
Ben narrowed his eyes, surprised. It was not often she made so direct a comment on a guest.
"So what does he want?" she asked, edging up onto one elbow and looking down at him. "What was the deal?"
"Why should you think there was a deal?"
"Because that's how he is. He wants, he takes, he uses."
"And what if he also gives something back?"
She laughed bitterly. "What could he possibly give *you* that you haven't already got?"
His silence worried her.
"Ben? . . . *Ben*! What is it? Tell me. Please."
"You want to know?"
"Of course I want to know."
"I'm going to work with him. Make him a shell."
She was silent a moment, then, in a tiny voice. "You can't."
"Can't?"
Meg lay her hand gently on his shoulder. "You mustn't. He's . . ." She shrugged.
"It's what I do," he said. "It's my art."
"But you can't," she said again. "Not for him."
He pulled himself up into a sitting position, facing her. "What is it?" he asked. "What are you afraid of?"
"That you'll lose your soul."
"Faust and Mephistopheles, eh?" His laughter was reassuring; the warm, self-mocking laughter she remembered of old, but still the situation troubled her.
"What does he want you to do?"
"It's as I said. He wants me to make a shell."
She shook her head. "No. That doesn't make any sense. He wouldn't come here just for that. He'd summon Jack Neville to him, or something like that. He wanted something special, didn't he? Something that only you could do."
He looked away, past her, his silence answering her.
"Ben," she insisted. "You have to tell me."
"Okay. I'll tell you precisely what he wants. He wants me to make something so good, so distractingly attractive, that it's instantly addictive."
"And he'll use that, right?"
"Yes."
"As a weapon?"
"I guess . . ."
"No, Ben. You don't guess. You know."
He hesitated, then nodded.
"Then it's as I said. You can't."

"Why not?"

"Because that's not art's purpose."

"Says who?"

"Oh, let's not play childish games, Ben. You know as well as I."

"*Do* I?" He wrinkled up his nose. "That's it, you see. Maybe I don't know, after all. Maybe he's right and art always has been a kind of weapon – one which has never quite achieved its true potential. And maybe I find that a challenge."

She huffed, exasperated with him now. "But you can't. Not for *him*. You don't know how he'll use it."

"What does it matter how he uses it? You've seen the world, Meg. You've seen what they've done to each other these last fifty years. So maybe it's DeVore's time. Maybe he'll finally put an end to all this chaos."

"I don't believe that."

"But you don't know . . ."

She edged back, away from him, then stood, her naked figure silhouetted against the moonlit window.

"You mustn't do this, Ben."

"Oh, but I will."

"Then you'll do it without me."

"Meg . . ."

"No, Ben. I tried to persuade you. Now I'm telling you. You have to make a choice – working with DeVore, or living with me. Which is it to be?"

He watched her silently; a silence she took to be dissent.

"Okay," she said, her voice tiny, almost inaudible. "Okay . . ." And, without another word, she turned and left the room.

PART ONE – SUMMER 2240

INSIDE THE GATES OF EDEN

"Charon, his eyes red like a burning brand,
Thumps with his oar the lingerers that delay,
And rounds them up, and beckons with his hand.

And as, by one and one, leaves drift away
In autumn, till the bough from which they fall
Sees the earth strewn with all its brave array,

So, from the bank there, one by one, drop all
Adam's ill seed, when signalled off the mark,
As drops the falcon to the falconer's call.

Away they're borne across the waters dark,
And ere they land that side the stream, anon,
Fresh troops this side come flocking to embark."

– Dante, The Divine Comedy, Hell, Canto III

CHAPTER·1

THE PATTERN OF THE DAY

The day was hot. On the mountain road, dust rose from the metal tracks of the troop carrier, smudging the perfect blue of the sky. The growl and trundle of the half-track filled the valley as it came down from the heights to the north.

In the back of the carrier, beneath a thin cloth awning, sat eight shaven-headed boys and two men – the boys in pale red fatigues, the men in full uniform, their automatic rifles resting lazily between their knees. Eight backpacks rested in the space between the boys. All but one of them were looking down, lost in their thoughts. As the half-track rocked and lurched, their heads moved loosely with the motion. All but one.

A boy of fourteen sat beside the tailgate, his expressive blue eyes taking in every detail of the landscape through which they travelled. The valley was filled with scrub and pine and a host of small, dark purple flowers. Lifting his head slightly, the boy sniffed the air. Through the stink of hot diesel and dust he could smell the rich scent of the blooms, mixed with the all-pervading pine.

It was not far now.

Daniel turned, looking back into the shadows of the carrier. Aidan was sitting down the far end, on the left, behind the driver who was just visible through the dusty glass that sectioned off the cab. At fifteen Aidan was the oldest and most experienced of them, the natural leader of their team. While the rest were physically still boys, Aidan was already a man, broad at the shoulder, his muscular chest showing through the tight cloth of his fatigues. Daniel smiled fondly, then looked down. This would be Aidan's sixth time in Eden, his own fifth.

Daniel pushed the thought aside, concentrating on the moment. Each day had its own texture, its own feel. No two days were ever the same. You had to try to identify the difference; to isolate those moments that gave the day its own distinctive shape and pattern.

He did not know where he had learned this, yet he knew it to be the truth. It was like ladybirds. They all seemed identical, yet if you looked carefully you might see how the pattern of six black dots on the red casing differed in each and every case, giving each tiny insect its own distinguishing touch of individuality.

So it was in this world. Even ants, he was sure, possessed such tiny differences.

The guard beside Daniel stirred and made a small, murmuring sound in his sleep. Like his colleague at the front, he had been dozing the last hour or so. If they had wanted to, they could have killed the guards, the driver and his mate, and fled.

It would have been easy. It was what, after all, they had been trained to do.

But they did not want to escape.

Strange, Daniel thought, looking down the line of boys until his eyes rested on the youngest, Ju Dun. Only nine years old, Ju Dun was a small but stocky boy, self-contained and quiet, with deep brown eyes that seemed much older than his years. But so it was with all of them. There were no real children here, only soldiers.

Even so, Ju Dun was young to be on a team; much younger than Daniel himself had been when he'd first come to Eden.

Eden . . .

Geographically, Eden was a twenty-five kilometre square piece of land in the Black Forest, south-east of Munich, but in truth Eden was not in the normal world, or, at least, not in the day-to-day world that ordinary men would recognise.

"Daniel?"

Daniel looked across to Aidan. The guards slept on, but the others were alert suddenly, watching their exchange.

"Yes?"

"Nervous?"

Daniel shook his head. When it ended, it ended. Until then the *nowness* of things was enough for him. "You?"

Aidan smiled. That smile said everything. Seeing it, the boys also smiled. This was a good team, and they all knew it. They had been together three months now and were as prepared as they could possibly be. That was, if one *could* prepare for Eden.

"We're almost there," Daniel said, as the carrier eased its way between two great shoulders of rock, the gradient levelling out as they came out onto the floor of the valley.

"Home sweet home," Aidan said, winking at Ju Dun. "I wonder what new surprises the Man has prepared for us."

Mention of DeVore sobered the younger boys. Benoit and Leon both looked down. Only the eleven-year-old, Christian laughed. "Something for the specimen jar, no doubt."

Aidan grinned and nodded. "Oh, no doubt of that at all."

Slowing down, the carrier rattled through a pair of gates and into a high-walled compound. It slewed around, then stopped.

The guards jerked awake.

"Okay . . ." the driver said, coming round and beginning to take the pins from the tailgate. "You know what to do."

As the tailgate swung down with a clatter, the boys jumped down, one by one, passing the backpacks down to each other, then began to unload the rest of their equipment from the storage area at the side of the carrier, working silently, efficiently, as a unit, while the guards looked on with eyes that saw but did not understand.

* * *

The blockhouse was an ugly, functional building. It rested against the outer wall of Eden like an undecorated clay box, its slit windows and single doorway like something a child might have drawn. Behind it, dwarfing it, the wall rose a further fifty metres into the cloudless sky, solid and black, stretching off into the distance on either side. Guard towers studded the top of that immense wall, every half kilometre of its length, their deadly lasers facing inwards. No one cared what went into Eden. The lasers were there to make sure that nothing came out.

In a long, low-ceilinged room inside the blockhouse, Daniel sat in the corner, looking on as the younger boys lovingly checked and re-checked their equipment. Leon, the twelve-year-old, looked nervy; he had an insular air that was not his normal cocky style. By comparison, Johann, the tall pallid eleven-year-old, seemed positively nerveless. Christian, his bunk mate, was smiling and whistling to himself as he checked the charge on his rifle, while Benoit simply sat on the edge of his chair, staring at his hands. Ju Dun, meanwhile, was limbering up, stretching his neck and shoulders, then his arms, flicking out his hands, warming up the muscles.

Everyone reacted differently to this. Everyone had their own way of coping, but Leon's nerviness was worrying. Daniel knew he would have to watch that.

As he looked across, Aidan came back into the room, trailed by Slaven. "Okay," Aidan said. "They've given us a slot. Two hours and we're in."

Daniel saw how the boys looked to one another at the news. Excitement and fear were equally mixed in those looks. For some of them – Ju Dun, Benoit, Christian and Johann – this was their first time in, but even for Leon and Slaven this was only their second time, and the second time – as Daniel knew from experience – was the worst. It was all theoretical until you'd been inside, but they knew now what to expect.

Daniel stood. As he did, Aidan came across to him. Briefly he held his arm, then leaned close, whispering in his ear.

"I'm glad you're here."

Daniel smiled. Eden had changed them both. You did not go through it once, let alone five times, without it changing you. It made you appreciate things. Without it, Daniel would never have discovered the *nowness* of each living moment.

He stared at Aidan's face a moment longer, then gave a single nod, conscious of the others watching them.

* * *

From where it hovered just beneath the curved ceiling of the approach tunnel, the tiny OP unit sent back its signal to the Core.

Other observation probes – none larger than a midge – floated nearby, some sending back wide-screen images of the waiting team, while others hovered much closer, their microscopic lenses peering through the darkened visors of the helmets, transmitting pictures of the individual boys' expressions as zero hour approached.

Meanwhile, in the Core, a specially sealed vault at the centre of Eden, buried a hundred metres below the surface, a second team of analysts and strategists, sat watching a bank of screens and making notes.

Three hundred seconds now and counting.

From his seat in the gallery overlooking the operations room, Core Leader Dublanc looked on, his face expressionless, his gloved hands resting lightly on the tilted desk.

The faces of the eight boys showed in a single line at the centre of the wall of screens, Aidan's to the left, Daniel's to the far right. They were looking good. Confident. Their body signals were healthy: pulse rates, perspiration, blood pressure. Even Leon had settled now.

"It's looking great," Dublanc said through his lip-mike, his voice booming through the speakers down below. "We're going to scale up the first assault. Beef it up a little."

There was a murmur at that, but no one argued. It was why they were here, after all; to test out the Man's soldiers. To put them through their paces.

On a single large screen to the right, the image sent back by the first probe dominated the room. It showed the eight boys standing in a group some five or six metres back from the Entrance Gate. They were dressed in full body armour, which glinted red-black in the half-light of the tunnel. Inside, it would change colour to match the backdrop, but right now it was inactive. The group were heavily armed. Two had flamers, another two rocket-launchers. Two of them carried special battery packs – like huge, black plastic bricks – strapped to their sides, while Aidan and Daniel had a whole range of weapons attached to them. Each boy had two large semi-automatics – each weapon equipped with both munitions and laser functions – clipped to his back. All in all, the boys carried the fire-power of a small army.

The long, reinforced helmets the boys wore gave them a strange beetle-like look, accentuated by the five wedge-shaped neck-protector gorgets that extended from the back rim of the helmet to cover the shoulders and upper back. All wore armoured gauntlets and special flexible knee-length boots, part steel, part plastic. These boys could step on a mine and not lose a toe . . . just so long as they didn't do it twice.

Dublanc smiled. In their combat gear they finally looked what they were – soldiers. Age did not matter now, only experience, training and skill. And there were none more skilled than DeVore's boy soldiers.

"Show me Daniel."

At once the individual images vanished, replaced by a single image of Daniel's face, spread over all sixty-four screens.

Dublanc studied that face a long while; noting how those deep green eyes watched everything, the intelligence behind them considering the texture and form of all they saw, more like a machine than the machines themselves. He had noticed it before; had seen how quickly Daniel, of all of them, adapted to conditions – how he read the pattern of events and acted on it.

If they could get a machine to do *that* . . .

Boys came and went, and it was rare for him to recall one specifically, but he had known Daniel was special from the start. He remembered standing there in the rain outside the entrance to the mine that day as the truck emerged into the daylight, grating along the iron rails with its freight of black-faced, exhausted boys. And there had been Daniel, standing at the front, watching, those bright green eyes staring out from his grimy face, meeting Dublanc's gaze fearlessly as the truck clanked by.

He'd had the truck stopped there and then. Had stood there, his long coat wrapped tight about him against the cold, as his men took Daniel down and put him in the half-track. Even then Daniel had not been afraid.

That had been the start of it. That day in the rain.

"Give me Aidan."

The image changed. Aidan's face now filled the bank of screens.

As the technicians and observers watched, Aidan turned to face his team, smiling broadly, nervelessly.

* * *

"We're the best," Aidan said, rousing the younger boys. "That's why the Man has given us this chance. And we're gonna make it through, *right*?"

"*Right!*" came the resounding reply.

"We're gonna blast them and paste them!" Aidan said, clearly relishing the thought. "We're going to blow three different kinds of shit out of the little bastards, right?"

"*Right!*"

"But most of all," Aidan said, his voice changing, becoming subtler, conspiratorial, "we're gonna *out-think* those little fuckers . . . right?"

"Right," came the more sober response.

Daniel smiled, then looked down at the gun he was holding, his thumb stroking the casing of the big semi-automatic with an almost loving care. It fired shells and grenades, but it was best used as a laser. With it, he could pick the eye out of a fly at fifty metres.

There was a low hum, the vibration barely discernible at first, and then it rose up the scale until it was a finely-tuned note; a middle C. At the same time the whole of the great circle of the doorway turned green.

The two half-circles of the doors hissed back into the wall. Revealed was an inner room, lit by red strip lights – an airlock – and on the far side of it the door that led through into Eden.

"Okay . . . let's go!"

At the sound of Aidan's voice they moved into action; as efficient as machines, each knowing what part he had to play.

It took less than five seconds for them to form up inside, Ju Dun, as pole man, taking his position at the front. Ten seconds later the doors hissed shut behind them.

The outer doors slammed shut, massive bolts falling into place, and then the inner hatch popped as the explosive hinges were fired. Even as the circular metal plate flew outward, so Ju Dun threw himself through the gap and rolled, opening up with his automatic.

Less than a second later and Johann was through after him, Benoit almost bundling him out of the way as he too pushed through.

All three were on the other side now, the sound of their gunfire deafening.

Daniel was next.

He slid through backwards then spun about, clicking the safety off his gun.

Ju Dun was two paces out, kneeling, Johann and Benoit formed up at his shoulders, firing with a machine-like efficiency at anything that moved. The Entrance Gate was at the highest point in Eden. From where the team emerged they had a panoramic view of the terrain. To the right was the ruined village, its walls shot away over the years, the remaining brickwork heavily pocked; to the left a sharply descending slope and, just beyond it, the river. Beyond that was woodland, rising to low hills in the near distance, but the eye barely noticed them: what it saw was a flickering cloud of mechanoid hostility, a host of winged and clawed creatures – cycloids and mechanopods, scarabs and homers, assassin bugs and tinflies, screw-whips and stingers. The unheard signal drew them to the Gate like a scent, triggering the preprogrammed malevolence within them.

Daniel felt the adrenaline rush hit him as he took in the sight. The sky in front of him was dark with insect life, yet nothing was getting closer than ten metres. Shattered fragments littered the ground on every side.

Twenty metres up, something small and black stopped fluttering and fell like a dropped stone, its jet-black facets glinting as it turned. Ju Dun was directly beneath it. Daniel blasted it into a million pieces then turned, shooting the wing off a crab-beetle that was poised to leap from a wall just to Johann's left.

Leon was through now, and Slaven. They took their places in the deadly line, their guns blasting away, filling the air in front of them with splintering forms.

Daniel, his back to the wall, fired over their heads, lobbing grenades into the seething mass of dark, crawling things that covered the ground just beyond the front wave.

Here were things that hopped and chattered, things that whirred and buzzed; here were a thousand different things that crawled and jumped and clicked with menace, and all much larger than life and ten times as deadly as the originals on which they had been so carefully modelled.

And whatever moved, they blasted, not letting anything get within ten metres of where they crouched, the circle of the hatch at their backs.

Christian was through and then, finally, Aidan. And as the eighth gun began to bear on the swarm, so they began to make progress, the numbers of their assailants steadily diminishing.

Daniel was conscious of the movement all about him, of bodies jerking and turning, as target after target was picked out, such that the team seemed a single creature with eight deadly snouts that spat fire and steel, not a single enemy drone getting through.

And then, as suddenly as it began, it ended, the swarm withdrawing with a desultory buzz and whine.

Daniel looked about him, seeing through the visors of their combat helmets the elation on every face. But Aidan knew that such respite was brief.

"Come on!" he yelled into his lip-mike, his voice resounding in their helmets, "let's get moving!"

At once the team moved on, keeping close together, tightly organised and in perfect step, like a machine with sixteen legs and sixteen arms, heading down the slope towards the river, the black wall receding behind them as they began to make the crossing.

* * *

There had once been a war, many years before, between the Man and his enemy, Lee Wan, the King of the Han. From his bases in the south, the Man had struggled to liberate the north from the T'ang's tyrannical grip. The main thrust of that lengthy War had been fought out in a great trench between the two great cities, a long, narrow zone that was known only as The Rift, a place so inimical to mankind that a new form of life had evolved, a whole host of artificial life-forms dedicated not to their own propagation and survival, but to the destruction of all other living forms.

Evolved, men said, yet in truth these forms were not a genuine part of the great evolutionary tide; they were more a breaking of the great chain, a perverse twisting to breaking point of that age-old process. A reversal. And as they became more complex and more subtle, so – though they mimicked evolution's drive to betterment and the fulfilment of some vague, far-future goal – they grew closer to the great Nullity from which they derived their being.

Of this the boys knew little, other than what they had been told by the education officers back in the training camp. Only Daniel, intrigued by what he had seen in Eden, had taken the trouble to seek out Commandant Dublanc and ask why such things were and how they had come about.

That query had produced no answers – only a long stay in the isolation cells. It was not, after all, the boys' place to question, only to act upon instruction. They were soldiers, not scholars. What they needed to know they would be told, and nothing more.

Looking down at the great bank of screens, Dublanc saw how Daniel turned and looked back at the Gate, a long, thoughtful stare, his dark eyes taking in everything.

"Close on his eyes."

The boy's head grew, filling the screens until, from the shadows of his face, only the eyes shone out, massive, each sea-green eye spread out over nine screens.

It was like staring straight into his head. One could almost see what he was thinking.

"Do you think he knows?" one of them asked, turning from his desk to look up at Dublanc.

"Not yet," Dublanc answered.

Yes, but he will, he thought, remembering Daniel's persistence. That spell in isolation hadn't cured him – he had still wanted to know. And finally – faced with the choice of indulging Daniel's curiosity or doing away with the boy altogether –

he had given him access to the camp library, such as it was. Yet if the boy thought he'd find all the answers there, he must have been disappointed, because these days *no one* knew the answers, least of all the scribes who had tampered with the ancient books.

The past was one huge fiction. And the future?

Dublanc turned in his seat, looking across at the map of Eden that glowed in the shadows to his left.

Inside the gates of Eden there *was* no future, only the endless present.

* * *

"Leon, go left and come out behind the wall! Benoit, cover his back!"

Aidan spoke urgently into his lip-mike, his voice sounding clearly inside their helmets as they crouched in the narrow road that ran through the ruined village. As he spoke, his instructions were punctuated by concussive thuds and bright laser flashes as one or other of the team fired off a gun, responding to the buzzing whine of some flickering, flashing attack.

"Joh, Christian, take anchor. Slaven, you go in first. Ju Dun and Daniel will back you up. Now go!"

At once the team moved into action, Benoit's flamer opening up on a coppice just to Leon's left as he ran, toasting a group of three metamoths even as they launched themselves, their tiny egg-like bombs sparking explosively.

Slaven had the worst job. At the centre of the village was a well, at the foot of which was an energy-tap. There were hundreds of them, scattered throughout the Garden, and the team could use the taps to recharge their weapons, but each tap had to be fought for, for they were also the main source of energy for the countless mechanoids that populated Eden.

There were three types of taps. The simplest and most numerous were the platform taps, that were situated at the centre of big bowl-shaped platforms. Then there were well taps and – rarest of all – dome taps, of which there were no more than six in the whole of Eden.

The taps themselves were energy spigots – small, studded posts onto which one might clip one's weapon, or, in the case of insects, one might squat and "feed".

Normally Aidan would have ignored this particular tap and pressed on, recharging further in, but the sheer intensity of the attack at the Gate had left several of the boys' weapons on low charge. They had to take this tap. But it would not be easy. Well-taps were never easy.

As Slaven ran towards the well, Daniel saw what looked like a billow of dark smoke lift from the well's mouth. But it wasn't smoke. Smoke didn't make that whining, drone-like noise. He saw Slaven hesitate, then open up with his automatic. At the same time, Daniel went down onto one knee and, flicking his visor to longsight, opened up with his laser, firing past Slaven's shoulder, squeezing short bursts that seemed to cut tiny holes in the drifting swarm.

The tiny insectile machines popped and cracked and, splintering, fell from the air like shattered crystal, but there were hundreds of them. Thousands. Both Ju Dun and Aidan were firing now – Aidan lobbing mortars into the air from his big gun, the circular shells fragmenting in the midst of that chittering, droning cloud of metallic bugs – yet more and more seemed to come up out of the well to replace those which had been destroyed.

Slaven was slowly moving to his right now, drawing the swarm with him. That was his job. Leon, meanwhile, had come out on the far side of the well and was stealthily approaching it. At the same time, Johann and Christian were moving into the gap Slaven had created. If all went well, the three boys – and Benoit, who was hurrying to move into position – would get to the lip of the well at roughly the same time.

The swarm was almost on Slaven now. You could barely see him. At any moment they would cease holding back and fall on him as one. A muscle in Daniel's cheek twitched. Timing was everything.

"Okay, Slaven, *seal!*"

Yet even as Aidan gave that crucial order, Daniel saw one of the bugs – a tiger-wasp, its bright orange and black markings distinctive – fall directly towards Slaven's back. He twitched his gun upward to fire, but the back of Slaven's helmet was directly in his line of fire.

Seal-damn you!

The material of Slaven's uniform shimmered and changed colour, becoming a simple metallic black. At the same time it changed shape, hardening into a kind of chrysalis. The tiger-wasp shattered against it.

Instinctively, Daniel turned his head away. Even so, the flash left him half-blind, while the concussion rattled his teeth and set up a ringing in his ears.

When he looked again the sky around Slaven was clear. At the well, Leon and Johann were climbing in, harnessed to their partners, their guns picking off anything that came up out of the darkness at them.

Not that there was much left down there.

Daniel looked back at Slaven. The black pupa-like shell of Slaven's uniform lay at the centre of a small depression in the earth. All about it, forming a perfect circle roughly fifteen metres in diameter, the earth was charred black. Faint wisps of steam rose up out of that blackness, drifting to the north.

The wind had changed.

Daniel turned, looking about him. Ju Dun was up, and Aidan. There was a shout from the well. The tap was secured.

He allowed himself a smile. They'd done it, and without a single man lost.

Hurrying across, He knelt beside Slaven. A moment later Ju Dun was at his side. Without needing to be told, the young boy put his hands beneath the shell and, with Daniel's help, turned it over.

Daniel studied the suit a moment. Good. There were no cracks. The seal had held. Looking to Ju Dun, he nodded. Lifting the suit between them, they carried it across and laid it beside the curved wall of the well, Aidan covering them all the while.

Slaven would be out of it for some while, but he was fine. The worst he'd have was a blinding headache.

But it had been close.

Johann and Christian were busy lowering weapons down the well to Leon at the tap. At once Ju Dun and Daniel joined Benoit and Aidan, taking their positions about the well, picking off anything that came in sight, whether it was a threat or not.

Some teams, he knew, did little else. They took a tap then held it, knowing that at the very least they had a constant energy supply. But it was a no-win situation. You couldn't live on energy alone. There was water in the suits – enough for two days – but you had to get across and out before you could eat again. Yes, and at some point you also had to sleep. And that's when they got you.

Inside the hardened shell of his uniform, Slaven groaned.

"Go help him, Daniel," Aidan said quietly, using a discreet channel to speak to Daniel alone. "I may be wrong, but I think he sealed late."

Daniel shivered. He'd not wanted to admit it before that moment, but he knew Aidan was right.

The groan deepened to a low moan of pain.

Even as he knelt over it, the shell shimmered again and, softening, changed colour once again. As the helmet visor cleared, Slaven's face was revealed, his eyes screwed tight in pain.

"What is it, Slaven?"

There was a sharp intake of breath, then, "My back."

Daniel stepped over him, and, gently easing Slaven up, looked.

The suit's sealing had concealed it, but there, just below the protective shielding of the neck-plates, there was a tiny rip in the softer back-plate. Protruding from it – broken off, no doubt, in the instant the suit had sealed – was the needle-fine sting of a tiger-wasp.

"Oh, shit . . ."

Slaven stiffened, hearing the words. "What is it?"

Daniel took a breath, knowing Aidan was listening. "A sting," he said. "We'll take it out and drug you up. I'll carry you."

He looked up as he said this last and met Aidan's eyes.

Both boys knew what this meant. You couldn't carry passengers in Eden, not without paying the price. But there was the morale of the team to consider. To abandon Slaven at this early stage would destroy team morale. It wasn't that the others didn't know how ruthless things were in here – they knew – it was just that to see one of their own simply left for the mechanoids to pick over would be too much, especially this early.

Aidan came over and, crouching, smiled at Slaven. "You'll be okay," he said, speaking on the open channel. "We'll get you through." But when his eyes met Daniel's they conveyed a different message entirely.

We have to deal with this, Aidan's eyes said, as clearly as if he had spoken the words. *And sooner rather than later, right?*

Right, Daniel answered silently. He unclipped the medic's kit at his side and snapped it open.

"Okay," he said, speaking to Slaven once more. "Let's give you something to numb that pain."

CHAPTER·2

CROSSING THE RIVER

It was not immediately discernible, but Eden was a place of subtle currents and pressures. Some paths were easy to follow, others fraught with difficulty and if one persevered, that difficulty tended to intensify so that it felt almost as if the air itself were thickening with danger. Most teams tended to gravitate towards the easier paths; to circumvent those places where the danger was most intense and look for trails where progress could be made quickly and at little cost.

So it was that they found themselves, at midday of the first day, crouched by the river bank on the outskirts of an ancient town, a long way further south than they'd intended.

While Leon, Christian and Ju Dun formed a perimeter guard, Aidan and Daniel took a moment to discuss tactics.

"They're pushing us out," Aidan mouthed, his visor pressed to Daniel's so that the watching bugs could not see what they were saying to each other.

"You think we're heading into a trap?" Daniel mouthed back.

"It's possible."

"Then maybe we should cross the river."

Aidan frowned. Here it was relatively easy to get across, but further east the land fell away between rocks and the current was much stronger. It would be much harder to cross back. And they would have to cross back if they were going to get to the Exit Gate.

"I'd rather not."

"Then we go north."

"Into danger, you mean?"

Daniel smiled. "I feel I've been pushed far enough, don't you?"

Aidan grinned. "Yes."

"Then let's go."

* * *

Dublanc was in the back room, lying on his bunk, half-dozing, when one of his assistants came in. He yawned, then opened one eye.

"What's up?"

"They're on the move again, sir."
"Across the river?"
"No, sir. They're heading north."
Dublanc sat up, suddenly alert. "*North*?"
He had expected them to cross the river, then try to re-cross further up, at Ebnet, maybe, or Brand, but north . . .
"They're going *through* the town?"
"It looks like it, sir."
Dublanc frowned, genuinely surprised. He stood, then walked out onto the gallery, seeing the team at once, there on the big screen, their backs to the remote as they moved in tight formation into the ancient, ruined town of Freiburg.
"Where's the nearest tap?"
At once a map was superimposed upon the right of the screen, a flashing light indicating an energy-tap a kilometre north of where the team were.
"Do you think they'll head for that, sir?"
"No." But even as he said it, he knew that if they were to survive at all, they would have to expend a great deal of their energy, so they'd need a tap.
He narrowed his eyes. If he could nudge them slightly east.
"Let them get in deep," he said, conscious of how his own team were watching him. "Hold back until they hit the high ground, then push them towards Breisgau."

* * *

The air was filled with an angry buzzing sound. Daniel turned, seeing at once a great swarm of hornet-like creatures with long glass bodies approaching from the direction of the Square below.
"Shit!" Daniel said, recognising the creatures. They were small but those long glass bodies were full of burning acid that could rot a suit in seconds. If only one or two got through the results could be disastrous.
But the rest of the team were already distracted, fighting off a nest of beetles that were threatening to overwhelm them.
Snapping a grenade from his belt, Daniel tossed it up onto the roof, where the beetles were coming from, even as Aidan did the same. The twin explosions threw dozens of the fist-sized mechanoids into the air and blew a hole in the tiled roof. But still they came, hundreds and hundreds of the black, scuttering things.
Daniel turned back. The others would have to cope now; the hornets were almost on them.
"Clench your teeth, Daniel," Aidan said, unclipping a big shovel-mouthed gun from his back and taking off the safety.
Daniel did as he was told. A moment later he felt the huge concussion in the air as the stun shell went off in the midst of the swarm, dropping instinctively as the wave of sharp glass shards swept over him.
There was laughter in his helmet – Aidan's laughter.
"Hey, Daniel!" he shouted. "Do you think someone's got it in for us?"

* * *

Dublanc slumped back in the chair, letting the tension ease from him. It was his job to distance himself from his charges, to test them as one might test machines, but sometimes – just sometimes – one found oneself getting involved. *Linked* somehow.

It didn't happen often, but when it did he found himself, as now, pushing harder to compensate, as if to prove to himself that he didn't really care.

He stood, pacing the gallery slowly, considering what he should do next. It was within his power to crush them – to make good and certain that they didn't stand a chance – but what was the point of that?

Unseen, he made a face into the darkness. Some days he wondered what the point was anyway? He selected these boys and trained them, and then . . . nothing. Those that came out alive were sent back to the camps, where they'd be trained yet more before being sent back here. Until, finally, they did not emerge from Eden.

There was a point. Of course there was. He'd been assured by Horacek many a time that DeVore had a good reason for all of this, even if that reason was not spelled out, but some days Dublanc's faith in the Man wavered. One did not train one's shock troops only to expend them in these endless exercises. So what did DeVore want? The perfect killer? A machine to outgun the machines?

Or was he just a sadist?

That answer did not satisfy. If DeVore *was* a sadist, why did he not ask for copies of the tapes? Why did he express no interest whatsoever in the fate of his charges?

Or was that true? Horacek, for certain, had expressed an interest in Daniel. And Horacek had the Man's ear.

Dublanc sat once more, looking across at the bank of screens, watching as the team regrouped.

The trouble was, it was hard to know precisely what DeVore *did* want. On the three occasions on which he'd actually met the man, he'd had the distinct feeling that – all reassurances to the contrary – DeVore didn't give a fuck what he did, nor how he went about it.

And yet . . .

Dublanc paused, coming, as he always did in this internal debate, to the nub of it.

And yet he's given over all of this time and effort to creating the camps and running them. And to building Eden, and the mechanoids, and . . .

He huffed irritably. There *had* to be a reason for it. It made no sense unless there was a reason. But even he, who was in charge of it all, could not say what that reason was.

"The Man has a plan," Horacek had said to him once, grinning that horrible feral grin of his, *"and it is not our place to question it. We do as he asks when and where he asks it and no more. You understand?"*

At times like this Dublanc wished he *did* understand. He sighed. Maybe Daniel understood. If anyone had an inkling of what was going on, it was the boy. Those eyes of his were so knowing, so *full* of seeing and understanding.

None of the other boys had that.

"Commandant?"

He went to the rail and looked down onto the floor of the operations room. His Duty Captain stood there, at attention, looking up at him.
"Yes, Captain York?"
"Do you want us to take any special measures, sir?"
"Not yet," he answered. "Besides, if they keep on in the direction they're heading, I think they're going to be busy enough, don't you?"
"Sir."
York turned back, facing his operatives once more, moving quietly from desk to desk, giving orders, while on the gallery above Dublanc paced slowly in the half dark, his gloved hands clasped together behind his back.

* * *

They faced a field of pods. Row after row of small, rounded pods. Or what looked like pods. Aidan stood there just in front of Daniel, the biggest of his guns clutched to his chest, staring out across the field warily, waiting for his scouts to return.
Slaven was on his feet now. He stood to Daniel's left, groggy but unwilling to be carried any further.
The town was behind them. Ahead, beyond the field, lay a low range of hills. To their left was a ravine, to their right a long slope covered in thick bracken through which a single path zig-zagged.
"What are they?" Johann asked, stepping up beside Aidan.
"I don't know," Aidan answered. "I've never seen them before."
Daniel lifted his gun and picked off an approaching hoverfly. "It's a minefield."
"You know that?" Aidan asked, glancing at him.
"No. But what else could it be?"
"Don't you think it's strange?"
"Strange?" Daniel laughed. Everything here was strange.
"No . . . that we've never seen this kind of thing before. It's different this time. Can't you feel it?"
Daniel looked about him, taking in the vista, then shrugged. It *was* different. He could *feel* the difference. But he wasn't going to admit it openly for the watching bugs.
"Here's Ju Dun," he said, nodding towards the path through the bracken.
Ju Dun was running at a squat, weaving from side to side and keeping himself very low, as if at any moment he would throw himself flat. Behind him, pursuing him, scuttled two large metallic machines – bombardier beetles.
"Guests," Aidan said, turning towards Ju Dun and lifting his gun. But even as he went to fire there were two sharp detonations and both mechanoids fell, large holes shot clean through their carapaces.
Johann smiled and lowered his gun, even as Ju Dun clambered up alongside them.
"There's no way through," Ju Dun said breathlessly. "There's a formation of defensive machines – mortar-flies and bombardiers – three, maybe four hundred of them blocking the pass."

Aidan nodded, then turned, his eyes scanning the ravine to his left. There was still no sign of Leon.

"I'll give him two more minutes then we'll press on."

Daniel smiled inwardly, knowing Aidan would as soon leave one of his team as shoot off his own balls. But Aidan was impatient and, faced with something he hadn't encountered before, a little edgy.

"Here he is now," Slaven said, his voice pained. "Looks like he's got company too."

Leon was now in sight, some two or three hundred metres away, running at full tilt, two large hoverflies – their wingspan two metres or more – idly shadowing him. Even as they watched, one of them swooped and dropped something that looked like a tiny cluster of eggs. Leon, sensing the creature's proximity, turned and loosed off a round that ripped the hoverfly's wing and brought it down, yet even as it toppled to the earth, the cluster of tiny explosives went off, throwing Leon off his feet.

"Get down there, *now*!" Aidan said, gesturing to Johann and Christian, then, taking sight, he took a shot at the second hoverfly.

The shell went off some three or four metres from the swooping machine, even as it went in for the kill, fragments of the exploding casing peppering its wing. It juddered in the air, distracted by the explosion, but it was not seriously damaged. It lifted, gaining a little altitude, preparing for a second swoop.

Leon was still down, stunned. Daniel saw him turn onto his back and look up as the shadow of the creature fell on him.

And then the thing exploded like a firework going off.

"Nice shooting, Daniel."

Daniel lowered his rifle. "I was lucky," he said. But he knew he wasn't.

As Leon rejoined them, Aidan quickly questioned him, then gestured straight ahead. They would have to go through it seemed. The ravine, like the pass, was heavily defended.

"Just don't touch anything," he said. "And move slowly. And *keep* moving. Right?"

"*Right*!"

* * *

Dublanc watched as the team slowly walked down through the waist-length grass of the slope and stepped out into the field.

Briefly the watching eye focused on Daniel.

"He can shoot, that one!" one of the operators said. There was a murmur of agreement.

"Yes," Dublanc said, acknowledging the comment.

It *had* been impressive. Two hundred and eighteen metres, and Daniel had shot the swooping hoverfly straight through its compound eye.

Another few seconds and the boy who was down would have been a steaming rack of bones.

"Let them get in deep," he said. "Let them almost think they're through."

Yes. Because it was time to put the pressure on. Time to start pruning them back. Because – reason or no reason – that was why they were here. To be pruned. To see just who among them was good enough – or lucky enough – to survive.

* * *

The pod was roughly fifty centimetres tall and curved at the edges, like a fat, fleshy cylinder that had been rounded top and bottom. It was blueish-white in colour, and across its mouth was stretched a tight, milkily-opaque membrane, beneath which something small and dark moved from time to time.

Daniel knew what it was. An egg. They were walking through a field of eggs. The eggs of insectoid machines.

The boys were spread out across the field in a straggling line, about five metres apart, Leon on the far left, Johann on the right. Slaven was with Aidan. Aidan had wanted to carry him across the field, but Slaven had refused. Nonetheless, Aidan kept close, knowing how close to exhaustion Slaven now was.

Daniel glanced across, knowing they would have to make a decision, and soon. But right now, getting across the field was paramount.

They were more than halfway across. Another two minutes and they would be clear of it.

But that wasn't how things worked here.

Daniel scanned the sky. It was still clear. Nothing had come near them for the best part of six minutes.

He looked along the line. Leon was walking circles, turning slowly as he walked to make sure nothing crept up on him. Beside him, Ju Dun plodded forward slowly, his gun lowered, the barrel covering each pod as he passed it. Benoit, nearest to him on his left, was doing the same, occasionally glancing up to check the sky.

Daniel stopped dead, listening. There had been a noise. A hiss, like air escaping, and a glopping sound.

A hiss. Another hiss.

All about him the pods were opening. From two or three of them tiny black feelers now extended.

He looked to Aidan.

"Move!" Aidan said, trying not to panic them. "Come on!"

All eight of them began to run, dodging between the pods. There was gunfire now as one or other of the boys let loose a round or two at the emerging "chicks": dark cockroach-like things, with short, transparent wings and long heads tapering into needle-fine beaks of steel.

There was a shout. A cry of fear.

Daniel turned. Slaven was down. He had slipped and fallen between two of the pods. But even as he began to pull himself up, something hopped from the top of a pod and settled on his back.

Daniel tried to shout a warning, but it was too late. He saw the sharp silver stiletto of the creature's beak flash in the sunlight as it rose then fell.

Slaven screamed.

"*Run!*" Aidan called again, jerking Daniel back into life. Yet even as he turned he found himself facing one of the needle-faced chicks. It eyed him with a pure machine malice, then launched itself at him.

His gun came up in time to knock the thing away. But it was quick. It leaped again.

Daniel slammed it into the ground then turned, opening up with his gun, hitting anything that moved.

After a moment he sensed rather than heard Aidan come alongside him, his gun chattering as it picked off anything Daniel missed.

Slowly they backed away, Ju Dun and Christian covering their backs. A minute, two minutes passed, then silence fell.

Daniel looked about him at the tall grass in which he now stood. The field was below them. Beyond it was a small barrier of rocks. He turned, counting. Seven of them. So Slaven was gone.

He blinked.

"Who's hurt?" Aidan said, clipping the red-hot gun to his side and taking another from his back.

There was a groan.

"Leon?" Aidan walked across and examined the rip at the shoulder of Leon's suit. "What happened?"

"It's okay," Leon said, "it's superficial. Just a scratch."

There was the chatter of Christian's automatic as it picked off two of the chicks that had tried to follow them. In the silence that followed, Aidan put his fingers into the rip and peered inside. He frowned, then pushed Leon away gently.

"Okay," he said quietly. "We'll find shelter, then you can bandage that and repair your suit, right?"

"Right," Leon said, relief in his voice.

Aidan winked at him then turned, looking to Daniel. *Eggs*, he mouthed, a sour look on his face.

Daniel looked past him at Leon; saw how the boy was smiling, pleased that he'd survived not just one close shave but two, and felt sick to his stomach. Leon hadn't survived. He only thought he had. Leon had just been injected by one of the creatures with a stream of nano-eggs: tiny pre-programmed machines, from which a host of new mechanoids would fashion themselves, feeding upon their host, converting his body tissue into matter they could use.

Daniel shivered and looked away. Leon had just become a walking pod.

* * *

At the head of the valley was a ruined chapel, built into the rock of the hillside. It was a good place to stop, if only because the floor and walls were made of solid rock and the chances of anything burrowing up under you were small. They rested there now, Aidan and Johann mounting the watch while the others grabbed what sleep they could.

Unable to sleep, Daniel stood on the ledge beside the shattered window at the top of the chapel, his gloved hand resting loosely on the crumbling brickwork as he looked out over the terrain they had traversed. The distant wall formed a black frame about a landscape that looked as peaceful as a picture from an ancient book, but there was not a square metre that was completely safe.

Seven hours they had been inside and they were still less than five kilometres from the Entry Gate.

He let out a long breath. This time was different from the rest, not just in its detail, its fine patterning, but in its general *feel*. On every other visit, Eden had been filled with an impersonal menace, but this time that menace seemed directed.

Just above him the tiny midge-like bug watched him, an unblinking eye that never left his side. Daniel stared at it, wondering just who was watching him at that moment.

Until today he had assumed that the bugs were there simply to observe; to make a visual record of their passage, but what if they were used for another purpose?

Daniel turned, looking back into the shadowed interior of the chapel. The four who were resting lay some three or four metres below the ledge on which he stood, slumped against the right-hand wall, their backs against the solid rock, their visors raised. Looking at their sleeping faces, Daniel felt a genuine fondness for them. They had accounted for themselves well so far. Ju Dun, particularly, had impressed him. The lad had handled himself like a veteran. Nothing had fazed him.

Christian lay to his right, his long body turned slightly on his side, one hand resting on his chest as he slept. Towards the end, in the field particularly, Christian's natural good humour had begun to slip. But that was hardly surprising. If Eden was a joke, then it was a bleak one.

Benoit, to his right, had shown surprising spirit. In training, Daniel had wondered about his temperament but he needn't have worried. Benoit's determination to protect his fellows was quite remarkable and that, as much as any other quality, was what got teams through. When you knew someone would cover your back when things got bad, then things could be borne. Just. And such spirit bred in a team, just as its opposite, despair, could take root and rot a team's spirit from within.

Leon stirred in his sleep, then reached up to scratch his shoulder.

Daniel studied Leon, knowing that they would have to do something about him before long. He had six hours at most, and in the last of those he would be in torment. But six hours was better than nothing, and the team could use that time. It would give them all a better chance.

It's hard, Daniel thought, knowing that in some more decent world he might have told Leon what was happening and let him make the choice. But they needed Leon. As long as Leon could walk and fire a gun he was useful to them. So it was essential – for the team – that he didn't know.

There was gunfire, then laughter. Johann's laughter.

"Six-four," Aidan said, keeping the score between them.

Daniel climbed down then went out the front, joining them on the narrow parapet that overlooked the valley.

"It's quiet," Daniel said, taking up position between them. Aidan was facing forward, his eyes watching the valley, while Johann scanned the rock above the chapel, making sure nothing came over the top and dropped on them.

"Can't you sleep?" Aidan asked.

"No," Daniel answered, his eyes scanning the valley for any sign of movement.

Aidan considered a moment, then: "Johann, go and join the others. Daniel will take your watch."

Johann did not argue. He disappeared inside.

Aidan looked back at Daniel. "You feel it too?"

Daniel turned, placing his back against the parapet, then nodded. Above the two the tiny camera-probes hovered, sending back their images to the Core. After a moment, Daniel smiled.

"Maybe we should talk to them," he said.

"The Watchers?"

"Yes. Tell them what it feels like. Maybe they'd be interested."

Aidan considered that. "Maybe."

A bug fluttered up above the ridge. Daniel shot it before it could settle.

"Then again," Daniel went on, his eyes briefly checking the charge on his gun, "maybe that would only help them. You know, stack the odds against us."

"I'd say the odds were pretty high as it was."

"Exactly." Again Daniel's gun went off. Another bug exploded in mid-air.

"Two-nothing," Aidan said, keeping the score.

There was silence for a while, punctuated by gunfire and the habitual keeping of the score. Then Aidan spoke again.

"What do you think he wants?"

"Wants?"

"The Man. Why do you think he keeps sending us through?"

Daniel watched the ridge above the chapel, conscious of the shape of the clouds, the colour of the sky and the sharp, jagged outline of the rock. The stock answer was that DeVore was testing them, preparing them for some future task, but he had begun to suspect there was another possibility. But what Daniel said was, "I don't know. I thought I did, but I don't any more."

Aidan was quiet then. "Leon . . ."

"I know."

"When?"

Daniel shrugged. His instinct was to leave it until the last moment. "Let's see, huh?"

"Okay."

And that was it. No ethical debate. No weighing of the moral arguments. Just a simple decision to deal with it.

Aidan's gun chattered – *pock-pock-pock* – as he picked off a bug that had come too close. In the silence that followed, there was a groan. Daniel lowered his gaze, looking through the open doorway at the sleeping boys. Leon stirred, then groaned again, scratching at the swelling behind his right shoulder blade.

Malice. It all came down to simple malice.

Looking up, Daniel saw the bright glint of insectile eyes staring at him from above the ridge. He smiled then blew it into a million tiny pieces.

* * *

Aidan gave them another hour, then woke them. They had three hours of daylight. If they were lucky they could get to the circle in that time. *If* they were lucky.

But the younger boys were rested now, which was good. Because there would be little chance for sleep when the sun went down. Then things would really hot up.

Ahead of them, just the other side of the ridge, was thick woodland – three, almost four, kilometres of it. There, they would be open to attack from all sides – including the ground beneath their feet. If they survived that, then they faced an even more difficult barrier, the river.

At present the river was off to the south of them, but about three kilometres upstream it changed course and turned back upon itself. Where they planned to emerge from the woods there had once been a bridge, with a tiny hamlet just beyond, but these days the bridge was down, and the river there was an icy torrent, rushing between two steep walls of rock.

On the far side of the river was a tap. And they would need to use that tap. If they could get across.

Daniel looked about him, seeing how the boys were psyching themselves up for the next stage of their venture. It would have been best, perhaps, if they hadn't stopped but had pressed on. That way they wouldn't have had to face things cold again. But then they would have had to face the problem of exhaustion sooner rather than later. Of nerves frayed to the limit and bodies that no longer responded as they should because they were just too tired. Aidan always rested his team as soon as he could afford to. It was one of the reasons why his teams got through and others didn't. But it was not only that. Today things weren't going to plan. Someone was pushing them – forcing them to take paths they wouldn't normally take.

Daniel turned suddenly. He had noticed something but wasn't sure quite what it was. Something peripheral.

Nothing had changed. The ruin was still precisely as it had been a moment before. *But.*

Aidan had stopped talking and was watching Daniel. The rest of them fell quiet. Aidan gestured, giving a subtle hand signal only they could read. *Get back*, it said.

Daniel stooped, as if he were flicking something from his boot, then straightened, throwing a handful of dust at the door.

As the cloud of dust struck it, the door exploded into life, the whole frame loosing itself from the surrounding brickwork and hurling itself at Daniel, its long claws flicking up to reach for him. But Daniel was already diving to one side as Aidan blasted the thing, blowing great chunks of it away.

As the dust settled, Daniel pulled himself up, shrugging off fragments of the mimic.

"Shit!" Johann said, and beside him Christian laughed nervously. They all knew about mimics – machines that looked like common objects but waited patiently, like living mines, to claim a victim – but none of the younger boys had ever seen one. Now, Daniel knew, they would find it hard to trust the appearance of anything.

Aidan was staring at it thoughtfully. After a moment he looked up at Daniel. "Why didn't it attack earlier?"

"I don't know."

But Daniel *did* know. It had been triggered, and not just by the handful of dust he had thrown at it. Whoever lay behind this had been after him. Had wanted to take him out – *specifically* him. And had wanted to do it when all the team were there to witness it.

He looked up at the tiny probe that hovered at the level of his eyes.

Why now? he wondered. *Are you tired of watching me?*

Or was he simply being paranoid?

That last thought brought a smile to his lips. Aidan saw it and frowned. *Don't crack up on me*, his eyes said.

"I won't," he answered out loud, wondering what they'd make of those two words.

"Then let's go," Aidan said. "And remember . . . call any earth-movements. There are burrowers out there."

* * *

"Leon . . . *Leon*! Sit down!"

Leon turned, glaring at Aidan, then, seeing from Aidan's face that he would brook no further argument, did as he was told. Even so, he sat there hunched forward, picking at the floor with his gloved fingers, unable to rest, his eyes twitching here and there as if he suspected the stones themselves to transform into sudden enemies.

Delirium, Daniel thought, studying him a moment, noting how the swelling behind his right shoulder had grown this past hour.

They were crouched on the rocks above the fall, the roar of the water filling the air all around them. Half a kilometre behind them was the bridge and beyond it the tap. But there had been a host of machines at the tap – many more than were usually there – and to attempt to cross there would have been foolhardy, even if they hadn't already lost Benoit in the woods. Aidan had decided to press on along the bank and cross further up, then double back, coming upon the tap from higher ground.

But it was as difficult to cross the river here as it had been back by the tap. More so, if anything, for the current seemed twice as strong and the sides of the ravine through which it passed twice as steep. And then there was the problem of Leon.

Leon stood once more, looking about him. A low growl escaped him.

"Leon?" Daniel kept all anxiety from his voice. It was important now to keep calm. To act as if things were perfectly normal.

Leon twitched round, looking at Daniel, his gun pointed straight at Daniel's chest. Stepping up to him, Daniel pushed the weapon's muzzle aside.

"It's okay, Leon. It's okay."

Leon seemed to shiver. Then, with a small, self-conscious nod, he squatted down again, his weapon balanced across his knees. But his eyes still flicked from side to side nervously, a deep anxiety in every line of his face. From the look of it there were poisons in his bloodstream.

Daniel stepped behind him and bent forward, looking at the swelling. As far as he could see, it now stretched right down his back. Through a crack in the armour Daniel could see how dark the flesh was, almost purple-black in colour, and as he looked he saw something within that darkness move, something small and mechanical, one tiny, fork-like limb showing its outline briefly as it pressed up against the outer skin.

Aidan, standing at the lip of the fall, had seen nothing. He was staring out across the mist-filled gulf, his head turning now and then to consider possibilities.

There was another tap, three kilometres to the west, but they would never make that. They had to recharge, and soon.

As it was they were low on shells and grenades, and the Exit Gate was still more than fifteen kilometres to the north.

Aidan turned, looking to him, then spoke into his helmet. "We need a rope."

"True. But we haven't *got* a rope."

"So how do we get across?"

"We blow it."

"What?" Aidan came across. "*Blow* it?"

"Sure. We can't wade it, and we can't jump it, and we haven't got a rope. But we *could* block it. Temporarily, that is."

"You mean, blow a chunk out of the bank?"

Daniel nodded. "And as the dust settles we quickly skip across. Before the water builds up again."

"You think it'll work?"

"I haven't a clue. But nothing else is going to, is it?"

Aidan smiled. "I guess not."

"Then let's not wait." And, taking a grenade from his belt, Daniel primed it and lobbed it down onto the bank some fifty metres below the ledge they were on.

"Come on!" he yelled, as the others scrambled to their feet, realising what he had done. "Let's get down there, before the whole lot comes down on our heads!"

* * *

"You think this is it?" Aidan asked, turning to Daniel.

"Looks like it," Daniel answered.

There had been rumours among the boys of an armoury, somewhere in the region of Buchenbach, but no one could swear to having seen it. Like much else it was thought of more as legend than true fact. But here it was, a strange bunker-like building, cut into the side of the mountain, below which ran a stream.

And astonishingly there was a bridge. A new bridge, made of solid wooden slats.

Daniel looked about him suspiciously. They were gambling now. The darkness was falling, and Leon was going mad, and . . .

He swallowed deeply. He had thought he was imagining it at first, but then he'd checked a couple of times and seen that it really was so. They had three camera bugs on him now. Three!

Was the Man himself watching? Was that it? Were they putting on a show for him?

He gripped his gun tighter, then looked to Aidan again. "Well?"

"Okay," Aidan said, his eyes briefly uncertain.

Aidan had not wanted to come this way. He'd wanted to go back and take the tap, whatever the cost. But Daniel had persuaded him. After his luck at the river he seemed to have been on some kind of a roll. So why not?

Because I was guessing. And that guess might cost us all our lives.

He did not know why he had persuaded Aidan, but he had. It had been the same kind of instinct that made him turn left and loose off a round even before he saw or heard the threat from that side – a "sixth sense" some called it. The same thing that got him through this living hell each time.

He stared hard at the building, certain now that it was the armoury. And even if it was a trap, they would survive it. He'd take them in and bring them out. And why? Because he had an instinct for it.

Aidan had not moved. Thirty seconds had passed and Aidan had not moved. Behind him the four boys waited in a line, stretched out, a good three metres between each of them as they faced the armoury.

"Okay," Daniel said, "let's go in."

So it's me now, Daniel thought, and wondered at how, in a single moment, command had switched from Aidan to himself.

Confidence, he told himself. *They see it in me. Pure self-belief, shining from me like a beacon. Why, even Aidan sees it and acknowledges it, for there's no room here for uncertainty. No mercy for the faint-hearted.*

Daniel smiled at the thought, knowing that somewhere they were watching him; smiling perhaps *because* they were watching him. Then, unclipping the rocket-launcher from his back, he stepped out onto the bridge.

* * *

"Fucking hell!" one of the operators said quietly as he watched the team cut their way through the guards and into the first level area.

"They don't stand a chance," another of them said, pushing back from his machine, his face registering a kind of awe at what he was witnessing.

All around the massive control room, men were sitting back from their screens, that same look – part shock, part awe – on every face.

"Seal us off," Dublanc ordered, coming down the metal steps. At once the great blast shields came down at either end of the room.

Standing beneath the bank of screens, Dublanc stared, then shook his head. It was true. They were used to watching these teams compete against machines that looked like insects and, though boys died, it was all a kind of game. But now, against human opposition, they were revealed for what they were – the ultimate predators. A nightmare with twelve arms.

"You want me to flood the level with gas?"

Dublanc turned to York and snarled. "I'll have *you* fucking gassed, you arsehole! *Look* at them! Just look at what we've made!"

And now he smiled. Smiled as Daniel reloaded, then blew away another pair of guards.

They shouldn't be anywhere near here, he thought. *That's why we built the Core here between the rivers, to make sure they didn't come anywhere near, but Daniel blew that safeguard away when he blew a path across the river.*

"Pull back!" he ordered. "Let them have the level."

"But the armoury . . ."

One look silenced his assistant.

Dublanc turned back, watching as the team broke down the armoured doors, then went to the racks and, with the care of experts, selected the weaponry they would need to go back out into Eden. Good NorTek weapons with heavy duty munitions.

Pride, he thought, *that's what I'm feeling. Pride in these little bastards.*

And the Man?

Maybe DeVore ought to see this, no matter what happened from here on. It was certainly unusual enough to warrant his attention. Then again, DeVore didn't want to know about failures. So maybe he *would* wait, after all.

"I was wrong," he said aloud, grinning as he looked about him at the crowded operations room. "There was I thinking Daniel was getting paranoid, when all the while he was getting smart."

* * *

The full moon was halfway up the sky when they came to the tap at Breitnau. In its light they could see the towering presence of the wall, no more than four kilometres distant. They had made good progress, but it had been at a price. Johann had been cut by a clipper-fly and Ju Dun had trodden on a spine-beetle. Both wounds would have to be treated, and soon, but most worrying of all was Leon.

Leon was on the edge.

Not only that, but it was night now, and at night Eden exploded into sudden, vicious life.

In an insane mimicry of life, the mind that had devised Eden and its occupants had chosen to stay close to the pattern on which it drew. In the insect world most bugs lay quiescent during the heat of the day, their shape and colour blending into the background, effectively hiding them from sight. Yet at night they'd come alive. So it was that machines that had rested throughout the day, drawing power and energy from tiny solar panels set into their wings and into the flanks of their long, segmented bodies, now buzzed or scuttled about, their infrared night-sights seeking out every source of body-heat.

Yet they too gave off traces of warmth from the tiny engines that powered them, and it was these the boys now depended upon, their guns locking on each bright flicker as it appeared in the darkness that surrounded them.

From the watch-towers on the wall, the guards, looking back into Eden, could mark the team's slow progress, not merely by the sound of gunfire and explosions, but by the display of pyrotechnics that accompanied the team, sudden bright coruscations lighting the sky briefly, then several vivid flashes and, a moment later, the *pock-pock-pock* of an automatic.

And at the heart of that, Leon, his eyes dark with pain, firing at anything that moved, real or imaginary.

The tap was just ahead of them. Through their visors, the boys could see it as a broad glow, constantly in movement where hundreds of the mechanoids clustered about it. The spigot of the tap shone like a tiny spire, poking up from the centre of that glowing, shimmering mass. From moment to moment it would seem to bulge, as if oozing a great blood-drop of light, then pulse, before resuming its sharp, needle-like shape.

Daniel glanced across at Leon. The whole of Leon's back now heaved and pulsed with the burgeoning life within. You could see the glow of the tiny, growing mechanoids through his armour as faint presences, yet where the plate was split, the glow was livid, shining out like a magma flow in rock. Every bug for kilometres around was being drawn to him. Yet Leon, mad as he was, dangerous as he was, had one final use before he was done.

Leon would get them the tap.

"Leon? Leon . . ."

Leon's gun swung round. Daniel could not see his eyes through the visor, but he could sense from his agitated movements just how close he was to doing for them all. One burst of rapid gunfire and they'd all be dead.

"Leon, I've a job for you."

Did Leon understand him any longer? And if he did, would he still respond to orders? Or had he gone beyond that now? Had they left it too late?

"Leon, listen to me carefully. I want you to draw the swarm from the tap. Do you understand? I want you to take them off and then, when I give the command, I want you to seal. You got that?"

There was a grunt. The gun swung away. Leon looked towards the tap.

So you are still in there, Daniel thought, feeling real pity for the boy now that the moment had come. *And maybe you even understand what's happened to you. But it won't be long now, I promise.*

"Okay," Leon said, the first word he had uttered in over an hour. "I . . ." He groaned as the teeming life inside him visibly shifted. "I'll go in."

The others were all watching now. They saw how Leon jogged toward the tap, his body hunched and weary; saw how the glowing mass seemed to shiver with a sudden agitation as it sensed his proximity.

Slowly Leon began to move to the right, and as he did, he opened fire, sudden gashes of pure white light exploding within that general numbing redness. Once more the glowing mass seemed to shimmer. Then, with an eerie silence, it began to lift into the air, a great flickering cloud of red that rose with an infinite slowness to hurl itself at Leon.

Yet even as it rose, a vivid pencil line of light streaked out, joining the bright-lit figure of Daniel to Leon.

The explosion ripped Leon's suit apart. Leon stood there a moment, flaming like a torch, then tumbled forward and lay still.

"Okay," Daniel said, as the brightly glowing swarm fell upon the fallen boy. "Let's take the tap."

CHAPTER·3

WHITE SPACE

Daniel woke to the *crump-crump-crump* of Aidan's rocket-launcher. Ju Dun was bending over him, shaking him awake.

"Bees!" he was shouting. "*Bees*!"

Daniel was instantly alert. "Where?" he asked, getting to his feet and drawing his gun, even as the first of the three shells detonated.

"Coming out of the sun!" Aidan yelled, a note of apprehension in his voice.

Crump-crump-crump.

Six shots left, Daniel thought, his visor darkening as he looked into the sun.

Johann and Christian were at the windows, their visors blacked to cut out the glare of a sun which seemed to be balanced on top of the wall, three kilometres off, like a searchlight beamed directly at them.

"I can't see the fuckers!" Johann shouted anxiously.

"Don't bother looking for them," Aidan yelled back, "just fire into the sun!"

"Aidan's right," Daniel said, his voice quiet but commanding. "Don't worry if you can't see them. They're there all right. Can't you hear them?"

They *could* hear them, even over the sound of gunfire. And once you heard that sound you couldn't really hear anything else – not if you'd fought against bees before.

Bees, the most innocuous of insects, the most *friendly* as far as humans were concerned.

Only these weren't cuddly little honey bees, these were ferocious fighters; soldier bees, ten to twelve inches long; semi-intelligent genetic machines, developed from an old GenSyn patent, which had only one idea in mind – to destroy unwanted intruders.

Daniel blacked his visor, then put his gun to his shoulder and fired blindly into the space directly in front of him, slewing the gun from side to side and not releasing the trigger until the chamber was empty. And still the sound of the swarm grew.

Dead.

He had only ever fought bees once before, and that had been on his second tour. There had been seven of them at the beginning of that brief encounter. At the end of it there had been only him and two other boys. Most teams weren't even *that* lucky.

Daniel unclipped another gun and opened fire again. There was a deep, circular shadow now at the centre of the sun, a dark spot, like the pupil of a golden eye. The bees were still several hundred metres off, but the intensity of the noise suggested they were right on top of them.

"Stun?" Aidan suggested.

"Won't work," Daniel answered. "We'll get some of them, but the rest will simply sit on us until we unseal, then pick us apart."

"Then what the fuck do we do?"

Keep firing, he thought, but he didn't know if there was enough ammunition in the Garden to bring a whole swarm down. Why, there could be anything up to a thousand of them out there.

"Back off!" he ordered. "Into the store room. We'll block the door and sit it out."

The store room had a packed earth floor and a solid stone ceiling. It wasn't big but it was large enough to hold the five of them.

As they began to back towards it, there was a scream.

Daniel cleared his visor and looked. Three of the bees were feasting on Johann. One of them had speared him straight through his visor. Another had landed on his back. As Daniel watched, Johann's visor slowly cleared.

His helmet was filled with blood, but Johann was still struggling, drowning in his own blood!

Yet even as Daniel took in the sight, a flash of orange-black filled his own vision. Instinctively, he ducked to one side, bringing up his gun, a satisfying thud telling him he'd connected.

And then he was inside, Aidan and Christian gasping for breath beside him.

"Where's Ju Dun?" he yelled, as Aidan threw himself forward to secure the door.

A bee poked its upper body into the space between the door and the wall, trying to prise its way around the closing door, one eye swivelling, searching the interior. Its mandibles twitched. As Aidan ducked to avoid it there was gunfire – loud in that enclosed space – and the bee's head was blown away.

"I'm here," Ju Dun said from the shadows, lowering his gun.

Daniel looked to Christian. The boy had his head down, his visor still blacked. He made no sound, but Daniel knew he'd seen what had happened to Johann.

Daniel turned. There was a second door, at the back of the room. They would need to secure that, too. Yet even as he stepped toward it, the wooden panels seemed to swell and groan.

Daniel pointed to the heavy wooden table to his right. "Ju Dun, help me! Let's barricade the door."

He had no plan except to survive. To get through a few more precious minutes. And maybe they'd go away.

Maybe.

The wooden panels of the door bulged again. There was a thud, the flutter of a wing against the roof. Lifting the table, they slammed it against the door. As they did, a solid steel sting rammed its way through both layers of wood, missing Daniel's arm by less than a centimetre, the poisoned tip quivering.

Bees. Of all the fucking luck.

"A hive," Daniel said, turning to look at Aidan. "We must be near a hive."

* * *

Bees were patient. They remembered their purpose. Only nightfall would draw them off, but that was half a day away.

And one thing was certain. They would not last half a day. For the bees were relentless. They did not give in until their purpose was achieved.

While Daniel paced the room, trying to work out what to do, Aidan made a check on what armaments they had left between the four of them.

Christian was slumped against the wall. He had cleared his visor now, but his head was down and he wasn't speaking. Ju Dun, standing close by, was watching him. The young boy frowned, then looked up at Daniel.

"We can't stay here," he said, unexpectedly.

Aidan looked round. He frowned, then looked up at Daniel, his eyes querying that.

"Ju Dun's right," Daniel said. "If we stay our chances are zero. I know them. They'll regroup and attack both doors at once."

"And if we go out, our chances are pretty slim, wouldn't you say?"

Daniel smiled. "So it's heads we lose . . ."

". . . and tails we lose." Aidan too was grinning now. He grabbed up his gun then turned to face Christian. "Come on, lad. Grieving's over. It's time to get revenge."

* * *

The first rocket blew down the door. Christian's flamer took out the dozen or so bees that thought to slip into the gap. Then Ju Dun ran through, spraying bullets right, left and centre. Daniel followed an instant later, picking off anything Ju Dun missed. Aidan, in the doorway, turned, aiming the big rocket launcher up at the main swarm that had lifted and turned toward them, the second rocket exploding in their midst. Then they were running, following a straight line to the nearest building two hundred metres away, forcing the bees to adopt a tight formation in pursuit.

The bees gained on them, step by step. They were almost on them when Daniel called the order and, as one, they turned to face the cloud of angry machines, the four of them in a line and kneeling.

If they were going to die, then they were going to go out in style.

Christian's flamer licked the edges of the swarm. *Crump-crump-crump* went the big rocket launcher.

Only one left, Daniel thought, conscious of Aidan discarding the launcher and opening up with his automatic.

The three explosions punched great holes in the tight-packed swarm. Normally the bees would have spread out more, to lessen the impact of rocket attacks, but Daniel's tactic had forced them into a basic error. More than a quarter of the swarm had been destroyed in those three explosions.

Suddenly, the odds had changed.

Now it was a simple bug-shoot. Get them before they get you. And the gods help the man whose nerve failed.

Christian, beside Daniel, was crying now. Daniel could hear him in his helmet. But he was also shooting like a man possessed and between them they were slowly driving back the swarm.

And then, suddenly – miraculously, it seemed – the bees lifted and turned, heading back the way they'd come.

Daniel's mouth was dry as he watched them, wondering if this were only a trick – a tactic to un-man them. To give them hope then snatch it away once more.

"Hold tight," he said, "they may be re-grouping."

But the truth was they were moving farther and farther away and that hellish vibration – the great pulse of insect wings that had seemed to fill the air – was also diminishing, until, a minute later, it was barely audible.

The day was suddenly quiet. The sun beat down on them.

Slowly the four boys stood.

It was not done with yet. In fact, it was far from over, but they had got this far. And they had survived a swarm.

Daniel looked about him, seeing how the others watched him, looking to him now for their lead. "Come on," he said. "The next tap's just north of here. We can be there within the hour."

* * *

Dublanc rubbed his eyes, then leaned forward, pressing the pad that lowered the blinds about his gallery office.

"Commandant?"

The voice on the communicator was York's.

"Yes, Captain?" he asked wearily.

"I'm sorry, sir, but what do you want to do?"

Dublanc hesitated, then. "We'll leave things be."

"But, sir . . ."

Dublanc brought his hand down, cutting the link, then sat back, closing his eyes. The drugs were wearing off. He would need to take some more if he was to stay awake for the final push.

I could end it now, he thought. *I could throw everything I have at them and end it.*

And what would that prove? Nothing they didn't already know.

He reached down into the second drawer of the desk and took out the box of capsules, shaking two out into his palm then swallowing them down. They'd keep him alert for another twelve hours if necessary. But he would pay for it.

He always paid.

None of his men knew just how much nervous energy he expended on these runs. They thought him indifferent to it all – a cold, maybe even callous, man – and he did his best to foster that illusion. But deeper down he paid for that outward lie.

Long ago, he'd had a son. An eight-year-old named Matthew. But Matthew had died in the plague, along with his mother and baby sister, while he – plain Captain Dublanc, back then – had been on duty on an orbital station above it all.

Now nothing remained of that former life. Only memories. All else – all physical trace of those he'd loved – had been destroyed on those great pyres which, glimpsed from geostationary orbit high above the City, had seemed to fill the land to either side of the Rhine like sunlight glimmering on the surface of a pond.

Dropping the box back into the drawer, he slid it closed, then opened the top drawer, taking out the file on Daniel.

Like much else that was secret, there was no computer record of this file. Officially it did not even exist. And much that had once existed on computer file, had been erased, to be placed here, where enquiring eyes might not see it.

Dublanc opened the file and quickly flipped through the handwritten pages to the latest entry. Then, taking a pen from the stand nearby, he began to write, setting down his most recent observations.

Here too were the maps of Daniel's past excursions into Eden, bright red ink markings tracing the paths he'd taken, the obstacles he'd faced, the friends he'd lost.

They were impressive documents.

He took them out now and studied them a while, wondering if there was a clue to Daniel in the meandering red lines. A *pattern*. Laying the thin, transparent sheets one upon another, he picked them up, looking at the transposition, but there was *no* pattern to it. Daniel had faced each crossing as if it was the first.

Or last.

And this time, well . . . this was the strangest of them all.

He set the maps aside, then took out the last of the sheets in the file. It was a sketch he'd done – a picture of Daniel's face, the visor of his helmet back, those deep green eyes staring out. And behind him two tiny midge-like cameras. Watching, always watching him.

Everything was here. A list of the books he'd borrowed from the camp library. A list of friends he'd made, transcripts of conversations he'd had, a note of his dietary preferences. But nothing that gave a clue. Nothing that told you about the real Daniel Mussida.

For that real self was locked away somewhere. Was buried deep inside his head where no watching camera could see.

Until now.

For something was happening inside the boy. Dublanc could sense it. And sometimes, for the briefest moment, he thought he could even see it, there in his eyes.

A metamorphosis.

Dublanc sighed, then closed the file, rubbing at his eyes once more. It would be a good ten or fifteen minutes before the drugs kicked in. Until they did, he'd lie down and take a moment's rest. Real rest, not the chemical variety.

He stood and walked across the room, then settled on the long bench-like bed at the back, closing his eyes, knowing that York would wake him if anything happened.

* * *

The valley was due north, about two kilometres from the wall. To their left, just above them, was a stand of trees. To their right the ground fell away, until, about five hundred metres distant, it rose again to form a hummock. On top of that was the tap. A platform tap.

There were no buildings here, only rock and scrub and here and there the splintered shape of a tree. The land was rough, untended. Rusting machinery lay everywhere. One could not take a step here without treading on the ruins of past campaigns.

And yet, right now, the valley was deserted, the tap – clearly visible from where they stood – unguarded.

"Flame the slope," Daniel said.

Christian stepped forward and, narrowing the aperture on the flamer, ignited it. As the long tongue of the flame licked over the surface of the ground, the others raised their guns, waiting.

Normally the flamer would make any hidden machines fly up, and they would pick them off, but this time the tactic was in vain. It really was deserted.

Daniel looked to Aidan, suspicious now. Aidan shrugged, then gestured at his feet.

Underground. Of course. That's where they were. Sitting down there, waiting. Burrowers, perhaps, or beetles, or . . .

He didn't like it. The situation made his skin crawl. If he could, he would have turned right round and headed for the tap to the east, but they couldn't do that. They were on low charge as it was. They *needed* this tap.

Only Daniel wasn't sure they could take the tap – not against stiff opposition. There were only four of them now, and though he knew what good fighters they were, it took only a moment's inattention and the odds against them would be shortened dramatically.

No choice, he thought, excusing himself. But it didn't make him feel any better.

"Okay," he said. "If they're going to come from anywhere, they'll come from underfoot. So watch out. And move quickly. Right?"

Without another word Daniel set off, jogging down the charred and steaming slope towards the tap, his armour feeling heavy now, unwieldy.

Every time he set his foot down, he expected something to happen. At every moment he expected the ground to explode in a fury of dark, snapping forms, but nothing . . . still there was nothing.

His heart was in his mouth. There was a pain of expectation in his gut that was indescribable. Behind him, the others tried their best to keep up with him, their heavy armour squeaking and rattling, the grunt of each breath they took sounding loudly in Daniel's helmet.

Ahead of him the hillock rose up, blocking his view. Slowing he began to climb it, the second finger of his right hand aching now from where he'd held it tight against the wire-fine trigger.

Come on you little bastards! Show yourselves!

He climbed up, onto the solid base that surrounded the tap. A moment later Aidan joined him there, quickly followed by Ju Dun and Christian. They were all gasping for breath.

For a moment they simply stood there, their guns raised, scanning the empty valley for some sign of life, but there was *still* nothing.

"What the fuck's going on?" Aidan asked, giving a tiny incredulous laugh. "Doesn't it work?"

Daniel whirled about, thinking that maybe Aidan had hit upon it, but the tap *was* working. As he brushed his fingers against one of the metallic teats it gave him a tiny shock.

"We *are* still in Eden?" Christian asked. "We didn't . . ."

"Charge the guns," Daniel said, with an uncharacteristic impatience. This emptiness – this lack of opposition – worried him more than anything he'd come across, for he knew it was not a chance thing. The mechanoids were not evenly spread, he knew that, but there were not – as far as he knew – whole valleys without any such life, and there wasn't a tap that didn't have a thousand or more of the little buggers crawling all over it.

So where were they? And why were they holding off?

As Ju Dun and Christian charged the guns, he and Aidan kept watch.

"Spooky," Aidan said after a moment. "Give me something to shoot at every time."

Daniel nodded, knowing exactly what Aidan meant. He didn't mind the fighting, it was the waiting that got to him. When you were fighting you could forget and let another, more ancient, part of the brain take over, but this . . .

This was sheer torture.

There was the faintest vibration, deep down.

The swarm?

Daniel listened. No. It was not in the air, it was in the earth.

Aidan too had noticed it and was looking down.

"Are you almost finished?" Daniel asked, not daring to turn his back and look.

"Almost," Ju Dun answered. "Two more guns, that's all."

A minute, then, at most.

Daniel swallowed. The vibration had become a steady shaking. Clods of earth were jiggling up and down on the slope just beneath them. The whole of the platform was resounding now like a struck gong.

As Ju Dun snatched the gun from the charge-nipple and turned, the whole of the bank just in front of them seemed to rear up, changing from black to red in an instant.

Daniel blinked, his mind not taking in what had happened. Then he understood. Ants. Red ants. Millions of the little fuckers. Not big, like the rest of the mechanoids, but tiny.

"Oh, shit . . ."

Christian's flamer roared momentarily, taking out the first wave of ants, but even as he went to spray them a second time, the fuel feed stuttered and went out.

Daniel turned and looked. Ants were all over Christian's back. They had chewed through the feed line. And in a moment . . .

He gave the order almost without thinking, knowing how much of a risk it was, and knowing that there was nothing – absolutely nothing – else he could do.

"Seal!"

And as the word died in his throat, he depressed the button on his chest and the world outside went white.

* * *

Daniel woke with a continuous high-pitched whine in his head. All about him piles of the ants lay inert where the sonic light-stunner had gone off.

He lifted his head a fraction. "Aidan?"

There was a faint groan on Aidan's channel.

"Ju Dun?"

The answer came back crisply. "Here!"

Daniel couldn't see from where he lay, but he knew, without having to look, that Ju Dun was already on his feet.

"Christian?"

There was a moment's silence, then Ju Dun answered. "He's dead. His suit cracked."

Daniel pulled himself up slowly, feeling as if someone had glued all of his limbs very loosely to his torso. He could still feel the shock wave in his bones. The same shock wave that had destroyed the sensitive mechanisms of the ants.

Turning, he saw at once what Ju Dun meant. Christian lay there, a great jagged rent in the back of his armour. And where his flesh had been exposed, it had a transparent, almost jellied bloodiness.

For the best, perhaps, he thought, wondering how, even if Christian *had* survived the journey across Eden, he would have survived living without his soul-mate Johann.

But he didn't give in. Not even after Johann's death. He grieved and then got on with it.

Daniel bent down and picked up one of the tiny ants between his thumb and forefinger. Taking a tiny pick-lock from the neck of his suit – one he normally used to adjust the visor mechanism – he prised the minute shell of the creature apart and looked.

Incredible, he thought, spilling it out onto his open palm. *Such workmanship.*

Shepherd's, he knew instinctively. *This has to be Shepherd's work.*

It was like the jewelled clock Dublanc had in his room – the one with the transparent back that let you see the workings. Only this was much smaller and more delicate and the workings were far more complex.

The whole of Eden was a warped creation. A land of wonders turned into a horror show. And why?

He kept returning to the question.

Why did The Man force his boys through such a violent rite of passage? Why, if he said he loved and cared for them, was he prepared to see them die in so cruel a manner?

Daniel turned. Aidan was on his feet now, dusting himself off. Ju Dun was off to the left, his gun at his shoulder, looking for anything coming in.

Daniel studied the terrain, comparing it to the map he held in his head. The Exit Gate was not far now. Two-and-a-half kilometres at most. If they headed directly north-east they could get there in two hours.

The map. He stared at the map in his head, realising suddenly that there was only one remaining gap in it, there at the very centre of it all.

A gap. Or was there something there. Something that Eden was designed to push them away from.

"Well?" Aidan said, gesturing towards the Gate. "Are we going or not?"

Daniel lifted a hand, signalling that he should be silent.

It was true, now that he thought about it. The nearer they got to that gap, the more intense the fighting became. Why, if the swarm hadn't attacked, they'd have walked straight through it.

Yes, he thought. *And that's why we've got to go back.*

But not with the bugs watching them and sending back details of their every moment.

Without warning, Daniel lifted his gun and began to blast the tiny midge-like probes out of the air. Eight shots later and it was done.

Aidan was staring at him as if he'd gone mad. "*Daniel?*"

"Come on," he said, gesturing for them both to follow him. "We're going back."

"Back?" Aidan asked. "Back where?"

"Back to the very centre of Eden."

"But we're almost out. The Exit's within reach now, Daniel!"

But Daniel shook his head. "Don't you see? Getting out alive isn't the point. If it was, then why send us back time and again? No . . . that's where it is . . . there, in the white space at the heart of it all."

* * *

Things flew at them and scuttled into position, almost like someone was hurling everything they could at them to stop them.

They had come almost five kilometres now, following the course of the river, heading north. Now Daniel took them directly west again, climbing, skirting the Hinterwaldkopf, the river ahead of them. When they hit the river they would go directly south, then turn west again at Notschrei and, taking the old road, head north.

Into white space.

They had no rockets and no flamers, and they were low on ammunition, but they were still fully-charged. If they had to, they would burn their way in.

Aidan's voice whispered in his helmet. "Daniel . . . remotes."

He made no sign that he'd heard. "Where?"

"Across the river. Two hundred, maybe two-fifty metres off. You can see them glinting in the sun."

"You sure they're remotes?"

"They're keeping parallel with us and making no attempt to come any closer. I'd say they were remotes, wouldn't you?"

"Then let's deal with them. We're going into the trees. If they want to see what we're doing, they'll have to follow us."

He scanned the hillside to his left. If there were any mechanoids in there, he couldn't see them, but they'd have to take that risk. The odds were much better if they weren't being watched.

"Ju Dun," he said. "We're going into the trees. Keep tight with us and watch yourself."

He glanced at Aidan. "Ready?"

Aidan grinned back at him. "Ready as I'll ever be!"

"Okay, then let's go."

As one they broke into a trot, coming off the river path and into the cover of the trees.

On the far side of the river the remotes slowed then, reacting to a distant command, came straight across, moving at speed, following the boys into the trees.

* * *

"Fuck!"

Dublanc slammed his fist down onto the table.

They'd lost them *again*!

The thought of it made him nervous – yes, and excited, too. This hadn't happened before.

"Send in everything we've got. And position them where they can't be blasted from the sky. I want to *see* this."

And Daniel doesn't want me to . . .

He knew why, of course. He knew that Daniel had finally put two and two together and come up with an answer. That was the only explanation for what he was doing. And though it was his role, as Core Leader, to stop Daniel, it was – paradoxically – also the *raison d'être* for Eden, if such a thing existed. Daniel was *supposed* to get through. Or someone like Daniel. The perfect killer. The machine to outgun the machines, as he liked to think of it.

Or so he guessed.

And the odds were that one or other of them would have worked it out sooner or later. The only trouble – as far as the boys were concerned – was living long enough to come to that realisation.

"Okay," he said, certain now that his earlier instinct had been the right one. "Send a message to DeVore. I think he'll want to see this."

* * *

There were eyes everywhere Daniel looked. He could make them out by the way they glinted in the sunlight. Distant. Too distant to bring down with any certainty. And they needed every last bullet now.

They were facing north, the sun to their left, its slanting rays casting their shadows long across the slope.

The centre was directly ahead of them now, below where they stood, at the heart of a broad valley. Daniel squinted through his visor then enhanced the enlargement, trying to make out something – *anything* – that might be "it".

Because he *couldn't* be wrong. It *had* to be there.

But there was nothing. Nothing but rock and tree and . . .

White space, he thought. *Nothing but white space*.

"Come on," Aidan said, a strange gentleness in his voice, as if he sensed Daniel's disappointment. "Let's go and poke about."

No blame. No recriminations. Daniel looked to his friend, loving him at that moment. In all of this, he could have had no one better at his side. And if this – this foolish errand of theirs – was it, then at least they had made the gesture.

They began to walk down, Daniel to the left, Aidan level with him to his right, Ju Dun walking slowly backwards, forming the apex of the triangle, some twenty metres behind.

Gunfire. A flash of laser. These were constants. It was almost over, yet still the artificial life of Eden sought to destroy them. They fought it off, slowly expending the last of their munitions, while, floating above everything, the probes looked down, sending back their signals to the watching Core, ten kilometres distant.

"Underground," Daniel said. "It *has* to be underground."

"Yes, but what?"

A *gate*, Daniel answered in his head, but he didn't want to say it aloud, just in case he was wrong.

Yes, and not just a gate. There had to be something else. Something besides a gate.

Two hoverflies, their wingspan a metre across, swooped down out of the sun.

And were gone in a flickering flash.

Aidan lowered his laser and looked about him. It was a fine afternoon. In the late sunlight Eden was beautiful. The grass had never seemed greener, nor the trees so lovely. The sky was clear and blue. Down below, a stream gurgled its way through the valley.

They walked towards it, the peacefulness of it sinking deep into them like a balm.

And then the stillness hit them.

It was as if they had stepped through an invisible glass wall and were now inside.

The cool breeze that had been blowing dropped abruptly, as if it had been switched off. The air felt suddenly heavier, more oppressive. And the sounds were suddenly muted, as if heard from the bottom of great depths of water.

The light here was different, too, as if it fell on them through thick glass, or from some distant past.

Daniel stopped, pointing down at the floor.

Aidan looked, then frowned. "What is it? What am I looking at?"

"No shadows," Daniel answered, turning a full circle to look about him, his every gesture wary now.

Aidan swallowed, the faintest hint of fear now in his eyes. "Where are we, Daniel?"

"In the centre," he answered, his own voice suddenly sounding strange to him, muted. "In the white space."

And then a voice sounded, seeming to come from all sides of them at once: "*Well done, Daniel. But there's one more hurdle to leap. One final test. Turn around. Turn around and look.*"

Daniel turned. There, not twenty metres from where he stood, the earth had opened up. A tunnel led straight down into the earth. A bare, inhuman-looking tunnel, the walls smooth and black like the inside of a beetle's wing-case.

Staring at it, he recognised what it was and felt a cold fear grip him. A nest. He was looking at the entrance to a nest.

"What is it?" Ju Dun asked, coming alongside.

"It's a nest."

He had a glimpse of himself, strung up and still alive, as the hellish little things crawled over his face while others fed from his guts.

No, he thought, taking a step backwards. *No*.

"Daniel?" Aidan was looking at him strangely.

"I'm . . ." *Okay*, he thought, the fit passing.

He shivered, then looked about him. They were under some kind of dome. He could see its shape in the air all about them. But what kind of dome was it that one could simply walk through?

A force-field, perhaps. One that had been triggered by their entry.

As he looked, the surface of the dome flickered and sparked as a bug tried to fly through it at them. The thing vanished as if it had never been. No tiny part of it had penetrated the dome's surface.

Daniel met Aidan's eyes. "I was right."

Aidan nodded.

"So shall we go in?"

Aidan's smile was as of old. "It doesn't look like we're going to get out any other way."

It was true. The only way out was in.

Daniel stared at the darkness of the tunnel's mouth, forcing himself to face his worst imaginings. For a moment or two he hung on a thread, as the wings of the mechanoids brushed against his face and the nano-grubs nibbled at his guts, then, with a determined little nod of his head, he gestured towards the tunnel.

"Okay. Let's see what's down there."

* * *

DeVore stood facing the bank of screens, his hands loosely on his hips, while all about him the staff of the control room stood, their attention divided between him and what was happening on the screens.

Four probes had gone in with the boys, two ahead, two behind, and the bank of screens was divided into four, so that each image lay across a section of four by four screens. At the top left, Daniel, crouched in the narrow tunnel, his visor lit, so that one could see his face in the darkness, moving slowly forward. To the right of that, the screens showed Aidan, also crouching, but seen from behind as he followed his friend in; and beneath that image, that of Ju Dun, standing upright, his much smaller figure fitted neatly into the circle of the tunnel.

Only one of the quadrants was dark. In that left-hand section of the screens – directly beneath the figure of Daniel – something moved, a shadow among the shadows.

"Do you think he knows?" DeVore asked. "Do you think he understands it yet?"

Dublanc, standing just behind him, answered hesitantly, his own misunderstanding clear. "No. I . . . I think he's still guessing."

"He's afraid now."

"Yes."

It was true. You could see it in his eyes. So this was true bravery.

Yes, or foolhardiness.

"Are you a gambling man, Dublanc?"

"Master?"

DeVore turned and looked at him. "What would you say his chances were of getting out?"

"Not good."

Again, true. But Daniel was an expert at beating the odds. A genuine survivor. And he had Aidan at his back, so . . .

"You want to wager with me?"

The thought of it shocked Dublanc. Wager with DeVore?

"Don't you think . . .?"

"I think he's going to make it," DeVore said, interrupting him. "I think that *whatever* we throw at him, he'll walk through it, or round it, or over it. Don't you?"

Part of Dublanc agreed. But then, he also knew what Daniel was walking into. And even Daniel would be hard pressed to survive that.

"A hundred *yuan* he doesn't," he heard himself say.

"Make it five," DeVore said.

He swallowed, then nodded his head. Five hundred *yuan*. Shit! It would clear him out.

Up on the screen, Daniel moved slowly forward, into the darkness of the nest.

* * *

The dart came whistling out of the dark. Daniel heard it and reacted instinctively, throwing himself to the side, his suit thudding against the tunnel wall.

There was a sharp crack just behind him, but there was no time to look. From that same impenetrable darkness came a clicking and a whistling and a fluttering rush of wings.

Daniel hit the pad on his arm, flooding the tunnel ahead of him with light from the lamp on his helmet.

And felt his stomach fall away . . .

Forty, maybe fifty, metres down the tunnel, a seething solid wall of glittering eyes and beaks and claws approached steadily like a great plug of living hostility being pushed up out of the darkness.

And even as he opened fire, Daniel understood. Corruption. He was being tutored in the reality of corruption, of the living darkness that lay behind the light, of the unending physical nightmare of existence.

In the end this was all there was. All else was surface.

The knowledge seemed to sap his will, even as he sprayed round after round into that advancing mass.

Daniel stepped back and almost fell, his foot catching against something on the floor behind him. He glanced down, even as his gun emptied and fell silent.

Aidan was down. The crack he'd heard was the sound of the dart going straight through Aidan's visor. He was dead. Daniel could see that at a glance. The dart had gone straight between Aidan's eyes and embedded itself in his brain.

Daniel looked up, tearing his eyes away from the sight. Just beyond Aidan, framed by the blackness, Ju Dun had crouched, his whole face intent, business-like as he fired past Daniel into the advancing mechanoids.

He turned back. That wall of living menace was now no more than fifteen metres distant. He had no bombs, no guns, no rockets to stop them. In a minute, maybe less, they would be overrun.

They could turn and run, of course, and maybe they would be fast enough not to be caught, but he doubted it. Besides, the twists and turns of these tunnels were labyrinthine, and who knew what lay back there in the darkness waiting for them?

"Ju Dun?" he yelled. "Are you ready?"

"Ready?" The boy laughed. "Ready to die, you mean?"

"No. We're going to go through. We're going to see what lies on the other side of that!"

"Then I guess I'm ready."

Daniel reached across and took Aidan's gun. They were almost on him.

As he swung the barrel up he almost rammed it into a pincered mouth – the mouth disintegrating in a shower of metal as the gun opened up. And then Daniel was inside that seething mass, flailing about, his head tucked down, the gun juddering in his arms as he held it to him, trying not to let them rip it from his grasp.

And pain, and pain, and pain . . .

* * *

"*Gods . . .*"

They had never seen the like. There was a silence in the control room that was a silence of shock and awe and . . . incredulity. All the operators were on their feet now, staring up at the single image that now filled the bank of screens, while DeVore, unnoticed in their midst, looked down, stroking his chin thoughtfully.

The boy was on the floor of the chamber, on his knees, his head fallen forward, his hands hanging loosely at his sides. His gun lay on the floor beside him, where he'd dropped it. Slowly his chest rose and fell, slowly his head came up. His suit was cracked and ripped, and there were smears of blood everywhere, but he was alive. And his eyes, which had witnessed all the horror and come through it, seemed now to see beyond the surface of all things.

Not a dozen paces from where he knelt was the Inner Gate, the polished circle of its hatch gleaming softly in the half-light.

As they watched, Ju Dun walked back into the picture and crouched, facing Daniel.

"Are you okay now?"

There was the vaguest of movements from Daniel. His eyes flicked up and met the other's, then glanced aside, looking past him at the Gate.

"There's something else," he said quietly. "Some final thing."

Ju Dun straightened, waiting for the other's lead.

Daniel gave a little shudder, then, putting his weight on his left hand, pushed himself up off the floor, getting to his feet.

The right arm hung limply where the tendon had been cut. Daniel had staunched the bleeding and sealed the wound, but the arm could not be used.

Not that that mattered now.

"Close," he said, speaking to himself, his voice a throaty whisper. "We must be very close now."

Across from them, positioned some ten metres either side of the Gate, were two tunnels, their dark mouths like the eye sockets in a skull.

Daniel limped across, every movement causing him pain, until he stood at the mouth of the left-hand tunnel. Lifting his visor, he leaned forward slightly, sniffing the air.

Warm earth and engine oil.

For a moment he held himself perfectly still, listening. Then, without a glance at the Gate, he hobbled over to the other tunnel and, standing there, half-crouched, sniffed the air again and listened.

There was a faint, yet distinct whirring sound.

Daniel turned his head, looking back at Ju Dun.

Down there, he mouthed, pointing with his good hand.

Back in the control room, Dublanc, seeing Daniel's gesture, looked to DeVore. "Shall I seal it off?"

DeVore shook his head. "No. Let him find out. He ought to have that much satisfaction."

"But he might . . ."

"*Destroy* it?" DeVore laughed coldly. "Yes, but we can make another."

Yes, DeVore thought, returning his attention to the screen, *but can we make another Daniel?*

Maybe Daniel was the one. Maybe – and it was a big maybe – this was what, unconsciously, he had been looking for.

If he could clone him, if he could somehow use those innate qualities of Daniel's – qualities DeVore was certain he'd find encoded in the boy's DNA – then who knew what he might create?

It was a big if. But he had worked with less before now and succeeded. And after all, it didn't hurt to try.

On the screen, Daniel reached out, steadying himself with his good hand against the curved edge of the tunnel's mouth. And then he stepped inside, hobbling slowly, awkwardly, his right arm hanging limp at his side, weaponless, undaunted, moving down, away from the safety of the Gate.

Down, into the darkness at the heart of Eden.

* * *

The tunnel dipped sharply, then levelled out again. Where it levelled, three great circular holes had been cut into the ceiling.

Daniel stood beneath the first, looking straight up, nodding to himself. Fans. Air extractor fans. That was the whirring sound he'd heard.

Glancing at Ju Dun, he walked on. Beyond the fans the air grew warm – uncomfortably so.

And then, suddenly, the tunnel ended. As Ju Dun stepped up alongside him, Daniel felt something scuttle over his boot. He looked down, seeing nothing, then looked up, hitting the pad on his chest.

In the momentary glare of the light he saw it all.

The cavern was huge, maybe five hundred metres to a side and fifty metres in height. And against one wall, filling that space, its top edge crushed against the rock of the cavern's roof, was what looked like a massive spider, its corpse-white flesh palpitating visibly.

Beside him Ju Dun let out a shivering breath. *"Aiya . . ."*

The floor of the cavern was alive. A million tiny spiders crawled and heaved, carrying eggs backward and forward.

Fifty or more teats lined the side of that great monster, and even as they watched, egg after egg was squeezed from those puckered apertures and swiftly carried away.

The light faded and died.

Again Daniel hit the pad. Again the cavern lit up with a sudden, intense glare.

It was a factory, a living factory. The end walls were pocked with holes. Tunnels, no doubt, that led to nurseries.

Daniel bent down and picked up one of the tiny spiders. It struggled between his fingers, a small, blind thing no more than three centimetres long, a tiny blue pupa clutched between its legs.

He made to put the thing down, then noticed the marking on the egg. Bringing up the magnification on his visor lenses, he studied it, then, with a tiny shudder, threw it from him.

A face. The marking was a tiny face.

He looked about him, noting how many different kinds of eggs the tiny creatures carried, then looked across once more at the bloated mother.

Here it was, then. This ugliness. This meaninglessness at the centre of everything.

Daniel held his hand to his chest, maintaining the light, staring across at the corpse-pale monstrosity that filled the far side of the cavern.

Was this the truth, then – this vision of blind process, this breeder of nullities? Or was it really the aberration he felt it was?

The floor heaved with tiny dark shapes carrying off the eggs. And on each egg a face. The same face, endlessly duplicated. *DeVore's . . .*

"What do you want to do?"

Daniel turned, surprised to find Ju Dun there. For a moment he had completely forgotten him.

"Do?"

Ju Dun smiled. "I've one grenade and a dozen rounds. It might not be enough, but . . ."

Daniel shook his head. He did not need to destroy it. Seeing it was enough. And even if he died now, at least he understood.

This was how DeVore saw things. He had suspected as much, but now he knew. Knew beyond all doubt.

Something buzzed over his head. A probe. Daniel stared at it a moment, then nodded to himself.

Understanding was a seed. A seed to be carried from this place of nullity and nurtured. A seed. To be tended and watered.

He looked back at Ju Dun and smiled. "Okay. Let's go."

PART TWO – AUTUMN 2240

THE SIX SECRET TEACHINGS

"*The eye values clarity, the ear values sharpness, the mind values wisdom. If you look with the eyes of All Under Heaven, there is nothing you will not see. If you listen with the ears of All Under Heaven, there is nothing you will not hear. If you think with the minds of All Under Heaven, there is nothing you will not know.*"

– T'ai Kung, *The Six Secret Teachings* [11th century BC]

"*It is to be inferred that there exist countless dark bodies close to the sun – such as we shall never see. This is, between ourselves, a parable; and a moral psychologist reads the whole starry script only as a parable and sign-language by means of which many things can be kept secret.*"

– Friedrich Nietzsche, *Beyond Good And Evil* 1886

CHAPTER·4

BLOOD AND IRON

Egan sat far back in the great chair, his expression dour, the thumbnail of his right hand poked between his teeth as he thought back over what had happened. Below the broad steps of the dais on which he sat, the stone-flagged floor of the Great Hall of Victory was empty, the colourful banners that lined the massive walls – tokens of a dozen victorious campaigns – obscured by heavy shadow. Hours earlier he had ordered all his servants to leave, the lamps in the hall still unlit, the day's business barely begun. Now the daylight slowly drained from the great window behind him with its panoramic view of the ocean.

Five years. Was that all it was? A mere five years?

Egan sighed heavily, then stood, looking about him at the growing shadows. Five years ago he had returned triumphant from the North-West, the tribes of Washington and Oregon subdued, his treasure chests filled with their tribute. To celebrate that triumph he had built this great castle, overlooking the modern high-rise city of Boston: a brutal place of ancient stone and metal, of twisting stairs and high battlements, but also of high-tech trickery and state of the art defences. Declaring himself "King of America", he had set out to subdue those other parts of his great continent that yet stood out against him.

A mistake. He knew that now. The old Han had been right, curse him. Yet, at the time . . .

Egan took a long breath, then slowly descended the steps. This morning he had returned from the scene of his former triumph, his tail between his legs, his armies thoroughly humiliated, the whole of the Western seaboard lost to him.

Five years . . .

"Master?"

He turned. A small wooden door had opened in the wall to his right. From its shadows now stepped a young man – a soldier; one of those who had made the long, tiring journey back with him from the battlefield in Spokane. Like Egan, he was still wearing the battle-soiled fatigues he had first put on four days ago.

"What is it, Alan?"

"It is your Chancellor, Master. He has been waiting to see you this past hour."

"Ah . . ." For a moment he thought of sending the man away; of making some excuse about tiredness, but he knew it would not do. The lesser men would do as they were told, but Harding was not to be put off. Besides, he had words for Mister Harding; things he wanted to get off his chest. "Give me a moment to compose myself, then send him in. And Alan . . ."

"Yes, Master?"

"Get some sleep now, lad. You, at least, can hold your head high."

The young man bowed deeply. "Thank you, Master." Then he was gone, the Great Hall empty again.

Egan sighed, then walked over to where the first of the great banners hung. The banners of his enemies. Well, now three of his own banners hung in enemy halls. And how many more before this year dragged to a close?

"How did it come to this?" he murmured. "How in God's name . . .?"

"I beg pardon, Master?"

Egan turned. Harding was standing there, at the foot of the steps, his wine-red cloak of office trailing almost to the floor, his grey hair cropped close to his skull. He must have entered the moment the young man left, yet Egan had not heard him.

I must watch that, he thought; *for with such stealth and silence do assassins tread.*

He walked across and held out his right hand, letting Harding kneel and kiss the heavy iron ring on the second finger.

"And how are things, Mister Harding?"

Harding straightened up, his grey eyes meeting his Master's. "Things here are well, Master. I came because I've heard disturbing rumours."

"*Rumours*?"

Harding hesitated, as if searching for the best way to couch what he was about to say, then came out with it direct. "Word is, our armies have suffered a setback and that our grasp in the West has been weakened."

Egan smiled bleakly. He had never liked Harding; had never really trusted him.

"The fact is, Mister Harding, our armies have been annihilated. The West is lost."

Harding blinked, as if taking in what had been said, then laughed, as if Egan had made a joke. "Oh, very dry, Master. Very droll."

Egan stared at him. Didn't he know? Hadn't his spies told him yet? Or did he – as was far more likely – know *precisely* what had happened? If so, was he here to gloat? To indulge in a little *schadenfreude* at Egan's expense?

"There's nothing droll about it, Mister Harding. I'm talking about a million men dead, four times that number taken prisoner. We have *lost* the West."

Again Harding blinked; yet there was no real shock there, as one might have expected. "Then . . ."

Egan looked past the man, focusing on the great gold and black banner that hung over the facing arch. "You are my chief advisor, Mister Harding, so *advise* me. Tell me what I should do."

"Do?"

"The gods help us!" He turned away, suddenly angry with the man; all of the frustration and disappointment he had been feeling these past twenty-four hours spilling from him. "Yes, Mister Harding. *Advice*!"

"But what can I say?"

Egan turned back, his face dark. "You could start by apologising."

Harding gave a laugh of disbelief. "*Apologise*? For what?"

"For counselling war against the Californians, when war was clearly not the best of options."

Harding shook his head, astonished. "But that was *your* decision!"

"Mine?" Egan laughed. "And my Counsellors said nothing, I take it? When the matter was discussed, you did not rush to oppose such a course. Indeed, if I remember things correctly, you practically *urged* me to take action!"

"We but supported you."

"Exactly!"

"I still don't see . . ."

"Don't *see*?" Egan walked back to the man and stood there, glaring at him openly now. "That's precisely what I meant. You *didn't* see. You *didn't* anticipate events. And now we're in the shit up to our necks!" He gave a great huff of exasperation. "You were my principal advisors, damn it! You should have *known* what was going on out there, *known* just how strong they were. But you didn't. Or if you did . . ."

Harding's answer was immediate. He met Egan's anger with his own. "That's totally unfair! You knew everything we knew! *Everything*! We held nothing back. Whatever intelligence we had, you were party to. If I had suspected for a moment. . ."

"Suspected what?"

Harding hesitated, and in that moment of hesitation Egan understood. He *had* known. In fact, come to think of it, Harding more than any of them had pushed him to declare war on the Californians.

"Get out."

Harding blinked. This time his shock was unfeigned. "What?"

Egan pointed to the door from which Harding had come. "I said get out. I do not wish to see you here again. As of this moment you are stripped of your rank!"

Harding glared back at him a moment, then pulled the narrow band of iron from the index finger of his right hand and threw it down. A moment later the wine-red cloak slipped from his shoulders and fell to the floor. Drawing himself up straight, he gave a tight bow. "As you wish . . . *Master*."

Then, without another word, he turned and left the Hall.

* * *

Egan was sitting back on the throne when his wife, Li Kuei Jen came to him. They had not seen each other in three months and had barely spoken in all that time, but now, sensing that something was wrong, Li Yuan's son – Egan's one-time lover, now his surgically-adapted wife, and mother of his three children – paused at the foot of the steps, then slowly mounted them, his long, feminine clothes whispering on the stone.

Li Kuei Jen stood there a moment, facing his husband, studying him, noting the worry lines there on his brow which had once been so smooth, so handsome, then lay a hand gently on his neck. "Mark?"

Egan did not look up. "Hello stranger."

Li Kuei Jen bent down, looking into his face. "Are you alright?"

Egan smiled wearily. "I think so. But things are bad, Jenny. We've lost the West. And now I've alienated Harding."

"Ah. I saw him leave. I wondered what had happened."

"He betrayed me, Jenny."

"Betrayed you?"

"Yes. He knew how strong the Californians were but never said. He urged us to make war against them. I suspect he may even have been in league with them."

"Maybe so. And yet the decision was yours."

"An informed decision, or so I thought. But my information was incorrect. We were told they had four hundred thousand men at most, and those poorly armed. The truth . . . well, we know the truth now."

"Too late."

"Oh, far too late." Egan took a long breath, then. "We must prepare ourselves for trouble. When news of this gets out . . ."

Li Kuei Jen reached out and held his shoulder tightly. "You mean to let the people know?"

Egan laughed forlornly. "You think we can conceal something as big as this?"

"Oh, we must. For a short while, anyway. We need to buy ourselves time. Time to regroup our forces. To bring troops back to the capital from the south and west."

"But how?"

"Call a meeting of the full Council straight away, and demand a full media black-out."

"But the satellites . . ."

"Jam the satellites. Shoot them down if you must. And lie. Give the people news of great victories in the south."

"But there are rumours . . ."

Clamp down hard on the rumours. Use your secret police. That's what they're for. Hold a great banquet to celebrate the victory. And as for Harding . . ."

"What of him?"

"You must reinstate him."

Egan stood, brushing his wife's hand aside angrily. "Never!"

"You must. He's an important man."

"He's a traitor!"

"Maybe so. But right now you need him, to help hold things together."

But Egan wasn't listening. His eyes flared with anger. "I'll make sure he won't talk. I'll arrange an accident . . ."

Li Kuei Jen huffed impatiently. "For the gods' sake listen to me, Mark! You *need* him. So go to him and apologise. Grovel if you must. But get him back on your side."

"I won't."

"You must. Don't you understand? With him at your back, you might just survive this crisis. Without him . . . well, I'd give us all a cat in hell's chance!"

Egan turned back, staring at his bride, then, letting his head fall, he nodded. "Okay. But it won't be easy."

"I never said it would. Oh, and one last thing."

"Yes?"

"You must bring my father home to Boston."

"Your father?"

"Yes. It's time you had a proper advisor."

* * *

Stirring on his silken bed, Li Yuan opened his eyes and looked up at the ornately-tiled ceiling overhead. The carriage was dark, the thick blinds drawn against the desert daylight. The motion of the monorail was smooth and soothing. At times it almost seemed that they were not moving at all, but floating, as in a dream. He looked across. His once-wife, Fei Yen, was sleeping in her chair, propped up, her mouth wide open, her pale, lined face framed by bright red pillows.

America. He was in exile in America, Land of a Thousand Wonders, as the natives liked to call it. A hard, cold-hearted land. A land without ghosts, unless one counted the ghosts of the seven billion Han who had died here in the aftermath of the City's collapse.

Such is my fate, he thought; *to be thirty thousand* li *from home and three thousand light-years from my heart's content.*

He let a sigh escape his lips, as quiet as an old man's final breath, then turned his head, staring once more at the ceiling.

It was not really that he minded the Americans, it was just that they had no humility, no sense of their place in the greater scheme of things. They were like children, delighting in their smallest achievement, and crowing like the farmyard rooster who had never heard of the Yellow Emperor who had once sat on his golden throne at the very centre of the world.

Children. Squabbling children. Maybe so, but they were now the bosses here. And to be truthful, his own kind had been no better when they had been in charge. They had not ruled wisely, and this was the result.

Four months now he'd been travelling, starting in the northern capital, Boston, and progressing down through the great cities of Providence, Bridgeport, Philadelphia, Baltimore and Washington, before moving on to the new enclaves of Charleston, Cincinnati and Louisville. From there he'd had taken the monorail south to the garrison at Nashville and on to the great urban sprawls of Birmingham, Memphis and Little Rock, finally arriving in the southern capital of Dallas three weeks back. Now he was heading south-west across the great desert of central Texas to the fortress-city of San Angelo.

It was all his son-in-law Egan's idea: to get "the old man", as he called him, out from under his feet by organising a tour. "It's time you saw something of this land," Egan had said, as if seeing it would somehow satisfy, or at least abate, the dormant urge in Li Yuan to meddle in events.

Not that I really blame him, Li Yuan thought, stirring restlessly on his pallet.

After all, he has a great deal on his mind, trying to fight wars on three separate fronts while satisfying all the various factions in his own camp.

Yes, he knew how that felt: to face enemies wherever one turned. He even felt sorry for his son-in-law, up to a point. But beyond that?

Li Yuan huffed with exasperation. Why wouldn't the boy listen just for once? Why did he insist on hearing only those who sang his own tune? Couldn't he *see* what was going on?

"Master?"

The soft voice of his servant, Chang, came from beside the bed.

"It is all right, Chang," he said quietly, loathe to wake Fei Yen, lest she begin with her whining and moaning. "I was merely thinking . . ."

Chang gave a small nod, then settled again, sleeping where he always slept, on the floor beside his Master's pallet, his legs tucked under him, like a folded marionette.

Li Yuan let out another sigh. It was the fate of all once-great men, to be taken from place to place and fed and watered like old horses that have been put out to pasture. Yet he was not old. Far from it. He could still have contributed a great deal. After all, who in the entire world had more experience of governing than he? But young Egan would not hear of it. He thought he knew it all, that boy. As if he had invented history!

His arrogance will be his downfall. And when he falls . . .

Li Yuan shivered, then rolled over, onto his side, trying to push the thought aside. For himself he did not fear death, but there were his sons, his grandchildren to think of. If *they* were to have a future, something needed to be done, before Egan pissed it all away.

You must come up with a plan, Li Yuan. You must find a way to make *him listen.*

But that was easier contemplated than attained. Even his sons had been shut out these past few months. Court life had made young Egan suspicious, even, perhaps, slightly paranoid. He listened now to no one but those who had been with him the longest – the old men from his Advisory Council, mainly, and a small coterie of six or eight young men who had been to the Academy with him. *Sons*, as they called themselves. Men who would as soon cut the throat of a Han as listen to one.

Even so, there had to be a way to make Egan listen. If not . . .

If not, the great chain will be broken, and the graves of our ancestors will remain unswept.

He understood now. It was not the loss of a world that mattered – of the power or the territory – it was that loss of continuity, of peaceful succession, father to son, that was so vital. He knew now that they had been right, those grand old men – those T'ang – who had once ruled this world. One had to hold tight to the reins of government, or chaos followed.

Yes, and now they lived in Chaos, like worms burrowing blindly in a rotten apple.

America. Li Yuan sighed, then closed his eyes again, letting the smooth motion of the monorail soothe him as they sped south-west toward San Angelo and the border. *I would as soon be in hell as in America*!

* * *

"Horton? You've a visitor."

Feng Horton, better known to his friends as "Meltdown", placed the weight back on the rests just behind and above his head, then sat up, reaching for a towel to wipe himself down. The gym was almost empty. Only Horton and his bodyguards were there. And Russ, of course. It was Russ who had brought the message.

"A visitor?" Horton asked, towelling himself down, conscious of Russ's eyes on his half-naked torso. "Who the fuck would want to see me this time of the day?"

"Guess," Russ said, his eyes never leaving Horton.

"Don't play fucking games," Horton said, pushing roughly past Russ, not caring if the little man fell or not. "I ain't got time for fucking games."

"It's Harding," Russ said, turning, rubbing at his arm where Horton's hand had made contact.

Horton stopped dead, then turned, his eyes half-hooded. "You're kidding me. Harding? Here?"

Russ nodded. "Says he wants to talk. Private. Just you and him."

Horton took four clear breaths, thinking about it. Russ counted them, watching that hugely-muscled chest rise and fall and imagining the big man in bed with him.

"Okay," he said finally. "But no tricks. And search the fucker, right? In fact, scan the fucker. If this is one of Egan's scams . . ."

"He's clean," Russ said, following Horton as he went through toward the shower. "I frisked him myself."

"I'm sure you did," Horton said, sliding the changing-room door across before Russ could follow him inside.

Russ turned, looking about him at the bodyguards; smiling at them, amused that they didn't return his smiles. At least two of them were gay. He knew that for a fact. But they wouldn't dare admit it openly, as if it might somehow demean them.

And Horton? Russ didn't know. Not yet. But it would be fun finding out. And in the meantime there was this business with Harding.

Now what the fuck could Harding want from Horton?

Whatever it was, it sure as hell wasn't a courtesy call. Something was going on. Something big.

Russ turned back, listening to the sound of the shower running inside the changing-room and imagining the sight of Horton stood there, proud and naked beneath it.

If I play things right, maybe I'll get to stand there with him one of these days.

Russ smiled and surreptitiously slid his hand down over his swollen manhood, giving himself a gentle squeeze.

Now there's a thought.

* * *

There was a soft rapping at the doorway to the carriage.

Li Yuan sat up, then gestured to Chang who waited, head bowed and on his knees, beside the bed.

"Go to the door, Chang. See who it is."

At once the servant did as he was bid. There was the creak of the door, a hurried exchange of whispers, then Chang returned.

"It is the young Captain, *Chieh Hsia*. He says we are approaching the city of San Angelo. He wonders if you would like to join him in the viewing gallery. He says it is a sight not to be missed."

"Ah . . ." Li Yuan stood and stretched. He had known even before Chang went to the door who it was and what they wanted, but it was easier not to let on than to try to explain things to the dark-eyed Chang. "Tell him I'll come," he said, walking across and taking a gold-handled brush from the side. "And tell him to wait. I'll only be a minute or two."

He turned, facing the mirror.

"Shall I summon your maid, *Chieh Hsia*?" Chang asked, hovering in the background, his back bent like an old man, his head bobbing up and down as he spoke.

"No," Li Yuan said, an air of tiredness in his voice. "I have little enough hair to brush these days and it would be a shame to wake her. Let her sleep. I shall have need of her later."

Chang bowed, understanding, then hurried back and pulled the door open once again. There was more low whispering and then the sharp click of heels as the captain came to attention.

Li Yuan drew the brush across his thin, prematurely grey hair, conscious of how narrow his face seemed, how his golden eyes seemed to shine inhumanly in the olive flesh of his face. Now fifty, he had worn a beard these past five years and but for those eyes might have closely resembled the head-and-shoulders portrait of his great-grandfather that had once hung in the Great Hall at Tongjiang.

All gone, he thought wistfully. *All of those wonderful, powerful images. And when I die, my memories of them will also die.*

"*Chieh Hsia*," Chang said, stepping to the side to give Li Yuan a clear view of the young captain standing there waiting for him.

"Ah . . . Captain Zelic. I must have slept longer than I thought."

"Not at all, *Chay Sha*," Zelic answered with his faint drawl. "We made up a lot of time. They opened the Abilene Crossing specially for us."

"I see," Li Yuan said, amused by the man's attempts to pronounce his language. Still, at least he *did* try. There had been one escort who had insisted on calling him plain "Mister Li".

"And what is on the itinerary for tonight, Captain?"

"A banquet, *Chay Sha*." Zelic answered, bowing his head respectfully.

"A banquet. Of course."

Yes, and more inedible Hung Mao *food*, he thought. *Never any attempt to prepare something Han.* Barbarians they were, even his son-in-law, though without Egan they would have been nothing in this land. Simply a few more Chinks. And everyone knew what had happened to the "Chinks" after the collapse. They had been eradicated, down to the last man, woman and child. To *purify* the land.

And so the Great Wheel turns.

Li Yuan sighed, then went out past Zelic, pleased by the young Captain's show of respect. Though young, he was a fine soldier and ran his élite squad of thirty men like an old hand.

"You would have made a good Han, Captain Zelic," he said, liking the young man.

"I beg pardon, *Chay Sha*?"

"Oh, nothing. Let us go. I am curious to see this city of yours."

That much, at least, was true; for San Angelo was a fortress city – one of nine that spanned the thousand mile frontier with old Mexico – and he had heard much about them these past few years. Up until ten years ago there had been nothing here. Nothing, that was, but desert and bleached bones.

And so it would be once more unless the war with the eighteen states of the Southern Alliance was won. Not that he had any doubt that it *would* be won. It was merely a matter of time. Unless, of course, those other wars – with California, and its ally Oregon, and with DeVore in Europe – bled America dry first.

He followed Zelic along a narrow corridor. Like the other three carriages that comprised his mobile "Court", it had been decorated in the Han style and smelled of incense. Past that, they came out into the part of the train that was not reserved for his entourage. The blinds were up and all was gleaming bright and thoroughly high-tech, the surfaces of shining polished steel and moulded plastics in a style reminiscent of an earlier age when the great American Empire – the 69 States as it had been known – had policed an ailing world.

He winced as his eyes adjusted to the late afternoon sunlight pouring in through the windows, then gazed about him at these signs of the new technological age.

And still the lesson isn't learned, he thought wryly. Or were empires themselves a necessity? A gathering-in of the human masses in a single moment of conformity before new growth, new dispersion? He smiled. Once he would have been unable to answer that, but now that his own empire had fallen, he had begun to see things with a clearer eye.

Guards snapped to attention as they passed through into a second carriage then mounted the set of twisting steps that led up into the great blister of the viewing gallery.

Here all was pure light and space. It was like being inside a giant lens, travelling fast above the ochre landscape. In the distance strange rock formations thrust up out of the desert floor, as if they were on Mars and not Chung Kuo.

Earth, he reminded himself. *They call it Earth these days*. Yes, and how strange that was, to name a planet after its most common aspect. Like calling a country Rain because it was wet and miserable.

He walked over to the front edge of the oval blister and rested a hand against the thick plastic wall. The sun was low and to his right, a great flattened ball of gold. *Like an eye*, he thought. And there, some ten or twenty *li* distant, was what looked like a great glass bowl, upended on the earth, a cluster of needle-fine glass pinnacles jutting up from it. The stanchions of the monorail – each one like a huge version of the pictogram, *Jen*, meaning "man" – swept in a great arc toward that glimmering, distant sight, while the rail itself was a thick, dark brush-stroke bisecting the landscape horizontally.

"Is that it?" he asked, sensing the young Captain just behind him.

"That's it, *Chay Sha*. Fortress San Angelo. Population four hundred and fifty eight thousand, including the garrison."

"Impressive," Li Yuan said, watching it slowly grow as the seconds passed. "But what do they do for water?"

"There's a massive lake on the other side of it and a huge desalination plant."

"And food?"

Zelic laughed softly. "That's the beauty of it. It's all self-contained."

Li Yuan turned, looking to him. "Self-contained?"

"You'll see, *Chay Sha*. But look . . ." he pointed out to either side of the city itself. "You see those things that look like studs coming out of the ground?"

Li Yuan turned, narrowing his eyes, then nodded. "Ah, yes. Now what are those?"

"Guard towers. Every half-mile. They stretch from Odessa in the west to San Antonio in the south-east."

"I see. And they're meant to keep your friends from the Southern Alliance out, neh?"

"That's right, *Chay Sha* . . ."

"In case they steal some of the sand you seem to have so much of, I presume."

Zelic laughed. "There are plans, *Chay Sha*. Once funds are available, all of these lands will be opened up again for farming. Until then . . ."

"Until then you put up guard towers to protect the sand from your neighbours, right?"

"It is not quite so simple, *Chay Sha*."

"No," Li Yuan said, relenting, deciding to bait the young man no more. "Nothing ever is."

Li Yuan looked back. The fortress had grown considerably in the past two minutes and he could now discern its details. It had to be five *li* wide at least and three, maybe four, *li* high. Twice as high as his own City had once been. But compact. And surrounding it was desert. Mile after mile of empty desert.

Self-contained indeed. But he still could not see how it could possibly sustain a population of close-on half a million. The other cities he had seen had had vast growing areas surrounding them, tended by robot farming machinery, but this had nothing.

He frowned, then smoothed his beard thoughtfully. "How goes the war, Captain Zelic? Are you still winning?"

Zelic smiled. It had been a standing joke between them these last six weeks, ever since Zelic had joined their party at Wichita. Every evening there was news of some great victory or other on the media, and yet the war never ended, the enemy was never finally defeated.

"You know how it is, *Chay Sha*," Zelic answered, conscious that his every word was monitored. "We are one against three. Our enemies seek to grind us down."

"But you are resilient." Li Yuan finished for him. "My cousin Wu Shih often remarked upon it when he was still alive."

Zelic bowed his head, embarrassed by that explicit reference to the past, when the Han were Masters and the Americans their humble subjects. It was not often their conversation touched upon such matters, but when it did, as now, an area of awkwardness opened up between them.

Li Yuan turned back. The fortress-city was now directly ahead of them, dominating the landscape, the dark rail running directly into it. To their left the chain of guard towers was now less than a *li* away, a line of massive concrete toadstools, their heavy armaments visible even from this distance.

And beyond them a thousand *li* of desert.

"Are there many encroachments?"

"Encroachments?" Zelic stepped across, then, seeing where Li Yuan was pointing, said, "Ah, *raids*, you mean?" He shrugged. "To be honest with you, *Chay Sha*, I don't know. But I shall ask, if you wish."

"It would be interesting to know."

"Then I shall find out for you. Incidentally, the Governor's name is . . ."

"Rogers. Cal Rogers, neh?"

Zelic smiled again. Fine teeth he had. Regular and white, like a well-bred horse. "You are well-briefed, *Chay Sha*."

"There is little else to do, Captain. Unless one actually likes the sight of sand and sky."

"You are bored, *Chay Sha*?" Zelic asked, suddenly concerned.

Caged, perhaps. Frustrated. Impotent, even, but bored? He laughed good-humouredly. "No, Captain Zelic. I am not bored. As I say, I keep myself busy, reading reports, watching your media channels, writing . . ."

Zelic, who had been looking down, now glanced up, a spark of genuine interest in his eyes. "Writing, *Chay Sha*?"

Li Yuan nodded. "I have begun a journal. A kind of . . . oh, what is the word for it?"

"A history?"

"Yes. But a history of myself. An autobiography. I find it soothes me."

"I see."

"I don't think you do, Captain. But never mind. I suppose you barely remember the world as it was."

"I'm afraid I don't remember it at all, *Chay Sha*. I am only twenty-six, you understand."

"Ah . . ."

Then Zelic had been born two years after City America had fallen. Two years after the death of his cousin Wu Shih. Li Yuan sighed heavily. How could it all have gone so quickly? How could such power, such strength, dissolve so rapidly and fade to nothingness?

It was a mystery. A mystery he strove to answer in his writing.

Ahead of them the great fortress had grown to fill the sky. As they passed into its shadow the monorail began to brake, the slightest judder in the viewing carriage reminding Li Yuan of where he was physically. For a moment he had been back there, standing beside Wu Shih and Tsu Ma in Rio more than thirty years before, when he'd been Regent, talking and laughing; he and Tsu Ma standing there studying a delicate lavender bowl and talking of ancient craftsmanship.

"Ingenious," he said softly as he took in the details of the approaching city, noting how the great glass exoskeleton curved outward from its foot for the first half *li* or so, until it stabilised and then curved inward. The tiny blisters of robot gun-emplacements studded that great upward sweep at regular intervals.

There were nine such fortresses, stretching from Laredo in the south, through San Antonio, San Angelo, Lubbock, Amarillo, Las Vegas, Trinidad and Pueblo, up to Denver. Beyond those, to the south and west, was the unclaimed wilderness. It was his son-in-law Egan's ambition to reclaim that territory and reunify the great North American continent, but things had not gone well for him these past few years. The strain of isolating DeVore was telling.

Like most aspiring Emperors, young Egan had been forced to face the fact that the more land one conquered, the more difficult it was to keep. Now he faced enemies not merely in Europe and the North-West, but from the South and West also. Indeed, the emergent power of New California was only one of several potential challenges to Egan's reign, and considering the strain on Egan's forces, one might have thought it politic to come to some agreement – even, perhaps, a treaty – with the Californians, but Egan's response had been to escalate the conflict.

But so it was. So it had always been. War, endless war. As if mankind could not exist without it.

I am well out of it, he thought, watching as a great circle began to form in the solid glass wall directly ahead of them, dagger-like shards slowly folding inward, like the petals of some strange Antarctic plant.

They swept in, following a steep curve around the inside of the city, great metallic stanchions flashing past them as they slowed to a halt.

"We are here, *Chay Sha*," Zelic announced, somewhat superfluously.

"Yes. And there's our welcoming party."

A small group of high-ranking soldiers and officials had gathered at the edge of an immense empty space that was more like a great hall than a platform. They waited uncomfortably, talking among themselves.

Seeing them, Li Yuan knew without being told that his visit here was no occasion for popular celebration.

But then, who could really blame them? For more than two centuries his kind – the Han – had kept them down. Now that they ran things, why should they treat their once-oppressors any better than they themselves had once been treated?

No. They would be polite because Egan had ordered them to be polite. Beyond that they would offer nothing.

"Well, Captain Zelic," he said, steeling himself, reminding himself that, despite all, he was still a Son of Heaven, "let us go and meet our hosts. I would not wish to keep them waiting."

* * *

"So what do you want?"

Harding sat forward, smiling. "I want to make a deal."

Horton laughed. "You know I'm taping this?"

"It doesn't matter. A time comes when a man has to take sides. That moment arrived this afternoon."

"I don't understand . . ."

"We've lost the West."

Horton sat back, shocked by the news. "But I thought . . ."

"You thought we were winning. Yes, and so did many. But that bastard Egan has pissed it all away. Three whole armies he's lost."

"And he blames you, neh?"

Harding blinked. "What have you heard?"

"Nothing. I'm just guessing. What did he do? Shout and scream at you?"

Harding looked down. "He stripped me of my rank."

"So you're no longer Chancellor?"

"No."

"So who . . .?"

"Li Kuei Jen."

Horton laughed. "He wouldn't dare! Why, half his court would abandon him!"

"I'm told he made the appointment immediately I left."

Horton's face slowly changed. "Li Kuei Jen? *That* half-man!"

Harding leaned forward, conspiratorially. "Precisely. Now about this deal . . ."

* * *

"Captain Zelic?"

The young officer got up smartly from his chair and turned to face Li Yuan, surprised to find the T'ang there in his room in the heart of the soldiers' quarters. "*Chay Sha*?"

"Are you *busy*, Captain?"

"Busy? No, I . . ."

Zelic glanced at the open journal on the table beside him. It was a large book with a thick, dark leather cover. Beside it, a quill pen rested in an ink pot. From the dark, wet look of the handwriting on the left-hand page, he had interrupted Zelic in mid-flow. But what had he been writing? A report for his superiors? His personal thoughts on events? Or was Zelic, perhaps, of a literary turn of mind?

In another place and time he might have walked across the room and looked, but he knew better than to do so now. He was no longer in a position of power. Besides, he liked Zelic, and even if the man were reporting back his observations, that was his duty and he could not be blamed for it.

"You want something, *Chay Sha*?"

Li Yuan turned away, his golden eyes scanning the room, conscious of its spartan, military feel. "I hoped you might show me around the fortress. While we've time."

"Of course." Zelic gave a single nod, then, turning to close the journal, took his tunic from the back of his chair and slipped it on. "What would you like to see, *Chay Sha*? The trays?"

"We could begin there."

Zelic paused, alerted by something in Li Yuan's manner. "*Chay Sha*?"

"I thought we might go outside, perhaps, and visit one of the guard posts. See the frontier."

"But *Chay Sha*, it would be most . . ."

"*Irregular*?"

Zelic nodded, then, in a much quieter voice, added, "Besides, I don't think we would get permission."

"And why is that?"

"They would say it was not safe, *Chay Sha*."

"And the real reason?"

"Security."

"Ah . . ." Li Yuan smiled. So his guess had been right. Something *was* going on out here. "The trays, then," he said, standing back to let Zelic move past him.

* * *

Yin Han Ch'in was eating his evening meal when his half-brother called on him at his modest quarters in the south of the city. Sending his wife and children into another room, Han rose from the table, then asked his Steward to send his brother in.

"Well, brother," he asked, as Kuei Jen stepped into the sparsely decorated room, "what brings you here so late in the day?"

Li Kuei Jen embraced his brother warmly. "The truth is, I need your help, Han."

"My help?" Han Ch'in laughed. "Have you debts, little brother?"

"Only one. And that is to my husband."

Han Ch'in made a sour face. "We owe him everything, neh? He's been so generous, after all. These quarters, for instance . . ."

"Forget that. We are to move into the castle, as his guests."

"*We*?" Han Ch'in stared at him a moment, then, in a quieter voice: "What has happened, Kuei Jen? Has there been an attempted coup?"

"No. But there might be, unless we intercede."

Han Ch'in laughed scornfully. "You think you and I can influence events? No. If anything, our intercession would only make things worse. These Americans hate us. They hate everything we stand for. Don't you understand that yet?"

"I understand full well, yet we must try. We know things you and I. Oh, and father, too. We know how to govern. How to ride the tiger. These things were bred in us. Are in our blood."

Han Ch'in sighed. "Things must be bad."

"Bad enough. A million men dead, four million prisoner."

"*Gods*! When?"

"He returned from the battlefield earlier this afternoon. No one knows . . ."

"*Everyone* knows. You can be sure of it. How can you keep a thing like that a secret?"

"We can try. Egan has called a full meeting of his Advisory Council. They are sitting even as we speak. In the meantime he has called for a total media blackout."

"And you think they'll obey him?"

"He has given Colonel Chalker the job."

"Ah . . ." Han Ch'in nodded thoughtfully. Chalker had a reputation for ruthlessness, and as newly-appointed head of Egan's Internal Security Force, he was not known for his restraint in carrying out orders. "Then your husband means to fight."

"You thought he wouldn't?" Kuei Jen put out his hand and touched his brother's arm. "You thought him an excellent soldier once."

"And a pig-headed, stubborn fool."

"You were friends."

Han Ch'in looked down. "Yes. But that is in the past. The things he said to me . . ."

"You must forgive him, Han."

"*Forgive* him? What, and lose face? Never!"

But Kuei Jen was insistent. "You *must*. Think of your children, Han. Is *your* face worth *their* lives?"

Han Ch'in met his eyes, his voice quiet now, subdued. "As ever you are right, little brother. You have an instinct for these things." He smiled, then reached out to hold his brother's arm. "No doubt it is the woman in you . . ."

Kuei Jen looked back at his brother, smiling now, letting the immense pride he felt show in his face. "Let me tell you clearly, Han. You would lose no face in my eyes. Besides, this is our chance to show these *Hung Mao* what we're made of, neh?"

"And what is that, Kuei Jen?"

"Blood and iron, elder brother. Blood and iron."

CHAPTER · 5

HOMECOMING

Stepping down from the cruiser, Daniel looked about him, conscious of how familiar and yet how strange the Camp seemed after all this time.

Massive black walls rose up on all four sides, great circular gateways set into the centre of each, their huge wooden doors studded with brutal metal bolts. The central yard was cobbled, two parallel lines of steel cutting directly across from the North Warren to the Outer Gate, while above all, six great blockhouses – watch towers – loomed, dark and threatening.

Daniel shivered. Three months. It wasn't long, and yet it had seemed an eternity.

And what had they found out about him that they didn't know already? Nothing. At least, nothing worth knowing.

De-briefing, they'd called it.

Torture was another word for it.

The long rectangle of the exercise yard was empty. Or almost so. The Camp Commandant, Schutz, stood not twenty metres away, between the railway lines, two of his senior guards lined up just behind him.

So the bastard was still here, was he?

Daniel smiled. That was one thing about de-briefing. If you survived that you could survive anything, even another spell back here.

"Mussida!" the Commandant barked. "Fall in!"

He fell in, legs apart, hands folded behind his back. After all, what point was there in disobeying orders? One fought when one had to fight, not over such stupid, petty things. But he could see how the Commandant thought even this a minor victory.

Daniel smiled inwardly. *Let him think what he wants. When it's important, he'll discover how things really are between us.*

He let himself be marched, quick-pace, across the cobbles, over the massive iron rails that cut across the yard, through a huge, circular doorway – "Camp Eickel: East Warren" on the noticeboard above the arch – and into the tunnel. And as the darkness closed about him, redolent with the smell of unwashed boys, so the past flooded back.

Home, he thought. Or as near home as he had ever known.

* * *

"So what did they do to you, Daniel? What did they *do*?"

The voices were unending. Whispering voices in the darkness of the long dormitory, wanting to know, always to know, more and more, gloating – so it seemed – on the details of his ordeal.

They tried to break me. They tried to crush my spirit. To destroy whatever it was they had created in me. But they failed. They couldn't break me. They could only kill me.

But they hadn't killed him, and now he was back. The oldest of them now. A veteran of five tours.

"Quiet now," he said, wanting only to sleep. "I'll tell you everything in time."

But they could not be quiet. They wanted to know.

"There's a new boss," one of them said suddenly. "In the North Warren. A boy named Raeto."

"Oh?" Daniel had turned to face the wall, meaning to ignore them, but this was interesting. "What's he like?"

"A bastard!"

And there was laughter at that. To be a "boss" in the Camp, one had to be a bastard. It went without saying. Only the biggest bastards became "bosses". It was why Daniel had never been a boss. Equally, he had never served a boss. After a while the bosses had known to leave him well alone. But a new boss might be different. A new boss might have ideas.

"Is he strong? Cunning? Cruel?"

"All of those things," one of the boys – Tom, he thought it was – answered him from the darkness. "On his first day here he killed a boy. Strangled him in the showers."

"Yes, but he buggered him first!"

There was some laughter at that, but it was uneasy laughter. Most there knew what Daniel thought of such cruelty.

"And since then?" Daniel asked, turning to lay on his back.

"Ten, maybe twelve boys have been killed by him," Tom said, becoming the spokesman for them all.

It was not many, really, not when you thought how many boys died of simple exhaustion, or malnutrition, or disease. Still . . .

"And the Commandant does nothing?" he asked.

"Nothing," came the answer from a dozen or so throats.

"I see."

There was silence, then, "Daniel?"

"Yes?"

"We're glad you're back."

* * *

"Ben? Ben, are you there?"

Shepherd turned from his workbench, surprised. He'd thought himself alone in the house. "*Catherine*?"

He heard her footsteps on the narrow wooden steps. A moment later her head popped round the door.

"I hope you don't mind. I'd heard . . ." Her face gave a little moue of sympathy.

"It's true," he said, dropping the pen onto the page and straightening up to face her. "She's left me. Not before time I guess."

"I'm sorry. I guess it must have hurt."

He shrugged, then went across and held her to him briefly, greeting her.

As she moved back slightly, she smiled at him. "You know, it's really nice to see you, Ben."

"Yes?" He looked at her sceptically, his eyes searching hers. "And how's Sergey these days?"

"Fine. But I hardly see him. He lives his own life."

Sergey was her first husband. The father of her first child, Sasha. Ben and he did not get on at all.

"So why are you here?"

"To see you."

He looked past her. "No surprise guests this time?"

She looked hurt. "I thought . . ."

"What?"

"I thought we might try again. You and I." She looked down. Her hands still held his arms. "I've been thinking. Remembering things."

He waited. After a moment her head came up and her eyes met his again, a question in them now.

"You want me to take you to the bedroom and fuck your brains out, is that it?"

She grinned. "It might be a start. It's been ages."

"Almost five years, to be exact."

A little tremor went through her. "Well?"

He stared at her a moment, then pulled her closer, his hands sliding down her back until they rested on her buttocks, drawing her close in against him. "All right," he said. "But no games this time, Catherine. I take you back, you stay, right?"

She smiled, then, placing her right hand about his neck, drew him closer, kissing him deeply, passionately, while her left hand travelled down his chest until it lay upon his crotch.

For an instant he tensed, as if some final barrier yet remained between them, then, with a shudder, he gathered up the soft fabric of her dress and tugged down her briefs, his movements rough, brutal almost. Freeing himself, he pushed her back against the bench and entered her, thrusting up into her with such violence that she cried out.

But Catherine did not try to push him away. She clung to him desperately, matching each thrust with her own, bringing her legs right up so that they pressed against his chest as he fucked her, her eyes wide and wanton, the moaning sounds she made inflaming him, so that he came quickly, violently, his whole body going into spasm, as she too came with a great groan and a shudder.

Later, snuggled up against him in the big double bed that had been his parents' and his grandparents' before that, she wondered how she could ever have left him. But then, that had been the pattern of their relationship, and doubtlessly she would leave him again despite what he said about her staying for good this time. He said it because he was hurting and in need. But when Meg came back . . .

When Meg comes back things will change. As they always did. For she's his wife. I know that now.

It would hurt. She knew it would. But let tomorrow take care of itself. For now she was happy to be with him once again. However long it lasted.

* * *

Commandant Schutz was angry. And when the Commandant was angry, someone usually got hurt. He looked about him at the crowded duty-room, then brought his fist down hard on the desk.

"How dare they send him back! How *dare* they!"

The rumours had been circulating for weeks now. Rumours that had begun to border upon legend. And now the central figure in that legend was suddenly back here, in Schutz's camp. The thought of what it might do to the carefully-established status quo was clearly too much for Schutz.

The cramped room was packed. Every last one of his senior officers was there, at Schutz's bidding. Above the door a single screen seemed dark, as if switched off, but if one looked hard, one might discern the sleeping figure of the boy.

From where he stood by the wall, to the left of the Commandant, Schutz's second-in-command, Raditz, glanced at his fellow officers, then quietly asked:

"What if he were to have an accident?"

"An accident?" Schutz blinked, and looked up at him. "You mean, kill the little bastard?"

"In a manner of speaking . . ."

Schutz snorted his derision. "And have the Man's agents crawling all over the place? No. Start using your brain to think with, Raditz, not your arse! If the Man sent him back into the Camps, the Man had a reason. Killing him's no answer. What we need is to get him transferred out of here. Personally, I don't give a fuck what happens to the boy, I just don't want him *here*, as *my* problem!"

"Then maybe he could get sick. Real sick."

Schutz seemed to like that better. He actually smiled. "I like that. But how do we go about it?"

"Inject petroleum into his leg," one of the senior guards suggested.

Schutz laughed. "You want to try and hold him down while we do that, Sergeant?"

"I thought . . ." The Sergeant hesitated, then, "I thought maybe we could get one of the bosses to do it for us. You know . . ."

"That's right," Raditz chipped in. "We could make it seem like it was all just part of our normal gang rivalry."

"Excellent," Schutz said, watching his man. "Now you're thinking. Okay, work on it, Raditz. But make it quick. The last thing I want is a fucking hero in the camp."

No, Raditz thought, still smarting from that earlier insult, *the last thing a cock-sucker like you wants is to have a bright light shone on his practices!*

"I'll get onto it straight away," he said, coming to attention and saluting. "In fact, I'll wake that little arse-lick Raeto right now and tell him we've a job for him!"

"Good. Then go to it. I want that little shit out of here before he's had a chance to shake things up. Remember, we've worked hard to get things the way they are. I don't want any of that hard work ruined, you got me?"

"I got you," Raditz said.

"Then go. And Raditz?"

"Yes, Commandant."

"Make me a tape of it, huh?"

* * *

They were woken at dawn and, after a cold shower and the briefest of inspections, marched to the meal hall at double pace. Coming out of the tunnel into the brightness of the exercise yard, Daniel closed his eyes, lifting his face to sniff the air.

For three months he had been locked in a tiny cell, his only escape the daily walk down the narrow corridor to another, bigger room where, beneath glaringly bright lights, they beat him or tortured him or found new games to play with his head.

He had almost enjoyed the last, if only for the relief it gave from the physical side of things.

Daniel flicked his eyes open. He was near the front of the column of marching boys. Up ahead was a pair of double doors. As they approached, the doors swung back. Guards – their guns ostentatiously on display – flanked the doorway, three to each side. That, he knew, was not normal. That was for him, to remind him just who was in charge here.

Inside the hangar-like hall, the stench of cooking hit him like a foul miasma.

Daniel made a face. "Nothing changes," he said, and there was laughter where before there would have been none.

They were all watching him now. Taking their lead from him.

He joined the queue, making no effort to push in as the other bosses did, patiently waiting his turn to take a tray, a bowl, a spoon and a cup, joining the slow shuffle towards the serving hatch.

They saw that, too, and whispered among themselves, surprised by Daniel's behaviour and wondering what it meant, for they were used to displays of power and privilege, and Daniel, surely, was a power now.

Slowly the queue diminished as the boys were served and made their way to the tables. Daniel was almost at the hatch when he heard a commotion at the door.

He turned, seeing at once the source of the disturbance – a small but thick-set boy with a wide, lumpy head – heading straight for him, several "heavies" – their faces familiar from Daniel's previous stay in the Camp – in tow.

Raeto, he thought, knowing it even before the whispers about him confirmed his guess.

Raeto stopped a metre from him, scowling at him, staring at him as if he were a steaming pile of shit and not another boy.

"They said you were bigger," he said, a sneer in his voice.

Daniel stared at him, his face expressionless, taking in the cold blueness of Raeto's eyes, the strange, almost waxy, smoothness of his skin, then turned away, facing the hatch again. Barely a second passed and then he was barged aside, as Raeto and his friends stepped in front of him.

Usually they would have gone straight to the front of the queue and taken what they wanted from the trays. But today was different. Today they were keen to make a point.

Daniel stood there, unmoving and unmoved, staring at the backs of their necks, dispassionately studying the blemishes in the pale flesh – the scabs and pustules that were the result of an unhealthy diet. At least his session in debriefing had had that going for it – they had fed him well.

Daniel looked in at himself. His pulse had not changed. He was calm, his breathing normal. Inwardly he felt clear and still, like a cool, dark pool at the bottom of a deep, deep well.

Good, he thought, pleased that he had come this far.

"You settling in, new boy?" Raeto asked, his back arrogantly turned. "You got a nice soft cushion for your head?"

There was a moment's silence. Raeto's head turned the tiniest amount.

"Maybe I come visit you," he said. "Maybe I come use your arse, eh?"

You can certainly try, Daniel thought, but outwardly he gave no sign that he had even heard the other boy.

"Yes," Raeto said, with a great deal of unpleasant insinuation. "I think you make a good cushion for *my* head!"

There was laughter at that from his lieutenants, but Daniel could sense how uneasy they were, having to stand there with their backs to him as the queue went down. It was clear they'd prefer to see what Daniel was up to. But Raeto was keen to give his machismo full rein.

"Maybe I let you lick me, eh? You could be my cleaner. You got nice long tongue, eh, boy?"

At any other time that would have been a step too far, for there were boys in the camp – runts and weaklings – who would provide just that service for a boss: who would suck his cock and lick his arse clean for him, too. But the insult washed over Daniel.

He looked out over the rows of tables, his gaze casual. You could almost feel the expectation in the hall. They wanted him to fight – to put down this smug little shitball once and for all. But what was the point? It would change nothing. Not while The Man was still in charge.

He'd learned that. One could fight all the little shitballs in the universe – could put every last one of them in the morgue – and there would still be The Man.

And one could not fight The Man.

Raeto's head was almost half turned now. He wanted to see what Daniel was doing – to see what expression was on his face – but pure machismo did not allow him to turn round. He had set up the rules of this encounter, but Daniel had not played by the rules.

Seeing it, Daniel almost – *almost* – laughed.

Insults. He knew a lot about insults these days. But an insult was not an insult unless it contained a grain of truth, and all in that hall knew that Raeto had as much chance of getting Daniel to be his "cleaner" as Schutz had of getting The Man to give him head.

"What's the matter, new boy?" Raeto said, the tiniest hint of desperation in his voice. "Too *scared* to speak?"

Again the shot was wide. Daniel looked to the boy beside him. The young lad – who was eight or nine at most – was hunched into himself, fearing a sudden explosion of activity at any moment.

Daniel smiled. "Hungry?" he asked.

The boy, afraid to make any comment, even the most innocuous, gave the tiniest of nods.

"Me, too," Daniel said, for all the world as if Raeto and his henchmen weren't there. "A few spoonfuls of camp food and I'll be feeling like my old self again."

Raeto had stiffened, listening, trying to make out whether there was an insult in the words. Then, his impatience finally too much for him, he turned, facing Daniel again.

"You arrogant sack of shit!"

Daniel looked to him, his expression bland. "If you say so."

Raeto laughed, as if he'd finally scored a hit; but then his eyes narrowed. "If *I* say so? Are you *challenging* my word?"

"I wouldn't dream of it," Daniel said urbanely. "You seem to know how things are."

Raeto had begun to nod, but again he caught himself and frowned. Was Daniel taking the piss? He tilted his head slightly, his eyes almost closed as he spoke again. His whole body was aching for a fight. But first there was this ritual to be gone through.

"You'll suck my cock, then?"

"And lick your arse? Sure . . ."

But there was the faintest smile on Daniel's face now.

Raeto tensed. Behind him his little crew of thugs bristled, ready for action.

"Tonight," Daniel said nonchalantly. "In your rooms. Oh, and Raeto . . . make sure it's nice and dirty for me, eh?"

* * *

There was a long silence at the table after Raeto and his boys had gone. Finally, Tom looked up from his bowl and spoke.

"Are you really going to go there, Daniel?"

Daniel stopped spooning up his soup and looked back at the boy. "Sure."

"And are you really . . . you know?"

But Daniel didn't answer. Daniel looked back at his bowl and began to spoon up the foul, thin liquid once more, while round the table the boys looked on with troubled eyes.

* * *

Ben brought her breakfast in bed, on a tray, with tea in the finest china and a single red rose in a tiny glass vase.

Lonely, she thought, looking at him as he sat on the edge of the bed, looking out through the open casement window. *Who'd have thought you would be lonely?*

But so he was.

She tucked in, eating with an appetite she had forgotten she possessed.

It's the air here, she reminded herself. *It always does this to me.*

And Ben, too. He had always known how to excite her, more than any other man. Even Dogo. And Dogo had been a warrior.

Of all her husbands and lovers, Ben had always been the strangest. No man had ever come so close to her, no, nor remained so far apart. Split, he was. As if he were two men, not one. There was this gentle, kindly man. And then there was the other – the violent psychopath with the camera eyes and the ability to mimic anything and everything.

No man could be more cruel. No, not even DeVore when it came down to it, and that was saying a great deal indeed. Strange, then, that they had become allies these past few months.

"Ben?"

He turned, looking at her, a faint smile on his lips. "Yes?"

"Why did Meg leave?"

He stared at her a moment, then stood and, turning away from her, walked out of the room. She heard his footsteps clumping heavily down the spiral steps, then he was gone.

Setting the tray aside, she got up and went over to the window.

Ben was outside in the morning sunlight, striding down the long garden, heading for the fields beside the bay.

"Wrong question," she said quietly, annoyed with herself – with that damned curiosity of hers. "Wrong sodding question."

* * *

Ben returned two hours later, his hair slicked back.

"Ben? Are you all right?"

He nodded. "I went swimming. Down in the cove. I . . ." He sat down on the other side of the table to her, facing her. "I'm sorry. It's hard, you know. I didn't think anything in life would be hard, but living without her is . . . well, impossible. I didn't think I needed anyone, but I do. She's my twin, Catherine. My soul. Without her . . ."

It was not what she wanted to hear, but she could not help but listen.

"She left," he said, looking down, "because of DeVore."

"Because you agreed to work with him, you mean?"

"Yes."

"Then . . ."

"Then *what*?" He met her eyes, defiant now. "I cannot *limit* myself, Catherine. Not the way *she* wanted me to limit myself."

"And yet you cannot live without her."

"No."

"Then you must choose."

He shook his head. "It isn't that easy."

"Only because you won't make it so."

"No!" He stood, real anger in his face. "It isn't easy because I don't *have* a choice! Can't you *see* that, Catherine? This is how I am, how I was made! God help me, I wish it were otherwise, but it isn't!"

She stared at Ben, astonished. He was usually so controlled, so absolutely lacking in emotion. To see him otherwise was a real shock.

And then she understood.

Meg. It's Meg who channels that, and without her . . .

It was a revelation. She had always seen Meg as a mother-substitute – as cook and mender, elder sister and lover. But she was more than that. Much more.

But then she should have known, for when Ben used words he did not use them flippantly as others did. *My soul*, he'd said. And truly that was so. Without her he was an empty shell. A nothingness. No wonder he was half insane.

"Where is she?"

"What?" Ben stared at her, half distracted it seemed.

"Meg. Where has she gone?"

He gave a little shrug. "I don't . . .

"You don't *know*?" Then, noting something odd in his manner, she understood. "You *do* know. You know *precisely* where she is, don't you?"

* * *

DeVore stood at the sink, naked, washing the blood from his hands.

Behind him, his head lolling forward, his arms hanging limp at his sides, the boy's eyes stared out into the great nothingness as he swung on the wire. His flesh was pallid, bloodless. Beneath him a drain was set into the tiled floor of the cell, the black metal grid almost blocked by congealed blood.

In the far corner of the cell, in shadow now, rested the saddle, a duplicate of that which Shepherd now owned, its smooth black and white seat smeared in the blood and faeces of the boy.

DeVore pulled the towel down from the rack on the wall then turned. His penis was still hard, almost painfully erect, and for a moment he thought of cutting the boy down and playing the game again. But there was little enjoyment where there was no pain, no crying out for mercy.

He smiled and went across, taking the boy's limp arm and pulling him round, then let go.

The body swung back and forth, imitating life.

He studied the boy a moment, as calmly and dispassionately as one might study the carcass of an animal, hanging in the window of a butcher's shop, then he nodded to himself and walked across to get his gown from the peg.

Stepping stones, they were, all of them. Bridges to be burned, like all the other bridges to his past. For his element was the future.

Soon now, he thought, renewing the promise to himself. Very soon and he would have done with all this. With men and their petty concerns. For this game was almost at an end. A new game called him. A bigger, better game, played with galaxies and whole new species of adversary.

Challenges. He needed challenges.

Yes, he thought, *and I need to get rid of this damn erection!*

He strode to the door and, pulling it open, gestured to one of the guards to go and clear up. Then, knowing he would not be able to settle to his work until he was purged of the sickness in his blood, he began to run. It was time he had the woman again. Time to give it to her up the arse.

* * *

Raeto stood as Daniel came into the room, clearly surprised. He had thought he would have to send his men to get Daniel – to drag him kicking and screaming to his fate.

"You wanted me?" Daniel said, looking to Raeto only, as if there were no others seated about that tiny cell.

Raeto looked past him. Boys crowded the corridor outside, looking on, but they were *his* boys, *Raeto's* boys. Daniel was alone, unarmed.

Glancing at his chief enforcer, Raeto came across the room until he stood face to face with Daniel. He was smaller than Daniel, but much broader at the shoulder. And besides, size didn't count much, so he'd discovered. It was all a matter of will.

The needle was prepared. It waited in the back room. When he was ready they would use it on Daniel, like Schutz wanted. But only when he was done with him.

Raeto studied Daniel a moment, trying to see if there was anything there in his eyes he should be warned of, but Daniel seemed passive, utterly compliant.

Maybe they beat it out of him, Raeto thought, surprised that it had been this easy. *They say they can destroy the very spirit of a man in there.*

"I had a good shit," Raeto said, smiling up into Daniel's face. "A nice messy one."

There was unpleasant laughter within the room. Outside, in the corridor, a low murmur ran through the watching boys.

Daniel had his hands at his sides, palms open. He seemed relaxed. "You want to show me?"

There was a flicker of uncertainty in Raeto's eyes, and then he smiled again. This was *his* room. If Daniel tried anything, *his* boys would sort the fucker out.

Unfastening the cord at his waist, he let his trousers fall, then turned. The stench of stale faeces wafted up at Daniel.

"You kept your promise, I see," Daniel said, his eyes taking in the sight. "Now let me keep mine . . ."

The movement was too quick for the watching boys. One moment Raeto was standing, grinning broadly at the thought of his triumph, the next he was lying face down on the cell floor, dead.

There had been a resounding snap.

Daniel was crouched now, facing the other boys, in the crane stance, his hands raised and tensed, ready to strike.

There was a long, low noise of breaking wind from the corpse, but no one laughed. Slowly Daniel backed towards the door. And still no one moved. Now that Raeto was dead, they had no reason to fight Daniel.

As Daniel stepped out into the corridor, the crowd gave way before him, letting him pass, boys touching his arms and back lightly, as if to win good fortune from the touch.

Daniel had seen to him. Daniel had killed the little bastard.

But Daniel himself felt nothing. Nothing but a sense of utter waste.

* * *

Catherine paused by the gate, pulling her cloak tighter about her. There was a cold wind blowing from the sea. The sky was grey and overcast.

So bleak a place, she thought, staring at the small clifftop cottage, and wondering why Meg should have chosen here of all places to run to. It was not even as if it was pretty – at least, not in the way Landscott was pretty. The grey slate roof was discoloured by orange lichen and the grey stone walls were bare, unpainted.

The wood of the gate was weather-worn and cracked, the stone path that led up to the front door covered in weeds that had poked up from beneath the earth.

So desolate, it seemed. Unexpectedly so.

She looked up at the two small quarter-pane windows that sat above the door, to either side of it, but there was no sign of life. The curtains were drawn, as if the house slept.

For a moment she was tempted to leave it – to turn about and go home. Then, steeling herself, knowing that it was important, she pushed the gate aside and hurried up the path.

She lifted the old brass knocker and let it fall. The sound seemed hollow, the silence from inside the house profound.

What if she's not here?

The wind whistled tunelessly through the porch, the sound of breaking waves just audible above it. And over everything the call of gulls, their echoing cries sending a tiny shiver up her spine.

Such a plaintive sound, she thought, turning to watch one climb the sky above the cliff, seeing how it struggled against the wind, its frail wings bending and turning in the changing air currents.

The sudden scent of woodsmoke broke into her reverie.

"Catherine?"

She had not heard the door open. Meg stood just inside the narrow hallway, in shadow. Beyond the hallway was a galley kitchen. Through its open door Catherine glimpsed a fire burning in a tiny grate.

"Meg . . ."

"You'd better come in."

She stepped inside, then followed Meg through, into the tiny kitchen, taking the seat Meg offered her.

All was orderly, she noted. All spick and span and organised. Not like her own apartment. She looked up at Meg, noting how the other woman was watching her, and smiled. But Meg seemed hostile. Her face was set, unsmiling.

"How did you find me?"

"I . . ."

Meg leaned towards her, strangely aggressive. "Even Ben doesn't know where I am."

Catherine laughed. "Of course he does. He watches you."

"Watches . . ." Meg stood up abruptly and went to the window, throwing it open, her eyes searching for something. There was a moment's tension in her and then she seemed to slump, as if defeated. Her head fell forward, her chest rising and falling agitatedly. Then she turned, looking back at Catherine, angry now.

"He has no right!"

"Maybe not, but . . ."

"Tell him to leave me alone. Hasn't he done enough already?"

"He needs you, Meg."

Meg shuddered, a fire of indignation burning in her. "No. Let some other poor bitch cook his meals and keep his bed warm. I did it long enough."

"I didn't mean that."

"Then what do you mean?"

"I mean . . ." Catherine closed her eyes momentarily. "It's like there's only half of him there."

"The self-indulgent, selfish half, you mean?"

Catherine hesitated, then nodded.

"So what's new?"

Catherine blinked, surprised by Meg's harshness. She had expected something other than this. "He hurt you, didn't he?"

"That's not the point. He always hurt me. Always. It's hurting others I won't put up with. When he started working with that man . . ."

"DeVore?"

Meg nodded.

"He won't stop, you know. Even if it kills him. He won't be told what to do. Not by you or anybody."

"I know."

"But if you love him . . ."

Meg exploded. "What in God's name has that to do with anything!"

Catherine looked down, then put out her hands towards the fire's warmth. "I just thought you might be a check on Ben. A brake against the excesses of his nature."

Meg was silent. The crackle of the fire and the wind from outside – for a moment these were the only noises in the world. Then she sighed.

"I can't help you, Catherine. I can't."

"But he needs you."

"Maybe so, but he made his bed, now he must lie in it."

"And that's your final word?"

Meg looked up, staring directly at the distant camera eye. "That's my final word."

* * *

"What's the matter, Daniel? Don't you want to run things here? Don't you *want* to be a boss?"

The voice came out of the darkness of the dormitory.

"Go to sleep, Tom."

"Don't you?" another voice said, taking up the question. "Things would be better here if you did."

"Yes," someone else said, "things would be different if you were boss."

Daniel sighed inwardly. If he had thought they would leave him alone, he had been wrong. He had tried to avoid trouble – to live a quiet life – but they wouldn't let him. He was a hero now, and every little prick and cocksucker wanted either to raise him up or pull him down.

"Let me sleep," he said, but he knew they would not leave him be until they had an answer. They were all too excited. Word of what he'd done to Raeto had gone around the camp in minutes. The boys had talked of nothing else all evening.

Schutz, it was said, was livid.

He would not, perhaps, have minded so much, had he not known now just how *diseased* it all was. Yes, and he knew now who that came from.

He makes us in his image.

"Daniel?"

"Yes?"

"*Why* won't you be boss?"

He hesitated, then, knowing that they would not be satisfied until he had explained it to them, turned and sat up.

"Tom, get a light. I need to talk to you."

Candles were brought and lit. In their faint, flickering glow, they gathered about Daniel. A hundred, maybe two hundred boys in all. Orphans, every last one of them, taken from the streets by The Man and brought here to the camp.

Daniel took a long breath, then, looking about him, began. "Listen to me carefully. Things are not as you think they are. It's all an experiment . . ."

"An experiment?" Tom asked, his blue eyes staring moistly up at Daniel in the candle-light.

"Yes. An experiment in enhanced evolution." He raised a hand to fend off questions. "I know you don't have a clue what I'm talking about. Evolution. It's a word from before the Time of Cities. They told me. In the cells. They . . . *showed* me what was happening. You see, it's make-or-break time, and not just in Eden. The whole of mankind is being tested – broken on the wheel. And The Man . . ."

Daniel shivered, remembering suddenly his one and only meeting with The Man.

"The Man is using us."

He could see from the blank stares they were giving him that they didn't understand.

"*Using* us?" Tom asked.

Daniel looked down. How, in a word or two, could he express the depth of cynicism he had sensed, the unfathomed malice he had glimpsed in The Man's dark eyes? How could he possible articulate in words that would bring it alive to their imaginations, just how vile The Man's great scheme for them was?

Using. That was all The Man was capable of. Not sharing or giving or enhancing – not in any sense other than in making a weapon better – but *using*. The same way Raeto would have used him.

Cleaners. The Man was making them all into a race of "cleaners" – of little arse-lickers and cock-suckers. Using them. Debasing them in the name of testing them. Humiliating them. Making their lives living hells.

Daniel stared out at the sea of expectant faces, then shrugged. "Okay," he said. "If that's what you want, I'll be boss here. But on my terms, right?"

"*Right!*" came the resounding answer as several hundred faces broke into a single beaming smile.

* * *

"Commander Horacek!" Schutz said, beginning to get up out of his seat, shocked to see his Commanding Officer there in the doorway of his office. "If I'd *known* you were coming . . ."

"You'd have shat yourself."

Horacek looked about him disdainfully, his black and melted face registering disgust. "I hear you've had an unfortunate incident."

Schutz swallowed. Who'd told him? Who, among his officers, was the little sneak? Or were they *all* in Horacek's pay?

"I was just making the report," Schutz began, gesturing vaguely at the papers on his desk.

"You should have called me, *at once*."

Schutz bowed his head. "Yes, sir."

"Is the boy all right?"

"The boy?"

"Mussida. Did any harm come to him?"

Schutz blinked. Just how much did Horacek know? "No, I . . ."

"Were you *behind* it, Schutz?"

Schutz glanced up. His senior staff were behind Horacek, filling the corridor outside, witnessing his humiliation.

"No, sir."

"I think you *were* behind it. I think you thought to yourself that if Mussida had an accident then maybe he'd be moved out of here and then he'd no longer be your responsibility, that's what *I* think."

Someone *had* told him. Told him everything. Raditz, perhaps. Indeed, now that he thought of it, Raditz had probably set him up.

"No, sir," he said, knowing that he had no choice now but to bluff it out.

"No?" Horacek sat down on the edge of the desk. The very proximity of him made Schutz's flesh creep. Horacek was like something that had crawled out of an oven. "Are you sure about that, Commandant?"

Was this a test of some kind? Did Horacek have a tape of that earlier meeting? Schutz weighed things up, then shrugged.

"I may have . . . I don't know . . . *suggested* my feelings on the matter. But I gave no order. Mussida was in *my* charge. He was *my* responsibility."

"Precisely."

Schutz felt himself squirm under Horacek's direct gaze.

"Do you realise what *care* The Man has put into raising the boy?"

Schutz kept his thoughts on that to himself. If *caring* was trying to have the boy killed five times, then The Man cared hugely for the boy.

"Yes, sir."

"Then I'd say that, at the very least, you have been . . . *negligent*, Schutz."

The word was like a slap. No, it was worse than that – it was like a cold hand closing over his exposed testicles. Schutz felt suddenly very very vulnerable. Horacek was so utterly unpredictable.

"Well?" Horacek prompted.

If he said no, that would be a contradiction of Horacek, and Horacek would not like it. But if he said yes, it would be an admission of his negligence, and neither Horacek or The Man liked any failings in their inferiors.

It was a classic no-win situation.

Schutz chose what he thought was the least bad of his options.

"No, sir."

Horacek's silence was awful. He got up and came around the desk, until he stood at Schutz's shoulder. Schutz could feel his breath on his neck – could smell the foul odour of its corruption.

"I . . ."

Horacek's right hand clamped about his throat, choking off the word. An instant later, Horacek's left hand joined it, the two hands attacking Schutz's windpipe with the ferocity of two wild animals.

Schutz's arms went out, feebly trying to reach behind him, a strange sound somewhere between a wheeze and a howl of pain escaping his grimacing mouth. His eyes bulged – literally bulged – in his face and his whole head seemed to go a strange, bruised colour. And still Horacek squeezed.

In the doorway, Schutz's staff looked on, both fascinated and horrified by the sight. And as Schutz fell lifeless to the floor, a collective shudder went through them, as if they had all just orgasmed at once.

Horacek looked across, businesslike again.

"Raditz, you're in charge now."

Raditz snapped to attention. "Sir!"

"And Raditz?"

"Sir?"

"Remember what you've seen, neh?"

* * *

There was meat in the soup the next day, little chunks of it.

Daniel took a spoonful of the steaming broth, then spat it out, pushing the bowl away abruptly. At once everyone at the long table stopped eating and stared at Daniel.

"Out," he said, distractedly, as if talking to himself. "We've got to get out, onto the streets. We've got to *see* what's going on."

"They won't let you," one of the older boys said.

"No?" Daniel said, meeting the boy's eyes defiantly, forcing him to look away. "Then Raditz can tell me that to my face, can't he?"

He stood, looking about him. "Who's coming with me?"

At that many looked down, not wishing to meet his eyes, yet Tom and several others – the older boy among them – got to their feet.

"Well?" Daniel asked, turning to look about the dining hall. "Anyone else? Or are you all shit-scared?"

Slowly, one by one, they got to their feet, until every last boy in the dining hall was standing.

There were no guards – the boys guarded themselves at meal-times – yet someone in the kitchens, seeing what was happening, pushed through the back door and hurried off, meaning to warn Raditz.

Thus it was that, as Daniel and the boys approached the main Guard House, Raditz and his men stepped out. They were armed with automatic rifles.

Daniel ignored the guns and walked straight up to Raditz. "Things have got to change."

Raditz laughed. "Says who?"

Daniel narrowed his eyes. "You can listen or you can fight. But if you fight, you'll lose. And then you'll all be dead. So what's the point?"

Raditz blinked. He had not expected Daniel to threaten him directly. This was a new Daniel, one he hadn't come across before.

"Okay," he said. "Talk."

"You've got to let us go outside."

"Outside?" Raditz shook his head. "The Man won't allow it."

"Ask him. Ask Horacek to ask him."

"But why?"

"Because it's time we did the job we were trained for."

This amused Raditz. He hadn't known they were training them for anything – unless it was as test-fodder for the new-generation mechanoids. Their job was to dig holes and cut rock, that was all.

"And what's that?" he asked, amused now.

"To patrol his City. To be his shock-guards when the time comes."

"He's got guards."

"Not like us."

That's true, Raditz mused. *Even the most corrupt of The Man's guards weren't as corrupt as these boys.*

Yes, but it was still strange that Daniel should be the one to make this request. Unless he had really changed. And who knew what was possible? He, for one, had not expected to see Daniel come out of de-briefing alive.

"Patrols?"

"That's right," Daniel said. "Six to a patrol. Eight hours, then back inside."

"And what's to *make* you come back?"

"These," Daniel said, tapping the back of his head where the wire was. "Oh, don't try and deny it, Raditz. I know what's in there. I've seen it dozens of times."

Yes, Raditz thought. *I bet you have.*

And in his mind he had the picture of a head, the skull half shot away, the silver threads of the implanted wire showing clearly against the grey of the brain matter.

"Okay," he said, "I'll ask."

"Good," Daniel said. "And while you're at it, Raditz, you can tell your cook something for me."

"Oh, what's that?"

"Tell him Commandant Schutz tastes like shit."

* * *

DeVore was amused. "Patrols?"

"Yes, sir. He claims they'd do it better than our guards."

"And so they would. But do we want them to?"

Horacek shrugged. "I don't see what harm it would do. Maybe it would even keep some of those golden-eyed cunts in line."

"Have they been troubling you, then, Horacek?"

"No, sir. But they give me the fucking shivers."

"Oh?" DeVore turned, intrigued. "I wouldn't have thought anything gave *you* the shivers, Josef."

"Oh, they don't scare me, if that's what you mean. It's just something about them. They seem to know all the time when we're going to act, and where. It's like someone's tipping them off."

"Then in all likelihood someone *has* been tipping them off. Purge your staff, Josef."

"I've done it."

Yes, DeVore thought, looking at the odious little specimen. *In fact, it's a wonder anyone will come near you, let alone work with you. But there's always a willing supply of lunatics, ready to serve a monster like you.*

Thank the heavens.

DeVore smiled. "Okay. Let Mussida have his way. Besides, it might be interesting, don't you think?"

"And if they get out of line, sir?"

"Then you'll blow their fucking little heads off, right?"

Horacek grinned like a gargoyle made of tar. "*Right*, sir!"

"Good. Now fuck off out of here. I've work to do."

* * *

The woman lay where he had left her, tied to the bed, blood smeared over her naked buttocks.

"There you are," he said, smiling tenderly, then sitting on the bed beside her, stroking her neck and shoulders.

"Who was it?" she asked, turning to look up at him, her face strikingly beautiful. The face of a much younger Emily Ascher.

"That little gargoyle, Horacek. He wanted to know if his boys could play games outside their camps."

"And you said yes."

"Why not? After all, it's all a distraction. What does it matter what they do?" He paused, then, "Does it hurt, still?"

"A little."

DeVore nodded. He had been, perhaps, too brutal last time. But the need had been so bad, the desire to hurt her so great, that he had not been able to stop himself.

Worrying, he thought. *To lose control like that . . . I must get a better grip on myself.*

Yes, or next time he'd end up killing her, as he had the boy.

He smiled. Maybe he would give Daniel a tape of that, if he stepped out of line. Let him know what had happened to his little friend, Ju Dun.

And what might yet happen to him, if he got too cocky.

For now he would indulge the boy. Build him. Maybe even set him up as a rival to Horacek.

Yes . . . he could see that working beautifully.

But in the meantime . . .

"Howard?"

"Yes," he answered, his hand pausing where it had been caressing the small of her back.

"Would you let me have some of your boys . . . to play with sometime?"

He smiled, his fingers drifting lower, caressing her buttocks, then slipping down into the gap between. "What kind of *games* have you in mind?"

And as he said the word "games" he pushed his finger deep into her, making her gasp with pain. A shudder passed through her whole body.

"Just games, Howard," she said, her voice almost a whisper. "Just something to amuse me while you're gone."

Wiping his bloodied finger down her back, he drew the letter D, then smiled. "Okay. But I want to see what you do, all right?"

"Okay."

"And Em. I can't let them live, you know. Not afterwards. You understand that?"

She turned her head again, looking up at him over her naked shoulder, and smiled. "I understand."

* * *

She found him in his room, his back to the doorway, painting.

"It's for you," he said, knowing she was there.

Meg stepped closer, looking over his shoulder at the canvas. It was a familiar scene – the rose garden at sunset, the cottage in the background bathed in golden light – but the picture seemed strange and threatening, for in the foreground, dominating the canvas, was a bee, a massive, beautifully-detailed bee, its gold-black shape framed by the blood-red mouth of an open flower.

She felt a ripple of apprehension pass through her. Catherine was right. He *had* changed. And not for the better. This painting had the air of rape.

"For me?" she asked.

He looked back at her, a slight edge of challenge in his eyes. "Why? Don't you want it?"

"No. I . . . don't like it."

He looked back at the painting, then set his brush down. "No, I guess you wouldn't."

She moved away from him, going over to the window. Outside the sun was low above the hills. Darkness filled the bowl of the bay while directly below her, still in sunlight, was the rose garden – the very scene he had painted – but anodyne, *innocent*, without his curious take on it.

"I knew you'd come back."

"Did you?" If so, it was more than she had known. She had begun to think she would never return.

"I . . . missed you."

Did you? But this time she was silent.

"Meg?"

She turned. He was watching her. Of course he was. He never stopped watching her. And maybe that was the problem. Maybe *that* was why she had needed to get away.

"*Meg*?"

"Not now, Ben," she said, a tiredness in her voice. "Not now."

CHAPTER·6

SIEGE MENTALITY

Li Yuan stepped back from the rail and looked across at Zelic. "I wondered how they managed to feed so many. Now I know."

The platform they were on was slowly descending. As it did, level after level came into view, like a series of massive baking trays in a giant's oven, only these "trays" were filled with soil to form huge fields, three *li* to a side, in which were planted wheat and maize and rice. Huge arrays of lamps set into the underside of each level gave artificial sunlight to the plants below, while special channels moulded into the trays provided irrigation. Workers could be glimpsed out in those massive fields; long lines of them, their backs bent, their heads protected by straw-woven hats. That much, at least, seemed timeless.

There were one hundred and ten levels in all, according to Zelic, though, owing to crop rotation, only four-fifths were functional at any time. That effectively took out twenty-two levels, but it still left a total growing area of eight hundred square *li*.

"Impressive," said Li Yuan, wondering not merely at the ingenuity of it, but at the paranoia – the siege mentality – that had devised such a system. The Americans had built themselves a string of castles to defend their border, like the kings of olden times. Yes, and like such kings they permitted no opposition. These were harsh times – how many times had he heard one or other of them say that? – and harsh times demanded harsh measures. Yet, as he knew from his own experience, one could not rule this way forever. One could only clench one's fist for so long. One day all this would have to change.

He sighed, thinking once again how hard it was to see another make the same mistakes he'd made and have his voice unheard.

"Are you tired, *Chay Sha*?"

He turned. For a moment he had forgotten Zelic. Tired? *Was* he tired? Maybe. But not in any sense the young Captain would understand. No. His was a weariness of the spirit. To continue after his useful time, like an old man playing chequers in the sun, that was his fate now. All he had seen, all he had done meant nothing now. For these young men it had no value, no . . . *significance*.

"No, Captain Zelic. I am fine."

The platform slowed then stopped. This was as far as it descended. Going to the rail Li Yuan leaned over, looking down. The levels went on, down into the earth itself, while beneath them, at the very foot of this great edifice, were the workers' quarters. *Workers* . . . He smiled at the euphemism. They were slaves, every last one of them, enemies of the state, taken in war, the flicker of the electronic collars about their necks a constant reminder of their status.

"Does it never worry you, Captain?"

"Worry me, *Chay Sha*?"

"The impermanence of things?"

Zelic laughed. "You think all this impermanent, *Chay Sha?"*

"Of course. The wheel turns . . ."

He stopped, looking past young Zelic. On the far side of the platform a door had opened and two men had stepped out. One wore the simple blue one-piece of a high official, the other the uniform of a Major in Egan's Southern army.

"Forgive us for interrupting you, Li Yuan," the official began, coming over to him, "but I'm given to understand that you'd like to visit one of the frontier posts."

Li Yuan glanced at Zelic, but Zelic merely shrugged. He turned back, facing the official. "If it would not be too inconvenient."

"Not at all," the man continued urbanely. "Whatever you wish to see. After all, we have no secrets here."

No secrets, eh? But Li Yuan kept what he was thinking from his face. "That is most kind," he answered. "And Captain Zelic here?"

The official did not even glance at Zelic. "It would be best if the Captain stayed here. Major Lanier will provide full security throughout your tour of the front."

"But *Chay Sha*," Zelic protested. "I have orders . . ."

"It's okay," Li Yuan said. "I am sure I will be perfectly safe in Major Lanier's care."

The Major straightened slightly at the mention, bowing his head the tiniest amount, more in acknowledgement of what Li Yuan had said than from any notion of respect.

A weakness, Li Yuan thought, remembering his own men, back in those days when ten million men had served him, doing his will, dying to his command. *Respect is the cement of a society. Without it, the arch falls, things fall apart.*

Those final words reminded him suddenly of Shepherd and of the gift Ben had given him that time – the book of proscribed poems by the man Yeats. So strange they'd been. So passionate. A violation almost. And yet true. True, in a way his own kind's poetry was not.

Barbarians, yes, yet even barbarians can sing . . .

As with all of the things Shepherd had given him across the years, it had been a lesson. An "eye-opener" as Shepherd had called it. And indeed it had opened his eyes, to a side of these *Hung Mao* he had never really guessed at, for all their proximity. Reading Yeats' poems he had finally understood what motivated them; what soothed and angered them; what fuelled their strange, irrational moods. They were not like Han. No, yet there was common ground.

"You will need to wear a suit," Lanier said, stepping forward, almost but not quite touching Li Yuan's arm.

He met the man's eyes directly, adopting a sudden tone of command in both his manner and his voice. "Is that really *necessary*, Major?"

The Major blinked, surprised, automatically reacting to the signals of tone and gesture. This time he bowed his head fully. "I . . . am afraid so, Master Li. I cannot guarantee your safety unless you wear a body-suit, and if I cannot guarantee your safety . . ."

"Of course," Li Yuan said, dismissing the matter. Yet the moment had been interesting. It was still there in him, that instinct to control and command. The plague had not devoured it, no, nor had time or lack of opportunity diminished it. When a man had been born and bred to rule – when one belonged to the seventh generation of a powerful ruling dynasty – one could take away the world and still that man would think himself an Emperor.

Yes, he thought. *I shall have to set that down.*

He looked down, smiling, amused by the thought. How often now he found himself contemplating his own thoughts and actions, as if at a distance from them; almost as though he were a clerk, following himself around, noting down each tiny utterance and gesture.

So a man becomes, when there is nothing else to fill his time.

As if a man were but a well, waiting to be filled.

He glanced up. Zelic was still waiting, his eyes uncertain, his whole manner anxious. Surprised, Li Yuan almost asked him what the matter was, but that would have been a mistake – a clear breach of etiquette.

"You may leave me now, Captain Zelic," he said softly. "I shall be all right. Major Lanier has given his word."

With a reluctant nod, Zelic turned and left. Li Yuan watched him go, wondering why he'd seemed so anxious. Then, steeling himself to make the best of things, he turned back, facing Lanier and the official.

"Well, Major, it seems I am in your hands. Lead on. I'm rather looking forward to seeing what you keep out there."

* * *

The room was arctic blue and chill, a huge, vault-like space, the walls of reflecting glass, the space between unfurnished. Overhead a sloping ceiling of smooth black ice, two hundred *ch'i* to a side, was supported by two lines of slender pillars.

Into this room now stepped two white-coated technicians, their faces masked, their shaven heads reflecting back the cool blue light. They paused, conscious of the entity embedded in the perspex at the far end of the room, then slowly, hesitantly, began to walk toward it. As they did, a disembodied voice filled the great hall with a low bass resonance, like the voice of emptiness itself.

"Is it ready yet?"

A dozen paces from the far end of the room, they stopped and bowed, the taller of them answering.

"It is ready, Master."

There was a pause, then an echoing reply. "Good. That is . . . good."

The wall facing them was dark. Now it began to glow, a dim cold light growing in its depths, like a firefly trapped in a block of ice.

As the glow grew, a tiny figure was revealed, more an emaciated mummy than a man. One side of its skull was larger than the other, the mottled skin stretched tight across the bone. One eye was fixed and focused, staring mad, the other rolled slowly in its orb. The arms were thin and tiny, like a child's, but the hands were big, the fingers brown and elongated, the knuckles swollen like dice. It had a belly like a young baby's and long stringy legs that dangled uselessly. At the end of them the feet were black and rotted, one of them almost a stump.

This was Josiah Egan, grandfather of the reigning king.

Slowly the two men set to work, freeing the great block of perspex from its position in the wall. That done, one of them turned and gestured to the camera overhead. At once six others entered the room at the far end – big, heavily-muscled men in black one-pieces – bringing with them a large flotation tray. As the technicians stepped back, the newcomers lifted the heavy block up onto the thick-based tray, then slowly manoeuvred it across the floor.

"I died . . ." the voice said, sending its low, bass echoes throughout the room. "Six times I died."

And now they would bring it back to life again.

Two hours and it would be done. Two hours and twenty years of intensive work would be concluded. The technicians looked to each other and smiled.

* * *

"Would you like anything, *Chieh Hsia?*"

Li Yuan turned from the painting he had been studying and smiled. "No thank you, Chang. I am fine. You see to your Mistress, neh?"

"*Chieh Hsia.*"

With a low bow, Chang backed away, returning to Fei Yen who sat in the corner of that massive anteroom, both of Li Yuan's maids attending to her. Behind her, through a great silk curtain of red, white and blue, he could glimpse servants laying the tables and making their final preparations for the banquet.

My Court, he thought, looking about the room at the nine people gathered there. Once he had maintained a great household of five thousand servants, now he was reduced to this: a steward, a cook, a barber, a seamstress, two maids, a serving-boy and a bootmaker who doubled as his taster.

Not that he really missed such luxury, for with it had come a stultifying sense of confinement, of being a prisoner to ritual and obligation, yet it was hard to come to terms with such a reduction in social status, especially when one had to deal with such *hsiao jen* as these Americans, who judged a man not by his innate qualities but by how many "coats" he could stand beside his dining table.

He turned back, looking at the massive painting once again, taking in its brutality, its heavy-handed symbolism, reminded, as he did, of his visit to the frontier post that afternoon, and experiencing again that same tiny frisson of shock he'd felt earlier.

Whatever it was he'd expected, it had not been that.

Their faces . . . He shivered, remembering his first sight of one of the border guards. The face had been rebuilt, the nose removed, the cheek bones restructured to house a fine-mesh metallic filter. The mouth and throat had also been refashioned, two thick ridges of new muscle surrounding the neck, so that at first sight it had seemed as though the man had been decapitated and a new, non-human head set upon his shoulders.

It was a blunted, dehumanised face, more mechanical in its appearance than any machine he had ever seen, yet human, for all that. Yes, and it had made him re-evaluate what he'd seen. The trays, for instance. The trays weren't a response to the threat from the south. They feared *something*, that much was certain, but it wasn't the Southern Alliance. No. It was something much closer to home; something they feared so intensely they would mutilate themselves to defend against it.

Li Yuan blinked, unable to see just what was missing.

I haven't all the pieces. Not yet, anyway. But they're scared. That I do know.

"*Chay Sha*?"

He turned. "Ah, Captain Zelic. I wondered where you had got to."

Zelic stared at him, bemused. "I don't understand, *Chay Sha*. Why are you here? The banquet does not begin for another hour."

"So I thought. Yet the Governor requested that we attend at once, and so here we are."

"But this is . . ."

"An insult?" Li Yuan smiled. "Oh, I have suffered worse, Captain Zelic. Far worse."

"Do you wish me to speak with the Governor, *Chay Sha*?"

Li Yuan smiled faintly. "Your concern is gratifying, Captain, but no. I have grown quite used to waiting these past few years. Besides, does it matter where I wait, in our rooms or here? Here, at least, I can study this magnificent example of your new art."

Zelic made a small sound of disgust. Li Yuan raised an eyebrow, then turned to contemplate the canvas.

"You do not *like* it, Captain?"

"Do you, *Chay Sha*?"

"The figures are a little . . . *chunky*, perhaps. And the colours a touch crude. But there's vigour there, neh? A . . . *vitality*."

Zelic lowered his voice. "Forgive me for saying so, *Chay Sha*, but I think the painting stinks."

"Oh, I would not go *that* far. It is far from subtle, I admit, but then a new culture must seek new forms. Must experiment. It would not do for you Americans to *imitate*, would it now?"

Zelic laughed. "I'll bow to your superior wisdom, *Chay Sha*."

"And to my far greater wealth of experience, neh, Captain?"

Zelic gave a little bow, like a swordsman acknowledging another's skill with the blade. Then, "And how was your visit, *Chay Sha*?"

"My visit?" Li Yuan considered a moment, then. "It was . . . most interesting, Captain Zelic, seeing the blunt face of frontier life."

"The blunt face . . .?"

Li Yuan's eyes flicked up toward the watching camera; a movement Zelic saw and understood at once.

"No matter," Li Yuan continued, his eyes meeting Zelic's for a moment longer than normal; conveying to him that this was something they would talk of later on. "Now tell me the latest news from Boston. Does the war go well?"

* * *

Harding closed the door firmly behind him, then came back, taking a seat across from his two white-haired visitors. Shelves of ancient leather-bound books surrounded them on three sides, while to Harding's left was a long window from which a clear view of the bay could be had.

"Well?" Stewart asked without preamble. "Is it true?"

"Is *what* true?" Harding asked, wondering how much he could trust either of them, and deciding immediately that it wasn't worth the risk.

"That we've been soundly beaten by the Californians," Warner said, leaning toward him.

"It's nonsense," Harding answered, sitting back. "Just mischievous scaremongering, put about by our enemies to try to undermine the king."

"But I heard . . ."

Harding's voice cut through Stewart's, loud and authoritative. "I repeat. All is well. The campaign in the West proceeds according to plan. News comes in daily of fresh conquests."

"And the satellite blackout?" Warner said, his eyes half-lidded with suspicion. "Are you being straight with us, Jim? I've heard all kinds of things today. Some of it quite outrageous. Why, I'd even heard that Egan had sacked you!"

"*Sacked* me?" Harding began to laugh. "Why, I've heard some things in my time, but . . ." Again he laughed; a soft, amused laughter that encouraged the others to join in after a moment.

"I guess we heard wrong," Stewart said, wiping his eyes, then glancing at his brother-in-law and shrugging.

"You did indeed," Harding said, standing, smiling down at them. "Now if you would forgive me, gentlemen, but I've a great deal to do before the banquet tonight."

Stewart had got to his feet. "Banquet?"

"You've not heard?" Harding looked from one to the other, as if deeply surprised, then. "Why, gentlemen, if you would be my guests?"

"Why, now, that would be most kind of you, Jim," Warner said, taking hold of Harding's hand as he lifted his huge bulk up out of the chair. "But could I ask the reason for this banquet?"

Harding grinned, then, in a conspiratorial tone, said, "It was to be a surprise. But as you're such close and trusted friends, let me tell you now. It seems we've won a victory. A great victory."

The old men's eyes lit up. "In the West?"

Harding nodded. "But not a word, eh? The king himself wishes to announce the news. There's to be a special broadcast."

"A victory . . ." Stewart looked to his half-brother and grinned, showing tiny yellow teeth in sunken gums. "At last, a victory!"

"Yes, yes . . . now if you would leave me, gentlemen . . ."

"Of course," Warner murmured. "You must have much to organise . . ."

"Indeed. My servants will collect you at eight."

"That is most kind," Stewart said, bowing his head, unable to stop grinning now that his fears had been put to rest. "We shall not forget such kindness . . ."

"No. Of course," Harding said, stepping to the door and opening it for them. "Until later, then."

* * *

Harding stood in the great hallway of his mansion, watching the servant bolt the great outer doors, then turned. He took two steps then stopped, noticing Horton in the doorway to his study.

"Have they gone?"

Harding smiled wearily. "Yes, thank the gods."

"You should have told them the truth."

Harding considered that a moment, then shook his head. "No. As it is, they'll serve us well enough. Two looser tongues couldn't be bought in the whole of Boston. If they're convinced, then so will all the other old fools. Trust me. Their tittle-tattle will buy us valuable time."

Horton frowned. "Time? I don't understand. Surely we want Egan to fall? And the sooner the better."

"We do. But do you want to inherit a bankrupt and defeated state?"

Horton laughed. "Have we any choice?"

"Maybe." Harding took a folded piece of paper from his pocket and handed it to Horton.

Horton read it, then looked up, wide-eyed. "Is this genuine?"

"As far as I can make out."

Horton whistled. "I was surprised enough when Egan reinstated you. But *this*!" Again he laughed. Then, handing the paper back to Harding, "Do you think we can trust the man?"

"I don't know. Maybe not. But it's worth a try, neh?"

Horton considered a moment, then nodded, a cold, unhealthy smile coming to his features. "DeVore, eh? Just *think* of it! An alliance with DeVore!"

"Yes," Harding said, keeping the doubt he felt from showing in his eyes. "Who would have thought it?"

* * *

The young man's body had a perfect roseate tinge. Lying there, naked on the operating table, it had the look of something godlike. Blond-haired and handsome of face, broad of chest and thick of arm, it seemed a veritable Son of Adam.

Looking down at it from the observation platform, Charles Bernadini, Senior Technician on the Project, felt an overwhelming sense of pride and achievement. For so long this had been merely a dream, frustratingly close and yet always, ultimately, unattainable. They had suffered so many failures, so many setbacks. Until now.

"Look at it!" he said to his assistant, who stood beside him at the rail. "We've done it! This time we've really, finally done it!"

Wiley laughed. "Not quite, Charles. Let's see how the transfer goes before we break out the champagne."

"A formality," Bernadini answered his old friend, turning to him and smiling. "We've done the transfer a hundred times."

"On psychotics and murderers, yes. But this is Old Man Egan. One glitch and we'll *all* be experiment fodder."

Bernadini laughed. "You worry too much, Dan. The gods are with us. I mean, just look at it! The perfect host. That's always been our trouble until now. I hate to admit it, Dan, but this Han biotechnology is a damn sight more advanced than anything we managed to come up with!"

Wiley nodded, but his expression was suddenly more sober. "I agree," he said quietly, "but don't let old Man Egan hear you say it. As far as he's aware we've done all this from scratch. If he got word that we'd plundered *Ching* techniques, he'd go up the wall."

"You think so?" Again Bernadini pointed to the sleeping figure. "Myself I think he'd have advocated *anything* that could get him out of that damn spider's body and into that!"

"Maybe," Wiley said. "But I'd not be too forthcoming with the information if I were you."

Below them a technician came into the operating room and, looking up at the pair in the observation gallery, gave a thumbs-up signal.

"Okay. Let's go down," Bernadini said. "It's time we made the transfer."

* * *

The body woke. Its eyes flicked open. For a moment it simply stared. Then, with a jerky little movement, it sat up. It blinked, then blinked again. Slowly it raised a hand up to its face, staring at it, *studying* it, flexing the fingers like a young child playing with a new toy.

It laughed. An old man's laugh; a mixture of surprise and understanding. Then, turning its head jerkily, it looked about it, taking in the details of the room. A sterile, undecorated room, the walls a pristine white, the floor a stippled cream.

Its gaze travelled upward, then stopped, meeting the eyes of the figure behind the glass of the observation balcony.

"Welcome back, Mister Egan," the stranger said, and smiled broadly. "I'm delighted to say that everything went perfectly."

Egan made to answer, but the sounds that emerged formed a slurred, incoherent groan.

"Take it slowly," the stranger said reassuringly. "At first you'll have to think each word clearly, individually, before you form it. The vocal chords haven't been used much, you understand. We can't exercise them like we do the other muscles. It'll be a while before it comes automatically."

Egan listened, then gave a peremptory nod.
"I . . . wa-an . . ."
He swallowed, the slightest flicker of pain crossing his face. Then he pointed down at the unmistakable erection he now sported.
Up on the balcony, Bernadini smiled then turned and spoke to Wiley, who sat behind him in the shadows, watching the brain traces on the bank of monitors.
"Dan. Get Mister Egan a woman."
Wiley looked up, shocked by the suggestion. "Are you sure? I mean, what if he's not ready for it?"
Bernadini looked back, seeing how Egan sat there, staring in clear awe at the fierce, proud stalk he had inherited, and chuckled to himself.
"I don't know about you, Dan, but after thirty years stuck in a block of plastic, I know *I'd* be ready for it!"

* * *

"So tell me, Li Yuan, how did you feel when Old Man Egan had your boy's balls cut off? Must have been some damn shock, *neh*?"
The speaker was a big, balding man with a pronounced southern drawl and a lazy, mocking manner. He had been goading Li Yuan all evening, offering minor insults which the T'ang had overlooked, but this was different – this was a direct slur upon his manhood.
As the laughter died, Li Yuan stood, staring coldly at the big man.
"Forgive me, *Shih* Tanner," he began, as if responding to some far more innocuous query, "but it surely helps if you *have* balls to begin with?"
The man's smug, mocking smile flickered, then died. "I beg your pardon . . ." he began, but Li Yuan was not finished.
"The fact that you feel you can discuss such matters openly shows not only how ignorant and ill-mannered you are, but also how totally unaware you are of the pitiful sight you make."
"Now look here, Mister Li . . ."
Li Yuan laughed; a cold, imperious laughter that seemed to chill the room. "Look where? At you, *Shih* Tanner? At the great pile of lard that dares to call itself a man? At the obese nothingness that occupies the chair in which you sit? Why, I would as soon contemplate a plate of steaming turds as look at *you* overlong."
There was a hiss of indrawn breath. The banquet room was suddenly deathly silent. In that silence, the big man's chair scraped back. "Now that's just too damn much! If you think . . ."
But Li Yuan had pushed his own chair back, quietly, delicately, with a fighter's sure touch, and had stepped around the table, slowly approaching Tanner. One or two of the other guests went to intercede, but others pulled them back. This was interesting. This was . . . *fun*.
A body's length from Tanner, Li Yuan stopped, two guests and the width of a table between them. Though he had pushed back his chair, Tanner had yet to get to his feet. He leaned forward, his plump hands gripping the edge of the table, his eyes wide with anger.

"Why, you jumped-up little Chink!"

But as Tanner tried to rise, Li Yuan jumped up, onto the table, scattering glasses and dishes, and, balancing himself carefully in the crane stance, placed his foot – toes pointed – in the centre of Tanner's chest.

There were gasps of disbelief. "Good God!" someone cried from close by. "The Chink's gone raving mad!"

Li Yuan stared down at his shocked adversary, a mocking smile on his own lips now.

"You want to fight me, fat man?"

There was a low murmur from all sides, but still no one made to intercede. What would Tanner do?

Tanner grunted, then made to snatch Li Yuan's foot away, but Li Yuan withdrew it quickly, delicately, then flicked it out again, giving Tanner's chest the tiniest of touches.

"You're fucking insane!" Tanner mumbled, clearly put out by this new situation. All of the bluster had gone from him. But there were others who were not so in awe of Li Yuan. One – younger than Tanner and far fitter – now made a grab for Li Yuan, lunging across the table at him . . .

And went down, groaning loudly, his nose broken, blood spattering his white silk tunic.

"*Enough*!" Governor Rogers shouted, standing up.

Li Yuan turned to look at Rogers. Behind the Governor a huge viewing screen was showing muted scenes of the latest victory against the Californians, but no one was watching the screen. All eyes were on Rogers now, wondering what would happen next.

The Governor's face was dark with anger, his eyes protruding from his face. "For God's sake, Mister Li! Return to your place!"

"Tell *Shih* Tanner to apologise," Li Yuan said, staring back at Rogers defiantly. "Tell him, or I'll kick his lungs out through the back of his ribcage!"

"Li Yuan!" Rogers yelled, close to apoplexy now. "If you don't desist, I'll have my guards arrest you!"

But Li Yuan seemed not to hear him. He looked down at Tanner, glaring now. "Apologise, you bloated bag of shit, or I'll crack your ugly face in two!"

That did it. With a furious gesture, Rogers signalled to his guards to intervene. As they began to squeeze their way between the tables, Zelic got up from his seat and hurried to the door.

Li Yuan, meanwhile, had slowly lifted his foot until it hovered before the mesmerised Tanner's face. "Apologise," he said once more, his voice almost gentle now.

"You mad fuckin' Chinaman," Tanner murmured. "You can go to fuckin' hell!"

The sudden crack surprised them all. Tanner sat there a moment, his eyes glazed, blood gouting from his nose and mouth, then slowly he toppled backward, dragging down two other guests as he went.

Pandemonium broke out. There were screams from the female guests, angry shouts from the men. Some tried to get at Li Yuan but most hurried to get away, pushing in the way of the guards. One young guard did squeeze through, and found himself face to face with Li Yuan, but a sharp blow to the abdomen doubled him up.

At the onset of trouble, Chang had positioned himself as close as he dared to his master, but in the first few seconds of the fight, someone had broken a chair over his head. The rest of the Han party sat where they'd been placed, looking on in astonishment as their Master went berserk.

"*Aiya*!" Fei Yen continually shrieked, her hands folded before her face. "*Aiya*!"

Li Yuan was backing away now, his feet clearing plates and dishes from the table as he went, his body crouched, his hands circling in the air before him. But he was surrounded now. A circle of eight men slowly closed in on him.

"Li Yuan!" Rogers barked, coming up behind one of those eight. "Surrender now or face the consequences."

"Consequences?" Li Yuan laughed. "As Tanner said. Go to hell."

Rogers bridled, angered by the continued defiance of the man. "You have killed a man, Li Yuan, and, honoured guest or no, you are not above our laws."

"Your laws!" Li Yuan's laughter was scathing. "I've read your laws! They would make an honest man weep!"

Rogers swallowed angrily, but before he could say another word, Chang, who had hauled himself back onto his feet, called out to Li Yuan.

"Master! You must do as the great man says. They will not hurt you. Remember whose protection you travel under."

"Protection?" Rogers shook his head. "You seriously think Egan will *protect* you when he hears what you did here tonight?"

Li Yuan gave a tiny shrug. "Maybe I choose not to let another fight my battles anymore. Maybe I have had enough of insults, of being treated like a dog by lesser men – *hsiao jen* – like you, Mister Rogers."

He paused, then nodded slowly to himself, as if something had been settled at that moment. "And maybe it is better to die an honest death than to live on one's knees."

"Fine words, Mister Li," Rogers answered, "but you'll be rotting in my cells before nightfall."

"Forgive me, Governor," Zelic interrupted, stepping up to him, "but I think you ought to read this before you act so hastily."

Rogers blinked, then took the paper Zelic was holding out to him and impatiently began to read. He looked up after a while, his lips parted in surprise.

Beside Zelic was another man, Rogers's own Master of Communications. Rogers looked to him, querying the genuineness of the paper. The man hesitated, then nodded. "It's real, sir. The codes match."

Slowly Rogers turned, facing Li Yuan, then, with an angry gesture, dismissed his men.

"It seems you are fortunate, Mister Li," Rogers said, crumpling the paper into a ball and throwing it aside. "Word is you've been recalled."

"Recalled?"

"To Court," Rogers answered. "It seems your son-in-law requires your presence there . . . as Advisor."

Li Yuan's laughter was brief and uncertain. "You jest?"

"No," Zelic said, as Rogers turned on his heel and left. "I went to try to contact Boston and found that the message had come through an hour back. It seems they did not want to disturb the banquet. But it's true. Egan's ordered you home."

"Home?" Li Yuan jumped down from the table and walked over to him. "Home is Tongjiang. You mean Boston, Captain Zelic. Boston, in America, not home."

And with that he walked past, letting Chang hurry after him, ignoring Fei Yen's whining shriek as he pushed through the door, making for his rooms.

* * *

Mark Egan stood at the window of his private quarters, watching the cruisers set down, one after another, on the floodlit roof of the Kennedy Barracks, half a mile distant, while behind him, General Armstrong finished giving him the latest report from the front.

Armstrong himself had set down on that same roof only an hour back and had come directly to see him. The news he brought was bad, yet not as bad as it might have been. The good news was that the war with California was over. The bad was that an entire army had been captured and would be slaughtered to a man unless they came up with five billion dollars.

"So?" Armstrong asked. "Will you sign?"

Egan half-turned, conscious of the two princes in the room beyond the General.

"Yes," he said wearily. "God knows where we'll find the money, but it must be done, neh? The alternative . . . Well, we all know the alternative."

"I was surprised they agreed so readily," Armstrong said, candid now that the thing was done. "One more push and they could have been in Denver."

"And after Denver?" Han Ch'in asked, coming over and standing by the General. "No. Coover's no fool. He knows that to win battles is one thing, to hold territory another. Besides, he has what he wants. Provided we guarantee the Rockies as a border between us, he'll keep the peace."

"And Harding?" Kuei Jen asked, looking up from where he cuddled the sleeping child. "Do you think Harding will go for this package? It will mean heavy taxes. He and many of his friends will suffer."

Egan turned, facing them all, looking in to the brightly-lit room, yet still conscious of the darkness of the night behind him. "He'll go for it, never fear. It'll cost him, yes, but better to keep something than to lose it all, neh? And if we do not make this peace there's no clearer certainty than utter oblivion."

"Even so," Han Ch'in said, "we must keep news of this secret for a day or two. Until our forces are in place. When news of this breaks . . ."

All were silent a moment, then Egan spoke again, reaching out to embrace Armstrong, giving him a strong, manly hug.

"You've served me well, John, both on the battlefield and off. Be sure I'll not forget it."

Armstrong laughed. "Be sure I'll not let you."

There was a sharp knocking at the door on the far side of the room. A young guard looked round the door, then came smartly to attention.

"Yes, Douglas?"

"Your Chancellor is here, Master."

"Okay. Give me five minutes, then show him in." Egan looked to Armstrong. "We'll speak later, John. But tell Coover I'll meet him when and where he wants."

Armstrong came to attention and bowed his head. "Sir!"

Egan watched Armstrong leave by the side door, then turned, facing the two princes.

"You want us to leave?" Kuei Jen asked.

Egan shook his head. "No. Harding will find out soon enough, and I'd rather he heard direct from me."

"He'll not like it," Han Ch'in said.

"Whether he likes it or no, it's how things are from now on," Egan said, "so he'd best get used to it."

The two princes looked to each other.

"You should take care," Kuei Jen said quietly. "It is not so much Harding as the faction he represents. Such a man cannot be dealt with as an individual. One must look to his friends . . ."

Egan turned upon his wife, his irritation clear. "You seek to teach me statesmanship, Kuei Jen?"

"No . . . no, my husband." He stood and, after setting the sleeping child down on a nearby sofa, came across to Egan and held his shoulders. "I merely wish to *remind* you. This is a critical meeting. You know that. So reign in your honest anger. See him not as a man, but as a colour."

"A *colour*?" Egan laughed, incredulous. "Kuei Jen, what in God's name are you talking about?"

"It is something that my tutor, Lo Wen, taught me long ago. Something I've always found useful. As a Prince one must deal with all manner of men. Some of them we will like instinctively, others we shall take an instant dislike to. That is quite natural. Unfortunately, such natural responses are inappropriate at the level on which we are forced to function. Personal feeling must always come second to political expediency, no matter the circumstance. In brief, it is not what a man is, in himself, that matters, but what he represents. Even so, that natural instinct remains and can sometimes colour our response, so it helps to consider each individual not as him or herself – a free agent, acting without responsibility – but as a colour; that colour symbolic of those views or that particular faction he represents."

"And Harding?"

"Pardon?"

Egan smiled. "What colour is Harding?"

Kuei Jen laughed. "Isn't it obvious? Harding is brown. Shit brown."

* * *

Egan was still laughing when Harding was shown into the room. He looked about him and smiled, clearly wishing to share the joke.

"Master?"

"Chancellor!" Egan said, rushing across to take both his hands in greeting. "I am so pleased to see you. Earlier . . ." He shook his head regretfully. "I was not myself . . . what I said . . ."

"It doesn't matter," Harding said, continuing to shake Egan's hands. "Let all that be behind us, neh? We work together from henceforth."

"Together," Egan echoed, grinning broadly. Then, turning, he put out an arm to indicate the princes. "You know Prince Han Ch'in, and my wife, Prince Kuei Jen."

Harding turned and bowed. "*Ch'un tzu*," he said. "Good friends are welcome in such troubled times."

The words were unexpected. Taking his cue from his brother, Kuei Jen spoke for both of them. "From adversity comes strength. You can be certain that my brother and I shall give our full support to all your efforts, Chancellor."

"It comforts me to think so," Harding answered, half-turning to summon his clerk. "But come. Let us catch up with the current situation. I have much to report, and a great deal to discuss."

* * *

"He didn't like it," Kuei Jen said when Harding was gone. "He concealed it well, but I could tell. He was too tense. And that smile . . ."

"Was a mask," Han Ch'in agreed. "It was the one thing he hadn't counted on, Father coming back. It threw him."

"Yet he was open with us," Egan said. "I thought, perhaps, he'd avoid mentioning the meeting with Horton, yet he came clean. That speaks in favour of the man."

"If his account of the meeting can be trusted," Han Ch'in said, somewhat sceptically. "He would have known, after all, that Security were tailing him."

"Maybe so. But why should he lie?" Egan said. "As for the matter of your father's return . . . well, perhaps he *was* put out a little, but he'll come round, surely?"

Kuei Jen sighed. "I counted on him doing so, but now I'm not so sure."

"He can accept us as Advisors," Han Ch'in said, "for we have never ruled. We were the seeds that never grew. But Father . . ." He shook his head.

Egan closed his eyes. "*Now* you say."

"So we were wrong," Kuei Jen said. "The answer is simple. Let us leave our Father where he is. Contact Harding straight away and tell him that you've changed your mind."

"Too late," Egan said. "I sent the summons an hour back."

"Then we must make the best of things," Han Ch'in said. "We must convince Harding that Father is no threat. That he will have no greater say in Council than any other man."

"You think that will be enough?" Kuei Jen asked, facing his brother, his full, feminine shape contrasting strongly with the angular masculinity of his half-brother.

"It will have to be," Egan said, coming between them and laying a hand on each. "But we must watch our brown friend carefully henceforth."

"Our shit-brown friend . . ." Kuei Jen said, and all three roared with laughter once again.

In the corner of the room, the young child, Egan's son, Samuel, conceived three years ago that day, stirred on the sofa and turned, putting his thumb into his mouth for comfort, his jet-black hair falling across his lidded eyes, while in the room behind him his future was decided.

* * *

Horton climbed from the bed and crossed the room, pulling on a gown before he answered the urgent beep of the vid-phone.

"What is it?" he asked, as Harding's face formed from the blackness.

"It's as you said," Harding answered. "He appointed me Chancellor once again. Not only that, but he's appointed both the Han as his Advisors."

"You see!" Horton said. "Didn't I tell you!"

"Yes. But all's not well, even so."

"Why?"

"He's recalled Li Yuan."

"*What*!"

"It's true. I checked myself. He sent the recall order an hour before he saw me."

"Without consulting you . . ."

Harding nodded. "And yet it will seem as if I had a hand in it."

Horton considered a moment, then made a sour face. "I don't like this. That bastard's up to something."

"Yes, but what?"

"Martial rule?"

"Mar . . ." Harding's mouth opened like a fish. Now that Horton had said it, the fact stared him in the face. The recall of the armies; the appointment of close family to key positions; the use of Colonel Chalker to subdue the media. It all pointed to the same conclusion. "So what do we do?"

Horton smiled. "You do nothing, Jim. Go home and go to bed."

"But . . ."

"Leave things to me. *Okay*?"

Harding stared at him uncertainly, then nodded. "Okay. But nothing that comes back to us."

"I promise." And with that Horton reached out and cut the connection. He turned, looking back at Russ, who was watching him from his bed. "What are you looking at?"

Russ smiled lasciviously. "You, you monster. Now make that call to Rogers, then come back to bed. I haven't finished with you yet!"

* * *

"*Chay Sha*! *Chay Sha*!"

The urgent whisper woke him. For once it hadn't been in his dream. This time he woke surprised, not knowing where he was, nor even who it was who was calling him in so strange a manner.

"Wha . . .?" He sat and knuckled his eyes as a light came on in the room.

"Quickly, *Chay Sha*!" Zelic said, handing him his robe. "There's no time to explain. We have to leave here now!"

He saw the guards at the door, their automatics drawn, and knew something was wrong. Maybe Rogers had had a change of mind about the incident. Or maybe it was something else.

"Where's Fei Yen?" he asked, as he slipped on the robe.

"Don't worry," Zelic answered, watching as Chang gathered up Li Yuan's essential belongings and bundled them into a bag, "my sergeant will make sure she's well looked after."

Li Yuan gave a little nod of understanding then, stopping only to glance around the room, followed Zelic out.

And stopped, staring down at the black-cloaked assassin who lay face down in the corridor, a loop of wire pulled tightly about his neck.

He felt a jolt of surprise and looked to Zelic, but Zelic was already hurrying on.

"Come on, *Chay Sha*!" he called back to him. "We've little time!"

Zelic had stationed his guards at every junction along the way, the men joining them as they ran towards the monorail, falling in to form a tight formation about Zelic and Li Yuan. For a time it seemed that they had made it without incident, yet as they came to the last turn of the corridor that led directly into the terminal, they heard raised voices up ahead. There was a shot, and then a burst of rapid fire, followed by a single explosion.

They had stopped at the first sound, the whole party dropping into a crouch. Now Zelic took control. "Green Two!" he barked, standing and waving six of his men through. "Go on ahead! Secure the entrance, then send a man back."

They waited, out of sight of what was happening, tensed in the sudden silence.

There was a shot. A second. Then footsteps hurried back. A visored soldier waved the all clear.

"Quick now!" Zelic said, sending two further men ahead. "Okay," he said, looking to Li Yuan once more. "Let's go."

Around the turn of the corridor was a scene of carnage. There were great gaps in the walls, the edges scorch-burned. A dozen, maybe fifteen men lay dead, most of them mutilated by the blast. From the look of it, one of Zelic's men had run at the defenders with a grenade.

Li Yuan glanced at Zelic, reappraising things. Whilst he had always casually assumed their protection, he had never wholly trusted them. But now he knew just how seriously they took his defence. Serious enough to lay down their lives.

The thought gave him strength.

They ran on, picking their way over the bodies and through the great entrance, out onto the massive concourse. The monorail was waiting, its doors open, a number of Zelic's men kneeling inside the carriages, their guns raised. But as he made to go across, Zelic took his arm and pulled him back.

"No, *Chay Sha*. Over here. We're going up onto the roof."

"The roof?"

Zelic nodded. "They'll pick the monorail off in an instant. A cruiser makes a far more difficult target, neh?"

He followed Zelic across, into one of the RRs – the Rapid Risers – grateful that at least one of them was thinking straight.

"How did you know?" he asked, facing Zelic as the door hissed shut and the lift began to accelerate.

"I didn't," Zelic answered, watching the ascending numbers on the wall.

"Then you were lucky," Li Yuan said.

Zelic smiled. "I guess so."

Or damn good at your job, he thought, liking the young man more and more by the moment.

"Why did you do that, by the way?" Zelic asked, looking directly at him.

"Do what? *Flip*?"

The smile came back. "You could call it that."

Li Yuan shrugged. "Because I'd had enough."

Zelic nodded. "I thought so."

As the riser slowed and weight returned to their bodies, Zelic took a large handgun from his belt. He handed it to Li Yuan, then drew a second gun – a smaller stunner – from inside his tunic pocket.

"We may have to fight."

Li Yuan nodded. The gun felt strange and heavy in his hand. Holding it, he realised that it was some years since he had held a weapon of any kind.

As the door hissed back, the cold night air hit them. They were on the roof, the darkness held at bay by the glare of arc lamps.

"Sir!" someone yelled, to their right. Looking that way, Li Yuan could make out the shape of a cruiser, its engines already warmed up and humming, its ramp open. Two guards stood at the top of the ramp, one with his arm raised.

"Come on!" Zelic said, yet even as they began to run, an automatic opened up from somewhere close.

Li Yuan threw himself down. A moment later there was an explosion.

"Shit!" Zelic said, from where he lay face down beside Li Yuan. "Crawl toward the cruiser. And keep going. My men will try to pin them down, whoever they are."

There was a second rapid blast of gunfire, then the *pop-pop-pop* of a gas-launcher.

"Okay!" Zelic said. "Let's go!"

He saw Zelic get up and begin to run, and began to do the same, but as he got to his knees, something warm and strong seemed to grab him from behind, lifting him up off his feet and throwing him forward.

* * *

Zelic woke and tried to sit up, but the pain in his head was too great. He could feel the vibration of the cruiser all around him, Wincing, he put a hand up to his brow. The bandage was wet.

"Soldier!" he called, keeping his eyes closed. "*Soldier*!"

Someone came across. He felt a hand touch his arm lightly. "It's okay, sir. You're going to be all right."

"Brevitt?"

"Yes, sir."

"Where are we?"

"In the cruiser, sir. Heading north-east towards Fort Worth."

"Ah . . ." he swallowed painfully, his throat dry. As if sensing it, the young sergeant lifted his head gently, then held a cup to his lips. He drank gratefully. "And Li Yuan?"

There was a pause. "I'm afraid he didn't make it, sir."

"Didn't . . ." The enormity of it hit him like a hammer blow. He had failed. Better to have died back there than this. He groaned.

"Are you okay, sir?"

But Zelic didn't answer, merely turned and lay, facing the wall as the cruiser flew on through the desert night.

CHAPTER·7

ACTS OF KINDNESS

Daniel stopped, his left hand raised. At once the patrol came to a halt, the younger boys looking about them nervously. It was midday and the town was directly below them, the river bisecting it like a line of molten steel. Behind them a wooded slope climbed to meet the lower slopes of the great range.

A road led down toward the bridge. For the first few hundred metres it was merely a strip of tarmac, running through the untended scrubland, and then the houses began, only one or two at first, and then, as the ground flattened out nearer the river, a solid mass of buildings – traditional Han houses with red-tiled roofs and high walls – intersected by endless little alleyways.

China on the Rhine.

Through the longsight of his visor, Daniel studied the streets alongside the river, noting how little activity there was down there. Normally those same streets would be crowded at this time of day, the traders' stalls surrounded by bustling life, but today there was barely anyone about. Something was wrong.

Rebels. It had to be.

Daniel turned, looking to his boys. It was hot in the suits and they were sweating, and not merely from the heat, but all eyes were on him now. He was their leader and they trusted him. Worshipped him, if the truth be told.

"Come," he said simply. "We're going down."

There was no need to tell them to be careful. They knew that. And they knew as well as he that something was wrong. You could tell that by the absence of the golden-eyed. *They* knew when something was about to happen – knew and got out of the way.

As they started down, the boys fanned out, two at the front, four in the middle, two at the back, forming a broad hexagonal shape, as Daniel had taught them. Daniel himself was on the right at the front, Robbie, a twelve-year-old, to his left.

If they were going to be ambushed, it wouldn't be here, it would be deeper in. The rebels would use alleyways and balconies and windows. Two, maybe three, of his patrol would be dead before they even knew they were in a fight.

Which was what made this worse, in many ways, than the Garden. There, at least, you knew that the threat was ever-present. Here it was the *longueurs* that killed. You could only remain tensed and alert for so long, and then you would relax. Your attention would drift. And at that moment they would hit you. Unseen assassins. Snipers.

They passed the first few houses. The town below them seemed deserted, but one could sense the people behind their shuttered windows, or lying on their floors, silent and fearful, listening as they passed by.

Daniel glanced back. They looked good. Confident. Professional. More like men than the boys they were. That much he could be proud of. But they had yet to face a real fire-fight.

Tests. That seemed to be all there was to their lives.

The thought brought back a memory, something from when Daniel had been in de-briefing. It was towards the end of the process when, his interrogation at an end, they had given him the freedom to exercise in the gym. Under the watchful eyes of the guards, he had spent that last month slowly working his way back to fitness. After the inactivity of the cells the exercise made him feel good; made him feel *human* once again. But there was another reason why he liked those sessions, for if he climbed to the very top of the rope he could see out through the narrow windows and glimpse the prison's cobbled yard and the gate.

That tiny glimpse of life – of a world carrying on outside – lifted his spirits after the long months of isolation. The world, for him, had shrunk to the length of a single corridor. Now it expanded again, hinting at unlimited horizons.

It was at one of those moments, while he hung at the top of the rope, gripping it tightly, that he saw one of the young guards – a blue-eyed young man who, while he'd never spoken to Daniel, seemed somehow less hostile than the others – go to the gate and, putting his hands to the bars, appear to take something.

For a moment Daniel hadn't understood. What the guard held was small and white, yet he didn't make any attempt to stash it away in a pocket. Only when the young guard lowered his mouth to it and kissed it did Daniel realise what it was. A hand. It was a young girl's hand. And now that he knew what to look for, he could make out the shape of her on the far side of the barred gate.

That moment's tenderness had shocked him more than if the guard had put a gun into the girl's mouth and blown her head off. Shocked him, because he himself had never known such tenderness. The nearest he had come was the comfort of another boy's arm about him as he slept, the brief physical pleasure of another boy's cock inside him. Nothing permanent. Nothing . . . *deep.* And certainly no love.

No love. Yes, that was what shocked him. The realisation that he lived in a no-love universe. That he existed . . . and nothing more. He and several thousand boys like him. Surviving day by day in the camps.

Again and again, he saw the young guard's lips come down and kiss that tiny white hand. And each time the shock of it seared him for, like the tiny glimpse of the world outside he got each time he climbed to the top of the rope, it hinted at a great world outside of himself that he did not know. A world filled to overbrimming with love.

In another universe to this . . .

"Keep tight," he said quietly, reminding himself where he was.

To either side the houses were closing in. A high grey wall was to their left now, on their right a row of shops, their shutters down. Just ahead the first of several alleyways criss-crossed the road.

Daniel raised a hand. At once they stopped.

Why go straight down? Why not cut across?

He narrowed his eyes, thinking it through. They had to cross the river, for their orders were to report to the camp at Abendorf, and that was on the far side of the river, but that didn't mean they had to go straight there. They could make for the great square beside the *yamen*, then head back along the waterfront. That way, at least, they'd have the river at their back and only one side to defend. If the rebels didn't hit them before they got there.

He decided he would take the risk.

Daniel gestured toward the left and made the signals which meant "form up tight" and "at a trot". There were nods.

"Okay. Let's go."

The alleyway was deserted. As they came out into the next street, they had a glimpse of someone disappearing into a doorway, otherwise it too was empty.

A single shot rang out. Distant. Down by the river, if he was any judge, though the echo from the surrounding hills made it hard to be sure.

Daniel pulled the patrol up. They crouched there, their eyes searching the surrounding windows and balconies, their gun barrels searching for movement.

For a moment nothing, and then another shot rang out.

Snipers, Daniel thought, a shiver going down his spine.

A count of five, and then the rapid stutter of automatics opening up, followed by the booming concussion of a grenade. A patrol. There had to be another patrol down there.

"Come on!" he yelled, turning and heading down the street, the river directly below him. "Someone's in trouble down there!"

As they came within fifty metres of the river, Daniel stopped. The gunfire had been heavy, but now, suddenly, it ceased.

Too late, he thought, unclipping a grenade from his belt.

"Stay there," he whispered, indicating that they should take cover and keep low. "I'll go look."

Crossing over to the nearest house, Daniel went through an open gate and up a set of stairs. Then, crawling along a balcony, he peeked out through a gap in the stone balustrade. Bodies. Two, no three of them, lying in the road between the Customs House and the river. They had already been stripped and were semi-naked.

Daniel moved a little, altering his view, and saw a fourth body, suited this time, two young Han crouched over it, removing the suit. Nearby was a cart. On it were several combat suits and a pile of weapons.

Careful to make no noise, Daniel eased back a little, slipping the barrel of his gun into the gap. His finger brushed the trigger, putting the most gentle pressure on it as he squinted through the sight. Two shots should do it.

"Lin Pei!"

One of the crouching Han looked up at the call, combing his black hair away from his eyes as someone came across.

Daniel felt a moment's elation. The woman was wearing a fighter's one-piece and her greying hair was tied back in a bun at the back of her head. Even so, he recognised her from the films they'd been shown. It was her! As she stepped into the cross-wires of his sights, he felt a little tremor go through him.

"Look!" she said, pointing down at the body. "Boys! The bastard's sending out boys against us now!"

Daniel tensed. One shot, through the head – that's all it would take. And then he'd be a hero. Again.

Unexpectedly, the body groaned. Daniel watched the woman kneel, her face filled with sudden concern.

"Get Wu Ye over here at once! This one's alive!"

Daniel moved the sight marginally, so that he now had it trained directly on the boy's head. He didn't know the boy, but he was determined not to let the bastards take him. He was about to fire when the woman did something strange. She put her hand under the boy's head and, lifting it gently, cradled it in the crook of her arm.

"Lin Pei, give me some of your water."

The young Han handed her a water bottle, then crouched, watching as the woman placed the lip of the bottle to the boy's mouth. He drank a moment, then lapsed back, against her.

As Daniel watched, she handed back the bottle, then, turning to look down at the boy again, began to gently stroke his brow.

"There," Daniel heard her say, "you're going to be all right now."

There was something about the way she said it, something about the way she looked at him and smiled, something in the movement of her fingers against the boy's sweat-beaded brow, that made Daniel groan inwardly. His hand trembled now, making the cross-wires joggle.

One shot. That was all it took.

He lowered the gun and sat, his back against the wall of the house. Lifting his visor, he removed his glove, then reached inside his helmet and rubbed at his eye. A slow, sighing breath escaped him.

So that was her. His enemy. The one they'd been taught to hate and despise.

He closed his eyes and saw her, cradling the boy's head and placing the water bottle to his lips, then, afterwards, stroking his forehead and smiling down at him. Only now the boy was Daniel.

He shuddered and flicked his eyes open, then crawled back to the gap and looked out.

She was still there. Still she cradled the boy's head and crooned to him, even as the doctor crouched over him, cutting at his armour to get to his bloodied chest.

Daniel watched, grimacing as the boy's body spasmed, one leg kicking, before he slumped and lay still, dead.

The doctor moved back slightly, shaking his head, and as he did, Daniel saw the woman's face, saw the loss there, and marvelled at it. Why, she hadn't even known the boy. And her eyes.

He caught his breath. She was crying. The woman was crying, holding the boy tight against her breasts and crying.

"You poor boy," she was saying, "you poor, poor boy."

Daniel jerked back, away from the gap, as if he was watching something that was forbidden. Then, trembling, afraid lest he drop his gun, he crawled over to the stairs, hurrying away.

* * *

DeVore stood on the balcony, his hands resting loosely on the stone balustrade, watching his creatures at play.

In the shadowy darkness of the ancient hall they seemed more like giant moving pillars than living beings, their great torsos bending and stretching, their great arms moving like whips as the tiny missiles flew between them, whistling in the half-dark.

It was a game they often played, and DeVore never tired of seeing it, for it demonstrated the skill and agility of the morphs as nothing else did.

There were six of them in all, and they had formed a circle in the centre of the floor, roughly ten metres from each other. At the start of the game each was given two tiny balls, made of sewn black leather and filled with tiny metal beads. Once the game began, they were to throw these at their fellows – each throw to be accurate, and between knee and shoulder height – the object being to try and force an error.

A dropped ball and you were out, and to signal that you were out, you dropped to your knees and lowered your head.

A simple game. Indeed, a child's game. But not when played by morphs. Between morphs this became a game of speed and dexterity . . . and cunning. For at times the attention of all might be drawn to one, and that one would find not two but ten balls hurtling towards him.

Right now only four of the six were standing and the whizz and whistle of the balls through the darkness was like the singing of bullets in the heat of a fire-fight. There was the *slap-slap-slap* of caught balls, the grunts and groans of the morphs as they hurtled them back at each other. Faster it went and faster, until another cried out in dismay and knelt, bowing his head.

Only three then, and the pace seemed to get faster yet, the whistle of the missiles like the circling of a bolas.

A groan. Only two were standing now.

DeVore leaned forward, excited, intent on seeing which would win as they hurled the missiles at each other like two ancient gun-fighters. Back and forth the missiles whizzed, back and forth at an ever-increasing pace.

Then, suddenly, there was the slap as a ball whacked off a cheek, and that was it. There was a cry of triumph, a groan of dismay.

"Bravo!" DeVore cried, making them look up at him as one. "Well done, my children! But I've another game for you. A better game."

He went down the broad marble steps. They were all standing again, shaking themselves loose after their exertions, yet as DeVore stepped out among them – their comparative statures making him seem like a child among adults – they stopped and turned to face him, watching him attentively, their heads bowed in respect.

"I think it's time we paid our friend, Emily Ascher a visit."

There was a murmur of delight at that.

"In the Wilds?" one of them – Jerud – asked.

"Yes," DeVore said. "I've decided to sweep the whole northern section, valley by valley until we find them. Then we go in . . . and *eradicate* them."

"It'll take a month at least," another – Hiuden – said.

"Yes. But once it's done, it's done. And then . . . America."

DeVore saw how they liked the sound of that. Via hidden cameras he had watched them talk among themselves and knew that they longed for action – that they hated being cooped up here in the city – but there had been little he could do until now.

But now, if what he'd heard was right, things were about to change.

America was in turmoil once again. Young Egan had lost the western seaboard and power was daily slipping from his hands. With the help of Coover and Horton – and others – he might destabilise things to the point where they'd have to call off their blockade of Europe's airspace. And when they did . . .

DeVore smiled inwardly. The moment they opened the skies to him he had won. For in that moment they would have surrendered their one and only advantage.

This, then, was the endgame. And in the endgame he was supreme. Why, even that great Master of *wei chi*, Tuan Ti Fo, had not been as good as him when it came to this final nip and tuck.

"Okay," he said, looking about him at his creations with pride and a grim satisfaction. "Go and shower. And after, meet me in the War Room. There we shall make our plans."

* * *

It was dark when they got to Abendorf and the gates of the camp were closed, but the Commandant seemed delighted to see them even so.

Daniel saluted, then walked straight past the man, wanting only to find a bunk and the refuge of sleep. Behind him his patrol sneaked in, tired and bewildered, not quite sure what was going on.

On Daniel's orders, they had hidden in the basement of a shop, waiting more than two hours before they ventured out to the sight of the ambush.

The bodies were gone. At first Daniel thought that maybe scavengers had had them. But then, walking over to the grass walkway that ran beside the river, he saw freshly-turned earth – a patch six metres by two – and understood. The rebels had taken the time and trouble to bury their victims.

That, too, he had found something of a shock, for they had been taught that the rebels often tortured and then ate their victims. They had been told that they were vicious and heartless and that *nothing* was beyond them. But he had seen her with his own eyes now. He had seen that look on her face – a look of such suffering and regret that it had reversed in an instant all he had previously believed about her.

Lies. He knew now. It was all lies.

Daniel sat there on the edge of his bunk, in full armour, staring straight ahead, while all about him the boys removed their combat suits, moving silently, loath to disturb him. He was still sitting there when the Commandant came in.

"Mussida? Are you all right?"

Daniel looked up, then stood, coming to attention. All about him his boys did the same.

"Well?" the Commandant asked, trying to make sense of his mood. "Did something happen out there?"

Daniel's eyes met the Commandant's briefly. It was impossible to tell the truth. "Nothing, sir. I felt . . . fatigued, that's all."

"Ah . . ." The Commandant seemed satisfied with that. "We lost a patrol," he went on. "At least, there's no sign of them yet."

Daniel nodded.

"Is there . . . anything I can get you, Daniel? For your team?"

He almost smiled at that. It was strange how things had changed since he'd come back from Eden. Now they deferred to him.

"They're hungry, sir. Maybe . . . something special?"

The Commandant grinned broadly. "Of course! I'll send something down from my own kitchen." He hesitated, then, "Well, we'll leave the report to the morning, neh? You must be tired."

"Sir."

When he'd gone, Daniel sat again. But if he thought that was it, he was wrong. Closing the door, his twelve-year-old lieutenant, Robbie, turned to face him.

"Daniel?"

Daniel sighed. He could sense all the others listening, and knew what they wanted. "Yes, Robbie?"

"What *did* happen out there?"

He looked up and smiled sadly. "Why should anything have happened?"

Robbie glanced about him, then, steeling himself, looked back at Daniel. "After the shooting. You left us to see what was going on, and when you came back . . . well, you were changed. It was like . . ."

"Like what?"

Robbie shrugged.

He hated lying to them. Even so, it was lie or tell the truth, and he dared not tell the truth. He might as well put a gun to his own head.

"The truth is," he began, "I saw something sickening. So sickening that . . . well, I'd rather not mention it. It . . . disturbed me."

They were staring at him now, shocked. Only a moment before they had thought him invulnerable, more a machine than a man, and now . . .

"What . . . kind of thing?" Robbie asked.

But Daniel shook his head. "You don't want to know."

But he knew they would speculate; would fill the gap he'd left with the most lurid imaginings. Something so hideous that it would instantly become "the truth". But the truth was worse in a way. For the truth was that they were all living a lie. It was not The Woman who was their enemy, it was The Man. The truth was they were all living in some hideous inverted mirror of reality, wherein black and white had been reversed.

Out, he told himself, looking down at his gloved hands. *I've got to get out.*

But how? And even if he did get out, how did he stop them following him? How did he get the tracing wire out of his head?

If there's a way to put in, there's a way to get it out.

He just had to find out how. Yes, and where it was done. And who did it. And then . . .

Daniel looked up. They were still all watching him, taking their mood from him – *patterning* themselves on him. He was their hero. Their model. What he did mattered to them.

"I'll be okay," he said, looking from face to face and smiling. "A good meal and we'll all be okay, neh?"

And slowly, tentatively, their faces began to mirror his, until everyone was smiling.

Daniel nodded, letting the smile remain on his lips. Yes. All was well again. All was . . .

* * *

DeVore cried out even as he sat up, the dream so vivid that for a moment he felt the blow strike the side of his skull and split it.

Emtu, sleeping beside him, sat up and, reaching across, held him as he calmed. "What was it?" she asked, her eyes searching his.

"Karr. It was Karr. He . . .

"Killed you again?"

DeVore nodded, then, shrugging off her arms, climbed from bed and went through to the bathroom, switching on the shower.

She went across and stood in the doorway, watching him. "What do you think it means?"

"It means nothing," he answered, annoyed that she should ask. "It's just a dream, that's all."

"But you've had it several times now."

"So?" He switched the water off and turned to face her. "Karr's light-years from here. Literally. We'll never see him again. So the dream means nothing."

"Dreams always mean something," she persisted.

"Bollocks!"

As he came to the doorway he stopped, staring angrily at her, his face pressed close to hers. "Just leave it, okay? It's a dream, and *only* a dream. If it worries you, I'll have the surgeon purge it, all right?"

She nodded, averting her eyes as he continued to stare aggressively at her.

"Good," he said finally. "Besides, if there's anyone who's going to be smashing skulls, it's me. I'm good at smashing skulls. I've smashed a whole fucking mountain of them in my time!"

And with that he turned away.

"Yes," she said softly, almost inaudibly, watching him walk over to the wardrobe and begin to dress. "You're the best. The very best, my love."

* * *

Daniel jerked awake. He was wearing only his breech-cloth, but for a moment he had thought he was still in full armour. He had been sweating profusely and his limbs felt like they were encased.

Sitting up, he looked about him at the tiny dormitory. On every side the boys

slept on, their faces innocent in sleep, their soft snores filling the half dark.
Something had woken him. Something . . .
He went very still, realising what it had been. The answer. He had the answer suddenly.
For a moment longer he sat there, letting his pulse return to normal, his breathing slow, then he slipped back beneath the thin cloth blanket.
Horacek. Horacek was the key.

* * *

A single huge arc lamp illuminated the yard, throwing its bright glare over the entrance to the barn. Both of the massive doors were thrown back, and as the big cart lumbered into the yard men came out from the darkness within to help unload.
As the cart ground to a halt, Horacek jumped down, immediately organising the men, gesturing and shouting in his strange, high-pitched voice.
At once they began their gruesome task, taking the bodies from the cart and stacking them inside, men to the right, women to the left, children and those too disfigured to make such distinctions, in the darkness at the far end of the barn.
It was still warm despite the hour, and as Horacek stood watching, he fanned himself, using the clipboard on which were written the latest figures.
It was going well. At long last, his campaign against the southern villages was having its effect. They knew now. If they sheltered even a single rebel, they would pay the price.
The probes were the key to it, of course. Since he'd been using them to spy upon the villagers, his success rate had rocketed. He had been able to go among them and, rounding them up, show them the unarguable evidence of their duplicity. But he had been careful to kill only a number of them. One in six. The rest were spared deliberately – so that word of what had happened would spread through the southlands.
Even so, there were still those who took the risk and defied him. And so he continued to go amongst them, like a vengeful god exacting justice.
As the last few bodies were carried inside, Horacek wandered over to the two white-coated men who were standing by the gates, looking on.
"Fresh tonight," he said, grinning his hideous, lop-sided grin.
"Good," one of them said, turning to him. "But you ought to think about refrigeration. On nights like this . . ."
"*You* think about it," Horacek answered him curtly. "I do my bit, you do yours. Besides, it's only for the camps."
The two men looked to each other, exchanging a glance that Horacek didn't quite understand. Were they providing meat for other markets now? If so, maybe he should up what he was charging?
"Here," the second of them said, as if reading his mind, quickly handing him a bag of coin. "Silver. As we agreed."
Horacek held the bag up in one hand, as if calculating its weight, then nodded. "Good," he said. "Tomorrow, then."
"Tomorrow."
He turned and walked away, past the cart and out of the yard, his six bodyguards

falling in about him as he walked down through the empty streets towards the centre of the town. His men would see to the cart. He had what he'd come for.

It wouldn't do, of course, to be too greedy. But no one would miss a few bodies. And if they all did well out of it, then why should anyone care if he made a profit or not, least of all The Man. After all, DeVore had more than he needed. Indeed, sometimes he thought DeVore had no interest in money at all, except in so far as it allowed him to continue his campaigns.

Horacek looked about him at his men. For once he felt like sharing his good fortune.

"Okay," he said, "you've worked hard for me today. It's time we had some fun. Let's go to *Ti Yu*, neh? On me."

There were broad grins and nods of gratitude. *Ti Yu*! It was well beyond their reach. This was unlooked-for generosity!

Horacek smiled. If you treated your men well then they looked after you. And little treats like this helped. But not too often. It wouldn't do to have them expect this kind of thing all the time.

No. Just now and then. When they'd done *particularly* well.

Grinning now, the heavy coin bag swinging back and forth in the pocket of his tunic, Horacek led them on down the empty, lamplit street, towards the glistening line of the river, and towards the great dungeon-like cellars of the *Ti Yu* club, where, if you had the money, you could buy anything.

Anything at all.

* * *

A great cheer went up from all around the exercise yard as Daniel marched his patrol towards the gate, boys crowding the mouths of the tunnels and hanging from the windows just to get a sight of him.

His own boys were grinning, their visors up, pleased to bask in his reflected glory – part of *Daniel's* team – and as they passed out under the gate, more than one of them raised an arm to acknowledge the cheers and whistles.

And then they were outside again, on the road that led down through Abendorf itself and out into open country.

Daniel turned, looking back at the camp. The land dipped here, going down into the valley before it climbed again, so they would be in sight of the camp for two, maybe three, kilometres. After that, however, thick woodland obscured the view from the camp walls. There he would leave the road and head east, because he wasn't going straight back. First he would pay Horacek a visit.

They walked briskly, keeping up a business-like pace while the sun was low and it was less than thirty minutes before they reached the point, deep within the cover of the woods, where he wanted to leave the road.

"Okay," he said, turning to face them. "I didn't want to say anything before now, but we're on a special mission.

Daniel saw how their eyes lit at that and felt a twinge of guilt, knowing they would believe anything he said.

"I had to keep quiet about this, but now I'll tell you. We're heading east, to meet up with Marshal Horacek."

That news, he saw, was less pleasing. None of them liked Horacek. And for good reason. They had seen his methods at close hand, when he'd visited the camp.

"And don't worry," he added, looking from one to another. "*I* shall be dealing with the Marshal. You have only to get me there."

Relief, and new determination.

"Okay," he said, smiling now. "So our brief is simple. We move quickly and try not to be seen. We rendezvous with Horacek and then we go back to the camp. If all goes well, no one will know about our little detour. Right?"

"*Right!*"

"Good. Then let's go. We've eight kilometres to make."

* * *

One of the golden-eyed, standing just back from the shadowed window of the ruined hut, saw them as they passed, moving quickly, silently along the gully that cut between the trees. Eight boys in heavy armour, the sunlight, filtering down through the branches, glinting off the hard edges of their suits.

Taking a step forward, he rested his hands against the cool stone of the window ledge, and as he did, he felt a strange yet familiar sensation grip him.

There was a flash of pure vision. The trees, the gully, the boys – all vanished. All, that was, but the largest of the boys, who now strode along alone on a grassy slope. And as he walked he appeared and then disappeared, time and again, his progress across the slope like a sequence of intercut films. There was laughter just out of vision and the clapping of hands. And then the boy turned and smiled.

Abruptly the vision faded and was gone.

Below him the gully was empty now. Only the faintest sound of booted feet on leaves came back to him, and in an instant that too was gone.

Daniel. The boy had been called Daniel.

He frowned, then turned, looking back into the room, wondering what the vision meant.

* * *

Daniel crouched by the wall, the boys spread out in a line to either side of him, waiting for him to give the order. Two big container vehicles – half-tracks with refrigeration units – were at the end of the lane, some two hundred metres distant. Beyond them men in bright green one-pieces were moving to and fro between the compound and the lane, loading the second of the vehicles.

Daniel ducked down, then unfolded the map and studied it again. According to the map, there was nothing here. Nothing, that was, except an old ruined barn.

So why the vehicles? Why the armed guards?

The vehicles belonged to SimFic, the entertainments company. At least, they had the double helix logo on the side. But what in the gods' names were SimFic doing out here at the edge of town?

Time was pressing, and he knew he really ought to be moving on if he was to see Horacek and get back. But this was intriguing. This was the kind of thing the patrols had been designed to observe.

If SimFic were working with the rebels, then maybe someone ought to know? Or maybe not.

Daniel looked down, frowning. Before yesterday, he wouldn't even have thought about it, but now he couldn't think of anything else.

What *was* he fighting for? To cleanse the world of rebels? To bring about that "New World" they had all been told so much about? But what kind of "New World" was it that had no compassion? And what kind of creatures were being bred to live in it?

Daniel looked along the line, giving the signal to hold position. At once the boys relaxed, turning to slump against the wall, taking the opportunity to rest, their weapons propped between their knees.

They were good lads, and in another world they might have made fine adults. But not in this world. Not in a world modelled upon Horacek and his like.

There was the sound of huge doors slamming shut, then a call. Boots clanged against the metal sides of the vehicles as men climbed up. Then, the two engines started up, sputtering into life, then giving a deep, throaty roar. There was a strong smell of diesel, the crunch of gears being engaged, and then the first vehicle started away.

He waited until it was silent in the lane once more, then waited a little longer, listening. Only then, when he was quite sure that no one had stayed on, did he poke his head up and look.

The lane was empty, the gate to the compound closed.

"Come on," he said, straightening up, "let's go and have a look."

* * *

At first he thought the barn was empty. There were dark stains on the bare earth floor, which, on closer inspection, might have been blood, but without analysis it was hard to tell. Then, in the shadows at the far end of the barn, they made their discovery.

At first glance Daniel thought that they were sacks of some kind. They were certainly stacked like sacks. But, shining a torch on them, he saw at once what they were.

One of the boys helped him carry one of the tiny bodies across and lay it down in the light.

Daniel raised his visor, then knelt, examining the corpse. The girl was five, maybe six years old. She had been killed by a single bullet to the side of the head. Her hands were still bound behind her back and there were bruises on her forearms. Her feet too were bound, at the ankles, and one of her fingers had been broken.

Daniel swallowed, strangely moved by the sight of her. Her long blonde hair was caked with blood and it was impossible to tell whether she had been pretty or not, so much of her face had been blown away, but he could imagine how she'd been. Could imagine her playing; could see her running, laughing in the sunlight.

Executed, he thought. *But why?*

They carried others across and examined them. They were all the same. All of them had been bound hand and foot, then killed by a single shot to the head.

Detaching himself from what he was doing, Daniel began to search the bodies, looking for papers. Almost at once he found an ID card.

The girl was from Lorrach, near Basel. One of the southern villages, bordering the Wilds.

He quickly searched the other bodies. Not all of them had papers, but those who did were all from the southern villages.

So what was going on? And what was SimFic's involvement?

He thought back to what he had seen in the lane and nodded to himself.

There had been shortages for years now. Indeed, he was hard put to think of a time when there had *not* been shortages, and not just in the camps. But if this was systematic, then things had worsened considerably.

Supposition, he told himself. *Maybe they're taking them off to bury them.*

Then why not bury them here? Why bother with the trucks, the guards and all? Why get SimFic involved in what was clearly a security matter?

Another thought struck him. If they'd left these then the trucks must have been full. There must have been no room for them. Or maybe they were coming back for them. Maybe . . .

He understood. This wasn't a one-off. This *was* systematic.

Business as usual.

"Okay," he said, "let's put them back."

"Can't we . . .?"

Daniel turned. Robbie was standing there, his gun hanging limply from his right hand as he stared at the tiny bodies.

"Can't we what?"

The boy turned, looking to Daniel. "They're just kids, Daniel. Can't we . . . well. *bury* them?"

Kids. And what were they?

"No," he said sternly. "We stack them back where we found them, and then we forget we ever came here, right?"

There was no answer.

"*Right?*" he insisted, looking about him.

"Right!" But the enthusiasm was rote, not real. This had touched them, *disturbed* them, the same way he himself had been touched.

He was glad that was so. Was glad that they saw what *he* saw. But it made things difficult.

"Come on now! Move!"

Daniel watched, pained by the looks they gave him, steeling himself against them. Personally, he wanted to burn the place down – to take the flamer and destroy all trace of it. But then questions would be asked. And if anyone was going to ask questions, it was going to be him.

"Come on!" he barked, angry now. "Let's stack them and get out of here!"

Children. The bastards were killing little children now. Tying them up and shooting them.

Yes, he thought. *But then, what's new?*

* * *

Horacek yawned and stretched, then sat behind his desk, staring at Daniel, who stood there at ease, his legs apart, his hands clasped behind his back. It was a cold, predatory stare that seemed to have nothing human in it whatsoever, and, facing it again, Daniel thought it strange that he had not understood things sooner than he did. It was not simply Horacek's physical appearance, which – after his experience in the furnace – was ghastly enough, it was the essence of the man.

Evil. This little bastard was evil incarnate.

To Horacek's left, suspended from the ceiling of the room, hung a view screen. On it, like a scene from hell itself, two naked men were laughing as they sadistically tortured a young boy, hurting him even as they used him to pleasure themselves.

"You'll excuse me, Daniel," Horacek said, yawning again, "but we had a long night." He gestured towards the screen. "*Ti Yu* . . . They let you take a tape of it away."

Daniel gave the slightest nod, as if all was normal.

"But anyway," Horacek continued, pushing back from the desk, "why are *you* here, Daniel? I thought you were meant to be out on patrol?"

"I am," he answered. "But I had to see you."

"Yes?" Horacek looked intrigued. "I can't see why. Or if you did, why not go through normal channels?"

"Because I don't think either of us would welcome that."

Horacek's golden eyes flickered momentarily. He was clearly trying to work out what this was – threat or offer – and it was just as clear that he couldn't figure it.

"I'd like to give you something."

"*Give* me something?" Horacek's face stretched in the parody of a smile. Then he laughed. "What on earth could *you* give *me*, Daniel?"

"What does *he* want . . . more than anything else?"

"To end the blockade?"

"Aside from that."

Horacek shrugged.

"The Woman," Daniel said. "Alive."

Horacek sat forward, suddenly alert. "How?"

"I go in and get her. And bring her out."

"And then?"

"I give her to you. And you . . . you give her to The Man. As a present."

Horacek's mask-like face split in a smile. "Only one problem with that. How do we control her?"

"We wire her. In fact, if you'll teach me how, I'll do it for you before I bring her back."

Horacek thought about it, then shook his head again. "Too risky. If something went wrong . . ."

"Have you lost your nerve, Marshal?"

Horacek stood, his whole body bristling with anger, his voice cold with threat. "What do you mean?"

Daniel faced him out. "I thought you were a man who liked taking risks. I thought . . ."

"You thought what?"

"I thought . . ." Daniel steeled himself inwardly, then said it. "I thought we might make a good team, you and I."

Horacek stared at him a long while, a smile slowly forming on his black and rigid lips. "You know, I think we just might. Why, with my intelligence and your talent for killing . . ." He stopped, then sat again, steepling his fingers before him as he looked at Daniel. "I've been watching you a long time now. Studying you. And you know what? You're the perfect weapon, Daniel. Smart, great instincts, but . . ."

"But?"

"But you need . . . *directing*."

Daniel felt a chill go through him at the thought. On the screen one of the men was kneeling over the boy now, grimacing as he tightened a loop of wire about the boy's neck. The boy's face was turning purple like a bruise, the veins on the side of his neck standing out like cords. And all the while the second guard continued to thrust hard into his narrow buttocks, until his brutal face contorted in an agony of pleasure.

My world, Daniel thought. *The universe I inhabit.*

He tore his eyes from the image of the dying boy and met Horacek's eyes again.

"So will you show me?"

"Show you?"

"How to wire her."

Horacek was silent a moment, then he nodded. "Okay. But you must do something for me first, Daniel. You must swear an oath to me . . . an oath of personal loyalty, to me before all others."

Daniel met his eyes unflinchingly, conscious of the immense darkness behind their golden surfaces. "And The Man?"

Horacek came round the desk and stood before him, looking up into Daniel's face. "You want to work with me, Daniel?"

"Yes."

"Then forget The Man. Now, will you swear?"

Daniel stared back at him long enough to read the ambition, the burning envy of DeVore that dwelt in the dark depths of those golden eyes, then, lowering his head, he knelt and, taking Horacek's outstretched hand, kissed the iron ring.

"I swear."

* * *

A cold wind blew across the launching field as DeVore stepped down from the tower and greeted his creatures.

Sixty of his morphs stood there, in lines of ten, their huge space helmets tucked beneath their arms, their long, massive bodies made to seem even more gigantic by the rust-coloured spacesuits they wore.

Beyond them, on the far side of the field, a dozen spacecraft waited, their hatches open, like huge metallic spikes pointed at the late evening sky.

Stepping up onto the platform, DeVore felt an immense pride. They had prepared for this for months, yet if they felt anything now that the time had come, they did not show it. In that they were the perfect servants, obedient to a fault.

Even so, like his boys, they were only a stepping stone to something better. Beyond them, in the future, lay other, finer creatures. And beyond those . . .

DeVore shivered, feeling the black wind at the back of him, like a gale blowing from the heart of nothingness.

His vision had no bounds. Exaggerated evolution, that was his aim. A perpetual pushing back of the frontier. And in that process these creatures that he'd made – fine as they were – were but a start, an inkling of what was to be.

Oh Brave New World that has such creatures in it . . .

He smiled at the thought. Shepherd had sent him the book only two nights back, and he had read it at a sitting, intrigued that someone – a mere human, who had lived before the modern age – could have seen how it would be. Even so, his own dreams went beyond that Brave New World, to a bright clean future in which his new creatures – his Neumann – had spread out to fill the entire galaxy. And galaxies beyond.

He recalled what Shepherd had said and felt a tiny ripple of satisfaction.

That's what I like about you, Howard. Your dreams are so modest.

But greatness had no call for modesty, as Shepherd himself well knew. And his own greatness lay in just this – that he could see beyond the day, to other, brighter days, far in the future. No. He was not limited as these time-bound creatures were limited, for he not merely dreamed, he could fulfil his dreams.

Worlds without end, Amen . . .

He looked out over the lines of earnest, expectant faces – long, inhuman faces that were almost abstract in their form – and nodded.

"The time has come," he said, raising his voice above the noise of the wind. "Tonight we shall smash the American satellites and end their blockade of City Europe. Tonight . . ." he paused, "tonight we start a whole new age."

He saw how they looked back at him, self-contained and proud, the very picture of determination. They knew that this was effectively a suicide mission; even so, they would do their best for him. And if they perished in the process, then they would do so without question.

So they were. So he had made them.

As you made the others?

Again they were Shepherd's words. And again the bastard was right. Briefly DeVore thought of Tybor and the other rebel morphs. Those too he had made. But something had gone wrong.

Well, maybe he would have Shepherd look at it sometime and see if *he* could put his finger on the problem. For he had looked long and hard and still he had no proper explanation. Not one that satisfied. Their genetic programming had been no different from these sixty creatures, nor were there special factors in their nurturing that could have made them different – and yet different they were.

Twisted, somehow.

He pushed the thought aside, returning to the task in hand.

"You know what you have to do," he said, his voice hard, his eyes gleaming now, as if he saw it all in his mind's eye. "Yes, and you know how difficult a task it is. But there's one thing I've kept from you until now. One final, tiny yet all-important piece in the puzzle. I couldn't tell you before now because I couldn't afford to jeopardise our operation but the fact is, we've breached American security."

DeVore smiled, noting their surprise. "That's right. We've agents inside the American command centre, and those agents have promised us an envelope of forty-five seconds in which the central control system will be down. For that brief time the crews of all eighteen satellites will be cut off from their command centre and operating on manual control only. They'll be confused and part of their attention will be on re-establishing a link to central command, so that's when we hit them. As many as we can. The more we hit, the better our chances in the seconds after the system comes back on line. I've had our strategists look at it, and they reckon that if we can hit ten of the eighteen in those first forty-five seconds then we've won."

DeVore paused, placing his hands on his hips. "That's the theory. But I know you can do better than ten. In fact, if I'm right about you – if you're as good as I *think* you are – then there won't be a single satellite functioning when their system comes back up."

There were smiles at that.

"Can you imagine it? One moment they've a fully operational security umbrella, the next . . . *nada.*" He grinned. "You know, I'd love to be there in their command centre when those screens come up again, wouldn't you? All that white noise coming through the speakers. All those fuzzy little white lines on the screens. And it'll all be down to you."

He paused, satisfied with the effect of his words, then nodded. "Okay. You know what to do. Go to it."

DeVore watched them turn and begin to make their way across to the ships, then jumped down, a feeling of pure elation flooding him. But that feeling had little to do with the waiting ships or the perilous venture on which they were about to set out.

No. He smiled now because a signal had come, at last, an hour back, from Charon, Pluto's cold twin, out there on the farthest edge of the system. There where he had spent long years of exile.

A signal had come, twisting, folding its way between the universes, tumbling in and out of existence until it reached him here on Earth. And following it, threading its way along the same existent/non-existent path, a ship.

DeVore grinned, then pushed through the door, mounting the steps of the tower, his cruiser waiting on the pad above.

* * *

"*Robbie . . .*"

The boy stirred, then rolled over. "Daniel?"

"*Shhh.*" Daniel placed a finger to the boy's lips, then eased back, away from him as he sat up.

"*What is it?*"

In answer, Daniel gestured towards the open doorway and the showers beyond. Robbie frowned. He'd been woken before now, by older boys, and taken to the showers. But Daniel? He'd not thought Daniel was like that.

A little shiver ran through him as he placed his feet on the cold stone floor.

Come on, Daniel mouthed. *There's not much time.*

He swallowed, then padded through, following Daniel into the shower block. A single dull light at the far end threw blurred shadows over the stalls. As he brushed past Daniel, Daniel quietly closed the door.

He turned, frightened now.

"*Quick now*," Daniel whispered. "*I can't trust anyone else.*"

He was holding a knife. A finely-honed stiletto with a bone handle.

Robbie took a step backward. "I . . . don't understand."

But Daniel seemed not to notice his fear. He walked past him and into one of the stalls. "*Come on*," he hissed.

His legs feeling weak now, Robbie went across. Daniel was kneeling now. As Robbie stepped up to him, he held out the stiletto.

"*The scar*," Daniel said, indicating the bright red line on his neck near the base of his skull. "*I want you to cut it open for me. But careful. Just part the surface, okay?*"

Robbie hesitated. What in the gods' names was going on? "*I . . . I can't.*"

"*You must. Now quickly. I can do the rest.*"

He noticed the mirror on the floor by Daniel's side, the towel.

Grimacing, his hand trembling faintly, he placed the tip of the stiletto against the top of the scar.

"*That's it*," Daniel encouraged. "*Now push. But gently.* Just enough to part the flesh."

He did as he was told, wincing as the blade cut neatly through, the flesh parting like an opening mouth. Blood weeped from the wound, but Daniel hardly seemed to notice.

"*Good*," he said, picking up the mirror and studying Robbie's handiwork. "*Now pick up the towel and hold it ready. I'll need it in a while.*"

Robbie watched, afraid and yet fascinated as Daniel, staring into the mirror, delved into his own head with the fine blade. At first he didn't understand. Then he gasped.

As the blade emerged, it drew out with it the finest of silver wires, and at the end of that wire a tiny bulb, no bigger than a five *fen* coin.

"*What* is *that?*"

Daniel snipped the wire, then signalled to Robbie to place the towel against his head. Blood was flowing freely now.

"*Can you sew?*" Daniel asked.

Robbie hesitated, then nodded.

"*Good. Then sew me up. There's a needle and thread up there on the tray.*"

CHAPTER · 8

TO NINEVEH

They had travelled all night, through the cool darkness of the desert. Now it was morning, and Li Yuan sat on a rock in the shade at the foot of the great rocky hollow, his hands bound, looking up at the two men who were guarding him.

He could see them just above him, standing on the uppermost ledge of the rocky depression, their slender figures silhouetted against the morning sky. They had their backs to him, but there was little chance of him escaping. Even if he overpowered these two, there were more close at hand. Besides, where would he run to? There was nothing but desert out here.

They were young men, clean-shaven, the youngest barely out of his teens, and they wore no uniforms, not even a sash or badge, only a strange tattoo, like a blunted spade or an upturned parasol, on their upper arms. There was no mistaking their earnestness, however. *Run*, they'd told him, *and you're dead.*

And so he sat there, listening.

"He's late," the younger of them said impatiently. "He said he'd be here by now."

"He's probably busy," the other answered. "A lot's been happening."

"Yes, but . . ."

"No buts, brother. We wait. And when He comes, we do his bidding."

The younger man fell quiet. The other turned, glancing down at Li Yuan, whistling to himself all the while.

Whoever they were, they were a strange lot. They talked often of "He", and always with a strange, awed reverence, as if they spoke of a T'ang or an emperor of old. Yet he, Li Yuan, was the last of the emperors. And beside this other, he, it seemed, was as nothing.

A cult. They had to be a cult of some kind. And they had kidnapped him. To ransom him, perhaps.

He almost laughed. Ransom, eh? Well, once he would have commanded a true emperor's ransom – his weight in diamonds, maybe – but now . . .

Now I'm not worth a piss in a rusty tank.

He looked down, smiling. It was strange how the expressions of these barbarians had rooted so firmly in his mind when so little else of theirs had taken hold. There was a blunt realism to many of their sayings that he found attractive, almost Han.

But when they found out his true worth? What then? Would they let him go?

Not a hope in hell, he thought, part of him already reconciled to his fate. *When they find I'm worth less than a bull's pizzle, then they'll slit my throat quicker than* . . . he searched for the name Zelic had used . . . *ah, yes, Jack Robinson.*

Briefly he had a vision of himself, there before the great white tablet in the walled garden of his father's palace in Tongjiang, in Sichuan Province, sprigs of white blossom in his jet-black hair as he stood beneath the Tree of Heaven, the wind blowing from the mountains to the north.

There where his father lay already, encased in pure white jade, his beautifully carved tomb beside that of his elder brother, Han Ch'in, who had been murdered on his wedding day.

Li Yuan shivered and looked down at where his hands grasped each other tightly.

They were wild lands now, in the control of some Warlord or another, while he sat here on a rock on the far side of the world, a prisoner of fortune.

And suddenly he knew. Knew, with a certainty that took his breath, that he would never see that ancient walled garden again, nor lie with his ancestors in the eternal silence of the family tomb.

No. And no son of his would sweep his tomb and burn incense to his departed souls, for the great chain was truly broken, and he was like a ghost in this land without ghosts.

Li Yuan looked up again, swallowing bitterly. How quickly his mood had changed, like a weather vane, blown this way and that by the wind.

So the mad felt, probably.

Not that he thought himself mad. Not yet.

Above him there was sudden movement. The two young men stepped back, into the shadow of the rock. A moment later Li Yuan heard the distinctive whine of a cruiser.

A reconnaissance craft, perhaps, out looking for him. That was, if they even cared where he had got to. In all likelihood these rebels – if rebels they were – had done his son-in-law a great favour in ridding him of such a burden.

The sound grew louder briefly, then diminished. As it fell quiet again the two men stepped out onto the ledge once more.

The elder turned, gesturing towards Li Yuan. "Whatever happens, we'll move him tonight."

"To Isis?"

"No. This one's being taken to Nineveh."

"*Nineveh?*"

Li Yuan saw how the young man turned, looking back at him, his eyes seeing him anew.

"Who is he?" he asked, after a moment.

The elder of them turned and smiled. "It doesn't matter, Jem. Who he is now is not important. It is who he will become. In the pit all men shed their former selves . . ."

"Oh, I know the words," Jem interrupted. "But a Chink. A fucking Chink!"

"Chinks are human, too, Jem. Cut them and they bleed."

"And so does a coyote. But Nineveh . . . are you sure?"

The elder seemed about to reply, then broke off. Someone was coming.

"Heather," he said, greeting a young woman who appeared on the ledge carrying a tray on which was a steaming bowl, some bread and a leather water bottle. "What's this?"

"For our guest," she said, letting them inspect the tray before they waved her through.

She came down the narrow steps and stood before Li Yuan, then crouched, setting the tray down. Then, as Jem covered her with a gun, she set about unbinding Li Yuan's hands.

Li Yuan looked up at her with a smile of thanks as he massaged each of his hands in turn. They had tied him tightly and there was a deep red welt about each wrist.

She had green eyes and, in her occidental way, an attractive face. And she too wore the tattoo – that strange bowl-like shape with a spike jutting up from it – on her upper arm.

"Eat," she said simply, handing him the tray and smiling. "You need to keep your strength up."

For a time he was silent as he broke the rough home-made bread and dipped it in the soup. He ate and drank and felt much better for it. Yet as he bent down to place the tray on the ground, he winced, a sharp pain shooting through his back. Seeing it, the woman hurried round behind him and, unexpectedly, began to massage his neck and shoulder muscles, her hands working their way expertly down his spine, the tension easing from him almost as if by magic.

"There," she said, straightening up, then came round in front of him again.

Li Yuan looked up at her, his eyes seeking an explanation.

"We don't mean to harm you, Li Yuan," she said. "You'll understand in time."

"Then why . . .?"

She placed a finger to his lips. "No questions." Then, with a gentleness neither of the guards had shown, she bound his hands once more, careful not to pull the ropes too tight.

"Later," she said as she picked up the tray and stood. "After Nineveh."

And then she was gone. Li Yuan stared after her a moment. Then, noting how the younger guard was scowling at him, he looked down, wondering.

* * *

That night they moved him. Four men – one of them masked, as if to hide his identity – came just before nightfall and, placing Li Yuan in a cart, bound his feet and tightened the bindings on his hands. Then, as the night before, there was a journey across the cooling desert, under a moonless sky that, to Li Yuan, lying on his back in the jolting cart, seemed dusted with a million bright stars.

He thought at first they were taking him to Nineveh – wherever that was – but from the few things he overheard, he quickly understood that things had changed. He was to go to Isis, after all.

There "He" would come and speak with him.

Li Yuan was tired and the motion of the cart lulled him; even so, he could not sleep. There were too many questions left unanswered.

Who were these people and what did they want with him? Were they rebels, or fanatics, or what? Certainly they had a seriousness to them – a sense of purpose – that he'd not witnessed among the Americans of the fortress cities. And certainly he had some part to play in their plans, or else why take him? Why keep him and transport him from place to place, unless . . .?

Unless what?

Always and ever he ran up against a point at which he knew nothing. And that was by far the worst of it. To be utterly in the hands of someone else. To have no say in where you went, or what you did, or what, ultimately, happened to you.

Li Yuan closed his eyes, feeling the bare wooden boards behind his head, and wondered how much further he could fall before the earth swallowed him up?

Down into *Ti Yu*, the earth prison, where the Great Warder of Hell himself presided.

The thought of it almost – almost – made him smile. Did he believe any of that any more? Hadn't he seen enough of the world to know that hell was not beneath the ground but up here on the surface? Or so Man could make it, just as Man could make a heaven for himself right here beneath the open sky.

Man lived between the dark earth and the dark sky, in an illusion of light, and all his life was shadowplay. And in an instant – in less time than a bird takes to ruffle its feathers – it was over, and the darkness was all.

So it was with illusions. Whereas reality . . .

Reality was this – this feeling of absolute powerlessness before forces over which he had no control. And even emperors – even T'ang – must bow to those forces ultimately. To the eternal processes of nature, and to the truth of entropy.

What did you do with your life, Li Yuan?

The voice seemed like his father's, but he knew his father would never have asked him such a question. His father had had little time for introversion.

I guess I lost a world.

The cart bumped on, over hard rock, climbing momentarily, then dipping down into a long valley.

The voice seemed surprised. *Was it yours to lose, then?*

He had to think about that.

It was given to me, by my father.

So it was his?

No. Not exactly. There were seven great Lords, you see, and between them . . .

But the voice interrupted him, impatient with that answer.

Who gave it to your father's father's father?

Li Yuan frowned. *No one gave it, exactly, he . . .*

Stole it?

Li Yuan's eyes flicked open. For a moment he had thought someone was there beside him on the cart, speaking to him. But the presence, like the voice, had been imaginary.

He dug his heels into the board and struggled up, wedging his back against the tailboard of the cart, then shook his head.

Voices. He was hearing voices now.

Tiredness, he told himself, conscious that the light had changed – that it was almost morning now. *The voices are only a product of your tiredness, Li Yuan.*

Yet for a moment, just before the end, it had seemed as if someone was really questioning him – pushing him to justify all that he was, and all that he had once been.

Thieves. Was that all that emperors were, when it came down to it? And was the Emperor merely the most successful of all thieves?

Li Yuan shivered, then flexed his fingers, feeling the ropes pull tight, chafing his wrists again.

And so the thief was caught, finally, and brought to justice.

The cart bumped on, jolting him, making him slip to the side and bang his head. Exhausted now, he lay there, staring up, up into the infinite night, and slowly the night came down into him.

And Li Yuan closed his eyes . . . and slept.

* * *

Egan stood facing the full-length screen, his hands on his hips, barely able to contain himself.

"How the fuck could you have let them take him, Major? Have you no defences whatsoever?"

Major Lanier lowered his head. "It was not our fault, Master. Captain Zelic . . ."

"Was acting to make up for your deficiencies!" Egan quivered with anger. "If you had taken proper precautionary measures in the first place, he would not have *had* to have interceded!"

Lanier glowered at that, but Egan wasn't having any of it.

"You'll scour the desert until you find him. And when you do – and it had better be alive and in one piece – you'll bring him directly here, to Boston."

"Master."

"Now is there any other bad news you have to relate to me, or are you finished for today?"

Lanier licked at his lips, then shook his head.

"Then get to it, man, at once!"

Egan cut the connection and turned. Li Kuei Jen was standing nearby, staring at him, his face filled with concern.

"Who could it be? Who would take my father?"

Egan came across and held his wife's arms. "Don't worry, Jenny. We'll find him. And when we do, we'll punish those who've taken him."

"Unless they kill my father first."

"Don't talk like that. Don't give up. We'll find him and we'll bring him back here, and then all will be well."

Li Kuei Jen looked up, meeting his husband's eyes. That was the thing about Mark Egan. In essence, he was a child, with a child's responses to the world. Oh, not a callous or whimsical child, yet still a child. His enthusiasms were as a child's enthusiasms and he hoped and dreamed – and was disappointed – as a child was.

"Come now," Egan said, smiling at him, "our friends await us."

The banquet was in full swing. Anyone of importance in Boston's élite was there, to celebrate their victory.

Egan paused in the huge doorway at the top of the stairs, waiting while total silence fell at the tables in the great hall below. Then he proceeded down, Li Kuei Jen on his arm. As everyone in the hall stood, Han Ch'in, who had thus far deputised for Egan, hurried across from the top table to greet them at the foot of the steps.

Han Ch'in bowed low. "Welcome home to Boston, Master," he said, loud enough for all in the hall to hear. "May I be the first to congratulate you on a historic victory."

It was over the top, yet it was clearly working. All about the hall faces were beaming now, as if a victory really had been won. Eyes glowed with excitement. All there wanted to be associated with this great success.

"Peace has been won," Egan said, smiling as he looked about him. "Now we must work to subdue the barbarians of the south."

A great cheer went up at that, but Egan raised his hands, begging for their silence once again. As he did, one of the stewards came across with a tray of drinks. Egan took two, handing them to Kuei Jen and Han Ch'in, then took one himself. He raised it.

"But first let us celebrate this great triumph. Let us drink a toast to our armies in the west. And to victory!"

The roar was deafening, as a thousand glasses were raised. "To victory!"

Egan drained his glass then turned and, whispering into Kuei Jen's ear, said: "I think you're right, Jenny. I think we might ride the tiger yet!"

* * *

Isis was a place between rocks. A natural circle of rocks that hid a bowl of dark water some half a *li* across. And beyond that, a village was cut into the rock itself, ledge after ledge of it, climbing the rock face.

It was morning, and the slopes above the village were in sunlight, but where Li Yuan sat in the cart it was still in shadow. He shivered, cold for the first time since he'd been taken, and looked across.

The men who had brought him were talking with other men; arguing, it seemed. Then, suddenly, it was resolved, and one he had not met before came across and, standing at the tail of the cart, stared at him as if to say, 'So this is what a T'ang looks like, is it?'

Li Yuan stared back at him. "Who are you?" he demanded.

But the man did not feel obliged to answer him. He turned away, walking back to those who had brought Li Yuan and making a dismissive gesture.

There was momentary laughter.

People were watching now, from the ledges and from windows.

If he could, he would have stood, defying them, but it was hard to be defiant when one's hand and feet were tied and one could not even move without falling over.

He closed his eyes, deciding he would wait, as the sages waited, with a patience born of inner strength. Yet after a moment he found he had to look again.

Someone was standing nearby, whistling a tune. Li Yuan laughed softly, then tried to turn his head to see who it was, for he knew that tune.

It was "*The Moon on High*."

Soft footsteps approached. The whistling stopped.

"Are you ready for me now, Li Yuan?"

He knew that voice. Knew it, but could not pin down whose it was. The same voice that had been in his head on the journey here.

"Unbind me," he said quietly. "There's nowhere I can go, after all."

A moment's silence, then, "Not yet. The place must be prepared. Then we shall meet . . . and talk."

"Who . . .?"

But the owner of the voice was no longer there.

* * *

The feast was going well. Very well. Indeed, from the air of celebration, no one would have guessed that at that very moment, on the far side of the continent, half of their once-proud army was in chains, being marched across the great desert that lay west of the Black Hills, towards Eugene, a thousand kilometres distant.

Four million men, of whom barely a third would reach their destination.

Egan, whose mind could think of nothing else, looked up, a pained expression in his eyes. Kuei Jen had nudged him.

"I beg pardon, I was . . ."

He saw who it was. The blunt, misshapen head could belong to no one else, nor that strange, disfigured torso.

"Colonel Chalker," he said. "You have news?"

Chalker raised his head, his cobalt blue eyes – the coldest eyes of anything, man or lizard, Egan had ever seen – meeting Egan's own.

"Horton's ours," he said quietly. "I took him an hour back. I have him in the cells downstairs."

Egan stood, then sat again, his hands still gripping the arms of his chair. He wanted to go immediately; to tear from Horton what part he'd had in Li Yuan's abduction, but there was still the banquet to think of. For once the public face mattered more than anything else.

"Well done," he said, keeping his own voice low. "Keep him safe for me, Colonel. And once things are finished here, I'll come."

Chalker's eyes widened slightly. "Shall I begin without you, Master?"

Egan considered, then shook his head. "This once, no, Alan. I want to hear every word he utters, every last inflection in his voice." He paused, then. "We need to know who are our enemies, and who our friends."

Chalker came smartly to attention, then turned and went.

Kuei Jen, at Egan's side, was quiet a moment, then leaned towards his husband.

"You called him Alan. Why? I've never known you use his name before."

Egan smiled. Nothing escaped Kuei Jen. He leaned towards him, whispering into his ear. "It's something you said, Jenny. We need every friend we can get right now, and who better to have on our side than Chalker. Gods, I'd hate to think of *him* in Horton's pay! But I knew he wanted to set about torturing our friend Horton at once, and as I'd have to disappoint him there, I thought I'd give him something."

"A name."

"Yes. Even the coldest fish likes to think he has friends."

Kuei Jen nodded, then put his hand over Egan's. "You are wise, Mark. Now, make the announcement. And don't fuck it up. Bad news first, good news second. Knock them down, then stand them up again. Take away something big . . ."

". . . and give back something small. I get the idea, Kuei Jen. Now quiet while your Lord and Master speaks."

Egan rose to his feet. At once there was the clashing of a gong. Silence fell once more over the long rows of tables in the hall. All eyes were on the king.

"Friends . . . citizens of the great state of America. Today we celebrate. Today we share in the joy of a great success. But the job is only half done. We have other enemies, other great battles to fight. And that is why I have decided to declare martial law . . ."

There was a shocked gasp, then uproar, but Egan simply raised his voice – a microphone at his lapel switching in, channelling his voice to the speakers all about the hall, so that his voice suddenly boomed above the rest of the noise.

"However, I make a solemn promise. That this situation will exist only so long as it needs to exist, and not a day longer."

"And how long is that?" called a voice from Egan's right.

"A year. Maybe less. Until we have subdued the southern barbarians and made a lasting peace."

"And DeVore?"

Egan looked to Harding, who had spoken.

"Nothing has changed," Egan said. "We shall continue to contain DeVore."

"But the expense . . ."

Kuei Jen could see the flush at his husband's neck and knew he was inwardly furious that Harding should choose this public moment to question him about policy. But Egan kept his temper. He answered Harding calmly, keeping all irritation from his voice.

"We must bear the expense. Or see that bastard sitting on the throne of America. Is *that what you want*, Chancellor?"

"No. But might we not come to some arrangement with the man?"

Egan smiled sourly. "One does not deal with DeVore. One fights or one rolls over like a whipped dog."

There was moment's silence, then Egan turned again, looking out over the main body of the hall, raising his arms.

"Friends, do not be afraid. I take these measures only for *your* good. To protect *you*. For you, as much as I, are the State. And you, I'm sure, once you've had time to reflect, will see how sensible this measure is in the light of what lies ahead."

Egan paused. "Great sacrifices must be made in the struggle to come. We will be stretched . . . stretched almost to breaking point, yet we shall prevail, if we stay strong. And that is why I ask for your support in this measure. For if you are behind me then we *must* prevail."

Maybe, Kuei Jen thought, looking up at his husband, immensely proud of him at that moment, *but first we must survive the next two days.*

* * *

They took him to a cave below the lip of the great rock and sat him on a rock ledge. There they removed his blindfold and unbound him, then left him.

It was a long, low-ceilinged cave. A single lamp burned in a cresset to his left. It was cool and dry and smelled of cinnamon and spice.

Alone in the half dark, Li Yuan sat and waited, listening to the slow drip of water from the far end of the cave. The very sound of stillness.

Outside it was night. A pitch black, moonless night. Even so, he could make out the outline of the entrance, above him and to his right, shaped like an inverted shield, jagged on one side, smooth on the other.

Li Yuan looked down, staring at his hands, remembering the heavy ring of iron he had once worn on the index finger of his left hand; a ring of power, symbol of the authority of the Seven who had once ruled Chung Kuo. His father's ring, and *his* father's before that. The same ring that now lay at the bottom of the Atlantic Ocean, where his son had thrown it.

Li Yuan frowned, recalling Kuei Jen's words that day when they had left City Europe. "*Chung Kuo is gone. We must learn to be ordinary people now.*"

So it was. But though he had not been happy when he had worn the ring, he still could not understand how Kuei Jen had thrown it away so casually.

"Oh, it was far from casual."

Li Yuan turned, startled. He had heard no one come into the cave. The voice – the same voice as earlier – came from the shadows behind him. He turned to face them, unable to discern a figure there.

"I *am* here, Li Yuan. But you cannot see me. Not yet. Not until you are ready to see me."

"What *is* this?" Li Yuan asked. But he felt shaken. How had his interrogator known what he was thinking?

"Oh, I know many things, my friend. All manner of things that you would rather have kept hidden."

Li Yuan took a long breath, then, "How do you do that?"

"Tell what's on your mind?" There was gentle laughter. "It is not hard, Li Yuan. You are a simple man when it comes down to it. Oh, maybe not as simple as these Americans, but certainly no wiser."

"You seem to take great pleasure in insulting me."

There was a brief silence then. "No. No pleasure. And I meant no insult. Yet we are not here to flatter each other."

"Then what *are* we here for?"

"To find out what manner of man you are, and why you have wasted your life."

"Wasted?" Li Yuan stood and took a step toward the voice. Still he could not see the figure of his interrogator. "How do you mean, *wasted*?"

"You wish to argue otherwise?"

"I . . ." He paused, then backtracked. "I heard your voice . . . out in the desert, coming here."

"That is so."

Li Yuan nodded to himself, then smiled, as if he suddenly understood. "Speakers. You are using hidden speakers, aren't you? It is all tricks. Illusions."

"If that explanation makes you happy."

"But it is the truth, neh?"

The same gentle laughter spilled out into the darkness, making Li Yuan go rigid with anger. He did not like being patronised.

"Too tense," the voice said, more familiar by the moment. "You were always too tense. Except with your maids. And there you had nothing to prove, neh?"

Li Yuan jutted out his jaw, an ugly expression on his face. "What do you mean, *lao jen*?"

"Only that a poor horseman always blames his animal . . ."

Li Yuan closed his eyes, anger burning in him. Insults. Nothing but insults.

". . . or kills it."

His eyes flicked open, surprised that the old man knew so much about him. He had indeed killed his horses, but only to stop his pregnant wife from riding.

"Rather drastic, wouldn't you say?"

Li Yuan shook himself, as if to wake himself from a dream. "How . . .?"

". . . do I know your thoughts?" There was the rustle of silks, then, "It is a power I have. To see clearly into the minds of others. For a long time I had forgotten how, but now my powers have returned. The time is almost upon us, and the way must be prepared."

"The way?"

"Of that I cannot speak. Not yet. But you are part of it, Li Yuan, and must be prepared for what lies ahead. You must be purged. Then, and only then, can you be reborn."

"It sounds . . ." he sought for the word Zelic had used for some of the Han beliefs they had talked about, ". . . *cranky*."

"Irrational, you mean?"

"That also."

"And you were ever one for rational explanations, weren't you, Li Yuan?"

"The world is what it is," he answered, "subject to fixed laws."

"That is true," the voice answered from the darkness, "but what if you do not understand those laws, Li Yuan? What if those laws make the universe quite *other* than you think it is. Your senses, after all, are limited."

"Even so . . ."

"Go to the pool, Li Yuan."

The voice was commanding. Li Yuan stood.

"Behind you," the voice said. "Can you not hear the water dripping?"

Li Yuan turned, then slowly walked across, stopping before what looked like a large, shallow bowl. The surface of it was black like ink.

Staring down into it, Li Yuan shivered, the memory returning to him of all the times he had stood beside the carp pond in Tongjiang, watching the dark shapes of the fish move slowly in the depths like circling thoughts.

A drop of water fell. The dark surface rippled, then settled again. It was like looking into the pupil of an eye.

"Well, Li Yuan? What would you like to see?"

He looked up, turning his head. It was as if the voice was at his shoulder now. More trickery, he guessed. Like this. This too, he suspected, was an elaborate trick.

"My mother," he said. "I'd like to see my mother."

A drop of water fell, the surface rippled. As it cleared, the pool began to glow. Slowly an image formed.

Two naked, sweat-wreathed bodies in the throes of passion, the man pressing down, the tendons in his arms strained and rigid beside the woman's head, his powerful buttocks thrusting like a blacksmith hammering iron, the woman's limbs embracing his flanks, her pert breasts moulded to his chest as she pushed up to receive each penetrating stroke.

And their faces . . .

Li Yuan gasped, realising what he was witnessing. He fell onto his knees, horrified, but unable now to look away.

A drop fell, rippling the surface, but still it went on.

Slowly their movements grew more urgent, like two riders urging their mounts on, each matching thrust more brutal and more desperate until, the muscles of their faces locking in mutual agony, their two bodies tensed and seemed to quiver against each other, their groins pressed as close as flesh permitted. And then a great spasm passed through them, making them shudder, as if an electric shock had been administered.

Their mouths groaned silently as they strained to break down the natural barriers of flesh, he into her, she into him. And then, when it seemed relief would never come, she fell back, he expiring upon her. And there they lay, her hand about his neck, caressing him.

Li Yuan shivered, astonished by the sight, amazed both by the brutality of the act and the tenderness that followed.

"Thus were you conceived, Li Yuan."

Yes, and thus had his father worshipped his mother, and she him.

"You understand, then, Li Yuan?"

He nodded, numbed by the knowledge. Oh, he had guessed how much his father had missed his mother, if only from his own feelings of loneliness, but never – until this moment – had he known just how finally his father's world had ended that evening in the floating palace, high above Chung Kuo.

Yes, *ended*, even as his own had begun.

Beside that single loss, his own losses – all of them, piled high, one atop another – were as nothing, for he had never loved like that. No, not even Fei Yen.

"Ah, then, you *do* understand."

Li Yuan felt a hand gently touch his shoulder. There was the rustle of silk and then the old man stood beside him. He turned, his eyes widening with surprise.

"Tuan Ti Fo!"

The old Master smiled. "So I am known to men. But I too have had to remember much that I had forgotten."

"Forgotten?"

"Look," Tuan Ti Fo said, pointing down into the darkness of the pool once more. "Look and tell me what you see."

* * *

There was a commotion at the main door to the hall. A group of stewards were blocking the way of three men who seemed keen to gain admittance. Excusing himself, Li Han Ch'in got up and went across to see to the matter.

After the initial shock of the announcement, things had gone well, particularly when it became apparent that martial law would affect none of those present in the hall. For them it would be business as usual, but without the risk of late night harassment by surly and dissatisfied citizenry. Kuei Jen's idea of "special passes" for the privileged few had gone down well, taking the edge off a measure that might otherwise have provoked bitter opposition. And when Egan had gone on to speak of the planned campaign in the south, Kuei Jen had felt the mood in the hall change dramatically, becoming bullish once more – unrealistically optimistic.

And that was the trouble in the first place.

Over by the doorway voices had been raised. Han Ch'in's voice sounded loudly.

"I don't give a shit what that says! You are not coming in, and that's that!"

Kuei Jen smiled at the person to whom he'd been talking, then turned, looking across.

Han Ch'in stood just in front of the line of stewards, arguing with one of the newcomers, a Senior Advocate whom Kuei Jen recognised from court. He sometimes worked for Chancellor Harding and others of the older generation.

Egan leaned across and gestured toward the group. "That's going on over there? Are we expecting anyone else?"

"Not that I know of," Kuei Jen answered, dabbing at his lips with the cloth. "I'll go and see."

"What is it?" he asked his half-brother, as he stepped up to the group, his long dress trailing on the floor behind him.

Han Ch'in glared, then shook his head, handing Kuei Jen the document he had been holding. It was a lawyer's affidavit.

Kuei Jen read through it quickly, then glanced up, shocked, looking past the Advocate to meet the young man's eyes.

"It is true," the young man said, a strange depth to his voice. "I am Josiah Egan, and I *demand* to be admitted."

Kuei Jen studied him a moment, noting the absence of wrinkling of the skin, the pure, almost infant freshness of its flesh tone. It was a perfect body, more like a sculpture than something genuinely human, and the face, if anything, seemed not handsome in itself, but a mask of handsomeness.

All this was evidence. Yet it was the eyes that convinced Kuei Jen. They were clear and bright, a young man's eyes, and yet something ancient stared out through them. Looking at them, Kuei Jen shivered, knowing that at last it had been done.

Lifting his dress slightly, Kuei Jen curtsied low.

"Mister Egan," he said, straightening up and smiling, raising his voice so all nearby could hear. "Welcome to our humble gathering. May I have the honour of escorting you to the top table. Your grandson will be delighted to see you again."

* * *

"Did you love your brother?"

Li Yuan looked up, meeting Tuan Ti Fo's eyes. Both men were seated now, cross-legged, facing each other across the ink black pool.

"I idolised him."

"And used him, too . . ."

"Used?"

"As an excuse, when things went wrong."

"No, I . . ."

Tuan Ti Fo's eyes were compassionate, yet his words, as ever, went to the nub of things. So it had been this past hour.

"Think back, Li Yuan. How many times, when things did not go as you desired, did you not say to yourself, it is not *my* fault, I was not born to rule. And again, with Fei Yen, did you not convince yourself that it failed not through any fault of yours, but because she was your brother's wife?"

"That is not fair!"

"No?" Tuan Ti Fo looked down. At once the pool began to glow. A drop of water fell. The pool rippled and cleared, and as it did, Li Yuan found himself looking at the image of the young Fei Yen, standing at the great window at Tongjiang, her face anxious. There was no sound, but he could make out the words she said as clearly as if he had heard them.

"*Why has he left me here alone? Why does he not come?*"

A drop of water fell. The pool rippled once more as the image faded into black.

"You neglected her, Li Yuan. She could have been everything to you. Yes, and would have been, did you but know it. But you did not value what you were given. You *never* valued it. It was always too easy for you."

"Easy?" Li Yuan laughed scornfully. "It was *never* easy. There were so many conflicting choices, so many enemies."

"True. But also many friends. And advisors, too. Good men whom you might have listened to." Tuan Ti Fo shook his head, like a father chastising an errant son. "You were given a world, Li Yuan. Yes, and the intelligence and compassion to govern it. But you did not value what you were given. You took it for granted. As with Fei Yen, you had to lose it before you understood its worth."

Li Yuan huffed impatiently, clearly put out by the old man's words. "And that is how you see it, is it, *lao jen*? It was as simple as that?"

"I did not say it was simple, yet the underlying causes . . ." He paused, then, leaning towards Li Yuan asked gently. "When did it start, Li Yuan? When were you first wounded?"

"*Wounded*?"

"Yes. When did the hurt begin?"

Li Yuan was silent a moment, then, very quietly: "It did not begin. It was always there. I woke to life with it."

"Your mother . . ."

"Yes."

Tuan Ti Fo watched Li Yuan a while, then nodded to himself, his dark eyes thoughtful.

"When a man is hurt – hurt in the way that you were hurt, his nature scarred from birth – he can inflict much damage on those about him. That hurt can be a poison, festering in him, making him a source of much corruption. Yet when an emperor – a T'ang – is hurt, how much greater the damage he can do. So it was with you, Li Yuan. Your hurt – that scar you were born with – also scarred a world. It damaged not merely those about you, but billions of ordinary lives."

Li Yuan's eyes flared. "So it was all my fault?"

"No. Not all of it. Yet you were thoughtless sometimes, callous even. As when you drew the line between the cities. That scar inside you made you blind to the suffering of others. You *did not imagine* what you were doing."

Li Yuan sat there, staring at the surface of the pool, his silence like a shroud about him.

"Well?" Tuan Ti Fo said, after a while. "Have I said too much?"

Li Yuan looked up, a weariness in his eyes. "No." He sighed. "I remember Karr mentioning it to me once. About the people falling. Like grains of pepper, so he said. But even then I did not see it. Not the *truth* of it, anyway."

"So you never saw the faces?"

"Faces?"

"The faces in the ice . . . where you drew the line."

"Ah . . ." Li Yuan shook his head. "You have to understand. It was hard. Very hard. We were riding the tiger. Each day brought new and greater troubles. Tsu Ma, Wei Feng and I, we tried. I swear we tried. But sometimes it was easier to lie between a woman's legs – to seek oblivion there – than face the problems of the day."

"You wanted something certain and unchanging, didn't you? You wanted that eternal summer moment in the orchard with your brother. And what did you get? You got Change. Endless Change."

Li Yuan's face creased with pain. "It *was* so . . ."

"Yes, but you were weak, Li Yuan. You could have been a beacon to men. Instead you hid your light and sought refuge far too often in that sweet and scented darkness."

"Perhaps."

Tuan Ti Fo sighed. "Such weakness in a man is understandable, but in an emperor . . . In an emperor it is fatal."

Again Yuan's eyes flared. "I did not choose . . ."

"To be T'ang? No. And yet you were. You were their father, Li Yuan. You were responsible for them. They were clay, to be moulded to your will, for good or ill. Such power you had."

"And now here I am, *neh*?" Li Yuan looked about him, a bleakness in his eyes. "*Such* is the fate of kings."

"Do you still wish to be a king?"

"No."

"Then you would be an ordinary man?"

Li Yuan looked up. "Is it possible?"

"Perhaps."

"And afterwards?"

"Afterwards, you may go."

"Go?"

"Back to your sons. But first you must be changed."

"Changed? How changed?"

But Tuan Ti Fo merely smiled. "Rest now, Li Yuan. The dawn is coming. Tomorrow you will be taken from here."

"To Nineveh?"

"Yes. To Nineveh."

* * *

As they came from the hall and stepped out into the narrow, half-lit corridor, Kuei Jen paused and, reaching out to touch Egan's arm, put a finger to his lips. Not yards away, the tasters were sitting in their room, beneath the glare of an overhead light, laughing and talking among themselves. It had been a good night for them: no one had died. Indeed, not a single case of poisoning had been reported.

"We live in paranoid times," Kuei Jen whispered, pulling him on past the door, before they were noticed by the men within.

Not that it was any different in my father's court, Kuei Jen mused. But there it had been a matter of long habit. Here, one's personal survival depended almost entirely upon taking such precautions.

Kuei Jen looked to his husband as they stepped out into the end hallway. Mark Egan was half-drunk. The shock of seeing his grandfather in a new young body – a body younger and stronger than his own – had been too much for him. Indeed, had Kuei Jen not been there to intercede between the two, it could quite easily have come to blows.

As it was, things were bad. Despite Kuei Jen's best efforts, he had not been able to reconcile the two men. Mark Egan had, in reality, considered his grandfather a dead man – no more alive than a programmed hologram of some long-dead ancestor – and he saw this new Josiah Egan as little more than an imposter. Whereas Josiah . . .

Josiah wanted it all back. He hadn't said as much explicitly, but she had seen it in his eyes. He wanted to be the power once again. To rule America, yes, and his grandson too.

It could not have happened at a worse time.

Their private rooms were on the far side of the pillared hallway. Yet even as Kuei Jen made his way across, walking slowly, supporting Egan and keeping him from falling, a man stepped from the shadows to their right.

Fearing he was an assassin, Kuei Jen pushed Egan away and stepped towards the man, crouched down, knife drawn. Then he straightened, seeing who it was.

"Colonel Chalker! What are you doing here at this hour?"

To Kuei Jen's surprise, Chalker fell to his knees and, bowing his head toward Egan, offered his dagger, pommel first.

"What is this?" Egan said, stepping forward, his speech slurred. "Chalker, explain yourself!"

"It's Horton, sir. He's gone."

"Horton?"

The events of the latter part of the evening had clearly driven the memory of Horton's capture from Egan's mind. He frowned, then shook his head.

"Sprung, sir, from the cells. I have the culprits. I've racked them. They were working for him. It seems he took a cruiser from the roof . . ."

"Gone?" Egan said again. "Gone where?"

"West," Kuei Jen said, before Chalker could answer. "Coover's behind this, right, Colonel?"

"That is so," Chalker said. His head was still lowered, the dagger still held out.

Egan waved at the dagger. "Put that thing away, Alan . . ."

"But I failed you, sir."

"You heard my husband," Kuei Jen said, surprised by this display of loyalty and honour from a man he had previously thought of only as cruel and ambitious. "We have need of every loyal officer, and there is no more loyal a man than you, my friend. Now answer . . . is there any chance of catching Horton?"

Chalker put away his dagger, then stood, raising his head. "I fear not."

"And his friends?" Egan asked, the situation sobering him more effectively than a gallon jug of coffee.

"Fled, sir. We had three dozen names. Of those we shall be lucky if we take five."

"I see." Young Egan looked to his wife. "Li Kuei Jen, what do you make of this?"

"In one way it is good, for it clarifies things. Yet word will get out. To lose so many prominent citizens at a stroke will create gaps. People will talk. They will ask questions."

"Then tell them the truth," Chalker said. "Tell them that the Sons were traitors to America and planned to sell us to the highest bidder!"

Kuei Jen stared at the Colonel of Internal Security, a new respect for the man filling her. "I think that's a good idea, Colonel Chalker. A very good idea indeed."

* * *

Alone in the cabin of the cruiser, Horton let his head fall back and shut his eyes, the vibration of the craft's engines lulling him. For a moment, back there, he had thought it was the end. When Chalker had smiled at him that way, his blood had frozen. But here he was, safe, and Chalker . . .

One day, he promised himself, he would have Chalker; he would strap *him* down on a butcher's block and make *him* babble like a frightened child.

Coover. Yes, he was Coover's man now, like it or not.

"Feng?"

His eyes flicked open. "Russ? What the fuck are *you* doing here?"

Russ took the seat facing Horton, then smiled. "What, no thank you?"

Horton sat forward, piecing it together. "So it was *you*."

"Of course. I couldn't let Chalker have your arse, could I? Not when it's such a nice arse."

Horton swallowed, dismayed by this turn about. Fucking Russ had been one thing, being in his debt was another. In fact, he didn't like the thought of it at all.

"Then I have much to thank you for," he said, keeping his thoughts to himself. "I'll not forget what you did."

Russ's smile broadened. "And I'll not let you." And, leaning across, he placed his hand over Horton's groin. "Until later, eh?"

* * *

Old Man Egan pushed open the door and stomped across the room, kicking a footstool out of his path. Throwing himself down into a chair, he scowled at the two men who stood in the open doorway.

"Do you want something, Josiah?" Bernadini asked.

"His miserable neck!" Egan answered, his old man's whine unmistakable, even from his new voice box. "Fancy keeping me waiting like that! His own grandfather! The nerve of the boy!"

"It must have been a shock for him," Advocate Richards said, trying to calm the old man, but Egan would not be calmed.

"Shock! I'd give him a fucking shock!" He made a face of purest disgust. "And that wife of his! Wife! Don't make me fucking laugh! Some half-man fucking Chink, that's all *it* is! How *could* he! I'd as soon poke a fucking pig!"

Bernadini looked to Richards, exchanging a meaningful glance, then he stepped across to Egan. "Are you sure I can't I get you something, Josiah? To help you sleep, I mean."

"You can bring me a couple of girls. Young ones. Fourteen, fifteen. No older. And then you can leave me be."

Bernadini swallowed, then glanced round at Richards. Richards nodded, then vanished to do his Master's bidding. Bernadini turned back to Egan, then knelt.

"You need to take things a bit more slowly, Josiah. You can't tread on toes the way you used to. It won't work."

Egan scowled again. "Why not?"

"You've been out of things a while, that's why. Things have . . . *changed*. You need to grow accustomed to how things are now. Then make your move."

But Egan waved that aside impatiently. "I've no time for all that shit. You saw him tonight. He'll do anything to shut me out. Anything. And I won't be shut out. I want power. And I want it now. Not later, when it's too late, when I grow old again. I want it right now, when I can best use it."

He stood, then ripped open his shirt, to show the powerful chest of his new host body.

"That's why I had you do this, Bernadini. Not so I could enter some body beautiful competition, but so that I could grab back what's mine by rights. This country's mine. I made it. And I'll fucking well have it back, whether my grandson wants it or not."

Bernadini knew his history and knew that what Old Man Egan said wasn't strictly true, but the old man was not to be denied in this mood. He smiled and placed a hand on Egan's arm.

"Okay. I understand. But let's do things a step at a time. Let's make sure, huh? Brain as well as brawn. That was always your way, right?"

Egan took that in a moment, then nodded, a self-satisfied smile coming to his lips. "Right."

"Then don't be hasty. Your grandson will come to you, when he's had time to recover from the shock of seeing you like this. And when he does, be a friend to him, Josiah. Be a good friend. And bide your time. For your time will come, I promise you. And then you will be king again. King of America."

* * *

Bernadini stood at the monitor, watching as Old Man Egan had the two girls strip and kneel before him. Then, unfastening himself, he had them take turns at sucking him off, before finally lifting up the younger girl and throwing her down on the bed. Ignoring her screams, he took her brutally from behind.

A king you might be, Bernadini thought, wincing at the sight, *but you're a barbarian, and no match for your grandson.*

Even so, he had to win, by hook or crook, for if he lost then all those who had helped him would lose too.

And that means me.

Indeed, if he was Mark Egan, he would be talking to the assassins even at this moment.

He turned, looking to the Advocate. "Jim. Hire more guards. People we can trust. And let no one into the inner sanctum without my word, okay?"

"You think the grandson will try something?"

Bernadini nodded. "He'd be stupid not to, wouldn't you say?"

"You don't think they can come to some kind of arrangement, then?"

"To share power?"

Richards shrugged. "I guess not." He was thoughtful a moment, then he looked up again. "You know, it surprised me tonight. I thought . . . I thought it would be different from how it was. I thought they'd maybe greet each other. I mean, the boy was always so respectful when he visited him."

"When he was effectively dead, you mean?"

Richards nodded. Then, "What did *you* think would happen?"

Bernadini turned and looked across. "I don't know. I thought maybe it would be enough for him, being young again. All the rest . . ." He shook his head. "I didn't think it through, did I? Power. That's all that ever drove him. Why should a new body change that?"

For a moment the two men watched the old boy as he spasmed and came into the first girl. Then, his penis still rigid, Egan withdrew and, pushing the girl roughly aside, turned and, reaching out, grasped the other by the wrist, dragging her, terrified, over to the bed.

"Which leaves only one option, wouldn't you say?"

Richards swallowed audibly. "War?"

Bernadini nodded, his eyes glued now to the screen as Egan began again, insatiable in his need to dominate.

Yes, war. And civil wars are always the most bloody kind of all.

* * *

It was three in the morning and Kuei Jen was finally about to retire, when his husband's Master of the Bedchamber came to his room.

"Forgive me, Mistress, but your husband asks if you would attend to him."

Kuei Jen looked at him, surprised. It was more than a year since he had been to his husband's bed. Not since they had argued.

"I need a while to prepare myself," he answered. "But tell my husband I shall come."

When the man had gone, he went over to the mirror and looked at himself. As a man he had never liked his figure, had thought himself too slim, too boyish; as a woman he admired his own curves, the much fuller look of his hips and breasts.

But Mark, she knew, had liked him as he was. Had liked *him*, before the change. That was part of it. Why they had quarrelled. For he had taken others to his bed. Not women. No, nothing so simple. But other men. Soldiers. Campaigners, like himself.

But now he had changed his mind. Now, after all this time, Mark had summoned him again, woman as he was.

Kuei Jen went across and, stripping down to almost nothing, chose something simple, something . . . masculine. It was time to be a man again. Time to be a brother as well as a wife.

He looked across, meeting his own eyes in the mirror. Was that what Mark had responded to? The memory of what he once was? The decisiveness? The aggressive masculinity that, despite all, still resided in him.

If so, he would use it. To rebuild the bridges that had been burned between them. For his children's and his father's sake.

Yes. And for my own. For I still love him. In spite of all.

* * *

"Jenny?"

Egan pulled back the cover, letting him slip in beside him.

"Hello stranger," Kuei Jen said, snuggling up against his naked form.

"I . . ."

He put a finger to Egan's lips. "No apologies. Just this."

Egan smiled, then turned to kiss him, his arms about him. As he broke from the kiss, he sighed. "I've missed you, Jenny."

"And I you."

"It's been . . . strange. I feel as if I lost myself."

"You did."

Egan was silent a moment, staring at him, his hands gently stroking Kuei Jen's back, straying down until they cupped his buttocks. "There was never anyone special."

"No?"

He shook his head.

"I missed you."

"Did you?"

"I missed this." Kuei Jen reached down, holding Egan's penis between the fingers of his left hand, finding it stiff with desire. Slowly he began to stroke it. "I dreamed of you, you know, fucking me. I dreamed . . ."

He shivered. "Jenny?"

His fingers stopped their movement. "What?"

"Do I *have* to kill him?"

"Yes. Now quiet, my love. I'll roll over, and we can pretend it's like old times."

CHAPTER·9

A NEGATIVE TWIST OF NOTHINGNESS

The sun was rising over the mountains as the tiny party made its way between the bare grey outcrops of rock and up the narrow track through the pines that led to the lower camp. Jagged peaks surrounded them on every side, snow covering the nearest slopes, while close at hand a stream cut deep through the ancient rock and fell, a narrow, crystal-white curtain of ice-pure motion, into the deep shadow of the valley below. They moved slowly now. Four of the five were dressed in the clothes of the alpine wilderness, thick sheepskins and heavy wool leggings, stout boots and woollen hoods. The fifth, a boy of fifteen, wore the thin silks of the city. From pity, one of the group had given the boy a thick blanket, which the lad had gratefully draped over his shoulders against the night's bitter cold.

They had walked through the night, climbing steadily, and stopping often along the way, for their leader, the nineteen-year-old, Lin Pei, had sustained a nasty wound to his leg the previous day and needed the constant support of one or other of his fellows. His face, as they made their way up above the rocks and into the camp, was ashen. The journey had exhausted him. Even so, he would not see the surgeon until he had fulfilled the promise he had made to the boy.

"Where's Chao?" Lin Pei asked, looking about him at the handful who had come out of their makeshift shelters at the sound of their arrival. Pain and tiredness made his voice uncharacteristically tetchy. "He said he'd meet us here. Where is he?"

"He is . . . *elsewhere*," one of them answered, a tough-looking, wind-tanned Han in his sixties called Yeh, reluctant to say any more in the presence of the stranger.

"It's all right," Lin Pei said, understanding the man's caution. "The boy is a good friend. He wants to join us."

Brief looks were exchanged. Again Yeh answered him. "Chao was called away. Something urgent. But he will be here. He promised. So be patient, young Pei. Have that wound tended to before it goes bad. You would not want to cause the woman more worries than she already has, would you?"

Pei did not like to hear his adopted mother called "the woman", no matter the circumstances, and made to answer Yeh sharply, yet as he looked about the familiar circle of faces he saw how their eyes told him to agree, how they gave the slightest nod as if to endorse Yeh's words. He let his head drop. He *was* tired, and the wound *did* need seeing to, but he had made a promise.

He turned, looking down the slope to where the boy sat among his men, shivering despite the sheepskin, then turned back to Yeh. "Could we build a fire, cousin Yeh?"

"That would not be wise," Yeh said. "The patrols have increased greatly in recent days. To build a fire out here in the open would be like waving a great flag. Our enemies would be upon us in an instant."

"But the boy . . ."

Yeh came close and touched Lin Pei's shoulder with a brown, sun-burned hand. "You rest now, Master Pei. I shall take care of the boy. And when your brother Chao comes, I shall wake you. Okay?"

Lin Pei hesitated, the urge to keep his word to the boy still strong in him; then, realising nothing could be achieved, he bowed his head. "Okay."

Yeh grinned his gap-toothed grin. "Good. Then go and have that seen to. Surgeon Wu is in the end shelter. It is time someone woke the lazy bastard!"

There was laughter at that. Lin Pei, grateful and yet frustrated, hobbled across. He bent down and rapped on the crude door of cross-woven branches.

"Wu Ye! Are you awake, Wu Ye?"

There was a grunt from within, and then the sleepy head of Wu Ye, his dark hair tousled, emerged. "Master Pei!" he said with surprise, then, seeing the bloodied bandage about Pei's left leg, pushed the mat door aside and bent down, quickly unwrapping the bandage and examining the wound with his fingers, all the while muttering to himself.

"*Aiya*!" he said finally, looking up at Lin Pei. "You should have had this treated earlier!"

Pei laughed sourly. "You think so? Like in one of our friend DeVore's hospitals, with a pair of armed guards keeping a careful eye on me?"

Wu Ye made a face. "At least you had the sense to clean it and bandage it."

"The boy did that," Pei said, wincing at Wu's indelicate touch, then looking down the slope to where Yeh was handing the boy a bowl of steaming soup, poured from a self-heat can.

"Then you have much to thank him for," Wu Ye said, nodding to himself. "But this wound's a bad one, Pei. I can't do much here. I need to get you back to the Eyrie. I need drugs, my instruments."

"You'll have to operate?"

Wu Ye was quiet a moment, examining the wound again, then nodded. "This is bad, Pei. Very bad."

"Then we ought to go at once. Take the boy."

"The boy stays."

Lin Pei turned, surprised to find his brother, Chao behind him.

"But we *must* take him, Chao."

"We can't," Chao said, matter-of-factly, stooping to take a look at the wound. "Not until he's been checked out."

"But he saved my life."

Chao looked up at that, surprised.

"I got hit and lost my weapon. Two of DeVore's creatures – his copies – chased me into a compound. They had me cornered. And then *he* showed up. Shot both of them dead. Two shots." Pei tapped his forehead, his eyes wide, remembering it. "Right here, between the eyes. Such shooting! And afterwards he cleaned the wound and bandaged it for me. Led me down back alleys and got me out of there. I'd have been dead without his help, Chao, or worse – prisoner in one of DeVore's cells."

"Even so . . ." Chao began, but Pei was impatient now.

"We *have* to," he said. "I promised him!"

"No," Chao said, in a tone that brooked no further argument. Then, lowering his voice. "You know the rules, Lin Pei. What if he's an assassin? DeVore would willingly sacrifice two of his creatures – even a hundred of the beasts – just for a single crack at her. You know that."

"Yes, but . . ."

"No buts, little brother. You might be right. He might prove to be a good friend. But what if you're wrong? What if it was all a set-up?"

"You really think . . .?"

"That DeVore's that devious? Yes. I do. And I'm not going to take a chance. Are you, Pei? Do you really want to take even the smallest chance with her life?"

Pei dropped his head, suddenly abashed. "No, . . ."

"Then leave it in my hands. I'll get him checked out. And if all seems well, we'll see what can be done. But for now he stays here, under guard. Until we can be sure."

Pei swallowed, then. "Thanks."

Chao reached out and ruffled his younger brother's hair. "Now let's get you seen to, neh? I'll have a stretcher made up and we'll carry you up. In the meantime . . ." he looked to the surgeon, "Wu Ye . . . have you anything to make my brother sleep?"

"I have."

"But Chao . . ." Pei began.

"No arguments," Lin Chao said, smiling at his brother, then, turning away, he walked slowly down the slope towards the boy.

* * *

DeVore stood on the balcony of the great amphitheatre in Bremen, watching expressionlessly as Horacek's troops marched by in tight columns of eight, their arms raised straight in salute, their leather boots and black uniforms reminding him of another, earlier time. Then he had stood among an admiring crowd, looking on as another took centre stage, but now it was his turn.

Inwardly he smiled. There would be no mistakes this time. No decisions born of anger or the effects of tertiary syphilis. This time he would control it all properly. And when it was done these men – through whom he sought to achieve his ends –

would in turn be eradicated; would "make way", as he thought of it. And in their place he'd put a much greater, finer race. A race better fitted to venturing out into the universe. A race capable of taking the stars.

To his left the dark-faced Horacek bristled with pride in his Marshal's uniform. DeVore turned slightly, smiling, bestowing the smallest of nods to him, as if to acknowledge what a fine job he had done. But in his mind DeVore was already dispensing with the young man, conscious of the threat he posed.

But not just yet, he thought. *Not while I still have uses for you.*

For a moment he let his eyes wander, looking out past the endless procession of troops, taking in the packed terraces, the cheering crowds, before they settled on the great white marble plinth at the centre of the stadium where a pile of cracked and fallen basalt lay.

It was the time of the endgame. Within the next six months, the fate of all would be settled. And when the last stone was laid and the points were counted on the great board of Chung Kuo, it would be he who would emerge the Master.

There was a brief, glancing touch against his gloved right hand. DeVore turned his head, meeting Emtu's eyes.

He smiled, thinking yet again how closely she resembled Emily Ascher; how that same strength and determination shone out from her eyes. Yet this copy – grown from the original's severed finger – was *his*. Obedient and deadly. The perfect partner, made to last a thousand years.

And when she was gone?

He smiled and laced his fingers into hers. When her flesh decayed he would make himself another, endlessly, throughout eternity.

"What is it?" he asked softly.

"The medals," she said, reminding him.

"Ah, yes . . ."

He turned back to Horacek. "Josef . . . let us go down. We must make the presentations."

Horacek came smartly to attention then bowed deeply. "Master!"

You're a proper little sewer rat, DeVore thought, smiling into the young man's burned and blackened face. *And yet you've proved by far the most useful of my servants. Brutal, excessive, and lacking a single redeeming quality, you were just perfect for me. A mark, a living stain upon the day, there to draw people's eyes toward some superficial shadow, blinding them to where true darkness lies. Indeed, looking at you now, it seems like fate that we met that day.*

As Horacek straightened up there was a moment's awkwardness as he realised how intently DeVore was staring at him.

"Master?"

"I was just thinking, Josef. Remembering how we met."

Horacek smiled broadly, showing feral, uneven teeth. "It was fate, Master."

DeVore nodded slowly, thoughtfully. "So it was, Josef. So it was."

Yes, and so it was fated that Horacek would die violently. Once he had served his use. When true night fell.

* * *

"What's your name?"

Daniel looked up from where he was sitting on a ledge of rock, and met his inquisitor's eyes. "Daniel," he answered, trying to read in those dark Han eyes what his fate was to be. "Daniel Mussida."

"And what district were you from, Daniel?"

"From Westerndorf," he answered, almost without thinking. "It's near Roseheim . . ."

"I know it," the Han said tersely, then crouched onto his haunches so that their faces were on a level. "So . . . what were you doing so far from home, Daniel?"

"I" He looked down. "I came to find you."

"To find us. What, so that you could claim a reward?"

He looked up at that, stung by the insinuation. "No! I'd never do that! I came to join you. I wanted . . ."

The young Han raised a hand. At once Daniel fell silent.

"I hear you saved my brother's life."

Daniel hesitated, then nodded.

"Well, for that I thank you, with all my heart. Even so, I'm still left wondering what a good boy like you was doing wandering in the backstreets with a loaded gun. Did your mother not warn you of the dangers?"

"I have no mother."

"And your father?"

"I have no father."

Lin Chao sat back a little, considering. "So where, exactly, were you staying? And with whom?"

Daniel took his ID card from inside his jacket pocket and handed it across. After studying it a moment, Lin Chao handed it back.

"So you're a cadet? No wonder you could use a gun. But I'm still wondering."

"Wondering?"

"Why you should want to join us. I thought they taught you that we were devils. Ruthless brigands who would as soon cut your heart out and eat it as talk to you."

"And are you?"

At that Lin Chao laughed; a pleasant, unaffected laughter that Daniel instantly liked. The laughter gave him sudden confidence.

"Who are you?"

"Me?" Lin Chao stood, looking past Daniel at the rock-littered slope. Beyond him the mountain climbed until it was lost among the other peaks in cloud. "Let's just say that I *could* be a friend. That is, if you are who you say you are."

"Then I can join you?" Daniel asked, standing for the first time.

"Hold on, boy!" Again Lin Chao laughed. "Did I say that? No. One thing at a time. First we'll get you some warm clothing, then . . . well, we'll see, eh? But for now, thank you, Daniel. Thank you for doing what you did for young Pei."

Not knowing what else to do, Daniel came smartly to attention and bowed his head, as if to the Captain of Cadets. There was laughter from the watching men, but Lin Chao did not laugh. Straightening up, he too came to attention, returning the bow. Then, as if he could find nothing further to say, he turned and hastened away, returning up the slope to where his brother now lay, wrapped in a heavy blanket on a straw bier, waiting to be taken up the mountain.

* * *

DeVore pulled off his gloves and dropped them on the table, then hurried through into the control room. Heads turned at his entry then quickly turned back, concentrating on the screens.

"Any news?" DeVore asked, taking his seat at the centre of it all.

"Nothing yet, Master," the most senior of his generals answered, coming across and standing beside DeVore's chair, head bowed. Behind him the remaining generals stood ill at ease, looking on.

DeVore glanced at the digital readout of the time in the right-hand lower corner of the biggest of the screens, then shook his head.

"Something's gone wrong. We should have heard by now. We should have *seen* something!"

On the screen there were a succession of tiny flashes.

"There!" DeVore said, leaning forward.

They waited, tense with anticipation, but that was it. There were no big explosions. The satellites remained untouched. The attack had failed.

DeVore sat back. For a moment he simply stared into the air, his face like flint, his right hand tapping out a rhythm against the arm of the chair, then he stood.

"Find out what went wrong," he said tersely, angrily. "Someone will pay for this!"

* * *

In the lift heading back up to the surface, DeVore allowed himself the luxury of a smile. Down below, his generals were running about and shouting at each other, trying to allocate the blame, but the truth was he had never expected the attack to succeed.

Emtu was waiting for him at the entrance to the San Chang, the broken tile roofs of the T'ang's ruined palaces dominating the late morning sky behind her.

"It worked!" he said exultantly, taking her arms. "Almost three minutes they were out, and we only needed two!"

She stared back at him soberly. "Don't get too excited. You do not know for certain yet."

He calmed. "No, no . . ." Then, smiling again, he took her hand. "Let's go and see."

Guards unlocked the gate to the north palace and stood back, letting them pass. Inside the central corridor was dark, sepulchral. All was silent. They walked through, their booted feet stirring the years-old dust, the sound of their footsteps echoing back from the high ceilings and massive rooms.

At the far end of the corridor was a huge set of double doors, panelled and studded. DeVore looked to his companion and, with a smile, pushed open the right-hand door. Inside was a massive hall, a row of stone pillars running away to left and right, stone dragons coiled about them. At the far end, beneath the great throne, there was movement.

Giant figures straightened, then turned, facing the newcomers. In their midst was a strange craft, identical to the ship DeVore himself had used to return to Chung Kuo; a translucent, capsule-like craft that could fold space and time about it.

Seeing who it was, one of the massive figures came across.

"Hannem?" DeVore asked, recognising his servant of old.

The big morph knelt, bowing his head low. "We have come, Master."

Behind him, his eight companions also knelt and bowed, subservient to their creator.

DeVore turned, looking to Emtu, a look of triumph in his eyes. "There," he said. "Now we are even. Now the endgame has begun."

* * *

From the air one could see nothing, yet some fifty metres beneath where the tree-line ended and the grey, rocky slope climbed to meet the first of the three snowbound peaks, tucked in among the ancient pines, was a slight indentation, a patch of shadow trapped between two twisted, limb-like roots. Here was the entrance they called the "High Door". Other hidden entrances were dotted about the surrounding mountainside, yet this was the quickest, the most direct route into the ruined alpine fortress.

More than thirty years had passed since Li Yuan's Imperial forces had bombed the Dispersionist fortress, leaving a massive crater in the mountain's flank, and for most of that time it had remained unoccupied and open to the elements, but for the past five years it had been reclaimed by rebel elements, the crater covered over with a mesh of high-tensile ice, upon which earth and rock had been piled. To add to this visual disguise, a web of anti-detection devices had been scattered over the fortress's new roof, so that to the camera eyes of passing craft it seemed that the mountainside was cool and solid.

It was mid afternoon when Lin Chao finally returned from the base camp. Normally he would have taken one of the lower entrances, down among the big boulders at the foot of the valley, but today he was late. The meeting would already have begun and he was keen this once to hear what was said and add his own voice to the debate.

Things were changing. The attack on his brother Pei said as much, but in truth he had known it for some time now. DeVore was losing patience. Not only that, but their activities had begun to hurt DeVore, especially since the Americans had agreed to back them.

A hundred metres from the entrance Chao paused, tucked in tight against the bole of a leaning pine. For a moment he stayed there, his eyes searching the slope ahead, flicking from tree to tree. There was nothing. Even so, he hesitated a moment longer. Old habits died hard, and he knew that one single mistake could cost them all dear.

Ducking low, he moved from tree to tree, following a zig-zag course towards the entrance. Ten metres from it he stopped again, looking up past the vee of shadow, then turned to study the slope beneath him.

He was alone.

Quickly now, he ran across and ducked inside, stooping to pass through the tight, dark entrance. Some five metres along a steel door barred his way. Reaching up blindly, he found the panel just above it and tapped out the coded sequence. The door slid quietly back.

Chao slipped inside.

Hidden cameras were watching him as he made his way through the narrow maze, following his every movement. In a control room in the heart of the mountain someone was watching a screen, their hand close by a pad, ready to flood the tunnels with gas if he set a foot wrong.

Necessary, he thought, as he waited at the end of the final tunnel, his left palm pressed to the pad as it took a tiny sample of his blood. For it was said that DeVore could copy anything, *anyone*. And the only way to stay alive was to keep one jump ahead of him. Paranoia had become a survival tactic.

At the count of ten the wall beside him slid back, revealing a well-lit, empty corridor. Chao stepped down, stretching his limbs as the wall slid back. There was the murmur of voices, the faintest click and whirr of machines. He walked towards them.

Doors led off to right and left. Most were closed. Through glass panels he could see his people at work, collating information, organising the vast and complex business of rebellion, or simply debating new "targets" among themselves. All would finally find its way to the room at the far end of the corridor where his mother had her office. He went there now, throwing the door open, expecting to find a dozen people seated about her desk, but the room was almost empty. Almost. At the far end of the conference table sat his mother, her gaunt, grey-haired head bent over a file.

She looked up at him from the document, surprised to find him there. "Chao?"

"I thought . . ."

"I cancelled it," she said, anticipating him. Then, closing the folder, she stood and came round the table until she stood by him. "There's a problem."

"A problem?"

"It's Michael. There's no word from him yet."

He reached out and held both her arms, the same way she had always held his own when he'd been a child and full of fears.

"He'll be okay. He's being careful, that's all."

"But he said . . ."

A look from him silenced her. "Okay," she said finally, the moment's weakness passed. "But I've sent Han Ye and Sung out to look for him. If they were ambushed . . ."

"He'll *be* okay," Chao said, insistently this time, but there was a small knot in his stomach at the thought of his stepfather being in DeVore's far-from-tender hands. Death was preferable. "How's Pei?" he asked.

"He's fine. The wound's clean. He had a lucky escape."

"Too lucky, perhaps?"

Emily had been about to turn away, but at his words she looked back at him. "You think the boy's a plant?"

"It's possible. I mean, it was rather a coincidence that he should be there at that precise moment."

"Maybe. But Lin Pei would have been a big prize for DeVore. He could have taken him back, copied *him*. Got to me that way. Besides, he lost two morphs. He can ill afford such losses, especially now."

"I'm sorry?"

She smiled at him. "You haven't heard, then?"

"*Heard*?"

In answer she went across and picked up the folder she'd been reading, then came back, handing it to him. Chao opened it, took out the slender document, then looked up at her, surprised.

"Is this true?"

She nodded. "We've had it confirmed from eight different sources. This morning at eleven DeVore attempted to break the blockade. Missile attacks on five of the stationary satellites were followed by an attempt to slip a number of ships through the High Barrier. Both the missile strike and the attempt to outrun the American blockade failed. All of his ships were blown out of the skies. Word is that they carried a total of more than sixty of DeVore's creatures. That's almost a fifth of his remaining strength."

"But what was he trying to do?"

Emily shrugged. "Who knows?"

"Then things really are desperate . . . for him, I mean."

"Maybe."

The way she said it made him look at her anew. "What are you thinking?"

"It's nothing."

"No. Tell me. I want to know."

"I don't know," she began. "It's just . . . well, with DeVore you can never take anything at face value. He's a master of feints and illusions. Such a direct action . . . it's unlike him, don't you think?"

He shrugged. "Go on."

"It made me think of the game . . . of *wei chi*. Of how a Master of the game might sometimes play a stone in a part of the board he isn't really interested in, as a decoy, to mask his true intentions."

"But we *know* DeVore's true intentions. He wants to break the blockade so that he can bring in reinforcements. Without them he's too weak to win this conflict."

"Or so he'd have us think."

Chao stared at his mother a moment, then shook his head. "No. His weakness is no bluff. If he were strong enough he'd destroy us all without a moment's thought. He'd not waste his time sending patrols out into the mountain passes, he'd destroy the Wilds themselves!"

"Maybe."

He huffed, exasperated with her. "And what does Tybor say?"

She smiled. "Why don't you ask him. He'll be here any moment now."

Chao nodded. If anyone could fathom DeVore's twisted mind, then maybe Tybor could, for Tybor had been made from DeVore's own genetic material, flesh of his flesh.

"You've spoken to the boy, I assume."

"Huh?" For a moment he was at a loss, then, "the *boy*."

"Yes." She laughed. "You've questioned him, I take it."

He nodded. "He seems . . . well, quite ordinary really. But who can tell? DeVore's so devious, I sometimes wake up wondering if I'm really me."

"I know. I dream of mirrors."

"Mirrors?"

"You know. What they used to call *ching*."

"Ah . . ." The thought of it chilled him. When the seven T'ang had ruled Chung Kuo, they had kept copies – *ching*, or "mirrors" – of each T'ang, ready for the day they died, so that their successors could symbolically kill their predecessors before becoming the new T'ang. These *ching*, made in the nutrient vats of the great genetics company, GenSyn, had been perfect copies of their originals but for one important aspect – their minds. For the *ching* were blank, unthinking creatures, born and maintained only to be ceremonially slaughtered.

The thought that such creatures existed was bad enough, but one further element gave the matter a much too personal twist. When his mother had fled Europe in the wake of the collapse of the *Ping Tiao*, it had been DeVore who had aided – some might say permitted – her escape. In return she had given him a single finger from her right hand. From that he had made himself a mate, a perfect copy of Emily Ascher. A *ching*, alike in all but her mental processes. A *thing*, not a proper human.

Like Tybor.

"Emily . . . Chao . . ."

Tybor ducked beneath the sill and came inside. Even crouched he was a good three feet bigger than Lin Chao, his smooth, hairless arms and head giving him the look of something moulded not grown.

Which was near enough the truth.

"Tybor," Emily said, embracing the creature. "Is there any news?"

"I'm afraid not," Tybor answered, pulling out a chair and sitting, so as to be on their level. "But it's early yet. They may have been caught in a storm. The weather's unseasonably bad."

"We were talking," Chao said, changing the subject. "About the attempt to break the blockade."

Tybor glanced at Emily, then turned his inhumanly large eyes on Chao once again. "Your mother thinks it may have been a bluff of some kind. A diversionary play."

"And you?"

Tybor smiled; a smile that could have swallowed up a small cartwheel. "I think she may be right."

"But what could he be up to? He can't do *anything* until he breaks the blockade."

"Or so we've been conditioned to think," Emily said, moving round the back of

Tybor and laying her hands on the creature's shoulders. "I learned an interesting thing the other day. It seems our friend DeVore paid a visit to Ben Shepherd back in the spring."

Chao frowned. "So?"

"So this. What does Shepherd have that DeVore might want?"

"You think DeVore wants something from Shepherd?"

"Of course. Why else would he pay a visit?"

"To be friendly?"

At that Tybor laughed. "Why, of course! I forgot. The man's a regular socialite!"

Chao looked down, trying hard not to smile. "So you think he's *using* Shepherd somehow?"

"Or trying to," Emily answered, coming round Tybor to face him. "I can't see anyone actually *telling* Shepherd what to do, even DeVore. But I can see the two of them coming to some kind of arrangement."

"But about what? Shepherd's an artist. DeVore . . . well, DeVore's just a homicidal maniac!"

"Yes, but a clever one. And a master of illusions to boot. I'd have let the observation pass but for one thing. Two days ago Ben Shepherd flew in to Bremen. It seems he's rented a studio apartment there, not five minutes away from DeVore's headquarters."

"Convenient, neh?" Tybor said, his huge eyes half-lidded.

"But I don't see . . ." Chao began, then stopped. "Shells? You think Shepherd is going to make special shells for DeVore?"

Emily half-turned, looking to Tybor. "I don't think anything . . . yet. But it might be useful if we could find out, don't you think?"

Chao nodded. "I'll see what I can do."

"Good," Emily said, touching his arm lightly. "Now let's go down to the control room. I want to be there when the news comes in."

* * *

Daniel woke, his eyes staring, unable for the moment to remember where he was. All he knew was that he was sitting up, his back against a cold, hard rock, and someone was shaking him.

"Soup?" a voice asked gently. "You want some soup?"

He focused on the face in front of him – a plump Han face with disconcertingly dark eyes – then looked past it at the vast and open sky, finally making sense of the huge shapes that surrounded him. Mountains. Of course! He was in the Wilds.

"Well?" the crouching man asked. "Are you hungry or not?"

Daniel nodded, then took the bowl from the man, grateful for its warmth. He had never been so cold, not even in the dormitories.

He looked about him at the camp. In truth, it was little more than a few crude shelters set up among the rocks. The sight of it, and of the roughly-dressed men who sat around, talking quietly among themselves, depressed his spirits. Whatever he'd expected, it wasn't this. As he spooned the soup into his mouth he began to wonder whether he hadn't made a mistake coming here.

Too late, he thought, concentrating his attention briefly on the soup. *They'd kill me if I went back*.

Or worse.

No. It was no use contemplating going back. He had burned his bridges now. He had seen with his own eyes what they did to those boys who'd tried to run away. Those who'd been caught, anyway.

Even so, he had hoped for . . . well, for something more than *this*, anyway!

"More?" the Han asked, coming over to him again and setting the soup pot down beside him.

"Thanks."

The Han took the bowl, then smiled. "You know, you're either very very stupid, or very brave, coming out here."

"What do you mean?"

Daniel watched the ladle dip into the dark broth and lift, tipping more of the tasty soup into his bowl. The Han handed it to him, then answered.

"Just that it's a dangerous place."

"The patrols, you mean?"

He shook his head. "The patrols are the least of it. Or were. No, I mean all of the other things. The rogue machines, the creatures."

"Creatures?"

"GenSyn stuff. Things that escaped from their factories after the war. This is where they came. To the Wilds. They made their lairs here."

"And the Machines?"

"Search-and-destroy machines. They date back to the conflict between Li Yuan and the White T'ang, Lehmann. Both sides used them to try to make this place a kind of no-man's-land. Most of them have rusted now, either that or their energy packs have run down, but there are a few that are active. Things that look like stones or rocks, that rest where they were dropped, their systems nine-tenths inactive, waiting for someone to come along and trigger them."

Daniel stared back at the young Han. "And then?"

In answer the Han rolled up his sleeve to show the burned tissue of his upper arm. "It took out four of our squad before we even got a trace on it. Lin Pei stopped it, but I was in the blast zone. So was my brother, Chan. He took most of the blast's force."

Daniel set the soup down. "I'm sorry."

The Han's smile was gentle, wistful. "So am I."

Daniel looked down a moment, embarrassed, then raised his head again, meeting the man's eyes. "What's your name?"

"Ho. Yueh Ho."

"I'm pleased to meet you, Ho. I hope we can be friends."

Yueh Ho nodded, then picked up the soup pot by its string and turned away. "I hope so, young Daniel Mussida," he said, over his shoulder. "I sincerely hope so."

* * *

DeVore looked up as his adjutant came into the room.

"Well?" he asked. "Is it true?"

The adjutant bowed his head. "Yes, sir."

"And when precisely did he disappear?"

"Two days ago, sir."

"And I wasn't informed."

"No, sir, they thought . . ."

DeVore leaned forward. "Who's this 'they' who've been doing so much thinking on my behalf?"

"The Camp Commandant, sir. He . . . he thought he could recapture the boy before the matter became serious."

"But now it's serious, eh?"

The adjutant hesitated, then nodded.

"And they've lost the trace, is that right?"

"Yes, sir."

DeVore sat back again, contemplating what that meant. The boy had been wired. But somehow – somewhere – he had managed to get rid of the wire in his head. Or mask it. And now he was missing, presumed defected.

"I've two of my best morphs in the morgue. Someone put them there. Maybe it was the boy."

"Maybe . . ."

But he could see that the adjutant was not going to make guesses of any kind.

"Okay," he said, relenting, not wanting to take things out on the man. It was the Commandant he should be angry with, not this messenger. "You can leave me now, Mark. I'll not need you 'til the morning."

"Sir!" The adjutant bowed exaggeratedly low, his relief palpable, then backed from the room.

Alone again, DeVore stood, then went to the window, looking out across the moonlit central courtyard of the San Chang and pondering what this meant. It was a blow, admittedly, for he'd had plans for the boy, but if he could find out where he'd gone, then maybe it could be turned around. The wire wasn't the only implant, after all; there *was* the boy's conditioning. And that he couldn't have removed.

Tomorrow, he told himself. *I'll deal with it tomorrow.*

Right now he would go and visit Shepherd. It was about time he found out what that mad bastard was doing in his rooms.

* * *

The moon was bright, casting sharp black shadows on the rocks as she made her way down towards the base camp. There was still no news of Michael and as she looked out across the valley, Emily wondered where he was at that moment. He had said he was onto something special. He'd sent a message six days back telling her he was going to investigate. But since then nothing.

She stopped, her hand pressing down tightly on the rough, cold surface of an upjutting rock as she looked south. *Be alive*, she thought, willing it fervently, her fear for him naked beneath the all-seeing moon.

And if he *was* dead?

Then she would endure that, as she endured all else.

A bitter smile crossed her lips. *Ah yes*, she thought. *I am good at enduring. As good as any Han peasant.*

The base camp was just below her now. As she came round an outcrop, it lay below her and to her right, tucked between folds of the descending slope. Knowing that DeVore had called off his patrols, they had lit a camp-fire. Within the golden-red pool of its flickering light she could see dark figures moving slowly, almost lethargically in the crisp night air.

If I could only touch you now and hold you, then I would be alright.

But that was the risk of loving. Once it had been easy to be a rebel. Once it had cost her nothing to be the firebrand that would burn whole cities down. Back then, alone and unattached, she had been driven solely by vengeance.

Now it was much harder. Now, every day was fraught with anxiety.

She waited, keeping herself perfectly still and silent, like a piece of the rock of which the mountain was composed, and after a while Tybor came up to her, like a huge shadow looming up out of the darkness.

"Emily," the morph said, his voice soft and warm, the bulk of him blocking out her view of the camp below. "You should have said you were coming."

"I didn't know," she said.

It was the truth. She hadn't planned to come down, but, restless for news of Michael, she had had to do something, and talk of the boy – the newcomer – had intrigued her. She had decided she would like to see him for herself.

"The boy?" Tybor asked, his saucer eyes shining in the moonlight, not a hand's length from her face.

Emily nodded.

He smiled. "Then I'll keep close by. Out of sight. Just in case."

Emily reached out, holding his arm briefly, glad he was there. Then, as he slipped away, heading back down into the darkness, she turned once more, looking to the south and wondering where Michael was.

* * *

Closing the door quietly behind him, DeVore crossed the room.

Ben was sitting beside the harness, hunched forward slightly, adjusting something with what looked like a small knife.

As DeVore bent forward to look, Ben turned his head, looking up at him, a half-smile on his features. "I wondered when I'd see you."

"Did you?"

"I thought to myself: I wonder how long he can contain his curiosity."

"And?"

"And here you are, bang on time."

DeVore shrugged. "So what is it?"

Ben moved back a little, allowing him a clearer view. "Something new."

DeVore studied the machine a while. "It doesn't *look* new."

Ah, but then looks aren't everything, are they? If we were to judge by simple appearances, then we'd still be back in the Dark Ages, wouldn't we?"

DeVore laughed. "I thought that you said that we were still in the Dark Ages."

"I did."

"Then the appearance of the thing . . .

"Is a paradox." Ben threw the screwdriver down, then turned, facing DeVore fully. "You wanted me to make something that would seduce people from their senses, right? That would, in effect, prise them from their grasp on the real world, right?"

"Right."

"But why should anyone risk losing their mind for the sake of an entertainment?"

DeVore grinned. "I don't know. *You* tell *me*."

"They would do so because, first and foremost, that experience was so wonderful, so . . . *desirable* that they wanted to repeat it time after time – in fact, had an overwhelming urge to go back to it."

"And secondly?"

"Secondly, because they hadn't a clue what was actually going on."

"And what *is* actually going on?"

Ben's smile was one of pleasure at his own ingenuity. "It's an imprint."

"An imprint?"

"Yes. Each time the participant goes back to the shell – to the experience – they receive not just the entertainment, but an imprint. False memories, if you like. Vague at first, but stronger as each layer of the imprint is added on."

"So the programme is cumulative, a . . ."

". . . sticky web . . . filled with insidious poisons."

"Rather a mixed metaphor, wouldn't you say?"

"Absolutely," Ben agreed, "but with good reason. If we showed them the spider in the web, who would enter it? What they don't know is that the poison is in the strands of the web. Simply experiencing this is enough."

"And what kind of symptoms would someone who's hooked on this show?"

Ben shrugged. "It depends what you're looking for. But generally you can make them believe anything you want them to believe – that they murdered their own mother, that they have a pathological hatred of someone they previously loved or revered, that . . . well, I'm sure you see the potential of the thing. Memory is a corrosive thing, particularly if it's been tampered with."

"And the Americans won't suspect a thing?"

Ben laughed. "They might. But not until it's too late. Not until half their country's fucking mad!"

* * *

Emily sat there a long while, watching the boy. From where she was, in the shadows some thirty feet back from the fire, to the left of the boy and almost in line with him, she could see his face clearly, the features carved in blocks of gold and black. The boy's clean-shaven head had begun to grow a fine stubble, but it was a good head and she observed how he held it up proudly, his eyes – bright, intelligent eyes – taking in everything.

Even so, he had not noticed her creeping up on him.

She waited while the others about the fire drifted off, then spoke to him, her voice pitched so that it carried no further than where he sat.

"Boy?"

There was no movement. No sudden turn of the head. For an instant she thought he hadn't heard her, but then he answered, his voice pitched no louder than her own.

"Yes?"

"Who are you, boy? Who are you really?"

He leaned forward and took a branch from the fire, lifting it and studying the glowing cinders at the end of it. Then he turned, looking in her direction. "Just a boy," he answered, moving the branch closer to his face and blowing on the tip, making it glow brighter.

"You served The Man, I hear."

"I was in his camps."

"One of his soldiers," she persisted.

He hesitated, then nodded.

"So why did you leave?"

Was that a smile? With his head tilted down it was hard to tell.

"I woke up. I saw, finally, what was going on."

"Ahhh." Did she believe that? "And what woke you?"

"You did," he said, looking directly at her. "I saw how you helped those wounded boys. Two weeks back. I saw . . ."

"You saw *that*?" Emily was surprised. "You mean . . ."

"I could have killed you. I had you in my sights."

"But you didn't."

He nodded.

Emily was silent a moment, thinking about that. Dead. She could have been dead two weeks ago. And then Michael would have been grieving *her*. And the boys.

"What's your name, boy?"

"Daniel."

"And what do you want, Daniel?"

Again he looked at her. "I want to know the truth. I want to know what's really going on."

CHAPTER·10

THE WELL AND THE SPIRE

"We're here."

"Here?" Li Yuan yawned, then sat up, noting through the blindfold that it was still dark. Hands reached up to him and took him down from the back of the cart. Then one of them removed the blindfold and stood back.

As the cart trundled away, Li Yuan looked about him, trying to make out where he was. They seemed to be inside a massive chamber, for the rocks surrounded them on every side without a break, rising to form the walls of a giant cavern, yet the roof of that cavern was the sky – a sky of velvet black, littered with jewel-like stars, most prominent of which was not a star at all, but the morning star, the planet Venus.

"Ishtar," someone said quietly from just behind him. Then, "Welcome to Nineveh, Li Yuan. May you find happiness."

The words surprised him and he turned, looking to the man, but the figure was in shadow, his face obscured.

Li Yuan turned back, looking, taking it all in. Buildings huddled against the walls of the settlement, low buildings for the main part, except for one or two that were on the far side of the cavern, including a great, seven-storey zigurrat.

Like Bremen, he thought, surprised to see such a structure there in the midst of the desert.

On a plinth before that building was a great statue. Of what, he could not make out at this distance. And in the centre of all, like a radio tower, was a massive spire, the tip of which was surrounded by a tiny platform.

There was a gap of some kind, which bisected the cavern, for he could see bridges crossing it, and just beyond that – close to the spire – there was a depression, but from this distance he could not make that out either.

As he looked, figures came across one of the bridges, a dozen or more in all, heading towards him.

"Go to them," his guide said. "They will prepare you for the ceremony."

He wanted to ask what kind of ceremony, but the man had gone, slipping away silently into the shadows, leaving him there as the welcoming party approached.

Li Yuan hesitated, then did as he was bid. Yet as he came close to them, he felt a tiny jolt of surprise. They were all women – young, beautiful women – wearing long, diaphanous gowns that both suggested and yet concealed their bodies. Surrounding him, they laughed and held his arms, brushing his back and shoulders gently, the sweet scent of them stirring something in him.

"You must not be afraid," one of them said, whispering in his ear. "We will not harm you, Li Yuan."

The words were similar to those the woman had used earlier, when she had brought him the food, and he felt now the same surprise, the same strange flaring of hope. He had thought himself at best a hostage, at worst a dead man. To be suddenly in the company of such sweet and gentle creatures was both strange and unexpected.

His spirits rose, yet his darker self suspected some deception.

He looked from side to side, seeing how they smiled at him, their eyes bright with laughter. And all the while their hands gently stroked him, comforting him, reassuring him with their touch.

As they came to the bridge, he looked up at the spire, which towered above him now. A narrow ladder climbed the steep side of it, while beneath it, not twenty metres from its foot, was a massive hole. A well.

"What is this?" he asked, slowing, taking in the strange grandeur of the sight.

"Later," one of them said, squeezing his hand. "You must not rush things, Li Yuan. First you must be relaxed."

Relaxed? Li Yuan frowned, unable to take his eyes from the spire and the great well that sat beside it. Somehow the juxtaposition of the two seemed significant, yet why or how he could not say.

He let them lead him on, the sweetness of their perfume filling his nostrils, the softness of their touch a strange, almost intoxicating delight, yet he felt a marked unease now, a tightness in his stomach that had not been there a moment earlier.

And all the while, above him, the evening star burned like a blind eye staring sightlessly from the centre of the darkness.

* * *

Old Man Egan closed the door, then turned, looking in at the bright-lit cell.

"Is this him?"

His men stood back, bowing low. "Yes, Master," one of them answered.

All three of them wore masks and butchers' aprons over their nakedness, and, incongruously, boots so that they would not slip on the bloodied floor. Between them, hanging upside down from the ceiling of the cell, was their victim, a young man of barely twenty years of age. He had been burned and cut, but thus far they had not badly mutilated him. Nor, it seemed, had they started on his private parts.

Egan walked across and, crouching down, put out a hand, gripping the young man's chin hard and twisting it, forcing him to look into his eyes.

"Well, you little cunt, what have you to say for yourself?"

The young man tried to spit, but hanging upside down, he could not raise the phlegm. Blood dribbled slowly from the corner of his mouth and along his nose.

Egan grinned, then spat fully in the man's face. "Is that what you mean?"

There was laughter from the watching men.

Egan released his grip, let the man's head fall, then, straightening up, put a hand over the man's exposed balls, letting his fingers rest there.

Fear contracted them.

Egan grinned, seeing that. He turned, putting a hand out. "Give me the pliers."

His man smiled as he handed across the heated pliers. An unpleasant, conspiratorial smile. Egan winked at him, then turned, crouching again, to show the pliers to the prisoner – holding them in front of his face.

"These are for your bollocks," he said. "Nothing personal, of course, but I'm going to pull them off, one by one, for what you tried to do to me. And then I'm going to put my hand up your arse and pull out your innards, bit by bit. And what won't pull out, I'll cut out. But I'm going to make sure you're alive for all this. We've got drugs that can do that, you know. Chemicals that will keep your body functioning, even as it's being torn apart. So is there anything you'd like to say before I start? Any names you'd like to mention?"

The man had blanched. But now, with a tiny shudder, he found his voice. "You c-can go to hell."

"Oh, come now," Egan said, touching the pliers to the end of his nose so that the skin there blistered, "you can do better than that. Hell? I've been to hell. I spent thirty years in hell. But now I'm back, I'm going to give my enemies a taste of what it was like. You understand?"

"I . . ."

Egan stood slowly, then, delicately lifting one of the man's balls, he applied the pliers to it, crushing it even as he began to stretch it.

The young man's screams were awful. But Egan was grinning now. He eased off with the pliers then stood back, admiring his work.

The man's screams were regular now. "A-oh, a-oh, a-oh . . ."

"So you're a singer are you?" Egan looked about him once again and winked. His men were looking at him now with new respect. Most bosses didn't like to get their hands dirty in this way. But he wasn't like most bosses.

Under their aprons, they all sported fierce erections. Egan looked down. He too was hard.

Fucking hard, he thought, then turned back, raising the pliers once again.

"One down, one to . . ."

The explosion knocked him from his feet. When he got up it was to find his chest and upper arms spattered with blood . . . and other things. He looked across and gaped.

"Shit!"

The prisoner's head had gone. Blown off like a ripe melon. Blood now gouted from his neck and his arms hung limp.

One of his own men was down, clutching his stomach. Clearly he had taken the full force of the blast.

"Master?"

Egan put a hand up, stopping the other two from touching him, from helping him to his feet. "It's okay," he said, "I'm not hurt."

He pulled himself to his feet, brushing the bits of brain and bloodied tissue from his apron, then shook his head and pointed to the injured man.

"See to him. Make sure he gets to a surgeon quickly. Then come back and clear this up."

They did as they were told, leaving him alone in the cell with the headless body. Egan stared at it a while, then, in a fit of anger, he stepped closer and kicked it hard in the chest.

The body swung back and forth, blood dribbling still from the neck, pooling on the tiles below.

"Egan, that's the fucking name you were supposed to say! Mark-fucking-Egan!"

Then, turning away, he left it.

Damn the boy! Damn him for ever existing!

* * *

They stripped Li Yuan and bathed him, then rubbed him down with aromatic oils, their touch so pleasurable that he felt he would burst unless he had one of them. But that, so they said, was not allowed.

Finally, when they were done with him, the eldest of them – the one who called herself Ishtar – came and knelt before him, offering him a bowl.

It seemed at first a perfectly ordinary ceramic bowl, dark blue in colour and round, like a cut section of a fruit, but as he handled it he felt a strange tingling go through his hands and arms and, looking inside, he felt a sense of vertigo, for it seemed as if he looked right through the bowl into the depths of the universe itself.

The inner surface of the bowl was studded with what looked like a ring of tiny metallic pegs, between which a silk-fine web of force seemed to dance, giving off the faintest glow. Beneath it, almost touching it, and yet it seemed a thousand *li* away, a second, equally insubstantial layer could be glimpsed, shimmering wetly in the half light.

He sniffed at it, then looked up at Ishtar. "But this is . . ."

She laughed. "Water, yes." Her dark eyes smiled at him. Still she offered the bowl. "You must drink, Li Yuan. It is important. Only then will you be ready."

"But . . ."

"No buts. The time for hesitation is past. A new life beckons you, Li Yuan. But you must first cross over. This will help you."

"Help me?"

"Yes. It will help you lose your old self. And afterwards . . ."

He stared at it a moment longer, uncertain. There was no scent to it at all, but could he be sure? What if it was a poison?

Ishtar waited, as patient as the rocks, holding out the flickering bowl. Again she smiled. "If we had wanted to kill you, Li Yuan, we would have killed you days ago. This *will* help. But only if you surrender to it."

It was true. And to be honest, he had nothing to lose. only his old self, and what good was that? Tuan Ti Fo was right. His old self had been responsible for the death of millions, yes, and had lost an empire in the process!

He took the bowl and, holding it to his lips, drained it at a go, then handed it back.

At once he felt the change. It was as if, suddenly, every part of him was doubled. And yet there was no physical change, no sense that he was drugged. The liquid had had no taste, no warmth to it, and yet he felt completely different, two bodies in the space of one, each coexistent with the other, their atoms shared.

"Good," Ishtar said, setting the bowl aside. "Now come. The ceremony can begin."

She stood, facing him, then, to his surprise, slipped off her gown, so that she stood there, naked before him.

Li Yuan stared, awe-struck. She was magnificent. Perhaps the most beautiful woman he had ever seen, Han or *Hung Mao.*

"Throw off your gown, Li Yuan," she said as he stood. "For we must come to the pit naked as we were born."

He did as she asked, letting his cloak fall from him.

She reached out, taking his left hand in her right, the simple touch of her making him shudder violently.

The drug – if drug it was – was coursing through him now, making his nerves spark and tingle, as if firecrackers were going off inside his blood. He felt his consciousness expand to take in not merely the room in which he stood, but the whole of Nineveh. And as it did he saw the spire and with it, next to it, the great pit into which we was to descend.

Yes, a voice inside him said. *You must go down inside yourself, Li Yuan. Only then can you make the journey up into the light.*

He laughed, but the laughter was only in his head. And then he was walking, Ishtar at his side, like the Queen of the Night, proud and terrifyingly beautiful. Out they went. Out from the caverns where they had prepared him and up into the great bowl of Nineveh.

Crowds had formed to watch his passing – a whole host of people, naked as himself – and as he passed so their hands brushed against him and on all sides faces smiled and voices wished him well.

And so they came to the pit. And there, as they stood beside it, a great hush fell – a quiet of awe and understanding. And then, with a tenderness that surprised him, hands lowered him slowly backwards into the dark. For the briefest moment he thought that he would fall, but other hands reached up for him, holding him, welcoming him, their bodies closing about him as he was embraced and taken, whole and naked, into the living darkness.

A mouth closed on his, soft hands caressed his buttocks while yet others gently stroked his legs and chest and groin. And as they did, he understood at last.

And shuddered, and let go, his old self slipping from him like a snake's discarded skin.

And with that last, bright-sparking moment of understanding came oblivion – that great darkness of the senses he had wished for all his life and never known.
And then the darkness swallowed him.

* * *

Harding threw on a gown, then went through to see who could have come at this hour.
His Steward, Levitch, was standing in the shadows of the hall. For a moment he did not realise that Harding was there, then, with a start, he turned and smartly bowed.
"Master . . ."
"What's happening, Levitch?"
Levitch took two steps towards Harding, then, bowing again, held out a book-sized package.
"This came, Master. From Shepherd."
"Shepherd? *Ben* Shepherd?"
"Yes, Master."
Harding took the package, frowning. He had never met Shepherd, yet he had had some dealings with SimFic in the past and had made some money out of distributing copies of *The Familiar* throughout City North America. But for Shepherd to send him something direct seemed unusual to say the least.
"Was there no note with this?"
"Nothing, Master."
"And you've screened it?"
"Naturally, Master."
And now that he looked, he could see that that was what Levitch had been doing. The scanner was on, its screen glowing faintly behind his Steward.
Harding studied the package and shook his head. It was in a strange covering that looked like paper – that may even have been paper – but was a curiously dark colour, his name and address written in a small neat hand directly onto the surface.
Turning, he walked through to his study and sat at his desk, switching on the lamp.
He stared at the package, surprised. It *was* wrapped in paper. Brown paper. As in the rhyme his mother had sung to him as a child. Now, how did it go?
And went to bed, to mend his head,
With vinegar and brown paper.
Fuck knew what vinegar was, but this . . . he recognised this, though he hadn't actually seen its like before.
Reaching across, he opened the top drawer of his desk and took out the knife he kept there, then slit the package open.
Tipping it out onto his desk, he felt a little shiver of excitement.
A shell! Shepherd had sent him a shell!
He picked it up and read the handwritten label, speaking the words aloud:
"A Perfect Art. A Tragedy in Three Acts."
Again he frowned. It sounded somehow . . . *archaic*. But a new shell, by Shepherd – that in itself was a major event.

He looked up, wondering who else had received such a package, or whether he was the only man in America to have a copy of this. Whatever, it couldn't have been many – not if Shepherd were packaging these up himself and sending them out.

The thought made him grin with pleasure. It was clearly a compliment to him. Someone – Neville perhaps – must have told him what he'd done for *The Familiar* out here, and this was his way of saying thank you, by getting a preview copy to him: for there was no doubt that this, with its handwritten label, was a preview.

And if it was even half as good as *The Familiar* . . .

Harding turned, meaning to switch on his screen and contact Neville, when the screen came on of its own accord.

"Jim?"

"Horton? What the fuck do *you* want?"

Horton's face smiled back at him. "I want what you want, remember?"

Harding, fearing they were being overheard, reached to cut the line, but Horton leaned towards him.

"No, don't cut me off. We're on a discreet line."

"Discreet, bollocks. He listens to everything."

"Not to this, he won't. I've made sure. Your house communications system developed a fault thirty seconds back. This is tight-beam, local. My man is switching the signal through from across the road to you."

Harding stood and went to the window, drawing down the narrow blinds momentarily. There, two hundred metres away, beyond the high security wall of his compound, a man squatted in the bushes, holding a receiver dish.

He shivered, realising suddenly that, just as Horton could get a message to him this way, so he could probably kill him if he wanted.

Sitting again, he composed himself, spreading his hands on the desk. "Okay," he said, far more calmly than he felt, "so what do you want?"

Horton grinned unpleasantly. "As I said. I want what you want. I want young Egan out."

"And Coover in?"

"Did I say that?"

"No, but he's your sponsor now."

"And yours. And don't forget it. But no. Coover doesn't want to make Egan's mistake. He's happy with what he's got. But he wants someone he can trust on his eastern border. Someone who's got no grudge against him, or doesn't feel he has to even the score."

"You, in other words."

"That's right."

"So where do I fit in?"

"Where you've always fitted in. As Chancellor. But with additional responsibilities. For a start, I'll need someone to run the new house."

Harding blinked. *What the fuck was he talking about now*? "I'm sorry. I don't follow you."

"It's simple. We're going to give the people the vote. And Representatives. The whole lot."

Harding was flabbergasted. Why bother to take power if you were only going to give it away? "But . . ."

"Don't you see?" Horton went on, speaking over him. "As things are, if push comes to shove and we've a civil war situation, people are going to stick with what they know, and that's Egan, even if they don't like the bastard. They'll see me as Coover's puppet and they'll resent that, especially if Egan finally lets them know just what Coover did to their precious Western Army. But if I put myself forward on a platform of reform – of power-sharing – then that's a whole new ball game."

"I see. And the House . . ."

"Will be a sham. And that's *your* job, Jim. To make sure that the fucking thing doesn't work."

Harding smiled. For a moment he had thought Horton was going soft on him. "Okay," he said. "I'll wait for instructions."

Horton winked at him. "Right. I'll be in touch. And Jim?"

"Yes?"

"Look out for the Old Man."

"Josiah? You heard about that, then?"

"Heard? Coover's full of it. Seems he sent his own man in to target the old fucker."

"And?"

"He failed. So mind your back. He's a malicious old cunt. I remember him from the old days. And he may still harbour delusions of grandeur. So look out for him, right?"

"Right."

The screen went black.

Harding sat there for a time, thinking through what Horton had said, particularly that last bit, about Josiah Egan. Perhaps he underestimated Old Man Egan. If the old bastard *did* still want power, then he could prove troublesome, and not only to his grandson.

Still, he would think about that in the morning. Right now he would see what Shepherd had sent him.

He picked up the tape and stared at the wording on the label a moment, wondering what it meant. *A Perfect Art*. Now what was *that* about?

Then, feeling a strange, almost intoxicating excitement, he got up and walked through to his Ents Room. There, beneath a silken sheet in the very centre of the dimly-lit chamber, lay his own personal shell-player; a great sarcophagus-like case with a finish of black and red lacquer inlaid with silver and pearls.

Throwing off the sheet, Harding touched the catch and stood back, watching as the huge, wing-like lid lifted back. As it did, the tape compartment emerged from the flank of the case. Smiling now, he placed the tape into the compartment; then, slipping off his robe, he slid into the interior of the machine, the electrodes attaching themselves automatically to the special nodes on his skin and at the base of his skull.

The machine hummed warmly about him, like a womb, embracing him. Slowly the lid came down, like an artificial sky, shutting out the mundane world. And then, with an abruptness that took his breath, he was there, in the garden, the sunlight pouring down on him as he crouched beside the flower's gaping mouth, watching the bee.

* * *

Li Kuei Jen yawned and stretched, then rolled over, putting his arm out across the massive double bed. But the sheets beside him were empty.

"Mark?"

He sat up, knuckling his eyes, then slipped from between the sheets, making his way across to the bathroom.

"Mark?"

There was no sign of him. Kuei Jen yawned again, then looked down at the timer inset into his wrist. It was not even seven yet. Where in the gods' names could he have got to at this hour?

He showered quickly, then dressed. As he was brushing out his long dark hair, the screen in the corner of the room came alive.

"Kuei Jen?"

He turned to face the screen. "So there you are. What's up? Couldn't you sleep?"

"My Steward woke me. It seems there was an attempt on my grandfather's life last night."

"And?"

"He thinks I was behind it."

"Were you?"

"You know I wasn't."

"But you were thinking of it."

"Yes, but . . ."

"Are you in the throne room?"

Egan nodded.

"Good. Then I'll meet you there in ten minutes. Have you summoned Han Ch'in?"

"Should I?"

"Yes, and Harding and Chalker, too."

"Chalker's here already."

"Good. But get Harding there, too. He knows your grandfather. If we need an intermediary he might be the man."

"Okay." He was about to turn away and cut contact, when something else occurred to him. "Oh, and Kuei Jen?"

"Yes, husband?"

"Watch yourself. We're all vulnerable now."

* * *

Zelic looked about him at the abandoned settlement, taking in the signs of a hurried departure. Perhaps they had heard the cruiser coming across the sands, or maybe they'd had a warning. Whichever, it looked as if they had simply left what they were doing and walked off into the desert.

He turned, looking back at the shadowed pool below where he stood, thinking what a pleasant place this was, and wondering what kind of life they lived out here, away from the cities. He would never have guessed that so many lived out here where life seemed impossible. Yet they seemed well-organised, yes, and well-fed, too. Certainly their store cupboards were well stocked.

Zelic raised the apple to his mouth and bit into it, savouring its sweet taste. There was a beautiful silence to this place, too. A silence that even the soft drone of the cruiser – a sound that was muffled by the barrier of rocks that surrounded the settlement – could not dissipate.

As he bit again, the communicator on his lapel crackled and a voice – scratchy, the treble turned too high – filled the air.

"Captain? . . . Are you okay?"

Unclipping the communicator, he answered Lanier.

"I'm fine, Major. There's no sign of life, but they *were* here. And recently, too."

The communicator clicked, then crackled again. "Then they can't have gone far. Twenty k at most, I'd say. Stay right there. We'll pick you up."

Zelic tucked the communicator back into the clip, then walked out into the open. Considering the circumstances, Major Lanier had been most helpful. For almost thirty hours they had scoured the desert, but until now they'd not found a thing.

Taking the gold stud from his tunic pocket, Zelic studied it a moment.

He had noticed this pinned to Li Yuan's ceremonial gown a number of times, and the Han inscription on its reverse was unmistakable. It was his, without a doubt, and to find it here seemed to suggest that he had dropped it here – by design or accident.

There was, of course, the possibility that it had been planted, put here to make them pick up a false trail, but he thought that unlikely.

No. The manner of Li Yuan's kidnap had been too direct. Whoever had done this – and he could not accept Lanier's simplistic description of them as malcontent rebels – they had had a special reason for targeting Li Yuan.

Or so he felt. He had no real proof of that, as yet, but the more he looked about him, the more unsatisfied he was with Lanier's simple political answers. This did not have the look of a terrorist training camp. In fact, there was something almost . . . well, *mystical* about the place.

The drone of the cruiser grew louder, becoming a steady whine as it lifted above the rock wall and then drifted towards him, slowly settling onto the flat rock platform fifty metres away.

He walked across, arriving just as the hatch hissed open and Lanier popped his head out.

"I've just been on the radio, Captain. I've re-directed all the other cruisers out here. We'll use this as our focal point and work our way out. If they're here we'll find them. And when we do . . ."

Zelic knew what the Major would *like* to do. He'd like to destroy the "rebels" for all the trouble they'd put him to over the years. But he'd been given strict orders not to do so. At least, not on *this* mission. His brief was to find and rescue Li Yuan.

Briefly Zelic wondered if Li Yuan were still alive. Certainly, when no ransom demand had come, they had begun to fear the worst for him, but who knew what these people wanted – Lanier least of all.

"Come on," Lanier said, beckoning him up into the craft. "You can tell me what you found when we're in the air. I feel naked down here."

Yes, Zelic thought, as he climbed the ramp and ducked inside. *In fact, if the truth be told, you don't much like venturing outside the walls of your city, do you, Major?*

But then, he didn't live out here on the edge of things, and he had – with his own eyes – seen just how efficient, and how deadly these "rebels" were. So maybe he ought to reserve judgement just now. Maybe he ought to see how things turned out before he grew too critical of the Major.

At least the man was trying.

"Well?" Lanier said, facing him as the craft began to lift. "What did you find?"

Zelic handed over the gold stud, watching as Lanier studied it.

"This is one of his?"

"Yes."

Lanier glanced at him. "And they'd just abandoned the place?"

"Looks like it."

Lanier turned toward the cockpit. "Okay. Take us up five hundred, then blast the fuck out of the place!"

Is that necessary? he wanted to ask. But it wasn't his place to comment on what the Major did. Apart from the difference in their rank, there was the matter of impertinence. This was Lanier's territory, after all, not his.

He felt the slight judder of the craft as the rockets were launched, then, a few seconds later, the whole craft swayed and shook, lifted by the concussion.

"Ok-ay!" Lanier said, grinning back at him. "Now let's go get your man, Captain! Before those bastards decide to make soup out of him!"

* * *

"Master? *Master*? Are you all right?"

Harding was sitting on the edge of the case, his gown loosely draped about him, staring straight ahead.

"*Master*?"

Slowly he raised his head and met his Steward's eyes. "It's okay, Levitch, I'm just . . ."

But how did he explain? How did he begin to put into words what he had just experienced. He shivered, remembering it, then turned his head, looking down into the shell's padded interior, a look of longing in his eyes.

He wanted to go back there. Not later, but now. He wanted . . .

Harding closed his eyes and groaned.

"Are you well, Master? Is there something I can get you?"

He opened his eyes again. "No, no . . . I'm . . ." Absurdly, he laughed. Fine was not the word for it. Wonderful? Enlightened? *Raised*? It was like . . . well, it was almost something spiritual. Not that all that business with the woman had been anything but grossly carnal, it was just that it had seemed to *mean* something for once. It wasn't just sex, it was . . .

"... sublime."

"I beg pardon, Master."

"Never mind," Harding said. "Now what is it?"

Levitch bowed, then handed his Master the handwritten note. Harding unfolded it and quickly read, then looked up.

"So the king wishes to see me, does he? Trouble, is there?"

Levitch hesitated, then, "Word is that Old Man Egan was attacked last night. An assassin. The attempt failed, but Old Man Egan's hopping mad. It might be war."

Harding nodded.

"And the king . . . he wishes me to intercede, neh?"

Levitch bowed his head. Like his Master, he kept himself well informed. "It would seem likely, my Lord."

"It would indeed."

Harding stood, his attention caught between the shell and this matter between the Egans. To be frank, it mattered little in the long run which generation triumphed, for both would be superseded in time. That was, if things went according to plan. But in the short term it was important to keep the younger Egan in his place, for he was the architect of these present troubles and the blame could be firmly placed upon his shoulders, whereas if Old Man Egan were to triumph, he might well claim to be the new broom that would sweep clean. And that could not be allowed.

"Coover should have bombed the old fucker."

"Pardon, Master?"

"You heard me, Levitch. If you want to kill someone, you make damned sure of it. None of this ninja stuff. A nice big bomb usually does the trick. Big enough to take out an estate and everyone in it. Something that'll leave a nice neat crater . . . and nothing else."

Levitch blinked. He had never heard his Master speak like this before. He swallowed, then, at a loss what to say next, asked, "Shall I bring your clothes now, Master?"

But Harding seemed barely to be listening. "Later," he said, waving Levitch away. "Tell him I'll see him later."

* * *

"He said *what*?"

Chalker kept his head low, embarrassed to be the bearer of such news. "He said he would come later, my Lord."

Egan sat back, astonished. "But I told him to come at once!"

"Yes, my Lord." Chalker hesitated, then. "Do you want me to go and get him, my Lord?"

"Yes I fucking do!"

But Kuei Jen was shaking his head. "No, Mark. I'm sure he has his reasons."

"Oh, I'm *sure* he has them, but I'm the king!"

"True, but you need him."

"Need him? I'll fucking wring his neck! Who the fuck does he think he is! Later! I'll give him fucking later!"

"Mark!"

He turned, looking to Kuei Jen, surprised by the tone of command in his voice. "What?"

"*Think*! Think what the situation is. Think what you need and why you need it. Do not feel. Feeling is dangerous, particularly now."

Egan stared at his wife a while, then nodded. "You are right, my love. Anger will get us nowhere."

"Good. Now send again, and this time don't simply summon. This time ask our friend Harding for his help. As a friend and confidant."

Egan looked down, then. "You should have been king, Jenny, not I, then we wouldn't have been in this godawful mess, would we?"

"Maybe not," Kuei Jen answered, smiling tenderly at him, "but here we are, nonetheless, and we must deal with the situation as it is, not with ifs and buts."

He sighed, then made to speak again, but as he did, one of his stewards entered hurriedly and, kneeling before his throne, bowed his head.

"What is it, man?"

"It is your grandfather, my Lord. He begs audience with you."

Egan stood, shocked by the news. "He's here?"

"No, my Lord. On the screen. From Providence."

Egan sat again, stroking his chin thoughtfully, then looked to his wife. "Well, Jenny? Should I speak to him?"

"You have no choice, my husband. But take care what you say. Do not let him goad you. And keep calm. Listen to what he says, but do not comment. Tell him you must consider what he says. He'll understand."

"You think so?"

"Oh, I know so. Your grandfather may be a malicious, greedy bastard, but he's no fool."

"No . . ." He turned back as the giant screen slowly descended. "Okay. Put him on."

Old Man Egan's face filled the ten by eight metre screen. Or rather, the new face that he wore: a lean, hungry-looking face that already seemed changed somehow from the face that had woken on the operating table, as if some inner force were moulding it.

"Mark . . . how are you, boy?"

Kuei Jen saw how his husband tensed at that "boy", how his fingers tightened about the arms of the chair, but his voice when he answered had an unexpected sweetness.

"I'm fine, grandfather. And yourself?"

"I am alive."

The reference to the assassination attempt could not be more pointed, but Mark Egan refused to be drawn.

"And I celebrate that fact. Now what can I do for you?"

"Do?" Old Man Egan laughed gruffly. "You can meet me, that's what you can do. Four days from now. I'll come to you, in Boston. But you must guarantee my safety."

"Grandfather?"

"Oh, don't give me all that shit, boy. We both know how things are. And unless we're going to be at each other's throats from here until Doomsday, we'd better sit down and sort things out between us, neh?"

Egan hesitated, then glanced across at Kuei Jen, who gave the tiniest nod. "Right," he said, clearly taken by surprise by this plea for conciliation.

"Good. And your guarantee?"

Again Egan glanced sideways at Kuei Jen, again she gave the tiniest nod. "You have it."

"Then we'll meet next Wednesday. At sunset, there in your throne room. And Mark . . ."

"Yes, grandfather?"

"No tricks, eh?"

As the screen slowly vanished into the ceiling, Egan sat back, giving a long whistle. "Aiya . . ." Then, turning his head to look at Li Kuei Jen. "Do you think he means it?"

"I don't know."

He sat forward. "What?"

Kuei Jen shrugged. "I don't know. I think he's on the level, but . . . I can't be sure."

"So what if he's not?"

"Then we kill the bastard."

* * *

Harding lay there after the programme had ended, staring at his hands, surprised to find them encased in wires and not, as he'd thought, stained with blood. He felt . . . exhilarated. Yes, and half in love. She was so beautiful. Perhaps the most beautiful woman he had ever met.

For I would rather owner be,
Of thee one hour, than all else ever.

Harding shivered, moved almost to tears. He did not know where those words came from, nor why they had come into his mind just then, but they described almost perfectly what he was feeling at that moment.

To have her, if only for an hour – that seemed a blessed fate.

He closed his eyes and the image of her face came to mind, those perfect features framed in the long dark curls of her silken hair.

Was she real? he wondered. Did the model for her exist in this world? Or had Shepherd conjured her from the air, to taunt such mortal men as he?

Shepherd had used his sister Meg in *The Familiar*, he recalled, but she was only fair compared to this beauty. A goddess this one was.

There was a whirring sound as the thick loop of tape rewound, then a tiny click.

Slowly the wires retracted into the sides of the machine. A moment later the catches of the lid clunked and the wing-like lid hissed open.

Harding sat up, the sense of doubleness he always felt after experiencing a shell particularly strong. It had been so real this time that he could not shake from his mind the thought that his memories of it were also real – that he really *had* met and slept with her. Yes, and killed his rival in a jealous fit. He could remember the sounds the man had made as he plunged the knife deep into his heart.

Harding looked at his hands again. Clean they were. Clean. Not a single spot of blood on them.

"I killed a man. I killed him and I *wanted* to."

Harding shook his head, confused now. He'd felt so good doing it. And afterwards they had made love again, his bloody handprints on her naked flanks and breasts, the dead man – her husband – in the room with them, lying there on the floor beside the bed, his staring eyes reproachful.

He shuddered. So powerful it was. So simple, yet . . .

There was a knocking on the door. "Master?"

Harding closed his eyes and groaned. It was Levitch. The man would have been monitoring things. He would have known when the machine stopped running.

Slowly, reluctantly, he stood. "All right!" he called, feeling a strange anger at this new disturbance. "I'll be out in a moment!"

He climbed out and pulled on his robe, then turned, staring longingly at the machine's interior. *Later*, he promised himself. *I'll come back later*.

Then, begrudging every moment he was away from the machine, he went across and, unlocking the doors, threw them open, storming from the room, all of the joy he had been feeling spoiled suddenly.

"Damn Egan!" he muttered as Levitch began to help him dress. "Damn him and blast his eyes!"

CHAPTER·11

BROWNIAN MOTION

"Sit down!"

Michael sat. He'd learned not to argue when the barrel of a loaded gun was jammed into his chest.

Through the open frame of the window he could see right down the valley to the distant mountains, their snow-covered peaks bathed in light. Outside the cabin, just out of sight, the villagers were going through the carts, looking for anything they could eat or use. He could hear them talking among themselves, their frustration rising by the moment.

The guard backed away, his ancient gun still covering Michael, and went to the window. Michael watched him take a furtive glance outside, then look back at him, scowling threateningly.

How old was the guard? Fifteen? Thirty? It was hard to tell. Living out here on the edge of the Wilds took its toll on a man. But there was a gauntness, a furtiveness, about him that Michael found all too familiar.

He looked about him, taking in his surroundings. It was an old log cabin of a fairly universal design, the walls undecorated. Apart from the chair he sat on, there was a small wooden table and, in the far corner, a chest; otherwise the room was unfurnished. On the wall just to his right someone had pinned up two posters. One was a printed list of rules and regulations – evidence that DeVore's patrols reached even this far out – the other was a Wanted poster, a side-on picture of Emily above the writing.

Seeing it there, Michael smiled. *Ten million yuan? You're worth a thousand million, my love.*

He turned back, looking at the young-old man. "Who do I speak to?"

Again, the guard scowled, the thinness of his face and his poor complexion making it the most ugly of expressions. "Shut up! Masso will see you when he's ready!"

Michael smiled, knowing it would infuriate him. "Thanks."

He could have jumped the boy and disarmed him. It would have been easy, but he had his men to think of. Robbers they might be, but murderers they weren't – not unless they were provoked. Best then to let them take what they wanted.

He looked down briefly, annoyed with himself. He should have taken the eastern path through Leukerbad. It might have taken longer but at least it would have been safe. Haste had forced him into a poor call, and here he was, sat in some draughty hut with Master Scowl, while some tin-pot Village Head went through his things.

Masso, eh?

Again he smiled. A muscle in the guard's cheek twitched. He clearly didn't like Michael's calmness. Nor did he like being left alone in the cabin too long with him.

There was a shout outside, a fierce exchange of words between two of the villagers, then the door crashed open. A big man stood there. He had dark hair that fell in long curls and a handsome face, but his eyes were small and greedy and his clothes were the clothes of a small-time bandit.

"What *is* this shit?"

He threw down one of the packets so that it split open on the floor, a faintly unpleasant smell coming up from it.

"You're Masso, I presume," Michael said, ignoring the question.

Masso's eyes flared with anger. He stepped across and grabbed the front of Michael's sheepskin. But before he could say another word, Michael had stood, pushing him away.

"Don't *touch* me."

Masso blinked, reassessing the situation. Then he laughed. "You're a proud one, my friend, but it'll do you no good. We've got the guns."

"Touch me again and I'll ram your gun up your arse."

Masso stiffened, then he relaxed. Whatever Michael said, he knew he had the upper hand.

"So what is it, Trader? You make drugs out of it?"

Michael smiled, deciding he'd tell the arse-hole the truth. "They're chemicals. We were going to make bombs out of them."

"Bombs?" There was a flicker of uncertainty in the man's eyes. "What you want to make bombs for?"

"To blow the shit out of the Man's soldiers."

He saw Masso put two and two together; saw how his eyes flicked toward the poster, then back to his face.

"You know the Woman?"

Michael shook his head. "No one *knows* her. But I work for her. I bring her things."

It was a lie, of course, but he wasn't going to tell this shit that he slept beside her most nights.

"Then she'd pay for this stuff?"

Michael shook his head. "This is hers. You steal it and you'll answer to her. You want that?"

Masso thought about it a moment, then, a flicker of anger crossing his face, he kicked the broken package across the room. "Just our fucking luck! Still . . ." His eyes went to Michael's sheepskin and again the smile – a smile of cunning – came into his eyes.

Michael, reading him like a tape, shook his head. "You take our coats we'll die."
Masso glowered. "*You* chose to come this way, Mister Trader, not me."
"Then kill us now."
Masso lifted his chin, responding to Michael's challenge. "Maybe . . ."
But the next word was choked off. Michael's hand had closed about his throat.
"Let me tell you something, little man. If I don't return on time, she'll come looking. And if she comes looking she'll find you, have no doubt about it. So back off, okay? Go bother some other poor bastard who's lost his way."
And with that he pushed Masso away.
Masso bent down, holding his throat, surprised by how strong Michael's grip had been, unaware of the prosthetic enhancement in the arm. His eyes were fearful now.
Michael glanced at the guard and saw at once how jumpy he was. It wouldn't do to push too hard right now.
"I'll tell you what," he said. "You help us and we'll help you, eh? After all, there's no need for us to be enemies. Life's hard and one has to make a living."
He saw how Masso's pride was mollified by that. He rubbed at his throat a moment longer, then shrugged. "So what's the deal?"
"You get us to Saanenmoser and I'll have the woman send you coats. Coats like these. And food."
Masso's eyes narrowed. "How much food?"
"Enough to feed fifty men for a month."
Masso shook his head. "It's not enough."
Michael laughed. "You're a greedy little shit, Masso. It's more than enough, and you know it. Now, have we a deal?"
He put out a hand.
"How do I know I can trust you, Trader?"
"Because you can't afford not to."
For a moment longer Masso hesitated then, reluctantly, he clasped Michael's hand in his own. "Okay. But you keep your word, eh, Trader-man? You keep your fucking word."

* * *

Emily looked up from where she was working at her desk, then set her glasses aside. "Chao? What is it?"
Lin Chao smiled, then came into the room. "We've news," he said. "It seems someone saw Michael three days back, at Chamonix."
Emily frowned. "Then he should have been back by now."
"No. It seems they've had bad weather. The Montets Pass was blocked. He would have been delayed."
She looked down, clearly relieved to have some kind of explanation. Then, pushing aside the report she'd been working on, she stood.
He watched as she pulled on her over-jacket and began to button it.
"Mother?"
She looked across. "I'm going to meet him."
"But . . ."

No buts. I'm going, and that's that."

He shrugged. "Okay. But I'm coming with you."

"Don't you think I can look after myself, Lin Chao?"

"Oh, I'm sure you can, mother, but I'd like to come, so humour me."

"All right. But what about your duties?"

"Tybor will fill in for me. He owes me a favour or two."

Emily looked at her adopted son sceptically, then shook her head. "Okay. Then gather together eight men and supplies for three days. If I know Michael, he'll head for Saanenmoser."

* * *

DeVore stood at the head of the stairs, looking out across the echoing chamber, his chest puffed out, his voice full of pride.

"There, Ben. What do you think?"

The four creatures at the far end of the chamber were massive – maybe eight times the body weight of humans – and their eyes . . .

"Can we speak to them?"

DeVore looked to him and smiled. "Of course. They'll be pleased to have some intelligent conversation for a change."

Ben laughed. "If these are what I think they are, then it ought to be interesting."

DeVore narrowed his eyes. "And what *do* you think they are?"

"The next stage in your plan."

"Which is?"

To populate the galaxy. To fill a million worlds with images of yourself. But all he said was, "I don't know. You tell me."

"Come," DeVore said, taking his arm, "let me show you them."

But Ben paused a moment, reaching out to touch DeVore's arm lightly. "Forgive me, Howard, but what exactly are they doing?"

DeVore looked to him and smiled. "They are making me a coat."

Ben looked back. *A coat?* He laughed, thinking of the tale of the Emperor and his new clothes. "But there's nothing there."

"Not nothing, Ben. Nothing*ness.* They are making a coat of nothingness, or rather, of folded space. It will fit over my normal coat, the field generated by my buttons and epaulets, and by tiny transmitters sewn into the arms and edges of the jacket. The field will be only microns across, but that will be sufficient enough to prevent anything from penetrating it."

"And your head?"

"My head, like all my vital functions will be inside the field."

"So how do you breath?"

"The field switches on and off at over three hundred times a second. That's enough to allow oxygen molecules to pass through the field. But anything larger and . . . *pfff* . . . it ceases to be in an instant."

Ben smiled, impressed. "Clever. Who thought of it?"

"Hannem. But come, let him tell you himself."

* * *

It was late morning when they came down from the passes and out into the valley. They were still high up, on the eastern slope, and the valley floor and the river that wound through it were still some six hundred metres below them, but the day was bright and visibility good. Saanenmoser was at most an hour away.

Emily was at the front of the group, flanked by two of the older rebels. Just behind her, walking alongside young Yueh Ho, was the boy, Daniel. Behind them were four more of Emily's most trusted men, and, bringing up the tail, Lin Chao.

Chao was unhappy. When the boy had asked to come, he had counselled his mother against the idea. *We can't be sure about him*, he'd argued; *not until we've made all the proper checks*. But Emily had overruled him. She'd spoken to the boy and liked him.

Which was why Chao was hovering at the back, watching him like a hawk. Why he'd insisted that the boy should be unarmed. For if this *was* DeVore's work . . .

He didn't like it. Not one tiny little bit. In fact, every instinct he possessed twitched at the thought of the boy. Something about him was wrong. Badly wrong.

Like the very fact that he had won his mother's trust so quickly.

You're jealous, a little voice inside him said. *You don't like him because your mother does*.

But even if that *was* true, it did not mean that he should abandon good sense. DeVore would go to any lengths to kill his mother. And *seeming* was his trademark.

The boy *seemed* harmless, and yet he'd shot two morphs dead with single shots between the eyes from over five hundred metres. If that was harmless then what precisely did he need to do to be thought a threat?

Besides, he'd watched the boy. He'd seen how his eyes took in everything, like cameras.

And who was to say that wasn't what he was? Why, even now DeVore might be staring through Daniel's eyes, watching Emily's back.

No, they ought to have checked him out thoroughly before trusting him on a mission like this. And that included a thorough medical check.

Why, for all they knew he could be a walking bomb.

Chao shook himself. *Paranoid*, he thought. *I'm getting paranoid*. But then, he had every reason to be. He had seen enough of DeVore's tricks to last him a lifetime.

He looked up. The sky was clear, not a cloud in the sky. Perfect patrol weather. But they would hear any cruisers long before they'd come close enough to spot their tiny group.

A hawk called, high and clear. Chao stopped dead, turning to look, his lips parting in a smile. Yet even as he saw it, circling high above the opposite slope, he heard an "ufff" and a muffled cry.

Chao looked back to see Yueh Ho down, his gun in Daniel's hands, the barrel aimed straight at Emily's back.

"*No-o-oh!*"

The gunshot echoed across the valley.

There was a moment's stunned silence, then Daniel threw the gun down.

Emily turned, staring at Daniel, her face a study in shocked surprise. Then, turning back, she walked across and stood over the shattered machine.

It fluttered and sparked, then lay still, smoke wisping from its splintered casing.

Daniel stepped up alongside her, then crouched, poking at the broken thing. "Mimics," he said quietly.

"You've seen these before?" she said, watching him.

He nodded. "In the Garden."

There was a murmur of surprise from all sides.

"You've been in there?" she asked, looking at him in a new light.

"Five times."

"Five . . ." Emily turned, looking to Chao. But Chao was staring past her at the shattered fragments of the machine that had almost – *almost* – killed his mother.

"This is new," Daniel said, looking up again.

"New?" Emily shook her head. "No, Daniel. These things . . ."

"It's new," he insisted. "He's been developing new versions of these things. This one . . . it's recent. No more than a year old at most."

"You must be wrong, Daniel. These are old machines. Leftovers from the War."

"No. He's making them again. And if they're here, they're here because he's put them here."

The thought clearly sobered her. She reached out and lightly touched his arm. "Thank you," she said quietly.

Daniel shrugged, then stood. Emily stared at him a moment longer, then, unclipping the spare rifle she carried on her back, she handed it to him.

"I think you've earned this."

Daniel smiled, then slung the strap of the gun over his shoulder.

Emily nodded, then looked about her at the surrounding slopes. "Okay. I guess we'd better hurry. We don't want Michael meeting one of *these* before we get to him."

* * *

"Well?" DeVore asked as they walked along the corridor, heading back to the North Palace. "What did you think?"

"I think I'd like to take one home to study it."

DeVore laughed. "It would beat you at chess."

"It could *try*."

DeVore pushed open the door and they went through. "They've a much bigger brain than the old model. It's quicker, too, and subtler. The creature's reactions are faster, too, and I've enhanced the musculature."

"I noticed," Ben said, slowing to let DeVore open the inner door. "Hannem looked like he could rip sheets of steel in two."

"Oh, he could. If I asked him to, that is. But they do nothing without my say-so." DeVore paused, taking a key from his belt, then looked back at Ben. "It's in here."

"Under lock and key, I note. You think someone will try to steal it?"

"If they could find it. At present it isn't there."

"Handy. Then why bother with a key?"

"Old habits."

But Ben sensed there was a reason. DeVore never did anything without a reason. But this intrigued him, more so perhaps than the new creatures. DeVore claimed he had a ship that travelled by folding space – now *that* was something he would like to own.

DeVore turned the lock then pushed the door open, stepping aside to let Ben pass. "There!" he said.

The ship rested on the floor of the chamber. It was a beautiful thing of silver and pearl and polished wood. Ben turned, surprised, looking across to where DeVore stood in the doorway.

"But I thought you said . . ."

"Go over to it," DeVore said, a teasing smile on his lips. "See if you can find out where it is."

Ben walked across, putting his hand out towards it. But even as he approached it, it seemed to go away from him, or disappear entirely, so that when he turned, it was behind him.

"I don't understand."

"It's a projection, direct into your retinas. The real ship is in a no-space between universes. In a space that isn't space at all, if you follow."

"And what powers it?"

"The differential between universes." DeVore smiled. "Put simply, it skips between the two, in the no-space that exists between their surfaces."

"A gap?"

DeVore shook his head. "No. There is no gap between realities. If one knew how, one could step through from one into another, as if one were stepping through an open door. But that secret has been forgotten, if ever it was known."

"By you, perhaps."

"Oh, if others knew it, then we too would know about it."

"Maybe." Ben smiled, then shook his head. "My father would have liked this. He loved to debate theories."

"This is no theory, my friend. The ship works. One like it brought me from Charon many years ago."

"Forgive me," Ben said, "but if that's so, why don't you use this same technology to defeat your enemies? Or at least to confound them."

DeVore looked away. "It is not that easy. The energy involved, if misdirected, could rip apart this tiny system."

But Ben was not happy with that explanation. If there was a way of harnessing this mysterious energy – and he had no real reason to doubt that this force, whatever it was, really existed – then it could be controlled. And if it could be controlled it could be fine-tuned. And used. For good or ill.

So why was DeVore so vague about it? Had he, perhaps, not *made* but *found* the ship? And was he lying when he said he understood the principles behind its function? For if he could make a craft that skipped between the universes, why could he not harness this power to break Egan's blockade or track down and kill the woman?

And yet DeVore had made Hannem, and Hannem and his fellow creatures *were* a genuine marvel. It was not that DeVore lacked intellectual substance – he was a clever man, and no doubting it – but one could never be sure just when he was lying and when he wasn't.

Standing outside the room again, Ben felt as if he had been given an insight into DeVore. He was powerful, certainly, but not quite powerful enough. Not enough to carry out his plans, anyway. And his need to wear a cloak of invisible power to protect himself spoke volumes.

DeVore was paranoid. And slowly, piece by piece, he was creating a world just as paranoid as he.

But his spell could be unwoven, by a single bullet or a knife. Yes, or a blow to the skull with the butt-end of a gun.

And what then? How would the world be without DeVore to give it a cutting edge?

Like a carp pond without a pike, he thought, recalling what Li Yuan had once said to him.

Back in his rooms, alone again, Ben sat, staring into space, thinking about what he had seen. It did not worry him that DeVore might do away with humanity and place some greater, finer creature in its place. If so, then that was mankind's fate, and what could individual men do about it? One could not build a dam against such evolutionary pressures. Yet it did worry him that, despite the morphs' evident intellectual ability, they might not be the chosen race, the natural successors of mankind. For a start they were too docile – far too compliant to the Great Man's will. As DeVore himself proudly boasted, there was no more obedient creature in the galaxy.

No. It seemed more likely that all this was but an act of extreme egoism – an attempt to people the galaxy with copies of himself. With mirrors. And what had vanity to do with evolution?

So what was the answer? Side with DeVore? Or kill him?

And if the latter, could he, personally, do it?

He smiled, remembering what Meg had said before he'd come here to Mannheim.

If you get at all close, Ben, slip a knife between his ribs and leave it there.

He had not thought his sister capable of such hatred. But so it was. Meg loathed DeVore with a passion he could not imagine.

And maybe she was right.

He stood, then went to the window, looking out. DeVore's woman, Emtu, was down there, walking in the gardens. He watched her a while, wondering just why DeVore had created her. Then, a strange smile forming on his lips, he nodded to himself.

That's it, he thought. *That's bloody well it*!

* * *

Masso had been as good as his word. He'd given back the carts and freed Michael's men. And then, he'd brought them here to Saanenmoser. But that had been the end of things, for having come so far, his nerve gave and, fearing that Michael might, after all, have duped him, he decided to take what he could get.

"Your coats," he said, his gun levelled directly at Michael's head, while his other men covered the rest of Michael's party.

"We've still a good day's travel," Michael said, as calmly as he could. "We'll not survive a night without our coats."

"Find shelter," Masso said, a sneer on his face now. "Huddle together. If the gods will it, you'll survive."

"You gave your word," Michael said.

"And now I take it back." Masso shook his head. "I don't trust you, Trader. Something about you rings false. So I'll take what I can and beg your pardon."

Michael stared at the man a long time after that, remembering his face, then, with an angry shrug, he pulled off his coat and threw it down at Masso's feet, his eyes never leaving Masso's face.

He heard the sound of his men pulling off their thick winter pelts and throwing them down.

Dead men now. For the weather was against them this far up, and there was little shelter in the hills above Saanenmoser.

"If I live I'll come back for you, Masso."

"If you live."

And there was laughter suddenly. Cruel gallows laughter. And there he'd been thinking them different from the other cutthroats and vagabonds who roamed the lower slopes. Michael swallowed bitterly, wishing he could have seen Emily once more before he died, then, with a bellow of rage, he ran at Masso, head down.

He heard the shot but didn't feel the bullet strike him. Then all hell broke lose. There was automatic fire and the sound of small detonations. Grenades or . . .

Gas . . . Where the fuck had they got gas?

And then he was falling down a long deep hole, his head as weightless as a leaf blowing on the wind . . .

* * *

Emily looked down at the corpses at the foot of the slope and shook her head, her voice trembling.

"The idiot. The impatient bloody idiot."

The strangers were all dead. She had killed two of them herself, and Lin Chao had shot another, but Daniel had picked off four of them with successive shots.

Even so, they'd come too late. Michael was dead. He lay face down in a pool of blood.

"Go help those two," she said, gesturing urgently towards the two wounded men who knelt beside the cart. Then, forcing herself, feeling like she was in a dark and awful dream, she began to walk towards her fallen husband.

She'd heard his bellow even as they'd come out of the trees, had seen him throw himself at the stranger, arms out like a diver.

Michael hadn't stood a chance. The gunshot had ripped into his chest from almost point blank range, and the way the body had jerked she knew it was bad.

Emily slowed, the blood pounding in her temples. For a moment she almost stumbled.

"Mother?" Lin Chao's arm was under her arm, holding her up. "Are you all right?"

"No, no I . . ."

She had to sit. Chao helped her down, then squatted, facing her, his face filled with concern. She looked back at him a moment, a look of pure desolation in her face, then let her head fall forward, beginning to sob.

I came too late. The stupid, stupid man! Why couldn't he wait?

For a moment nothing. Then she looked up. Daniel was crouching close by. He had been saying something to her.

". . . bad," he said.

"What?" she said, slurred, like a drunk.

"He's hurt bad. We have to get him back at once. He's lost a lot of blood."

"Who?" she said, blinking. "Who's hurt?"

"It's Michael," Chao said, cutting in. "He's still alive, mother. He's still alive!"

* * *

The journey back across the mountains was the worst she'd known. She felt every bump, every painful little jolt. From time to time she would have them slow, so that she could place her ear against his chest to check he was still breathing, then would make them hurry on, her haste to get back to camp balanced against a desire not to hurt him too much.

Michael's chest was a mess. It was a miracle really that he was alive. But then she reminded herself of what he'd been like last time – after the bomb that had killed his best friend. Thirty years ago, that had been, in America. Back then he had survived against the odds. And so now. If only they could get him back in time.

When darkness fell they were still an hour from the camp and Emily began to fear the worst. To come this far and fail would be dreadful, and yet it seemed they must fail, for Michael's breathing grew laboured, and with each breath he groaned, as if he wanted to be gone from this world of pain and suffering. But she would not let him go.

"Hold on," she murmured, walking beside the makeshift stretcher, her hand resting on his arm. "We'll get there soon, my love, I promise you."

Ahead of them now was a small ravine, crossed by a narrow rope bridge. Beyond it the path sloped down again. Yet, as they climbed the steep path something rattled down the slope to meet them.

The explosion knocked the two stretcher bearers off their feet. Emily too went down. The stretcher fell, tilting to the side.

Daniel and Lin Chao had opened fire. As the things came down the slope at them, they picked them off.

Emily rolled over, bringing her gun up to her shoulder, even as another of the spider-like things scuttled over the rocks towards her. She blew a hole in its pot-like belly.

For a moment there was nothing in the world but gunfire. Then stillness. A sudden, awful stillness. And then a groan.

Emily turned her head. The groan had come from one of the stretcher bearers who lay there, his body hunched into itself, like a caterpillar arching its back, his hands holding his ruined stomach. He had taken the worst of the blast. By the look of it, shrapnel had embedded itself in his stomach. Emily took this in at a glance, then clambered up, looking for Michael.

"Michael . . .?"

She saw him almost at once, lying face down on the ledge nearby. He was still. Ominously still. Even as she made to go to him, Lin Chao crouched down beside him, placing his hand to his stepfather's neck to check for a pulse.

Emily shivered. She knew, even before Chao turned and looked at her. Knew because, even before that moment, they had been using up their luck. But knowing was not *knowing*. She went across and knelt beside the body, her hands gently cradling his head, caressing the soft mantle of his hair.

"You should have waited," she said, whispering the words into the unhearing shell of his ear. "You should have known I'd come."

* * *

The broken packet lay upon the floor of the hut where Masso had thrown it only the day before, a vivid orange glow thrown up into the shadowed room. Close by, stretched out upon his back, one hand frozen into a bloated claw, lay the guard, his bright yet sightless eyes staring at the ceiling. He too glowed, his flesh, where it jutted from the ragged cloth pulsing with a faint blood-pink light.

Pollen danced in the darkness of the cabin, glowing gently, each spore diseasedly alive.

Brownian motion.

The randomness of particles.

The clawed hand trembled then burst like a pod, spewing a cloud of glowing pollen into the shadows.

Sudden agitation, and then stability. The eternal pattern of nature.

And then silence. A long, inhuman silence.

* * *

DeVore threw the door open and stormed from the room. Behind him, his personal staff looked on, white-faced with fear.

He half-ran down the corridor, past the open lift and down the concrete steps that led to the morgue. There, on a slab in the centre of the main dissecting room, lay one of his morphs – one of the new generation Neumann – dead.

White-coated technicians, their faces masked, cowered against the far wall, their eyes frightened. DeVore looked to them then gestured for one of them to come to him. The man came, his legs almost failing him, until he stood before DeVore, his body half-bowed.

"What *happened*?" DeVore said, a strange twisted tone in the second word.

"W-we d-don't know . . ." the technician began.

DeVore reached out and lifted the man from his feet with one hand, then sank a knife deep into his heart.

"Wrong answer."

He let the body fall, then looked to the others, showing them the knife. "*What . . . went . . . wrong?*"

"It's diseased," one of them offered; a young technician at the very end of the line. "The nervous system . . ."

DeVore stared at him hawkishly. "What *about* the nervous system?"

His Chief Technician answered him. "It's rotted away."

Devore shook his head. "Impossible. It was fine this afternoon." Then, more quietly. "So what caused it?"

The Chief Technician answered quietly. "That's what we don't yet know. We need to do a proper autopsy . . ."

"Twenty-four hours."

"I'm sorry, Master?"

DeVore's eyes were like steel. "That's how long you've got to find out. Twenty-four hours. And then I start dissecting *you*."

* * *

Ben found DeVore in his rooms, seated in a chair beside the open window, staring out into the moonless dark, his right hand restlessly stroking his chin.

"Howard?"

DeVore looked round distractedly. "Oh, it's you . . ."

"What's the matter?"

DeVore gestured towards the chair beside his own, then shook his head. "They're diseased."

"Your creatures?"

DeVore nodded. "I've put the others in isolation, but two others have already gone down with it. It's their nervous systems. It seems they're simply rotting away."

"Impossible."

"Yes."

"But there must be some explanation for it."

"You think so?"

Nothing happens without a reason."

"No . . ."

"And your coat?"

DeVore's eyes met his blankly. "My coat?"

"Your special invisible force-field. Did the creatures finish it?"

"They . . ." DeVore stopped dead, sitting forward suddenly, his eyes, which had been lifeless, now brightly alive again. "You don't think . . .?"

"What?"

"The field. You don't think the field affected them?"

"Why? Could it?"

"I don't know." DeVore frowned, then shook his head. "No . . . If it was harmful Hannem would have known."

"Maybe he did."

"Impossible."

"Why?"

"He would have said there was a danger."

"Would he?"

DeVore bridled. "Of course he fucking would!"

"Why? You told him to make you a coat of power. It wasn't his place to question that decision."

"But that's stupid. If he knew . . ."

"Then he would have said nothing. You said it yourself, Howard – there's no more obedient creatures in the galaxy than your morphs."

"But that's . . ."

"Crazy?"

DeVore nodded, but Ben could see he was already half convinced.

Ben gave a little push. "Which of them have sickened?"

DeVore turned and looked at him. For a moment he was silent, then he made a little shrug of acceptance. "You're right."

"None of the others have been affected?"

"Not one."

"And the coat?"

DeVore looked to him, then smiled. "Try touching me."

* * *

As the morning sun slowly climbed the sky they buried Michael under the lawn beside his favourite stream, the branches of an ancient elder overhanging the mound. They were all there – at least, all of them that were still alive after six years of campaigns against The Man.

Emily was the last to leave the graveside. Lin Chao waited for her some little way off, then walked across and put his arm about her shoulders, letting her weep against his side. But his face too was wet. Michael had been a good man, yes and a good father too. He had been a "Mender", like Lin Shang before him. Mender Lin, who had first taken him from the streets and cared for him.

Three fathers he had had now, and each in turn had been taken from him violently. Such was the world he lived in. Yet he did not despair. Not while she was there. Not while she yet strove for a better, kinder world.

Daniel was waiting for them beside the tiny wooden bridge that crossed the stream. Seeing him, Chao smiled. If any doubts remained, they were not significant. Daniel had proved himself twice over on the journey. Now he was a brother.

At the head of the valley, Emily turned, looking down at the stream and at the tree-edged lawn beyond it. You could barely see where the mound was from this high up, yet she seemed to see it clearly. Once more her eyes misted.

That's where her heart is now, Lin Chao thought, watching her face, finding a real beauty in those deep-carved lines of hers, in the fine-spun grey of her hair.

They said DeVore kept a copy of his mother. A younger, fairer copy, made from the finger she had lost to him that time. But no copy could match this original. To his eyes there was no finer sight in all the universe than this.

Emily turned, looking to him, her eyes gentle now, a faint smile on her lips. "What were you thinking, Chao?"

He lied. "I was wondering what was for breakfast."

She laughed. It was what he always said. "Come," she said, taking his arm and holding it overlong, letting the love she felt for him pass between them. "Let's go and find out."

CHAPTER·12

WAKING

Waking, he found her in his arms, her naked breasts against his chest, her body folded along the length of his body. Bodies surrounded them; soft, warm bodies, their sleeping forms filling the shadows of the well.

Sighing deeply, he stretched like an animal, the feeling of relaxation, of utter satiation, so strong that for a moment his mind was dark and without thought.

Nameless he was. A leaf drifting on the great swell of the ocean's tides. All will, all struggle had been washed from him. For the moment he was complete, enclosed.

Adrift. He was adrift upon the dark tide. Sleep took him once again and he turned, folding himself back into the contours of her body, her limbs and his interlocked, their breath a single sound, a single motion. Adrift.

And then a noise, like the lapping of a wave against a rock.

Consciousness.

Slowly, memory returned.

Li Yuan opened his eyes and yawned. The light was above him. A bright curve of light that was slowly travelling down the side of the well.

Morning.

He looked about him, remembering the long night's pleasures, a tiny shiver of astonishment rippling through him.

I never guessed.

Need. Sex had always been a matter of need, and the more intense his need, the more intense the experience. Until last night.

Last night had been surrender. Last night he had found at last what he had been seeking all his life.

Obliteration.

The smile he now smiled was like a child's, wholly innocent; a waking smile that came from the great well of contentment deep within him. Contentment . . . and love.

Yes. He was loved. Even as he lay there, he felt that love all about him, there in the bodies that lay against his own, flesh to his flesh, enveloping him.

He had lived his whole life in ignorance, unaware of the depths within himself, lacking even the vaguest notion that this other self – this vast oceanic being – existed within the narrow compass of his human frame.

He had spent his time staring at sunlit surfaces, his inner eye blinded by the winking light. But now he saw.

Halfway, a voice said, or rather, did not say, except in his head. *You have come but halfway.*

Li Yuan narrowed his eyes, looking up into the brightness above him. "Tuan Ti Fo? Is that you?"

A rope fell softly from above, brushing his upper arm.

Climb up, the voiceless voice said. *Climb up and meet your other self.*

"Must I?"

There was laughter. A gentle, healing laughter.

You wish to stay there, Li Yuan?

He reached out and took the rope, grasping it with both hands as it tightened, letting himself be pulled up out of that soft mound of naked bodies.

Dangling on the rope, he looked back, a sigh of happiness escaping him.

They will always be there for you.

"I know."

There was no jealousy, no discord, none of that awful, hateful nonsense that normally accompanied the sexual act. This once it had been pure, unselfish. He had given and taken without thought.

As it always should have been.

The old man slowly hauled him up, then put out a hand, pulling him up onto the flattened earth beside the well.

Li Yuan looked at the sage, seeing him properly for the first time. He was both there and not-there. Light passed through him, and yet he was solid.

"What now?" he asked.

"You must climb up."

Li Yuan looked past Tuan Ti Fo to the spire. In the morning's light it seemed to spear the heavens. He stepped forward, meaning to go across to it and climb, but Tuan Ti Fo put out a hand, gently touching his chest.

"Not yet, Li Yuan. First you must rest and bathe."

* * *

Egan stepped from the bathroom and stopped. Li Kuei Jen stood in the doorway, his face clouded.

"What's up?"

Li Kuei Jen shrugged. "Maybe nothing. Then again . . ."

He finished towelling himself then threw the towel aside and walked across to where his clothes were laid out.

"Rumours?" he asked, stepping into his pants.

"No."

Kuei Jen came across and sat on the edge of the dressing table, watching him dress. "Something's happening, Mark, but I'm not sure just what it is. I heard it from one of my servants first. It seemed incredible, but, now that I've checked on it, it looks like it's true."

"True?"

"The clubs. Last night they were empty. Not a soul in them."

"*Clubs?* What clubs?"

"You name them. Ectogenesis. The Kitchen. Blake's. Yes, and the rest. Not a soul in any of them."

Egan had begun to turn away, now he turned back, facing her. "Impossible! The world could be ending and those places would still be packed out!"

"That's what I thought."

"So what the fuck's happening? Someone throw a party or something?"

Kuei Jen shook his head. "No. And no one's gone down sick, as far as I can make out."

"Then maybe it's got something to do with our declaration of Martial Law?"

"It crossed my mind. But anyone who can afford to go to The Kitchen is going to be exempt from current legislation anyway. Oh, a handful might have been worried about the reaction of the common citizenry and not ventured out, but *all* of them?"

"So maybe they know something we don't."

"A coup?"

Egan nodded. "Are the palace defences in place?"

"It was the first thing I checked on."

Egan stood there a while, thinking it through, then shook his head, more confused than ever. "No. It still doesn't make sense. Why tip everyone the wink, then do nothing?"

"I don't know."

"My grandfather?"

"Is in Providence still."

"Horton?"

"With Coover in Reno."

"DeVore?"

Kuei Jen shook his head. "They'd not stay indoors for DeVore."

"Then *what*?" He was getting twitchy now. "What in the gods' names is going on?"

There was a knock. Egan stared at the door a moment, then went over to a drawer and took out a gun. He walked across, standing just to the side of the door. "Who is it?"

"It's me. Li Han Ch'in."

Egan turned, looking to his wife. Kuei Jen nodded, then walked across and pulled open the door.

Li Han Ch'in stepped in, then turned, giving Egan a little bow. "Here," he said, holding out a package for him to take. "I think this might explain what's going on."

* * *

It seemed a long wait, but finally the lid swung back and Egan sat up, looking dazed, but clearly none the worse for the experience.

"Well?" Kuei Jen asked anxiously. "What is it like?"

Egan climbed out, then sat on the edge of the shell, staring at his hands and frowning. "It was . . . *wonderful.*" He shivered, then looked up at his wife. "I . . ."

Kuei Jen came across and wrapped a cloak about Egan's shoulders, then sat beside him. Li Han Ch'in stood across from them, looking on, his face creased with concern.

"You what?" Li Kuei Jen coaxed, his arm about him, his face looking into his.

"I . . . killed a man. A rival in love. I . . . wanted to."

Li Kuei Jen looked to his half-brother and frowned. "What do you mean? It was a shell, Mark. A fiction. You didn't really kill a man."

"No, but it was so real. So . . ."

Again he shivered, not from cold, as Kuei Jen had first thought, but from something else. Mark's eyes were staring now, as if he could physically see something there in the air before him.

"I've never met anyone like her. She was so surprising . . . so funny, and . . . so beautiful."

"She?"

Egan turned his head and looked directly at her. "Helen. Her name is Helen. She . . ."

"She doesn't exist, Mark. She's a fiction"

"No. She exists. Somewhere. She has to. He couldn't *possibly* have invented her."

Again Kuei Jen looked to his half-brother, his concern growing. Then, standing up, he turned and stepped down, removing the tape from the slot.

"What are you doing?" Egan asked, his eyes suspicious.

"I'm going to destroy it."

"No!" He stood, making a grab for it, but Han Ch'in interceded, holding his arms.

"Kuei Jen is right, Mark. It must be destroyed. Look at the effect it's had on you. And the others, too. Think, Mark. *Think!*"

But Egan was trembling as he watched Kuei Jen smash the tape against the side of the shell again and again. His eyes showed real pain.

"No," he moaned. "No-oh-oh!"

Kuei Jen threw the broken tape aside, then faced his husband once more, gesturing to Han Ch'in to release his arms. Egan staggered, then fell to his knees, holding his head in his hands.

"Aiya! You don't understand . . ."

"Oh, I understand right enough," Kuei Jen said, looking over his husband's head at his half-brother. "Shepherd may have made this, but this has the mark of DeVore all over it. It's a trap, Mark. A silken web. And it's got most of Boston's élite strung up in it. But if we act quickly we can do something."

Egan glanced up, something like sanity returning to his eyes. "Tell me what to do."

"Do? You must ban the tape, that's what you must do. And you must confiscate every copy you can find and burn them. And then you must find out where they've been coming in from and plug that gap."

"And then?"

"Then you have to try to forget what you've just experienced."

But that, Kuei Jen knew, was going to be the hardest part of all.

* * *

Chalker came smartly to attention in the doorway to the Throne Room, bowing his head low.

"Master."

"Ah, there you are, Colonel. How goes the search?"

Chalker raised his head, his eyes taking in the extraordinary sight of Egan, sat upon his throne, thick ropes bound tight about his chest and arms. To the left of the throne, just below the steps, was a wire brazier, smoke curling up from the smouldering coals.

"Master?"

It's okay, Colonel. This is for my own good."

Chalker looked to Li Kuei Jen, a query in his eyes, but Egan's wife stayed silent.

"I'm sorry, I . . ."

"The tapes, Colonel. Have you found any more tapes?"

"Hundreds, Master. But . . ."

"Bring them," Egan commanded, gesturing towards the smoking brazier. "Place them there, beside the brazier."

Chalker hesitated, then turned and signalled to two of his men who stood outside in the long corridor.

"Quickly now!"

He turned back, standing aside as his men wheeled in a cart piled high with copies of Shepherd's tape.

"It was as you said," Chalker said, watching his men set the cart beside the brazier. "Nearly every Mansion had a copy."

Egan's eyes followed the cart, a strange light in them now. "Are they all . . . the same?"

"It seems so, Master. We've not checked them all, of course, but . . ."

"Then maybe I should . . ."

"No!" Li Kuei Jen said, stepping across and standing between his husband and the cart. "You have ordered these destroyed, *remember*?"

"Yes," he said, a strange wheedling tone in his voice now. "But it wouldn't hurt to check, just in case."

Chalker watched the exchange, astonished. What in the gods' names was going on?

"Burn them!" Li Kuei Jen said, turning to face the two men who stood to attention by the cart. "Do it! Quickly now!"

"No . . ." Egan said, groaning, his body straining against his bonds as he watched the soldiers throw the first of the tapes into the fire. "Please, don't . . . *Please* . . ."

Li Kuei Jen turned back. "We *must*, my love. For your own sake. And for the sake of City America."

Chalker took a step towards his king. "*Master*?"

But Egan was not even aware he was there. Egan was staring wide-eyed at the flames that now leaped from the burning pile of tapes, such pain and longing in his face – such loss – that Chalker shuddered to see it.

* * *

Egan was sleeping now, heavily-sedated. Stepping from his room, Kuei Jen looked to his half-brother and grimaced.

"Have you ever seen the like?"

Han Ch'in frowned. "Once, back in Sichuan, when my stepfather, the Warlord, took me to one of his clubs. There were addicts there. I tell you, Kuei Jen, they were like beady-eyed, soulless machines. But *that* . . ." He shuddered.

"What could have been on that tape to do that to him?"

"I do not know, and I do not *want* to know." Han Ch'in fell silent, then. "Did he sign the Edict?"

"Yes."

"Then maybe there's a chance."

"You think so? You think the threat of death will stop someone who's already experienced the tape? You saw what it did to him after only a single viewing. Why, he almost tore himself out of his bonds trying to save those tapes!"

"I saw," Han Ch'in said, his eyes troubled.

"And if I know DeVore, Boston won't be the only City to have been seeded with those things. We can only pray that Chalker and his men will root them out . . ."

"Before the damage is done?" Han Ch'in shook his head. "If you ask me, the damage has already been done. While we slept."

Kuei Jen slumped into a chair. "I should not have let him sample it."

"You could not have known."

"No. But I ought to have suspected it. We have tasters taste our food to make sure it is not poisoned."

Han Ch'in crouched, facing his half-brother. "Do not blame yourself, Kuei Jen. You were not to know. And when you did, you acted swiftly and decisively. No more could have been asked of you."

But Han Ch'in could see that Kuei Jen was unconvinced.

"So what now?" Han Ch'in asked quietly, when the silence had dragged on.

Li Kuei Jen looked up and sighed. "I don't know. But let us hope they find our father, neh, and soon. Let us pray to Heaven that he, at least, is safe."

* * *

Locking the door behind him, Chalker quickly crossed the room, setting the tape down on the edge of the machine.

It had not been hard to trace the company who had delivered the tapes. EC – Elite Couriers – had their offices in the Hartford Enclave, near Bradley Spaceport. But on arriving at their offices, he knew at once that he'd come too late. The fire crew said it was an accident – an electrical short – but he knew better. All the delivery records had been destroyed, *and* the computer back-ups.

As he'd picked over the smouldering debris he had felt more and more certain of it. This had been a professional job. A covering of tracks. Now he'd never know who'd smuggled the tapes in, or how.

But he had found this one final copy, among the half-burned bits and pieces in one of the bins. A return, perhaps, or a misdirect. Its plain, brown-paper cover had been ripped and charred and the address label was missing, but the tape itself was untouched. He'd felt a slight twinge of guilt as he'd slipped it into his tunic pocket, but he told himself it was for the good of all.

At least, he hoped it was.

It was almost four hours now since he had witnessed those extraordinary scenes in the Throne Room; four hours in which he'd brooded on the matter, his initial feeling of frustration at not being trusted by his Masters growing until it had become a full-blown anger. He had thought he'd done enough to earn that trust; to have made himself much more than a mere "fixer" – more than the man who tidied up their messes after them – but it seemed not. No, they had not even given him the courtesy of an explanation; he had simply been told to collect up the tapes and burn them, like a common servant.

But he wasn't a common servant. Nor would he allow himself to be treated as such. Not by the likes of Egan and his half-man wife, anyway!

I need to know, he told himself, as he shrugged off his uniform and climbed into the shell. *It is my duty to know.*

And when he knew?

Then he could effectively combat this, whatever it was. It was the first rule of combat, after all: know thine enemy.

As the lid hissed into place, Chalker lay still, letting the wires attach themselves to his flesh. Closing his eyes, he surrendered to the embrace of the machine.

I need to know.

* * *

That evening they bathed Li Yuan and anointed him, then led him to the tower and bid him climb. There, at the very top of that great spire, the deep-shadowed bowl of Nineveh below him, he sat cross-legged upon the platform and waited for the dark, the faintly glowing bowl beside him, the great ocean of the night surrounding him.

And as the sun set, he remembered what Tuan Ti Fo had said:

There is a duality to everything, Li Yuan. You have known it all your life, for it is there in the teachings of the Tao, but you have never really felt *it. Until now. Now you will understand, and see. And when you have seen, you will never stop seeing.*

It was true. He had known of that duality all his life; had read of it and paid lip service to it. *Li* and *Ch'i* it was – the outward form and the inner energy. As the great sage, Chu Hsi had said, three thousand years before, "Throughout the universe there is no *ch'i* without *li*, nor *li* without *ch'i*." Yet he had never included himself in that great universal equation, as if somehow, merely by existing, he was outside of it all, his self-awareness something special, something different and apart from the rest. But all things were a part.

Yes, even a man's consciousness was divided, split between the darkness of sensuality and the searing light of intellect.

This too was old knowledge. Yet each individual man forgot. Time and again he needed to be reminded – to be immersed both in himself and in what was outside himself. To look in both directions and be made to face both ways.

For vision was not a singular thing. One needed both one's eyes to see.

As darkness fell, so he lifted the bowl and drank deeply, feeling the drug that was not a drug course down his throat, the scentless, tasteless liquid changing him, *doubling* him, placing him both within and outside of himself, contiguous, each atom aligned and fused, a two-in-one.

Letting the bowl fall from his hands he sat back, resting his head against the top of the spire, and stared up into the star-filled void.

He hadn't long to wait. There was a prickling sensation in his spine and at the base of his neck. That prickling grew, until his whole body felt numbed and swollen, and then he felt a strange rushing sensation and the stars seemed to leap down at him and spear him – a thousand million points of light piercing him, so that where, a moment before, there had been nothing but the endless darkness of the void, suddenly there was nothing but light – piercing, shining light.

Burning him. Filling him. And as he encompassed it all within the fragile bowl of his skull, so his mouth opened and laughter spilled from his lips. The joyous laughter of understanding.

So there you are, Li Yuan.

* * *

The body lay on the bed where the servants had laid it, the skin so pale it seemed like wax. Looking across at it from the doorway, Levitch could not help wondering what his Master had been feeling in those last few moments before he'd died, for he had never seen a smiling corpse before – never seen such joy on the face of a dead man. And that erection!

Chalker's men had come an hour back to confiscate the tape, but it had been too late to save Harding.

Six times he'd visited the shell. Six times! And each time more feverishly, as if he could not live unless he were back there, inside that awful, suffocating box.

It had killed him. Levitch was as sure of that as he could be. Harding had been a fit old bastard and had no history of heart trouble, so the seizure was totally unexpected.

Unless that too had been part of the programme.

The idea hadn't occurred to him immediately. He'd been too shocked to find his Master dead in the shell with that grin on his face. But the more he thought about it, the more it troubled him.

He had seen Harding use the shell before. The old boy had at least two dozen tapes, Shepherd's *The Familiar* among them, but he had never acted the way he had last night.

Like someone driven. Someone who had totally lost control.

Levitch shook his head then turned away, heading back to his room. The surgeon's report was on his desk, along with the death certificate. "Natural causes," it read.

Natural causes, my arse.

Sitting down behind the desk, Levitch pushed the surgeon's papers aside, then reached across to take the house journal from the tray. He knew already what he would write for this evening's entry: "Master found dead." There was no need for any further details. No, nor time to write them, really. The old man's death had created an administrative headache that would eat up his every waking hour. Even so, he felt he ought to mention his suspicions to *someone*.

Chalker, perhaps.

Opening the big, leather-bound book, Levitch reached across, took the pen from the inkstand and began to write, even as the dawn's light began to filter through the blinds.

* * *

Tuan Ti Fo was waiting for Li Yuan when he came down, standing in the sunlight at the spire's base, his white hair glistening. Greeting Li Yuan, he smiled and handed him a peach.

Li Yuan stared at the dew-beaded fruit a moment, astonished by how different it appeared, how differently he *saw* it, then looked back at the old man, realising at that moment that he was standing with one of the Immortals.

The sage's smile was filled with gentle amusement. "You see now."

"I see," Li Yuan answered. And it was true. Before now he had seen only the shadow form of the old man, but now Tuan no longer lacked substance. He was there before Li Yuan, rooted to this reality like a tree.

And yet there was still a part of him that was elsewhere.

"Why is that?" he asked.

"Soon," the old man answered, his eyes letting Li Yuan know that he would have his answer. "The time is almost upon us."

He understood. Something was happening. Something . . . so vast, so all-encompassing, that it would transform everything, just as he had been transformed.

"What do you want?"

"Nothing but what you yourself want. You have experienced both the loss of self and the mirroring of the self within the cosmos. These two are integral and yet apart, both inside and outside of the great unthinking One."

Li Yuan was quiet a moment, then he nodded. "I think I understand. You want me to go back?"

Tuan Ti Fo nodded. "There will come a time when what you now know will be of use to you. Until that time, keep safe, Li Yuan. And remember what you learned here. We are dual creatures, possessed of two directions within ourselves. Those directions should not be at war with each other. That was never our Creator's purpose. They are there to be expressed and enjoyed – yes, and celebrated!"

Li Yuan stared at the old man a moment, then, smiling his thanks, he turned and began to walk away.

It was time to go back. Back to the human world.

* * *

There was a great flash, and buildings falling, and bodies burning like matches, gone in an instant in the great wind.

And the air like molten glass.

And behind it all the figure of a young man laughing. A young man with old and bitter eyes.

Li Yuan straightened, the vision still with him, then put up a hand to shield his eyes against the sun's glare.

They were coming. He could hear the drone of their engines across the sands.

He turned, looking back. Nineveh was far behind him now, yet he could still make out the dark outline of its caldera against the desert sky.

Nineveh. Where he had lost and found himself again.

He closed his eyes, remembering. He had been a broken bowl, a half-man in a world of half-men, but now he was complete.

What I should always have been.

He turned back, squinting into the sunlight as the ships came on towards him. Three cruisers, flying in low formation.

Smiling, he raised his arms in greeting.

* * *

"What the . . .?"

"Slow down!" Zelic barked, leaning over the pilot. "That's him!"

The cruiser shuddered as it decelerated, the flanking cruisers out-running them a moment, then beginning to decelerate themselves.

"Gods," Lanier said, coming alongside. "It *is*. What the fuck is he doing out here?"

Zelic shrugged, then, remembering their guest, looked at Lanier. "You want to tell him, or shall I?"

Lanier shrugged. "You know these Chinks better than me."

Zelic raised an eyebrow, then turned away, making his way back through the cabin to where Li Han Ch'in was sleeping.

Or had been, for even as he went to knock, the door swung open and Han Ch'in stepped out.

"Are we landing?" he asked.

"Yes," Zelic said, smiling, liking Li Yuan's son immensely. "We've found your father."

"Found . . .?" Han Ch'in whooped, then gripped Zelic's arm. "Is he all right?"

"I . . . don't know. We've only just spotted him. But he was on his feet."

Han Ch'in grinned, then. "Well, come on, Captain! Let us go and greet my father!"

* * *

Li Yuan stood with his arms at his sides, waiting as the ships landed all around him, sand whipping up into the air in great swirls from their engines.

One by one, the drone of the engines faded.

In that sudden silence, the *thunk* of the hatch locks being sprung was like the sound of an arrow hitting a target.

He smiled, looking back down the years to a moment when his elder brother Han Ch'in, had squinted down the arrow and let fly. It had been a spring day full of sunlight, down by the stream at Tongjiang, and he had sat beside the beautiful Fei Yen looking on as she wagered with his brother.

And now his son, his brother's namesake and that woman's progeny, stepped out from the hatch to greet him.

"Han Ch'in," he said, stepping towards him, his arms out.

"Father!"

Han Ch'in ran to him and almost picked him up, he was squeezing him so hard.

"Father! We thought you were lost!"

"I was," he said, "but now I'm found."

Han Ch'in stood back a little, holding his upper arms. "Where have you been?"

Li Yuan laughed. "If I could but tell you."

"Father?"

"Never mind. I'm here now. Is Zelic . . .?"

"In the cruiser," Han Ch'in said, smiling again, pleased – clearly pleased – to see him. Again he hugged him, and again Li Yuan found himself thinking of his brother and how like him this Han Ch'in was.

Lost, but found . . .

He smiled, acknowledging what Tuan Ti Fo had said. *And my mother, too,* he said silently. *She is here, within me.*

Yes, Li Yuan. She has always been there. You had only to wake to her presence.

"Han Ch'in," he said, returning to the moment, "how fares my other son?"

"Kuei Jen is well, father, or was when I left him. But young Egan is not well. The truth is, our armies were crushed in the Californian campaign, and then there was a shell . . ."

"Then we are needed, neh?"

Han Ch'in blinked, then bowed his head, responding to something in his father's tone; something that had not been there a moment before. Suddenly it was not simply his father who stood before him, but a T'ang, a Son of Heaven.

"Come, Prince Han," he said, smiling and laying his hand upon his son's shoulder. "To Boston. Before night falls."

* * *

They flew direct to Baltimore, then changed cruisers, flying in one of Egan's own, north across Chesapeake Bay and along the Delaware valley, heading for Boston.

It was there, seated at the window, looking down across the burned-out wastelands between Baltimore and Philadelphia, that Li Yuan had the vision again.

Han Ch'in leaned across. "Father? Are you all right?"

"Boston . . ." Li Yuan said, recognising it this time.

"What? What about Boston?"

Li Yuan looked to his son, concerned. "Contact Kuei Jen and Egan. Tell them to get out of there at once."

"But they can't. They're meeting Old Man Egan in two hours."

"Old Man Egan? You mean *Josiah*? But . . ."

"They gave him a new body."

"Yes . . ." He nodded. "I see that now. The young man with the ancient eyes. I wondered why."

"Father?"

"Do as I say, Han. Tell Kuei Jen that it's a double-cross. Old Man Egan won't be there. The only reason he's arranged the meeting is to make sure his grandson *is*."

Han Ch'in looked troubled. "How do you know this?"

"I *saw* it. In a vision. With *these*." He pointed to his golden eyes. "Has no one ever told you, Han? We see things, all the time. Small things mainly. Things that *will* come to pass. That's what the plague did to us. What it gave us."

Han Ch'in looked shocked. Even so, he bowed his head and, turning, hurried through to the cockpit. Two minutes later he was back.

"Kuei Jen wants to speak to you, father. He says . . . well, he asks if you are all right?"

"In the head, you mean?"

Han Ch'in made an apologetic shrug. Li Yuan got up and went through to the cockpit.

Kuei Jen's face was on the tiny screen.

"Father? Oh, how good it is to see you. How are you?"

"Clearly not well in the head, according to you."

"I didn't mean . . ."

"No, but I did. You have to get out of there, Kuei Jen. And everyone who's dear to you. Josiah means to bomb Boston out of existence. I've seen it. It *will* happen."

"Then we must stop him."

"No. You can't. But you can save yourselves. So get out of there. Now!"

Kuei Jen hesitated, staring at Li Yuan, then gave a nod. "All right. We'll evacuate the court. But what if you're wrong?"

"Meet me in Providence two hours from now and we'll see who was wrong."

* * *

They carried Egan from his bed to the waiting cruiser, his hands and ankles bound, a gag about his mouth, as if they were kidnapping him.

Chalker arrived late, a look of real distress on his face. But there was no time for that. Getting him aboard the last of the five cruisers, Kuei Jen gave the signal to go.

The cabin was packed. Baby Yuan slept in his nurse's lap. Beside him, young May Ji stared wide-eyed into space. She had been woken from her bed to be brought here. Squeezed in beside her was her elder brother, Samuel, his sullen face showing his displeasure at events.

All those he loved and cared for were here in the cruiser. All, that was, but his father and half-brother.

As the engines roared into life and the cruiser lifted from the pad, Kuei Jen turned, looking out through the cabin window, watching as the great fortress diminished below him, its distinctive towers merging into the massive high-rise sprawl of City Boston. The sun was low. Soon it would be night.

And if her father was right . . .

"Impossible," he said softly, speaking to himself.

"What?" Chalker said.

Kuei Jen looked to him, noting the strangeness in his eyes.

"I said, 'impossible'."

"Yes, but what's impossible?"

"My father reckons Old Man Egan's about to nuke Boston."

Chalker laughed. But then his face grew long again. "Oh, god," he said, letting his head drop, his left hand coming up to grip his brow.

"Colonel? Are you all right?"

Chalker looked across, then shook his head. He looked as if he was suffering from a very bad migraine. "I experienced it."

"The bomb?"

"No. The shell. Shepherd's thing. I . . . I got hold of a copy and experienced it. I wish to god now I hadn't."

Kuei Jen stared at him. *Oh shit*, she thought, *it's infected Chalker, too. I can see it now.*

"I'm sorry," he said. "I . . . I destroyed it afterwards. That was the hardest part. It was . . . well, like murdering the woman you love. It was . . . *horrible*. But a part of me knew it was only a tape. A tiny part. Heaven help someone of a more . . . *passionate* nature."

"Like my husband?"

Chalker met his eyes and nodded.

Kuei Jen looked down at the timer in his wrist, then looked up again, concerned. "How far out are we?" she yelled, looking past the crowded cabin towards the open cockpit door.

"Four and a half k and accelerating."

"Shit!"

"What is it?" Chalker said quietly.

"The meeting with Old Man Egan was set for sunset. That's four minutes from now. If there *is* a bomb . . ."

"We'll be okay. We'll be ten k out by the time it blows up. Tell the pilot to climb. If we can get above the concussion zone."

He stared at Chalker, then, with a nod, stood up and went out to talk to the pilot. A moment later he was back.

"I'm afraid," he said. "I've never been afraid before, but I am now. If my father's right . . ."

Even as he spoke, the whole cabin lit up as if someone had shone a dazzling light through every window.

"*Aiya . . .*"

Kuei Jen made to turn and look, but Chalker stopped her. "No!" he yelled, taking charge. "Close your eyes everyone and don't look! It'll burn your eyes out! Just sit still and strap yourselves in."

Kuei Jen looked to her frightened children, seeing that both May and Samuel had their eyes squeezed tightly shut, then sat, letting Chalker strap her in. The light had faded, but he could still see its after-image.

And then the wind hit them, lifting the craft, juddering it roughly for a long, long while.

Boston's gone, she thought, picturing in her mind the smouldering waste the bomb would have left. *The mad old fucker's nuked it!*

Kuei Jen shook his head, unable to believe it. And then it hit him. His father had seen it. He'd had a vision. Not only that, but he'd told them it was going to happen. Now what in the gods' names did *that* mean?

"He saw it," he said, shaking his head slowly as the craft returned to normal. "He really *did* see it, after all."

But Chalker was not listening. Chalker was staring at his hands and rubbing them one against the other, as if to wipe the blood away.

* * *

Li Yuan was waiting for them in Providence, on the roof of the Imperial Barracks. As Kuei Jen's cruiser landed alongside the row of other craft, he walked across to meet them, standing there beneath the glare of the arc lamps as the hatch opened.

"Well?" he asked sombrely, embracing his son. "Did I not tell you?"

Kuei Jen stood back. "Are all the golden-eyed like you? Do they all have . . . *visions*."

He shrugged. "I cannot say. Yet I sense it must be so."

"It's strange," Kuei Jen said, looking at him with something akin to wonder. "I can't help wondering what it means."

"And I. But we *shall* know. Soon."

"You had another vision?"

Li Yuan smiled. "No. A friend told me."

"A friend?"

"Never mind, Kuei Jen. How is your husband?"

Her face told him the answer. "Not well," he said finally. "The tape is eating away at him like a disease. There's such a need in him. The gods know what was in it."

"Can I see him?"

"He has changed, Li Yuan. He will not even recognise you."

"Maybe so, but can I see him?"

Kuei Jen shrugged, then, "Come, he's in the second cruiser."

* * *

Egan lay there on the narrow bed, sweat covering his face and neck and chest. He was held down by four thick, broad leather straps, but he struggled constantly against them, while his eyes looked this way and that, as if searching for something that was not in the cabin.

Li Yuan studied him a while, then shook his head. Now that he had seen it, he understood. Someone had closed Egan's eyes.

No. Not someone. Shepherd. My old friend Shepherd.

Li Yuan turned, looking at his son. Kuei Jen had changed his sex to be with this man. He looked closer and saw the loving concern there in Kuei Jen's eyes and, for the first time, understood – and sympathised.

And shivered, a feeling of pure indignation coursing through him.

What evil was it that cut a man from his senses and made him believe in ghosts?

It was the evil of inwardness. Not the inwardness of self-knowledge but of illusion. Of displacement.

Shepherd was snipping the threads that held humanity together. He was isolating them. Giving each his own padded, silken cell, in which was kept the image of what that person wanted. A mate. Someone to lock oneself away with. Someone to kill for.

There were no flames, no devils with implements of torture, yet all the same it was hell. *Ti Yu*, the earth prison. And Shepherd was casting them all, one by one, into the fire.

Li Yuan stepped forward, placing his palm on young Egan's forehead. It burned, as if some inner fever were raging. But the contact seemed to calm the younger man. His movements slowed, then stilled, and his eyes, which had been unfocused, now looked straight up at Li Yuan.

"It is not real, Mark. *She* does not exist. She is but light and air. You know this. Deep down you know it."

Egan groaned. "No . . ."

"Open your eyes, Mark. Open your eyes and look. *This* is reality . . . this out here."

"Go away . . ."

Li Yuan turned, signalling to the guards. "Remove the restraints."

"But, father . . ."

"Be quiet, please, Kuei Jen. I shall do only what is best for your husband."

Kuei Jen bowed his head, obeying his father.

Li Yuan turned back, watching as the guards removed the straps.

Egan lay there, still and silent.

"Can you hear me, Mark?"

"I hear you."

"Good. Then you know I am right. You must give up these ghosts. You must find the strength in yourself to give them up."

"But I want . . ."

"Perfection? . . . I understand. But perfection is a dream."

"She exists."

"No."

"She . . ."

". . . is light and air. A signal on a tape. A fantasy. But you, Mark Egan, are real."

Again Egan groaned, yet it was a groan of despair – of realisation – not of pain.
Li Yuan leaned forward, placing his hands either side of Egan's head, pushing down forcefully. "Return to yourself now. Return, and be the man you were."
Egan shuddered, a great spasm rippled through him like a shock through the earth. He grimaced, his eyes closing, his lips parting, and then . . .
"What . . .?"
Egan looked about him, clearly surprised to find himself there in the cabin of the cruiser. "Where in the gods' names are we?"
"Providence," Kuei Jen said, smiling now, looking to his father in gratitude. Then, knowing Mark knew nothing of the bomb, his face changed.
"I am afraid we are at war."
"War?" he sat up, instantly alert. "Has Coover attacked again?"
"No," Kuei Jen said, taking both his hands. "We are at war with your grandfather."
"With Josiah? Then why in heaven's name aren't we in Boston?"
"Because Boston's gone, my love. The Old Man nuked it half an hour back."

CHAPTER·13

A TRAIL OF SMOKE

Hannem lay on the slab, barely conscious now. It was four days since he'd been "infected" and he had suffered a slow and painful deterioration. He had been blind these last two days and as his nervous system slowly rotted, so the natural functions of his body had switched down, one after another.

Coming into the lab, Ben paused, wrinkling his nose in disgust at the sickly, stale stench that wafted across.

He walked over and stood beside the slab. Hannem was naked, and in the dim light from the wall lamps his flesh looked so pale it was almost grey. He no longer seemed real, more like a clay model, moulded to resemble a man.

Yes, clay we are, Ben thought, noting the sheen of sweat that covered the skin wherever he looked; *flesh puppets, dancing on glistening strings of nucleopeptides.*

And when the dance was done the spirit fled, leaving a rotting hulk, a wreck upon the ebbing tide of time.

Ben stared at the creature's massive, bony skull, wondering what yet remained of that vast and powerful intellect he had witnessed; whether some tiny flicker of awareness yet remained. Or was this all? This putrid mimicry of life?

Machines. Machines of flesh and blood, of bone and nerve and sinew, the whole thing animated by a force that utterly defied analysis. A force that came and went and left no explanation for its existence, other than the fact that it had once been and was no more.

The fact of death.

Ben smiled at the thought. Death worried some people, yet when the force that animated *him* finally left *his* corporeal frame, then he was happy to know that he would be broken down and used again, his atoms eternally recycled, until the universe ran down.

And that was, in essence, why he could not understand his sister's anger; why he felt he had more in common with DeVore and his love of eternal process – of the long view – than in her petty vision of the individual.

For, after all, what did it matter if mankind did die out? Would the universe be diminished by man's passing? Not at all. For a finer, better creature *would* evolve in time. And that too would have its day before it died and was replaced. For that was how things worked, *ad infinitum*, until the great game ended.

Death. That was all there was when it came down to it. Death.

Death before and death after. And in between, the bright, flickering illusion of life.

He stared at the body a moment longer then turned away. There were no answers here, only patterns of force, holding out briefly against dissolution. Or until Newton's second law prevailed.

Ben smiled. Yes, in the end, entropy was all.

* * *

"Howard?"

DeVore looked up from the *wei chi* board, his eyes distant.

"Howard, you've a visitor."

As Emtu moved aside, Ben stepped forward, but seeing the abstracted look on DeVore's face, he hesitated. "Look, if you're busy, I'll come back."

"No," DeVore said, dismissing the woman with a nod, then looking back at Ben. "In fact, sit down. You play, don't you?"

"Chess is my game, but yes . . . I can play if I'm pushed."

"Then take black. We're into the endgame."

Ben nodded, as if he understood, then sat, taking in the pattern of the board at a glance. "Whose turn is it?"

DeVore put out a hand, indicating that he should take a stone. Ben did so, placing it seemingly without thought in the top left of the board, by DeVore's right hand. DeVore studied the move a moment, then gave a grudging nod.

"So you *do* play."

"If pushed."

DeVore ran his right forefinger along the length of his bottom lip, then looked up at Ben once more. "So what do you want, my friend?"

"Hannem."

DeVore raised an eyebrow, surprised. "I thought you wanted one of the living morphs."

"You'd have given me one?"

"No."

"Then I'll take the next best thing."

"He stinks."

"I know. But I can cure that."

DeVore took a white stone from his pot and placed it, extending his line in the north of the board and threatening one of Ben's stones. "Out of interest, what will you do with him?"

"Make him live again. Like Lazarus."

"Lazarus?"

"It's a tale from one of the old religions. From before the City."

"Ah . . ." But DeVore showed no signs of recognising the name. Then, "You think you can?"

Ben slapped down another stone, defending the stone DeVore had just threatened. It was a necessary *sente* move. "Oh, I'm sure of it. I'm good at repairs."

"Is there anything you aren't good at?"

"Relationships."

DeVore laughed at that. "You should build yourself a mate."

"Like you did?"

DeVore nodded. "You and I . . . we need compliance, neh? That sister of yours, I bet she's a handful."

"She hates you, you know."

DeVore grinned, showing his teeth. "Oh, I know. I could *feel* it. What's that saying you English have? A 'look like daggers'?" He laughed. "I was well and truly stabbed that night."

"That's why she left me."

"So I understand." DeVore met his eyes, no sign of any remorse or contrition in his own. "Your move."

Ben looked. DeVore had placed another stone in the same group, pushing him into yet another defensive move. That was, unless he decided to relinquish that small group and go for something bigger.

"By the way," DeVore said, "I've heard your tapes were a great success. You're the toast of America. Or would be, if anyone bothered to climb out of their shells."

"Really?"

"Absolutely. It's worked like a dream. My agents tell me that Boston was a ghost town."

"Was?"

DeVore looked up, surprised. "You mean you haven't heard?"

"Heard what?"

"Old Man Egan nuked the place. Yesterday at sunset. Took out the whole damn government at a stroke."

Ben sat back, astonished. And here was DeVore, playing *wei chi* as if nothing had happened!

"So why haven't you made a move?"

"Because I'm waiting . . . for the dust to settle, if you like. I want to see if anyone makes a move to fill the void."

"Coover, for instance?"

"Or Old Man Egan himself."

"And if they do?"

"I make a deal with them."

Ben nodded then placed his stone. A *sente* move again. Defensive.

DeVore looked at him, then gave a little shrug. "Strange," he said. "I was sure you were going to make a more aggressive play."

"And if I had?"

The smile was predatory. "I would have bitten your fucking head off."

* * *

Seated at the far end of the crowded table from her son, Emily frowned, surprised to hear such bitter words from him.

"Lin Sung? Do I hear you right? Do you *really* think we've achieved *nothing* these past eight years?"

"Well, it's true," Lin Sung said, refusing to meet his adopted mother's eyes, his face almost scowling as he spoke. "We're just pissing in the wind! We kill one corrupt official and DeVore replaces them immediately with another, equally corrupt! We destroy one munitions dump and he builds two in its place!"

"So what do you suggest?" Lin Chao asked gently. "You want to bomb Frankfurt, maybe? And Bremen, and Munich?"

Sung swallowed, then. "It would be a start. At least he'd know he had a fight!"

"I see." Chao looked about him at the others gathered round the table. Most, like himself, seemed saddened by this suggested escalation, but one or two met his eyes challengingly, his young brother Lin Han Ye among them. "And what about the innocents who would die? The mothers and children? The old people and the sick? Don't you care about *them*, younger brother?"

"Does *DeVore* care?"

"That's not what I asked. Don't *you* care?"

Sung struggled with the notion a moment, then. "Of course I care. You know I do, Lin Chao. But DeVore's just taking the piss out of us, can't you see that? He's using the fact that we care to stifle our effectiveness. To nullify and castrate us!"

"I see. So what you're saying is that we should become more like him. Adopt *his* rules, *his* ways?"

"That's not what Lin Sung is suggesting at all," the stranger on Lin Chao's right answered, turning to face him, his grey, steel-like eyes staring humourlessly at Chao. "We merely want to widen the conflict."

Looking into those eyes, Chao felt himself go cold. He had only been marginally conscious of the stranger until that moment, but now it seemed as if he sat alone, facing the man. "I'm sorry," he said, after a moment, "but we have not been introduced."

"Horton," the American said, putting out a long, sparsely-fleshed hand. "Feng Horton. I represent my good friend, Coover."

Lin Chao took a mental step backward. *Horton*. Now that he had the name, the face slipped into place. He had seen the file on this one. His full name was Feng Horton, otherwise known as "Meltdown". Horton had been a "Son" once; one of those who had been incarcerated by Wu Shih back in '07. If the rumours were right – and who could tell what was true and what false in the chaotic aftermath of the collapse of City North America? – it had been Horton who had been behind the "Campaign for Racial Purity", Horton who, so rumour had it, had boasted of eating "nothing but good Han meat".

And now here he was, sitting at *their* table, discussing policy. Chao looked to Emily. "Mother?"

"What is it, Chao?"

"May I speak with you, in private?"

Emily looked about her, then nodded. "You will excuse us a moment, *ch'un tzu*. We shall not be long."

They went through, into Emily's own rooms, then closed the door.

"Well?" she asked.

Lin Chao kept his voice low. "Why is that man here?"

"Because Coover is the power now in America. Word is he has destroyed Egan's Western banners and all the land to Denver is his. Horton is his man."

"You know what is said of him?"

She nodded. "I too was once the subject of such rumours, don't you remember?"

"Yes, but that's different. What they say of Horton . . ."

"May or may not be the truth. But we must deal with him now if we wish to throw down the tyrant."

"And put another in his place?"

"It is a risk we take."

Chao shook his head. "I do not like it. It feels wrong."

"Like Daniel felt wrong?"

"There I was wrong, I concede. But this . . . to embrace such a one, I feel, would be a grave mistake. Already he speaks of widening the campaign, of bombing cities and hurting innocents. I, for one, would vote against it."

"And I too, Chao." She smiled. "I'll not be Coover's puppet, if that's what you fear. Yet it would be well if we came to an agreement with the man. He can give us weapons and supplies, and the gods know we are in dire need of both right now."

"And in return?"

"In return we continue to be a pain in the arse to The Man."

Lin Chao hesitated, then, encouraged by Emily, smiled a reluctant smile.

"Now come," she said. "Argue strongly, but also listen."

They went back. In their absence Tybor had arrived. He sat now next to Lin Sung, his tall figure looming over the table as he spoke quietly to one of Emily's lieutenants.

"Tybor," Emily said, greeting him. "Have you any news?"

Tybor had taken three men and gone to bring home the carts. For the last three or four hours he had been in the labs, analysing the strange-smelling powders that had been in the sealed plastic wrappers.

Tybor met her eyes gravely. "I'm afraid there was nothing we could use."

"Nothing?" Emily felt a strange little tremor inside at the thought. Had Michael died so needlessly then?

"Nothing *useful*." And the way he said it made her understand that this was not something he wished to pursue in an open meeting.

She made to move things on, but Horton interrupted.

"Are you speaking of the powders Michael was bringing back from the old GenSyn works in Milan?"

Tybor looked to Emily, who shrugged. "Yes," he answered.

"And you've destroyed them?"

Again Tybor hesitated, then, "Not yet."

"Good," Horton said. "Because I'll take them off your hands."

"I'm not sure . . ." Emily began, but Horton interrupted once again.

"I'll pay you well. Enough equipment to launch a new campaign and whatever supplies you need."

Lin Sung's eyes lit up at this offer. He looked to his mother, expecting her to be equally enthusiastic, but she was looking down.

"Forgive us, *Shih* Horton, but we shall have to consider your kind offer." She raised her eyes to meet his. "We need to consult . . . you understand?"

"Oh, perfectly. But if it helps persuade you, we can provide you with cruisers. And artillery."

Emily stared at him, astonished. What *had* Michael brought back that he wanted so much? "Cruisers?" she asked, her voice almost a whisper.

Horton nodded. "We could supply them within a week, from Africa. Would six be enough? You'd get spares, of course, and expert back-up."

With that many cruisers they could take on DeVore's patrols and make the Wilds their own, and that, in itself, would make them so much more effective. But at what cost? Horton seemed far too keen to close this deal.

Besides, how did *he* know what Michael had brought back? Or was he guessing, gambling on the reputation of GenSyn's big Milan plant? Of course, none of it was in the plant itself. If it had been, DeVore would long ago have plundered it. But much remained – hidden away – that had once been produced there.

Like the cache of powders Michael had stumbled upon and bought.

"Let's call this meeting to a close," Emily said, her thoughts racing. "Tybor, Lin Chao . . . Daniel . . . come through, we need to talk."

She saw the flicker of frustration in Lin Sung's eyes, the way he glared at Daniel, who'd been included in the decision-making process rather than himself, and knew she would have to deal with that. But not now. Right now she had to find out what was going on.

* * *

Emily waited until the others had gone, then, closing the door behind her, she turned to face Tybor.

"Well? Just how dangerous *is* it?"

Tybor hesitated, then. "It's hard to say. In its sealed form it's not harmless at all, but when it's activated . . ."

"What do you mean, *activated*?"

Tybor spread his hands. "The packets are vacuum-sealed. That means that the contents have been kept at a constant temperature – not cold exactly, but low enough for them to remain dormant. But when I cut open one of the packets – under the proper conditions, naturally – the temperature quickly rose."

"And?" Lin Chao asked.

"It's organic. Or rather, *genetic*. The pure building blocks of life. Magic dust, you might call it. Living change. Whatever it reacts with it transforms."

"You know this for a fact?"

Tybor nodded. "We experimented. You should have seen what it did to one of the birds we put into the iso-box with it."

"Did the bird die?"

"No. But it would have been better for it if it had. We had to incinerate everything in the iso-box. But I've kept a tape if you really want to see how lethal this stuff is."

Emily shook her head. "I'll take your word. But earlier, when I asked how dangerous, you said that it's hard to say. Why?"

"Because in laboratory conditions the thing just keeps transforming itself. But out in the open it might . . . just *might* find a natural, stable form. Then again, it might just keep on metamorphosing."

"Meaning what?" Lin Chao asked.

"Well," Tybor said, turning to face him, "imagine a landscape so transformed that it was like an alien planet. Every single form changed. And that change going on at every single level of existence from the smallest bacteria to the largest mammal. A great soup of change. That's one possibility."

"Then we burn it. All of it."

"And Horton's offer?"

"You think I'd give this to him, Chao? No. We'll have to make do without cruisers." Emily shuddered, then. "What madman would have thought of such a thing?"

"Klaus Ebert."

"Hans Ebert's father?"

Tybor nodded. "He was a great man in his way. He used the stuff in controlled experiments."

"Are you guessing now, Tybor?"

"No. There were two small notebooks in one of the sacks. Ebert's notebooks. He used these substances in minute amounts to unlock normal genetic structures and re-structure them."

"Skeleton keys," Daniel said, speaking for the first time since he'd come into the room.

"Exactly," Tybor said.

"Then we're lucky," Emily said. "Extremely lucky. Imagine if these had fallen into other hands."

She was silent a moment, then, "Tybor, go and arrange the incineration at once. Chao, give Tybor whatever help he needs."

Tybor and Lin Chao stood and, with a small bow to Emily, left. Daniel too had stood, but Emily gestured for him to sit again.

"No, Daniel. You stay. You and I need to talk."

* * *

Late afternoon, Ben always took a nap – a doze of an hour or so, so that he'd be refreshed and ready for a long evening's work. Today, however, that nap had been broken. He had woken with a jolt, blinded and in pain, gasping for air, then, blinking, looked about him.

Slowly the vision passed.

The night-coloured pearl. After all these years he had seen it again, in a dream – a dream so realistic and powerful that it had seemed almost like one of his shells. But this time, instead of being a thing of beauty, of wonder, it had seemed to emanate an air of horror, creating in him a sense of dread so overwhelming that, in the dream, he had whimpered and cried out.

And still the thing had grown, blotting out the depths beneath him as he floated there, immersed in the cool blue water, rising towards him all the while, like the swollen abdomen of a giant, female spider, its dark skin bloated as if a thousand awful creatures moved beneath the thick skin of its outer covering. And even as that thought suggested itself to him, so he saw that it did move, like a nest of dark maggots.

He had struggled up, hauling himself up to the surface, even as the great egg-like pearl brushed against his feet, making him cry out yet again and lift his feet, afraid lest they be contaminated by it.

And then, even as he glanced back at it, it split open, a great rift of pure light leaping like a spear from its heart to pierce his eyes, the pain so fierce it took his breath away.

Which was when he woke.

Ben sat up, trembling. He was covered in sweat and his head ached, as if he had a migraine.

That light. It had been so real.

He looked about him again. No wires, no tapes. It had only been a dream. Just a dream.

And now he recalled what had woken him, and shuddered, for as the light had spilled from the splitting pearl – in that last moment of vision before it blinded him – he had seen faces on the tiny maggots that filled the great dark pearl. Hundreds of faces, and all the same.

DeVore. Howard DeVore.

Ben walked across the room, slowly, unsteadily, like an invalid recovering from a fever that had laid him low, then stood beneath the shower for some time, letting it flow ice-cold on his flesh, his eyes closed against the pain in his head.

He knew what the dream meant, of course. He was far too self-aware *not* to know.

Yes, and he knew what Meg would say, were he to tell her. But did that mean the dream was right? *Was* he repressing this? Forcing himself not to feel what, perhaps, naturally – as a human being – he ought to be feeling.

Which was what?

The words came easy. Aversion. Repulsion. Appalled. Sick. And so on . . . A nice long list of responses to DeVore and his schemes.

Decent responses, or so his sister claimed. Not sickly ones, like fascination.

I am a camera.

For too long now he had lived in his eyes, in the landscape of his visual memory, shutting out anything that did not slot into the great library of images he'd stored over the years. Emotions were untidy. One did not know what shelf to put them on. Whereas images . . .

Maggots. Hundreds of squirming black maggots, and every one possessed of that bastard's face. Enough maggots to fill the galaxy.

He shut off the flow and stepped out, beginning to dry himself.

Meg. I need to see Meg.

Yes, even if he didn't mention this, it would be good to go home for a while. To see the Domain again and walk down to the bay.

He looked about him, as if fragments of the dream still clung to the edges of his vision, then, with a tiny shudder, went through to his bedroom and began to pack.

* * *

DeVore sat in Li Yuan's chair, the two handwritten notes laid side by side on the desk before him, and smiled.

He had got what he wanted. An alliance. And not just one, but two.

Picking up Coover's note, he read it through again and laughed. Coover acted the humble peacemaker but he was a greedy son-of-a-bitch. He wouldn't rest until he had a map of the world on the wall above his desk – a world marked out in his own colours.

He let the paper fall from his fingers then reached out and picked up Egan's. Egan's note was more grudging, as if every word had been forced from him – as probably it had been. Rumour was that he'd taken on Li Yuan as his advisor. If that was true, then he could prove a dangerous enemy. But as an ally . . .

As an ally he could be made to agree to all manner of things he might otherwise baulk at.

So which would he go for? Coover? Or Egan? For the two were sure to slog it out from here on in, winner take all.

Or so they thought.

Egan looked the least likely victor. He'd lost all his Western armies and now his capital. But he was tenacious. And now he had the experience of Li Yuan to guide him.

Then again, there was his grandfather, Josiah, to contend with. He had to win that battle even before he took the field against Coover. In the meantime, if accounts of the treaty they had made were true, Coover was bleeding Egan dry.

Egan's only chance was a swift, decisive strike against Coover. And Coover knew it and was wary of it. That was why he had sent Horton over, to see The Woman.

DeVore smiled. Coover thought he'd kept that secret.

Not that I blame him, DeVore thought. After all, a successful card player always stacks the deck in his own favour.

Trouble was, Coover was playing the wrong damn game.

And all the while I'm slapping down stones in his territory.

DeVore laughed aloud, amused by Coover's naivety. But what could one expect? He had not been bred to intrigue, and though he was both cunning and greedy, Coover was neither a subtle nor an intelligent man – not in the way that, say, he and Shepherd were intelligent.

And that, alas, would be Coover's downfall.

So Egan it was.

He sat back, surprised by how right the decision felt. He would answer Coover in the affirmative, of course, for it would not serve his purpose to make an enemy of him straight away, yet he would let Egan know of his dealings with Coover –

maybe send him copies of everything that passed between them, to create a sense of openness between them. And in time he would send Egan a token of his friendship.

Horton's head, perhaps.

For now, however, he would keep it simple.

Setting down Egan's note, he took a sheet of his own headed paper and penned a quick response. Then, satisfied that he'd got just the right tone, he folded it in half, then half again.

As he finished, he looked up, to find Emtu standing there in the doorway.

"What is it, my love?"

"It's Horacek. He's called from Dusseldorf. He wants to see you tonight. Says it's urgent. Life or death."

"Life or death, eh?" DeVore considered a moment, then shrugged. "A plot, perhaps?"

"He would say nothing more."

"Then tell him to come. And Emtu . . . is it true that Ben has gone?"

She nodded. "It's true. He went an hour back."

"How strange. Did he leave a note?"

Emtu shook her head.

"Well," DeVore said, "I'm sure he had his reasons. But if he calls, put him through, even if I'm sleeping. There's something I want to talk to him about."

She nodded then withdrew.

DeVore sat there a moment longer, then stood. Horacek, eh? The rat-boy he'd made Marshal. Now what in the gods' names did that little creep want?

A plot. I bet you it's a plot. Some of my generals, I'll warrant, want to do away with me. Or so he'll claim.

DeVore smiled. Maybe one of them insulted the little monster and this was his way of paying them back – to blacken their name the same way the fire had blackened his face.

If so, he would play along . . . this time. But Horacek was running out of rope. Daniel might have fled to the Wilds, but there'd be another boy who'd fit the bill. And he, in time, would replace the odious Horacek.

For there were always replacements: an endless line of them, hungry to serve.

The messenger waited just outside the door. "Here," he said. "Take this to Egan's man. You know where."

"Master!" The man took the folded note and bowed low, then backed away, hastening to run his errand.

Servants, everywhere he looked servants. Even Emtu, for all she looked like Emily Ascher, was but a servant – a plaything.

And that, more than anything, was why he wanted the real Emily, alive. Because she had defied him. For the very fact that she had refused to serve him, as others had always served.

And when he had her . . . what then?

He did not know. Indeed, he had never known. Yet he *would* have her. In time.

Yes, everything would come to him in time.

* * *

"Well?" Daniel asked after an awkward silence. "What do you want to know?"

"What it's like in there?"

"Like?" He gave a tiny laugh, then looked down, his face sober. "You must know what it's like, surely?"

Emily watched him, her eyes noting every nuance of his body language. She could see that even talking about this was painful, but she needed to know. She needed as complete a picture of what DeVore was doing as she could get if she was going to come up with a half-decent strategy.

"It's different," he said. "I mean, not just different, but *different*. When you go in through those gates it's as if you were in another universe entirely. Even the sky overhead seems different. And the boys . . . the boys are like machines. *Jou chi ch'i*, the guards call them sometimes."

"I know the term," Emily said. "Meat machines."

"Right," Daniel said. "But it's like everything in there's deliberately reducing the boys to that state. To the suppression of the instinct of decency."

Emily sat back a little, surprised to hear him say that. Surprised not by the idea so much as the way he articulated it. "Daniel, can you read?"

He hesitated, then nodded.

"And you learned that in the camp?"

"No." He looked down, the smallest hint of vulnerability in the gesture suggesting to Emily that she had hit upon something.

"Then how . . .?"

She stopped, understanding coming to her. Was *that* why Daniel was different from the rest?

"Daniel . . . were you quite old when you first went to the camps?"

"Older than most."

She waited, but he would not go on, nor would he look at her.

"Then you *knew* your parents?"

He hesitated, then gave the tiniest of nods.

Emily closed her eyes, wondering if she should really push this. She knew from her own experience how tender such wounds were and how they never really healed, for all the care – all the *mending* – one lavished on them.

She looked at him again, seeing at once how he held himself, his shoulders set, as if to fend off the whole world.

No wonder he's fucked up.

But then they were all fucked up, those who lived in DeVore's world. There was no normality in *his* universe.

"I'm sorry," she said quietly.

"It's okay."

"The camps . . ."

He looked up suddenly, the hurt in his eyes surprising her.

"I've done things – terrible things – simply to survive. Things that I can't believe I was capable of doing. But every time it was as if I hurt myself. Every time it was a . . . a *violation*."

Emily saw how he shuddered and knew that it was no exaggeration. She could imagine it. A young, sensitive child, torn from a loving home environment and thrown into a living hell. It was a wonder he was even half sane.

"And Eden?"

Daniel laughed, then looked at her. "They never understood. Five times they watched me and they never once saw it."

"Saw what?"

"They thought I was brave, but it was easy in there compared to the camps. I didn't have to *feel*, you see. I could exist on a single level. No complications. I wasn't . . . torn."

She nodded. So torn, in fact, that he had cut into his own head to get out DeVore's wire.

"*I* think you're brave. But not for the reasons they'd think you brave. I think you had to be brave simply to get here, to this moment."

"What do you mean?"

"To come through and still be able to feel, to still be able to make real choices about what you should and shouldn't do. That must have taken a great deal of courage. Almost your whole store, I'd say."

He looked down. "I don't know." But she could see his eyes were moist now. Something in him had relaxed – something he had kept clenched all these long years was finally untensing in him.

Emily stood, then went round the desk.

"Stand up," she said gently, "then turn around to face me."

Daniel stood, then turned, facing her, the uncertainty in his eyes now so marked, so prominent, that she knew she had been right.

"Here," she said, stepping close and embracing him, mothering him, her arms tight about him. "Come here, my darling boy."

* * *

"So?" DeVore said, watching his Marshal cross the room then snap to attention before him. "What is it that's *so* important?"

Horacek held out an official scroll canister, offering it to DeVore. "I intercepted this, Master."

DeVore took it lazily, making no attempt to remove the scrolled message from within. "Let me guess. From Horton to my generals."

"To General Lodge," Horacek said, his eyes registering surprise. "You *knew*?"

DeVore smiled. "Of course I knew. So what are you going to do about it?"

"Arrest him?"

"And torture him, no doubt?"

"I . . ." Horacek hesitated, then. "Forgive me, Master, but is something wrong?"

"No, Horacek. Everything's *exactly* as I thought. It's rather reassuring, actually."

"Reassuring? But they were planning to kill you, Master."

"Kill me?" DeVore roared with laughter. "You really think that's possible, Josef?"

Horacek blinked. There was something strange about his Master's manner and he could not work out what it was.

"Take this, for instance," DeVore said, lifting the scroll canister slightly. "It seems innocent enough, neh? Yet what better way to smuggle a weapon in."

"Master?"

"Everyone who comes into my presence is searched . . . for weapons. But what if some innocent-looking thing – like this – was actually a weapon. A bomb, perhaps, or a means of poisoning my blood. Why, I might already be dying."

Horacek's mouth opened in astonishment.

"Only it wouldn't be possible," DeVore went on, "You see, I wear special skin-tight gloves to protect against such a possibility. And as for bombs, why this whole room could be destroyed and I would not be touched."

"But, Master . . ."

DeVore's smile was steady now. "Do you wish me dead, Horacek? Speak freely now. You *may* speak freely."

"No, Master. You know I'd give up my life for you!"

"Go on then . . ."

"What?"

"Here," DeVore said, taking the knife from his belt and holding it out to him. "*Prove* your loyalty, Josef. Slit your throat."

Horacek stared at the knife in horror, but made no move to take it.

Slowly DeVore's smile changed into a snarl. "Take it!" he barked, jerking forward so that the hilt of the knife brushed against Horacek's knuckles.

Horacek took a step backward. His eyes met DeVore's briefly, then looked about him, like a cornered rat about to run.

"You heard me," DeVore said, beginning to enjoy the game. "I said, take the knife. I order you to slit your own throat."

A shiver went through Horacek's frame, then his expression changed, becoming a snarl that mirrored DeVore's own. Snatching the knife, he crouched, facing DeVore.

"Ah . . ." DeVore said, relaxing back into his seat. "And so we come right down to it, neh? The truth. You hate my guts, don't you, Josef? And if you could you'd stick that between my ribs, wouldn't you?"

Horacek's eyes flared, then, with a sudden little movement, he thrust the knife at DeVore, aiming for his heart. Yet even as he did, the air about DeVore seemed to shimmer and the knife-blade melted like smoke.

Horacek cried out, then sank to his knees, clutching his damaged hand. He had lost the tips of all four fingers down to the first knuckle, but there was no blood. They had been neatly cauterised.

He stared at his hand a moment longer, then looked up at DeVore, expecting to die. But DeVore had other ideas.

"Get out," DeVore said. "Get out before I kick you out."

Horacek blinked, then began to back away.

"Oh, and Josef . . . send General Lodge to see me. It seems I need a new Marshal."

* * *

Horton made to pass Lin Chao, but Lin Chao blocked his way.

"Lin Chao? What's happening?"

Chao's face was stern. "You must turn back, *Shih* Horton."

There was a flicker of suspicion in Horton's eyes. "But I need to go this way, Lin Chao. I am expected, at the labs."

Again he tried to step past Lin Chao, but again Chao blocked him off.

"I am afraid that is not possible, *Shih* Horton. The laboratories are out of bounds for the time being."

"What's going on?" Warning bells were clearly sounding in Horton's head.

"We are merely implementing a decision."

Horton narrowed his eyes. "What decision?"

"To destroy the powders."

Horton's face went ashen. Then, with a bellow of rage, he tried to shove Lin Chao out of the way, but Chao, anticipating his response, stepped back and fended him off.

Drawing his sidearm, he levelled it at Horton's chest. "Go back to your rooms, *Shih* Horton. I will not ask you a second time. This is *our* affair, not yours."

Horton glared at him, openly hostile now. "You'll regret this, you Chink bastard!"

Chao's eyes widened, but he did not respond to the insult. "So it's true."

"True?" Horton stared at him sneeringly.

"The Campaign for Racial Purity."

Horton laughed. "You bet your fucking life it was."

Chao stared at the man, feeling a cold hatred, then gestured with his gun. "Go. Now. Before I shoot your fucking bollocks off!"

* * *

Emily was still talking to Daniel when Lin Chao burst in.

"You'd better come. Horton's got into the labs. Him and four of his thugs."

She stood, alarmed. "*Aiya*! What happened?"

Chao shrugged. "I'm not sure. I stopped him earlier, but he must have gone back and got his men. It looks like they went through the west tunnels."

"Anyone hurt?"

Chao grimaced, then nodded. "They've killed young Cho."

Emily's face creased with pain. For a moment she rested her weight on her arms, then, nodding to herself, she straightened up again. "Okay. We need to play this carefully. Have they got into the inner labs yet?"

"We don't know. But I can't get through to Tybor."

"How far along was he?"

"When I left him he'd only just begun. I'd say he had three or four hours work incinerating it all."

Emily looked to Daniel. "I'm sorry, Daniel. We'll have to finish this later."

Daniel nodded. "Can I come along?"

"It might be best. . ." Then, changing her mind, "Okay. But don't do anything rash."

Daniel smiled, then stood. "I won't."

* * *

It was bad. Horton couldn't come out – not without having to come through them – but equally they couldn't get in. Not unless Horton let them in.

What's more, he had Tybor.

Emily stared up at the screen, seeing how Tybor tried not to flinch as Horton tightened the loop of cord about his throat, and swore to herself that she would kill the man when this was over.

"What do you want?"

"You know what I want," Horton answered her, a cockiness in his manner now; all pretence at politeness shed like a skin. "I want you to refuel my cruiser, then I want a safe passage out of here."

"I can't do that."

Horton smiled sourly. "I think you can."

"I can't let you take that stuff away."

"No? Then how about if I open a packet or two and sprinkle it into your air-conditioning system."

"I'll shut it down."

"Then you'll all suffocate."

"Eventually. But that'll get you nowhere, will it?"

There was a flicker of irritation in Horton's eyes. Again he tightened the cord. "I'll kill him," he said.

Emily nodded, her eyes meeting Tybor's, understanding in them. "Tybor knows the risks."

"You're bluffing."

"I was never more serious. I'd rather we all died than you took a speck of that stuff out of here."

Horton's expression slowly changed. It was clear he couldn't comprehend the notion that someone would rather sacrifice themselves than make a deal.

"You *are* bluffing," he said, an ugly grin appearing on his face. "And I'm going to call your bluff right now."

Emily looked down, unable to watch. She heard Lin Chao, just behind her, gasp then cry out. Daniel, she saw, had clenched both fists.

There was an awful noise, somewhere between a sigh and a choked swallowing sound, and then she heard the huge body fall.

Dead, she told herself. *That bastard Horton's dead.*

"Lin Chao," she said very quietly, so Horton would not hear, "cut off the air."

As Lin Chao turned away, she looked to Daniel. The boy was watching the screen, his eyes narrowed. Noting he was being watched he glanced at Emily, something in his eyes.

What is it? she mouthed.

He stepped back, out of view of the overhead camera. *Let me take him*, he mouthed back. *I can do it.*

Emily looked back at the screen. Horton had stepped back. Now he was snarling up at the screen.

"Well?" he said. "Are you going to let us go, or are you going to die? You'd better make your minds up. Time's running out."

"Okay," she said, letting a false resignation sound in her voice. "You've got your cruiser. Give us fifteen minutes."

"You've got twelve," Horton said. "Now move!"

Emily nodded, then turned away as the screen blanked. "Okay," she said, looking to Daniel. "He's yours."

* * *

Horton looked about him at his men, then nodded. "Good," he said. "Now let's see those bastard Chinks try and trick us!"

They had taped packets all over themselves, covering their chests and backs and the tops and backs of their heads. Horton grinned, then picked up his rifle and hung it by the strap over his shoulder. It was like wearing a bomb. The rebels didn't dare shoot for fear of splitting open one of the packets. But as a precaution, Horton had saved one packet, which he now picked up, holding it in his left hand, then unsheathed his hunting knife.

One wrong move and they'd *all* be dead.

But there weren't going to be any wrong moves.

"Jeffers? Is the cruiser ready?" he asked, speaking into the button mike on his lapel.

"Ready and fuelled," came the reply.

His man. One of two left in the craft.

"Have they backed off?"

There was a pause, then Jeffers answered again. "Looks like it. There's no one in sight."

"Good." He turned, checking his men were ready, then gave the thumbs up signal. "Okay. We're coming out."

* * *

Lin Sung leaned forward, putting his left hand over the mike, then smiled at the pilot, pressing the gun a little harder into the man's temples. "Good boy, Jeffers. Now start the engines."

* * *

The corridor was clear. There were two doors leading off, but both were closed.

"Check those out," Horton said, gesturing to two of his men. "If there's anyone inside, shoot the fuckers."

They hurried off. A moment later a head popped round the first doorway. "It's clear."

"And this one," a second voice came back as its owner reappeared.

"Good." But Horton was still wary. The woman had capitulated too quickly for his liking. Not that she had any choice, but . . .

"Up to the end," he said, sending the two forward. "Take up position in the next corridor."

He was used to this. Many a time they'd fought the Chinks, corridor by corridor in the old City. Yes, and winkled the little fuckers out, too.

He smiled at the memory.

Yeah, and maybe I'll leave our friends here a little something to remember me by.

Or, better yet, give *DeVore* a little something. A grid reference, maybe.

Not that his patrols wouldn't be able to follow a trail of smoke.

Getting the thumbs up, he hurried forward, then sent his men on again, commando-style, as they'd been trained, back in the Sons.

He had the map of the tunnels in his head. Up ahead they turned sharply left, then climbed a set of concrete steps and out, onto the roof.

"Jeffers? All clear up there?" he asked, speaking into the lapel mike once again.

"All clear," came the answer.

So far so good. But just in case . . .

"Ascher? You listening to me, woman?"

There was a pause, then, "I can hear you."

"You ain't gonna try any tricks now are you? Because if you are . . ."

"I don't like you, Horton, but I'm not stupid."

Horton grinned, then gestured to his men to move on to the next turn. "Good. because I've got a packet right here in my hand and if you try *anything* . . ."

"As I said, I'm not stupid."

"Good. *Ve-ry* good."

He glanced back down the corridor behind him, listening, then nodded to himself. Coover would pay him well for this little lot; maybe even give him a command.

General Horton. Yeah. He liked the sound of that.

They went left and along the final stretch of corridor. Just ahead of them the steps climbed steeply into daylight. A cold draught came down at them, bringing the reassuring hum of the cruiser's turbines. He sent one of his men up.

Almost there.

Mind, if she was going to make a move, it'd be here.

He looked about him. "Keep alert now. No mistakes. Anyone sticks their head up, pop them, right?"

"Right!"

"Jeffers?"

"Sir?"

"All okay there?"

"Hunky dory, sir."

His man had reached the top of the steps. Horton waited, tensed, as the man looked round then turned back, giving the thumbs up.

"Come on," Horton said, sending the other three up in front of him. "Straight up and into the craft."

He turned, looking back. Good. Not a sight or sound of anyone.

Horton smiled, then spoke into the open channel. "Looks like you kept your word, Ascher."

"Pity you didn't keep yours."

"I'd have given you a good deal, you know. Cruisers. Yeah, and artillery. I'd have delivered them, too, but you gave me no choice."

"You killed two of my men, Horton. I won't forget that."

"Necessity," he said tonelessly. No way was he going to apologise for killing Chinks and mutants.

"You better watch your back, Horton, because one of these days . . ."

But Horton cut in irritably. "Just cut the shit, woman. I'm out of here."

He took the steps in twos and threes, exultant now. At the top he paused briefly, looking about him at the empty landing pad, letting his eyes accustom themselves to the daylight, then, seeing the cruiser twenty feet away, began to walk towards it.

A single shot rang out.

Horton staggered a moment, then fell, his legs buckling, the packet tumbling from his open hand.

Daniel watched a moment, ready to squeeze off a second shot, then – seeing that Horton wasn't going to get up – lowered his gun and stood, steadying himself against the top of the cruiser's cockpit.

Dead.

"Daniel?"

He hesitated, then, "I got him."

There were cheers, sounds of jubilation on the open channel.

"Well done, Daniel."

But Daniel didn't feel as if he'd done well. Daniel felt sick. He'd *felt* the bullet pass through Horton's eye and out through the top of his spine. Yes, even a no-good bastard like Horton and still he felt it.

He jumped down, then threw the gun away.

To hell with it.

Lin Sung popped his head out of the cruiser's hatch, grinning. "We got them, Daniel. Trussed up and sedated, just like you said."

He nodded, but he felt faint now. Was this all he was good for?

"Daniel?"

He looked across. Emily was standing at the top of the steps, where Horton had emerged from only a minute before. She was not far from where Daniel stood, yet it seemed as if she were a mile away.

"Daniel?"

The voice receded, as if it were travelling away from him.

Daniel . . .

* * *

"Daniel?"

Daniel opened his eyes. For a moment he had been back in the camp, the smell of unwashed bodies all about him.

Turning, he looked up, meeting Emily's eyes.

"You had me worried, Daniel."

"Did I?"

"I thought . . ." She shook her head and smiled. "We all owe you a lot, Daniel. If that stuff had got to Coover . . ."

He was silent a moment, then. "I can't do it any more."

"Can't do what?"

"Kill. I can't do it. I . . ." He closed his eyes again. "It was horrible. Like killing myself. I felt it."

"Sometimes it's the only answer."

There was a long silence, then he opened his eyes and looked up at her again. "Emily?"

"Yes?"

What if it never ends? What if this is all there is?"

"What do you mean?"

"Killing. Wars. Strife. What if that's all we're good for?"

"I can't believe that."

"No?" A look of real pain crossed his face. "It's all I've ever known. Or almost all. And sometimes I think . . . well, that maybe DeVore's right."

"No. *Never* think that."

"But . . ."

"Normality," she said, taking his hands and squeezing them, "that's all we're fighting for. Not for some high-sounding ideology, but for simple, everyday normality. That and the possibility of not having to fight any more."

He gave a faint smile. "I wish I could believe you."

"Do you?" Then, relenting, she nodded. "If it helps any, I've been where you are now, Daniel. I too ceased to believe that I could change anything. But it's not true. We *can* change things. We can make it better, even if it's only in the tiny circle that surrounds us. And we can't give up. We can't *ever* give up, because if we do then DeVore's won – and what he stands for . . . that's all there'll ever be."

Daniel sighed, a long, weary sigh, then, giving Emily's hands a final, tiny little squeeze, he turned and faced the wall.

Emily watched him a moment, her eyes sad, her own heart heavy, then, knowing she could do no more, she left the room.

Outside she stopped and leaned her back against the wall, sighing deeply, knowing that Daniel was right. Killing. They had had their fill of killing. But it would not be over, not until DeVore was dead.

Only then could *she* rest. Only then could she put away her gun.

PART THREE – WINTER 2241

THE KING OF INFINITE SPACE

"O God! I could be bounded in a nut-shell and count myself a king of infinite space, were it not that I have bad dreams."

– Hamlet.

CHAPTER·14

BEHIND THE WALL OF SLEEP

In the blink of an eye the snake swallowed its tail.

Kim, lazing on his back on the surface of the pool, stared up at the animation and smiled.

So it was, in that first instant of forever. Nothing before that moment, and nothing – absolutely nothing – outside of it. For the universe was an island, infinite in size, yet strangely still an island.

Now that *was* a paradox.

Normally the great dome above him showed an image of the star field into which they daily sped, yet today he was problem-solving. Or so he had told Jelka. What he was really doing was playing – toying with an idea he had had only the other evening, while he was washing out his equipment at the sink.

An island, yes, but what if there were other islands, close by – so close that you could almost touch and penetrate them? And what if there was a membrane – some kind of field – between the universes, that one could push back and therefore use, just as one could push back and use the surface pressure of the water?

It was so simple – so *direct* – an idea that he had known at once that it was true.

He had been washing out the beakers and, pushing one down into the water, had felt it slip between his soapy hands and spring, like a rocket being launched, up into the air. For a moment he had simply stared, his mind seeing, in that instant, how one might push the craft he had been making down into the surface of another universe and, using the pressure of the membrane between the universes, launch it at high velocity.

No, at a *phenomenal* velocity.

If one could only find where that surface membrane lay.

And so, today, he floated here, watching the programme he had made for his daughter, Mileja, on how the universe began – the story of the snake that swallowed its tail – a story of infinite repetition, infinite regression.

He smiled sadly, recalling what he'd said to her, all that time ago. Imagine, he'd said, a firework display. Only this firework display was so quick the eye could not even register it, while the slow fade of the fireworks' traces in the air took . . . well, forever.

Or so it seemed. But even forever could be measured.

The trouble was that the human mind was forever trying to visualise – to form metaphors for the complex processes of physics – but the truth was that he was working within a realm where such visualisation was not a help but a positive hindrance – a distraction. One spent one's time trying to make such metaphors fit, to put flesh on the bare bones of numbers, yet in doing so the mind would constantly reach for a visual handhold and find . . . nothing.

Kim stretched then flipped backwards, under the water, bobbing up beside the steps. In two quick movements he was up, reaching for the towel that hung beside the blackboard.

While he towelled his head and shoulders with his left hand, his right hand worked at the calculation that had flipped into his mind, chalking the figures on the board. He stopped a moment, considering what he'd written, then jotted down a further two equations, drawing two long horizontal lines between the figures. There was no connection . . . yet. But that would come. It always came.

He tossed the chalk into the basket, then turned back, facing the pool once more.

"Opaque," he said, speaking to the house machine. At once the dome ceased to be a screen, showing – through a second, larger dome – a perfect view of space and, surrounding that second dome, the bare, red-brown surface of Ganymede.

Kalevala was behind him where he stood, the house and its tower raised up on its promontory. Still towelling himself, he turned to face it, never tiring of the sight. Against the backdrop of interstellar space it looked almost Wagnerian.

"Kim?"

Jelka's voice sounded all about him, transmitted by a dozen hidden speakers.

"Yes, my love?"

"Have you finished now?"

He smiled. No doubt she had been watching – had seen the surface of the smaller dome become translucent.

"For now."

There was a pause, then. "Only you have a visitor."

Kim raised an eyebrow. It was unusual for Jelka to be so indirect. Was something wrong?

"I see." He stared at the blackboard for a second or two, then looked up again. "Take them through to my study and have them wait there. I'll come up."

In that moment, between looking at the blackboard a second time and answering Jelka, he had seen the connection. Or rather, he had seen that there *was* no connection. And that was it. The mathematics of alternate dimensions was a different kind of mathematics altogether – a broken maths with holes and gaps and . . .

Kim's face broke into a grin. *And snakes swallowing their tails.*

* * *

The tree was singing. It seemed as if every leaf and branch was singing. Chuang Kuan Ts'ai stared up at it amazed, and shivered.

Birds, the voice inside her head told her. And at once she had an image of birds, and saw their strange, sharp beaks opening and closing and a shrill, high-pitched noise emerge. Birdsong. How strange.

"But I thought there were no birds."

There weren't. But now, it seems, there are.

She looked again at the strange tree that stood before the house, then stepped through the massive doorway into the entrance hall. She turned, looking about her. A broad staircase went up to the first floor of the house. From there carved wooden balconies looked out over the tiled square of the hallway below.

The hall itself was brightly – artificially – lit, as though by sunlight, yet the whole house had a feel of shadows, as if it were still embedded somewhere deep in the heart of an ancient wood.

In a week's time – at *Ta Hsueh*, the Time of Great Snow – Chuang would be sixteen, yet she was strangely small for her age; her slender, almost elfin figure giving her the appearance of a child some four or five years younger. The furniture in the hallway – the great grandfather clock and the massive oak chair, dwarfed her tiny figure.

Seeing her there, Jelka came across, her golden eyes smiling; a warm, welcoming smile.

"Kim says he'll see you. He's been bathing in the star-pool, but he's finished now. He won't keep you long. You can wait for him up in his study."

Placing her hands together, Chuang bowed. "Thank you."

"Come then. I'll show you through."

Chuang hesitated, then. "I liked the birds . . . in the tree outside. Are they new?"

Jelka laughed. "Quite new. Kim made them last year. It was an old GenSyn formula. You should ask him to show you one sometime."

"I shall."

She followed Jelka, not up the main stairway, but along a corridor and up a flight of narrow wooden steps at the back of the house.

Kim's study was at the end of another long corridor, past the library and what was clearly a laboratory of some kind.

On the wall behind Kim's desk was a portrait.

Marshall Knut Tolonen, said the voice in her head. *Jelka's father*.

In an instant she knew all that was important to know about the man whose likeness hung there. That knowledge added a whole dimension to what she saw.

Before she could stop herself, she heard herself say, "Do you miss your father?"

Jelka turned, surprised, then, with a little nod, answered her. "Yes. But part of him's still here, inside me." And she touched her brow with the forefinger of her right hand.

Chuang studied Kim's wife, almost as if she had not seen her before that moment, though the truth was she had known her nine years now. Her hair, which had once been long and blonde, was now cut short about her face, and her eyes which had once been a startling blue, were now a dull, burnished gold, but her face was still strong and beautiful.

Unbidden, the Machine gave Chuang a picture of Jelka as a child, displaying it so that the two images – one real, one memory – were superimposed upon Chuang's eye.

Chuang gave a little shiver. At once the older image faded.

Why did you show me that? she asked silently.

Because you wanted to know.

And that was probably true. It was just that sometimes she would rather chose what she saw and what was left mysterious.

I'm sorry.

You're not, she answered. Then, suddenly conscious that Jelka was watching her, she walked across and sat in the low chair by the window.

"Would you like a drink?"

Chuang shook her head, then, realising how rude that seemed, quickly added. "No, thank you. I . . ."

She wondered briefly if she should mention why she'd come. Wondered if Jelka too had had the dream.

Jelka seemed to hover a moment, then, when there was nothing more, she smiled again. "Well . . . I'll leave you. I've things to do."

"Of course . . ."

Left alone, Chuang looked about her at Kim's study, noting how even in the apparent disorder of things there was a logic.

You see it too, then? the Machine asked.

Yes, Chuang answered, standing and walking to the desk. *He connects things that seem to have no connection.*

She picked up a tiny ivory box and turned it in her hand, wondering what it was, then turned it over. There was a word scratched into the ivory on the bottom in a neat and tidy hand. Kim's writing, she supposed. A.N.N.A.

Chuang looked up, expecting the Machine to enlighten her, but it was silent.

"My mother," Kim said.

Chuang turned, surprised, to find Kim standing in the door. There was a strangely wistful look on his face. He came across and gently took the box from her, doing something to it – twisting it somehow.

At once a faint, ghostly figure filled the air.

"Blinds," Kim said, speaking to the house machine. Swiftly, the window blinds came down, throwing the room into darkness.

In that sudden dark, the hologram shone clearly. It was a woman. Kim's mother, Anna.

"But I thought . . ."

"I *was* an orphan," Kim answered, anticipating her. "My father was executed before I ever had a chance to meet him. My mother . . . well . . . she died in the Clay, back on Chung Kuo. I was six when I last saw her. Oh, and she never looked like this. This is a computer extrapolation, based upon my own and my father's genetic material. But the resemblance *suggests* her. Indeed, in my mind she has come to look very much like this. Any real memory of her is hidden from me. Walled-off."

Chuang frowned. "Why?"

Kim shrugged. "I don't know. Perhaps it's just that I don't like to see her as she really was."

Kim turned and snapped his fingers. At once the room was filled with light again. With a small twist of his hand, the hologram vanished from the air.

"I'm sorry."

Kim shrugged. "It's okay. Now . . . what did you want to see me about?"

"I've had another dream."

"Ah . . ." Kim went round his desk and sat. Chuang had come several times before to tell Kim of her dreams, and most times the dream had proved significant. Not prophetic in any *direct* fashion, yet meaningful enough for Kim to sit up and listen attentively.

"In the dream I was back on Chung Kuo," Chuang said, staring away, her eyes recalling the dream. "It was the time of the Spring Festival, when the earth is renewed, but this time there was to be no renewal. The ritual plough lay broken, its metal harrow rusted and rotten. And the earth was not earth at all, but ash. Deep drifts of ash. And in the distance a host of sickly white flowers had bloomed, huge things that towered above the trees and houses, their black and snake-like roots seeking out every tiny nook or crack in the rock beneath the ashes. And their scent . . ." She shuddered. "Their scent was like the stench of rotting flesh."

She fell silent.

"Was that all?"

Chuang lowered her head and nodded. "It seems very little in the telling, but I woke in a panic, my whole body covered in a sheen of sweat. I felt . . ." She swallowed, then continued. "I felt as if I had been buried alive."

Kim nodded. "And did you have this dream once or many times?"

"Just once."

"Ah . . ." Reaching across, Kim touched a pad on the side of his desk. "Jelka? Would you join us, please?"

Chuang turned as Jelka appeared in the doorway. She looked to Chuang, then walked across to Kim. "Yes?"

He looked up at her. "Have you been dreaming lately?"

There was a tiny hesitation, then she nodded.

"Has Chuang Kuan Ts'ai spoken to you of her dream?"

"No."

"Or you to her of yours?"

"No."

Kim narrowed his eyes, then looked to Chuang. "Tell Jelka your dream, Chuang. Just as you told me."

Chuang began to repeat her dream, then stopped, conscious that Jelka was staring at her open-mouthed, her eyes appalled.

"What is it?" Chuang asked.

"That dream, Jelka said. "That is the dream *I* had two nights ago. And in the dream."

"You died?"

Both Chuang and Jelka looked to Kim. He stood, then gestured to them. "Come," he said. "Let's see who else has had this dream."

* * *

Deep in the rock, in the great engine room that serviced the six great shafts, Ikuro Ishida turned to his brother Tomoka and smiled broadly. Behind him a row of screens showed images of the massive engines that drove the moon through space. Just above them were a further row of screens, each giving a separate readout.

"It looks good, elder brother," Ikuro said, raising his voice above the constant pulse of the engine room. "At this rate we can begin slowing down long before the year's end."

Tomoka stared back at him, his demeanour serious. "You think the Council would agree to that, Ikuro?" he half-shouted back. "You know *their* feelings on the matter. They would rather we travelled faster and braked harder."

"And tear this planet into rubble!" Ikuro huffed his impatience. "No, the new engines Kim designed for us have done their work. We've cut our journey time by more than sixty per cent. Isn't that enough for them? We have to start decelerating soon or we'll overshoot! We've passed the halfway mark as it is!"

Maybe," Tomoka said, conceding the point. "Even so, the matter must be debated formally. You cannot decide for everyone, Ikuro."

"I know, I know . . . but . . ."

"No buts. You put your case and the Council will vote on it. It is our way now. No single man – not even Kim – can have it otherwise."

Ikuro bowed his head. "As you say, elder brother."

"Good, now let us . . ."

Tomoka stopped mid-sentence. One of the screens was flashing. Someone was trying to contact them. Tomoka reached across and touched the screen.

It was Ward. "Tomoka? Ikuro?"

"Yes, Kim?"

"Urgent meeting. Kalevala. One hour."

"Has something happened?"

"Something and nothing," Kim answered cryptically. "I'll tell you when I see you."

And then he was gone.

Ikuro looked to his brother. "What was that about?"

Tomoka shrugged. "Maybe he overheard you, little brother."

"And agreed, no doubt," Ikuro said. Then, more soberly, "He looked troubled."

"Yes."

"Do you think something's wrong?"

"Do I read minds, little brother?"

"No, but . . ."

"Then wait. We will find out what it is soon enough."

* * *

Karr was washing – sluicing water up into his face – when Marie called him from the next room.

"Gregor, it's Kim. He says it's urgent."

Karr reached out and took a towel, then wandered through, standing before the vid-screen.

"Kim . . . what is it?"

"Gregor . . . do you dream?"

"Dream?" Karr laughed. "Are you serious, Kim?"

"Never more so. Well . . . do you?"

"Sometimes. I . . ." Karr hesitated, then gave a little shrug. "There was one . . . the other night. It . . . disturbed me."

"Go on."

"I was back on Earth. On Chung Kuo. Only it was all changed. There was this awful stench, I recall, and when I looked . . ."

"There were flowers. Great white flowers everywhere you looked."

Karr stared.

Marie came over and took her husband's arm. Her face was white with shock. "*You* dreamed that too, Gregor?"

Karr nodded.

"It's like I thought," Kim said. "Marie, Gregor, get dressed. Then meet me at Kalevala within the hour."

* * *

A series of long transit tunnels linked the northern colony towns of Ganymede, like wormholes in the skin of a frozen apple. Athens, where Tom and Sampsa lived, was only half an hour from Kalevala, and as they sat there in the carriage of the fast-link, answering Kim's summons, they spoke to one another silently, each voice a low murmur in the other's head.

Do you think it's about the dreams?

Sampsa shrugged. *I guess so. What else could it be?*

A signal? From Eridani?

No. We would have heard.

That much was true. Word travelled quickly through the townships. But the dream was something else; something that no one was too keen to talk about too much. Even so, they knew at least a dozen people who had had the dream.

What do you think it means? Tom asked.

I think something's wrong, Sampsa answered, his eyes staring straight into Tom's, seeing both himself *and* Tom at that moment. *Back home.*

They still both called it home, even though they were many hundreds of millions of miles from it now.

But how will we know? We're much too far out to communicate with them. And even if we did, what could we do?

Nothing.

I thought it wouldn't matter, Tom said after a moment. *I thought we'd severed our connections with all that.*

It seems not.

No . . .

The carriage began to slow, climbing as it did. Kalevala was just above them now.

What do you think your father will do? Tom asked.

Brilliant lamplight spilled through the windows of the carriage suddenly. They were inside the dome.

Nothing, Sampsa answered. *There's nothing he can do.*

* * *

Kim gathered them all together in the Marshal's old study, Hans Ebert and Aluko Echewa the last to arrive. Sitting there on the edge of his desk, he looked about him at his seated guests while beyond him, through the window, could be seen the wooded slopes of Kalevala and, beyond them, the pure night sky of interstellar space.

They numbered twelve in all, thirteen if you counted the Machine, where it rested in young Chuang's head, looking out through her eyes. Jelka had brought chairs in from nearby rooms to form a rough semi-circle about the big oak desk, but some, like Karr, preferred to stand.

"Okay," Kim said, smiling at Ebert as he took his seat, "let's delay no further. We all know why we're here."

There was a sudden uneasiness in the room. Kao Chen – his right hand raking over the stubble of his iron-grey hair – looked particularly disturbed.

"Is there any . . . *precedent* for this?" he asked, his blunt Han face wrinkled with concern.

"None that I know of," Kim answered. "Chuang Kuan Ts'ai?"

Chuang blinked, concentrating a moment, then shook her head.

"So there are two explanations," Kim went on.

"Two? You know what this *is*, then, Kim?" Karr asked, crossing his arms over his chest.

"No. But either it's a real phenomenon – one we've no precedent for – or we're being manipulated somehow."

"*Manipulated*?" Karr clearly did not like the sound of that.

"Yes," Kim continued, "and the first thing I suggest we do is to check all transmissions for the past week."

"You think there have been subliminals?" Sampsa asked, from where he sat on Kim's left.

"It could be one explanation. Certainly it couldn't have been a normal transmission, else someone would have remembered it and put two and two together. Besides," Kim said, "it's the consistency of detail in the dream that I find strange. It isn't just that we've all dreamed the same thing, but that we've all dreamed about it in the same way."

"And you, Kim?" Karr asked. "Did *you* have the dream?"

"No."

"That's strange, don't you think?" Marie Karr asked, from where she sat at her husband's side. "Why should we all have it and not you?"

"I don't know."

"You dream, don't you, Kim?" Aluko Echewa asked.

"Of course." Kim met the old Osu's eyes. "In fact, I keep a very detailed dream diary."

"But you didn't dream *this* dream," Ebert said, sitting forward slightly. "That's *very* strange."

Kim laughed, then shook his head as if to clear it. "No. Let's get this right. What's strange isn't that I didn't share *your* dream, what's strange is that you all *did*. That's not natural."

"No," Ebert said quietly. There was a murmur of agreement from all round.

"So what does it mean?" Sampsa asked.

"Wait, wait . . . hold on," Kim said. "Before we ask that, let's check on the other matter first. Let's see if there *is* a rational explanation for it."

"You mean, sit through a week's transmissions?" Karr asked.

"No," Kim said. "It won't take that long. I've already asked the central computer to analyse the pattern of the past six days' internal transmissions – on all frequencies and all channels – to see if there are any unusual breaks in transmission that might suggest the use of inserts or subliminals."

"So what has it come up with?"

Kim smiled. "We'll know any moment now. I've asked it to interrupt us with its findings."

"Then let's discuss non-rational explanations," Sampsa said, taking up the matter once again. "Why would dozens of us – hundreds, maybe even thousands of us – dream the same dream if it didn't *mean* something."

"I'd like to know what triggered the dreams," Jelka said, and once more there was a murmur of agreement.

"They began three nights ago, right?" Kim asked.

There were nods.

"And the last was last night? And that was you, young Chuang, correct?"

Chuang looked about her, then nodded.

"Hmmm . . ." Kim considered a moment, then turned, looking at the chart on the wall behind the desk. "Three days ago we went past the halfway mark on our journey. Eridani is now closer to us than Earth."

Ebert laughed. "And you think the two events are connected somehow?"

Kim shrugged. "I don't know. But I'd say we ought to look at *any* possible connection, however odd it might seem, wouldn't you? That is, if this isn't someone having a prank."

"Who would do that?" Tomoka asked, his long face deadly serious.

"I don't know," Kim answered, "but maybe a little bit of boredom is creeping in? Maybe someone has thought to fill the idle hours with a practical joke or two."

"A joke?" Tomaka looked horrified.

"In bad taste, admittedly," Kim said, "but it makes a lot more sense than the other explanation. If this *is* real . . ."

"Then what?" Jelka asked.

Kim looked to her, then shrugged. There was a tiny chime in the air and then the house computer spoke.

"Search completed. No trace of any interruptions in transmission."

Kim looked about him at the thoughtful faces that surrounded him. "So . . . not a joke."

"No," Aluko Echewa agreed, nodding his grizzled grey head, his dark face splitting in a smile. "Unless the gods are playing with us."

* * *

"So what are we to do?" Ikuro asked after a further hour of talking.

"Turn back," said Sampsa, Tom's voice an echo in his head.

Karr laughed. "Impossible!" He looked to Kim. "You said yourself, not a week back. It would take us several years to slow down to the point where we could even make a course adjustment. To turn completely about would be . . ."

"Impossible," Kim said thoughtfully.

"Then isn't there another way?" Chuang Kuan Ts'ai asked, speaking for the first time in a long while. "Some way we could get back there *without* turning Ganymede and the other ships about?"

"Possibly."

All eyes were suddenly on Kim.

"What do you mean?" Ebert asked.

Kim smiled. "I've been working on something. Something . . . interesting, I guess you'd call it." He stood, looking about him, then gestured toward the door. "Come. I'll show you."

* * *

Kim's workshop was in a deep cellar beneath the house – a cavernous place he had had hollowed from the icy rock of Ganymede. The walls were sealed. Wall-mounted heaters kept the temperature at a comfortable sixty degrees Fahrenheit. Overhead strip lights revealed a clutter of standing shelves and benches.

"There," Kim said, ushering them into the central space between the benches. "What do you think?"

"I think I'd like to know what the hell it is," Kao Chen said bluntly, bringing laughter from all sides.

"It's a spacecraft," Kim said, walking up to the strange-looking apparatus.

"It looks more like a dentist's chair," Karr said with a slight grimace.

"Three dentist's chairs," Marie corrected him, indicating the basic trefoil pattern of the machine.

"Where's the hull?" Ikuro asked, completely puzzled now.

"And where's the engine?" Tomoka added, frowning deeply.

Karr shook his head. "If that's a spacecraft . . ."

Yet none of them were willing to be too sceptical. This was Kim, after all, and if Kim said it was a spacecraft – however odd it looked – then in all probability it *was* a spacecraft. Unless *he* was joking now.

But Kim never joked. Not about things like this, anyway.

"The top part of the frame," Kim said, indicating the curious, leaf-like canopy, "is the field-generator. Or will be, once I've worked out how to tap into the field, and where precisely the field is."

Ikuro shook his head. "You mean, it doesn't work?"

"Not yet."

"But surely you need a hull of some kind?" Ebert said, one hand reaching out to gently brush the fine web of wires that curved out from the top of the central pole, surrounding the three skeletal-looking recliners.

Kim smiled. "Perhaps I should be more specific. I say spacecraft, but what this is – or will be – is a space-time craft. A folder."

"A *what?*" Tomoka asked.

But Ebert was staring now. "You mean . . .?"

Kim nodded. "When you told me about the craft DeVore was using, that time on Mars, I knew it must be possible. It was only the *how* of it that remained to be answered."

"Then this is a kind of channel," Chuang said quietly.

"That's right," Kim said. "The central pole is the important thing. It's a basic energy conductor."

"And the wires?" Karr asked.

"They're the hull."

Karr laughed. "A bit draughty, wouldn't you say, Kim?"

Kim smiled. "Not when they're working, Gregor. You see, they generate a force-field. When that's working, *nothing* will pass through it. Not even the cold of deep space."

"I still don't understand," Marie said. "I mean, how can you build the craft before you know how it's going to work? That doesn't make any sense to me."

"Oh, I know how it's going to work. I just don't know how to tap into the energy source yet, that's all. But maybe I had a clue to it, this morning."

"Then you could go back?" Sampsa asked, from where he stood on the far side of the machine. "To Earth, I mean."

"Possibly."

"And you said space-time. Does that mean you could go back in time?"

Kim shrugged, but this time he seemed much more uncertain. "I don't know. But I'd guess no. If one could . . . well, none of it would make sense. Physical process has to have a direction . . ."

"Talking of which," Tomoka said, "which is the front and which the back of this thing?"

Kim grinned. "You don't need a front and a back. You don't even need up and down. You see, it doesn't work that way. It's like a snake – a snake swallowing its own tail."

* * *

For the first time in years, Kim dreamed of the death of Ravachol, the humanoid morph he'd made, to whom he'd given life.

Or, at least, a kind of life.

In the dream, as in life, he had aimed the gun and killed his progeny, conscious that, in that last moment, the mad gleam had left the eyes and something sane had stared out at him, begging to be killed, to be released from its suffering.

But why *that* dream? And why now?

And why had he not shared the dream of flowers. The *common* dream.

He sat up, looking about him at the shadows of the room. The familiar shadows of a familiar place. Beside him Jelka slept on, her soft snores filling the darkness.

Impossible, he thought, going over it for the thousandth time. He could think of no rational explanation for it. And yet . . .

Be scientific, he told himself. *If such a thing is possible, then what follows?*

For a start there would have to be something in the brain of each of them – a receptor of some kind – that could pick up on this "signal", this triggered dream.

Something in the hypothalamus, perhaps.

Okay. But if that were so, why had *he* not received the signal? Or was his turn to come? For the dreams had been strangely staggered.

And why was that?

Part of his difficulty in accepting this was to do with the imprecision – the symbolic *fancifulness* – of the dream. Flowers and ashes. Why could the deeper mind not speak in less dramatic – less *theatrical* – tones if it must speak at all. Why such indirectness?

And if a signal, then from whence did it come? For every signal had an origin.

Yes, and a purpose, too.

And why had it been sent to *them*? And why had he specifically been excluded?

It made no sense. Unless . . .

Walled-off. He had said it himself, earlier, to young Chuang.

Maybe that part of him that *could* receive the dream was walled off. Or maybe his shadow self – *Gweder*, the dark mirror in which his deeper nature was reflected – *had* received it, and never told him.

The thought frightened him.

He stood, then went to the window, staring out into the eternal night of space.

It had been a long time ago, but who was to say he had changed? Maybe that darker, shadow self yet existed in him, subdued and submerged, yet there all the same, influencing him in unknown ways.

And the dream itself? What *did* it mean?

Kim drew a circle on the pane, then turned, looking back into the room.

It was no good; he wouldn't sleep now. Nor was it fair on Jelka to disturb her.

Moving quickly, quietly, he crossed the room and out into the corridor. The old house was dark and silent. Blindly he made his way along to the library and, softly closing the door behind him, switched on the lamp.

Against that warming glow, the great panelled window on the far side of the room seemed to be backed by a sheet of tar, it was so black.

Again he walked across, as if drawn to it, and stood there for a time, looking out into that blackness.

Home. Back there was home. He felt it call to him.

Yet something in him denied that call. He had set his face against return – had rigged it so that return was not an option.

Or so he'd thought.

We made our choice, he thought. *That's why we're out here in this awful, inhuman place. Because there's no option for our species. Not if we want a long term future.*

Or was he thinking like DeVore now?

He huffed, exasperated with himself, then turned from the window. Books. The walls were filled with shelf after shelf of books – *real* books, not tape-script. Old, leather-bound books from before the time of the City.

Kim walked across and took one down at random, opening it halfway through. He read aloud:

"The sign is always less than the concept it represents, while a symbol always stands for something more than its obvious and immediate meaning."

And when the symbol had no obvious and immediate meaning?

Kim slipped the book back and chose another, then sat in the chair beside the window, opening the book up.

Answers. He was looking for answers. But what if there *were* no answers? Then he might trawl all the books on all of the shelves in the entire universe and not find what he was looking for.

He looked down at the page, then smiled.

The Kalevala. He had taken down the Kalevala.

* * *

Sampsa pushed the door open quietly, then peered in from the shadows of the corridor.

"Father?"

Kim was sitting by the window, a book open in his lap, but Sampsa could see he was not looking at the words. He was thinking.

Kim turned his head, looking towards him.

"What is it?"

Sampsa went across and sat on the low stool, facing his father. Physically he was much bigger than Kim in every way, yet he had never felt bigger. Not in any meaningful way. His father could encompass whole universes in that imagination of his.

Beyond Kim, through the panelled window, he could glimpse the blackness of space.

Your dimension, Sampsa thought, wishing for something less grand, something far more human than that eternal sight.

"Well?"

Sampsa smiled. "I just wondered what you'd decided."

"Whether to go back or not, you mean?"

"Yes."

Kim pondered that a moment. "You think that's what the dream *means*, then, Sampsa?"

"What else *can* it mean?"

"I don't know. It's a dream. It could mean that we were right to get out when we did. Maybe it's ended back there. Maybe we're all that's left of the story of humanity."

"Doesn't that worry you?"

Kim frowned, then, "I thought we'd made this choice."

"Did we?"

"I thought we had."

"Then maybe you were wrong."

Kim laughed at that. "Maybe. But what would be the point? What could we do?"

Sampsa sighed. "I don't know. I just feel that we ought to do something. If we can."

"Like go back and fight DeVore?"

"I didn't say that."

"No. You kept it nice and vague. But think, Sampsa. If we *could* go back, and we *did* decide to go back, then why would we do it? For what reason?"

"Because we have a duty."

"A duty?"

"To those we left behind."

Kim huffed and shook his head, but Sampsa could see he was thinking about it. And that was what was ultimately good about his father. Kim would never dismiss what was put to him. Never.

"Let me think about it, okay?"

"Okay."

"And Sampsa?"

"Yes, father?"

"Try talking to your mother more. She gets very lonely sometimes."

CHAPTER·15

A FRAYING CLOTH

After the meeting at Kalevala, Karr and Marie had gone back to Kao Chen's apartment in Fermi, where they'd stayed, talking long into the night. Now, as the lights came on again all over Ganymede, Karr stood in the corridor outside the upper-level apartment, while Marie said her goodbyes to Wang Ti and the children.

Standing beside him, Kao Chen looked to Karr and smiled. "You know, I wish there was something to do."

"Heads to break, you mean?"

Chen hesitated, then. "There were *three* chairs, Gregor."

"What do you mean?"

"Just that *if* we went back . . . well, Kim would have to be one . . ."

"And you and I?"

Kao Chen smiled. "Like old times, neh?"

Karr nodded, his smile mirroring his friend's. "Like old times."

"You think we can persuade Kim?"

"To go back?" Karr shrugged. "I don't know. But Kim's the key to it, neh? Without his acquiescence we can do nothing."

"You think a vote in Council would not be enough, then?"

Karr laughed. "Will a vote make his machine work? No, Kao Chen, for once we must be patient."

But Kao Chen, he could see, was anything but patient. The dream had troubled him far more than most.

As Marie broke from embracing Wang Ti for the dozenth time, Karr reached out and held his friend's arm briefly. "I must go now, Chen. I've a duty shift on the *New Hope* two hours from now, but if you need to talk, call me there. Or come up. The gods know there's little enough for a man to do up there."

"Maybe."

"And Chen. Don't brood on it."

Kao Chen gave a little laugh. "Okay. Now you'd better go." He turned, looking towards where the two women were still embracing, still talking, then shook his head and sighed. "Wang Ti! Let her go now. And Marie, come now, woman. Your husband's waiting for you!"

* * *

As the transporter slowly slid along the massive wire, Karr looked back at the diminishing circle of Ganymede. Once a month he came up here, to take his turn on the bridge of the great starship, and once a month he found himself confronted by the same sights and thoughts.

Nowhere. It was as if they were in the middle of nowhere. All about them was the darkness – a darkness so vast that some days it scared him as nothing else had the power to scare him. Here, in the sealed pod of the transporter, it felt as if he was the only thing moving in the entire universe, for though both the moon and the four great starships that were tethered to it were travelling at a speed that defied the imagination, it still felt as if they were not moving at all, for there was nothing to gauge their rapid progress by. Even the nearest stars were so distant that they did not change from day to day, but sat like painted jewels upon the black.

To get any sense of the reality of his situation, he had to close his eyes and imagine himself within the bright-lit transporter, like a bead on a thread between the spaceship and the moon, the two, and their three companion craft, hurtling through the dark between Chung Kuo and Eridani, their velocities matched.

And even then . . .

Karr sighed heavily. The vague restlessness he had been feeling for the past few months had now taken a clear and distinct form. He was homesick. More than that, he had begun to think he had made the wrong decision coming out here.

Yes, and he was not the only one. More than half the people he spoke to these days expressed private doubts about the venture.

Yet what else could they have done? If they'd stayed, they would have had to fight DeVore, and this time, probably, they'd have lost.

To survive at all, they had had to come out here. To make a fresh start. But what none of them had counted on was just how long it would be before they could make that start. Seven and a half years they'd been travelling now, with the prospect of at least five more.

It was time enough for a man to go stark staring mad.

Back on Ganymede, lights were coming on all across its surface, as the domed cities woke to another artificial morning. Watching it was like watching bubbles forming on the dark sphere.

They had achieved a lot these past few years. More than any of them had thought possible. Even so, the restlessness remained and the doubts, as if this constant building and expansion of their world were no more than a distraction.

Which is unfair, he thought, feeling the transporter slow as it came up under the starship's massive hull.

For one day, if Kim were right, their world would be a proper world, orbiting a proper sun and possessed of a proper atmosphere. Yes, and their children and grandchildren would thank them for the opportunity they had given them.

He knew that. Knew it almost as if it were an accomplished fact. But it did not help him when he felt like this.

Kao Chen is right, he thought, turning to face the hatch as the transporter docked. *We need to go back. To break heads and create mayhem among our enemies.*

He shuddered. Aiya, but he'd missed that! Missed the adrenaline flow that came as one went into action, the sense of danger and the comradeship.

Soldiers! he thought, and shook his head, as if saddened by this sudden attack of sentimentality. But deep down he felt not a sadness at his inability to change, but a strange comfort. A soldier. He was a soldier before all else. And circumstance had stopped him being what he was. But now . . .

Now he could go back. If Kim was right. If his machine could be made to work.

The thought of it sent a tingle of pure excitement through him.

There was a sudden hum. The hatch hissed open.

"Marshal . . ."

The two crewmen stood to attention beyond the hatch, their heads bowed as he stepped through.

Karr straightened, feeling a sudden pride course through him at the thought of what he'd been.

To be a fighter again, and not just a man in a uniform – that was what he wanted. Before his joints got too old and too stiff, his hair too grey. One last time before the darkness took him.

And in his mind's eye he saw DeVore, and smiled.

Enjoy the coming days. Make use of them well. For you've not seen the last of me, Howard DeVore. Not by a long chalk.

* * *

Ikuro set down his helmet on the long table by the window, then turned to face his elder brother, his eyes shining with excitement.

"Imagine it, Tomoka! A machine that can take you anywhere you want, and at once!"

Tomoka, who had sat down to pull off his boots, merely grunted. "I will believe it when I see it."

"But you *saw* it, brother. Yesterday, in Kim's workroom."

"No, Ikuro. I *saw* a strange apparatus, and I *heard* a very strange theory. What I did *not* see was a machine that can travel anywhere."

"But *Shih* Ward said . . ."

Tomoka gave his younger brother a hard look. "*Shih* Ward is a very talented man, and a good man, too, but this time he has allowed his imagination to roam too far."

Ikuro stared at his brother, shocked to be hearing this.

Tomoka went on. "What Kim does not know about engineering is not worth knowing, and his grasp of physics is beyond the sages of old, but . . . when I hear him talk of snakes swallowing their tails, then I begin to doubt."

Ikuro's mouth had fallen open now. If Tomoka had claimed that their mother and father had never existed he could not have been more astonished.

His belief in Kim was absolute. There was nothing Kim Ward could not do.

"You cannot mean that, elder brother."

But Tomoka's face was hard and unyielding. "Mysticism . . . that's all this is. Otherwhens, otherwheres. Jumping through folded space."

"But we know it's possible. DeVore's ship . . ."

"May or may not have existed. And anyway, I for one did not see it."

"No one *saw* it," Ikuro said, "but it was there. They sensed it. And as Kim says, if it exists, then there is a way to make another such craft. Maybe even a better one."

Tomoka grunted. Standing, he unbuckled his suit and stepped from it, then went across and hung it in the wallspace. Turning he looked directly at Ikuro, who stood now at the long, curved window, staring out across the great bowl of Sparta Town which was waking to the day.

"Besides," Tomoka said, "there is another question to be answered. Do we *need* to go back? Do we really want to get embroiled in all that nonsense once again? Surely that is why we came – to get away from all that foolishness? To go back now . . ."

Ikuro stood where he was, his shoulders slightly hunched. Tomoka waited a moment, expecting him to answer, but Ikuro was silent.

"I am right, Ikuro. In your heart you know that I am right."

"Do I?"

"Of course you do. And given time you will understand that. Oh, I understand it well, Ikuro. Kim's words have fired your imagination. That is good. But you must not let them rob you of your common sense. There is only *this* universe, *this* reality. And we must deal with that, not with some flight of fancy. We cannot go back, and even if we could, we should not." He smiled. "There. I have said all I have to say on the matter."

"And yet all is not yet said."

Tomoka shrugged, then went across and put a hand gently on his brother's shoulder. "You will see, Ikuro. Give it time. Then we shall talk again."

* * *

Out here, between the stars, time seemed frozen. Though they moved now at a phenomenal speed – almost one fifth of the speed of light – still it seemed that they stood still. True, Ganymede still span upon its axis, displaying the surrounding stars, yet without the presence of sun and moon in that pitch-black sky, it seemed almost a painted thing, no more real than the computer-generated display on the inside of the dome of Kim's pool.

Out here, one could quickly lose one's grasp of what was real.

Kim stood at the window of his study, thinking about the earlier meeting. He could hear himself now, sounding off confidently about the possibility of going back, yet for all his talk he had not mentioned the single greatest problem that he faced.

Energy.

Enough energy to make a dent in the space-time fabric.

To launch his tiny ship he would need an almost unthinkable amount of energy.

And he would need to control that energy, for what he wanted was a fuel-source, not a bomb.

But how did he get that energy?

His first thought had been to make a black hole, but how would he get rid of it once the craft was launched? How control it? How prevent it from devouring all of surrounding space?

So black holes were out.

Resonance, folding, compression . . . his mind trawled through a hundred possible solutions. But nothing. Nothing yet, anyway.

Given time, he knew, the answer would come to him, like a gift from the ether. But this once he was impatient. This once – and who knew why? – he felt that he could not simply stand back and let the answer come to him: *he* had to pursue *it*.

He had five equations now, and a diagram. And who knew if they were right or totally wrong? They were glimpses and no more than that. Nothing definite yet. Nothing . . .

Kim shook his head. The trouble was that normal rules no longer applied in these circumstances, and all of that vast accumulated knowledge he possessed counted for nothing; not even the methods he had developed to solve problems. If there *was* an answer to this, then – or so he sensed – it was not to be had by normal deductive reasoning. A new kind of logic had to be developed – a logic that, to a human mind, didn't seem logical at all: a logic that did not "link" but "jumped", that did not build brick upon brick, but hung suspended, as if by pure magic.

But how did you get there? How *did* you step through the looking-glass?

Mirrors . . .

The word filled his mind. Unattached. Nothing trailing from it. Just itself. As if it were an answer of itself.

"Mirrors?"

Before he could stop himself he began to play the old, old game – his mind pushing at the word, cracking it open like a nut to pick at it and analyse it, turning the full glare of his intellect on it as if it were a specimen on a slide.

Kim stopped and squeezed his eyes tightly shut.

"No," he said, talking it through for himself. "It's as I said, normal means won't do this once. I need a logic that isn't logic at all."

He paused, grimacing in his effort to get to what he wanted. "What I *do* know is that the reflection is . . . not a *true* reflection. It *can't* be, else we'd have the answer already. So . . . it's not simple *mimicry*. In fact, it's not . . ."

His eyes popped open, his mouth forming a small Oh of understanding.

It's not even a surface at all.

Mirrors. Mirrors had depth. Depth of field. Of course! And there he'd been thinking only of the face of the thing!

* * *

Ebert stood in the darkness at the centre of the bowl of rocks, the great dome of Fermi, greatest of Ganymede's fifteen cities, a mile distant, the great curve of glass glowing softly like pearl.

All about him stood the Osu, more than a hundred in all, their suited forms mere shadows beneath the sky.

Stepping up onto the platform of the rock, Ebert raised his hands towards the darkness overhead, his voice filling the silence.

"The night is our mother. She comforts us. She tells us who we are. Mother sky is all. We live, we die beneath her. She sees all. Even the darkness deep within us."

"So it is, Tsou Tsai Hei. She sees all."

There was a murmur from all sides at Echewa's words. Ebert spoke again.

"We must decide, my people. The time approaches and we must make our choice."

A voice came up to him from close by. "Is it the dream, Walker?"

"It *is* the dream," he answered, "but there is something else. There is a way to go back."

"Back?"

He looked towards the hidden voice. "Yes, back. Back to Chung Kuo. But only for a few of us. The rest will go on, to find the new home promised us."

Again, a murmur ran through the gathered Osu, like a sigh. Then the same voice spoke again.

"Will you go back, Efulefu?"

Efulefu, the Worthless One. So the Osu Elders had named him. Ebert smiled at the use of his pet name, then answered the query.

"It is not chosen yet. Yet we must decide. If I go back, I cannot go forward. I cannot be your Elder."

"I do not understand," another voice said, more distant than the first. "Is that, too, to do with the dream?"

"Yes and no. As you know, I had the dream. The same dream we all had. Yet I also had another dream, this past night. A dream that is clearly linked to the first. A dream in which I saw myself, as if from above. And when I looked down I saw my still and silent figure shrouded in a mist of white."

"Then you must not go back, Efulefu."

"Oh, I *must* go back."

"Then the decision is already made," another said, and there was laughter; a gentle laughter which slowly spread to all those in the shadowed bowl.

"Yes . . ." Ebert grinned, then bowed his head to all of them. "Yes, I suppose it is."

* * *

A wood surrounded Kalevala. It was an ancient place, a place of earth and rock and pine bordering the great lawn, and Sampsa, stepping in among the trees, felt, as he always felt, how even this simple act had meaning – as if, in entering the wood, he shucked off his ordered, rational self.

He moved quickly, silently, until he stood at the edge of the clearing. For a moment he stared up at the solitary tall pine that dominated that open space, recalling how, as a boy, he had once jumped the circle, leaping from stump to stump – a leap of six or eight feet onto a platform less than two across – before launching himself into the centre.

Now, looking up that long, smooth bole, into its branches, he felt an overwhelming sense of loss. The moon, that had once shone so brightly through the branches, was gone, and in its place was a darkness so intense – a gap so huge – that nothing, *nothing* could ever fill it.

Unless his father found a way.

His eyes, one blue, one brown, flicked round, sensing another presence there.

"Father?"

Kim stepped out from between the trees and took a step into the circle. He was wearing a dark one-piece, as if he had been exercising, and his feet were bare. In the light from the house his hair shone silver.

"I thought you'd gone home."

"I meant to," Sampsa began. "But I've been thinking."

"Me too."

Sampsa smiled at that. "You never *stop* thinking."

Kim smiled, then came across to stand beside Sampsa, looking up at the pine. "You think I was wrong, bringing you all out here, don't you? You think we should have stayed and seen it through."

"Yes."

"And maybe you're right. But nature has its way . . ."

Sampsa frowned. "You think this is natural?"

"Absolutely. Trees launch their seeds on the wind, insects deposit their eggs. And that's no more than what we're doing. Sending out seeds. In time those seeds will grow and send out their own seeds. And so the galaxy will be filled by humankind."

Sampsa shook his head. "Bearing in mind our past record, I'm not so sure that that's such a good thing."

"Good thing, bad thing, who are *we* to say?"

"But surely we *must* say?"

"Must we?" Kim looked down, meeting his son's eyes again. "Are we really that big then, Sampsa, to so buck destiny and the urgings of our own DNA?"

"I didn't mean that. I meant . . ."

Sampsa huffed from pure exasperation. This was the trouble with arguing with his father. Kim didn't think on the same plane as ordinary people. His parameters were just so much bigger.

"Would you rather humankind died out, then, Sampsa? Is that your argument? Would you rather DeVore got his way and wiped out the lot of us and put his morphs – his *Inheritors*, as I'm told he calls them – in our place? Would you rather *they* got the prize?"

"But it doesn't have to be like that."

"Doesn't it?"

And now there was a hardness in his father's voice he had never heard before. Sampsa looked at him, surprised.

"Father?"

"Let me tell you something, Sampsa. For a long time I tried hard *not* to get involved. I tried to argue that it had nothing to do with me – that I ought just to get on and live my own life and look after those in my narrow little circle. But after a while I realised that I couldn't fool myself any longer. There really *was* a war going on. And not just any war. This was a war that could decide whether mankind would survive or go under. Once I saw that, the rest was easy. It was a question of taking sides, of choosing which *direction* I would ultimately follow: *for* life, or *against* it. You see, I *did* care what happened to other people. Just as I care now – despite what you think – about what's happening back on Earth. That's why I brought us out here. And that's also why I've decided to try to go back. Why I'm willing to risk my life trying out a machine that could, for all I know, blast me into a thousand million tiny little pieces!"

Sampsa smiled. "And what will you *do* when you get back? Have you decided *that* yet?"

"No. But I will."

"And DeVore?"

Kim looked away thoughtfully. "I'll let our friend Karr deal with DeVore. If and when the time comes."

* * *

Ebert unscrewed the helmet of his suit and, lifting it off, set it down on the table and turned, looking about him at his tiny apartment.

Once, back on Chung Kuo, he had had everything a man could wish for – a great mansion, a massive company, and command of a great army of three million men. He had been betrothed to a beautiful woman and had had the trust of emperors. Now he had only this.

To some that might have seemed a great descent. His old self, certainly, would have felt it so. That self would have equated such a loss of material power with a loss of vitality and strength. Yet in the years since, Ebert had discovered where true strength lay in a man. Yes, and had been richer for it.

He had embraced *wuwei*, the path of inaction. He had become as the stream that flows. But now he had to turn his back on things and become once more a man of action.

One last time.

Ebert smiled. It was strange the peace he'd felt in the dream, seeing himself dead. Such peace as he had only previously imagined.

Unclipping the fastenings at his wrists, he pulled off his gloves and went over to the window, looking out through the toughened ice at the ancient surface of the moon.

It was a magnificent view, and his apartment was only one of many that overlooked the surface, but few were occupied these days. His last near neighbour had moved out almost five months ago now, and no one new had moved in.

I should say something, he thought, wondering if Kim and the others had noticed this, or whether only he was sensitive to it.

Anxiety, that was what it was. His fellow travellers were anxious. And as each month passed, that anxiety grew. At first it had manifested itself in small ways – a reluctance to venture outside the domes or look up at the open sky – yet as the journey lengthened it had taken on more definite forms. They had begun to dig, deeper and yet deeper into Ganymede's surface, as if to hide away from the void that surrounded them.

Two years back they had begun to build long tunnels between the cities, and the old ways – the surface routes – had fallen into disuse.

He had listened without comment to the arguments they gave, and no doubt some of them were true. It *was* safer to build below ground, for there was less chance of decompression. Yet that was not *why* they did it.

There were exceptions, of course. Kim, for instance, and Karr. But the rest were slowly turning inward. Burrowing into themselves just as they burrowed into Ganymede.

And maybe that was necessary if they were to protect themselves psychologically from that void. For if that void reached them and touched their hearts, what then would transpire?

It was all uncharted territory.

Ebert stretched his neck and shoulders, feeling weary now. But his thoughts were restless. Since he'd had the dream – since he'd glanced behind the wall of sleep and seen his fate – he had thought of little else.

At times like this he wished for his old unconscious self; wished that he did not feel so much for those who suffered. To be blind to all that and at peace again.

And that, perhaps, was why his own death did not trouble him, for at least with death would come rest and a cessation of this constant ache. The ache of responsibility.

In a fit of frustration he smashed his fist against the glass. "I am *not* my brother's keeper!"

But it was not so. Kick as he might against it, his fate was set. He had to go back. Yes, and die, if what he'd seen was true. Because he was *Tsou Tsai Hei*, the Walker in the Darkness, and he had been granted a vision of the path's end.

And as he thought that, so Tuan Ti Fo's words came to him, from that time on Mars when he had first met the old man:

"*Am I to tell you everything? No, Tsou Tsai Hei, that is for you to learn. Study them. Be as them. The truth will follow. You are to stay here, to finish the work that time has begun in you. To wait here, among these hidden works of darkness. Until the call comes.*"

* * *

Karr slumped down into the chair, then sat back, stifling a yawn. This was the worst of it – the inactivity; the feeling that it didn't matter what one did or didn't do. It undermined him. Slowly, day by day, he felt himself *eroded* by it.

He stared at the screen. On it was a table of figures, showing their relative position to the nearest stars, their speed, the temperature of the engines, and other things. The figures had not changed for three hours now, or if they had, it had been so minor a change – a decimal point or two – that he hadn't noticed.

"*Aiya*!"

The two young guards on the far side of the bridge turned, looking across at Karr, surprised.

"Marshal?" one of them asked, thinking that something must be wrong.

But Karr simply shrugged. "It's okay, boy. It's just . . ."

The screen changed suddenly. The tables vanished, replaced by a familiar face.

"Hans? . . . What in the void's name do you want?"

Ebert smiled. "I need to talk, Gregor. I've had another dream."

Karr frowned. He didn't like these dreams. No more than Kao Chen did. "Was it like the first?"

"No, no it . . ." Ebert shook his head. "The thing is, I've seen into the future, Gregor. I've seen my own death."

"Impossible."

"I know. I realise how it sounds, but I've seen it, as clearly as if I was there. And I've seen other things, too. I've seen you and Chen standing together in the courtyard of a strange building. A strange structure of jet-black stone that looked as if it had been built into the walls of a giant well."

"I don't know any place like that you describe."

"No, but you were there, as you look now. And Chen, too, with his fine white hair."

"And you? You say you saw your own death?"

"Yes. I was with you, back on Chung Kuo. There were six of us, in two craft."

"But Kim has . . ."

". . . only made one, I know. And yet I saw it, as clearly as if I was remembering it."

Karr closed his eyes a moment, rubbing at his temples as if he was suffering from a migraine. Then he looked back at Ebert again. "I'm sorry," he said, "but I find all this hard to take in. It's . . . well, it's as if reality were coming to an end. These dreams . . . they're like the fraying of an old cloth."

"Yes," Ebert said. "So it is, old friend. And we shall be there for the weaving of the new."

* * *

Jelka stood at the window of the tower, her hand resting on the chair's back as she looked out over the stand of trees. From where she was she could see the clearing of the seven pines and, through the trees, the figures of Kim and Sampsa. She had been wondering what had been said between them earlier to make Kim so quiet, and had thought that perhaps they'd argued, but things seemed all right now between them. She saw them smile and laugh and felt herself relax.

She was about to turn away, when the fit began. The sensation was familiar – it had happened many times since her illness – but she had not been troubled by it for some time. Now it swept her up, like a great wind rushing through her head and overwhelming her senses.

She staggered, then held onto the chair back. Yet even as she did, she saw the vision, there above the clearing where Kim and Sampsa stood. They were still there, but now, in the sky directly over them, maybe half a kilometre up from the moon's dark surface, burned a massive wheel of fire, its fierce light reflecting back off the curved surface of the dome and illuminating the whole of the plain surrounding Kalevala.

"*Aiya!*" she whispered, her golden eyes flaming fiercely in that unearthly light.

It was not, she knew, a dream – leastways not a waking dream – but a real and genuine stochastic vision. A glimpse of what would be.

She wanted to cry out, to warn Kim and Sampsa, but they seemed to know. They pointed at it, laughing, then turned to look up at her.

Jelka stared at them a moment, then looked back at the fiery circle, shielding her golden eyes against its glare. Through her fingers she could see that it was not a solid, sustained image. It seemed to flicker . . . to somehow oscillate even as it turned, like a film that has had every second frame blanked.

And then, as suddenly as it came, it was gone.

Jelka dropped onto her knees, a sudden cold throughout her body. The darkness of the sky outside now seemed a shock. She groaned, then put her hands up to her head, the pains in her head – yet another familiar symptom – beginning with a vengeance.

What was that? What in the gods' names *was* that?

She had seen many small things in the past; little things that subsequently came to pass. But this time she would have to tell him.

And risk him thinking you mad?

Yes, even that. For she had never had a fit so strong, so . . . *vivid.*

Even with her eyes closed she could still see it, as if the image had been burned onto her retinas.

Like a snake, she thought, remembering what Kim had said. *A great snake of fire, swallowing its tail.*

* * *

Ikuro sat alone in his room, staring at the diagram on the screen. He had spent the last two hours designing what he was looking at and still he was not happy with it. It looked vaguely like what he had seen in Kim's workshop, but there was still something about it that was wrong. Something he'd overlooked.

It was at times like this that he wished he had a memory like Kim's, that once he had seen a thing he could not forget it. *Eidetic* they called that.

But it wasn't only that that made Kim a great man. He had watched him often these past six years and seen how – like a magician – he conjured answers from the air. Or from within himself, which was the same.

Ikuro shivered. It was cold in the room. No doubt Tomoka had been turning down the heating once again. Getting up, he walked over to the cupboard and got down a sweater, pulling it on.

Better, he thought, sitting back in front of the screen, half frowning at it in his attempt to work out what he'd missed.

A spaceship with no engines and no hull. A craft that, in essence, was but an array of seats.

He laughed. Who else but a madman or a genius would think of such?

There was a knock. Ikuro turned in the swivel chair, facing the door.

"Who is it?"

A head popped round the door. "Ikuro? Can I have a word with you?"

It was Ebert. Ikuro smiled and got up.

"Of course. Come in."

Ebert stopped, looking blindly at the screen, then nodded. "There. That's how I saw it."

Ikuro shrugged. "It's not quite right. But I can't figure out . . ."

"No," Ebert said, with a certainty Ikuro found strange. "That's it exactly. I saw it. Like that, without the fans."

"The fans!" Ikuro slapped his forehead, then went to sit down and change the image, but Ebert stopped him.

"No. Save that, as it is. Or better still, print up a copy. We'll take it to show Kim."

"Kim?" Ikuro turned back, looking up at Ebert. "I don't understand."

"No," Ebert said. "But you will. Just trust me, Ikuro. You will."

* * *

Back in his study, Kim set to work at once, gripped by a sudden and immense excitement.

Going over to the big touch-screen in the corner of the room, he took the stylus and began to write down the three equations he had jotted on the blackboard by the pool, only this time he did not write them one atop the other, but spaced them out, so that they formed a triangle.

Three points on a circle. Or almost so, for he saw now that he had only half the picture. The rest . . .

Kim laughed aloud, surprised by the simplicity of it, amazed now that he had not seen it before. But that was always the way of things. What afterwards seemed obvious was – before that all-important moment of insight – as opaque as death itself: a barrier that no man's mind could cross.

But cross it he had.

Taking the first of the equations, he reversed it, changing two of its elements and transforming it in the process. Satisfied, he wrote it down to the right of the original, just below it. Now that he'd done so, he could see how it linked directly to the second of his equations that lay at the next point clockwise about the emerging circle.

Again he reversed the equation, changing two of its elements. Once more the new equation fitted like a link in a chain. And then the last, again more or less a reversal of what he already had, yet at the same time a total transformation of the original.

He stepped back, staring at the great circle of equations in wonder, seeing suddenly the connection not merely between each point on the circle's edge, but between every single part. It was not *just* a circle, it was a web. And each strand of that web contained a distorted mirror of each other strand, harmonics in a great chord.

Kim felt a shiver go through him. Whatever else he had done in his entire life, none of it matched what he had achieved here in this single diagram.

"Save and store," he said quietly, almost afraid to speak.

"Kim?"

He turned. Jelka was standing there, just inside the doorway.

"This is it," he said. "What I've been looking for."

"A wheel of fire," she said, looking at him, not the diagram. "I saw it, Kim. I saw it in the air above Kalevala. A great wheel of fire in the air, and you and Sampsa laughing and pointing up at it.

"You *saw* it?"

"Yes. And it *will* happen. I know it will. I've seen things before. Things that have subsequently come true."

"Ahh . . ." He didn't know quite what to say.

"I know it seems like madness, Kim, but . . . it happens. It really *does* happen. It's to do with the sickness. At least, I think it is. I didn't have them before."

"And the dream?"

Jelka shook her head. "No. The dream was something different."

She walked across and stood before the screen.

"It's like the *Ywe Lung*," she said.

Kim nodded. He had not seen it before, but now that she had pointed it out to him, it was curiously like the great wheel of dragons of the Seven which had once been the symbol of their authority over Chung Kuo.

"Maybe they knew," he said. "Knew but . . . didn't know."

She laughed at that. "How can you know but *not* know?"

"It's easy," he said. "I knew. But I didn't *know* I knew until just now. Even so, it was there inside me. And you – if your vision was real – knew that it was."

"That's too deep for me, Kim. But this . . . if *this* is true . . . if this *works* . . . well, what does it mean?"

"I'm not sure," he said. "But if I'm even vaguely close with my guesses, then life is going to get a whole lot more complicated round here."

"Yes, but how?"

He hesitated, not wanting to tell her what had been going through his mind, then shrugged. "Let's wait and see, huh? Let's just wait and see."

* * *

That night, as Jelka lay beside him, sleeping, Kim found himself returning to the thought he'd had while talking to her earlier.

All the while he had thought only of the practical use of the equations – of how to find a power source for his craft. Energy. It had all come down to energy. But now that he had the answer, all manner of other things – peripheral things – had popped into his mind.

He had thought only of using that surface between realities to launch his little ship. But if one could unlock the door to another universe, then what stopped one from stepping through and entering that other space?

And what exactly would one find there?

Mileja, perhaps . . . And my mother, Anna, too. Only a different Anna, an altogether different Mileja . . .

The thought disturbed him.

Just how different would it be? Or would it be different at all?

The truth was, he didn't know. And he couldn't begin to guess. Only by going there would he know.

The equations aside, he wasn't even certain that he *could* just step through. Maybe something in the composition of himself – something beyond simple cell structure, something implicit in the reality in which he existed and of which he was a part – prevented him from slipping across that great dividing line.

He did not know. Nor *would* he know, until he tried.

But did he dare?

That was the big question. Did he dare? Was he confident enough to risk taking that single step that changed the rules of everything?

I'll sleep on it, he thought, conscious of Jelka's soft breathing, of her warmth pressed against his side.

And as he slipped down into the dark well of sleep, he had a momentary vision of himself, elsewhere – in that other place, perhaps – tucked in beside another Jelka, the same and yet entirely different.

Mirrors, he thought once more, and, yawning, turned onto his side. *It's all done with mirrors . . .*

* * *

It was night on Ganymede. Beyond the dome of Kalevala the stars burned down, peppering the interstellar blackness.

In the shadows of Kim's study, the silence was profound. One moment the room was empty, the next two figures stood before the corner screen.

The screen, which had been dark, now glowed with a low, dull light, in the midst of which Kim's diagram burned with a strange dark brilliance.

"*Finally*," one of them said, speaking in a tongue that was unlike any that had been heard by human ears.

"*Yes*," the other agreed, studying the elegant equations.

The two figures seemed to flicker, like a film in which every second frame has been removed. They were unearthly tall – tall beyond human measure – and vague in the sense that a human eye would have found it hard to discern exactly where their outlines lay. Moreover, they seemed not merely colourless but *without* colour, though not transparent. If colour there was, it was of a hue outside the normal spectrum. A colour out of space.

The two looked to each other.

"*It's almost time*."

"*Almost*."

The screen glow died. The room was empty. Outside, beyond the silent dome, the eternal stars burned down as they had since time began – like a thousand million tiny windows breaching the living dark.

The darkness shimmered.

It was almost time.

CHAPTER · 16

The Place of Inner Dark

"Friends! What an unexpected pleasure."

Kim stood back, smiling broadly as the three men came into the room, Ikuro and Aluko Echewa first, Ebert the last to enter, the two tiny camera probes slowly circling his head.

"You've timed it well," Kim went on, going over to the screen and switching it on. "I've something to show you."

"We know," Ebert said. "The equations."

Kim turned, astonished. "You *know*?"

"I saw it. In my dream."

Kim blinked. "I don't understand. First Jelka, then . . ."

"Here," Ebert said, handing Kim a folded slip of paper. "This will explain."

Kim unfolded the paper and looked. Slowly his eyes widened. He turned, looking to the circle of equations, then shook his head. "And there I was thinking it was complete."

"No," Ebert said. "There's more. Much more. But that's the key. The key that unlocks the door."

Kim's mouth was open. He blinked, once, twice, then began to smile. "Yes . . . I see it now."

"It's breaking down," Ikuro said. "The cloth is fraying. Hans thinks that we're coming to a cusp."

"A cusp?"

"A point where it all changes."

"Ah . . ." Kim looked at the screen again, then nodded. "Then this . . ." He stopped and looked to Ebert. "I was going to make another craft," he said. "Did you see that, too?"

Ebert nodded. "Ikuro . . . give Kim the printout."

Ikuro handed Kim the diagram of the craft he'd drawn. Kim looked at it, then laughed. "That there – where you've removed the fans – that's exactly the amendment I thought of this morning. But this and this . . . these are new. That looks like some kind of generator, and that . . . well, it could be a heater of some kind. And these, underneath it . . ." He looked up at them. "But how . . .?" Kim stopped, staring fiercely into the air a moment, then he laughed. "Do you think . . .?"

"What?" Ikuro asked, glancing at Echewa who stood beside him, concerned by Kim's sudden strangeness.

"All of this . . . coming together like this. Dreams and clues and visions. It all seems . . . well, like we're being *given* this. And if we're being given it, then someone is doing the giving. Someone *higher* than us, perhaps."

"Higher?" Ikuro looked perplexed.

But Ebert seemed to understand what Kim was saying perfectly. "Yes. I felt that too. We're being directed. To go back and face DeVore. To determine our direction."

"You think so?" Kim asked.

Ebert smiled. "Oh, I'm certain of it, Kim. As certain as of anything in my whole life."

* * *

They decided to hold a meeting of all the colonists, to discuss the dreams and all that had arisen since. Kim scheduled it for that evening at eight, yet even as he prepared for it, events overtook him.

The first Kim knew of it was when Karr called him from the bridge of the *New Hope*.

"Kim? Where are you right now?"

"In my study, why?"

"Look out of the window."

Kim turned and looked. For a moment he saw nothing. Then he gasped. Nothing. He really *did* see nothing.

"*Gods* . . ."

The stars had gone. The sky was black, unblemished. His voice, when he spoke again, was a whisper.

"*What's happened*?"

"I don't know," Karr said. "One moment they were there, the next they weren't."

"But they *must* be there. They *have* to be."

"Our sensors no longer register anything. The nearest star is an infinite distance away according to the figures on my screen. Which is another way of saying that there *aren't* any stars."

"Impossible."

The machine had to be wrong. And their eyes . . . their eyes obviously weren't seeing what was out there, because the alternative . . .

The alternative was mad. Madder than doors into other universes. Madder than shared dreams. Madder than people seeing things that hadn't happened. Madder than . . .

He stopped and closed his eyes. It was possible, just possible, that he was hallucinating – dreaming all this even while he thought he was awake. Like Chuang

Tzu and the butterfly. But if so, what did *that* mean? And besides, if this *was* a hallucination, it certainly didn't feel like one.

Unless it was a shell.

For a moment that possibility – that Shepherd had somehow tricked them all – dominated his thoughts. Then he opened his eyes.

"Kim? Are you all right?"

"Am I dreaming, Gregor?"

Karr laughed. "Maybe. But if so, then we're all dreaming the same dream. And that's as good a definition of reality as I can think of."

Kim nodded. *So if it wasn't a dream . . .*

The screen began to buzz. Someone was trying to get in touch with him urgently.

Kim lifted the flap of skin and looked at the timer inset into his wrist. It was five fourteen, Ganymede time.

"Okay," he said. "Here's what we'll do. We'll bring the meeting forward two hours. Something's happening, and it won't do to wait and see what it is."

"And the stars?"

Kim shrugged. "I don't know, Gregor, but do you recall what you said, about the old cloth fraying."

"So?"

"I'd say we'd just fallen through a tear in the cloth."

* * *

They met just after six, gathering together in the Circles, the great meeting places that had been built at the centre of each of the fifteen domes. The colonists were frightened and not a little confused by events, but as yet they were calm. So it was that they watched – some in person, most on the great screens that surrounded them – as Kim Ward climbed up onto the platform in Fermi Circle to address them.

"Friends, fellow citizens . . . I have asked you to gather because something is happening. Something strange. Something that even I can find no explanation for."

He paused, letting the significance of that statement sink in.

"The facts are simple. We are still travelling – or, at least, the engines are still firing as before, still pushing us on – but we are going nowhere. Eridani is no longer directly ahead of us. Indeed, from all we can make out, we are no longer within the relativistic universe."

There was a strange collective sigh. Kim raised his hands, as if to fend off objections, even though there were none.

"I can think of no theory which would explain these facts, only a metaphor. It is as if we have fallen down a well. Yet even this is unsatisfactory, for a well has a bottom, and from the bottom of a well one might glimpse the sky, but we can see nothing."

Ebert, standing just below the platform, now spoke up. "Is there *anything* we can do, Kim?"

Kim nodded. "There are several things we *might* do. For a start we might send out a probe. If we *are* still moving relativistically then the probe will quickly fall behind us at this speed. We might also consider closing down the engines."

There was a worried murmur at this suggestion and Kim, looking about him, could see that this troubled them almost as much as the situation itself. To close down the engines was a major step. To many it would seem like an admission of defeat.

He could see they wanted to go on, even if they were going nowhere.

A big, grey-bearded man named Baker now spoke. "I say we do nothing. I say we wait and see what happens."

Kim smiled. "I'd say that was a good suggestion, Jed. But how long do we wait? And what if this situation is permanent? What if we *have* fallen down a well in space?"

"Not a well. A pocket."

Kim turned, surprised to find the old man behind him. Then, with a gasp of astonishment, he realised who it was.

"*Tuan Ti Fo*!"

Old Tuan bowed low, then, smiling patiently, stepped up beside Kim and, raising his arms, spoke to them all.

"Forgive me, my friends, for coming among you unannounced, but you must know now how things are. Kim is right. You are no longer within the relativistic universe, but in a pocket, a no-space between the universes. Eridani is still before you, and you travel towards it hourly, yet there is no trace of you in your universe. This *we* have done."

"*We*?" Kim was staring at Old Tuan in disbelief. He had thought him dead, or back on Chung Kuo. He had certainly not been on Ganymede. Not until a moment or two ago.

"I can say little now," Tuan answered. "Only that you are in no danger." He paused, then, "You must be patient. You must remain here in no-space for a while, for *he* must not see you. Not yet. Things are changing, and just as we have woken, so *he* in time will wake."

"Can you not tell us more?" Karr asked, his own face filled with wonder at the sight of the old man.

"Only that you have work to do. You have come right to the edge. To the time of change. Beyond it everything will be different. But you must first step over. Until then we can say nothing more."

"The equations?" Kim asked. "Has it to do with the equations?"

But Old Tuan would not be drawn. "Do your work, Kim Ward. Go where you must go – where the visions show you *will* go. Then, when things are clearer to you, we will talk."

They had not seen him arrive, but all there saw him leave. For a moment he seemed both to be there and not be there, his form shimmering, as if every other frame of a film had been removed. Then he was gone.

Again a sigh ran through them.

You have come right to the edge. To the time of change.

Kim stared a moment, then turned back, looking out across the upturned, awe-struck faces of his fellow travellers.

"Well . . ." he said, finding no words to describe what he was feeling, "let us do as Master Tuan says. Return to your homes and wait. When something is known, I shall contact you again."

He could see how they hung back, reluctant to go; how they looked to him for some kind of explanation. But for once he had nothing to give them. Nothing but his own bafflement.

* * *

"So what exactly *is* happening?"

Ebert laughed at the bluntness of Karr's question.

"Do you think I'm holding out on you?" Ebert shook his head, as perplexed as they for once. He knew Tuan Ti Fo's tricks of old, but this once Old Tuan's appearance had shaken him; so much so that he could not think straight. "The gods know what happened back there. One moment we were in the normal universe, the next *nowhere*. And I've no how idea how they did it."

"But where are we?"

"The place of inner dark . . ."

Karr frowned. "Pardon?"

"That's where we are. The place of inner dark." His blind eyes looked about him at the others who were packed into the room with him. "That's what the Osu call it. It is a place outside of time and space."

"A dream time," his son, Pauli offered, but Ebert shook his head.

"No. It is a real place, a *physical* place."

"And do the Osu go there?"

Ebert smiled. "No. It is a place of the gods."

"Then . . ." Karr hesitated, "what you're suggesting is . . ."

"That Old Tuan is a god. Or an immortal. Like those in the old Han tales. Kim told us how he claimed to be as old as the rocks. What if that was true? It would explain a great deal. Like how he manages to walk through locked doors."

"Yes," Karr said, "and travel between Chung Kuo and deepest space in the blink of an eye."

Ebert nodded. "And you, Kao Chen, what do *you* think?"

Kao Chen made a face. "I feel as if I must have eaten something that disagreed with me. If this is not a dream, the gods know *what* it is!"

Ebert nodded. "I understand. I've been questioning my sanity, too. But it looks like it's real. Unless we're all hallucinating."

"So what are they, then?" Pauli asked. "Gods? Immortals? Or are they aliens in human form?"

"Tuan said he was born," Ebert answered. "He told Kim that DeVore was his twin – that they found him in the afterbirth, the cord wrapped about his throat."

"Pity they found him," Karr said, making them all laugh. But they quickly grew serious again.

"Maybe it's true but not true," Ebert said.

"How do you mean?"

"Just that he might be a twin, and he might have been born at the same time as

DeVore – if DeVore's another of these beings – only they might not have been born to a human mother, on Earth. That might have been the part of the tale he'd doctored, to make it acceptable to you."

Karr shrugged. "I think I'd have believed it *more* if he'd said he and DeVore were aliens, not less. Aliens I can believe in, just about, but immortals . . ."

"Whatever Tuan *is*," Ebert said, "he seems to have powers beyond our present understanding. Yet he talks of having woken slowly to those powers."

Karr nodded. "Yes, and this business of it being almost time. Of us being on the edge. What do you think he means by that?"

"He means the equations," Ebert answered. "I'm sure of it. As I said, we have the key now."

"Then surely Kim is where he wants to be. In the doorway."

Ebert looked to Chuang Kuan Ts'ai, who had spoken. "What do you mean?"

Chuang smiled. "Kim said that he wasn't sure in which direction he had to look, to seek the door between the worlds. Well, now we know. In fact, Old Tuan has brought us right to the spot. All Kim has to do now is make it work."

Karr looked about him. "Where is Kim? He ought to have come back by now."

Kim had gone away while they were talking, but he had not returned.

"Kao Chen," Karr said, "did you see where he went?"

"Into the wash room, I thought. I'll check . . ."

Kao Chen disappeared. A moment later he was back, his face ashen. "Quick! Kim's collapsed! I found him slumped over one of the stalls. He looks in a bad way!"

* * *

Kim's room was dark. As the doctor stepped outside into the corridor and closed the door behind him, five anxious faces stared back at him.

"Well?" Jelka asked, her voice a whisper. "How is he now?"

"No change," the doctor – an elderly Han named Ji – answered quietly, his concern mirroring their own. "Physically he seems fine. His breathing's normal and his heartbeat. But these voices you say you've heard. What kind of thing is that?"

Jelka looked down. "It's nothing . . . just murmuring, that's all."

"Ah . . ." Surgeon Ji considered a moment, then shrugged. "I can only suggest that you be patient and wait. It strikes me that this whole business has been quite a shock to his system. Kim is a very rational man. What we've experienced . . . well, it would shake the faith of any rationalist, neh?"

"But surely, to sleep this long . . .?"

"Is not unusual," Ji quickly reassured her. "Sixty hours is not long, *Mu Ch'in* Ward. And we are not talking about a coma. All that's happened is that Kim's conscious mind has switched itself off. It's having a rest. And long overdue, I'd say. No, let nature take its course."

After Ji was gone, Jelka turned, looking to the others.

"What voices?" Sampsa asked.

Jelka shrugged. "It was nothing . . ."

"No," Sampsa said. "Whatever they were, it certainly wasn't nothing. I can see they disturbed you."

She hesitated, then. "It's just that it hasn't happened in a while."

"What?" Karr asked impatiently, his voice raised momentarily. Ebert touched his arm.

"Gweder and Lagasek."

"Gweder and . . .?" Karr shook his head, looking to the others for an explanation.

"It goes back to his days in Rehab," Sampsa said. "When he first came out of the Clay. They are the two sides of his nature. His two selves, if you like. For a long time Lagasek – Starer – has been in control. But it seems that Gweder – Mirror – is back."

Karr stared at Jelka open-mouthed. This was the first he'd heard of any of this. "You mean Kim is schizophrenic?"

"Not technically," Sampsa said, answering for her. "But Gweder – his darker self – has been walled off all these years. Inaccessible."

Jelka shook her head. "That's not true."

"Pardon?"

She looked to her son. "I said that's not true. After Mileja's death, Gweder came back. Sometimes he was only a voice, in the night when Kim was fast asleep, but sometimes he would make Kim get up and go out, to walk beneath the trees. I'd see him out there, prowling, and I'd know it was Gweder."

"You could tell?"

Jelka shivered, then nodded. "He would go on all fours."

"Ah . . ." Karr looked aside.

There was a moment's silence, then Sampsa spoke again. "And the voices?"

Jelka met her son's eyes. "He was arguing with himself."

"Arguing?"

She nodded. "His face would change. It was quite striking. And frightening, too. Gweder . . . well, Gweder's how I imagine Kim would have turned out, had he remained in the Clay."

"If he'd survived."

"Yes . . ." Jelka looked thoughtful a moment, then. "It's strange. Kim – the waking Kim, that is – is so determined, yet Lagasek, supposedly his rational self, is so passive. Whereas Gweder. Well, Gweder's a bully. He pushes."

"And what did Gweder push *for*?" Ebert asked, staring at her blindly.

"He wanted Kim to step through."

"*Through*?" Both Sampsa and Karr said it as one.

"Yes. Into the other universe."

"And Lagasek?"

"Lagasek's unwilling. I think he's frightened."

"Frightened?" Sampsa asked. "Frightened of what?"

"I don't know."

Again, a silence fell. Then Karr let out a sigh. "So what are we going to do? Without Kim . . . well, the equations are just so much mumbo-jumbo to me."

Ebert laughed. "For once I agree with you, Gregor. I thought my maths was good, but those calculations are quite beyond me."

"And me," Sampsa said.

"Well," Jelka said, looking about her. "It seems, then, that we have but one course, and that's to do as Surgeon Ji says, and wait."

"And if he doesn't wake?" Kao Chen asked.

"He'll wake," Karr said, putting a hand on his old friend's shoulder reassuringly. "Jelka's seen it, remember?"

* * *

The wind was up and waves were crashing against the rocks below his bedroom window. Kim lay there, listening, the sound of the wind rushing through the trees lulling him. In his mind's eye he could see the great branches stretching in the wind, their leaves streaming out like bright green banners in the sunlight. He turned lazily and smiled, for a moment not remembering. Then, with a jolt, he woke.

Silence.

Nowhere. He was nowhere.

Kim opened his eyes. It was dark; a shadowed darkness that quickly resolved itself.

My room. I am in my room at Kalevala.

But how had he got here? He could not remember. The last thing he could remember was standing in the Circle at Fermi, waiting to speak.

And after that?

Nothing. Absolutely nothing.

He stretched, then sat, conscious for the first time how rested – how totally rested – he felt. As if he'd slept for days on end.

He laughed at the thought, knowing that he was a creature who needed little sleep.

"Jelka?"

When there was no answer, he stood and walked over to the door, throwing it open.

"Jelka?"

Nothing. The house was silent.

Throwing on a robe, he went down to the kitchen. It too was empty, no sign of Jelka anywhere.

Strange.

He went to the larder and opened the door, looking in to see what he could eat.

Starving. He was absolutely starving.

Taking a hunk of bread, he buttered it and crammed it into his mouth, chewing it voraciously. Then, taking another bite, he went over to the window and looked out. The lawn was empty, and the garden.

He turned, making his way back to the larder, taking down meat and apples and cheese. Then, sitting down at the great wooden table, he gorged himself, his mind empty of anything but the hunger he felt.

Finally he sat back, replete.

He reached across and picked up a cloth, wiping his mouth.

It was strange how vivid his waking dream had been. So vivid that, for a moment, he had been back there on the island, the waves battering the shoreline, the wind streaming through the trees.

Strange indeed.

Kim made to stand, then stopped, his mouth falling open.

"Old Tuan . . ."

It flooded back.

He sat again, shaking his head. So *that* was what had happened.

For a while he simply sat there, letting his breathing normalise, his mind grow accustomed to the strangeness of his new situation.

They put us here, to keep DeVore from seeing us.

The thought of it awed him. To have such power. It was unthinkable.

Or almost so.

For a moment longer he sat there, his mind flicking over the possibilities, then he stood and hurried from the room.

It was time he did some work.

* * *

How large was nothingness? How wide? How deep?

Kim drew a circle on the screen, then drew a line through it, cutting it in half.

They were *within* the line. Beyond that he knew nothing. Or almost nothing.

He closed his eyes, concentrating. If this place existed, then it was governed by a set of physical laws. But how could such laws exist in a place that had no measurements?

Or was that so? Could it not be that their instruments were unreliable here?

The trouble was, he imagined this place to be not infinite, but like a tiny bag of velvet cloth, tied with delicate draw-strings at its neck. A minutely-small universe, designed for the pocket of a giant. Or a race of giants. The kings of infinite space.

Kim swivelled on his chair, facing the blackboard again.

Within the larger circle of the first equations – the six he had figured out – he had set a second circle, on which were written out the three equations Ebert had given him. They fitted perfectly, enhancing and enlarging the totality. He could see how – mathematically – it all connected up, but how did they work? How – physically – did the one relate to the other?

And, on a more practical level, how did one *enact* the equations? How use them and test them?

One could not accelerate them, as one could atoms, nor collect them in a tank, as one did photons.

Energy. That was the key. Any physical event required energy. And so here, surely?

Kim stood, looking about him at his laboratory, seeking some clue as to how to proceed, his eyes finally resting on the looking-glass at the far end of the room.

Doubleness. That was it. Mirrors.

Tuan Ti Fo had said as much. Though they seemed not to be moving, they were. In reality they were still heading for Eridani, their speed and direction unchanged.

And if that were so, then whatever he did here in the lab, even if it seemed to have no effect here, would have a genuine effect – if hidden – in his own universe.

Kim looked at the equations once again, staring and staring at them until his eyes blurred and the things took on the look of a mantra.

Jelka was right. It *did* look like the *Ywe Lung*.

A ring. A ring of power . . .

He laughed. Of course. It was *that* simple.

He didn't need a lot of energy. No more, in fact, than he'd need to power a simple circuit, for once the thing got going it would feed upon itself – an energy spiral, switching between the two universes, feeding upon the transition between them to power itself.

Feeding, yes, and growing.

Growing uncontrollably, unless . . .

Kim reached out to touch the three equations at the centre.

The problem was not *creating* the doorway, but limiting its size, for this process, once begun, had no natural controls. And that was where the second set of equations came in. They were there to set the limits of the thing – to create a web of power in which to ensnare the doorway.

A snare not to catch a rabbit but a rabbit-*hole*.

It was *Alice* all over again!

Grinning, Kim began to set up his equipment, seeing precisely what he needed for the task.

Two hours and it was done.

He watched it through special protective lenses, the arch of light – a half-circle like the hoop of a tiny rainbow – shimmering as it grew above the apparatus, getting bigger and bigger with each oscillation, tiny flames flickering within that glowing ring, until – *snap!* – nothing.

Kim laughed. It worked! The snare worked!

He felt a shiver go right through him at the thought of what he'd done. What he'd seen was only half of what had been there. But the other half – half of that ever-growing spiral – had protruded elsewhere, in another universe entirely.

A hole. He'd made a hole. A gateway between universes. And if he made it large enough, he could step through, into another reality.

"Did you see that, Master Tuan?" he asked, speaking to the air. "Did you see that?"

* * *

Ebert groaned and rolled over. Someone was shaking him awake.

"Hans! Hans! Wake up! I've something to show you?"

"Kim?" He put his hand to the tiny panel on his chest, activating his eyes. As they rose up into the air, to take up their positions above his head, so he saw Kim standing there, a broad smile splitting his face.

"Are you all right?" he asked, sitting up.

"Never better," Kim answered. "But come. I want to show you what I've made."

He stared at Kim. "Then it works."

"Like a dream."

Ebert was quiet a moment, then. "Have you thought about it, Kim . . . I mean, about what this means? About how it will change things?"

Kim's smile faded. "The truth is, since I knew it was possible, I've thought of little else. If *I* can do it, then *everyone* can do it. And if everyone can do it . . ."

"Do we all become gods?"

Kim stared back at him. "What do you mean?"

"Only that we're men, not gods. And these powers . . ."

But Kim was adamant. "We can't back away from this, Hans. We can't refuse this knowledge. That's what the Seven did. They tried to put an end to change, and look what happened! We can't go back. We have to go forward, whatever the consequences."

"Is that what you believe?"

"I do. Besides, I sense we're not the first to pass along this road; to come to this gate and seek admittance. Old Tuan, for certain has travelled it before us."

"And DeVore?"

At that Kim shrugged. "What DeVore is is dark to me as yet, but Master Tuan I trust, as I trust Jelka and yourself. It was Tuan, remember, who found me when I was lost."

"And I," Hans said, nodding his agreement.

"Then let us go. My cruiser is waiting up above. We can be in Kalevala within the hour."

"All right," Hans answered, smiling now, his blind eyes sparkling mischievously. "But first let me rinse the sleep from my eyes. If I'm to be a god, I'd like to see clearly where I'm headed."

* * *

In the hours between his first experiment and this, Kim had built a bigger, more permanent version of his apparatus.

Six powerful horseshoe-shaped electromagnets formed one half of it, arranged in a kind of ladder, in steadily decreasing size, like the levels of a loosely-linked Tower of Babel, or the spinal column of some strange metallic creature. Facing them, like a mirror image, were a second, identical set. In the gap between, their faint traces reminding Ebert of sunlit water-drops on a thread, were six lines of laser light that zipped back and forth between two lines of silver studs on twin generators.

All in all, it had the look of a musical stave.

Looking closer, Ebert saw that there were, in fact, twelve threads, for each thread was a double thread of light.

Ebert gestured towards them. "Why are they twinned?"

"They oscillate," Kim said, waggling his finger as if to demonstrate. "When it's functioning properly, each of the six pulses switches from one thread to the other two hundred times a second. In effect, the whole thing resonates like a plucked harp."

"And the electromagnets?"

Kim smiled, then, donning his protective glasses, reached out to touch the switch. "Watch . . ."

As the lights dimmed, the electromagnets began to hum.

At first, nothing, then, like a tiny whirlwind, a spiralling cone of light began to grow in the space between and just above the tips of the two magnet-towers, burning with a searing brilliance, a fine needle of light vanishing into the blackness above.

Then, with a suddenness that was shocking, the air above the needle split, a circle of crystal clear air opening in the darkness. And about that crystal circle was a tiny ring of fire.

Moment by moment that circle grew, its edge oscillating to the same fast flickering rhythm as all else.

For a moment Ebert stared through the gap, seeing, on the far side, another place, so like to the room in which they stood, that it could easily have been its mirror image.

And then – *snap!* – it ended.

Ebert shuddered. His nerve ends trembled. In that final moment before the light had died, he had seen himself there in the room, staring back at him, and beside him, Kim, or someone who looked a lot like Kim.

"*Mirrors . . .*"

Kim nodded, then pressed the pad to raise the lights again.

"It's us, or as near to us as makes any difference. But that's how it has to be, if you think of it, Hans. There must be endless universes, one next to another, pressed close like the flimsy skins of an onion. And the nearest will be very similar, while those further away will begin to differ."

"Hold on," Ebert said, "you mean that was another reality?"

"Yes," Kim said. "Or, to be accurate, another no-space, but one so similar to ours that the me that's there is experimenting just as I'm experimenting – holding this self-same conversation with you even as I'm holding it."

"Then what's the use of that? If it's the same . . ."

Kim laughed. "Don't you see? If we can cross through into that other universe, we can cross through into others. Indeed, we can't help but do so. The bigger the gate, the more layers of the skin peel back. We could set up a whole series of gates, like a tunnel, and travel into a universe where the difference *is* significant. Or . . ."

But Ebert raised a hand, as if to calm a fretful horse. "Wo-ah. One thing at a time. You say we can travel through these holes? But they're tiny."

"Then we build a huge great big version of it and suspend it in the air – a massive wheel of fire – and fly through it."

Ebert laughed. "Now I know you're mad. Fly *through* it? You mean, in the craft you've made?"

"Why not?"

"Because it has no hull, no engine. When you came out the other side, you'd emerge into a freezing vacuum."

Kim smiled. "You're thinking that the apparatus has to be outside of the field, framing it, but it doesn't. It can generate a field about itself. That's the beauty of it. At the same time you can generate heat and oxygen inside the field."

"Yes, but even if we can get through, how does that help us? We'll still be out here, between the stars."

"Yes, but in one of those universes, I've *solved* the problem. I've *made* a ship that can fold space. Or a machine that can do it, anyway. In one of those universes we *can* get back. Not a year from now, nor even in a month, but immediately."

"Now?"

"Well, not right now. But soon. Just as soon as I've re-jigged the craft."

"Re-jigged it?"

Kim beamed. "You saw Ikuro's sketch. That's *it*. I realise it now. That's the little beauty that'll take us back to Chung Kuo!"

* * *

Kim was standing at the pool's edge, looking out across the shimmering surface of the water, thinking about what he'd said to Ebert and the sheer difficulty of doing what he'd claimed he could do, when he became aware that there was someone else in the dome with him.

He looked across, then smiled. "I wondered how long it would be before you came."

Tuan Ti Fo stepped over and stood beside him, looking out across the pool. "We have lived this moment before, Kim. This and many other moments. But the time is coming when all things change, when *nothing* will be predictable."

"How do you mean?"

Old Tuan's smile was filled with a thousand years of patience. "You, and many of your other selves, are about to change the rules by which man lives. All creatures, if they are intelligent enough, come to this point. Beyond it they must make new rules for themselves, or abandon their quest for knowledge."

"You heard, then, what I said to Hans."

"I heard and understand. You must go on. It is in your nature, Kim. But not all of your species are like you."

"My species?" Kim laughed. "You talk as if you yourself were not a man, Master Tuan."

Tuan turned his head, looking steadily at Kim. "You wish to see my real form, Kim?"

"I . . . Kim shivered. "I'm not sure."

"Oh, it would not shock you, Kim." He laughed gently. "Indeed, it was more of a shock to me, remembering what I was. I have been a man so long, you see. Much longer than I ever expected."

"Then that tale of your birth . . ."

"Was a metaphor. A way of making you understand. DeVore *is* my twin, but not as you humans conceive the word."

"A doppleganger, then?"

"My dark self? Yes, but more than that. Much much more. He was not merely my twin but my mate, the kindred of my soul. So it was, long ago. There was a time when whatever pained him would pain me and vice versa. But we have been apart so long now that I but feel only the faintest echo of what he feels. And he . . . well, I think he has come to feel nothing. Nothing but the dark wind blowing at his back."

"What do you mean?"

"We are not creatures like you, Kim. We were not born and bred in the sunlight, but in the vast spaces between the stars. Such powers as we have were forged there – coded into us, if you like. You do not sense it, for you have not developed the means of sensing it, but there is a dark wind blowing behind reality, behind it and underneath it. Oh, and within it and around it, too. A nothingness. DeVore – forgive me if I call him that and not his true name – senses that. He feels it still, at times. But he has forgotten what it is."

"And what *is* it, this dark wind?"

"It is the nullity that destroys all. The eroding force."

"Entropy, you mean?"

"No. It is a force that, if allowed into this universe of yours, would destroy it in an instant, just as, in those first nanoseconds of your universe, all was created."

Like a light switch in a vast room, Kim thought. *Switch it on and you have Creation and all its vast complexities. Switch it off and Nothing. Not even darkness. For how can the dark exist without the light*?

"A dreadful pun, Kim, but true."

Kim laughed. "You see all and hear all . . . even my thoughts. Why, then, do you need me?"

"Because it was decided thus, long ago."

"Decided? By whom?"

"By ourselves. We met and . . . *debated* it."

"There are more like you?"

"Oh, many more."

"And DeVore?"

"You think he is unique? You think this is the only universe this is happening in?"

"It's . . . difficult. Getting one's mind around the concept of endless realities, endless struggles."

"It is a great war. And the outcome will determine the very shape of existence."

"A war?"

"Yes. A war of directions, not unlike the war you yourselves have been fighting these many years. But our war has been going on for long millennia. When you were yet apes, we had long pursued this struggle."

"But now the time has come, eh? The time to decide it all?"

Old Tuan nodded.

Kim hesitated a long while, then. "I find that strange. My mind . . . well, *rebels* against it. Why now? And why me? I'm too small, too . . . *insignificant*"

"You remember the vision you were given, Kim, down in the Clay? The web of light?"

Kim nodded.

"Do you think just anyone is given that?"

Kim stared at him, astonished. "*You* gave that to me?"

"Not I. I, remember, was asleep. Yet it *was* given. And, when I woke, I saw the reason for it. Yes, and I saw clearly what you would do with that vision. Up to a point."

"When the rules change."

Tuan Ti Fo smiled, then gave a single nod.

"So?" he asked, after a moment. "Would you like to meet the real me, or are you still not sure?"

Kim grinned. "You know the answer, Master Tuan."

"Of course. Yet politeness is its own virtue, neh?"

"Then show me, please, Master Tuan," Kim said, and bowed, his hands pressed together, palm to palm, in the ancient gesture of respect.

"Then get suited up, Kim Ward. I cannot show you here."

* * *

Jelka met Kim in the corridor outside the airlock.

"Kim? What's going on?"

Kim hesitated, then. "Get suited up. We have an appointment with an old friend."

Recognising the teasing tone, she laughed. "Friend? What friend?"

"He calls himself Old Tuan, but he has other names, I'm sure."

"You're meeting Master Tuan again?"

"I've met him, and talked. And now I am to meet him again. As he truly is."

Slowly Jelka's eyes widened. "You mean . . .?"

Kim nodded. "Get ready, my love. Old Tuan is waiting to reveal himself."

* * *

There was a disturbance in the air above the dome. It was as if the darkness blew a kiss. And then Old Tuan appeared. Or rather, something strange and yet familiar.

Kim stared at it a while, then gave a single laugh.

"You sensed it," Tuan's voice boomed down at them. "Part of you always knew."

Jelka took Kim's arm. He could feel a faint trembling in her.

"You must not be afraid," Kim said, staring up at the giant figure in the sky above them. "It is only Tuan Ti Fo."

She was silent a moment, then. "I see why you had to mask your true form, Master Tuan. It is . . . fearsome."

The giant spider, its lower abdomen larger than Kalevala itself, its metallic-looking, jointed legs like massive cranes, quivered.

"It is very strange," Tuan said, "You humans consider your form – bipedal, humanoid – the norm, yet this shape I now wear existed long before your own, and when all other forms die out, ours will remain. It is the most common in all the universes."

Kim smiled. "I have no doubt, Master Tuan. Indeed, I'm sure you find us ugly."

Tuan Ti Fo laughed at that, a booming, rasping laughter. "I've grown accustomed to it, let us say. But you, Kim, you've always had an affinity for us. That too, it seems, was coded. Perhaps it's even why you were chosen."

"You see that far, Master Tuan?"
"I see so far . . ."
". . . and no further." Kim laughed. "So what now, old friend?"
"Ahead lies a time of waiting, and frustration and failure."
"Failure, Master Tuan?"
"Oh, yes. Did you really think you were there yet, Kim?" The great spider's voice boomed in Kim's helmet. "You have but begun to toy with the potential of what you have uncovered. The real task – the using of what you have found – will not be so easy."
"But the equations . . ."
"Are but a beginning. A framework for what follows. But do not give up, Kim. Though I cannot see that far ahead, I sense you will triumph in the end. If anyone can succeed, it will be you."
Kim frowned. "You say you cannot see, Master Tuan. I don't understand. I thought you could see everything up to the change."
"So I can. But ahead of us things grow unclear. The single path of vision splits and splits again, until it is like staring down a hall of distorting mirrors. In some one thing happens, in another something different."
"So it is not written then that this will come about?"
"Not at all. Only that you would come to the gate. And knock. But whether you will enter . . ."
Old Tuan shrugged. At least, it seemed a shrug.
"And now?"
"Now I must go. Kim . . . Jelka . . ."
"Master Tuan . . .?"
But he was gone. The darkness above Kalevala was empty.
Kim turned, looking to Jelka, then drew her close, holding her tightly to him. Only minutes ago he had been elated – full of an optimism that seemed unbounded – but now . . .
Now he was afraid. Failure. Old Tuan had seen him fail.
But I made *a gateway.*
A small one. Easily controlled. A tiny hole that was gone within seconds. A toy.
Making the real thing would be much harder.
"You say you saw it, my love," he said, moving his face back and staring up at Jelka.
"I saw a wheel of fire burning in the sky above Kalevala, and you and Sampsa laughing."
"Then why did Master Tuan not see it?"
"Maybe he did."
"Yes. And maybe he saw other things. Things too horrible to mention. What if your dream is not the only dream?"
Jelka smiled, then placed her palm softly against his cheek. "Then we shall find that out, neh, my love? But I shall be here with you, whichever way chance falls."

PART FOUR – SPRING 2243

AND THREE DARK FLAMES

"'We see,' said he, 'like men who are dim of sight,
Things that are distant from us; just so far,
We still have gleams of the All-Guider's light.

But when these things draw near, or when they are,
Our intellect is void, and your world's state
Unknown, save some one bring us news from there.

Hence thou wilt see that all we can await
Is the stark death of knowledge in us, then
When time's last hour shall shut the future's gate.'"

– Dante, The Divine Comedy, Hell, Canto X

CHAPTER·17

FLOWERS

Daniel stepped up onto the ledge of rock, then gazed down the length of the valley, his eyes pausing at the stark, dividing line between the green and the black. That blackness was an ugly scar that stretched for two kilometres east, like a fighter's belt about the waist of the world. The rich greenness of the valley tumbled down towards it with the full weight of Spring, only to falter.

Devore had poisoned the land. Burned it, then sprayed it. And now nothing grew. Plants stretched their roots out into that blackness, only to see them shrivel up and die, while pollen, drifting in the sunlit air, hissed as it touched that barren strip, flickering briefly, like leaves in a fire, transformed to smoke and air.

The strip had not existed when last they'd been out here. It was four, maybe five days old at most.

Daniel turned, looking back at the other members of the patrol. In their heavy suits they looked like they were on an alien planet. Not that that was so far from the truth these days.

The two boys were staring past him at the blackness, their eyes wide, their lips parted, while the girl was looking at him. Staring at him, as if to read his thoughts.

As always, he thought, looking away, disconcerted by her constant attention. What did she want, always staring so?

It was awkward in the protective suits, and hot, but necessary. Despite Devore's efforts, the floraforms were rife in this part of the mountains. It made no sense to take chances.

"Okay," he said, speaking for the first time in a long while. "Let's go down there. See what's to be seen."

They followed without a word, keeping a tight formation as they made their way down through the trees, their eyes searching the nearby trees and rocks, lingering on the long beds of brightly-coloured flowers that lay between the tall young trunks.

It all looked so innocent, so paradisaical, yet one never knew. Things changed so fast out here. Even the insects were not always what they seemed. There was not a single thing the floraforms did not know how to mimic.

They came to a stream. It ran swiftly between the rocks, a crystal clear torrent rushing down from the mountain slopes high above, its flow swollen by the spring melt. Daniel stared at it a while, then jumped across. An easy leap, even for a child. Yet even as he landed, his instincts twitched. Something was wrong here.

He turned full circle, looking, trying to place what it was. Nothing. Only the peacefulness of the morning, the cool, clean rush of the water down the gully. He watched the girl jump the stream, and then the first of the boys.

"What is it?"

The other boy, Anders, had held back. He had turned, looking back into the shadows between the trees.

"I don't know," he answered quietly, his attention focused on that patch of darkness just in front of him. "I thought something moved."

Was that it? Had he sensed that peripheral movement?

"Wait there," Daniel said, meaning to jump back and investigate, yet even as he took the first step, the whole of the far side seemed to shimmer and close up, as if a wall had formed, running tight against the edge of the gully – a great wall of leaf and flower that stretched up into the treetops.

Daniel blinked and took a backward step.

There was a stifled cry and then a sudden thrashing sound. The wall of verdancy trembled then was still.

It was silent again. Peaceful. The sunlight beat down upon the rushing stream. Like a dream, the wall shimmered and was gone. Beyond where it had been was only tree and shadow. There was no sign of the boy.

Daniel shivered. He did not know which was worse, this living green or the annihilating blackness of DeVore. Both gave no quarter.

What made it worse was that one could not fight these things – not in any meaningful way. They were not like DeVore's mechanoids. One could not simply blast them into oblivion and move on. Blow a floraform apart and it would simply reconstitute itself in a different form. It was mutability gone mad. And even when one burned and poisoned them, still they thrived, as DeVore was finding out. One could cut great swathes through the Wilds and still it made no difference, for after a while they would ingest and change the poisons used against them. And then the black would blossom with new life.

"Come on," he said, his sudden decisiveness bringing them all out of the daze they had fallen into. "Let's do what we have to do."

He knew they were scared now. They had not lost any of their fellows in quite that way before. It was as if the floraforms were learning day by day. Experimenting with their powers.

Them? Or It?

That was the trouble. You never knew whether there were a whole number of different floraforms, or just one single creature. But one thing was no longer in doubt. The floraforms were intelligent.

Coming out into the floor of the valley, Daniel paused a while, letting them rest in the shade. In an hour the sun would be directly above them and, unless they travelled beneath the tree cover, their suits would begin to feel like ovens.

"Daniel?"

He turned, looking towards where the girl sat on a small rock watching him. "Yes?"

"Is it always going to be like this?"

Daniel shrugged. The truth was, he could not answer her. If he had, it would have been to express his doubt, or rather, his firm conviction that their days were numbered. No matter what they did, the floraforms were spreading, day by day, week by week. Already the whole of the southlands were theirs. Nothing human remained down there. Africa, it was said, was one writhing mass of green.

Full circle, he thought, remembering what he'd read and imagining a world before humanity, before even the insects came. A green world. A world of silence and sunlight and growth.

And us? What happens to us? To humankind?

He wanted to ask the question, to have someone answer him and reassure him, but he was afraid they would merely mirror his darkest thoughts.

"Okay," he said. "Let's take our samples and get back."

Yet even as he turned to make his way towards the edge, towards that place where the green tide broke upon the black, he saw, through the trees, the boy he'd lost.

Daniel stood, rooted to the spot, waiting as the boy turned and made his way back, the sample case held out before him.

"Here," the boy's voice said, a ghostly echo of itself, "is this what you wanted?"

The boy was green. Where his eyes had been were tiny buds. Where his tongue once was now flicked a tiny stamen. His hands, where they poked from the gloveless sleeves of the suit, were like rolled leaves.

Slowly Daniel shook his head. If it wanted to take him now it could do it. Easily. In a moment. Yet still it stood there, holding out the sample case, its bud-like eyes sensing him.

"What do you see?" he asked.

The boy smiled, the inside of its mouth like glistening sap. "Only the green."

Daniel nodded. "And us?"

For a moment longer it stood there. Then, as if a great sigh had shuddered through the valley, it shimmered, scattering like a pile of windblown leaves.

Daniel stared at the case where it lay on the ground two paces from where he stood. Unlike the boy, the case was real. He stooped, examining it. The sample tubes were full.

He frowned, then, slipping the leather strap over his shoulder, turned to face the others. They were frightened. He could see at a glance just how frightened they were.

"Come," he said, no longer masking the tiredness he felt from his voice. "Let's get back."

* * *

The cruiser came down slowly, blowing cut grass and petals across the well-kept lawn. The back door to the thatched cottage was open, yet the shutters were pulled across at every window, and as DeVore stepped down from the craft, the engines whining down into silence behind him, he had the feeling that the house was empty.

Where was he? Out fishing on the river? In the fields?

DeVore walked through the house, going from room to room, his black leather boots creaking on the polished boards. The wardrobes were empty of clothes. Ben's journals were missing from the workroom. He had gone. There was no doubting it. He *had* gone.

"Damn him!"

DeVore stood in the ancient dining room, looking about him at the panelled oak walls, then nodded to himself. He would destroy this. He would destroy it all, in fact. If Ben would not stand with him, then *nothing* was worth saving.

He strode out onto the sunlit lawn and gestured to his pilot. At once the engines came to life again.

For a moment DeVore stood there, watching the rose bushes dance violently in the wind from the engines' exhaust, then, with a sneer, he made a dismissive gesture at it all.

Games, that's all it ever was. Just games.

As the cruiser lifted, he took over the controls. At five hundred metres, he steadied the craft and turned it to face the cottage. With a smile he released two rockets, watching them streak down into the hillside.

The craft rocked gently in the wind of the detonation. His smile broadened. There was gas on board, and a quantity of the special poisons. Turning to his pilot, he ordered him to mask up, then, donning his own mask, he began the sweep, the deadly mist trailing the cruiser as it progressed up the western bank of the Dart, then back again. And where the mist fell, the green shrivelled up and died.

As he came out over the town, he banked the craft, firing off two more rockets into the old hotel, then flew through the plume of smoke, laughing now, beginning to enjoy himself.

Games. The kind of games that gods allow themselves.

He sat back, letting his pilot take over, feeling the form within his form relax. Right now he only guessed at what that shape within him was.

Sensed it as the pupa senses the unfolding form within. But soon he would know. Soon he would wake and *know*.

Meanwhile he played these games with lesser forms.

"Turn back," he said, as the pilot began to climb. "I want to see it all. But take us up. High enough so I can see it at a glance."

From two kilometres above, the Domain stretched out like a tiny map beneath him, dark plumes of smoke roiling across its surface. And beneath that misted darkness was the blackness of the now-poisoned land, the blue surface of the Dart dividing it. Two burned lips about that mirror smooth blueness.

DeVore laughed. "Serves the fucker right!"

Then, wondering briefly where Shepherd could have gone, he gestured to his man to take them back. It was time to face things. Time to make big decisions.

* * *

Emily stood on the high balcony, looking out across the snow-covered slopes towards the south. Daniel was late. He should have been back two hours past, but still there was no sign of him.

Her gloved hands tapped the frosted metal rail absently, her breath pluming in the crisp air, then she turned and ducked back inside, impatient now. She would send a patrol out to search for him, for if darkness fell and he was still outside . . .

She stopped and leaned against the sloping wall of the narrow corridor, her heart beating rapidly, her chest rising and falling.

He'll be okay. You know he will.

The trouble was, she didn't know. Since Michael had died she had lost the confidence she'd once possessed. Besides, the world was changing hour by hour, becoming less human. That was, if it had ever truly been human.

There had been a time – at the height of the great world-spanning empire of Chung Kuo – when it might have been possible to claim that mankind had triumphed over the elements. Back then, inside their mile-high cities, men had been the masters of their environment. Not a breeze had entered their domain unless they willed it, not an animal or insect. They had lived in splendid isolation, independent from the world that had bred them – like laboratory specimens, cut off from any harmful influence. Yet harm there'd been – a purely human harm, a corruption – and, like an infection, that corruption had spread among the levels of their great global city. Year by year the great experiment had faltered, until it could be sustained no longer. In a frenzy of blood-letting Chung Kuo had ripped itself apart. There had been long years of death and destruction, of widows grieving and orphans weeping. It had been an awful, hideous time.

What, then, if the flowers inherited the earth?

"If it were only so simple . . ."

Emily walked on. The trouble was, these were no simple flowers. Indeed, if their latest tests were right, they weren't even flowers at all. They were as human – and *inhuman* – as man himself.

Emily smiled, then stepped into her office. Seating herself behind the desk, she leaned forward and touched the communicator pad.

"Gunnar? Are you there?"

There was a moment's pause, then the young man's voice filled the room. "Yes, Ma'am?"

"Daniel's late. I want a search party sent out. Lin Pei knows the details."

"Yes, Ma'am."

The communicator clicked off. She sat back, taking a long breath, then reached out and took the map book from the side. It was an old thing, from before the time of cities, and had all of the old alpine villages marked on it. Opening it, she flicked through to the map of Luzern and its surrounds and spread it out on the desk, studying the marks she'd written on it.

There was little now that the floraforms did not control. In a year, maybe less, they would control it all. Unless . . .

She raised her head. *Unless what? Unless a miracle occurred?*

Publicly she did not allow herself to be despondent about the future, but privately, as now, she had to admit, struggle seemed futile.

All her life she had fought. Even when she had been with Mender Lin – even then she had countered the apparent futility of events and *done* something, taking those orphaned boys and giving them a life. But this time it seemed there was nothing she could do. The green tide swept all before it, transforming all it touched, feeding upon what opposed it.

"Mother?"

She started at the unexpected voice, then touched the comset's pad again.

"Yes, Lin Pei?"

"It's Daniel, mother. He's back."

"But . . ." Her relief was mixed with puzzlement. He couldn't have got back yet; she would have seen him, surely? Unless he came from the north.

Emily frowned. "Where are you, Pei?"

"In the corridor outside Isolation."

She nodded to herself. "Okay. I'll come down." A pause, then, "Is everything all right, Pei?"

Silence, then. "I'm not sure. Anders didn't come back."

"Wait there. I'm coming."

* * *

Lin Pei greeted her outside Isolation, then stood back as she looked through the toughened glass window. Daniel was inside, along with young Jurgen and the girl, Siri. They were naked, their arms raised away from their sides. One of the morphs – Amenon, it looked like from the back – was spraying them. Not that it did a lot of good, but they felt they had to take some kind of precaution against the floraforms.

Ritual, she thought. *It's all mere ritual now. They could take us when they liked, if the truth be told.*

At once the answering thought – the thought that always came to her mind when she got to this point – filled her head.

Then why don't they? Why don't they simply end it, quickly and painlessly? Why tease us and torment us in this fashion?

She didn't know. Moreover, it worried her that she didn't know.

Activating the microphone, she spoke.

"Daniel?"

"Yes, mother?"

Emily smiled. Mother. Yes, she was mother to them all. But for how much longer?

"What happened out there?"

Daniel gave a little shrug. His face seemed momentarily pained. "I spoke to It."

"It?"

"The floraform. I'm fairly certain now. It's one being. It took Anders. Transformed him."

"Ahh . . ."

"And then it used him. To speak to me. And to give me the samples we wanted."

"It *what*?"

Daniel nodded. "That's what I thought. But I think I understand it now. It knows what we're doing. It *knows* we're analysing the poisons DeVore is using against it. I think it's its way of letting us know that nothing we do will affect it. Whatever we do, it will adapt itself and counter it."

"And yet it let you go."

"Yes." Daniel's eyes slid away, then met hers again. "That I don't understand. Not yet."

"No. Nor I." She shook her head, then, "Amenon, forget that. Daniel, get dried off and back in here. We need to talk."

* * *

The scene on the screen was familiar to Daniel. It showed the great parade square in Heidelberg, the marching columns of uniformed boys swelling into the distance as the camera panned across, then focused on the three figures on the balcony.

Daniel gasped.

"Yes," Emily said, from where she sat beside him in the darkness. She covered his hand with her own. "It shocked me when I first saw it."

For a moment he simply stared, taking in the sight of himself, standing there between DeVore and Horacek as, below, the young boys cheered and cried his name.

Daniel . . . Daniel . . . Daniel . . .

A copy. DeVore had had him copied.

Daniel swallowed. "When did this come?"

"Two days back."

His head turned. "Then why . . .?"

"I wanted to think about it. I wanted to consider whether it would do more harm to show you this than to keep it from you."

"But . . ." Daniel thought about that a moment, then gave a tiny nod. "I see. And you decided I ought to know. Why?"

She squeezed his hand. "Keep watching."

There was a set of double doors behind the three men. As the camera moved past them, it closed in on the doors even as they opened.

"There," Emily said, feeling the same frisson of surprise – and shock – she'd had the first time she'd seen it. Herself. But no longer young. Herself as she was now. Grey-haired, her flesh lined with age.

Daniel was quiet a moment, then he nodded. "So he's finally going to come for us."

"Yes."

She was glad. He understood. It made it that much simpler.

The film ran on.

"It's strange," he said finally. "That creature on the balcony. I can't help feeling that that's the real me. At least, the person DeVore meant me to be. The one who *ought* to have emerged from the camps. But something went wrong. As with his morphs."

"Yes," she said, smiling now. "It's very strange, don't you think? How good comes from such evil. And not once, and not always, but . . . well, occasionally. Enough to make things unpredictable."

"Like the floraforms, you think?"

It wasn't what she had been thinking, but now that he'd mentioned it . . .

"I don't know. Maybe. Maybe that's why they let you go. Because they sensed something in you. Maybe it means we can come to some kind of arrangement with them."

Daniel turned, his face halved by the light from the screen, and stared at her. "Do you think so?"

She shrugged. "I don't know. I don't know anything any more. Maybe DeVore's right to try to poison them."

"But you don't think so."

Emily nodded. "It makes no sense, when you think of it. If the only way to fight the floraforms is to destroy the earth, then what's the point? If they can't survive, then we sure as hell can't."

He smiled. "So we go under. Become transformed."

"Maybe."

"Without a fight?"

"We've tried fighting. It didn't work."

"Then maybe you're right. Maybe we have to come to an arrangement. Live alongside the floraforms."

"You think they want that, Daniel?"

"It's possible."

"And DeVore?"

Emily sat back slightly. "I don't know what DeVore wants. I used to think I did, but I'm not so sure any more."

She leaned forward, switching on the light. Daniel was watching her closely now.

"He'll fight," he said. "You know he will. He doesn't like competition."

"No . . ." Emily was thoughtful a while, then. "Do you like them?"

"Like them?"

"The floraforms. The girl, Siri . . . She was speaking to me about how you look at them. She thought . . . well, that maybe you liked them."

Daniel laughed. "She's always watching me, that one. Like she's spying on me. Sometimes . . ."

He stopped dead, then looked away.

Emily frowned. "Go on."

"Well, sometimes I even think that maybe – just maybe – she's working for DeVore. It's silly, I know, seeing how she's lived here all her life, but . . ."

He stopped. Emily was shaking her head, a faint amusement in her eyes. "Don't you see, Daniel?"

"See?"

"She's in love with you."

She saw the surprise in his face and smiled inwardly.

"No," he said, as if that simple denial could alter things. Yet his face was clouded now. He was so quick to understand things. Even this.

"You want me to speak to her? To reassign her, maybe?"

"No. No . . . I'll speak to her. Tell her . . ."

She saw how he came to the gap. What *would* he tell her?
"Think it over," she said gently. "If you need my help, just say."
He let out his breath, then shook his head. "I didn't know."
No, she thought. *But now you do.*

* * *

Beth was laughing; giggling uncontrollably, as if she would burst apart with happiness. With her half-toddling run, she tried in vain to get away from her father, but he was on her, swooping suddenly, lifting her up in his great big hands and holding her high, high above his head and whirling her about.

"Stop! Sto-op!" she shrieked breathlessly, but he wasn't going to stop, and besides, she didn't really want him to stop. Around and around she went, her head spinning now, the ground turning and turning beneath her until, with a swoop that made her head feel funny, she plummeted down, landing soft as a pillow on the grass.

She lay there, eyes closed, feeling her head go round and round, still giggling, the sound of her father's breathing mixed with the ebb and flow of the tide on the shingle beach below the garden.

"Beth! Beth! Do you want a drink?"

Her eyes popped open. Her mother was standing at the half-door to the kitchen, looking out at her, a tumbler of juice held out in one hand. Closer, almost upon her, her father's face, staring down at her, was smiling.

"Go on," he said. "We'll play some more in a minute."

Beth rolled over, onto her back, staring up at the pure blue, cloudless sky, then pulled herself up. For a moment she felt as if she'd tumble back. Gravity tugged at her like a hand. The ground whirled. And then, slowly, very slowly, it grew still. She jumped up and ran, arms out, towards the house.

The drink was fresh and sweet, the glass misted. Ice cubes chinked about its edge. She drank deeply, then wiped a hand across her mouth and looked up.

Her mother was looking out, past her, toward the garden's end. Beth turned, following her gaze. Her father stood there at the fence, his arms leaning loosely over the wooden bar as he watched the tide slowly turn.

They had gone swimming earlier, when the tide had been coming in, her hand in his as they leapt high to greet each incoming wave, the cold water splintering about them, taking her breath, even as she squealed with excitement. She shivered now at the thought, then looked down, poking her index finger into the cool, clear depth of the drink, twirling the ice cubes round and round and round.

Tomorrow was her third birthday. And her father had promised her a special surprise.

She grinned at the thought, then looked up again. Her mother was looking down at her now; looking down with those deep brown eyes and smiling.

"Tomorrow," her mother said, as if she could see each thought in her head like one could see the crabs scuttling about at the bottom of a rock pool. "We'll have a cake and everything."

Beth's grin widened. *Tomorrow . . .*

* * *

The latest map confirmed it. The stuff was spreading like a plague, despite the stepping up of his containment strategy.

"Fuck it!"

DeVore crumpled up the map and cast it aside, then stood, glowering at his advisors who waited like so many puppets – the strings that held their heads upright severed – about the half-lit War Room.

It was over. He knew it for a certainty. There was no way of destroying the floraforms, not without destroying it all. Lashing out, he caught the nearest of his men with the back of his hand, the square-cut ring on his second finger gouging a chunk of flesh from the man's cheek.

The man went down, groaning, clutching his injured face. DeVore watched him a moment, his eyes dispassionate, then began to pace the room slowly, a sudden calmness overwhelming the anger, the frustration he'd been feeling. A clear, *pure* feeling.

He laughed. Heads lifted then quickly tucked back down.

"I'll kick the fucking legs away, one by one!"

Yes. But first he had to win the game, else it would seem like pique – like a novice who, seeing he had lost, threw board, pieces and all into the air.

No. He would play out the endgame. He would destroy the woman. Would kill her. Or better yet, have her *then* kill her.

He grinned, as a hyena grins, then looked about him.

"Gentlemen, I need your help."

* * *

Meg stood in the doorway, looking on as Ben knelt beside the bed, cooing a lullaby to their almost-sleeping daughter.

He had changed so much this last year. Changed beyond recognition. Gone was the coldness, the distance.

Yes, and the thoughtless cruelty, the madness, the darkness behind each day.

She shivered, her love for him so full at that moment that she wanted to go across and kiss him. To hold him and *show* him what she was feeling.

It was like the day outside.

Happy. For the first time in her life she was happy, without a cloud in the sky. And Ben . . . Ben too was happy. Transformed. Now he spent his time worrying over simple things, like whether the roof leaked, or whether they'd enough to eat. He farmed and fished and made repairs to this old stone house.

And sketched . . .

Yes, he still sketched. But that was all that remained of his old self. The rest had fallen away, or rotted, like the equipment in the barn.

She watched him reach out and gently stroke his sleeping daughter's brow, the look of love in his face so intense that she bit her lip. Where had *that* come from? With Tom . . . well, Tom might as well have been another's child for all the notice Ben had taken of him.

She turned away, going out into the kitchen, then stopped, facing the wall of sketches. Twenty, thirty sketches, and every one of Beth. Beth laughing. Beth thoughtful. Beth laying on the study floor, playing. Beth sleeping. Beth, always Beth. No other subject for him now.

Ironic . . .

Meg ran her fingers through her hair, then turned. Dinner. She ought to be making dinner. But suddenly, from nowhere, the darkness had descended.

And there I was thinking it had gone away for good.

She frowned, surprised by the suddenness of the change. It was as if a cloud had drifted between her and the sun.

And yet nothing – *nothing* – had changed.

Except that she had reminded herself of what lay beyond them. Except that she'd forgotten for a moment to forget.

The world was ending. The world was fucking ending and here she was, playing Adam and Eve with her brother and their child, and . . .

"Meg?"

He came across, his face concerned, his fingers gently wiping the tears from her cheeks.

"Hey . . . what is it?"

But she couldn't tell him. Couldn't spoil it all with her *realisations*. The nowness of this, that had to be enough, even if it ended tomorrow. The *nowness*. It was what she'd wanted, after all. What she'd *always* wanted.

She huffed out a sigh, then smiled. "I'm okay. Really, I . . ." She shrugged. "Just seeing you with her. It broke me up."

Ben smiled. "I love you, you know."

"I know."

"And I'm happy. You know that? Really happy. I . . ."

He paused, then shrugged. There was a look of wonder – of sheer astonishment on his face.

"*Yes*," she said softly, almost whispering the words, "*I know*."

* * *

The room was silent. A single lamp lit the board. In its pearled light DeVore's face leaned towards the pattern of white and black stones, studying the play.

For a long time he was still, then, reaching across, he slapped a stone down in *ch'u*, the West. Only then did he turn, acknowledging the presence of the messenger in the room.

"What is it?"

"Forgive me, Master, but there's a new prisoner in the cells."

DeVore raised an eyebrow. "There are *always* new prisoners. What makes this one so special?"

"It is Lin Lao."

DeVore felt a surge of pure elation at the name. "Lin Lao? Are you sure?"

"Yes, Master. His retinal patterns match the record."

DeVore turned back, looking at the board. The signs were clear. It was *his* moment. The tide of fate flowed with him. He stood, then bowed to his opponent. "Forgive me, Master Chung, but there is an urgent matter to attend to."

The old man bowed where he sat on the far side of the board.

"Please take your time," DeVore said, knowing that an eternity would not help him win the game. "I *shall* return."

"Master . . ."

* * *

"Where is she?"

"In the cells . . ."

"And where did you say you found her?"

"On the lower slopes. She seemed . . . lost."

Emily pulled her cloak tighter about her. It was cold in the lower levels, especially at this hour of the night, and she had not had time to dress properly.

"Okay. Let me see her."

Lin Pei shrugged. "She's . . . sleeping. Besides, I thought you would want to see what she was carrying."

"Carrying?"

Pei nodded. "On her back. The gods know how she managed to get this far with all that weighing her down."

Emily stared at her son a moment, then. "You'd best show me."

Lin Pei led the way, down the narrow corridor past the cells and on, to where the guards slept.

"Here?" she asked, surprised. Two guards slept in their bunks. Another looked up at her from where he was cleaning his boots.

In answer, Pei pointed to a stack of books that were piled in one corner beside a heavy steel-frame-and-canvas backpack.

Emily went across, then bent down and picked up one of the heavy, leather-bound volumes, standing again as she opened it.

"But these . . ."

"Are handwritten, yes. They're a history. A history of our world."

Emily nodded vaguely, but her attention was on what she was reading. After a moment she turned, her eyes wide with surprise. "This is like the thing Ward wrote, but . . . bigger, fuller."

Lin Pei nodded. "She claims that it's hers. That she wrote it."

Emily looked down at the stack of volumes. Why, there had to be at least thirty of the big, leather-bound books. As Lin Pei said, the gods knew how she had managed to carry them this far.

"What's her name?"

"She calls herself Hannah."

"Hannah?" Emily thought a moment, then shook her head. She knew no one of that name. "And does she say what she wants?"

"To see you. And to get these to safety."

"*Safety?*" Emily laughed at the thought. That was all they needed right now – a true history of a world about to be taken over by the floraforms. In a year, maybe less, all this – this long and patient effort – would be transformed. Would become part of the greater greenness of the world.

And history itself would end.

"You say she's sleeping?"

Lin Pei looked down, then met his mother's eyes again. "I called Surgeon Wu. I had him give her a sleeping draught. She looked exhausted."

She smiled at him. "You're getting soft, Pei."

There was a moment's alarm in his eyes before he saw that she was teasing him, and then he smiled. "No softer than you, mother. Had you seen the state she was in, you would have done the same."

She nodded. "You're a good man, Pei. Your father would have been proud of you."

He bowed his head, moved by her words.

"Well," she said, looking back at the book in her hand. "I'll speak to this Hannah in the morning. In the meantime I think I'll take this to bed with me."

Pei grimaced. "It is not cheerful reading, from what I've seen."

She looked up at him. "No, yet maybe we would not be in this mess had we come face to face with what we were. Knowledge is power, so they say."

"So they say."

They both laughed, the darker knowledge of their fate behind their laughter. They lived in shadows now, in darkening days. Their laughter was a candle against such darkness.

"Good night, Pei." Emily stepped across and, one hand gently holding the back of his head, kissed his brow. "Sweet dreams, my darling boy."

"The gods protect you," he answered, pecking her cheek. "And don't read too long. You need your sleep."

"I won't."

Turning, she made her way back along the corridor, the book held tightly in her hand, a burning curiosity filling her.

Fate. Fate was playing tricks with them all in these final days, like a player moving the stones.

And in her head she saw the woman struggling along a mountain path, the heavy backpack weighing her down, and wondered why.

* * *

Daniel was dozing, not quite asleep, yet dreaming, when the door to his room opened and someone crept in. There was the rustle of something falling to the floor, then someone – warm and quite definitely female, slipped in beside him.

Surprised, he edged back slightly, then sat, turning on the bedside lamp.

"Siri?"

She looked up at him, the sheet pulled up about her neck, an uncertain smile on her lips.

"What are you doing here?"

It was, he knew, a silly, senseless question. He knew what she was doing there. One did not come to a young man's bed in the middle of the night – one did not cast off one's clothes and slip in beside him – if you wanted only to talk. But her simple presence there threw him. He found himself blushing, and holding the sheet to himself, as if to conceal his own nakedness.

"You can't stay," he said, when she didn't answer. "You . . ."

She reached out and touched him, her soft, warm hand resting on his hip. It made him feel strange. The cloth had fallen away from her slightly, revealing one of her breasts. He stared, as if he had not seen her naked before, surprised by the hardness of the nipple, knowing instinctively what it meant.

He took a small, shuddering breath, then reached down, removing her hand. "Siri . . . you can't stay. *Really*."

She blinked, surprised. There was doubt in her eyes now, and disappointment. Meeting those eyes, Daniel frowned, surprised to find her close to tears.

He eased back, away from her, then turned and, bending down to retrieve it, pulled on his cloak, fastening it tight about his waist.

He turned back, looking down at her. She was crying now. Tears dropped one after another from her bottom lids, running down her cheeks and into the hollow of her neck. Yet still she was silent.

Daniel walked round the bed and picked up her sleeping robe, then held it out to her.

"I'm sorry," he said. "I'm very flattered. You're very beautiful, but . . ."

"It's true, then," she said bluntly.

He frowned.

Siri looked down, then wiped the back of her hand across her cheeks. "Still, I guess it's not your fault."

"I'm sorry?"

She met his eyes again. "All those boys and no girls. It must . . . *change* you."

He laughed. A short, humourless laugh. So that's what she thought. And yet even if it were true, why should he be ashamed of that? It was the comfort, the feeling of being loved – of loving – that mattered, nothing else.

"Is that what you think? That I prefer boys?"

"Well, don't you?"

He shrugged. "I don't know. I've never had the chance to find out. Before tonight, that is."

She looked down again, swallowing, then, raising her head defiantly, threw the sheet aside. "Well? Do you want to find out?"

He stared at her, aroused by her arousal. Wanting her, despite his qualms. Even so, it felt wrong. "No," he said finally, holding out her cloak to her. "Not now. Not like this."

He saw how much his denial hurt her, and wished – truly wished – he could be selfish and just have her. Fuck her, the way he'd been fucked, or had fucked others. The way it was in the camp. But he didn't want that. Not here.

"I'm sorry," he said again. "Really I am."

She stared at him, then, standing abruptly, snatched the cloak from his hand and pulled it on. For a moment he thought that she would strike him, there was such anger in her, but then, unexpectedly, she stepped close and, pressing her mouth to his, kissed him.

"There," she said, standing back. "Now you know." She was trembling faintly. Her hands clenched and unclenched.

And then she was gone. Without another word, another look.

Daniel turned, staring at the open door. He could hear her footsteps departing down the corridor.

A door slammed shut.

Daniel closed the door then went across and sat. Drawing aside his cloak, he stared down at himself, surprised.

At least he had learned that much about himself.

For a moment he closed his eyes, imagining it, remembering the warmth of her body against his. It would have been so easy.

Easy, yes, but wrong. A violation.

Yet still it troubled him. Was he right to spurn her? Wasn't that a kind of selfishness? After all, all she wanted was a little comfort. A little love.

He shook his head, confused now. He'd made her cry. He hadn't meant to, but he had, when he could so easily have made her happy.

"*Aiya*," he said quietly, knowing that he wouldn't sleep. "Why now? Why *now* of all things?"

Yet he knew why. They all knew why. They were coming to the end of time. The end of human history. And at the end people did such things, took such risks.

So maybe he was wrong. Wrong to be so fastidious; to reject such a simple, heartfelt offer of love.

Emily. Yes, Emily would know.

He stood up, then crossed the room, determined to go to her at once.

And stopped.

What if she was asleep? What if she didn't think this was such a major thing? To wake her over a . . . a *nothing*.

Then again, why had she brought his attention to it in the first place if it wasn't important?

Okay, he thought. *I'll go and see her. But if she's sleeping, I'll come back. It can wait, after all.*

It *could* wait. Then again, the world might end tomorrow.

Pulling open the door, he hurried down the corridor, heading for Emily's private rooms.

* * *

"Daniel?"

He stepped into the room, then pulled the door closed behind him. "I'm sorry. If it's too late, I'll . . ."

"No," Emily said, setting the book aside, then patting the bed beside her. "Come and sit with me. You want to talk, I take it?"

Daniel nodded, then went across and sat.

"So?" she asked, reaching out to take his right hand in both of hers. "What is it?"

He seemed embarrassed, awkward for once. "It's Siri," he said finally, not meeting her eyes. "She came to my room, just now. She wanted . . ."

"Ah . . ." Emily nodded. So it had come to this. "How old are you, Daniel?"

"Seventeen."

"Yes." She smiled and squeezed his hand. "Seventeen. Gods, it seems so long ago since I was seventeen. Some days I feel ageless, like the rock that's all around us."

He met her eyes, curious to know where this was leading. "And?"

"And I know that some things are difficult, no matter how old you are. Love, for one. It never gets any easier, Daniel. Never. And no one knows all the answers, not even me. But I do know that you're a good person, and that if you sent her away – and I assume you did, or you wouldn't be here now wearing that hangdog expression – then it was for a good reason, even if you don't understand what that reason is."

"You think so?"

She nodded. "We are sexual creatures, Daniel. All of us. But sometimes that physical side of it isn't enough. Sometimes there's something much more important to us."

Daniel sighed. "Maybe. Yet I feel so confused about it. I . . . I want her, mother. I mean, my body . . ." He blushed. "But I can't. Something stops me."

"That's okay," she said. "It's nothing to be ashamed of. Indeed, I'd say it was something to be proud of. You want her, but you don't feel that you want to commit to her, and you sense that if you sleep with her she'll expect that kind of commitment, right?"

Daniel hesitated, then gave a single nod.

"And you don't want to simply use her, right?"

"Right," he said quietly.

"Then you're right not to, Daniel. Simple as that. Siri's lovely, but she's not what you want."

He frowned. "But I don't *know* what I want."

"Oh, you do, but you haven't met her yet."

He laughed. "That sounds . . . well, *mystical*."

"Maybe, but it's true. We each of us carry the pattern of the other – the intended other – within us. Many of us never find that intended other, but she, or he, *is* there."

"I wish I could believe that."

"Oh, but you do. Otherwise you'd be back in your room right now, with Siri."

He looked down again. "What you say . . . maybe that's so. Maybe there is a special someone for me. But I'll tell you what I felt. I felt . . . well, I felt that it was somehow important *who* I slept with. So much else about my life has been ill, I don't want to spoil this."

Emily was watching him, a tender smile lighting her features. "You know, you're a very kind person, Daniel. Siri will be hurting now. She's probably in her room right now, crying into her pillow at your rejection of her. But it would have been much worse if you had used and then discarded her. Even now, in these final days, we need to remember such things, and act to minimise the hurt we cause to others."

"And what I feel . . . physically?"

Emily released his hand then pushed him away playfully. "I don't think you need me to tell you what to do, young Daniel."

He stared at her a moment, astonished, then, seeing the teasing expression in her eyes, looked down, blushing.

"I may not have lived in the camps, Daniel, nor seen what you've seen, but I've raised a dozen boys of my own. And there's not a single one of you who doesn't seek solace in that fashion at one time or another."

He swallowed, then, returning to the subject, asked, "And the girl?"

"I'll see to Siri, Daniel. In fact, I'll go and see her now. Oh, and don't fear. Nothing of what was said here will pass my lips."

He grinned, grateful for her tact.

"And Daniel . . . here. I doubt you'll sleep, so take this and read it. You can return it to me in the morning."

* * *

After he'd gone, Emily sat there for a long time thinking, her mind filled not only with what Daniel had said, but also with the history she had been reading and her thoughts on the slow encroachment of the floraforms.

Time was ending. She had no doubt of it. For Time was nothing without some conscious mind to mark its passing. And though the floraforms seemed intelligent, she could not believe that, once man had passed from this planet, it would concern itself with hours and minutes and seconds. In the place of Time would be an endless Now, a green unmeasured haze. As there had been before human consciousness evolved, six million years ago.

Hannah's words had surprised her. She had not known – had not even suspected – that Man had been on earth so long, nor that so little of Man's history had been charted. It was almost as if nothing had happened but for those last few moments of Man's existence – ten thousand years out of a period six hundred times as long. There had been a blink of frenetic activity – of frantic exponential growth – and then . . .

"Nothing . . ."

She breathed the word, trying it out on the air. It was a frightening thought. But maybe not as frightening as the triumph of DeVore. At least *he* would not inherit. Not now.

Beneath that vague unfocused fear, she felt a sadness that her adopted sons and their children would not live to see a brighter future. But so it was. They had unlocked Pandora's box and this was the result.

Emily stood and, pulling on her cloak, went out. Outside Siri's door, she stopped and listened. There was no sound. No sound at all. She tried the door. It was ajar. She pushed it and stepped inside, listening once more.

"Siri?"

There was a sound from her right, from the bathroom. She walked across and gently tapped.

"Siri? Siri, are you in there?"

There was a heavy sigh, then. "What?"

"Siri, can I speak to you?"

There was a long pause, then the door opened a crack. Siri's face, puffed and swollen, looked out from the brightness within.

"Siri?"

Siri stood back, letting Emily enter. She waited until Emily had sat on the edge of the long, narrow bath, then, sighing, said, "He told you, did he?"

"Who?"

"Daniel. He told you I went to him."

Faced by the direct statement, Emily found she could not lie. "Yes," she said. "He was worried about you. He thought . . . he thought he'd hurt you."

"He did. But maybe it's for the best, neh?"

That "*neh?*", with its edge of cynicism, surprised Emily. She looked at Siri anew, recognising in that moment just how much Siri had pinned her hopes on winning Daniel's love.

"I'm sorry," she began, but Siri put up her hands, as if to fend her off.

"I don't want your pity," she said, her face hard now. "No, nor your advice. So you can save all of your rehearsed speeches for someone else. I don't need them."

Emily looked down, then shrugged. "I'm sorry," she said again. "Really I am." She paused, then, "You want some time off?"

Siri shook her head, then walked over to the sink and began to wash her face, attending to the task with an exaggerated concentration, as if to negate Emily's presence there in the room.

Emily watched her a moment, then stood. She would need to keep an eye on Siri these next few days. Who knew what stunts she'd try?

"All right," she said finally. "I'll leave you then."

Siri gave a little grunt of acknowledgment, then carried on washing.

Aiya, she thought as she closed the door behind her. Then, knowing she would not sleep unless she did something about it, she turned and began to walk towards the nearest guard room. It wouldn't hurt to have someone check on the girl every few hours or so. Just in case.

* * *

DeVore walked from the cell, a faint smile on his lips. At last! At-fucking-last! As guards bowed low or hurried to open doors for him, he began to laugh, a gentle yet triumphant laugh.

The prisoner was dead. He'd heaved a sigh and died, like a gutted fish expiring on the slab.

Dead but he won't lie down . . .

He felt calm; strangely, abnormally calm. Stepping into the darkened suite of rooms which once had housed Pei K'ung, Li Yuan's fifth wife.

DeVore sniffed the air and smiled. *The dirty little dog!*

He tiptoed across and looked. Yes, there they were, their naked bodies entwined about each other's. He stood there, studying them a moment, then reached out and tugged at the boy's big toe.

Da-neel grunted and turned his head slightly, one sleepy eye half-focusing on DeVore.

"Oh, it's you . . ."

"Yes, it's me," DeVore said. "And I've a task for you, if you've finished fucking my woman."

The boy sat up slowly, disentangling himself from the woman's limbs. "What's happening?" he asked, yawning as he reached down and picked up his shirt.

"I've been playing a game."

"A game?"

"Yes, with a poker and a map."

"Ahhh . . ." The fake's eyes widened with understanding. "Who was he?"

"Lin Lao."

"Lin *Lao*?" Daniel pulled on his shirt, then whistled. "Then you know where she is."

"Precisely. But we've not got long."

"I see that." The young man turned, looking down at Emtu. "Then you'll need her, too."

DeVore smiled. "Yes." He sat beside the woman, then ran his left hand slowly up her flank until it cupped her breast. Slowly the nipple hardened. She turned, murmuring vaguely in her sleep. DeVore leaned forward and nuzzled his tongue against the hardened bud. An eye flicked open. The woman smiled.

"I've a job for you, my sweet. A very important job. Indeed, you might say that it's the job you were made for."

* * *

It is night. A field of lucent blooms, pale, long-necked lilies, stretch beneath the circle of the moon, their radiance like the glow of living death. Tall-stemmed blooms that tremble in the chill wind from the west.

A sigh ripples from bloom to bloom, from stamened mouth to mouth; an utterance of darkness, uillean. There is a moment's perfect stillness and then they walk, black earth tumbling like pepper grains from their roots as they slowly climb the steepening slope, the faint rustle of their leaves filling the silence of the valley.

From space nothing, yet the truth is, in a thousand valleys the blooms are on the move, their faint corpse-light shimmering across the dark yet moonlit lands, slowly extending their domain, even as humankind sleeps.

A sigh and then they rest once more, leaves folded, awaiting the day and the sunlight from which they take their strength.

Fields of lilies, beautiful pale white lilies shining beneath the moon, filling the high ground of the alpine valleys, while beneath them lie the great plains of central Europe.

They rest. Tomorrow they will begin the descent. Tomorrow.

CHAPTER·18

THE SONG OF NO-SPACE

Chuang walked slowly around the edge of the circular pond, raised on her toes like a dancer, her arms out for balance, her back straight, her head back. Below her feet the fish circled slowly, a mix of dark and orange carp, their well-fed shapes appearing and disappearing among the bright green lily pads.

Returning to her point of departure, Chuang looked across.

Kim was sitting on the top step of the first tier, a notepad in his lap, writing. Behind him the great transparent dome of Fermi curved sharply upwards five hundred metres then levelled out. Through it she could see where the blackness of no-space met Ganymede's dull, orange-red surface in a sharply drawn arc.

Kim was dressed formally, the dark austerity of his cloak a sharp contrast to his normal, casual attire. It was almost three months since she had last seen him and he had changed a great deal in that time; his face was thinner, his hair grown steely-white. Chuang walked across and stood there, looking down at him.

"What are you writing, Uncle?"

Kim glanced up, as if noticing her for the first time, then looked back at his pad. "It's nothing, just . . ."

She went round and stood just to the side of him, looking down over his shoulder.

Equations, the Machine said, its voice sounding clear in her head. *He's developing new notations for the folded-space equations.*

To her eyes the marks Kim was making seemed little more than complex doodles – for they lacked the clean line and simplicity of normal mathematical symbols – yet the Machine quickly showed her how their shapes reflected their use; how each corresponded to a certain mathematical formula. They were symbols. Symbols in a new mathematics.

She smiled. "It's like music."

"Yes . . . Yes, it is."

He pointed to one of the marks, which resembled a flatfish being speared by an electrical charge. "Besides its mathematical value, each symbol contains an element of what you might call resonance and harmony. Factors that normal maths don't have. It's a kind of language. I'm using it to try to express the physics of No-Space and Folding, but its base, as you say, is musical."

"Like a song?"

Kim grinned. "Precisely."

"And does it help? I mean, does it make your task any easier?"

He shrugged, his large, dark eyes thoughtful, his forehead deeply furrowed. "I don't know, to be honest with you, Chuang. I *hope* it will. As I get more fluent – as I find subtler ways of expressing the equations – I'm hoping that something will jump out at me . . . will, if you like, *open* to me. But who knows? It's been a long time now."

She saw the tiny flicker of doubt in his eyes and looked away, pretending that she hadn't. Kim had been stalled on this problem for more than fifteen months now. It was the longest he'd ever taken to solve any problem, and it was beginning to look as if this once he had over-reached himself.

He could breach the membrane between realities, certainly – time and again he had created brief-lived, tiny windows between the universes – yet he could not make them big enough, nor permanent enough, to be of any use. Every attempt of his to create a larger, more stable window – one that was of practical use; that one could use to travel through – had failed. And with each new failure, Kim's confidence had visibly diminished.

"He's late," Chuang said, changing the subject. "I told you he'd be late."

Kim lifted the flap of skin over his wrist and glanced at the timer, then shrugged again. "If he's late, he's late. I can't be blamed for that. Besides, they can't start without him, can they?"

"No, I . . ."

There were hurried footsteps just below them, then a shout.

"Father?"

"Up here, Sampsa," Kim said, standing up and pocketing his notebook. He put a hand out for Chuang to take. "Come."

Sampsa met them at the foot of the steps. He looked flustered.

"You've remembered everything?" he asked impatiently.

"Everything," Kim said, patting his cloak pocket. "Now come. Ai Lin is waiting."

* * *

As they stepped out into the arena of Fermi's smaller dome, where the ceremony was to take place, Ai Lin looked across from where she stood on the raised podium beside her sister, Lu Yi, and Tom, and gestured to them to hurry.

Kim looked to Sampsa, seeing how nervous he was, then leaned close, whispering in his ear.

"She looks beautiful, Sampsa. Don't keep her waiting any longer."

Tom was smiling. He had clearly known all along where Sampsa was, but, mute as he was, he had not been able to communicate it to the twins.

As Sampsa stepped up onto the podium, Ebert detached himself from the little group he was standing with and walked across, taking his place before the two couples. A moment later Kim and Jelka joined him there, standing either side of him as the ceremony commenced.

"People of City Fermi," Ebert began, the twin probes above his head circling much slower than usual, "We bear witness today to the solemn joining of these two couples. We shall hear their vows and give our communal blessing, as is our custom. But before we begin, let me say a word or two about the young men and women standing here before us today."

There were smiles from the crowd of two to three hundred who had gathered in the arena. There had been few weddings these past two years, so this was an especially joyous occasion. Things had not been going well for the colony – a spate of recent suicides not the least of their problems – and so most found this occasion not merely welcome but almost an affirmation of faith in the future.

It was also the first time in more than six months that Kim had made a public appearance, and many in the deeper levels of the domed cities turned on their screens to watch for that alone; to look at Ward and judge whether there was any substance to the rumours of his illness.

For now, however, the cameras switched between the blind-eyed face of Ebert and the two couples who stood transfixed before him.

Ebert looked directly at Sampsa and smiled benevolently.

"Our friend Sampsa we all know and love. No one, I believe, has worked harder for the colony these past two years. Nor has anyone, I feel, done more to raise our spirits under trying circumstances. It would be no exaggeration to say that he has carried an immense burden, yet carried it with good cheer and without complaint."

Kim looked up, surprised by the words, then glanced across to where the giant, Karr, stood with his wife and daughters, beside Kao Chen and his family. Karr was looking down, slowly nodding to himself.

"What most of you will not know, however, is just how hard he works. Indeed, so concerned is he with the personal problems of our citizenry, he almost did not make it here this morning."

Sampsa gave Ai Lin an apologetic smile.

"But now that he is, let me move on quickly and say a word or two about his assistant on the Council, Tom Shepherd."

"You'd best," Lu Yi said, grinning, "for he certainly won't!"

There was laughter. Tom grinned.

"So it is," Ebert said, smiling, "yet as the old saying goes, actions speak much louder than words, and by his actions Tom has shown himself to be a good friend to all of Ganymede's citizens. His work with children, especially his classes on signing, has been of benefit to all and future generations will surely profit by having a language that can be used in vacuum conditions."

Tom nodded to Ebert, making the hand sign for "thank you", which Ebert returned with a gesture of gracious emphasis – "thank *you*."

"But before we think that the men alone are worthy of praise, let me mention the long hours of work that Ai Lin and her sister Lu Yi have put in supporting their partners. Moreover their visits to the sick and injured have been greatly appreciated by many. In a small society such as ours such actions are the cement that binds us together and we should not forget their importance."

Ebert paused, momentarily speaking beyond the small circle surrounding him.

"These past few years have been difficult. It is not easy to live without a sense of movement, of *destination*. It is hard to maintain faith in a condition of No-Space. Yet we shall come out of this, and today's ceremony is not merely a matter of personal joy for these two couples who stand before me, but a more general celebration of faith – that we shall come through. That we shall arrive at Eridani. And the children of these unions – for I hope there will be children – will come to stand upon a new world, beneath a new sun. And so the race of man will continue."

Ebert was silent a moment, then, looking to Kim, he held out his hand, palm open. Kim stared a moment, then, understanding suddenly what he meant by the gesture, fished in his pocket for the rings, spilling all four out into Ebert's palm.

They were simple gold rings, like the rings he and Jelka wore. A symbol so old it seemed almost to predate history.

The circle forged. The halves made whole.

He watched Ebert turn and smile at the two couples, and felt a great flood of warmth wash through him. Reaching out, he took Jelka's hand behind Ebert's back, squeezing it, conscious of the look of love and pride in her face.

If only Mileja were here to see this, he thought, his eyes suddenly moist. But Sampsa seemed unaware of any shadows. He glanced sideways at his beloved Ai Lin, his face lit with delight, then looked back at Ebert as the words of the ceremony began.

* * *

Afterwards, Karr came across to him and taking him aside, said quietly,

"Can I see you, Kim? We need to talk."

"Of course," he began. "If you want to come over tomorrow evening."

"No," Karr said, his face stern. "I meant right now. There's a room nearby."

"*Gregor*? What's going on?"

"It's important, that's all I can say."

"Important?"

But Karr would say no more. Taking Kim's arm, he led him away. And Kim, looking about him, saw how several of those gathered there glanced at him then quickly looked away.

"Well?" he asked when they were inside the room, the door locked behind them. "Is there a reason for this cloak-and-dagger stuff?"

"A very good reason," Karr said, indicating that Kim should take a seat. "We think there's a plot to overthrow the Council. A plot that involves killing all of us then turning round and going back to Chung Kuo."

Kim gave a laugh of disbelief. "But that's impossible!"

"You know that and I know that, but there are some here who think we've been lying to them."

"Lying?" This got more incredible by the moment. "Are you serious, Gregor?"

"Never more so. Your life . . . all our lives . . . are in danger. We must act soon, Kim, or go under."

"Now wait a moment. You say there's a plot, so I suppose there is one. But are you sure about this? Are you sure they mean to kill us and supplant us?"

"Not certain, no. But if what we've heard is right . . ."

"If what you've heard? Then why have *I* heard nothing?"

Karr gave a bleak laugh. "When did you last speak to me, Kim?"

Kim thought. "Two weeks ago? No . . ."

"That's right. Five weeks. And Sampsa, when did you last see Sampsa before today?"

Kim looked down. "Have I been that engrossed in things?"

"Obsessed is more the word."

"Then why didn't someone say something?"

"Because we thought what you were doing was important. But right now this is more important, hence the hastily-arranged ceremonies. You see, we are all being watched. And had we gone to you at Kalevala, they would have known. As it is, they'll probably suspect. So maybe we've not long at all in which to act. Maybe they'll choose to strike tonight."

"A coup?"

Again Karr nodded.

"So what do we do?"

"We round them up."

"And then?"

"We place them on board one of the ships and cut them loose."

Kim gave a low whistle. "Are things that bad?"

"Worse. There's not a single citizen who doesn't feel somehow imprisoned. We're suffocating, Kim. Not literally, but psychologically. And maybe that's worse. Maybe that's far worse in the circumstances."

"Then I must find the answer."

Karr sighed. "You think there *is* an answer?"

"Don't you?"

"I don't know any more. When you got so close, I thought . . . Well, I thought it would be days, not years. I thought . . ."

Kim nodded. "I understand." He was quiet a moment, then. "Okay. Let's do what must be done. But no violence unless we must. And give them all they need on the ship. I would not have them come to harm. It was not their fault that we came into this No-Space."

Karr looked to him then bowed, as if taking orders from his general, then turned and, unlocking the door, went out, leaving Kim to ponder how far things had degenerated.

I didn't know, he thought. *Why, I didn't even guess!*

* * *

Back at Kalevala, Kim went to his study and sat down in the big leather chair behind his desk, brooding. He was still brooding when Jelka came into the room.

"I heard," she said.

He looked up, his dismay etched in his face. "It's falling apart, isn't it?"

She went to contradict him, to somehow lift him, but she could see from his eyes that he didn't want that; this once he wanted the truth, whether it hurt or not.

"Maybe," she said, fearing to say an unequivocal yes. "But Gregor's no fool. If anyone can hold things together, he can."

"Yes, but at what price?" Kim sighed, forlorn now. "I knew there'd be times when spirits would flag, but this . . . I never imagined this."

She laughed, making him look up at her.

"What?" he asked.

"What you said," she answered, a faint smile on her lips now. "What did you imagine, Kim? That we'd meet a giant spider and be whisked off into No-Space? Did you imagine that?"

"No, but . . ."

"Then hold fast, my love. The answer's close. Remember my vision. You'll get the answer. I promise you you will. And when you do . . ."

Kim stared at her a moment, then shook his head. "I'm not sure I believe that any more. Remember what Master Tuan said. From this point on nothing is certain, not even the visions. I mean, if it was to have come true, it would have by now, surely?"

Jelka made to answer but he spoke on.

"And then there's these latest notations. Try as I might, I can't get them to work. It's as if there are still pieces missing. But that can't be so."

"You're sure of that?"

"No. To be frank, I'm not sure of *anything* any longer. The more I stare at it, the vaguer it seems to get. It's like . . ." He raised a hand then let it fall, unable to complete the image.

"You need a rest, Kim. You're tired. Mentally tired."

He laughed. "Nonsense. When was I ever tired, *mentally*."

Jelka stared at him a while, then shook her head. "You know, I've watched you these past few months and kept from commenting, but I can't keep silent any longer. You're ageing, Kim. Growing old before my eyes. It's like it's eating away at you from the inside. Those lines at your brow and about your eyes – were *they* there before?"

Almost comically, Kim put his fingers to his forehead, his eyes, tracing the deep furrows there, then frowned deeply. But it wasn't comic. Not for Jelka. Kim was destroying himself, day by day grinding himself against the rock of this No-Space problem, and day by day she had to watch him.

"Won't you take a break? Please, Kim?"

For a long long while he stared back at her, then with a shrug, he looked away. "Okay," he said. "I will."

* * *

Kim sat there a long time after Jelka had gone, then stood and, going through to the bedroom, quickly changed out of his formal clothes into the wine red one-piece he more normally wore.

Old Tuan, he thought. *I have to speak to Old Tuan.*

He left the house by the back door and, crossing the lawn, stepped out under the thick branches of the surrounding wood. There was a silence here, a darkness that one found nowhere else, that was profoundly different from the absolute nullity beyond the dome. It was a deep, primeval darkness, like a rich loam, from which, he knew, his own kind had come, a billion years before.

And to which he would eventually return. Unless space took him first.

"Tuan? . . . Tuan Ti Fo?"

He stepped out into the clearing, remembering as he did all those other times he had stood here beneath the windswept branches, the moon shining down like a polished mirror, the stars like the dust from a cut diamond, the waves breaking on the rocks below the tower . . .

Kim shivered, feeling a sudden homesickness. A longing, so pure, so overwhelming that it sent a tingle through every nerve end.

"Was I wrong, Master Tuan? Was I wrong to come out here?"

Out into the pitiless dark.

He waited, calling now and then, but Old Tuan did not come. Sighing, Kim turned, meaning to leave the clearing and return to the house. Yet as he did, he saw, peripherally, a movement between the trees just to his right.

He whirled about.

"Who's there? Who's . . .?"

Kim caught his breath, astonished.

Kim? his mirror-self mouthed from where he stood, a shadow among shadows, on the far side of the clearing.

He took a step toward the form, but even as he did the other raised a hand, as if to warn him to come no closer. The air about him seemed not so much clear as translucent. It shimmered, as if an unseen fire were burning under it, heating the air and making it waver.

He found his voice. "Kim?"

The other nodded, then made a gesture with his hand.

Kim frowned and shrugged, and the other repeated the gesture, describing the shape he'd made with an exaggerated care.

This time Kim understood. It was one of the new notations he had come up with. Fascinated, he watched, as his other self described a dozen or more of the symbols in the air, writing each with a clarity that could not be mistaken.

Kim laughed. "Of course," he breathed. "Of *course*!"

Seeing that he understood, the other raised a hand in a gesture of parting. The air about him shimmered and grew solid once again.

He was gone.

Kim walked across, looking about him at the place where his other self had appeared. There was no sign, no mark of any presence having been here, and yet he knew that what he'd seen was more than just a vision.

Yes, but was it real?

In answer, he saw the symbols once again, then formed them with his own hands. The other had been like him, very like him, but not *exactly* him. Which meant . . .

Kim laughed. This was *it*. This was the moment he had been waiting for. Turning he ran towards the house, his bare feet making no sound, his eyes looking inward as his mind already began to fit the new pieces into the equation, seeing how the original equations were doubled – twinned with these new equations.

Of course, he thought. *Of course!*

* * *

"Kim? Kim, are you there?"

Jelka walked over to the bed and peered into the shadows. No. He wasn't there. The bed was empty, the sheets untouched.

She turned, looking back at the doorway. He couldn't be . . . not after he'd promised her.

Angry now, she walked quickly through the ancient house until she came to the stair that led down into his workroom. The door was open, the light on the stairs was on.

She went down, slowing on the final few steps, realising that the big room beyond the doorway was in darkness. And in that darkness something shone with a ghostly presence.

Jelka stepped inside. Kim was standing with his back to her, operating the hologrammic viewer. Just in front of him and slightly to his left, was the source of the light, a large hovering sphere of silver light in which danced a whole series of golden symbols.

Even as she watched, Kim added element after element, each locking into its correct place, until the thing was finished, the structure of it a solid, complex shape of gold within the gleaming silver.

Now that it was complete she could see the pattern of it. In its new twinned form it was aesthetically much more pleasing than before, but she knew it was more than that. In its new form, it had the sleek, functional look of a complex molecule.

"That's it," he said, sensing her there behind him. "That's *it*!"

"Yes, but how do you use it?"

Kim turned to face her, the moist surface of his eyes lit with the gold and silver light, his face more alive than she'd seen it in months.

"Call Sampsa," he said. "Tell him to come at once. Oh, and call Gregor, too. Tell him to call off the dogs. And tell him I've something to show him. Something to show everyone!"

* * *

Sampsa turned, then reached across in the darkness to cut the summons. Sitting up, he took a moment to come to, then, pulling up the sheet to cover Ai Lin, he spoke.

"Vision only."

The screen at the far end of the bedroom immediately lit, showing his mother's face.

Fearing that something bad had happened, Sampsa slipped from the bed and pulled on his robe, then went across and stood before the screen.

"Full sound. Vision both ways."

At once his mother's eyes registered his presence. "Sampsa? I'm sorry to disturb you, especially right now, but . . ."

"Is father all right?"

Her laughter answered him. "Never better. In fact, he wants to show you something."

His eyes widened. "He's *done* it?"

"It looks like it."

He whooped, then, hearing Ai Lin stir behind him, said more quietly. "I'll be right over."

Sampsa cut contact, then went through to the bathroom to shower. As he dressed, he could not keep from smiling. So Kim had done it. He'd finally done it. One could not overestimate the importance of the moment.

"Sampsa?" A sleepy-looking Ai Lin looked round the door at him. "Is something the matter?"

"Nothing. It's dad. He's finally cracked it!"

Her face lit. "He's done it?"

Sampsa nodded, then. "You want to come along and see?"

"You just stop me." And, pushing past him, she began to shower.

There was a tickle in his head. Tom was waking.

Tom? he said, feeling Tom's mind come into focus.

He felt as much as heard Tom's laughter, as Tom read what was in his mind; experienced Tom's exultation. *I'll be there*, he said. Then, as an afterthought, *Don't let him start without me.*

I won't, Sampsa said, turning to look at Ai Lin, the image of her naked back superimposed upon a vision of Lu Yi asleep on her back beside Tom, her nakedness the very image of Ai Lin's. *And bring Lu Yi. She won't want to miss this.*

* * *

Kim was out there on the surface when they arrived, suited up, his equipment already in place. As Karr's cruiser set down, Kim waved up at it, before he turned and busied himself once more.

Karr cut the engines then turned to Kao Chen who sat beside him at the controls. "Are you nervous, Chen?"

"I guess I am," Chen said, his smile uncertain. "But then it isn't every day that you quell a rebellion then get to see someone punch holes in the walls of reality."

Karr laughed. They had been up all night rounding up suspected members of the coup, and had barely finished when Jelka's call had come. Leaving the prisoners in Aluko Echewa's charge, they had hurried here.

Chen sighed and looked down, drawing one hand over his smooth and mottled pate.

"What is it?" Karr asked.

Chen shrugged. "I don't know. I don't feel *easy* about this. Call me a simple peasant, Gregor, but I don't feel it is for the likes of us to be tinkering with reality. What if Kim succeeds? What if he *does* find a way to travel between realities? What then? Does it all unravel?"

"Unravel?"

He looked up and met Karr's eyes, his own deeply troubled. "If we can travel there, then they can travel here."

"So?"

"So it's like being suddenly in a room with no walls. Open to attack from any side. And how can one defend against that? How can one make sure one's children and grandchildren can ever be safe?"

Karr nodded. He hadn't thought of that. "Yet we must do this. To defeat DeVore."

"So Master Tuan says. But even he admits that he cannot see what will transpire. And if even Master Tuan is uncertain, then we should exercise great care."

"And what do *you* suggest, old friend?"

"That we use this knowledge sparingly, and then – once we have achieved what must be achieved – we lose it, for good."

"Lose it?"

Chen nodded. "Or hide it, where it can never be found. For someone like DeVore to have this knowledge . . ."

"Then we must make sure we kill DeVore."

"In every world?"

Karr looked away, his gaze resting on the dome of Kalevala and the eastern airlock, from which two suited figures were emerging. "You think he's everywhere, then?"

"I think it's likely."

"Then there will be other Chens and other Karrs, willing to do battle with him. In every place he exists, we shall be there, too."

Chen frowned. "I wish I could believe that. But I feel . . . exposed."

"Yes," Karr saw that. He nodded slowly. "Yet we must do our best, neh?"

The two suited figures had made their way across and now stood beside Kim, who was leaning forward over a temporary control board, making last minute adjustments.

Karr looked to his friend. "Shall we suit up and join them, Chen? Or do you want to watch from here?"

"We'll go down," Chen answered, suddenly more like the old Kao Chen – the one who got on with things and did not question why. "If it's our fate, so be it. We cannot change it now."

* * *

They stood in a little group beside the airlock, a dozen or more in all, as Kim began the experiment. Jelka had stayed in the house, explaining to everyone that as she had seen the vision from the window so she had to be there, to help it to come true.

Sampsa stood beside his father at the board, helping as he'd helped these past twenty years, acting as his father's hands as the apparatus began to glow.

The apparatus was like a great hoop, long gleaming twists of silvered metal reaching up almost twenty metres, like massive coils of DNA, one final spiral twist growing thinner and thinner until it seemed to vanish like a wisp of smoke. So it had been all along, but Kim understood the structure now – knew why he'd had the instinct to make it so. It had needed only the finest of fine adjustments to incorporate the new equations.

The glow intensified. Initially, they were tapping power from the line that ran from Kalevala to the grid in Fermi, yet once the thing was working it would generate its own power.

If the theory was correct.

"Slowly," Kim said, noting the strange ripples of light that were beginning to form about the arms of the hoop. "We want to push the door open, not blast a hole in it."

Sampsa laughed. "If I went any more carefully we'd be here until Doomsday!"

"We cannot be too careful," Kim answered him, remembering the worst of his failures. There was still a great crater on the far side of Kalevala from that one.

The ripples intensified. The metal arms were glowing bright red now, a mist of atoms forming about them where they were reacting against the vacuum that surrounded them.

"Look," Kim said quietly. "Look at that! A double pulse."

It was true. The apparatus was taking the single pulse that Sampsa was feeding it and doubling it, pushing it out again like a heartbeat, the first pulse more intense than the second.

With infinitesimal care, Sampsa increased the feed.

For a moment nothing, and then there was a great whoosh, as if a match had caught a stack of bone-dry kindling. A massive flare of light rushed up each arm of the hoop and met with a great crackle.

The air overhead seemed to darken and then explode with light – a great circle of light that, in a blink, became a hoop, five hundred metres above where they stood – a great wheel of fire that roiled and boiled as it circled.

For a moment or two pure shock paralysed Kim. He stared up at the fiery hoop, one hand shielding his eyes against the glare, his mouth open, eyes wide. And then he laughed, his laughter joined after a moment by Sampsa's.

"It's stable!" he shouted, a feeling of intense excitement washing through him. "Look at it, Sampsa! Look at how it balances the energy within itself!"

He turned, looking back at the house, knowing that Jelka was watching him, then pointed at the wheel, feeling almost drunk with the power of what he'd done.

"There!" Sampsa shouted back at him, his voice ringing in Kim's helmet. "What mother saw was true!"

"Yes," Kim said, turning once more to stare, awed by the reality of it.

* * *

Banton sat at the back of the cell, on the unmade bunk, his head down, his hands resting on his knees. Kim, looking at the shadowy image on the screen above the door, wondered what had brought the man to contemplate such a desperate measure. Banton had been a fine man once, a responsible citizen and a good father to his three sons, but the past two years had clearly worked a change in him.

"Open up," Kim said. "I'd like to speak to him alone."

"Do you think that's wise?" Kao Chen asked from where he stood between Ikuro Ishida and Karr.

"We must begin somewhere," Kim said. "And where better than with the ringleaders? We must build bridges now. Yes, and give these men hope, if that is still possible."

"Do you want this?" Ikuro asked, offering Kim the comset he'd recorded the experiment on.

Kim hesitated, then took it. A moment later the locks clunked open and the cell door hissed back.

Kim stepped inside.

Banton looked up wearily, then made a face of disgust. "Have you come to gloat?"

"You don't deny it, then?"

"What's the point? Even if I did, you'd not believe me."

"So you're innocent, eh?" Kim shook his head. "I think Karr's right. I think you meant to kill us all. It would have been pointless, you know. You couldn't have gone back, not without me."

"No?" The word registered a profound mistrust.

"I know you don't believe that, but it's true. Or was true. Now we can all go back."

Banton laughed bleakly. "You think a lot of yourself, Kim Ward."

"*You* used to think a lot of me."

"Well, maybe I was wrong. Maybe we were all conned by you."

"Is that what you think?"

Banton looked away, his expression sour.

Kim shrugged, then sat beside him, offering him the comset. "Do you want to see what I've been doing?"

Banton met his eyes, then looked down at the comset. "What is it?"

"The thing I promised you. The door between the universes."

Banton laughed. "How do I know it's real? For all I know it's some elaborate computer simulation."

"You don't. But if you want, you can come with me and try it. We're testing it a few days from now."

"Testing it? You mean, like stepping through it?"

"Flying, more like. But yes. Into a different world. Like this world, but different."

"With stars in it, you mean."

Kim nodded, then. "Is that what bothers you most? The lack of stars?"

"That's part of it. But it's in here . . ." Banton touched his forehead. "That's where it's darkest. It's like . . ."

"Like what?" Kim coaxed, his voice quiet now.

"Like I don't exist. Like none of us exist . . . or that we only think we exist. This life . . . it's like a dream. No motion, no stars, no sun or moon. Even the City was better than this."

Kim let out a long breath. "Yes. I can see that . . . But things will change now. I promise you."

"You *promise*?" Banton stared at him a moment, then shook his head, his former bitterness returning. "And you think this is the answer?"

Kim shrugged. "I don't know. But I plan to find out. Now will you come with me, or will you languish here in this cell?"

Banton laughed. "It's not much of a choice, is it?"

Kim stood, leaving the comset on the bed where Banton might look at it. "No. But it's better than the choice you'd have given us." He walked over to the door and rapped on it with his knuckles. "Think it over. I'll give you until tomorrow to decide."

"And if I say no?"

"Then you stay here, Mr. Banton. Until the ship's ready."

"The ship?"

Kim nodded, even as the door hissed open once again. Karr stood there, barring the way in case Banton tried to make his escape, but Banton did not even get up from his bunk.

"That's right," Kim said, as he stepped outside then turned, looking back inside. "Either you're with us or you're not. And if you're not, you can leave. We'll give you your own ship and supplies to last you a lifetime. And then it's up to you."

Kim saw the shock on Banton's face, but even as the man made to respond, the door slammed shut again.

In the cruiser heading back to Fermi, Karr turned in his seat to speak to Kim.

"You're too soft," he said. "He'd have killed you in your bed. Cut your throats, you and Jelka both."

"Maybe," Kim said thoughtfully. "Yet he's still a man. Besides, the fault's not his."

"Not his?" Karr snorted his disbelief.

"No," Kim said, insistent now. "This *is* an unnatural life. The gods know it is. So *be* soft, Gregor. We are not dealing with DeVore here, but with frightened people. Banton spoke of a darkness in his head. I *know* that darkness. I *lived* in it for many years."

Karr made to speak again, then stopped. "Okay," he said finally. "But we do not release them. Not yet. And not without guarantees."

"Guarantees?" Kim laughed, then, relenting, reached out to hold Karr's shoulder briefly, his small, childlike hand dwarfed by the giant's heavily-muscled stature. "We are beyond guarantees, Gregor. It's a looking-glass world out there and we had best get used to it."

"You think we can?"

It was Ikuro who had spoken. Kim turned, looking across at him.

"You talk of Banton being frightened," Ikuro went on. "Well *I* am frightened by *this*. I am used to making holes and taking risks, but this scares me."

"I agree," Chen said, from where he sat in the co-pilot's chair. "We are talking of something we know nothing about. You talk of knowing the equations, Kim, but do you also know the rules? Or is it all guesswork?"

"We'll learn," Kim said.

"And if we don't?"

"We'll learn. I'll learn *for* you. That's my purpose."

That certainty – a certainty that had been absent this last year – calmed them. Karr, in the pilot's seat, nodded, then smiled. Beside him, Chen grinned.

"Okay, but Gregor's right. Let us keep the ringleaders under lock and key until things are much clearer. *Until* we've some rules."

"Absolutely," Ikuro said, with a nod of his head. "We need rules, Kim. Especially now. You can't make holes in things without also making rules."

Kim looked about him, then shrugged. "Okay . . . *okay*, I hear what you're saying. But let's not lose sight of what we're doing here. Remember what Tuan said. This is a war. A war to determine our ultimate direction. And we *must* take risks. It is not death we should fear but resignation. *That* has been our enemy. It is that which has undermined us this last year. But now we are free of it. Now we can move forward once again."

"Maybe," Ikuro said, articulating the doubt they all still felt. "But I would still be happier if there were rules."

* * *

Later, back in his study, Kim found himself thinking about the uncertainties the others had expressed. If he was to be honest with himself, there was every reason to be frightened; after all, no one had ever punched holes in reality before, not unless one counted the folding-ship DeVore had brought from Charon, and he wasn't totally sure whether that had breached the barrier or, like them, had merely shunted itself into no-space.

Even so, what he personally felt was not fear but genuine elation. They had kept the gateway open for almost twenty minutes before they'd killed the power.

Stable as it seemed, however, they had not as yet sent anything through. They had not *tested* it. And what good was a door unless one used it, unless one stepped beyond the threshold?

Karr had wanted to, of course, but Kim had not let him. If anyone was going to test the gateway, it would be himself. But first he needed to get the F-ship, as he now called it, right.

So that was his next task. To redesign the ship.

Kim sat forward, stretching out his hand to take a sheet of paper. Yet even as he did a piece of hardened paper materialised on the desk before him. He blinked. The writing on it was in his own.

"*Kim*," it read, "*It seems I am ahead of you, but now we can work together*."

A variant on the equation followed. Kim stared at it, then realised with a start that it was a space-time coordinate.

He laughed. That was where he was! – where his other self was! He hesitated, then, taking a stylus, wrote, "*Should I come to you?*"

Kim pushed the paper away slightly, repositioning it, then watched it vanish before his eyes. He waited, expecting it to reappear, then heard a noise behind him.

He turned, then caught his breath. The other was there, not shadowy this time, but real – as solid as himself.

"Come," the other said, holding out his hand. "You only have to take my hand."

CHAPTER·19

DEAD GROUND

The sunlight, slanting in over the flanks of the mountains, drew stark dividing lines between what could be seen and what was mere blackness. Crisp, curved lines delineated where the land seemed to fall into an abyss, a great pool of blackness that was like the liquid pupil of some giant eye. Looking out across it from where she stood, high on the mountain's upper slope, Emily felt a small thrill of recognition. Taking a deep breath of the cold, pure air, she pulled her furs close, then walked on, her booted feet trudging crisply through the virgin snow.

Just below her, the snow gave way to bare rock. Climbing down, she found herself thinking over what had happened in the night. The business between Daniel and the girl was tricky. Siri would have to be watched. Nor would it make sense to keep her in Daniel's squad any longer, disruptive as that would be. But so it was.

And rightly so, she thought, glad that her problems were human, emotional ones. Glad that, after all that had happened, something simple and basic, like a young girl falling in love, could yet be a problem, for in the world DeVore proposed there would be no such complications, no shadows on the spirit. In *his* world there would be no shadows at all. Only darkness.

The ground levelled out briefly, a long ledge of rock curling about the elbow of the mountain. Emily rested a moment, getting her breath after the climb, then looked up suddenly, her eyes narrowed, listening.

Voices!

Unclipping her gun, she quickly checked the charge, then edged along the rock face.

There were two voices. One was deep and male; the other higher – a child's voice possibly, or a woman's. As she rounded the elbow of rock, they seemed to drift up to her, much clearer suddenly, their varying tones distinct against the morning's silence.

Just ahead of her the ledge broadened. A rough wall of fallen rock lay along its edge, forming a kind of natural balcony. Beyond it was a drop of four, maybe five hundred metres. Going across, Emily crouched down, then peered between the rocks, looking through the sight of her rifle, trying to make out who was down there.

She saw them almost at once, two or three hundred metres down, on the far side of the valley. The sunlight picked out their figures against the bleached rock of the valley wall – two tiny human figures that seemed dwarfed not merely by the great mass of rock above them, but by the depthless pool of stygian darkness which began just below where they sat.

Daniel. She recognised at once that it was Daniel. But who was with him? It was not Siri, as she'd briefly thought, but it *was* a woman.

For a moment she was perplexed. Then, with a tiny "oh" of understanding, she recognised her. It was the newcomer, Hannah.

Strange. She had finished reading the file only an hour back. Hannah's real name was Shang Han A, and she was daughter of Minister Shang Mu, devoted servant of the shadow Ministry, the "Thousand Eyes" and of its Head, the notorious *I Lung*, or "First Dragon". She had persuaded her father to go to the then T'ang, Li Yuan, with word of the traitorous activities of the "Thousand Eyes." But Shang Mu was assassinated – before her eyes – and Han A herself had only just survived. That had been thirty-one years ago. Since then she had dedicated her life to the task of writing Chung Kuo's true history, even as the great Empire of the Han disintegrated about her.

And now here she was, among them.

Emily frowned. Daniel was talking again, his voice a low, confessional murmur, and though she could not make out what he was saying, she could see that the woman was making notes; stopping now and then to nod, or ask a question.

For a moment she wondered if she should let them know she was there. Being there so secretively she felt something of a spy, a sneak. It seemed only fair somehow that she should hail them. But she was intrigued. She wanted to know what they were saying. There was something about them – something about the sheer intensity of the way they sat there facing each other – that puzzled her.

Emily turned. Just behind her and to the right, the ledge narrowed, then tilted into the rock face, a narrow passage cutting down through the mountainside into a network of caverns. The mouth of one of those caves could be seen some fifty metres or so above where the two of them sat talking.

She hesitated a moment longer, then went across, ducking inside, into the darkness, making her way down, blindly following a path she'd taken hundreds of times before.

And then out, into a cave, the mouth of which was a wall of brilliant, blinding light. She tiptoed across, then stood, one hand pressed against the damp surface of the wall, keeping her balance as she listened.

". . . not at all," Daniel was saying. "To be honest, we never even thought about it. The camp was all we knew. Few of the boys remembered any kind of life before the camp, so we accepted everything they told us. I mean, we had no reason to think they were lying. In our experience liars got found out, and who would dream of lying on such a phenomenal scale?"

"So when *did* you suspect that something was wrong?"

There was a long pause, then. "I guess it was that first time in Eden. You know, the experimental place. We were halfway across and resting and I suddenly looked about me. I mean, really *looked.* It was as if I had my eyes open for the very first time. I guess that's when I saw it. Saw that it wasn't only Eden that was an experiment. It got me thinking – wondering if it had always been so, or whether the lie was something new."

Hannah laughed. A pleasant, sympathetic laugh. "You know, I've tried all my adult life to distinguish between what's true and what's a lie, and I'm still not sure whether I've got it right. True history . . . some days that term seems the biggest lie of all. Not that it really matters any more."

"So it really is all over for us?"

A pause, then: "Yes. I think it is."

"You don't think we can coexist?"

"That's not how it works. Not in my experience, anyway. It only remains to be seen whether DeVore will triumph – and by that I mean whether he destroys this world – or whether these plant things, these floraforms as you call them, will assimilate it all. Either way, things look pretty bleak."

"So why did you come here? I mean, if everything *is* going to end, then one place is as good as another, surely?"

"Maybe. And then maybe not. Maybe I was tired of being alone. Maybe I wanted to end my days among good people."

Emily, who had been listening, felt a shiver run through her at the words. *Among good people.* The phrase resounded in her. Yet she herself was not resigned. Within the greater context, her little act of defiance might well seem meaningless, and yet she would fight on, for it was all she knew. She had tried to be a good Taoist and follow the path of *wuwei,* but at the last that path had failed her. Faced with annihilation she had chosen to fight back. And even now, when things were at their bleakest, she did not flinch from that fight. It was in her nature to oppose fate – to defy it; perhaps even to seek to change it.

The talk went on, yet she had heard enough. Turning, she stole away silently, the voices fading to a murmur behind her, retracing her steps until she came to the turn in the passageway that led down to the west door.

Lin Lao should be back by now, and he'd have news. She'd sit in on his debriefing, then see to whatever needed to be seen to. And then, if there was time, maybe she'd pay Hannah another visit; borrow a few more of her books.

Emily smiled. Hannah was far too modest. If anyone saw things clearly, then Hannah did. And if Hannah thought it was over, then, in all probability it was.

But not yet. And not without a struggle.

* * *

"Which way now?"

Lin Lao paused, then felt his head jerk about. The question had come from just behind him. It was the boy, Da-neel, who had spoken.

Lao's gaze was fixed on the mountains directly ahead of him now. He could not speak nor move a single muscle unless they willed it. He had been dead and now he was alive. He did not understand it, but so it was. And now they used him.

His mouth opened, compelled to answer, the words coming slowly from his mouth, slurred yet comprehensible. "Wee go riih . . . Heah for gaah 'twee two tawh pea. Vah-lee is bee-yawn."

"And the door?"

It was the woman this time. Lao felt his nerve ends bristle. The tone of her voice was so familiar, yet beneath it was something utterly alien. Alien and cold.

"Door is there," he answered, hating himself for the betrayal, but unable to prevent it. "At fahr enn."

"Good," the boy said, his tone warm, like a master to his dog. "Then lead on. You know the way."

He felt the restraint signal ease and began to walk again, a ghost in his own body, only tenuously in touch with his physical self. It was chill, but he felt the cold only in a distant, abstract way, for his mind kept returning to what had happened to him on the slab – to the way he had betrayed them all.

And the worst of it was that Emily would forgive him. That was, if she ever got to know what he had done. If she wasn't dead first – killed by the two fakes who walked along behind him.

The thought of it tormented him. It was unendurable. He wanted to cry out, to scream a warning to the surrounding hills, but it was impossible. He was wired like a puppet.

A butterfly settled briefly on his chest. He was conscious of it at the edge of his vision; a beautiful bright gold butterfly with vivid red markings. And then it was gone.

Behind him Da-neel cleared his throat, then laughed.

"Did you see his face when he found me fucking you? He pretended it didn't matter, but it did."

Her voice was cold. "You want to be careful, Da-neel. He doesn't like being crossed. You cease being useful to him and . . ."

Lao did not see the gesture, but he could imagine it. A knife being drawn across a throat, perhaps, or something like.

The image of DeVore's face looming over him came to mind. At the time he had wondered why the man had spared his face, for he'd heard tales of men's eyes being burned out, hot wires poked through the soft pupils, or of their tongues being sliced like liver while still in their mouths. But DeVore had taken great care not to touch his face. Not that he'd lacked inventiveness elsewhere on his anatomy.

That pain was still in his body; anaesthetised but there beneath the glass-like numbness that he felt.

And when they've finished using me, do I die again? Do they switch me off, like a machine that's been discarded?

Of course they would, for that's how they thought. They were not human in any proper way, for what made one human was compassion.

He felt a sudden sadness that it should have to end this way.

You taught me well, mother. But now they're going to kill you.

There was a tiny tremor in his body, the last faint remnants of what he'd been, and then it was gone. Like a machine he walked on, climbing the slope toward the gap, the door ahead of him.

* * *

The butterfly fluttered across the rock face, then settled. It stretched its wings, as if basking in the sun, and then it trembled.

Slowly it changed, the surface of its wings contracting to become a perfect circle which lifted, tilting towards the south.

It had noticed immediately how strangely the boy was moving, more like an automaton than a normal human being. It was that which had attracted it. And staring up into the boy's face it had seen how fixed the stare was, how pale the skin.

Dead he was. A corpse. And yet he walked.

It was a mystery worth mentioning to the main mass.

At once it began sending, the circular membrane vibrating delicately as the high frequency signal went out. Something was happening. Something the main mass ought to know about at once.

It sent again, duplicating the message, making sure; then, with a tiny shudder, it transformed itself again, a fleck of gold and red, fluttering off across the mountainside.

* * *

"Impressive," Hannah said, handing Daniel back the paper target, "but not unexpected."

"No?"

She smiled. "Your fame precedes you, Daniel. I was told you could pick the eyes out of an insect at a hundred paces. It was no exaggeration, was it?"

"No." Daniel grinned. He clicked on the safety, then set the gun aside. "It used to be a useful skill."

"But now?"

"Now history's ending. There'll be no need for guns any more."

"No . . ." She glanced at Daniel, conscious of how he looked at her, then asked: "Did you never think of trying to kill DeVore?"

"Oh, I thought about it. But the problem was getting close enough to do it."

She nodded, then shivered. It was cold down here in the target rooms. "Do you mind if we leave here, Daniel?"

"No. No, I . . ." He stopped, awkward suddenly.

"What?"

He shrugged. "No. Forget it . . ."

"No. What is it? Tell me. Please."

"It's just that I . . ." He looked away, his awkwardness now painfully obvious.

"Oh," she said, realising at last. "And there was I thinking you were interested in my work." She laughed. "I guess I ought to be flattered. I mean, I'm years older than you, Daniel and . . ."

"It doesn't matter."

"No?" Then, "No, I guess it doesn't."

"And I am interested. In fact, I read one of your books . . ."

She blinked. They had been talking all morning and this was the first time he had mentioned it. "I don't see . . . I mean, it's history. What has that to do with this?"

"You're there," he said, staring at her now. "You're everywhere, in every line, like a great calm presence behind it all."

"And you fell in love with *that*?"

Daniel nodded. There was a moment's awkward silence between them, then Hannah spoke again.

"So what now?"

"We could go to my room . . ."

Her laughter shocked him. Seeing that, she relented. Reaching out, she gently took his hands. "I'm sorry, Daniel, I forgot. I guess you didn't have much time for subtlety in the camps."

But he was blushing now, ashamed of his directness.

"Besides," she went on, "maybe you're right. Maybe it's best to be this open. After all, we've not much time left, have we?"

He looked up at her, hopeful. "Then you feel the same?"

She smiled. "No . . . No, I don't think I do. But I like you, Daniel. So let that be enough."

* * *

Just ahead of them the trees thinned out and the river that ran to their right twisted across their path, following the towering wall of rock that lay just beyond. Some fifty metres on, an old stone bridge crossed the deep gorge. A barrier had been pulled across the far end of the bridge. Behind it stood two men, rebels by their mountain attire, laser rifles slung over their shoulders.

Deep within the wood, Emtu and Da-neel crouched, peering through their long-sight lenses at the rebel patrol. Nearby, the corpse of Lin Lao stood among the trees, his unblinking eyes staring towards the north.

"It's Lin Pei," Emtu whispered, gesturing towards the figure who was coming down the path to join the two men at the barrier.

"Perfect," Da-neel answered.

"What do you mean? It's Lin Pei."

"Exactly. So we use that. Watch."

He scuttled across until he stood directly behind Lin Lao. "Okay, Lin Lao," he whispered, "this is what you do . . ."

* * *

Lin Pei blew into his cupped hands then straightened, looking toward the wood, suddenly alert.

Beside him, his two men had also turned and had taken their guns from their shoulders. There was a double click and then a hum as the guns warmed up.

Lin Pei drew his hand gun. He took a step towards the barrier then stopped, relief flooding him.

"Lin Lao!"

As Lao emerged from the trees, Pei frowned, noting at once how awkwardly his brother moved. He gestured for the barrier to be pulled aside, then hurried out onto the bridge.

Lao looked bad, as if he'd suffered some deep, penetrating wound that he was trying not to antagonise.

"Lin Lao?"

Pei hurried across, holding Lao's arms and staring into his face. Lao's face was strange, the muscles slack. He was pale and drawn, as if he'd lost a lot of blood. But it was his eyes that caught Pei's attention. They seemed in torment.

"Are you hurt, Lao?"

Lao groaned. It was a tiny sound, almost inaudible, yet so filled with pain that Lin Pei gripped him, certain now that he'd sustained some awful injury. Yet there was no outward sign of any hurt.

"What happened, Lao? Where are your men?"

Lao's mouth opened. There was a *haaah.* A nothing sound. The flesh inside Lao's mouth was dark, black almost.

Certain now, Pei turned, looking to his men. "Quick! Help me, now!"

Yet even as he turned back, Lao's legs gave and he fell.

"*Lin Lao!*"

* * *

Three shots rang out. As their echo faded, Emtu stood. Slipping her rifle back over her shoulder, she began to dust herself down, brushing leaf mould from her knees.

"That was good shooting, Da-neel."

He smiled, then stood, his attention still focused on the fallen figures fifty metres off. "You didn't do badly yourself."

They walked across.

Lin Pei lay on his back, his arms splayed out, one leg buckled under him. The bullet had gone straight through his forehead, leaving a neat entry hole, but his brains had been spattered all over the earth path behind him. Ten metres further on lay the second man, slumped against the side of the bridge, his skull half shot away. Beyond him lay the third of them, on his face, a trail of blood dribbling down from his shattered head, pooling on the cracked stone of the bridge.

Emtu watched as Da-neel checked the first two bodies, then, pausing over the last of them, placed his handgun to the back of the man's head.

She felt the detonation in her blood. Deep down in her groin.

As Da-neel straightened up, she grinned.

"What?" he asked, puzzled.

She walked over to him, then reached down, covering his swollen crotch with her hand. "This."

"You noticed?"

Pushing her face against his, she kissed him, her hunger unmistakable. Breaking from that kiss, he shivered, surprised by her. "Here?"

"Right here."

He stared at her a moment longer, the hunger in her eyes matched by his own, then pushed her down, his hands tearing at her clothes.

* * *

Lin Lao lay there, motionless, facing his dead brother, his eyes locked on his brother's face, trapped by that dark and tiny hole in the pale expanse of the forehead.

The sight burned him; seared him to the depths of his soul. Wretched he was; in hell as living memory flooded back to him. Pei, who had nursed him through sickness. Pei, who had loved him and looked after him. Pei, who'd made his heart swell with pride. His big brother, Pei.

A muscle in the dead man's face trembled, then lay still. Slowly a tear trickled down his cheek.

Quietly, the dead man cried.

* * *

DeVore speared a radish with his fork and popped it into his mouth, then set the plate aside, his eyes never once leaving the screen.

Emtu's face was flushed now, her lips drawn back in an animal rictus as Da-neel fucked her. She was close now. Very close.

"Shit!"

Unzipping his fly, he raised his buttocks, easing his trousers down over his hips, then gestured impatiently to one of the serving boys who stood nearby.

"Boy! See to me at once!"

As Emtu's face began to contort, he felt the boy's mouth close over the tip of his penis. Grasping the back of the boy's head, he pulled him closer and began to thrust. The boy gagged and tried to pull away, but DeVore merely gripped him tighter, ignoring his discomfort, pushing up into him, harder and harder, as it to poke his way out through the back of his head.

Emtu's face was wracked in agony now, and as she came, so did he, his groin grinding into the boy's face, like a broken bottle gouging out an eye.

With a gasp, he pulled back, letting the boy fall from him.

The boy lay there, choking, his face tinged blue, his bruised and bloodied mouth gasping for each breath, his chest heaving.

But no one saw. All eyes were carefully averted. No one dared see.

A great shudder passed through DeVore. He stood then, tugging up his pants, began to zip himself up once more.

"Yes," he said, a low chuckle escaping him. "Yes, indeed, my lovelies. You make a fine couple. Maybe I'll let you live after all, boy. Maybe I'll even let you keep her. But first you get me the real Emily Ascher, you understand? First you do that."

* * *

Da-neel pulled up his trousers, then turned, looking back at the woods with narrowed eyes.

"Get up!" he hissed. "Come on. Let's go."

Emtu sat up, frowning at him. "What is it?"

"Look!"

Da-neel pointed. There, among the trees, where before there had been nothing but grass and shrub, was now a host of flowers. Lilies. Gleaming, ghost-white lilies.

"Gods!"

She hastened up, fastening her clothes with fumbling fingers, while Da-neel got hold of Lin Lao by the shoulders and hauled him to his feet.

"Okay," he said, turning to look at her. "Are you ready?"

She nodded, but her eyes were looking past him at the whiteness that now lay beneath the distant branches.

"Do you think it's dangerous?"

He shrugged. "I don't know. But I'm not staying to find out. If our friend Lao is right, we're less than a kilometre from their base camp. Even with this zombie we can make it in an hour."

Lin Lao made a noise. *Haaah*, he said.

"Gas," Emtu suggested, answering Da-neel's unspoken query. "The little fucker's decomposing."

Da-neel laughed, dispelling the tension that had fallen on them. "That's all right, then. Just so long as he doesn't start falling apart before we get there."

* * *

It came down from the heights, like snow, covering the verdant slopes. Only this snow did not fall, it walked.

With a faint rustling, a sound not unlike that of the wind blowing through the branches of the trees, the great host of lilies entered the ruined village, spreading in a slow avalanche between the crumbling walls and along the weed-strewn paths, until there was nothing but ancient brickwork poking from a great sea of white.

There was a brief moment of perfect stillness and then the whiteness shimmered. Drawing memories from the stones, the floraforms began to change, to transmute themselves into roofs and doors and windows, until the ruin was no longer a ruin but a perfect replica of the place it had once been, two centuries before.

In the old graveyard dark earth heaved as its pale, lithe roots delved with an unsuspected strength among the caskets, unearthing bone and rotted cloth. For a moment it was a charnel scene, a scene of chaotic disinterment, and then those bones stood tall and straight, sprouting leaves and buds. Strange trees that resembled men.

They trembled and in an instant flowered, a season passing in the blink of an eye. Ancient codes were read and replicated.

Petals fell away, leaving the bare branches of human limbs. Men and women who had not drawn breath for two centuries and more now stood upon the surface of the earth, their pallid flesh tinged green, their eyes the unbroken white of lilies.

There was a sigh, an almost silent exhalation from that newly-resurrected host, as they turned to view the transformed landscape. The ancient village was embedded in a great ocean of white that had no end but filled the land from horizon to horizon; valley and slope, gorge and peak, lush meadow and barren rock face.

For a moment they dreamed an ancient, human dream. A time-locked dream of summers long ago.

But it was a new age, a new time. The beginning of a time without time. And as they turned and went into their houses, so they turned their backs upon that human past. The last vestiges of human memory – of ancient, coded instinct – slipped from them as the DNA within them was transformed, becoming something other.

Something greater.

There was silence, an utter, perfect stillness, and then the lilies in the graveyard shimmered, as if a flame had passed across them. Some glowed with a vivid brightness, while others withered, a strange darkness consuming them.

For the briefest instant they formed the image of a face; a perfect, almost photographic image. Daniel's face.

Again the lilies shimmered, and then, like the ripple of the wind passing across a cornfield, the petals fell, transforming as they fell into a mist that lingered briefly and was gone, leaving the dead ground green.

* * *

The feel of him laying there naked in her arms in the darkness was unreal, dreamlike. She had had lovers before, of course, but none so young, nor half so gentle. Besides, those other men had not stayed long – not when they'd discovered that her first love was for the truth of history and not themselves.

But now there was Daniel.

She brought her hand up and gently brushed his cheek, laying her fingers softly against his forehead, smiling to herself.

So surprising; to find a lover, here at the end of the world. Here, where she'd thought at best to find companionship in these final days.

Daniel stirred. "Hannah?"

Her fingers ceased their soothing motion. "Yes, my love."

"That part in your book about historical cycles and recurrence. What did you mean by that?"

She laughed. Had ever any of her lovers asked her such a question? No. At best it was "Was I good?" or "Can I see you again?" Never such interest in her work, her essential *self*.

"Just that there are recognisable patterns in history, and sometimes – just sometimes – it is as if all past history had not happened, and men were doomed to live through the same events again."

"How do you mean?"

She traced the shape of his jaw with her fingers, remembering as she did how he had kissed her in the darkness that first time. "Well, take the First Emperor, for instance."

"Ch'in Shih Huang Ti?"

"Yes." She smiled, pleased by his quickness. "One might say that he was a great man, yet he was also an ogre, an absolute tyrant, who made the lives of those beneath him utterly unbearable. Many millions died simply to glorify his ego, in the fulfilment of his schemes and in the building of his palaces and tomb. In his reign we can identify a number of dominant features: the drive to unify the world he knew – ancient China; the less admirable and yet no weaker drive to burn the history books and rewrite history, again to his own self-glorification. Further, we might note how, in his reign, ego came to outweigh wisdom, such that the man finally thought himself a god and sought to make himself immortal. In doing so he undid much of the good work he had brought about."

"And?" Daniel turned, snuggling into her, his cheek nuzzling against her breast, against the sensitive bud of her nipple, making her almost want to forget the history lesson and make love to him again. But this was important. As important as anything she might teach him.

"Two thousand years later, another great man arose in China. His name was Mao Tse Tung. He ruled a land much greater than his predecessor, the First Emperor; a land with maybe ten times the population. Unlike Ch'in Shih Huang Ti, Mao spurned personal adornment. He built no great palaces and tombs in his own honour. And yet the pattern of his days was much in accord with those of the Prince of Ch'in, for like the First Emperor, Mao let ego outweigh common sense. He thought himself a kind of god and one day decreed that men could grow five times the crop that they had previously grown on their land. They warned him, but he would not listen. In a single season he overthrew the wisdom of two thousand years. And, of course, disaster followed. Twenty million died of starvation."

Daniel looked up, intrigued. "Was Mao a T'ang?"

Hannah shook her head and smiled. "No, Daniel. Mao Tse Tung was Ko Ming. A rebel."

"A rebel?" Daniel laughed with disbelief.

"Oh yes," she said, serious now. "Perhaps the greatest rebel the world has ever known. Yet, just like the First Emperor, he sought to burn the books, to bury alive those scholars that opposed him and rewrite history to suit his purposes. Yes, and so in love was he with revolution that he even set his people against one another, to keep rebellion alive. He destroyed the people's love of knowledge and again millions died. And for what? To feed a vain man's ego!"

"And is that the pattern of history?"

She sighed. "It is. The greater the man, the greater the damage he can do. The finer his purpose – and what finer drive is there than to unify a people and give them stable laws? – the more chance there is of him falling into the pit of hell and taking all with him. So it was with the great Tyrant, Tsao Ch'un."

Of Tsao Ch'un even Daniel knew, for Tsao Ch'un had built Chung Kuo from the ruins of the old world. Had *unified* that world.

"And DeVore . . . is he another of this kind?"

"Far from it. DeVore is something new. DeVore is a breaking of that chain. Ch'in Shih Huang Ti, Mao Tse Tung and Tsao Ch'un . . . they are like spans in a great bridge that crosses time, but DeVore . . . with DeVore there is a gap. A breach. Why, I suspect that he isn't even human!"

Daniel sat up, then wriggled round to face her.

"Not a man? Then what *is* he?"

She reached out to trace the shape of his face with the fingers of her right hand. Her nipples were hard now and looking at the beauty of him she wanted him again. "I do not know, Daniel. Yet I know he is the end of history. With him the story finally ends."

For a moment he stared back at her, his eyes on hers, then, noticing her arousal for the first time, he laughed.

"We should not be talking. Not if time is ending."

"No," she said softly. "No, my love. We should not."

* * *

Da-neel pushed Lin Lao over, then, taking the butt of his rifle, smashed Lao's right leg just below the knee.

"Da-neel?"

He met Emtu's eyes and grinned. "I want him to limp. It's better if he limps."

She gave a small "ah" of understanding, then looked back at the slope facing them. For all she knew they were already being watched, but Da-neel said no. From what Lin Lao had spilled to DeVore under torture, the rebels didn't work that way. The faint glow of infrared from camera eyes could be seen from above, so the rebels didn't use them. No, they used camouflage and sophisticated entry gates underground.

Finding a gate was hard. But not so hard as using one.

Which was why they'd brought Lin Lao. His retinal print would be their key. Using him, they would walk straight into the heart of the rebel headquarters.

Or so they hoped.

Da-neel hauled Lin Lao to his feet again and had him walk backwards and forwards a moment, then nodded, satisfied. "Okay," he said, "this is what you say. 'I'm hurt. Let me in.' You've got that? Nothing more. 'I'm hurt. Let me in.' And you keep saying it, like you're exhausted and it's the only thing that's in your mind. Right?"

Against his will, Lin Lao nodded.

"Okay," Da-neel said. "Let me hear it."

Lin Lao's mouth opened silently, then, a moment later. "I hurr . . . Lehr mee i."

"Again."

"I hurr. Lehr mee i."

Emtu laughed coldly. "You think they'll understand that?"

Da-neel looked to her. "It'll have to do. Besides, it's the retinal pattern that'll convince them. This is Mamma's boy and she wants him back. She'll let him in, don't fear."

"And then?"

Da-neel grinned. "And then mayhem."

* * *

"I hurr. Lehr mee i."

Mo Teng looked away from the screen, facing his fellow guard, then shook his head. "I don't like it, Hun. Something's wrong."

"But the print matches."

"Sure, the print matches. But there's something about him. His face. That look in his eyes."

Hun made a noise of exasperation. "Yes, because he's hurt! Like he says. Look at him. The poor boy's barely holding himself together!"

Mo Teng looked back and shrugged. "Maybe. But I'd be happier if Emily made this call."

"*Aiya*!" Hun shook his head. "And have him bleed to death?"

"I don't see any blood. Do you?"

"No, but . . ."

Outside the gate, Lin Lao seemed to shudder, then he fell head first.
"Oh, shit!" Mo Heng leaned across and placed his hand on the release pad. Hun smiled and slapped his own, then stood.
"Come on. Let's give Lao a hand!"

* * *

"Not very original," Emtu said, lowering her lens and looking to Da-neel.
"No, but it works."
She watched him lift his gun and, as the first of the two figures emerged, fire the bolt.
It flew straight and true into the dark mouth of the gate, trailing the super-fine ice-wire thread that would cut in two anything that crossed its path, be it rock or flesh.
There was a cry from within the gate. The second man was hit. Throwing aside the thread-gun, Da-neel lifted his rifle and, taking only a moment to aim, picked off the other guard.
He stood, turning to Emtu with a smile. "Come. It's open."

* * *

There were gunshots, explosions. Daniel sat bolt upright, then slipped out from beneath the sheets and crossed the room, quickly stepping into his fatigues. He buckled on his gunbelt then straightened up, listening to the distant noises, trying to make out what part of the great underground warren they were coming from.
"Daniel?"
Picking up his gun, he turned, looking across at her. "Something's happening . . ."
"I know. Should I come with you?"
"No. No, I . . ."
Daniel realised suddenly that it could all be over soon. That in a while he might easily be dead and that would be it.
Putting his gun down again, he went across and sat beside her, holding her to him, kissing her and stroking her hair, afraid suddenly to leave her. What if someone came while he was gone?
He took a handgun from his belt and, quickly checking it was fully loaded, handed it to her.
"In case."
She nodded. Then, with a final kiss, she pushed him from her. "Go on, Daniel. Emily will need you."
He grimaced. "Yes." Then, "I love you, you know that?"
Hannah smiled. "I know. Now go. And take care. Take good care, neh?"

* * *

Emily stopped and crouched, sniffing the air. The tunnel up ahead of her was dark. The lights had either failed or been shot out. From what she could make out there were only a handful of DeVore's men at most, but they were good. They had to be to survive more than ten minutes in this deadly warren.

The air blew cold from the darkness up ahead. Cold but not pure, for there was the stench of cordite and burned flesh.

So at last he's found us, she thought. The hour she'd feared was finally upon her. Now it was simple. Kill or be killed. Survive or die. The most brutal of equations. No love in it, and no compassion.

And no deals. At last, no deals.

She crept forward, listening for any sound, wishing now that she had remembered her helmet, knowing that if DeVore's men had infrared they would be able to pick her off like a walking neon sign.

Careless. How unlike her to be so careless.

She stopped. Was that a noise, or had she imagined it?

Silence. A long silence, and then . . . yes, a faint shuffling, as if someone were crawling forward on their knees and elbows. The sound of cloth on stone.

Emily raised her gun, meaning to fire, yet even as she did there was a gunshot. A bullet whistled past her ear.

She threw herself flat.

Silence. Once more, a long silence. But now she knew there was someone there. She let out a long, shivering breath, then spoke into the darkness.

"You missed."

There was laughter; curiously familiar laughter, though she could not make out why.

"You have a sense of humour."

Emily blinked, trying to make out where she'd heard that voice before. "You think this is funny, then?"

"Hilarious. You see, he doesn't want you dead. But I do."

The knowledge of who it was went through Emily like a shock. It was her double. Her other self, grown from her severed finger just as Eve was supposedly grown from Adam's rib. DeVore's plaything. His "woman".

"You're not *jealous*, surely?"

"What do you think? He made me so he could have you. Or someone who looked like you. Do you know what that does to a woman? Why, he even aged me so I'd look haggard like you."

"Haggard?" Emily laughed. "Well, looks don't matter much in the dark do they, my pretty? And a corpse looks like a corpse, however much rouge you apply."

"Do you think that's what I am?"

Emily's voice was cold now, hard. This thing was what she could have become. What DeVore had wanted her to be.

"Why? What do you think you are? *Alive?* You were never that. Nothing he makes is truly alive."

Two shots rang out, one high, one low. Both missed. Emily smiled. She hadn't been sure at first, but now she was. It was even between them. They were both blind.

Emily closed her eyes, concentrating, preparing herself, then, steadying herself on one elbow, raised her gun and aimed.

There was another shot, but this time no bullet whistled past her.

There was a groan; a deep, anguished noise, tinged with pain. There were booted footsteps on the stone, and then the distinctive click of a gun-hammer being drawn back into the firing position.

The second shot was muffled; a wet, spattering sound.

Even in the darkness she could imagine it.

Emily swallowed. "Who's there?"

Two steps, then. "It's okay. She's dead."

"Daniel?" Relief flooded her. Clambering up, she took two steps towards him, then stopped. "*Daniel?*"

The dart hit her right shoulder and knocked her backwards, her gun spinning away from her in the dark.

Booted footsteps, and then someone leaned over her, his breath warm on her face. "Almost right."

* * *

DeVore had landed cruisers on the northern slopes and flooded the entrance tunnels with his men. Now Daniel and a handful of survivors crouched in the trees below the western gate, waiting to see if anyone else would come out.

A huge pall of black smoke filled the sky above the mountain. A great roiling mass that threw its shadow over everything. The great roof of the rebel headquarters had buckled in that savage conflagration and caved in. Now only a massive blackened hole existed where their living quarters had once been.

The sight of it plunged Daniel into despair.

Emily was dead. He knew it for a certainty. And Hannah too. And soon he also would be dead, for there was no way they could defeat DeVore. Not now.

But he would not go easy into the darkness. And if DeVore dared show himself – to gloat or simply to claim victory – he would have him.

He looked about him. There were only fourteen of them left, himself included, and three of those were wounded badly. But they were well-armed and determined. They might yet prove a thorn in DeVore's side.

"Okay," he said. "It's time to hit back. We have two advantages. First, we know the tunnels better than they do. Second, they think they've won. They think they've only mopping up to do. They've relaxed. If we do this right, we could be in among them before they know what's going on."

He saw one or two of them look down and frowned.

"What is it?"

"They're boys," one of them mumbled. "They're only boys."

"Boys with guns," he answered. "Boys trained to hate. To kill."

"Yes, but . . ."

"But nothing," he said, more harshly than he'd meant. Then, relenting, "Look. I know it's hard. I know it's against your instincts. But we can't simply lie down and let them bury us. Not now. Not ever. We *have* to fight."

"I don't know," the first of them said, shaking his head despairingly. "We've lost. What point is there? They've taken Emily."

The words jolted Daniel. "They've *what*?"

"They've taken her. Ho Jen and I saw it. They must have drugged her. But we saw them carry her onto one of their cruisers."

Daniel closed his eyes. Dead was bearable, but *taken*. He did not want to imagine what DeVore would do with Emily.

"Did it leave? Did the cruiser go?"

The man nodded.

"Aiya . . ."

Then DeVore had her.

Grimacing, Daniel tore the rifle from his shoulder and began to load it.

"So what are we going to do?"

He turned to stare at the man. "We're going to do exactly what I said. We're going to go in there and kill as many of the little fuckers as we can."

"But why? It's over. He's won."

Daniel swallowed bile. It was true. He even knew it was true. But the anger he felt would not be assuaged until . . .

"Daniel! Look!"

He glanced up, then turned, looking to where one of the men was pointing.

"What in the gods' names . . .?"

To the north-west three peaks dominated the skyline. Between the first and second of them the sky was slowly turning black.

A swarm. He'd swear it was some kind of swarm. Then he understood. Cruisers. Hundreds upon hundreds of cruisers.

Daniel felt his heart sink. He threw the gun down, then sat, watching them come on, the drone of their engines growing by the moment.

As the first wave roared overhead, he looked down, thinking of Hannah, hoping she had not suffered. Not that it mattered now. Not that anything mattered.

There was the sound of rapid gunfire, of rockets exploding. The ground trembled beneath him. Frowning, Daniel looked up.

"What the . . .?

Immediately in front of him, on his eyeline and barely five hundred metres away, three cruisers now hovered. Daniel swallowed, then stood again, his hands on his hips, facing them.

"Come on, then," he said quietly. "Come on you bastards . . ."

Behind him the mayhem went on; explosion after explosion.

"Well?" he yelled, his voice echoing across the slope. "Don't you want me?"

The central cruiser detached itself and drifted slowly towards him. Stooping, Daniel picked up his gun then straightened again.

DeVore. It *had* to be DeVore. Well, let the bastard show himself.

A hundred metres off, the cruiser began to settle, turning slightly to the side as it touched down on level ground. The engines died, whining down into silence.

Daniel smiled. If he'd only had a rocket-launcher.

The other two cruisers still hovered there, their wing-mounted guns covering him, but Daniel was barely aware of them. His eyes were fixed upon the hatch, even as it hissed and fell open.

He raised the rifle to his shoulder and looked through the sight, taking aim. One shot, that was all it would take.

If they let him.

But he doubted that they'd let him.

Daniel tensed, waiting.

The rounded rectangle of the hatch was dark, no shadows in it. For a long, long time nothing happened, and then someone stepped out, their shaven head emerging into the light.

Daniel narrowed his eyes, surprised.

Not DeVore . . . Then who?

Golden robes. Flowing golden robes patterned with blood-red dragons. Beautiful Chinese dragons that floated on the golden silk like living creatures.

The man walked towards him, then stopped, a faint smile on his oriental features, his open palms spread, his golden eyes burning like suns.

"Daniel? It is the *real* Daniel, isn't it?"

Daniel blinked. The man was unarmed. Completely unarmed.

"Who are you?"

The Han grinned. "Me? I'm King of America. Or so they tell me. And now I'm King of Europe, too. And King of the Wilds, come to that. But enough of me. It's *you* I'm interested in."

"Give me one good reason why I shouldn't shoot you?"

"Hmmm . . ." The Han scratched his chin, then. "Well, for a start it might annoy your mother."

"My mother?" Daniel shook his head. "My mother's taken. DeVore has her."

"DeVore *had* her. But now I do. She's inside." The Han half turned, indicating the cruiser. "She's a little groggy, I'm afraid, but she'll be okay. Once the drugs have worn off."

Daniel swallowed, steeling himself against believing it. He knew the tricks such people played. To give you hope and then snatch it away. To break you with despair. It was pure Sun Tzu.

"I don't believe you."

"No?" The Han shrugged, then sadly. "Well, I guess I might be cautious, too, if I were you. But I'm not lying to you, Daniel, I swear. This is no time for lies."

"I don't . . ."

Daniel stopped. Behind the strangely-dressed Han, someone had stepped out from the hatch and onto the top of the ramp. Daniel blinked, then shook his head.

Was it her, or was it just the copy?

Noticing his gaze, the Han turned and smiled. "Ah . . . *Mu Ch'in* Ascher. You should not be up."

She hobbled across, clearly in pain, her shoulder tightly bandaged.

"Daniel? Daniel . . . put down the gun."

Despite himself, the sight of her filled him with joy. He wanted it to be her. Wanted it desperately.

But what if this were some final little torment? Some subtle, nasty twist?

Games. The Man loves games . . .

Though it ached now, he kept the gun steady at his shoulder.

He saw how she shook her head with exasperation. So familiar that gesture. But what it really hers?

"Come now, Daniel. Either shoot us or throw the gun down. Which is it to be?"

He nudged the rifle barrel slightly to the side, gesturing at the Han. "Who is he?"

"You mean you don't know?"

"Should I?"

Her eyes were suddenly strange. She turned, looking at the Han as if seeing him anew, then smiled. "This, Daniel, is Li Yuan, Son of Li Shai Tung. I fought him once. But now . . ."

"Li Yuan?" Daniel gave a laugh of disbelief. "The T'ang?"

Li Yuan gave the slightest bow of his head. "The same."

"But you . . ."

"Were dead? No. Were exiled? Yes. Were wrong? Often. But now I'm back, Daniel, and I want you to come with me. Now do as your adopted mother says and choose, for I for one am growing cold and would as soon be dead as stand here on this mountainside in my silks!"

* * *

They rounded up all of their captives in one of the lower meadows, then sent a messenger up the mountain to let Li Yuan know.

He came down, still dressed in his golden silks, and stood before that silent, bare-headed host. Beside him, Daniel looked on, impressed despite himself by the demeanour of the man who had once been ruler of Chung Kuo, and who now, at the end of that world's days, was once again at the centre of it all.

There were morphs here – the last of DeVore's once great army of 40,000 creatures – and men, but mainly there were boys. Boys from the camps. Boys who, like Daniel, had never known anything but brutality. From their eyes Daniel could tell that they expected nothing now but death.

Li Yuan went among them fearlessly, a piece of plain white chalk in his hand, meeting the eyes of each of them in turn, chalking the men and morphs, ignoring most of the boys.

When he was done, he looked to his General – a tall, stern-looking American with white hair and a neatly-trimmed goatee beard – and smiled humourlessly.

"Those I've chalked die," he said quietly. "The rest you release."

The man nodded and gestured to his waiting lieutenants, who at once turned away, to begin the work of separating the living from the dead.

"Is that it?" Daniel asked. "Are we finished now?"

Li Yuan looked to him. "Far from it. There is one final battle to be waged before we go."

"Go?"

"Didn't she tell you?" Li Yuan smiled. "I guess it must have slipped her mind. We're leaving here, Daniel. I've had a spaceship built."

Daniel stared at Li Yuan a moment, astonished by the news, then he looked down. "I don't want to. Not now she's dead."

"*She?*" Li Yuan's eyes were suddenly concerned. "There was someone you loved?"

Daniel nodded.

"And you're certain that she's dead?"

"As good as."

"And if she isn't?"

But Daniel shook his head. "You saw what happened."

"Maybe. And yet there *were* survivors. *You* came out."

"I knew my way."

Li Yuan stared at him a moment longer, then he turned and snapped his fingers. At once a messenger came across and, kneeling, bowed before him. "*Chieh Hsia?*"

"Go at once and find out whether there were any more survivors from the rebel headquarters. Any women, particularly." He turned, looking to Daniel. "Her name?"

Daniel sighed, then shook his head.

"Her *name*, Daniel."

"Hannah."

Li Yuan turned back to his messenger. "You heard. Now go. And return as soon as you have news."

* * *

There were eight of them in all, sat in a ragged circle about a fire that had been built beneath the ruins of the eastern gate, their figures hunched forward, hands stretched towards the comfort of the flames, rough blankets thrown about their shoulders.

As Daniel stepped up onto the brow of the slope and looked down on them, he felt a tightness in his stomach and knew it was fear. Fear that, having allowed himself to hope, that hope would now be dashed.

He had never known fear before. Never needed to. Before now it had been him alone, and he'd had nothing to lose, but now . . .

Daniel closed his eyes, trying to block it out, but it was impossible. Once one started feeling there was no stopping it. It was not a tap one could turn on and off.

She's dead, he told himself yet again. *She couldn't have got out*. But his heart didn't believe that. His heart wanted the impossible.

He looked from figure to figure, trying to make something of their stooped and dejected shapes. Three of them had their backs to him, but that one there . . .

One of them lifted her head. *Her*, definitely a her despite the shortness of the hair. Hair that had been burned from her head, or so it seemed. He knew her.

"Siri . . ."

The disappointment was immense. And yet he ought to have been pleased. Pleased that at least *someone* had survived that carnage. But if Siri's death had meant that Hannah lived . . .

Daniel swallowed bitterly. The very idea of it was appalling, and yet he could not deny it. If he could have made a deal with the gods, it would have been that, and he'd have made it without a moment's thought.

Love. The sheer brutality of love.

He trudged down, despondent now. Most of them had their heads down, from weariness or injury, yet as he came closer, Siri saw him and half rose, recognition in her face.

Her smile almost broke Daniel's heart.

"Daniel . . ."

Hearing the name, one of those with their backs to him half-turned. He barely noticed them, preoccupied as he was with Siri. Then he stopped dead, his mouth falling open. As the blanket slipped from her shoulders, he took a step towards her.

"Hannah . . .?"

Her face was black, her clothes scorched and soiled, but those eyes were unmistakable. There was a movement of her lips – charred lips that oozed blood through the cracks – then stumbled towards him, her face creased with pain.

"*Hannah!*"

He gripped her to him, grimacing as he did so, all of his hurt and fear and pain transformed suddenly. For a moment longer he simply held her, then, moving back, he stared into her face, putting his hand up to wipe away the tears that now streaked her fire-blackened face.

"It's gone," she said, the effort of making the words clearly hurting her. "It's all gone."

"I know."

"No," she said, the pain in her eyes so deep it seared him. "My work, Daniel. It's all gone. Burned."

He stared at her, smiling now, then kissed her brow, her neck, her blackened cheeks. "No, my love. You brought it out with you."

"But I saw it burning. I tried to save it, but . . ."

"It's all in here," he said, touching her brow with his fingertips. "As long as you're alive, it too survives. Every last word of it."

Her eyes widened. But this time as she made to speak Daniel placed a finger gently to her lips, careful not to hurt her.

"Hush now, my love. Hush. There will be time for words later. Now come. The King of America would like to meet you."

CHAPTER·20

ROOM A THOUSAND YEARS WIDE

It was a different place.

The same and yet different. In small ways different. Small ways that made Kim think that perhaps it *was* his room, and that intruders had come and not so much taken things as replaced them. *Realigned* them.

The workroom and its contents were so familiar, yet so far from his own room – his own space and time – that even to think of the distance he had travelled made his mind reel.

And yet it was no distance at all.

Across the room from where Kim sat, in a chair identical in every way to his own chair back in his own reality, his other self busied himself gathering together papers that would explain to Kim just how the trick had finally been done.

Kim's eyes went to that strange distortion of himself. To his *otherness*, as he had come to think of him. This other Kim was marginally taller than him – an inch or two, he'd judge – and broader at the hips and shoulders, too. Not knowing what the reason for this was, Kim nonetheless felt a momentary twinge of envy.

And suppressed it.

Buried it . . .

Kim smiled. That was the trouble with this kind of acute self-consciousness. Others could fool themselves – could pretend they had not felt what they had felt – but he could not. He was much too self-aware.

"Well . . ." the other said, looking across at him finally. "I think that's all. You can read them later. And the journal of course."

Kim sat forward. "Journal?"

"This." The other walked across and handed Kim a bound leather notebook and a file of papers. It was the closest they had come since that first joining of hands, and as the other made to draw his hand away, Kim reached out and held it, examining the ring that rested on the knuckle of the forefinger. A gold ring, but with a band of jet embedded in it, as if a cat's-eye had been distorted topographically.

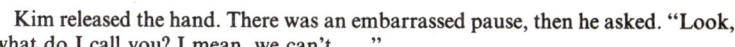

Kim released the hand. There was an embarrassed pause, then he asked. "Look, what do I call you? I mean, we can't . . ."

". . . both be Kim?" His other self frowned, his eyes briefly studying the ring, as if it were the first time *he* had seen it. "No, I guess we can't. Call me K."

Kim gave a brief laugh. "It sounds Kafkaesque."

"You've *read* Kafka?" K. stopped, then: "Silly question."

"No," Kim said, serious suddenly. "Ask, even if it seems pointless. It's clear that we don't map. Not exactly. It's like this room . . . like our physical selves. If we're to work together, it'll help us enormously if we know where we're similar . . ."

". . . and where we're not."

"Yes." Kim grinned. "So what now?"

"What do you want to see?"

Kim answered almost without thought. "Her."

K. stared at him a long time. Silence. A strange, almost eerie silence, then a sigh.

"Well?" Kim prompted. "Don't you?"

K. nodded, but it was the vaguest of nods.

Kim stared at K. a while, puzzled by his reaction, as much as by his general air of sobriety. He had never met anyone quite so sombre. But sensing that this was something that would be explained in time, he changed tack.

"Am I the only one you've been in touch with?"

"So far."

"So far? But I thought . . ." Kim looked down at the cover of the journal. "I thought you'd been to a number of worlds."

"I've been travelling for six months now," K. answered. "But you are the first I've come across."

"The first *you*."

K. nodded, his eyes looking inward. "You see, we inhabit a very narrow spectrum of possibility, you and I. Perhaps that's why the Edderiminaru chose us."

"The *who*?"

"Master Tuan and his merry band of men. That's their real name. Or an abbreviation of it, should I say. In its full form it's a description. A very full description, so I understand."

Kim nodded. "They're giant spiders . . ."

"Yes. I know."

There was a moment's eye contact; an exchange of understanding so deep, so profound that, released from it, Kim felt giddy.

He knows me . . .

That fact, so obvious and yet so unexpected, was perhaps the most frightening thing of all. Even Jelka did not know him one tenth as well as this stranger did.

This stranger who was himself. Or all but.

"It's strange, isn't it?" K. said, coming across and sitting on the edge of the desk beside him.

Kim shivered, then asked what was on his mind. "Your physique . . ."

"This?" K. stood, turning about, as if to let Kim study him, as he'd studied the ring. "Vanity, I'm afraid. It's a special drug treatment I concocted."

Kim frowned. "Why?"
"To see if I could . . . be normal, that is."
"Normal?"
"Physically."
"Ah . . ." Kim looked away. In recent years he had barely thought about it, but there had been a time when it *had* worried him. To be thought of as some stunted, large-eyed dwarf all the time – it was hard not to let that affect you.

Even so, he had never once thought of actually doing something about it. That seemed such a waste of his talent when there was so much else that needed to be done.

Vanity. Kim looked up again. "I'm surprised."

"Yes. I knew you would be. But then you don't know me as well as I know you."

"Clearly not."

"Then perhaps you should get to know me a little better before we decide what's to be done." K. nodded towards the journals. "I tried to be as candid as I could. You see, I knew you'd read them. Or someone like you."

* * *

Kim opened the journal to the first page and began to read:

"*To be truthful, I did not know what to expect. My death, perhaps; the soft tissues of my body imploding under vacuum conditions, flesh and bone freezing even as they shattered; cold sculptures, drifting for eternity. But no. I did not die. There was no searing cold, no pain beyond enduring. Passing through that burning hoop I stepped out into a place I knew. Or had known, in another life.*

The Clay. Its stench so awful that I almost gagged.

And dark. A darkness unimaginable. That, too, I had blocked off in memory. It was like being blind. And yet, all about me, I could hear the scufflings of a thousand unseen creatures.

Why here? I asked, wishing even as I did that I had brought some kind of light to pierce the stygian gloom.

A wish at once fulfilled, for even as I turned, the darkness just behind me split, a shaft of burning, shimmering light spilling out across those dead lands.

The Gateway! And there before it the pool! And finally – there at the pool's far edge – myself, a stick-like creature of sinew and bone, sat back upon its heels, both hands shielding those obscenely bulging eyes against the blinding light, the mouth gaping, an expression of pure awe on the emaciated face.

I knew the moment. Knew that in that one instant the vision had been imprinted in me; the seed of light sown deep in the rich, dark earth of my psyche – the same seed that would one day drive me up and out until I finally reached the stars.

Back I'd gone. Back in time. But why?

It did not see me there. Did not, or maybe could not, it was so bright. Yet the three who came down from the Above – Lehmann, Berdichev and Wyatt – he did see. Oh yes, he saw them and trembled, thinking them gods, gaping as the unrelenting light glittered off the glass of their tall, domed helmets and the silvered metal of their contamination suits.

The child's screech – my screech, I guess it was – surprised me. It was a raw, high-pitched sound that seemed almost to have been torn from deep within the stick-like creature. Yet even as it faded, two shots rang out, the sound of their concussions deafening in that enclosed space.

I stared, shocked, at the smoking gun in Berdichev's hand.

Horrified, I took a step towards myself. 'No-oh!'

But already things were losing substance. Even as the life-blood pumped from my other self, even as the three men turned, surprised, to stare at me, so the world about me – the three men, the Gate, the Clay itself – shimmered like a film that has had every other frame removed.

And then, with a suddenness that literally took my breath, I was back here, in this room, the image of the burning hoop fading in the air."

Kim looked up thoughtfully, giving a little nod to the air, then read on, devouring the pages.

After a while he sat back, rubbing at his eyes. He was beginning to understand, to see what K. had meant about the narrowness of the spectrum in which they existed. Gates. The gate by the pool had been the first, but there had been endless gates in his life. In this existence he had passed through all of them unscathed, or relatively so, yet in another life . . .

No, he corrected himself; *in other lives*.

In other lives he'd failed. In some he had not even begun. Oh yes, he saw it clearly now. Endless worlds in which he had not existed. Worlds where he had not met and married Jelka and so had not conceived Sampsa or Mileja. Worlds where DeVore had triumphed because *he*, Kim Ward, had not been there to counter him.

Or was that the truth? Had he *really* made a difference?

He looked back down, reading on, the hairs rising on the back of his neck.

It was almost two hours before he looked up again. K. was sitting just across from him. Kim blinked, surprised. He had not even noticed him return.

"So?" K. asked. "What do you think?"

What *did* he think? The accounts that had followed the first were all equally graphic. And always, without fail, he'd died. It was as if his life had been a maze and at any point along the way he might have made the wrong turn and come upon a dead end. His end. His death.

His tutor, T'ai Cho, who in this life had loved him and cherished him, yes and saved him many a time – particularly that time after the fight with Janko when Director Andersen would have trashed him without a second thought – in other worlds had gassed him, unable to see the light of intelligence that burned within him.

And even when he'd made it through – to Rehab and beyond – it was to die in stupid, silly ways, in accidents, or at the hands of overzealous guards. Or, in the worst case, at the hands of Marshal Karr – executed on Li Yuan's palace steps as an uncaring Jelka looked on with dispassionate eyes.

To have survived at all was a miracle of kinds.

So what *did* he think?

"I think someone must have trod these paths before us. To find us, I mean."

"Master Tuan?"

"He certainly implied as much."

K. blinked, surprised. "Did he?"

"You mean he hasn't spoken to you?"

"Yes, but not of that. Not of seeking and finding us."

Kim sat back. "I remember him telling me something once, about that time after the attack on SimFic's labs, when he found me and looked after me. He told me that he'd first dreamed of me, and then, how he had later followed the dream, step for step, and how it had come true, almost though if he were still dreaming. And yet it *was* real. It really had come to pass, almost as if there were but a single path to follow. But now . . . well, now we are in a hall of mirrors, and who is to say which path is the right path, and which dream the reality?"

"Then maybe that's our purpose, Kim. To make things singular again. To unify the universes, so that there's only one. Maybe it was never meant to be like this, fragmented like the veins of a leaf into a thousand million pathways. Maybe we're meant to be the glue that bonds it all together again."

"And maybe not."

"Maybe not. And yet I feel certain that we have *some* purpose."

Kim glanced at the open pages of the journal, then met K.'s eyes once more. "Can I finish reading this?"

"Of course. But look, I'm being a very poor host. You must be hungry. Can I get you supper?"

"Supper?" And then he remembered. Jelka. Jelka would be worried if she went down to his workroom and found him gone. She would think . . .

What *would* she think? That he had gone without telling her?

Well, so he had, only . . .

Only what?

"Okay," he said. "But then I must get back."

He said it as if it were a simple thing, as if he only had to catch a train, perhaps, or go through a door and walk down a hallway, whereas the truth was he would have to trust to that device again – to pass through a wheel of burning fire into another universe entirely.

It hit him. Until that moment he had been sleepwalking. Drifting. But suddenly . . .

Kim held on to the desk.

K. stared at him, concerned. "Are you all right?"

"Yes. Yes, I . . ." He laughed, dismissing it. "I felt giddy, that's all. I felt . . ."

". . . like a ghost of yourself?"

Kim nodded. "All those other worlds. Their very existence seems to drain you. To rob you of your essential solidity."

K. smiled; a faint smile, but the first he'd given Kim. "It's okay. I call it the Existentiality Effect. It wears off, after a while."

"Does it?" Kim paused then. "For a moment then, I felt like a painted figure on a canvas. I felt . . ."

The same gap. The same words. I *felt* . . . And then a gap. Because what he felt wasn't like anything he'd felt before. Was something there were no words for. Kim felt . . .

As if I were both here and not here.

Which was impossible, and yet the physical truth.

"You need to eat," K. said, getting up. "There's something very real about eating."

"Yes . . . yes, I guess there is."

"Then come. There's some stew on the hob."

* * *

There was a moment before he knew. A moment when he had all of the pieces he needed, but hadn't yet connected them. The ring. The abnormal, almost psychotic moroseness. That driven quality in the eyes.

And that single word he'd uttered when K. had asked him what he wanted to see. *Her*. By which he'd meant his mother. But K. had not meant *her*. No, he had meant *her* – Jelka.

Kim stood there in the kitchen, staring open-mouthed at the picture on the wall, struck by the significance of the black frame that surrounded that familiar face, filled with a sudden, gut-wrenching understanding.

"*Aiya* . . ."

K. turned and saw at once where Kim was looking. "She didn't make it back," he said, continuing to ladle the steaming lamb stew into a bowl. "It was the virus. You know, Golden Dreams. She was too weak. Her and Mileja both. There was nothing we could do."

He came across and offered Kim the bowl. "Do you want bread with that?"

Kim shook his head. For a moment longer he stood there, stunned, trying to imagine how *he* would have felt had Jelka died that time; how he'd have coped, that was, if he'd have coped at all, for he could not imagine a life without her there at the still centre of it all. There like a rock to which his soul was anchored.

He could simply not imagine it.

But then, he did not have to. He had only to look at his other self, there on the far side of the kitchen. That strange, unhappy man.

"I'm sorry," he said. "I . . ."

A moment's sudden realisation stopped him dead in his tracks. He had what this man had lost. Had lost and thought irredeemable. The most important thing in his life. And he had it. Identical in all respects.

"The gods help us . . ." Kim whispered.

K. turned. "Pardon?"

Kim sat, the bowl unregarded on the table before him. How did he even begin to broach this?

K. came across and sat, then began to spoon up his stew. After a moment he stopped and looked across at Kim. "Aren't you hungry, Kim?"

Not now, Kim thought, but in lieu of an answer that would suffice, he picked up his own spoon and began to eat in a desultory fashion.

Strange thoughts were filling his head. Indeed, the strangest thoughts he had ever had. And pictures, too. Images . . .

Squeezing his eyes tight shut, he let his spoon fall with a clatter to the table.

"Kim?"

He felt K.'s hand upon his arm.

"Kim, are you all right?"

Kim nodded, then opened his eyes again. K. was leaning right across the table, staring into his face. "Is it about that?"

His head gestured past Kim towards the painting.

Kim nodded, afraid to say what he'd been thinking. Afraid because, once said, it could not be retracted.

"Are you afraid of me?" K. asked, his eyes staring into Kim's candidly. "Because if you are, you have no reason to be. I would not harm you. No, nor your Jelka."

Kim shivered. So he understood.

"It must be hard," Kim said after a moment. "I mean, this situation."

"Yes . . ." K. relaxed back into his seat, but his eyes remained locked with Kim's. "I've tried not to think too much about it. Tried not to . . . well, *picture* things."

Again Kim shivered. *Too close*, he thought, finding this intimacy of understanding almost unbearable. Yet at the same time he knew it could not be helped. This was the price of their doubleness.

"I know what you mean."

K. nodded. "Myself, I would be guarded. Oh, and jealous, too."

Kim swallowed but did not answer. He did not have to answer. It was the truth, after all.

"All the same, I would like to see her again. Or should I say, I would like to meet her . . . as she is now. With your permission, of course."

How could he deny such a request? If their fates had been reversed, would he not have wanted precisely that? To see the woman he'd loved – the woman he'd thought lost forever? Of course he would. Yet he feared it. Feared it more than he'd feared anything in his whole life.

Kim looked away, knowing that what he felt showed in his face – that the other could read him as clearly as one read a page. But he could not help it.

"You must not be ashamed of what you feel, Kim. I understand. You do not want to share her with me."

Kim looked to him. It was unfair. He knew it was unfair. But that was how he felt. He nodded.

Yes, and saw the disappointment in the other's face. And behind it, the longing. Oh gods, the longing. How he understood *that*.

"I'm sorry . . ."

But K. waved the apology away. "It was some while before I got up the courage to visit you, you know. I found you months ago. I spent one whole evening watching you from the shadows of your workroom. But then she came into the room. Until then, you see, I thought you'd lost her too. I thought . . ."

K. looked down, then pushed his bowl away, as if he too had lost his appetite.

"I imagined how you'd feel. Or rather, how *I'd* feel if I were in your place. How I'd rather die than share her, even with myself. Strange that, eh? I mean, where's the logic in it? But then, when it comes down to feelings, there is no logic is there, only gut reaction. Which is to say, my soul's brother, that I understand. Yet if I could meet her once and talk with her."

Kim hesitated, then nodded.

"Then let that be enough."

* * *

They went back to Kalevala. Back to Kim's reality. And there, while K. waited in the workroom, Kim went up to speak to Jelka.

As he came into the kitchen she turned, smiling at him. "How's it going?"

Kim went across and, without a word, held her, closing his eyes, drinking in the wonderful smell of her, the warmth of her body against his own, knowing in those few instants that he was blessed. Blessed beyond all imagining.

He moved back a little, his eyes studying her eyes. "We've a visitor."

"A visitor? But I didn't hear the bell."

"No . . . I mean I've brought someone back with me."

She laughed, confused. "Back?" Then her expression changed. "You mean . . . *back*?"

He nodded. "But there's something you have to understand. Something very important. You see, it's me."

"You?"

"Yes, me. Or almost me. Like me, but not exactly me."

He saw her mouth fall open, the lips parting in shock. "You."

"That's right. But that's not all. In his universe, he lost you. Lost you to the Golden Dreams plague."

Her eyes widened. He saw the understanding there, the deep compassion, and felt again that awful stab of jealousy. Pure jealousy.

He was trembling now. "But I'm afraid."

"Afraid?"

"About you . . . and him."

"But he *is* you, Kim."

"No, he isn't. And that's the point."

"Ahh . . ."

Jelka sat, then shook her head, trying to think it through. "So you're afraid I'll fall in love with him? And maybe want to leave you for him?"

"Or share you with him."

Jelka's eyes met his. "Is *that* what you're afraid of?"

He nodded.

"And still you brought him?"

Again he nodded. His mouth was dry now. "I told him that I wouldn't."

"You *told* him." There was a flicker of a smile, quickly suppressed. "And what about me? Did you consult me before you told him?"

"I . . ." He looked down, ashamed of himself. Gods, it was a mess. And there he'd been thinking it was all a simple matter of equations. But where was the mathematics of love and jealousy? Where was the graph that charted the movements of the human heart?

"I love you, you know."

His head came up. He swallowed, then nodded. "I know." But it didn't help. He was still afraid. Afraid of himself! It was ridiculous, but he couldn't help it.

"And if I find that that love extends to him too, that would be no betrayal, Kim. Honestly. Indeed, it would be the most natural thing, don't you think?"

He gave an embarrassed laugh. "Do you think Tom and Sampsa have these problems?"

"Undoubtedly."

"Only . . ." he paused, then carried the logic of the thing through, "they both have their twins. Ai Yin and Lin Yu are both alive. But if one of them were to die . . ."

"*Kim*!"

Her tone startled him. She was staring at him sternly now. "This isn't like you."

He bridled. "No? You forget who I defied to win you."

"I don't forget. But *he* defied my father, too. Remember that, Kim." She sighed. "You must trust yourself, Kim. Literally so. Would *you* hurt *him*?"

"No . . ."

"Then trust to that. You are a generous man, Kim Ward. It's one of the reasons why I love you. Maybe the greatest reason. So be generous this once. Give him this moment with us."

"With *you*."

She smiled. "Okay. With me."

He sighed, then gave the briefest nod.

"Then go," she said, watching him with kindly eyes. "I think he's waited long enough."

* * *

It was, perhaps, the strangest moment of her life, to see the two of them emerge from the door at the top of the steps and come towards her down the shadowed corridor.

Strange, yes, and dreamlike, too. And for a moment she wondered why she had not dreamed it beforehand.

She saw at once how alike they were, even as she saw the differences of build and height.

And then he saw her.

He stopped dead, almost as if he'd walked into some unseen barrier, his eyes visibly widening. And then he smiled. A great beaming smile of awe and love that had in it such depths of hurt and loss that her heart went out to him.

For how could it not? This was her man. Through all eternity and in every universe, her soul mate.

She opened her arms and embraced him, hugging him to her, feeling him begin to sob, his arms wrapped tight about her, the way a lost child clings to his mother once she's found.

She stroked his hair and petted him, then kissed the side of his head, murmuring reassurances.

"There . . . it's alright now. Everything's okay . . ."

Her eyes met Kim's, who stood there looking on. And saw, to her surprise, that tears were streaming down his cheeks, as if whatever fear he'd had had crumbled in that instant. She put out a hand, gesturing for him to come and hold her too. And so he did, and so they stood there for a while, the three of them, holding tight to each other in the very strangest of embraces.

"It's alright," Kim said, after a moment, reaching out to touch and hold K.'s shoulder. "You're home now, brother. Home."

* * *

Karr waited at the door, his helmet under his arm, frowning down at the patterned marble beneath his feet.

As the door swung back, he looked up and smiled. "Ah, Jelka . . . I came as quickly as I could."

She embraced him, kissing his cheek, then stood back, a mischievous glint in her eyes puzzling Karr.

"Well?" he asked, as she closed the door behind him. "What's going on?"

"Wait and see," she said, taking his hand and leading him through to the kitchen.

As they entered, Kim looked up from where he sat at the long table and smiled. "Gregor . . ."

Again that same secretive smile, as if some joke were being played on him. Karr huffed and, setting the helmet down on the table, demanded, "Come on, you two, what *is* going on?"

"Gregor?"

Karr turned, looking to the doorway, thinking for a moment that maybe Kim had learned to throw his voice, and then did an almost comic double-take. He turned, astonished, looking from one Kim to the other, then gave a little laugh, understanding in that instant what had happened.

"It works!"

Both Kims nodded, with an eerie synchronicity. The new one – taller, Karr noted through narrowed eyes – came and stood behind the Kim he knew and placed his hands on his shoulders.

The new one spoke. "I understand you've problems, Gregor."

"I've dealt with them."

"Temporarily. But you haven't solved them."

"And you can?"

K. nodded.

"How?" Karr asked.

But K. merely smiled. "I want you to set up a broadcast, for this evening. I want it to go out on every channel and into every set. We use the override and make sure every set is working."

Karr looked to Kim, but Kim merely nodded. "It's okay, Gregor. You can trust him."

Karr looked to Jelka, appealing to her. "Won't *you* tell me what's going on?"

She smiled. "I can't."
"Can't?"
"No. Because they won't tell me. But I trust them. I'd trust them with my life, wouldn't you?"
Karr hesitated, then nodded. He looked back at the strangely doubled image of his friend. "Tonight?"
"At eight," both Kims said, the movements of their mouths so perfectly synchronised that Karr found himself blinking at the sight, surprised.
"I feel . . ." He laughed, as if it were too stupid a thing to say. "I feel like I'm dreaming, only I can't wake."
"I understand," K. said, coming round until he stood before the giant; looking up into his face. "Then it's time for us to make things real again."

* * *

At precisely eight that evening, every screen in Ganymede, in every room and every public place, on the four great spaceships and in every transit vehicle, switched on, showing the image of Kim's face.
"Friends," Kim began, without prelude. "I am sorry to divert you from whatever you are doing, but something very important has happened. The breakthrough has been made. We have forged a door into another universe."
He paused, letting that sink in, then continued. "That door is stable and it works. Yet we must use it wisely and expeditiously."
Kao Chen, who had been relaxing in his living room, dipping into the second volume of the *San Kuo Yan Yi* and reading his favourite episodes, now sat forward, spilling his wine over the rug.
"Wang Ti!" he yelled. "Come see!"
". . . to introduce a friend," Kim was saying as Wang Ti hurried from the kitchen, wiping her hands on a towel. "In fact, more than a friend. Fellow colonists and travellers, may I introduce my close friend, K."
"*Aiya*!" both Kao Chen and Wang Ti said as one, astonished by the vision on the screen.
Indeed, throughout Ganymede there was a sharp intake of breath as a second Kim stepped into view and stood beside the Kim they knew.
"I am Kim Ward," the newcomer said, "and in many ways I share a common history with my brother here. Yet our universes are not identical. There are many differences. And those differences will prove useful in the days to come. But I believe – and my brother here shares my belief – that it is our task to put an end to all such differences. To unify reality. And tonight we take the first step in that process. Tonight we return to our own space and time. To our own universe."
The camera pulled back until it showed the window behind them and the perfect blackness of the sky.
"Look!" two voices said as one. "We return!"
And as if it were some great conjuring trick that blackness was suddenly alive – alive with shimmering points of light.
Again, throughout Ganymede there was a gasp.

They had left no-space. They were back inside the universe of stars and motion. And they were sailing full-tilt towards Eridani.

One could almost feel the relief.

"Our journey continues," Kim's voice said, speaking over the image of the star-spattered sky. "But some of us must go back, to face our old adversary, DeVore. And defeat him. And thus end all divisions. It is our purpose to make things whole again."

The broadcast ended, as abruptly as it had begun. But back in the room, unseen by the watching thousands, Kim turned to K.

"And you? What will happen to you when that happens?"

K's smile was bleak and knowing. "Then I will vanish from this world of yours, as if I'd never been."

Kim stared at him, understanding that K. knew much – had considered much – that he had not yet even begun to think of. And reaching out, he held his mirror-self to him.

"Then we must use these moments well, neh, brother?"

* * *

That night, in the silence before midnight, Kim climbed from his bed and went to K's room.

K. sat up, a shadow among the shadows. "What is it?"

Kim sat beside him, reaching out to take his hand. Steeling himself to take it. "I couldn't sleep. I kept thinking . . ."

"Thinking, eh?"

Kim nodded, unable to see the other's eyes in the dark.

"And?"

In answer, Kim tugged at K.'s hand, making him follow him, out of the room and down the passageway until they stood before the room where Kim and Jelka slept.

"Are you sure?" K. asked, knowing without being told what Kim meant by this.

"No. But I know it's right. You *are* me. I *am* you. And to keep her from you, or you from her . . . I couldn't do that."

"Yes, but . . ."

Kim put a finger to K.'s lips. "There's so little time. Let's make the best of it, eh?"

K. reached out, embracing him. Then, hand in hand, they walked over to the bed where their wife awaited them.

CHAPTER·21

THE FEATHER IN THE COFFIN

Li Yuan sat in the chair at the far end of the table, listening as Emily recounted what had been happening in the Wilds and itemised the details of her long guerrilla war against DeVore. The conference table was crowded. This was a full Council of War and besides Emily's own people, Li Yuan's full staff were in attendance, including both of his sons, the latter disconcertingly wearing a long, flowing dress over a very full bosom.

Hannah, standing by the door, looked on, part of her thrilled at being there on this momentous occasion, part of her watching analytically as Emily came to the end of her account and fell silent.

Li Yuan sat forward slightly, steepling his fingers before his nose, then began to speak.

"Thank you, *Mu Ch'in* Ascher. It seems we have much to thank you for. It could not have been easy for you. But now we have a chance to rid ourselves of this disease called DeVore. To cleanse this world – and others – of his malice."

Li Yuan paused, looking about him, a real authority in every glance and gesture.

"But before we come to the matter of what actions we shall take, let me – if briefly – advise you of our own recent history. As you might know, the bombing of Boston led to a brief but very bitter civil war – a war from which we were fortunate to emerge the victors. But at a great cost. My son-in-law, Mark Egan, was assassinated and one of my grandchildren – Samuel – taken hostage."

Hannah noted how Kuei Jen looked down at that, a tightness in her face.

"For those crimes we captured Old Man Egan. I personally saw that he burned for them. Then, in the months that followed, thinking us weak, Coover made his move, attacking us in Denver and pushing east. We let him come on, two thousand *li* and more, until, at Memphis, we turned on him and annihilated his Banners, destroying every last man. Which left our enemies in the south."

There was a brief smile before he spoke again.

"We invited them to a meeting, on neutral ground. There we offered them terms, but they sought to trick us. All of which my spies knew, of course. They meant to assassinate us in our seats, but they did not know that their assassins were already dead, garroted in the cell beneath the floor of the room in which we met. And so their plans misfired and now their bones lie rotting in the desert."

Hannah shivered. Though she had heard much and read even more of Li Yuan's life, this aspect of him – the sheer brutality – surprised her, and for a moment she found herself astonished that he should be sitting here at table with the woman who had once been his greatest enemy.

But then, necessity makes strange bedfellows.

Emily, she saw, had lowered her head. Li Yuan was now looking at her, a strange expression in his eyes.

"I say all of this not by way of boasting, but to explain how things were. The past few years have seen much ugliness and much brutality. Nor is it easy to steel oneself to do those things that one must do. Yet they had to be done. For there was always a greater enemy to face, and if I had not triumphed in America, he would have gone unchallenged. And time, I knew, was running out. Though we held the high ground of space, we could not keep him contained much longer."

Emily looked up. "I understand."

"Do you?" Li Yuan was suddenly like a rock. Like T'ai Shan itself. "I am not proud of what I have done in my life, Emily Ascher, and looking back I can see every reason for you to have opposed me. I was not always a good man and many times I claimed necessity as an excuse. But it is not always necessary to be brutal, or callous. Only now, at the end of the world, do I understand that."

Emily narrowed her eyes. "Then you really think it is ending, Li Yuan?"

"Assuredly so. The only question now is whether it is DeVore or these new forms – these floraforms, as you call them – who inherit. That is why, yesterday, I launched a full scale assault on DeVore's forces. We struck from space, targeting his main nerve centres. We hit his camps and factories, his warehouses and spaceports. But in doing so we left ourselves open to counter-attack, and DeVore was quick to retaliate. He hit our satellites. Put out our eyes."

"And the Three Palaces?" Emily asked.

"Have survived, it seems. They were too heavily defended. None of our rockets got through. Yet his strength is broken."

"So now it's cat and mouse."

Li Yuan nodded. "Our time on this planet is over. We must seek our destiny elsewhere. But I will not go without a fight."

Emily smiled. "Nor I."

"Then let us talk of strategy." Li Yuan paused. "I believe that DeVore means to destroy it all."

It was Daniel who interrupted. "*Everything*?"

Li Yuan nodded. "Everything. And the quickest way to achieve that would be to destroy the oxygen generators. It would make this planet a barren, lifeless waste." He sighed. "Indeed, if my information is correct, he has begun already."

The news clearly shocked Emily. "What have you heard?"

"That the Iceland Station was hit, yesterday, just after dark."

And now Hannah felt that same shock reverberate within her. So it was finally happening. DeVore had finally had enough of the game. He was kicking away the legs of the board by systematically destroying Chung Kuo's atmosphere.

"So what's to stop him?" Emily asked, her voice much smaller than usual.

"Us," Li Yuan answered. "I've set up temporary defensive positions about the remaining eight generators in Europe. But they are only temporary, and were DeVore to make a concerted effort against any of those forces, he would succeed."

"Then what is to be done?" Daniel asked.

"We must outguess him. Work out where he means to strike next and be there." Li Yuan smiled. "And then it will be him or us. A battle to the last."

"And if we win?" Emily asked. "Do we then turn and fight the floraforms?"

"No," Li Yuan answered her. "If we win we leave here. Find a new home."

"So you have become a Dispersionist in your old age?" Emily laughed at the irony of it. "Then Ward was right."

"So it seems," Li Yuan said, smiling in agreement. "Things change. We cannot stand still. That is the lesson of history, neh, Han A?"

Hannah, addressed directly, blushed. She gave a little bow, acknowledging the truth of what Li Yuan had said, then looked to Daniel, who was staring at her, a mixture of love and pride in his eyes.

"Then we will do as you say," Emily said, giving Li Yuan a tiny bow of respect. "The years have given you great wisdom, Li Yuan."

"Maybe," Li Yuan acknowledged. "But then I have had a good teacher."

* * *

Tuan Ti Fo sat in the sunlight in the space between the palaces, the board before him, the game balanced at a crucial stage.

It was there that DeVore came upon him.

"Master Tuan?"

Old Tuan looked up. "Will you play, Howard?"

DeVore stared back at him, astonished. "How did you get here? The guards . . ."

"Are only human." Tuan smiled calmly and gestured to the seat facing him. "Come. You've time to play one last game with me, surely?"

DeVore sat, bemused, then, with a tiny shrug, focused on the board. At once his attention was drawn into the pattern of the stones.

"Ahhh . . ." he said, the noise like the sighing of the wind. For a long time after that he was silent, concentrating, then he looked up, meeting Tuan's eyes once more. "You are white, I take it?"

But Tuan Ti Fo shook his head. "This once I am black."

"But . . ." DeVore looked back, surprised. "Then who have you been playing?"

Tuan laughed, a gentle, mocking laughter. "Why you, of course. Do you not recognise your own play, Howard? Or have you forgotten everything, brother?"

"Forgotten?" And then he noted what Tuan had said. "What do you mean, *brother*?"

"Then you have indeed forgotten."

Tuan seemed to swell, to extend himself backwards, changing even as he did, until a huge, giant spider squatted in his place – a great metallic beast with two abdomens and long, steel spikes for legs.

DeVore's eyes were wide now, but not with surprise; his expression was one of recognition.

"*Aiya!*" he said softly, putting a hand to his brow. And even as he did, his human form seemed to split like a husk and his true form emerge. Yet whereas Tuan's form was beautiful and polished, like a sculpture of burnished steel, his own was mottled and cracked, as if it had been subjected to intense heat.

The two Edderiminaru glared at each other across the tiny board.

"*So now you know,*" Tuan said, speaking in his own tongue. "*So finally you remember.*" He laughed, then gestured with one long, spindly arm towards his twin. "*It is a pity you did not look after yourself better.*"

DeVore was silent for a time, then tried to speak, but his voice, like the great shells of his twinned abdomens, was cracked and brittle. What came out was a squeaky whine, like the sound two pieces of metal make when they are ground together. He tried again.

"*Why did you wake me?*"

Tuan's smile was a yard long. "*So that you would know. At the end.*"

"*Know?*"

"*Why you had to die. Why there was room for only one of us in the universe.*"

Tuan vanished. With a great shudder, DeVore returned to his human shape. But now that shape was creased and torn, the frail flesh barely held together where the great Edderiminaru shape had burst from it.

DeVore stood, blood dripping from his hands and chin. He staggered forward, spilling the stones from the board, then went down onto his knees, a great groan ripped from deep inside him.

For a moment he stayed there, his head down, eyes closed. Then, slowly, he lifted his head again and his eyes popped open. Steel-blue eyes that now remembered everything.

"*Of course . . .*"

* * *

Li Yuan stood on the slope above the meadow, watching as the last of the teams prepared to depart. They had decided to concentrate on just three of the generators; those in Norway, Southern Spain and – closer to home – the central generator beneath Geneva, sending a force of five thousand men and heavy armaments to bolster the current defensive strength.

DeVore could easily hit elsewhere. But the chances were that he'd hit one or other of those three, and when he did, they would attempt to keep him there – to pin him down – until they could bear such strength upon him that he would break.

We are fortunate my ancestors considered everything, Li Yuan thought, recalling what he'd been shown – long ago, when he was but a boy – about the generators.

Unlike their Martian equivalents, Chung Kuo's oxygen generators had been buried deep in the crust of the earth, where even a nuclear strike could not destroy them. Moreover, they vented over an area of several hundred square miles. To destroy one, you had to take the "tap" – the head of the great shaft – and then travel down almost a mile.

It was possible, of course, that DeVore had already mined them. Possible, but not likely. Not if what Li Yuan's spies had told him was true. No, if his information was correct, DeVore had thought he could defeat the floraforms. Until two days back.

And that was why he'd come. To stop DeVore. To keep Chung Kuo alive, even if humankind were not to benefit. For the floraforms were life, if of a strange, transmuted kind. And life – life of *any* kind – was preferable to the nullity DeVore wished for.

It was all a question of direction.

Li Yuan sighed, then began to make his way down towards his own cruiser, which waited, the ramp extended, the hatch open, not fifty metres away.

All was arranged. Li Han Ch'in and Emily knew what to do. He was not needed now. He had led them to this point, now it was up to them to carry out his strategy.

It was time for him to make his peace with an old friend. To see him and talk with him one last time before he left.

Li Yuan smiled, then stepped up onto the ramp, making his way inside.

Yes, and maybe we'll have rabbit stew for supper.

* * *

Li Han Ch'in frowned, then scratched his head, amazed.

"Master Tuan? What in the gods' names are *you* doing here?"

"I was hoping to speak to your father, but it seems he has already gone."

"Gone?" Han Ch'in looked about him. "You must be mistaken, Master Tuan. He said nothing about going."

Tuan smiled benevolently. "I think you'll find he's gone to see Shepherd."

"Shepherd?" Han Ch'in shook his head. "But Shepherd's with DeVore."

"Again, I think you'll find . . ."

". . . that I am mistaken." Han Ch'in huffed. "What *are* you doing here, Master Tuan?"

"I'm here to bring you a message."

"A message?"

"From Ward. You do remember Ward?"

"But isn't he . . . well, out *there* somewhere."

"Yes. But he's coming back."

Han Ch'in laughed. "Then he'll be too late, I'd say, unless he's already in orbit." He paused, narrowing his eyes. "Is he?"

Master Tuan shook his head. "Not at all. In fact, he's close on eleven light years from here right now. But he says to watch for him."

"To watch . . ." Han Ch'in roared with laughter. "Now I know you are teasing me, Master Tuan!"

* * *

A log fire crackled in the grate, throwing patterns of golden light across the shadowed room. The polished frame of the fireguard gleamed. Outside, beyond the open casement window, the day was ending, the sky slowly fading from blue to black. Inside the two friends talked, reminiscing over a world that seemed as insubstantial as a dream.

"Chung Kuo is ending, Ben."

Ben laughed; a soft, amused laughter. "It ended long ago, Yuan. What we've been witnessing are post-mortem effects."

"You think so?"

"Oh, I know so. I was fooled for a while. I thought . . ."

"What?"

"Oh, that history would go on forever. But I forgot how frail we are as a species. Silly really. I always prided myself on my sense of perspective."

"You think it's futile, then, leaving here?"

"Not futile. Nothing's futile, except suicide. But it will only delay things. I like the idea of the floraforms: of something better than us, *bigger* than us, inheriting the world. It's a better idea than DeVore's. Evolution, not devolution. It has to be applauded, don't you think?"

Li Yuan shrugged. "I'm not so sure. I liked human beings. They were . . . *troublesome*, I guess, but their capacity for love was great."

"You always were sentimental, Yuan. It was your weakness."

"And you were always hard. That was *your* weakness. But you've changed. You've changed a great deal since we last met. I was . . . well, uncertain what I'd find."

"I am less mad than I was."

Li Yuan laughed, then sipped from the glass he held. For a moment he stared into the bright red liquid, watching the flames dance within it. Then he sighed.

"There is so much that I would have done differently, if I could."

"You did as you were fated to do."

He looked up, meeting Ben's eyes. "No. I used to believe that, but it was an excuse. I *could* have chosen differently, but I didn't. I governed Chung Kuo badly. I let emotion rather than reason govern my actions."

"Well . . . I won't argue with that. Fei Yen, for instance."

"An obsession . . ."

"Yes. But understandable. It must have been wonderful making love to her . . ."

"Ben!"

Ben looked across. Meg was standing in the doorway, the baby asleep on her shoulder.

"Well, it's true," he said, grinning at her. "Not that I'm envious in the least. I have been the most fortunate of men in that regard."

"And selfish," Meg said, mollified somewhat by his comment.

"Oh, that I *don't* deny. Yet I do question whether we could have acted other than we did. My obsession with death, for instance. What was that but an expression of my deep mistrust of existence? I was an experiment, damn it! A clone! Why should I not think myself unreal?"

"Do you really think it was that, Ben?" Li Yuan asked, a strange compassion in his tone.

"Part of it," Ben answered. "And there the floraforms have the advantage over us, I feel. They can control the DNA they have inherited from us."

"You think we've been controlled then?"

Ben laughed. "Of course we have. Machines, that's all we were. Machines of flesh. Mere sensory keyboards." He looked into the flames of the fire. "When you think how many generations there have been. Six million years, and what was the result? An orgy of self-destruction."

He looked up again, meeting Li Yuan's eyes. "I'd say that whoever made us played *wei chi*. Not only that, but he was a lover of the long game. But he got bored. The experiment turned sour and he abandoned it."

"You believe that?"

Ben grinned. "Not entirely. But it's one explanation."

Li Yuan frowned. "You've not entirely changed, then?"

"Not entirely. I didn't grow dumb when I grew kind."

"No . . ." Li Yuan paused, then drained his glass. "I really ought to go."

"What's happening?" Ben asked. "I mean . . . out there."

"A war. Another war."

"The last?"

Li Yuan smiled. "I think so."

"And when it's over?"

"We either leave or we don't." He paused, then. "You can come, Ben. In fact, I came deliberately to invite you."

Ben smiled. "I'm grateful. It was . . . well, nice of you, I guess. But . . ."

"We'd love to come," Meg said, coming across and standing beside Li Yuan, looking down at him, even as she rocked the sleeping child. "Your offer is most graciously accepted."

"Meg . . ."

She turned. "No, Ben. We have the child to think of. And Li Yuan's right. There is no future here. This world – this *human* world – is ending. It's time we left. Time we sought a new home."

Ben stared at her a while, then shrugged. "Then so be it."

Li Yuan laughed and clapped his hands. "But that's tremendous news! We could leave at once. We could be there in two hours."

But Meg was staring now at Ben, her dark eyes mirroring his own. "Tomorrow," she said, soothing the child's head with her hand. "We'll leave here on the morrow."

* * *

Ben woke to hear voices out in the garden. He went to the window and, drawing back the curtain, looked out. Li Yuan's cruiser was still there – an extraordinary sight in that rough uncut field of grass, its emblematic golden dragon embossed upon the old flag of the American Empire.

The hatch was open and Ben could see Li Yuan himself standing just within the shadows, talking. For a moment he stood listening, then, with a word or two of Han, he turned and came back down the ramp, gathering up his long silks with one hand as he hastened back to the house.

Ben threw on a wrap then went down to the kitchen.

Meg was standing at the hob, making breakfast. Li Yuan sat nearby, cradling a cup of steaming apple *ch'a.*

As Ben stepped into the room, Li Yuan looked up. "Ben . . ."

Noting his despondency, Ben went across and sat, facing Li Yuan across the scrubbed pine table. "What is it?"

"It's DeVore. He's hit two of the generators. One in Northern Poland and another in Lapland."

"Destroyed?"

"Totally."

Ben nodded thoughtfully, then. "Do we know what kind of effect this is having?"

"There have been violent storms. With each generator he knocks out, the strain on the others grows. Air flows out to fill the gaps." Li Yuan shuddered. "It is as if he is poking holes in the planet's lungs."

"Hmm. Then maybe you should adopt a more aggressive policy. Don't wait for him to come to you. Go to him."

Li Yuan smiled bleakly. "And if in the meantime he takes out yet more generators?"

"Then that is a risk you must take, Li Yuan. He must be stopped, and stopped quickly."

Li Yuan sighed heavily. "I wonder if it's worth the death of any more of my people. I wonder if we shouldn't just go and let DeVore fight it out with the floraforms."

"And leave him here, triumphant? You want that?"

"No, but . . ."

"Then fight, Li Yuan. This one last time. Make sure he doesn't have a base to extend from. If DeVore survives here, you will be safe nowhere. Not even if you cross the galaxy."

Li Yuan thought a moment, then nodded. "All right. But you will come with me, neh? And be my advisor, like old times?"

Ben looked to Meg, who had turned to watch them. She smiled and gave a tiny nod.

"Okay," Ben said and, smiling, reached across to take Li Yuan's hands in his own. "Like old times."

* * *

The cruisers drifted in, like bees on a summer's day, their lazy drone filling the valley long before their shadows fell upon the outpost.

Bombs fell, hanging in the air like rows of chimes before they exploded with a flash and huff, a rapid succession of detonations, earth and trees thrown up amidst the roil of smoke and flame.

And then the hidden guns opened up. Rockets streaked across the burning valley, homing rapidly upon their targets. More detonations. Craft exploding in mid-air or tumbling, flaming to the valley floor. And then a kind of silence, with only the roar and crackle of flame.

Dense smoke drifted across the valley. The burning pyres of ruined craft littered the Edenic scene.

And then cheers. Cheers from the hidden gunners. Elation from the defenders of the generator. They had won. They had beaten off the attacking force.

They wandered out from beneath their camouflage nets, clapping each others' backs as they looked out over the burning ruins that dotted the length of the valley. Not a single craft had escaped. They'd nailed the lot. Broad grins gave way to whoops of excitement.

And then a faint rumble. A rush of wind. From the far end of the valley something dark and sleek whizzed past them like a bullet.

Heads turned, mouths open in shock. And then the mountainside lifted, as if a dark wall of earth and rock had emerged from deep beneath the surface. The shock wave rippled through the earth to where they stood, knocking them from their feet, throwing their guns – their feeble rocket-launchers – fifty metres into the air.

And then it fell on them.

For a minute, two minutes there was silence. And then there came the faint yet distinctive drone of cruisers.

Only this time there would be no opposition.

* * *

DeVore stepped down and looked about him at the burning valley.

"Perfect," he said, the word muffled by the breathing mask he wore. Already the weather was changing, great cyclones sweeping across the central plains of Europe as the air slowly gave out. One by one he was picking them off. And all Li Yuan's attempts to second-guess him were futile.

When it came to the endgame there was no better player. Besides, he remembered now. He knew now just why he had to win this game.

Ward. Ward was the stone that turned it all.

Yes, and he must be drawn back here. Must be enticed to come. For sentimental reasons if no other.

And he *would* come.

As they brought the great excavator across, he stretched and yawned, feeling the stitches pull in the wounds where his surgeons had sewed him up.

He did not need this form much longer now, but for a while longer it would serve him. Until he had Ward in his web. And then he'd show himself, even as the sticky strands wrapped about his adversary.

The thought of it made him grin. He could feel his true shape buried within him, just there, on the other side of reality. Less than a breath away. Closer than the width of an atom.

There where the black wind blew eternally.

And soon it would blow here too. The breath of the vacuum, into which he had been born, and in which he had had his being.

How strange that Tuan should seek to deny that heritage. But so it had ever been among his kind, the weaker of the twins drawn always to the sun's misleading warmth, while the stronger . . .

Blood seeped from the wounds. DeVore relaxed. His time would come. Soon. Very soon now. Until then he'd play the Man.

* * *

Emily stood in the doorway, weeping for the last of her sons who now lay dead upon the mortuary slab.

And so she had lost them all. All whom she had loved. All but her last adopted son, Daniel.

The thought of it made her want to lie down beside them and embrace that long, cold sleep. She kept seeing them in her mind, picturing them laughing and happy, as they'd been but days ago. The very best of sons. Dead now. Cold and pale and dead.

And she still alive. She who had survived the worst the world could throw at her.

Pained, she pressed her hands together, then, whispering a last "farewell", turned and left them there.

Her boys. Her beautiful boys.

Daniel met her just outside and held her, embracing her, his hand at her neck, his voice mumbling soothing words into her ear. But her grief was beyond words. Seeing them thus had finally brought home to her the price she'd had to pay all these years. The endless loss. The endless grief she had been forced to endure.

Eat bitter. So the Han said. *Eat bitter and endure*. And so she had. But now she'd had enough of it. Now it was time to end this struggle, one way or another.

The news was bad. DeVore had now hit six of the twelve generators. Great storms were raging, blowing like a dragon wind across the continent. And still there was no word from Li Yuan.

Where is he? she wondered, easing back out of Daniel's embrace. *Where in the gods' names has he got to*?

"What is it?" Daniel asked.

"Li Yuan. He should be back by now."

"He's on his way. We got a signal ten minutes back."

"Ah . . ." She hesitated, then. "We should send ships out to meet him and escort him back. If DeVore intercepted that signal . . ."

"I've already done it."

"Yes . . ." She patted his arm. Of course. Daniel thought of everything. "Come then, let's go and see Han Ch'in."

Han Ch'in was waiting for them in the tent they'd set up in the meadow. He was leaning over the map table, checking the positions of his forces against the latest reports of DeVore's movements.

"So where is he?"

Han Ch'in turned and bowed respectfully. "That's what I'm trying to work out,

Mu Ch'in Ascher. According to our spies in the field there have been three sightings in the last two hours. But it doesn't make sense. There's no way he could have got from one location to another so quickly."

"Then he's using copies."

"That's what I thought. But that contradicts my father's information."

"Then perhaps Li Yuan's spies were wrong."

Han Ch'in hesitated, then shook his head. "Our information was the best. The very best. If DeVore had copies, we'd have heard. No. Something else is going on. Something we don't quite understand just yet."

"Hmmm . . ." Emily took the report from Han Ch'in and studied it, then looked to the map. "I see what you mean. It's as if he's jumping from place to place."

"Wearing seven-league boots, eh?" And Han Ch'in laughed. But then he grew serious again, listening to a report coming in on the transmitter in his ear. He gave a tiny nod then looked to Emily.

"Father's coming in. Right now. But they've been attacked. Two of our ships were hit."

"*Aiya* . . ." Emily turned, looking to Daniel. "Daniel, go and organise a welcoming party. Stretchers and surgeons. And be quick . . ."

But Daniel was already gone. Emily turned back, looking to Han Ch'in, then, without a word, both of them hurried from the tent, heading for the makeshift landing pads at the far end of the meadow.

* * *

As it limped in over the brow of the hill, Emily could see at once that Li Yuan's cruiser had been badly hit. There was a great dark gash down one side of the craft, and as the sunlight glinted against its hull she could see the tell-tale pock-marks of shellfire.

As it settled awkwardly on the pad, the hatch hissed open. Medical crews, standing to the side, barely waited for the ramp to unfold before scrambling on board.

Emily waited, heart in mouth, staring at the darkness of the hatchway. For a moment nothing, then a figure stepped out into the sunlight. A woman, clutching a child to her breast. Behind her, one hand resting lightly on her shoulder, was a middle-aged man.

Shepherd! It was Ben Shepherd and his sister!

As they came down the ramp, Emily went across to greet them. But even before she could say a word, a mobile stretcher rattled out and down the ramp, four orderlies hastening to get the stretcher's occupant to the tent where they could give him attention.

"It's Li Yuan," Ben said, even as Emily recognised the ring upon the hand that lay outside the blankets. "He took a piece of shrapnel. I staunched the bleeding, but . . ."

And now that she looked at Ben she saw how the whole front of his shirt was covered in blood.

"He's dying," Ben said.

"No," she said, over-insistent. "No, we can save him."

"You can keep him alive, yes."

Emily stared at Ben, frightened by his words. "What do you mean?"

"Half of his brain's gone, that's what I mean. So even if you did save him, it wouldn't be Li Yuan you're saving. You'd do better to reactivate his *ching*."

The coldness in Shepherd's voice surprised her, yet there was something in his eyes that contradicted that. This had hurt him. Hurt him badly.

"It can't . . ." she began.

"Can't what? End like this? Of course it can. You think he was immortal?"

"No, it's just . . ."

But she couldn't say. Not to Shepherd, anyway. To have been reconciled – to have found such a good friend in such awful times; an unexpected friend, and then to have had him snatched away like this. It was unfair.

But then Shepherd was right. The world wasn't fair. The world was as it was. It was up to them to make it fair or unfair.

She wiped away the tear that had rolled down her cheek, then nodded. "Is that why he went? To fetch you?"

"So it seems."

Emily shivered. "I thought you were enemies."

"We were. And then we weren't. Something changed him. Changed him profoundly. He was . . . different."

"Yes," she nodded. It was exactly how she'd felt in his presence. As if Li Yuan had somehow found the thing each one of them was looking for. Yet even then he'd fought. Even then he'd still concerned himself with the business of the world. To put things right. Yes, and to stop DeVore from triumphing, because unless he could be stopped nothing mattered.

Against DeVore, inaction was not an option.

But now Li Yuan was dying. Li Yuan, who had been their beacon of hope in these final days.

And when he dies, will hope die too?

Touching Ben's arm again, Emily hurried past him, heading for the operating theatre, wishing as she'd never wished for anything before that Ben was wrong.

* * *

A faint mist swirled about the pit and then was gone, sucked outward it seemed, like a tide receding, and as it did, so the greenery about the pit began to shrivel up and die, a false autumn making the trees shed their leaves with an unheard sigh.

It was cold now. A frost rimed the bare earth. And overhead, where a hole was slowly forming in the atmosphere, one could see the stars winking mercilessly in the blackness of the vacuum.

At the far end of the valley a cruiser lifted and, banking as it rose, headed south. Towards the Wilds. Towards the final confrontation.

* * *

The wind was blowing strongly now, tearing at the thorny shrubs that clung to the mountain's slope and threatening to prise Emily from the rocky crevice in which she stood, peering out over the edge of the valley wall. Huge black clouds had formed on the horizon. There was a distant rumbling. Flashes of lightning regularly lit the darkening evening sky.

She was still standing there, one hand shielding her eyes, when Daniel came to her.

"It's over," he said, raising his voice to combat the noise of the growing storm.

"Ah . . ." She felt an immense sadness. It was as if the world itself had ended with his death. The last T'ang. The last great ruler of the Earth. The last aristocrat.

There was a time when she would have applauded that. But not now.

Daniel nudged her gently. "Look," he said, pointing down the slope and to the left. She looked. There was a swirl of dust and grain and then a man appeared, as if he had stepped from the air.

"Floraforms," Daniel said, leaning close and speaking into the shell of her ear. "They've been forming all afternoon."

Emily turned, wide-eyed, to stare at Daniel. "Why didn't you say?"

He shrugged. "I wasn't sure what it meant."

They both watched a moment as the man-like shape walked on a pace or two, small swirls of black wisping from his arms and legs and back. He stopped, looking down at the palms of his hands, then he shimmered and was gone, a great swirl of seed and dust and grain marking where he'd been.

Emily shivered. The world was growing strange. Stranger than she could ever have imagined as a child.

"What do you think they want?" she asked, shouting across at Daniel.

"To be," he answered. "I think they're trying out their powers. Seeing what they can do."

She watched a moment longer. Saw how it tried the shapes of animals and birds, each time reverting to a swirl of dust, then looked to Daniel again. "Okay," she said. "Lets go back. It's time we paid our respects."

Daniel nodded. But he did not say what he'd been thinking. Emily, he knew, had not seen it properly, but he had. The shape the floraform had made had not been just any man, it had been Michael. Somehow it had sensed Emily's presence there and – who knew how? – had drawn the memory from her.

But why? What did it mean by it?

He walked on, following her back up the mountainside, his eyes flicking from side to side, looking for any sign of threat among the stones and shrubs.

Not that it mattered now.

* * *

They had made him up and dressed him in his finest robes, then placed him in his coffin. The same coffin he had brought with him from America.

Han Ch'in stood to the left of the coffin, Kuei Jen to the right as Emily entered the tent. They half turned to look at her and smiled – the same sad smile that made her realise for the first time how close in blood these two men were, though one was now a woman.

"I'm sorry," she said.

Han Ch'in met her eyes, a great dignity in his own. "They say he did not suffer."

"No . . ."

She walked across, then stood beside the dead man's head, looking down into his pale, uncaring face.

And so it ends.

Each man a story. Each man a patchwork of things known and things hidden from the sight of others. Though few men lived as much within the public eye as a T'ang, an Emperor.

She looked up, meeting Kuei Jen's eyes. "Your father was truly a Son of Heaven."

Kuei Jen stared back at her strangely, then shrugged. "He was a very *human* man. With human frailties. I would remember him thus, not as an Emperor."

"But in the end . . ." she began.

"In the end he *was* a great man," Han Ch'in said. "And yet Kuei Jen is right. Indeed, my father knew it at the last. A stronger man might have done better with the burden he was given. A more determined man."

Emily sighed. How strange, at this moment, to find such words in the mouths of Li Yuan's sons. At such a time one might have expected even the most honest man to fall into platitudes.

"It was his request," Kuei Jen said, noting the puzzlement in Emily's eyes. "That we spoke honestly of him after his death. No lies. No plastering over of the cracks. And it is better thus, I feel."

"Perhaps."

She looked back at Li Yuan's face, so peaceful now that it was freed of all responsibility. How dreadful that must have been, to have carried that burden all those years. To find oneself responsible not just for oneself and one's immediate family, but for all men.

Father to forty billion orphans.

Emily shuddered, seeing it for the first time as it must have seemed to the young T'ang. No wonder he had turned his back on it, for to face that every day would have broken even the stoutest spirit. No wonder he sought consolation between a woman's legs.

It was only human, after all. One needed to be a kind of god to take on such a burden.

Or not to care at all. Like DeVore.

She bowed respectfully, then backed slowly away, nodding to each of Li Yuan's sons in turn.

And then out, out into the late evening air, past the flickering torches and the bare-headed guards. Out into the flickering light of the growing storm.

Out. On the last night of the world.

* * *

Dawn came bleak and white, a thin mist veiling the mountainside. Down in the meadow there was the cough and whine of turbo engines starting up, the bark of orders as the dead T'ang's forces were loaded into the waiting craft.

Han Ch'in stood on the brow of rock overlooking the meadow, Kuei Jen at his side. He was to lead the attack today. They were only waiting for the word and they would go.

"Come on . . ." Han Ch'in said impatiently. "He can't hide a whole fucking army."

"Be patient, brother," Kuei Jen said. "They'll find him. And then we'll have him."

But Han Ch'in's patience had run out. "It's wrong," he said, making a fist of his right hand. "He should have seen it, Jenny. He should have been there to see DeVore strung up, all justice done."

Kuei Jen looked down, affected by the naked violence of his brother's emotion. It was how *he* felt. At least, how the dormant male within him felt.

"He will be watching us."

Han Ch'in shuddered with indignation. "I wish I could believe that . . ." He stopped and turned, then relaxed. "Oh, it's you, Daniel."

Daniel hastened down to them. "It's come."

Han Ch'in's face lit. "We know where he is?"

Daniel grinned fiercely. "We have a fix on him."

"*Where*, dammit, boy! Where is he?"

Daniel laughed. "He's coming here. The fucker's coming here!"

* * *

Kuei Jen buckled on his body armour, kissed his children goodbye, then walked over to the tent where his father's coffin lay.

Guards formed a human barrier about the tent, their heads bowed in respect for the great man who lay dead within.

Kuei Jen pulled back the flap and stepped inside. The lamps had burned themselves out long ago, yet in the dawn's light he could see the coffin clearly.

He took two steps then stopped.

"*Aiya . . .*"

The word was a breath of disbelief. The coffin was empty. Or almost so. For where his father's body had lain was now a single white feather.

He stepped across, gaping at the sight, then turned, looking about him, as if at any moment his father would step from the air.

But Li Yuan was gone.

Kuei Jen swallowed, then reached in, picking up the feather almost reverently, feeling how soft its down was, like silk, the white so pure it almost hurt the eyes.

He knew what this meant. Knew because, like all Han, he had learned the legend as a child. Even so, some rational part of him was loathe to believe that it was true.

An immortal. His father had become an immortal. That was what the feather meant.

He let it fall, then, turning, hastened to the flap and stood there, bellowing across the field, calling for Han Ch'in.

CHAPTER·22

NIGHTFALL IN THE PARADIGM WORLD

The head lifted out of the blackness of the desktop and smiled.

"Yuan? You fancy lunch?"

Li Yuan grinned back at his elder brother, then eased back in his hydraulic chair. "I've a few things to do here, but yes. Where d'you want to meet?"

"Yang's. In Kennedy Avenue. I'll be there at one."

"Make it half-past."

"Okay."

The head winked, then reformed back into the blackness of the surface. Li Yuan looked up, across the busy trading room. Nearby his partner, Cho Yi, was hard at work, head down, the lead that connected him directly to the terminal flexing and unflexing as he ducked this way and that. He was a big man, a southerner from Hunan, and like all of his uncles on his mother's side, he had gone bald in his late twenties. Now, in his early seventies, he seemed eternal, unchanging.

Yuan smiled. Cho was one of those people who had a very basic approach to things. When he read a letter, his lips formed the words, when he talked, he spoke as much with his hands as with his mouth, and when he was plugged in, his whole body responded to the datastream, as if all those computer-simulated images really existed somewhere.

But for all that, Cho was a genius, and more than half the reason why Spring Day was so successful. It was Yuan's father's firm, but Cho was senior partner. And rightly so. Without him they'd have been sunk long ago.

Cho looked up and, finding Yuan watching him, did a double-take. He raised a hand, as if to say "I won't be a minute", then, with a flourish on the keyboard in front of him, cut connection, the wire snaking back into the console with a swish and a clunk.

"What is it?" Cho asked.

"I'm meeting Han Ch'in for lunch. Half one at Yang's. You want to come? We could get the *ching* to cover."

The *ching* was a computer simulant, designed by Cho and programmed to operate the way Cho operated, complete down to the last idiosyncrasy. When the *ching* was running there was no way – in the short term – that anyone could tell the difference from Cho himself. But Cho, Yuan knew, did not like to leave things in the hands of mere machines.

"I don't know," Cho said, frowning, the lines in his forehead like the lines in a piece of old carved ivory.

"This once," Yuan pleaded. "You know how much Han loves your company. Put a limit on the *ching*'s transactions. An hour, Cho. What can go wrong in an hour?"

Cho answered him sternly. "A tremendous amount. But this once I'll come. It's ages since I saw Han. What's he doing now?"

Yuan smiled. Even this – this small chit-chat – was a concession on Cho's part. When the market was open he liked to be dealing one hundred per cent of the time. Making money. Building their tiny empire. While he talked they missed out on deals, and on the commission on those deals. While they talked, Spring Day stood still.

"He's a Major now," Yuan answered; then, gesturing to his own wire, he said. "But let him tell you. Come Cho. Let's make money."

* * *

Across town, in the eastern suburbs of Beijing, DeVore was sitting in the back of a glide, his legs stretched out in front of him, the plush white leather and silk interior extending for yards in every direction. The screen between him and the driver's compartment was blacked out, the screen showing the state of the markets, the colourful 3-D diagrams changing every moment.

All was stable. World trade was flourishing. And with the arrival of President Newell in Beijing tomorrow, there was every indication that things would stay that way, especially if he and President Wei agreed to extend the bilateral agreement. And that seemed almost a formality.

Yet things were not as they seemed.

DeVore spoke to the air. "Tell Wyatt to meet me at the Park. And tell him to bring the woman. I want to check her out myself."

The woman would be crucial. President Newell liked only a certain type. And if Wyatt was right, the woman was just that type. Getting her into the reception was the easy part. Getting her into Newell's bed would be much harder.

Or maybe not, if what he'd heard was right.

DeVore steepled his hands before his face and smiled. All was in place now, every stone set in its proper place on the board. All, that was, except the last.

He took a long, relaxing breath, then spoke again. "Opaque the windows."

As the ice of the windows cleared, he found himself looking out over a sprawl of ancient Han buildings, six to eight levels high, each level smaller than the last, like the steps of a giant pyramid. *Hutong*, they called these nests of alleyways and rat-runs. They were crawling with life beneath their protective meshes – five, six, sometimes even eight families to a living unit, wallowing in their own filth. If he'd had his way he would have had them cleared years ago. They and the teeming hordes who inhabited them. Yes, he'd have gassed them and bulldozed the district flat. And then he'd have built something better. Something *cleaner*.

Below him the airlanes were packed with barely-moving traffic, but up here he was alone. Not that that surprised him. He had paid for exclusive use of this lane.

He sat back, smiling now, imagining the panic – the pure fear – that would run through that nest of tiny alleyways.

If it worked.

DeVore grinned fiercely. Of course it would fucking work. He hadn't spent the last twenty-five years setting this up for nothing. Why, once it got going, it would be unstoppable. The bastards would feed upon themselves like wounded sharks.

Fear. That was the key. That was the engine that would drive the world to self-destruction. Simple naked fear.

And now he laughed. "Tomorrow," he said, making a toast in the air with an imaginary glass. "Here's to tomorrow!"

* * *

Kim sat there watching K. at work, feeling his own frustration mounting by the moment. At last, unable to help himself, he stood.

"Are you *sure* I can't help?"

K. stopped and turned, looking at him. "I'm almost done now. But if you want . . ."

"No . . ." Kim smiled, then slowly sat again. "No, you're right. Please, carry on."

It was true. It would have taken K. much longer to teach Kim how to recalibrate the machine than for him to do it himself, and time was of the essence.

Even so, he watched, trying to make sense of the tiny alterations K. was making.

"Earlier, when you were speaking of it, you called it the paradigm world. Why?"

K. frowned with concentration a moment, then, "You'll see. The moment you enter it. It's different."

"How?"

But K. was saying no more. He gave the machine one final little tweak, then straightened up, a look of immense satisfaction on his face.

He had changed a great deal these past few days. Gone was the moroseness of former days. And no wonder. It was not every day a man got his dead wife given back to him.

Kim stared at his twin admiringly. It was narcissistic, he knew, but he could not help it. It was like seeing himself in one of those distorting mirrors that gave back a flattering image of oneself. Only this mirror was real. Was himself.

"Don't you think we ought to tell the others? I mean . . . what if something goes wrong?"

K. glanced at him again. "We'll be in and out of there before anyone realises we've gone. Besides, they'd only argue against it. You know they would."

"And rightly so." Kim sighed. He was still not sure about this. "Can't we let Karr know? Swear him to keep it a secret. Then if something *does* go wrong, he could come after us."

K. shook his head. "Karr would just go and tell Kao Chen. And Chen would tell Ebert, and then . . ."

Kim raised a hand. "Okay. Just you and me. But we find out what's happening and we get back. Okay? No risks, no danger."

"Okay. And then . . . and only then . . . we have that strategy meeting. Agreed?"

"Agreed."

"Good. Then are you ready, Kim? It's time to go."

* * *

Yang's occupied the whole of the 135th floor of the old Tiananmen building on Kennedy Avenue, overlooking the Imperial Park, Lung Tan Lake to the left, the *Tien Tan* – the Temple of Heaven – to the right. Beyond it, less than three miles south, began the megalithic sprawl of the new city, its walls like a breaking wave of glass that reflected back the clouds that drifted past its upper storeys.

From his seat beside the massive wall-length window, Yuan looked down, his eyes resting briefly on the ancient three-tiered temple. From this height it seemed to jut like an erect nipple from the centre of its great circular base. Yuan smiled at the thought, and found himself momentarily wondering what it had been like in those days.

If he'd been Emperor he would have fucked every beautiful woman in the land. A new one every night.

As it was . . .

He looked away, determined not to dwell on the break-up of his latest marriage. Across from him, Cho Yi was scanning the desktop comset, checking that all was well back at the office.

As Cho looked up again, he smiled. "All's well."

"Good," Yuan said, then turned, in time to see his brother Han come striding across the floor of the eating hall towards him, his huge, muscular frame seeming to strain the seams of his uniform.

Han Ch'in was wearing his full military regalia and as he moved between the tables, Li Yuan saw how heads turned, giving a tiny bow of respect as they saw the three golden stars on his bright red epaulettes.

Yuan stood and gave a bow, then, as Han stepped closer, embraced him in a hug that was returned with equal warmth.

"Yuan!" Han Ch'in said, showing his perfect white teeth in a wide grin. "How are you, little brother?"

"I'm fine," Yuan said, beaming delightedly. "And you?"

"Hungry," Han Ch'in answered, and laughed. Then, noticing Cho Yi for the first time, he whooped. "Master Cho!"

Cho Yi stood and gave Han Ch'in a deep, dignified bow, only to be grasped and hugged by Li Yuan's bear-like elder brother.

"How good to see you, Cho Yi! Are your mother and father well?"

"They are very well, thank you," Cho said, smiling with pleasure at the politeness.

They sat, looking to each other and smiling, letting the waiters fuss about them a moment, fixing the sound baffle that would keep their conversation private. As the glass screen came up about their table, Han Ch'in leaned forward, speaking in a confidential tone.

"I had to see you, brother. To tell you the news."

"News? Are you engaged, Han Ch'in?"

Han laughed exaggeratedly. "Gods! Perish the thought! No, little brother. My Masters have given me a special task. I am to look after the American President when he arrives later this evening."

Li Yuan's eyes widened. "President Newell?"

Han Ch'in nodded. "It is a great honour and may lead to other things."

"Other things?" Cho Yi looked doubtful.

"A posting," Han said. "To the American Empire. As Consul."

"But you're a soldier, Han," Li Yuan said.

"As was President Wei."

"You are to be Wei's protégé, then?" Again Cho's eyes held a depth of scepticism.

"Not at all. It will be an army appointment."

"Then that is different," Cho said with a terse nod of approval. "But let us order now. There will be time to talk while our meal is being cooked."

Han looked to his brother and smiled, a look passing between them, then he turned back to Cho Yi and gave him a tiny bow of respect. "You know the menu here, Cho Yi. I would be honoured if you would order for us all."

Cho Yi looked up over his menu and nodded, pleased by Han Ch'in's courtesy. "As you wish, Han Ch'in. As you wish."

* * *

The smell of chrysanthemums was overwhelming. Kim, who had just stepped through the burning hoop, reeled and then sat abruptly on the bed, gasping, his eyes watering. The air seemed thick and rich, as if he could taste each molecule of oxygen.

K. turned to him and smiled. "You see?"

"I see," Kim gasped. Yes, and *felt* and *smelled* and *tasted* the difference.

The blinds were down over the windows, yet his eyes still smarted from the brightness. As if a giant searchlight was focused on the window outside. And that scent!

He was drowning . . . drowning in his own senses!

"Here," K. said, pressing something into his hand, "take these."

Kim blinked, then held the capsules away from him. They seemed to glow in his hand, mauve and yellow, like the abdomens of some strange species of insect.

"Am I hallucinating?"

K. shook his head. "Not at all. This is Reality with a capital R. Where you and I come from is but a pale shadow of it. This is the real thing. Full strength."

Kim put out a hand to steady himself, and felt the texture of the fabric against his flesh. He felt a shock ripple through him, almost as if *it* touched *him*, and felt that he could almost see its surface, its presence was so vivid.

Like braille against a blind man's palm.

Everything here seemed to shout at him, announcing itself, glaring at him in startling neon colours.

He closed his eyes. Then, trusting that K. knew what he was doing, he popped the two tablets into his mouth and swallowed. Even so, he could feel them move down his gullet, as if he'd just gulped down a pair of bullets.

He could feel the flex of the muscles in his chest and abdomen, the tingle of the nerve ends in his fingertips.

Alive. This world was vividly alive. And he . . . he was like a radio receiver in its midst, tuned in to everything.

Or like a child, new born to the world.

For a moment longer he felt the throb of it pulsing all about him, and then it began to fade.

The smell of chrysanthemums slowly became less prominent.

He opened his eyes again and sighed. "Why didn't you give me those before?"

K. smiled. "Because I wanted you to know. To experience what *I* experienced. And to understand. This is it, Kim. The primary world. The most real of realities. This is the one we have to win in. This is the one we've got to make all of the others conform to."

Kim nodded, then looked about him. It was a very ordinary room, now that his senses had dulled. There was a single bed, a chair, and a small table on which there was a lamp and a bowl of flowers.

Chrysanthemums.

He turned. There was one window, with a blind, and, on the far side of the room, a single door. And nothing else. Not even a painting on the plain white walls.

"Where are we?"

"Beijing."

"And the year?"

"It is April in the year two thousand two hundred and forty two."

"Ah . . ." Kim hesitated, then. "And we are dead here, I take it?"

"We were never born."

"You know that for a fact?"

K. nodded. "I've checked the records. The woman who, in our worlds, was our mother, here died childless twelve years ago. And our father, Wyatt, also had no children. They never met. We were never conceived."

Kim shivered. "You've been here a number of times?"

"Eleven in all."

"And yet you never wrote about it."

K. smiled bleakly. "I wrote about it several times, and at length. But then I tore the pages out and burned them."

"*Burned* them? Why?"

"In case he followed me and found out what I was doing."

"And what *were* you doing?"

"Planning how best to stop him."

Him. It could be no other. "DeVore?"

"Yes."
"This is his world?"
K. hesitated, then shook his head. "No. Not yet. But it will be. Unless we act."
"Okay," Kim said, feeling more comfortable by the moment. "I think you'd better tell me exactly what's going on here."

* * *

Cho Yi had gone to relieve himself. While he was gone, Han Ch'in took the chance to speak to his brother of a private matter.
"I did not know you were going to bring Cho Yi," he began, "else I would have said something. But I wanted your advice, Yuan."
"My advice?" Yuan laughed. "Since when did you start listening to advice, elder brother?"
Han shrugged, as if admitting the mild criticism, then. "What you said earlier, about getting engaged . . ."
"Then it's true."
"No. And yet I am in trouble. I have been seeing this woman."
"A married woman?"
Han looked dawn, troubled. "I wish she were. It would make my present problem much easier to deal with. No . . . she is pregnant."
"Ah . . . And she will not *relinquish* the child."
Han's eyes came up. "Kill it, you mean?"
"I was trying to be sensitive . . ."
Han raised a hand, acknowledging that. "No. Nor would I have her kill it. It is my child, after all. But the woman is common."
"Common?"
"All right. She's a whore, damn it! I've been seeing her for several years now."
"But whores . . ."
"Take precautions, yes, but this one didn't."
"So pay her off. Give her an allowance."
"I offered, but she refused point-blank."
"Then cut her dead."
"I cannot, I . . ." Han looked down, embarrassed deeply. "I like her, Yuan."
"Enough to marry her?"
Han Ch'in nodded.
"Ah . . . I see now. The man in you wishes to marry her, but the Major . . . the Major is worried what his superiors will say. And as for your chances of becoming Consul . . ."
"They would cut *me* dead."
It was true. For a Consul to marry a whore was impossible. It would be effectively an insult to every wife of every man he met and had dealings with.
"*Aiya* . . ." Li Yuan slowly shook his head, then, seeing Cho Yi coming back across, leaned across and laid his hand over his brother's. "Let me mull this over for a while, dear brother, and consider what would be best to do. Tell her you will give her your decision in a week."

"And if she will not wait that long?"

"She will wait, Han Ch'in. I assure you. In the meantime write down her address. I will go and see her."

"Do you think that's wise, brother?"

"If I am to advise you properly in this matter, I had best meet the woman, neh?"

Han frowned, then. "I guess so." Taking a napkin, he scribbled down a name and an address, then handed it to Li Yuan. "There," he said, with a slightly shamefaced expression. "But please . . . do not say who you are, Yuan. Not yet. I . . ."

But Cho Yi was back and no more could be said. Li Yuan pocketed the napkin, then looked up, smiling as Cho Yi took his seat again.

"I've made my mind up," Yuan said, smiling at his partner. "I think I'll have the boiled monkey."

* * *

Kim looked down at his hands and frowned. "Eighty-four billion?"

"Eighty-four billion."

"But how do they feed them all?"

"They don't. Several billion – three, some say four, billion – are starving in this world."

"But that still leaves . . ."

"Eighty billion."

"So?"

"Mars is a farming world. There are massive greenhouses out there. And nine-tenths of its output is shipped back here. And then there are the floating factories. Great orbital farms many times the size that you and I are used to."

"But why? Why did they let it all get out of hand."

"For the same reasons it happened in our worlds. Because mankind's urge to multiply obeys no laws of reason. And because it suits the people of this world to let it be so. Imagine the size of the markets here! The five Presidents are powerless beside the Heads of Companies. They are the real rulers of this world, and that's why DeVore has chosen the marketplace as his battleground."

"The stock markets?"

"Yes. And he's about to strike. Tomorrow, if I'm right. There'll be a trigger event of some kind, no doubt, but it was all prepared long ago."

"Prepared?"

"As on our worlds." K. looked at the surprise in Kim's face and laughed. "You mean, you didn't know? You think the great economic collapses that struck our worlds were accidental? No. They too were DeVore's doing. But in both those cases he struck too soon. Despite the Century of Blood, as it was known, mankind survived that body blow."

Kim's eyes widened. "Tsao Ch'un?"

"That's right. Ironic, isn't it? That the great Tyrant should have been the one to save us. I've looked upon him with kinder eyes since I've known. But here Tsao

Ch'un never got his chance. He lived and died in obscurity. His moment never came. And DeVore kept his nerve, building his own economic empire – a shadow empire – within those of the great Merchant Lords." K. sighed. "Little do those great and powerful men know it, but the majority of their holdings – vast as they are – are in the hands of their chief enemy. The man who would bring it all tumbling down on top of them. He has built a great web of companies, connected in such complex ways that even the subtlest-minded analyst would never guess who was the Puppetmaster behind them all."

"And yet you did."

K. shrugged. "It was easy. I knew what I was looking for."

"And what was that?"

"DeVore himself. Once I found him, I found the main root. After that I merely had to dig."

"But why tomorrow?"

"Because it is the last day of this world."

Kim felt a shock ripple through him. "You know that for a fact?"

"Not for a fact, but I asked the Edderiminaru, and they sense nothing beyond tomorrow."

"Then we shall fail."

"Only if we do not try to change things."

Kim laughed sourly. "That seems a quantum leap of faith. A 'will we, won't we?' kind of affair at best."

"Maybe. But it's the best we've got. I know what DeVore plans. So maybe we can prevent it. If we can only find out what will trigger the collapse."

"It seems a long shot."

K. grinned. "It *is* a long shot. But we've twelve hours at least in which to do it."

"And if we can't?"

"Then we kill DeVore. If we can."

* * *

The girl was very pretty. That was, if you liked that kind of full-blown, curvaceous look to a woman. Personally, DeVore liked his women slim and breastless, like boys.

"She'll do," he said, looking to Wyatt, who was standing close by, looking on nervously. "You'll get her to the reception at eight. Oh, and Edmund."

"Yes, Howard?"

"Don't go buying any stocks and shares."

Wyatt laughed then winked at his old friend. "I shan't."

DeVore watched them depart, Wyatt pushing the girl before him into the black windowed glide. As the sleek Min Chang III climbed into its airlane, DeVore turned away, walking back across the sunlit park towards where his own white executive glide hovered beside the lake.

It was all in place. All organised. The thought of that made him laugh. How ironic it was – that one needed to plan so carefully, to organise so efficiently, to bring about such chaos.

And there was no doubt in his mind that there *would* be chaos, for once the props went, it would all fall down, like a pack of cards. And there would be no building it again.

No phoenix would rise from these ashes.

And no one would know why. That was the beauty of it. The *humility* of it, in fact. Let others gloat over their petty triumphs. He would destroy a world and have no one there to see it.

That was humility indeed.

The glide sank to the floor. A door hissed open.

As he stepped inside, he wondered for a moment whether he shouldn't keep Wyatt alive. As witness. Then he dismissed the notion.

"No survivors," he said quietly. "Not a single one."

"I beg pardon, sir?" the driver said, his sapphire-blue eyes meeting DeVore's in the driving mirror.

"Nothing," DeVore said, sitting back as the glide began to climb. "Just take me home, Haavikko. I think I need to rest."

* * *

As they crossed the huge square that marked the intersection between the east and west cities, Li Yuan leaned across and, nudging the dozing Cho Yi, said:

"There's something I have to do, Master Cho. A favour for my brother. I'll get the driver to drop me, then meet you back at the office in an hour."

Cho Yi yawned and stretched, then smiled at Li Yuan. "A favour?"

Li Yuan nodded.

"Okay," Cho Yi said. "I'll mind the fort."

"Thanks."

Li Yuan looked away, smiling, as much at Cho Yi's attempt at the American colloquialism as at Cho Yi's condition.

As ever, Cho Yi had eaten far too much, and now all he wanted to do was sleep. But Cho Yi would never admit that. Cho Yi would rather sit there at his desk, plugged in, and snore aloud, than admit he needed an hour's nap.

But this once it wouldn't harm. And it would give Li Yuan the opportunity to sort out this mess his brother had created for himself.

A whore! Who would have believed it of Han Ch'in? Han Ch'in who could have talked the silk briefs off of any woman in the city!

Unless, of course, he'd met her through his work.

Li Yuan leaned forward, speaking softly to the driver, getting him to set him down three blocks from where he needed to go, conscious of Cho Yi sitting there beside him, eyes closed yet listening.

He sat back, closing his hand over the napkin in his pocket even as the driver began to take the glide down.

What was she like? Was she pretty? Was she young?

Li Yuan closed his eyes, trying to imagine how his brother had reacted to the news. He ought to have asked at dinner, but there had been so little time.

He gave a tiny, shivering sigh. *What a mess! What a goddam awful mess!*

The glide descended, moving into denser air traffic, while Cho Yi, beside him, began to snore again.

* * *

The Madam, it seemed, was her mother. A thin-boned, hard-faced woman who, he imagined, must have been quite pretty in her time.

"Are you sure you would not have another of the girls?" she asked, her fan fluttering agitatedly before her heavily made-up face. She seemed quite reluctant to let Li Yuan have his specific request.

"I am quite sure, Madam Yin," he answered, standing his ground. "And if it is a question of the fee, I will happily double it. Now show me to her. I am growing impatient."

Madam Yin hesitated a moment longer then folded up her fan. "Wait there," she said and ducked back inside.

A minute later she returned. "All right. But nothing kinky, you understand?"

"I understand." And Li Yuan bowed, even as the Madam's fan started up agitatedly once more.

"Then follow me."

He followed her, through a corridor that stank of perfume and sweat and out through a small ante room into a hallway that had three doors leading off it. She stopped at the second of them and knocked.

"Fei Yen! You have a visitor!"

Flying Swallow. It was such a pretty name. He commented on it now to the mother.

She gave a grudging nod, a faint colour appearing at her neck where the line of make-up ended. "I am pleased you like it, for she was named after myself."

"Then it is doubly pretty," Li Yuan said, and only afterward, as he turned back to face the door, did he think how crass a comment it had been. And yet she had seemed pleased by it, as if she received few compliments.

Yin Fei Yen. Both the name and the face seemed familiar. And yet he had never met her in his life before this moment.

As the door opened, the girl, who was sat upon the bed in a desultory fashion, looked up. A moment's hope died as she saw how old he was. He saw how she looked to her mother, a pleading look, then looked down, in an instant accepting her fate.

And Li Yuan, watching the tiny play in her eyes, felt sickened by it all. Was this what his brother wanted? *This*?

The mother hovered behind him. He turned and pressed the credits into her hand – four times what had been agreed – then stepped through and pulled the door shut behind him.

"Well," he said, staring at her again. "So *you* are Fei Yen."

She looked up, a brief defiance in her eyes. But she knew the score. Her mother had sold her to him. For the next hour she was his, to do with as he wished.

Did Han Ch'in think of that? Did he picture her with other men every time he made love to this woman?

Oh, she was pretty. A real head-turner, and no mistaking it. But . . . there was a cold, sour knowledge in her eyes right now that no games of pretence could ever wash away. She had seen awful things; maybe had awful things done to her, for all the mother spoke of doing "nothing kinky".

And then there was the child.

"Stand up," he said, no tone in his voice.

She stood.

"Now turn around."

She slowly turned full circle, then looked to him, wondering what he wanted from her next. The child – if child there was in her belly, and as yet he had no proof – barely showed. She looked, if anything, underweight. The only clue to her predicament was a tightness about her mouth, a redness about her eyes – as if she had been crying earlier.

So what now?

A customer – a real customer – would fuck her. But this was his brother's future bride.

Talk, then. He'd talk to her.

He went across and sat on the edge of the bed, then patted the space beside him. She sat, uncertainly, he saw. As yet she hadn't fathomed him.

"What do you want me to do?" she asked.

He stared into the darkness of her eyes a moment, understanding in that instant how his brother might have fallen for this woman; but his purpose was to check her out. To *test* her.

"What do *you* want?"

There was a frown, then: "Sexually, you mean?"

He shook his head, his mouth suddenly dry. "From life."

Her laugh was bleak. It told him much more than he wanted to know. She didn't think his brother was going to marry her. She thought he was only using her, and that now she was carrying his child he would discard her.

As well he might. For she was a liability to such a man as Han Ch'in. His brother might as well spit in his General's face as marry this one.

"Well?" he insisted. "What *do* you want from life, Fei Yen?"

He saw how she hesitated, then backed away from the truth that had been on her lips. She wasn't going to tell *him*, that was for sure.

"My own place . . . and the means to live."

"I'll give you it."

She had begun to look down, but now she met his eyes again, startled by his words. "What do you mean?"

"Whatever you want. I'll give you it. And no strings attached."

Slowly her eyes narrowed. "What are you doing?"

"Nothing," he answered. "Only being kind. Giving a young woman what she wants."

She stared a moment longer, then shook her head. "It's a trick, isn't it? A game. To make me grateful to you. To get me to do things for you."

"Why?" he asked, chilled by her train of thought. "What *would* you do?"

In answer she stood again and took off her top, revealing pert white breasts, the nipples of which stood out like tiny almond buttons.

Despite himself, Yuan felt his penis harden. Desire coursed through him. She was beautiful. More beautiful than any woman he had ever slept with.

As she slipped from her briefs, that hardness at his groin became painful. He could not tear his eyes away from that small dark patch between her legs.

"No strings?" she asked, her voice suddenly seductive. "Are you sure there'd be no strings?"

Li Yuan swallowed. It would be so easy. There was nothing – nothing, that was, but his loyalty to his brother – to stop him.

She stepped close, her warmth pressing against his knees, then leaned into him, so that her breasts pressed against his chest.

He felt her lips close upon his own and found himself responding, found himself placing his hands upon her back, his fingers slowly smoothing their way down the length of that silken flesh until they rested on her buttocks.

Her kisses were like wine. As she lowered herself into his lap, her legs wrapped about him, he groaned and, unable to stop himself, pulled her tight against him, beginning to rub himself against her.

"Slowly now," she said, moving her face back from his, her smile as different now as any smile could be from the first look she had given him.

He was a customer now. And she a whore. An actress.

Yet even though he knew that, even though he knew what he was doing was wrong – as wrong as anything he had ever done – he could not pull away. He *wanted* her. Wanted her more than he had wanted anything, or anyone, in his life.

"*Aiya*," he moaned, as she reached down and freed his penis from within the cloth of his *pau*. As her fingers gently caressed the tip of it.

The feel of it was indescribable.

She chuckled, then leaned into him again, her lips on his once more, her movements against him making him whimper now.

And then, suddenly, she lifted herself up and he was inside her, fucking her, pushing up into her as if nothing else in the universe existed but this.

He came explosively, shuddering against her, his hands gripping her buttocks, pulling her down into him, as if he could tear her in two, or push through her. And she, he knew, had come, too. He could feel it, and knew it was no act.

And as they surfaced from that darkness, he saw the surprise in her eyes, the unfeigned shock.

"No strings," he said, moving his hands up onto her shoulders, his fingers gently caressing her neck. "No strings at all."

* * *

They went down by lift, then crossed the hall and out onto a crowded walkway that, so K. later told him, was reasonably empty by the standards of this world.

Kim paused a moment, noticing the heavy metallic meshes that surrounded every building, every balcony, then looked to the traffic in the skies and understood.

Different ways, different rules.

He walked on, keeping up with K.

A walkway took them up into the heart of another massive building, on the twenty-seventh floor of which K. had hired an office.

"I don't understand," Kim said, once they were safely inside the tiny room, the door locked behind them, the "silence baffle", as K. termed it, in place around the desk.

K. smiled. "First time I arrived here, I stepped out into the middle of a park. I almost didn't get back. But after a few visits I decided I'd have to buy my way into this world and so I stole a few things. Took them back and forged them. Then I came back and hired this place, and the apartment. Made myself an identity in this world."

Kim laughed. "So who are we?"

"Culver. George Culver."

Kim narrowed his eyes, searching his memory, then nodded. "DeVore . . . he used that name once, didn't he?"

"In our worlds. Not in this. Here he has no need for aliases. He has pawns enough to do his business for him."

As he spoke, K. tapped out a code on the keyboard that was embossed into the desk's surface. Almost at once a pair of screens rose from the surface, lighting up as they did so.

"First, however, let me show you what he's up to. But bear with me. This gets somewhat technical . . ."

K. turned, looking to him, then laughed. "Forgive me, Kim. Sometimes I forget I am talking to myself."

Kim smiled. "No matter. Just show me how he means to make it all collapse."

* * *

As the exhaust from the great rockets cleared, the band started up, playing a vigorous Chinese version of the Star-Spangled Banner, the anthem of the 69 States of the great American Empire.

As the ramp came down and President Newell stepped out onto the platform of Airforce One, a cheer went up from the invited crowd. Han Ch'in, watching from his position at the front of that crowd, smiled, then began to walk across.

He had met Newell on several occasions, though not since he'd been elected President. A nice man, if ineffectual: that was the official view. But Han knew better. Han knew how hard Newell had fought to keep Sino-American relationships on an even keel, especially after the Nebraska incident.

Showing his pass to the two guards at the barrier, Han Ch'in stepped through, then walked across, getting to the foot of the ramp even as Newell stepped from it.

Han Ch'in stopped directly in front of Newell and bowed low.

As he straightened up, Newell smiled broadly and put out a hand.

"Major Li! How good to see you again! It's been three years, almost!"

"Two years, eleven months," Han said, returning the smile even as he grasped Newell's hand firmly. "It's good to see you again, Mister President."

"Call me Bob," Newell said quietly, leaning closer. "Let's cut the shit while we're here, eh, old friend?"

Han Ch'in laughed. "Whatever you say, sir."

Newell raised his head, grinning for the cameras, then walked on, speaking through the side of his mouth. "I've managed to leave the wife at home this once, Han Ch'in, so see what you can do for me, okay? I hear your army fellas are about to announce their choice of Consul for Washington, so you scratch my back, I'll scratch yours. You understand?"

"I'll see what I can do."

"Blonde and busty. You know the type."

Han looked down, trying to keep from laughing. "Whatever you say, sir."

Newell lowered his head, as if he'd given the cameras quite enough of his grin, and looked to Han Ch'in again. "You know, I often wonder just how many of those bastards out there watching this on their screens actually bother to read our lips, or whether they just think we're talking matters of state."

"Does it matter?" Han asked, interested by this insight into the man.

"Hell, no. So long as my wife ain't one of them!"

* * *

Kim stared at the screen long after it had been cleared, then shook his head.

"Amazing. And you think no one suspects a thing?"

"I *know* they don't. If they did, they'd do something. His set-up breaks the market's rules in every possible way."

Kim nodded. DeVore owned major companies and their subsidiaries, and their subsidiaries' subsidiaries. He also owned certain trading companies – those who specialised in buying and selling shares – and commodities agents. He owned suppliers and retailers, and the security companies that serviced all of these people. But most important of all, he owned the communications companies through which all of these people traded.

DeVore owned the numbers on this world. And tomorrow he would set off a chain reaction in the system.

"I'm only guessing," K. said, but if I were him I'd start low down, among the little companies. Get a few of them to sell at a loss, just as if they know something that the rest of the market doesn't. Then I'd use my buyers to stoke up the process – have one or two bigger companies involved. A couple of the top hundred. Start a mild panic. Then I'd hit with one of the big boys. Botch, perhaps. Or UCM. Or, best of all, Murdoch Inc. Something basic. Something essential to everybody's lives."

"A slitting of his wrists."

"His and everyone's, because once this gets going there'll be no stopping it. The markets will drop like stones, especially if, at first, people's attention is drawn elsewhere."

"But where?"

K. tapped at the pad a moment, then the screen lit up again. It showed the main Murdoch news channel, Channel 96. A newscaster was talking, a panel on the wall behind him showing a steaming rocket ship that had just set down at Tientsin Spaceport. Two great banners flew together behind the ship. One was the red dragon on a golden background of the Chinese Empire, the other the red white and blue of the United States, the 69 stars boldly emblazoned in one corner. As the picture grew to fill the screen, a caption came up in English and Mandarin, even as the newscaster spoke again in his best mid-Pacific accent:

"United States President Robert Newell arrived this evening at Beijing Spaceport on his way to tomorrow's meeting with President Wei. They will meet at noon at the Imperial Palace to sign the latest draft of the Sino-American trade agreement . . ."

"Oh, shit!" K. said, clearing the screen then looking to Kim. "We'd best get back immediately."

* * *

Han Ch'in saw her at once, there at the far end of the crowded reception hall, beside the trader, Wyatt. Blonde, extremely busty, and with the kind of bored look on her face that said "escort" as clearly as if she'd had it tattooed on her forehead.

Excusing himself momentarily, he made his way across.

"Edmund . . ."

Wyatt turned, then smiled. "Han Ch'in! How are you? I hear you're escorting the President."

"That's so. And that's why I've come to speak to you. I have . . . well, a little proposition, shall we say."

Wyatt's smile broadened. "You want to deal, Han Ch'in?"

"There's a room," Han answered, maintaining his dignity, "just along the corridor. If we could talk there?"

Wyatt looked to the girl. "Wait here, Susan. I'll be two minutes maximum."

She stared at him doe-eyed and nodded, then went back to sipping at her drink and looking about her, a glazed expression returning to her features.

Han Ch'in studied the girl a moment, wondering what an intelligent man like Newell was doing fucking bimbos like this, then, turning back to Wyatt, he gave a tight smile and put out an arm, inviting him through.

* * *

Li Yuan took off his jacket and threw it down on the chair, then went over to the sink and, turning the tap full on, sloshed water up into his face.

What am I doing? What in fuck's name am I getting involved in? If Han Ch'in should find out!

But it was too late now. He'd had the girl. And not just once, but three times. No. He had to go through with it now. Had to. And then, for the first time in his life, he'd have to pretend. To Han Ch'in of all people!

"*Aiya* . . ."

Li Yuan turned and looked back through the door at his luxury apartment. He had lived here fifteen months now, ever since Hu Sho had thrown him out. Not that he blamed her. It couldn't have been nice to come home and find your husband shagging not only your best friend, but her daughter too!

And now, once again, his dick was getting him in trouble. Only this time he could not afford to be caught. This time he had to set things up so that he *couldn't* be caught.

He went over to the comset and punched out the number the woman had given him. For a moment there was no reply, and then the screen lit up.

"Ahh . . . Mister Huang. Have you made the arrangements?"

Li Yuan nodded, then sheepishly read out the details.

He had bought an apartment in Shanghai, using a company account. At the same time he had set up a fund to pay the woman and her daughter enough to live on for the next thirty years. And not just subsistence living, but a comfortable sum – enough to allow them many little luxuries.

But if he knew the mother, she'd find other ways to supplement her income, promise or no promise.

The girl, however, was another matter. He was determined not to share her. Not now.

No strings. The girl had been right to question that, for all relationships – even of this crude, mercantile kind – had strings. That was how it worked. Maybe it was even *why* it worked.

"You'll leave tomorrow morning," he said finally. "The tickets will be waiting for you at Central Station, in your name."

"First Class?" the woman asked, a tightness born of greed in her face.

"Of course. And you will be met at the other end and taken to your new apartment. You will receive a decorating allowance. And there will be special payments."

"Special?" The woman's eyes lit.

"For your silence. Which will cease the moment that a word is said about this agreement between us."

"I understand."

"Make sure you do, Madam Yin. Make doubly sure you do."

Li Yuan broke contact, then slumped down onto the sofa. He sniffed his fingers. He could still smell her on him. The very thought of what they'd done made him stiffen again.

No wonder Han Ch'in had wanted her; whore or not. Such a woman could rob one of all sense.

Yes, and he would raise his brother's son as his own. Would do well by him. Make sure he had nothing but the best.

But the thought slipped into the background as he thought again of the woman and the way she had of presenting her breasts to him, that teasing light in her eyes, and the noises she made.

"Aiya . . ." he said, going across and beginning to strip off, knowing that nothing but a cold shower would cure this. "The gods help me for what I've done!"

* * *

The President lay on his back, the girl astride him. As he came, he reached up, burying his head between her breasts.

As he relaxed again, the girl straightened up a little, then giggled. "That better, honey?"

"Fucking wonderful . . ."

"You want me to stay? I can, if you want."

Newell looked up at her. In the light from the single bedside lamp she looked magnificent. A *real* woman, not like those tight-arsed frigid little bitches that manned his office back in Washington. That lot didn't have a decent pair of tits between them!

"You stay as long as you want, sweetheart. I sure as hell ain't kicking you out!"

"That's good," she said, giving him a lascivious smile. "Because I know one or two tricks you just might like."

"Oh yeah?" He raised an eyebrow, interested.

"Yeah," she said lazily, reaching up to cup her breasts, her erect nipples drawing his eyes. "And I ain't talking about tricks you can teach your kids."

"I didn't think you were . . ." He paused, then. "You ever thought of settling in Washington?"

"You offering me a job?"

"I might be. Depends if you pass the interview."

She grinned, then reached down, gently taking his flaccid cock in one hand, beginning to coax it back to life. "Well now, let me see if I've got this right . . ."

* * *

Li Yuan was dozing in the chair by the screen when it came alive.

"What the . . .?"

Cho Yi's ancient, timeless face stared back at him. "Yuan! Wake up! It's me. I'm in the office. You must come at once. Something's happening. Something big. I need your help!"

"Master Cho?"

The screen went dead.

Yuan shook himself, then stood, feeling unsteady. He was tired. To be honest, he was knackered after being with the girl. But Cho Yi had sounded desperate.

Walking across, he took his jacket from the back of the chair and pulled it on, then, responding to the urgency in Cho's voice, he went back to the screen and tapped in the code for Rapidcabs.

"Yes, *Shih* Li? You want a glide now?"

"Yes, Hung," he answered, recognising the young man. "To go to my office. Fast as you can."

The young man looked down, checking something, then looked up again, a wide grin on his face. "One minute. He'll be there by the time you get up onto the roof."

"Great!" Yuan said. "Bill me double, Hung, okay?"

Hung bowed, hands together. "Very generous, *Shih* Li. Any time you need us . . ."

". . . I'll phone you."

He cut the connection, then hurried across, turning off the lights behind him. Something big, eh? Now what could that be?

* * *

Turner, Newell's Security Chief, was a big, uncompromising man. He stood now nose to nose with Li Han Ch'in in the corridor outside the President's suite, bellowing at the Han, his face and neck bright red with exertion.

"I don't give a shit what the President wanted! I'm not here to satisfy his fucking carnal needs, I'm here to stop the fucking asshole getting topped!"

Han Ch'in glowered back at the man.

"You want to do something about it, you knock the fucking door down and drag her out. But I don't think the President would be very pleased about that, do you?"

"I may just fucking do that!" Turner bellowed back at him. "But from here on you butt out, alright, Major Li? You keep your fucking nose out of our fucking business!"

Han Ch'in raised his hands, as if to make peace, but Turner still wasn't satisfied.

"Shit knows what went through your fucking head, man! Why, you didn't even check the fucking woman out, did you?"

Han Ch'in bristled. "She was with a reputable gentleman, who assures me he got her from one of the top escort agencies. The woman's been with them five years, and not a hint of trouble." He sneered. "What's your problem, Major Turner. You think she's going to fuck the President to death?"

Turner lifted his chin a little. He clearly wasn't used to be answered back, and besides, Han Ch'in was theoretically his equal in rank. But he was *still* not happy.

"Okay. But you *ask* me from now on. In fact, you get my fucking permission before you do *anything* that involves the President, *okay?*"

"Okay."

Turner eased back a little. "Then good. I'm glad we're agreed on that."

Han Ch'in stared at him a moment, then asked. "What does he usually do on these kind of trips, go in his room and wank?"

Turner's lips curled slightly at that, amusement replacing anger. "Hell no. Usually he doesn't have sex at all."

"No?" Han Ch'in sounded incredulous. "But the guy's got a libido that'd take two firetrucks to put out!"

"What I mean is, usually he's got Mrs. Newell along with him. The Ice Queen, we call her."

"Ah . . ." Han Ch'in stared at the man a moment, admiring his loyalty to Newell, then. "Hey, I'm sorry. If I'd known I was treading on your toes . . ."

Turner gave a little nod. "It's in the past. We go forward from here, right?"

"Right!"

There was a crash. Distant but loud. Both men turned and frowned.

"What the fuck . . .?"

The door to the President's rooms flew open. A security guard, gun drawn, looked out at Turner. "It was inside, sir! From inside his room!"

Turner rushed through, followed closely by Han Ch'in. Two men were already at the door, trying to break it down. Turner charged it with his shoulder. The hinges gave and popped as he slammed into it.

Han Ch'in, stopping in the doorway, saw at once what had happened.

Newell lay on the bed, his mouth gagged, his hands tied behind his back. His throat was cut from ear to ear, blood pooled darkly on the pillows and sheets. Beyond him, on the far side of the room, the curtains drifted in and out in the breeze from the shattered window.

The girl was gone.

Han Ch'in felt his stomach drop away. This was *his* fault. One hundred per cent down to him. The visiting President was dead, assassinated in a safe house, and he had introduced him to the killer.

He dropped to his knees.

Turner examined the body quickly, then turned. His eyes took in the kneeling form of Han Ch'in by the door, then looked past him at his own men, who stood in the doorway, wide-eyed with horror.

"Hansen, Josephs . . . go down and get the body. Then get the mess cleared up. And don't say a fucking word to anyone, right? Not a fucking word!"

They nodded, then turned and disappeared. Turner shivered, then looked to Han Ch'in again. "As for you, Major Li, you'd better contact your people at once and find out what you can about this Wyatt fellow. And you'd better let President Wei know while you're at it."

Han Ch'in glanced up, distraught. "I'm sorry, Major, I . . ."

"Just fucking leave it!" Turner barked, all of his pent-up tension in those four words. "He was a good man. And now he's dead, fuck it! So don't give me sorry, Major Li. I don't wanna hear."

Han Ch'in gave the smallest nod, then, standing, hurried from the room.

Aiya, he thought, thinking of what his superiors would say when they found out. *Ai-fucking-ya!*

* * *

Cho Yi was alone in the trading room. As Li Yuan closed the door and walked across, the old man looked up.

"It's happening," he said, as if Li Yuan should understand what he meant. "I can't believe it, but it is."

Yuan sat on the far side of the desk, puzzled by the look on Cho's face. He didn't seem troubled so much as bemused.

"Okay, what is it? We bought some valueless stock?"

"You might say," Cho answered, vague to the point of irritating Li Yuan.

"Look . . . I could be in bed now, Master Cho. Have we a problem, or haven't we?"

Cho laughed. Again, it was strange, because Li Yuan could not grasp what was meant by it. Was he amused or not? And if he was, then *why*?

"Well?" he asked, when Cho did not answer.

"Look for yourself," Cho said, sitting back and folding his arms across his chest. "See what you make of it."

Yuan frowned, then activated the screen in front of him. For a moment he simply stared, then his mouth fell open.

"*Fuck* . . ."

"Yes, fuck. Fuck times eighty billion neh?"

"Eighty . . .?" Li Yuan looked up and met the old man's eyes. This time he *did* understand. "But can't we . . .?"

"Stop it?" Cho Yi laughed again. This time Li Yuan had no difficulty placing Cho Yi's laughter. It was the ironic laughter of a man who saw that his time was up.

"But there are controls, surely?"

"Whoever started this removed them."

"*Removed* them? That's not possible, *is* it?"

"Oh, I'd say *anything* was possible, if you wanted to commit financial suicide. You simply have to bribe men, or threaten them, or have them killed. And then replace those you've had killed. Until you control the system. And then . . . see, Yuan? . . . see how it's happening before our eyes? . . . you just kick away the props."

Yuan stared at the screen, bemused now. "But who would do that? Who'd have the power? And if they *had* the power, then *why*? It would be like shooting oneself in the head!"

"Exactly. But someone has. Someone big."

Li Yuan shook his head slowly. "You've made projections?"

Cho nodded.

"And?"

"Freefall," Cho answered, smiling a beaming smile at Yuan. "Straight to the bottom and out the other side."

"But why? I mean, surely someone's spotted what's going on? Surely someone's taking action?"

In answer Cho Yi turned and switched on the news screen just above him and to his right. As it came alight, it showed the image of a woman lying on top of what looked like an airduct of some kind. She was quite clearly dead, blood oozing from her in a dozen different places.

As the commentary switched in, the camera travelled up the external window-wall of what appeared to be a plush hotel of some kind, until it focused on the shattered window of a room.

"*. . . of what was President Newell's own suite in the prestigious Eight Dragons Hotel. While the President's spokesman refuses to give details of the incident, it is understood that the President himself was not involved, and was actually at an official reception across town in Ching Shan Park . . .*"

Cho cut the sound then looked back across at Li Yuan. "Rumour is that Newell's dead. Assassinated by the girl. She too committed suicide. Threw herself out of a thirty-eighth-storey window. Strange that, neh? A curious synchronicity, wouldn't you say?"

"You think the two things are connected?"

Cho laughed. "Don't you, Yuan? What better distraction than the assassination of a visiting President? What better way of keeping eyes off one screen and on another?"

Li Yuan gestured towards the screen. "But this is more important, surely?"

"You know that, and I know that . . . but our friends in the media don't. Not yet, anyway. They're still speculating as to whether Newell has been killed, and if so, whether there will be a war."

"A war?"

Cho nodded, then looked down.

And then it struck Li Yuan. "Oh, shit! Han Ch'in!"

* * *

Kim followed K. into the lift, a sense of real urgency gripping him. He had seen the pictures on the news screens in the lobby of the apartment block, and heard the commentary, and knew now that time was running out for them.

As the doors slid closed behind them, he looked up at the screen in the corner of the lift, then spoke to the air:

"Channel 96. With sound."

At once it switched to the news channel, showing the latest pictures from outside the Eight Dragons Hotel.

". . . *and whilst the woman cannot be immediately recognised after falling thirty-eight storeys, it has been confirmed by eye-witnesses that she was naked and that, according to one, she appeared not to scream as she fell.*"

The image cut to the view from a news glider, positioned in line with the shattered window of the Presidential Suite. Armed men were gathered in that window, blocking any view into the room, but that only served to stoke up speculation.

"*It is now almost twenty minutes since the incident, and still no word has come from President Newell's spokesman, or indeed the President himself, about the affair, but it has now been confirmed that earlier reports from their office that the President was at a reception in Ching Shang Park were erroneous, and that President Newell was not seen by anybody at that reception. Which leads us to ask just what* has *been going on at the Eight Dragons Hotel, and what are the implications for relations between America and China if – as rumours have it – President Newell has been assassinated. It must be recalled that no American President has ever been murdered in a foreign country . . .*"

The lift stopped. The doors slid open silently. Ahead of them lay their corridor. Their door was the third on the left.

K. looked to Kim as they stepped out onto the plushly carpeted floor. "I'd say the shit's really hit the fan, wouldn't you?"

"So what do we do now?"

K. stopped in front of their door and took the door key from his pocket. "Simple. We get Karr and Chen and Ebert. And then we get the bastard."

"And the markets?"

"That depends."

"On what?"

K. turned the key and began to open the door. "On whether we can get back in time. If we can get back in an hour . . ." He stopped dead. Kim, following him in, cannoned into the back of him, then blinked, astonished by the sight that met his eyes.

The hoop of fire was gone. And DeVore . . . Kim swallowed . . . DeVore was sitting on the bed, a semi-automatic in one hand. He beckoned them in with the other hand, then grinned.

"I'd say that was a rather big if, wouldn't you?"

CHAPTER·23

TIME'S LAST HOUR

The storm had passed. Ragged clouds drifted about the edge of the great depression in the earth. Only an hour back the dark earth had steamed; now a great carpet of white flowers covered it; lilies, their tall, elegant white throats turned to the sky, spilling oxygen into the air.

Fifty kilometres away, to the south of the ruined generator, the sun shone on a different scene. On the gentle slope of a wooded hill, a cruiser lay on its side, its port wing crumpled, smoke wisping up from its damaged engine. The hatch was open, the inside of the craft in darkness.

Nearby, hidden beneath the trees, the entrance of a cave gaped black.

Silence. Not even the call of birds or insects. And then, far off, a muted drone, growing louder by the moment.

A second cruiser, smaller than the first, flew over the valley, its shadow flitting over the canopy of the trees. It banked then circled back, slowing until it hovered over the fallen craft. Then, edging back and across, it descended, settling in a patch of meadow by the stream at the foot of the valley.

The engines died. There was a hiss as the hatch opened; the clank of booted feet upon the ramp.

Daniel stood there a moment, squinting out at the wooded hillside through the visor of his helmet, his senses twitching, then he jumped down and began to make his way up the slope towards DeVore's cruiser.

They had beaten him. They had destroyed his army and broken his power.

Now only DeVore himself was left.

Coming closer to the cruiser, Daniel stopped and crouched, looking between the narrow boles of the trees at the craft. It seemed abandoned. There was the fizz and pop of electrics shorting, then, incongruously, a snatch of music.

Daniel blinked, then understood. Music. DeVore had been playing music even as he fled from them.

He moved forward, slowly, cautiously, his gun raised, the barrel covering the hatch.

The music flared up momentarily, the great sweeping sound of strings briefly filling the valley, then cut out.

The smell of burning circuitry was stronger now. To his left the tree cover was broken, the hillside gouged up where the craft had landed.

Daniel stopped, his eyes narrowed, taking that in. DeVore was some pilot to have landed his damaged craft without destroying it.

But why here? Why go down here?

A voice started in his head. Emily's voice. "*Daniel? What's happening there? Daniel? Do you read me, Daniel?*"

Daniel switched it off. The cruiser was less than ten paces from him. He raised his visor, listening intently. Nothing. Nothing but the faint crackle of burning circuits.

Silently he crossed the narrow space, keeping to the left of the open hatch. Now that he was closer, he could see that the hatchway had been forced. The ramp, which ought to have emerged automatically when the hatch was opened, had jammed. The whole side of the craft had buckled when it came down.

Daniel turned, looking at the ground beneath the hatch, and saw them at once. Footprints, leading away up the slope.

His eyes followed their line.

Daniel hesitated, then tongued the switch. "Listen," he said, speaking into the open channel. "I'm at the craft. There's a cave nearby. I think that's where he went. I'm going to investigate."

Emily's voice came back at him at once. "*Daniel? I know you can hear me, so listen. Stay where you are. Don't do anything until I get there.*"

Daniel's tongue brushed the switch but did not turn it off. He itched to go inside and get the bastard, to put a bullet through his head and end it all, but Emily was right; it made no sense to take risks. Not now that they'd come this far.

"Okay," he said. "I'll wait."

"*Good,*" came the reply. "*And Daniel . . . you've done well.*"

Daniel smiled, relaxing momentarily. None of them had slept these past twenty-four hours. A combination of drugs and adrenaline had kept them going. And now they were close. Close to a victory that had seemed impossible only a few days back.

Even so, they would be leaving soon. Leaving and never coming back.

The simple thought of it surprised him, making the hairs at the back of his neck stand on end, because until that moment it had all seemed academic – something that *might* happen *if* they beat DeVore. But now it was close. Why, if he closed his eyes he could see it. Could picture the earth, swathed in flowers, white beneath the sun, white beneath the moon. And silent. A silence broken only by the sound of the wind, the inward rush of waves breaking on an empty shore.

Daniel shivered, then spoke: "And when the lamb opened the seventh seal, silence covered the sky."

"*Daniel?*"

He blinked. "What?"

"*Those words . . . where did you hear them?*"

"I don't know. I . . ." And then he remembered. Remembered sitting there at his desk in the library, back in the training camp. "It was in a book I read. It was written by a man named Pasek . . ."

He felt as much as heard the sigh that echoed in his helmet. "*I knew him*," Emily said. "*He was in the Black Hand with me. Back before he created* The Sealed."

And now Pasek was dead. Yet the world he had foreseen had come to pass. A world without men.

Alas, alas for the human race. Alas for the kings of separation.

How strangely resonant those words had been when he'd first read them. How bleak and yet how moving. As if they spoke to something buried deep within him.

"*Daniel?*"

"Yes?"

"*Hold tight. We're almost there.*"

Daniel smiled and nodded to himself. Yes, he could hear the drone of their engines now. Yet even as he made to turn and look back down the length of the valley, he glimpsed, out of the corner of his eye, the faintest movement in the darkness at the cave's mouth.

There was a noise. A low whine, like the sound of an insect rushing through the air. Too late he saw it, not an arm's length from his visor. Saw it and jerked back, trying to move his head aside.

And then the top of his helmet blew away, as if someone had just cleaved it with an axe.

* * *

"Daniel? . . . *Daniel?*"

Emily crouched, looking through the trees, trying to make out what exactly it was she was looking at. The craft was some twenty metres to her left, the cave some way beyond it. Between the two was a tangle of greenery. Little else could be made out.

She turned slightly, signalling to the three men to her right to move up, then began to move forward herself, the big rocket-launcher clutched against her chest.

Where was he? Where in the gods' names was he?

One moment he'd been transmitting perfectly, the next . . . nothing.

This once she should have trusted to her instinct and ordered him to pull back. Or told him to seal the entrance to the cave and leave DeVore to the floraforms. But she, like Daniel, had wanted to make sure.

I should have killed the bastard when I had the chance, all those years ago when we went to visit him in his mountain hideout. Back when I was in the Ping Tiao. I could have done it then, and saved the world an immensity of grief.

Yes, but back then she hadn't known what he was.

A voice sounded in her helmet; a sharp, sibilant whisper. "*There's something there. On the ground beside the craft.*"

Emily stopped, then lifted her head slightly, moving it this way and that, looking through the tangle of leaf and branch. Yes, she could see it now. The humped shape of something. Could see the way the sunlight glinted off the angle of a protective flap.

Daniel, she thought, feeling her heart sink.

She straightened up, then moved quickly between the trees, anger making her fearless. And then stopped abruptly, wincing at the sight.

Daniel lay on his side, where he'd fallen, bits of his shattered helmet littering the ground just beyond him.

She groaned. Yet even as she made the noise, Daniel's right hand twitched within the protective glove.

"*Here!*" she yelled, turning and beckoning urgently to her men. "Quick now! He's still alive!"

There was a sudden rustling as men hastened to her. Emily stared a moment longer, pained deeply by the sight of Daniel's injuries, then, turning back, she stepped over the fallen boy and raised the launcher to her shoulder, taking aim.

Revenge. It would have been nice to get revenge. But saving Daniel was more important. Far, far more important.

She squeezed the trigger, bracing herself against the jolt as the rocket rushed away from her, haring into the dark mouth of the cave.

* * *

The hatch hissed shut, the bolts slid into place. Inside the shuttle, a siren was sounding urgently as the survivors strapped themselves into the restraint webs, special harnesses locking about them automatically to support their necks and backs against the massive g-forces they were about to face.

Daniel too had been strapped in, his bandaged head encased in a specially-adapted restraint harness into which were fed the various tubes and electrodes that would keep him alive during the launch.

Emily was the last to take her place, her concern for Daniel keeping her by his side until the very last.

The countdown began, the voice of Han Ch'in sounding throughout the craft.

Ten . . . nine . . . eight . . .

Outside, unseen by those within, a great tide of brightly-coloured flowers breached the outer walls of the spaceport and flowed in towards the ship, even as that voice boomed out across the concrete apron, a massive breaking wave of blooms that engulfed buildings and vehicles as it rushed towards the waiting shuttle.

The engines flared and then fired. *Slowly the vehicle lifted from the pad, even as the flowers met and merged beneath it.*

For a instant or two they roiled and flared, burning away in that intense fireball. Then, like a ripple, they withdrew to form a circle about the scorched and steaming earth. In a blink of an eye, they transformed into a crowd of people, green-faced yet strong of limb, who waved and yelled a silent farewell.

As the shuttle climbed, the circle rippled and then closed upon itself, swallowing up that single patch of darkness, those mimic human forms becoming simple flowers once again; a great ocean of flowers that stretched from coast to coast; a thousand billion blooms that now turned as one, lifting their long, elegant throats towards the sun.

The time of names had ended.
The long age of silence had begun.

* * *

Emily stood by the hatch, looking on as the two medics eased the unit through the umbilical that joined the shuttle to the mothership, calling on them to make sure that they didn't move too quickly.

They knew their job, however, and were careful in those nil-gravity conditions not to let the massive unit brush the side or jolt against the hatch. It slid through gently, easily, a third medic joining them, leaning on the end of the capsule to brake its momentum.

As the unit came alongside her, Emily stared down through its transparent lid at Daniel's pale, unconscious face and prayed to Kuan Yin herself that they were not too late to save him.

And then they were taking him away.

"You should not blame yourself, Emily."

She turned, almost putting herself in a spin. But Kuei Jen's hand reached out and held her arm, stopping her.

"I was responsible for him," she answered soberly. "If not me, then who?"

"Maybe the bastard who shot him."

She stared back steadily at Kuei Jen, then shook her head. "No. DeVore was finished. It was stupid to pursue him."

"Stupid?" Kuei Jen seemed surprised. "And yet DeVore was evil. Is it not right to crush evil?"

"Right, yes, but . . ." Emily shrugged. "Look, is there somewhere we can go . . .?"

"To be near to Daniel?" Kuei Jen smiled gently, understanding Emily's concern. "Of course. Come, I've prepared a room for you."

The room, as it turned out, was in the medical centre itself, just down the corridor from the theatre where, even as she settled in, they were operating on Daniel.

It was there that Han Ch'in came to her.

Sitting on the edge of the chair, which was bolted to the floor in one corner of the cabin, he stared down at his hands a moment, then sighed.

"How bad?" she asked.

"Six thousand. Maybe six two."

Her eyes widened. "Is that all?"

Han Ch'in nodded. "Three of the shuttles didn't make it off the ground. Another malfunctioned on the way up here. Or was tampered with. We'll never know."

"But they're all our people, I take it?"

"Yes. Everyone's vouched for."

Emily nodded. She could still feel the hard shape of her handgun against her hip, and realised that even now she had not relaxed; had not given up the habit of suspicion. She looked back at Han Ch'in. "What do you think the floraforms will do with DeVore?"

Han Ch'in shrugged. "If they're wise, they'll not try to assimilate him."

Her eyes met his, startled. "Do you think . . .?"

"That DeVore is bigger than the floraforms? No. He has the capacity to twist whatever he touches but the floraforms will know that. They seemed to know everything, didn't they?"

She nodded, then frowned. "Gods, it's strange, isn't it? All those years fighting one enemy, and then . . . well . . ."

Han Ch'in was smiling. "Kuei Jen thinks it's nice. Poetical, or so he says."

"You call her him?"

Han Ch'in laughed. "Of course! Tits or no tits, he's still my brother."

"And mother of your nieces and nephews."

"Thank the gods for it!"

"And what do they think?"

Han Ch'in looked away. "That it's all an adventure."

"And you?"

"I miss it already." He met her eyes again. "To be honest with you, I fear that I will die on board this ship. I fear . . ."

"The years ahead?"

"Yes. It's a long journey. And no certainty of arrival, whatever my father said."

She nodded, then, noticing someone standing in the doorway just beyond Han Chi'in, stood up, her face suddenly concerned. "What is it?"

The medic grinned at her. "It's Daniel. He's conscious and he's asking for you."

* * *

Daniel smiled at her as she walked into the room. He was propped up into a sitting position beneath a blanket, a pile of cushions plumped up behind his back.

"Di' yoo thin' yoo gor ri' oh me?"

Emily glanced at the surgeon, concerned, but he shook his head. "It's the drugs that are making him slur the words. The brain's relatively untouched."

She walked across and sat beside Daniel on the bed. Taking the gun from her belt, she slipped it onto the tray beside her, then turned to clasp his hands, surprised by the firmness with which he clasped them back.

"How are you feeling?"

"Groh-ee." Daniel wrinkled his nose. "I fee' li'e I wahnna scrah my 'eah."

"Your head?"

Daniel made to nod, then winced. Emily raised herself a little, looking at the back of his skull, then grimaced. The bone at the back of his skull had been ripped open and a large chunk of it stripped away.

She sat back. "Not pretty."

"Nah. Bu' o-kay, neh? I 'live."

Emily shivered. Yes. He *was* alive. It was a miracle, but there it was. When she'd seen the damage she'd thought it only a matter of time before he died. But here he was, sitting up and talking to her.

She turned, looking to the surgeon. "Do you have to operate?"

"No. We just need to put a plate in, to knit together the skull at the back and protect the brain. Otherwise . . ."

The surgeon's face went from earnestness to shock in a matter of a second. Emily blinked, then understood that he was staring at something behind her. She turned, then gasped.

DeVore stepped from the doorway, then smiled. "Emily, how nice . . . And Daniel. I'm surprised to find you here. I thought I'd killed you back on earth."

She stood, turning towards him, then saw he had a gun.

And Han Ch'in . . . where was Han Ch'in?

"How did you . . .?"

"Get on board?" The smile was urbane, polite; the smile of a Major in the T'ang's security forces. "Oh, we boarded your craft five minutes back."

"*Boarded?*"

DeVore nodded disinterestedly, then walked across, his gun covering Emily all the while. His eyes took in Daniel's injuries a moment, then he looked back at Emily.

"Why, did you think you'd seen the last of me, Emily Ascher?"

She hesitated, then nodded.

"I ought to be cross, you know. That rocket. Spoiled a good body. But fortunately I had another I could slip into." His smile widened briefly, then disappeared. There was a sourness now to his appearance. "But there's a lot you don't know, isn't there? Whole levels, in fact."

"Levels?"

DeVore nodded, then gestured towards the porthole on the far side of the theatre. It was shielded, but as he pointed towards it, the protective shield lifted.

"Go on . . . look. Tell me what you see."

Slowly Emily went across, then stared out through the narrow, oval window. Through the thick layer of translucent ice she could see a second craft, tethered alongside their own. And beyond it . . .

"Gods! What is that?"

"What does it look like?"

She shivered, then answered. "It looks like a hoop . . . a great wheel of fire."

He came across and stood just behind her. "It's a door. An opening into another world."

"Another . . .?"

She stopped, tensing. There had been the sound of gunshots.

"Tut tut," DeVore said, moving back slightly. "It seems that some of your people don't like their new masters. But maybe it's best, neh?"

"Best?"

"To deal with them now."

She saw the coldness in him, the void behind his eyes, and knew that she only had this one chance.

As her arm came up, the hand that he'd cut a finger from closing into a fist, he laughed.

Her hand struck coldness; a red-hot cold that seemed to splinter her hand and freeze her arm, so that she collapsed onto her knees, groaning with the pain of it, her useless arm giving beneath her so that she fell to the side.

DeVore knelt over her and smiled, his warm breath blowing over the landscape of her cheek. Laying there she felt bloated and unreal suddenly, as if, in that instant in which she had struck him, she had entered some strange, hallucinatory realm.

"You like my coat, Emily? I had it specially made. It cost me several of my best morphs, but it was worth it, neh?"

And now she saw the glow that surrounded him; a glow that emanated from the jacket he was wearing and seemed to form a cowl about his head.

"Em-ah-ee!" Daniel yelled from his bed. "Em-ah-ee!"

A cry that DeVore took up mockingly. "Em-ah-ee! Em-ah-ee!"

And with that he leaned into her and kissed her cheek. A kiss that seemed to burn with the same red-hot coldness that she had felt when she had struck him.

"Are you ready?" he asked quietly.

She felt the sudden vibration of the ship's engines. A moment later there was movement, a sense of drifting sideways. And then a brightness at the window that, with a shocking suddenness, engulfed them.

Emily gasped. It was as if the air all about her had suddenly grown dense. Its richness pulverised her senses, making her head swim.

I'm passing out, she thought, but unconsciousness did not come. She could hear Daniel's laboured breathing across the room – hear it with a needle-sharpness that seemed hallucinatory. And then laughter – laughter that boomed in her ears. DeVore's harsh laughter.

"We're there," he said, matter-of-factly, and, placing one hand under her elbow, lifted her up and took her to the porthole.

There, below them, was a great ball of green and blue. Planet Earth. But even as she looked she knew, with some instinct beyond simple explanation, that it was no Earth she had ever trod upon.

"Where are we?" she asked, her own voice strange in her ears.

DeVore turned his face to her and smiled. "We're at the centre. The very middle of it all."

"The middle . . .?"

He nodded, then turned, gesturing to his men who now stood in the doorway. "Take her and lock her up. And keep an eye on the boy. I don't want him causing *any* trouble."

CHAPTER·24

THE MARRIAGE OF THE LIVING DARK

"Gregor, Chen, thank you for coming."

The two men stepped past Jelka into the entrance hall, then turned, concerned to see her in such a state.

"Still no sign of him?" Karr asked.

"No."

"And the gateway?"

"Is still open. Come, I'll show you."

They went down, into Kim's basement workroom. The lamps were off, but the light from the burning hoop that hovered above the middle of the floor was enough to see by.

Karr walked over to it, then crouched down, staring into the dark space at its centre. A faint mist seemed to be gathered there.

"How long has he been gone?"

"I'm not sure. The last time I saw him was five hours back."

Kao Chen grunted. "And the other one? Did he go too?"

Jelka looked to him, surprised by the faint tone of hostility in his voice. "Yes. K.'s missing, too."

"And you're sure they're nowhere else?"

"Well, they're not in the house, and Kim would have said if they were going into Fermi. He always does."

Karr turned his head. "And yet he said nothing about going into another universe. That's strange, wouldn't you say?"

She hesitated, then nodded. It *was* unlike Kim. He was usually so thoughtful, so considerate.

"And you don't know where this leads to?"

Jelka shook her head. "All I know is that it disappeared an hour or so back, then reappeared shortly afterwards."

"That makes sense. The power's been fluctuating all morning." Karr sighed, then: "Damn it. I should have brought my gun."

"Gun?" Jelka looked alarmed. "You think they might be in trouble, then, Gregor?"

"Who knows? But it might be best to prepare for the worst, neh? You wouldn't by any chance have a weapon?"

"A weapon?" Jelka hesitated, then turned and left the room.

Karr watched her go, then looked to Kao Chen. "Are you up to this, Chen?"

Chen stared back at his old friend, wide-eyed. "You mean, step through that?"

"That's exactly what I mean."

Chen swallowed. "I don't . . ." Then, steeling himself: "If you go, I go."

Karr smiled. "Good. Then maybe I should ask Jelka for another weapon."

"You think we'll need them?"

"Who knows? But my guess is that if what's through there is anything like this world, then we'll find *him* there."

"DeVore?"

"Or whatever he calls himself there."

Chen appeared sobered by the thought. He was silent a moment, then shook his head. "You know me, Gregor. I fear no man. Yet the merest thought of this sets my flesh creeping. If we should lose our way in there . . ."

Karr nodded. "I understand. But we'll be together, Chen. Whatever's there on the other side, you'll not be alone. And we *shall* come back. I promise you."

Chen nodded, yet for once he did not seem cheered by the big man's reassurances. That worried look remained in his eyes, which flitted from time to time to the darkness at the centre of that roiling circle of flame, as if at any moment something horrific would emerge from it.

There were footsteps on the stairs outside. A moment later Jelka came back into the room. She was carrying two weapons. Big automatics that were clearly not Kim's.

Karr stood, then took one of the guns from her and hefted it, putting it up to his shoulder to look through the sight. "Gods!" he said enthusiastically, stroking the casing of the weapon almost lovingly. "A JPK-4! Best gun ever made!" He lowered it and looked at Jelka, shaking his head. "I didn't know any of these had survived."

Kao Chen was staring at his own gun, as if at a long-lost friend. Looking up, he grinned. "You know. I feel better already, Gregor." He met Jelka's eyes. "These are beautiful. Real works of art. Were they the Marshal's?"

But Jelka was staring at the weapons coldly. "No, Chen. Those were assassins' weapons. I don't know why we kept them, but my father insisted."

"Assassins?" Chen looked at the weapon in a new light.

Jelka nodded, her eyes looking back, as if seeing it all again. "They tried to kill me. I got one of them, and then my father came home. He shot the others dead." She sighed, then shook her head. "It was a long time ago. I . . . I'd almost forgotten."

Karr gave a sympathetic nod, then, more practically, asked, "We'll need munitions."

Jelka nodded and, reaching into her pocket, pulled out six slender clips of bullets. They were still packed in their ice-wrap covers, as if new.

Karr smiled. "Ever the Marshal's daughter."

"Of course." She was quiet a moment, then. "Bring them back, Gregor. Please. Just find them and bring them back."

* * *

The man sat before the bank of screens, watching the figures change moment by moment as the markets went into free fall.

"So . . ." he said quietly, drumming his fingers on the edge of the desk. Then, conscious that, at that very moment, measures he had set in place long ago were being activated, he leaned forward and began to tap out the pre-prepared codes that would set the second stage of his scheme into operation.

That done he sat back, a faint smile on his lips. DeVore would never know. Why, he'd never even guess. And even if he did, it would be too late. Much, much too late.

He turned slightly, looking at the portrait of his mother that hung on the wall to his left. She had died over twelve years ago now, but his memories of her were still fresh.

Five hundred dollars. That's what she sold me for. A mere five hundred dollars.

Not that he blamed her for it. After all, she'd been a mere serving-girl, not even sixteen years of age, when she had fallen with him. It must have seemed a good deal, to have the fertilised egg removed, her indiscretion expunged from the records. Why, he could imagine that she'd hardly felt a thing when she signed the paper that gave over legal custody. After all, it was not like giving up a baby.

And so he'd been implanted in another's womb and raised as their son. But she was the mother. Not that he'd known it until his first "mother" had died and he'd inherited her papers.

The knowledge had come as a shock to him.

And the father?

His real mother hadn't wanted to say at first, but slowly he'd wheedled it out of her. It had been at a ball at the great house where she had lived and worked. The man had been a mere five years older than her, but already an important man. A rich young man with influential friends. Beguiled by him, she had let him have his way with her in one of the small storerooms that led off the servants' quarters. She'd thought that was it, but five weeks later she found out she was pregnant with his child.

Not that she'd ever told him. As far as he was concerned, she had been just another meaningless fuck. An evening's entertainment and nothing more. No, Edmund Wyatt hadn't an inkling that the son he'd conceived that night was now the most powerful financier on the planet. More powerful even than his friend DeVore. Yes, and more secretive.

He looked back at the screens. Already the rate of fall was slowing as the great web of companies and agents he had set up to counter DeVore, bought shares and stocks at inflated prices. Already he had lost more than fifteen billion dollars. Not that it mattered now. All that mattered was to stop the sharp decline.

Lifeboats, that's what he called them: lifeboat companies, designed for one purpose only, to save as many as he could from the great financial flood.

News was coming in now of bombs going off prematurely, of foiled assassination attempts, of important men having fortunate escapes.

This too was his doing.

Information. Oh, he knew his Sun Tzu as well as any man. Information was the key, and he had gathered every snippet of information on his foe that he could.

And today it all paid off.

He pushed back, away from his desk, then stretched and stood.

"Mister Joseph?"

He turned, then frowned, surprised to find one of his junior partners there. "Emily?"

"I thought you'd gone, Mister Joseph. I was working late, I . . ." Then, seeing what was happening on the screens, she gasped. "Kuan Yin! What's going on?"

He smiled. "I've been playing a little game, Emily. Me and him. Only he doesn't even know I'm on the board."

"Him?"

But Joseph barely heard her. The tide had turned. Slowly, very slowly, the figures were rising once again.

* * *

DeVore was laughing, toasting his own success in the back of the glide, when the news came through.

"Howard . . . you'll not believe this . . ."

As the screen lit up, he blinked, then gasped. "*Impossible* . . ."

"That's what I thought," Wyatt went on, "But it's true. And that's not all. Wetton's alive. And Sinclair. And Beaton."

"But . . ."

"None of the bombs hit target. Not a single assassin got through."

DeVore felt his mouth go dry. Someone had betrayed him. Someone had fucking stitched him up!

Wyatt! It had to be Wyatt!

He kept his voice calm. "Meet me, Edmund. At the Yellow Emperor. Go there now and wait for me."

"But Howard . . ."

"Just go there!"

He cut the connection and sat back, fuming now. Impossible. It simply wasn't possible.

DeVore spoke to the air. "Gemma?"

Immediately his personal assistant was on the line. "Yes, Mister DeVore?"

"Get me a computer analysis of what's been happening in the markets."

"Over the last month, sir?"

"No, dammit! The last hour! In fact, make that the last half hour!"

"But Mister DeVore . . ."

"Don't argue with me woman, just do it!"

Again he cut connection. He had never spoken to her like that before – had been careful never ever to speak to any of his staff with anything but the utmost courtesy before – but now the gloves were off. Someone was fucking with him, and he wanted to know who and how, and no one – *no one* – was going to get between him and that knowledge!

"Sir?"

It was his chauffeur, Haavikko, speaking on the internal line. DeVore bristled, feeling a momentary anger, then answered him. "What?"

"There's a call, sir. On your private line."

"A call?"

"Yes, sir. I . . . I think you ought to take it."

He hesitated, then. "Okay, Axel. Patch it through."

A moment's pause, then, "Howard?"

The voice was familiar, but he couldn't quite make it out. "Do I know you?"

Laughter. Laughter that made the hairs on the back of his neck stand on end; that sent a ripple down his spine. DeVore leaned forward, punching the pad that would give him vision. As he sat back a face appeared on the screen. His own face.

"Yes, Howard, it's me. I've come to help you in your hour of need."

* * *

Karr staggered and almost fell. The smell of chrysanthemums was so overpowering that it felt as though he were breathing cotton wool. And the brightness of everything! As Chen came through, he almost fell against Karr, then straightened, looking about him wide-eyed, like an animal that has fallen into the steel mesh of a trap.

The rasp of Chen's breath was like the sound of an iron bar grating against a rock.

"Where *are* we?"

The words boomed at Karr.

"I don't . . ." Karr stopped abruptly, his eyes focusing on what lay on the bed. "*Aiya*," he groaned.

Chen turned, then gave a cry of pain. "Oh, gods . . ."

Kim lay on the bed, naked and unmoving. His eyes were open, but they saw nothing. His hands and feet were bound with wire, his flesh so white and waxen that it seemed to glow, but in the middle of his forehead was a single bright red hole, like the hole a worm might have made in an apple.

Chen dropped his gun and fell to his knees, beginning to retch.

Karr stared a moment, mesmerised – horrified – by the sight, then turned. Where was K.? Where . . .?

He took two steps then saw him, hanging from the light-fitting in the tiny bathroom. A piece of wire had been tightened round his throat. His eyes bulged, but like Kim's they saw nothing.

The sight emptied him; took away his courage. Thinking of Jelka, he groaned, wondering how he would ever break the news to her.

Oh, he had seen men die before, and broken the news to more widows than he cared to remember, but this . . .

This was the death of hope.

His head swam. Something was wrong here. It felt like he'd been drugged. Behind him Chen retched and retched, the sound and the smell of it so awful it made him gag himself.

Dreaming . . . he had to be dreaming. Forcing himself he walked across and touched the limp hand that dangled at K.'s side. It was cold; colder than anything he had ever touched, but real.

He shivered. Out. He had to get out.

Karr stumbled back, almost falling over his friend, then turned. He took a step towards the hoop, then stopped dead, realising with a start that it had gone. He whirled about, turning full circle, staring wildly at the walls, certain that there must have been a mistake, but the air was empty, the gateway closed.

"Kuan Yin preserve us!"

Chen looked up, wide-eyed. "Gregor?"

"The gate . . ."

Chen turned to look, then gave a whimper of fear. Karr stared at his friend, astonished, then understood. Kao Chen's worst fear had just come to pass, and the poor man was petrified. The thought of it dispelled Karr's own fears. It was up to him now.

"Kao Chen," he said, speaking as a commander speaks to one of his foot-soldiers, "stand up!"

Chen struggled up onto his feet, then glanced at Karr uncertainly. But Karr was staring back at him sternly.

"Good. Now pick up your gun, Major Kao. We've work to do."

* * *

As DeVore's glide touched down on the southern edge of Tientsin spaceport, his assistant, Gemma, patched through to him again.

"Well?" he asked unceremoniously, raising a hand to ensure that Wyatt, who sat beside him on the long, luxurious seat, kept silent. "Do we know what's happening?"

She smiled confidently. "It looks like there's been a concerted effort to stabilise the markets, sir. A lot of buying at highly inflated prices. Companies taking massive losses with no thought to their own economic survival. Eco-altruism, as one of our brokers has termed it."

"And do we know who owns these companies?"

She hesitated, then, frowning, shook her head. "No, sir. As far as we can tell, they're subsidiaries. But who owns them . . ."

"Get someone on it. Jenner, maybe. Or King, he's good at burrowing into other peoples' databases. I want to know who's behind this. I want a name, you got me?"

"Sir!"

As the screen blanked, he turned and looked to Wyatt. "What do you think?"

But Wyatt seemed as nonplussed as the woman. "I don't know. I can't see why anyone should do it. Why, looking at those figures, I'd say that whoever it was must have sustained massive losses. Twenty, thirty billion, maybe more." He paused, then shook his head. "I don't know about you, Howard, but I can't think of a single financier in the market who could take that kind of beating and survive. So why do it?"

"To beat me, that's why."

Wyatt laughed. "But no one knows . . ." He stopped, seeing the look on DeVore's face. "You don't think . . .?"

"Think what, Edmund? That you betrayed me, perhaps? That you've been feeding insider information to one of my enemies?"

Wyatt laughed, but he was clearly uncomfortable. "You can't be serious, Howard. How long have we known each other? Forty years? And you think I'd do something like that to you?"

"I don't know," DeVore said coldly. "But I'm going to fucking well find out. And when I do . . ."

The screen clicked on again. DeVore turned back, finding himself looking at his Head of Security, Hart. The man looked troubled.

"What is it, Don?"

"Those men you wanted sent to the apartment building in Beijing . . ."

"What of them?"

"They're dead, that's what. They stumbled across a couple of assassins in the lobby. The local police have the place surrounded. I thought . . ."

"Don't think," DeVore said, interrupting him, "just get on to the Head of Police . . . his name's Ch'ang San . . . and tell him not to precipitate anything until I get back. I don't want any of his men going in there, guns blazing, you understand? Containment."

"But what if he says no?"

"Then that big fat cheque he gets every month isn't going to arrive anymore. You understand?"

Hart grinned. "I understand, sir."

"Then see to it."

DeVore sat back, sighing deeply. "Just what the fuck is going on?" he glanced sideways at Wyatt, but Wyatt was brooding, chewing on a thumbnail thoughtfully.

"I said," DeVore repeated, raising his voice, "just what the fuck is going on?"

"A player," Wyatt said after a moment. "Someone you pissed off years ago, but who's kept a low profile all this time. Someone who's been waiting to pay you back."

"Are you talking about yourself now, Edmund?"

Wyatt looked to him and glared. "Leave it, Howard. *Okay*?"

DeVore raised a hand. "Okay. I believe you. But fuck it, *someone* must have let slip, and who knows more than you?"

Wyatt's eyes narrowed suddenly, as if he suddenly saw it. "Your AI. Your so-called discreet system."

"Bollocks! Why, I'm more likely to have given the game away than the computer's DS. It's programmed to self-destruct before anyone can tamper with it."

"Then what if someone hacked into it and re-programmed it?"

DeVore gave a laugh of disbelief. "No. They'd have to be some kind of super-genius to do that!"

"Right! The kind of super-genius who'd not worry about losing thirty billion in an hour just to stop you."

"And the rest? Are you saying that he's behind it all? The bungled assassinations? The mistimed bombs?"

Wyatt smiled. "That'd be my guess."

"Then who the fuck *is* he? And why don't we know him?"

"Maybe we do. Maybe he was one of those guys you killed in the apartment building."

"No. They were just messengers. Hackers. Else they'd have covered their tracks a damn sight better than they did."

"You should have kept one of them alive. Then you could have tortured him. Found out what he knew."

"Maybe. But I didn't have time."

"That's not like you, Howard."

DeVore shrugged, then said casually, "No . . ." But he was thinking, *No. But I won't make the same mistake twice. I'll make sure I take my time over you, my erstwhile friend. I'll make sure I rack you well and good.*

He laughed. "Do you recall that fat Chink I introduced you to . . . Wang Sau Leyan?"

Wyatt turned, a faint amusement in his eyes. "The one who liked fucking Western women two at a time?"

"That's him. I had him tortured. He owed me money. Arrogant bastard wouldn't pay me. Said I'd have to wring it from him. So I did. His brothers were furious – wanted me dead. So I racked them, too. All four of the fuckers in one room. Sang like a choir."

"And the money?"

"Oh, fuck the money. I had more fun than I'd had for a long time. Had to dump them when I'd finished, mind. Couldn't let them loose to tell the tale, could I?"

"No," Wyatt said, looking away thoughtfully. "No."

There was a knock on the partition between them and the driver's seat. DeVore opaqued it.

"News from the tower, sir. It seems the shuttle's due down any moment."

They felt the rumble. As DeVore opaqued the outer windows of the glide, they saw – far off to their right, almost a mile away – the shuttle descending on a point of flame.

"There," DeVore said, grinning suddenly. "There he is."

"Who?" Wyatt asked, intrigued.

But DeVore merely smiled. "Just wait and see."

* * *

Joseph stepped out from the lobby of the Tung Chan Building and stepped into his glide, which hovered five centimetres above the surface of the transit pad. It was a fairly modest machine; enough to confirm his status as a top financier, but not grand enough to mark him as a player.

Which was exactly how he wanted it, for the idea was to blend in, not to stand out. That was how he'd evaded notice all these years.

As the glide lifted and he relaxed back into his seat, Joseph recalled his first sight of DeVore.

He had not gone there to see DeVore, but to get a glimpse of his genetic father, Wyatt. To try and discover just what kind of man Wyatt was. And there, standing right next to Wyatt, talking to a group of leading businessmen, was DeVore.

He had sensed at once that there was something wrong. The man was charming – he went out of his way to be charming – but Joseph could see the brutality that lay beneath every gesture.

Certain that he was imagining it, he had wandered away. But later in the evening he had come across DeVore in one of the corridors leading off the central hall, speaking quietly to one of his minions, such casual threat in his voice that Joseph had felt a small ripple of fear run up his spine.

He had said nothing. He had not even let on that he'd seen a thing. But that brief glimpse of DeVore had intrigued him enough to want to know a little more about this man who was his father's constant companion.

Alarm bells had rung almost instantly. One could not make a computer query without triggering counter-queries of the "Who wants to know?" variety.

Which was when he began to get devious, and to use those skills he had been born with: the ability to take a system – any system – and turn it inside out.

DeVore had never known. He hadn't even guessed. Until tonight. But now he would be looking for him.

The thought of that ought to have chilled him, for he knew exactly what DeVore was capable of, but sitting there he felt a strange confidence in his own abilities. Besides, he had his "coat".

"Daniel . . . turn on the news for me, will you? Channel 96."

At once the wavering light of the screen filled the back of the glide.

First up was the latest on the business at the Eight Dragons Hotel. The Americans, it seemed, were vigorously denying reports that President Newell had been shot, but the President himself hadn't been seen now for almost four hours. The dead woman had now been identified as Susan Callaghan, an "escort", while reports from Washington revealed intense activity there, with Vice President Wetton arriving at the White House for an unscheduled meeting with senior aides.

Bad, Joseph thought, yet without his intervention it could have been so much worse. Wetton would have been dead, yes, and half his cabinet. And then the Generals would have been in charge and war would have been a certainty. A war that, on top of the economic collapse DeVore had triggered, would have wiped out ninety-five per cent of humanity.

It was hard to imagine any man wanting that. Which was why Joseph had developed his pet theory. That DeVore was not, in fact, a man.

A fact he could not prove, yet which seemed to be borne out by the record. For he could find no trace that DeVore had ever been born. Oh, there were strong indications that the man was in his forties, but no specific date was given for his birth. Not only that, but the man seemed to have been in his forties now for well on forty years.

Stranger yet was something he had stumbled upon one rainy afternoon three years back.

Idly trawling the web for new information, Joseph had come upon the file of a man – one of DeVore's employees – who seemed familiar to him. It was some facial characteristic that had made him sit forward and frown at the screen. It wasn't, of course, who he thought it was, but the idea that one might perhaps trawl the historical record for a specific face – *DeVore's* face – occurred to him in that instant.

Over the following week he had written a programme that would do just that. And then he'd let it run.

The results were astonishing. Not one or two, but hundreds of sightings, going back over not eighty years, but close on eight hundred, the oldest of them a figure in Piero della Francesca's painting, *The Recognition of the True Cross*, which was painted no later than 1460.

It was possible, of course, that these faces were simply similar. Were the natural result of genetics. Until one started to place them side by side and saw the unchanging nature of them. They were never young, never old. And always – *always* – there was that look in the eyes: that cold brutality that contradicted the smiling lips.

Which raised the question: could a man live eight hundred years and never age?

On the screen the news ran on. Joseph blinked then sat forward slightly, suddenly attentive again.

"*. . . have confirmed that the starship is of human construction and manned by a human crew, but as yet no one has claimed ownership of the craft . . .*"

Joseph cut in, speaking to his AI. "When did this happen?"

"An hour back," the computer answered him. "It's currently in geostationary orbit immediately above Beijing. A shuttle from the craft touched down at Tientsin spaceport two minutes back."

Joseph nodded thoughtfully. "When you know anything more, let me know."

He raised a hand. At once the sound from the news screen began again.

"*. . . leaving two dead and one seriously injured. The two men are still holed up in the lobby of the apartment block, which has been surrounded by armed police . . .*"

As the camera zoomed in on one of the men inside the lobby, Joseph gave a strange laugh of recognition.

"But that's impossible . . ."

The face on the screen had been that of Kao Chen, one of his men. But right now Chen was in Washington, along with Karr. It was they who had saved Wetton's life.

Again he spoke to the air. "Where are Karr and Chen?"

"Washington," came the immediate reply. "You want me to patch them through?"

"No." Joseph shivered. What was going on? Starships . . . and now this. "Where is that building?"

"Central Beijing. It's called the Tang Li Building."

"Buy it."

There was no argument, just a pause, then. "We now own the Tang Li Building."

"Good. Now let's divert there. And get security there at once. Two dozen of our best men. And make sure the police don't do anything stupid."

A pause, then. "Done."

Joseph let out a breath, then sat back again. Something was happening. Something he didn't yet understand. But he would. He had only to fit the pieces together and it would all come clear.

On the screen, the camera panned across until it came to rest on the face of Gregor Karr, who squatted behind a barrier, a huge gun clutched to his chest.

That's you, Gregor, he thought, narrowing his eyes. *That's unmistakably you. Yet if, at this moment, you're in Washington, how can it be? Unless . . .*

Joseph spoke to the air. "Emily? What have we got on multi-dimensional physics?"

* * *

"So what do we do now?"

Karr, crouched down behind the reception desk, glanced across at his friend. "I guess we wait and see. If they wanted us dead, we'd be dead by now."

That much was true. The cover in the lobby was poor. A good marksman would have had no trouble picking them off. And without exposing themselves fully, there was no way they could change that situation.

"Who were they, do you think?"

"I'd say they were working for whoever did that, upstairs."

Chen gave the tiniest nod. One thing was sure. The men they'd run into weren't Security. If they had been, they'd have been dead by now, because Security looked after its own.

Then again, there was little chance they'd get out of here alive. The only possible reason they were still alive was that someone wanted to know who they were, and where they'd come from. And as they had no intention of being taken, that left pretty few other options.

What would I do? Karr asked himself.

He'd use gas, of course. Or stun guns. Or . . .

He swallowed, saddened suddenly by the thought that they would die here, in a strange universe. And for what? Why, they wouldn't even get the chance now to take a pop at DeVore.

Outside, beyond the security cruisers that surrounded the front of the lobby, a craft was setting down: a big, black, shiny thing that was different in kind from the bulkier, armoured Security vehicles. It looked the kind of thing a businessman might fly.

Karr raised his gun, looking through the sights as the craft's door hissed open then folded back into the roof.

A big man stepped out, a multi-coloured coat draped about him, its surfaces seeming to wink like a prism in the late afternoon sunlight. The figure was unfamiliar, but the face, even without its bulging eyes, was unmistakable.

"*Kim!*"

Chen raised his gun and looked through the sights. "It can't be. Look at the size of him. He's got to be six-six easily."

But Karr was certain of it. Staring at the man, he saw what the Kim he knew could have been under different circumstances. Saw just what physical handicaps he had overcome in their own world.

Whereas *here*, in this world . . .

Kim was talking to the Security chief. Karr saw anger on the man's face, but Kim stared him out, then gestured for him to go.

There was a moment's tense eye to eye confrontation between the two, then, furious, the Security man turned on his heel and, gesturing angrily to his men, began to leave.

At the same moment craft were setting down. Men spilled out. Armed men, who looked to Kim for instructions.

"What are they doing?" Chen asked.

"I don't know. But it looks like he's taken over from Security. Maybe he owns the building."

"Well . . . it looks like we're about to find out. He's coming over. What do you want to do?"

Karr looked to Chen and shrugged. "I guess I'd better speak to him. Cover me. But don't fire unless they fire first."

Lowering his gun, Karr stood, then stepped out from behind the reception desk. Up ahead of him the outer glass doors of the lobby hissed open and the man in the many-coloured coat stepped through. He took a further couple of paces towards Karr then stopped, frowning.

"Gregor? What the hell are you doing here? I thought you were in Washington?"

Karr narrowed his eyes. "Kim?"

The man shook his head, then. "Do you know me?"

"I think so. In my world your name is Kim. But you are not half the man you are in this world."

At the mention of different worlds, this other Kim nodded, his eyes widening. "So you *are* from elsewhere."

Karr hesitated, then. "If you're not Kim, then who are you? What do you call yourself?"

The man smiled, then put out a hand to Karr. "My name is Mister Joseph Josephs. But you can call me Joseph."

* * *

The girl's mother was surprised to see him back so soon.

"Mister Huang . . . Is something wrong?"

"We have to leave here earlier than we planned. Pack two bags, Madam Yin. Essentials only. I can buy whatever else we need when we get there."

The Madam looked alarmed. "Where are we going?"

"To Tientsin spaceport. I have a craft there. From there we'll fly out to my country place, in Sichuan Province."

"*Sichuan?*" She stared at him, highly dubious now.

"Sichuan. Now get ready. And send the girl to me!"

The tone of command in his voice – one he but rarely used – did the trick. She turned and disappeared inside. A moment later the girl appeared. Her eyes looked tired, as if she'd just been woken.

"What is it?" she said, coming across and putting her arms about him, as if he had been her lover months and not a single day. "Mama says we are to go to Sichuan."

"I have a summer place there. An estate. Up in the hills. You'll like it. I've horses . . ."

"Horses?" She looked excited. "I *love* horses."

The closeness of her aroused him. Despite the urgency of the moment, he wanted to fuck her once again. He reached down and placed his hands over her buttocks, the thinness of the garment she was wearing letting him feel the warmth of the flesh almost as if he touched it.

She looked up at him, wide-eyed. "You want to? Now?"

He shivered, recalling how she had bewitched him the last time he'd been with her. "Not now," he said, denying the need he felt. "Now go and help your mother pack. We must be gone from here."

Fei Yen clung to him a moment longer, then turned and disappeared back through the door. Li Yuan stood there, staring at the doorway, then sniffed the air. *Mei mei.* Plum blossom. He shivered, then turned, confused momentarily.

Tongjiang. If they could get to Tongjiang they would be safe. Even if the world collapsed about them.

* * *

The two men met on the apron just beneath the shuttle. Though they were dressed differently, they looked identical, and Wyatt, looking on, stared in disbelief.

"Howard!" the two men said as one, embracing each other warmly.

"You're looking good," the newcomer said, standing back a little. "So what's happening here?"

"A little setback. But I'm dealing with it."

The newcomer nodded, then looked past his double.

"Wyatt! How good to see you. You're dead back where I came from. They had you executed in public. Big fucker with an even bigger sword took your head from your shoulders. I'd have brought a tape if I'd known."

Wyatt had blanched, but the paradigm DeVore seemed amused by the news. "Executed, eh? Who would have thought it? And you, Howard?"

"My world is dead. Or as good as. That's why I came to lend a hand."

There was a narrowing of eyes. Both men looked at each other intently a moment, then, as if they had come to some perfect understanding, grinned again.

"So who are we fighting?" the newcomer asked. "Ward? Li Yuan? Karr?"

DeVore shook his head. "None of those. Our enemy here is a man named Josephs. Joseph Josephs."

"Never heard of him."
"Nor I until five minutes back."
"You got a picture of this guy?"
DeVore nodded. "Come over to my craft. I'll brief you as we fly back in."
"And I'll brief you," the newcomer said, putting his arm about his twin's shoulders. "There's something you ought to know about yourself. Something rather important."

* * *

Joseph sat on the bed beside the naked body of his other self and wept. He had not dreamed – had not even guessed – what he would find in the apartment, nor had Karr thought to warn him.

To find he had two brothers, and to find them dead, horribly murdered in this way. It was too much.

He looked up, wiping away his tears, and saw the sympathy in Karr's face. "You say there was a gateway, here in the room?"

"Yes."

"So where is it?"

Karr shrugged, then, remembering something, blinked. "It went before . . . Jelka said so."

"Jelka?"

"Your wife . . ." Then, realising that Joseph was looking at him blankly, looked down. "Kim's wife. She's back on Kalevala."

"Kalevala?"

"Their estate. On Ganymede."

Joseph stared at him, then huffed out a sigh. "I think you'd better start at the beginning, Gregor. Ganymede? The Ganymede that's Saturn's moon?"

"Yes," Karr said, "only right now it's halfway to Eridani . . ."

Joseph gave a short laugh, then looked back at Kim. Frowning, he took the edge of the sheet and wrapped it over the corpse. "I wish I'd known him."

"He was a lovely man," Kao Chen said, his own eyes misted. "A real giant."

Joseph met Chen's eyes, and saw that he meant nothing ironical by the comment. He nodded, acknowledging what was said, then stood. He looked about him, as if in a dream, then looked back at Karr.

"You know nothing about the gateway?"

Karr shook his head. "Only Kim and K. knew how it worked. The equations were . . . well, difficult to say the least."

"Hmmm." Joseph seemed to sniff the air, then frowned. "Why would it shut off?"

"Pardon?" Karr said.

"The gateway. If it powered itself . . . why did it shut down?"

"I don't know. Maybe someone *switched* it off."

"Jelka?"

Karr shook his head. "No. She wouldn't know how."

"Then who?"

Joseph turned, then walked through to where they had laid out K's corpse. His clothes lay nearby where DeVore had thrown them. Bending down, Joseph went through the pockets, then looked up, smiling.

"There! Look, Karr. This has to be it!"

It looked like a marble. A simple piece of coloured glass. But inside the tiny transparent sphere was a tiny flaming snake – a snake that was swallowing its tale.

Looking at it, Karr shuddered. It was the key!

Joseph stared at it a moment, as if to try to fathom how it worked. And then he laughed and, holding it in his hand, gently squeezed it.

From the other room came a cry of surprise. "It's back!" Chen yelled, poking his head round the door. "The gateway's back!"

Joseph looked to Karr. "Will you go first, Gregor?"

"To break the news?"

Joseph nodded, but he saw how much the thought of it troubled Karr. The giant stood there a moment, staring at the prone figure on the floor, and then he nodded. "Alright," he said, an anger in his eyes as he looked up. "But then we come back here, *okay*? We come back and finish the bastards!"

* * *

The morphs clearly considered him no threat. And why should they? They had seen the damage to his head. And so Daniel found himself alone in the operating theatre, the faint vibration of the constantly revolving ship the only sound.

Slowly he sat up, wincing, the pounding in his head threatening momentarily to black him out. He closed his eyes and counted. By forty he was okay again. Opening his eyes he carefully looked about him, making the tiniest movements of his head, careful not to set it off again.

He had to bandage it up somehow. To hold himself together long enough to do what he had to do. There was surgical tape on the trolley nearby, and a scalpel.

He slowly swung his legs around, then stood. The pounding returned. Again he closed his eyes. Only thirty this time and the giddiness went, but the back of his head felt as if it was about to fall out through the gap in his skull.

Okay. One thing at a time. First he'd tape his head together. He tore strips from the roll of plaster and, gingerly – almost as if he was doing it to someone else, it felt so strange – he formed a tight web of tape about the back of his cranium.

There! That should do.

He turned slowly. Now he needed something to kill the pain. Because there would almost certainly be pain, and he wanted to feel nothing.

Daniel limped across to the dispensary, each step a small agony. Grimacing, he reached up and, slipping the catch, pulled the cupboard door open.

Pills. Endless pills. But which ones?

He saw a name he recognised and took the packet down, staring at the label. Shit! They were injection only. He looked about, then saw an injector-gun on the second shelf. He took it down and loaded it with four of the capsules, then held the nozzle to his arm, pulling the trigger twice.

Relief was immediate: a flood of warmth and reassurance.

He slipped the injector into his pocket. Two was enough for now. He'd save the others for a top-up if he needed it.

Daniel turned, resting his back against the cupboards. If what he'd heard was right, there were less than two dozen morphs on board. The very last of DeVore's once glorious forty thousand. That meant they'd be stretched thin. And that meant that they would be keeping their prisoners in as few places as possible, to make it easier to guard them.

If they'd kept that many prisoners . . .

Not the bridge. And not here. Which left only a few other possibilities. One was the recreation hall at the very centre of the craft, and that wasn't likely while they were in orbit, because it would be difficult to mind prisoners in a nil-gravity situation.

It was more likely that they had them in the cargo holds. There was room enough and more down there.

But would they have kept Emily and the others with them?

He decided not. DeVore would want his prize prisoners kept apart. Not only so that they could be specially looked after, but also to break down the morale of the rest of the contingent.

Daniel limped across and took the scalpel from the trolley, then, after wrapping it in a cloth, slipped it into his pocket. He crouched, drawing the cloth back and looking on the shelf underneath.

"Kuan Yin!"

There was a gun! He remembered now. Emily had put it there. And there it had sat all this while, hidden beneath the hanging cloth.

Daniel reached in and took it out, studying it. It felt like it was loaded. He checked. Yes, there were a full fifteen rounds in the cartridge.

Enough to do what he had to do. Enough to give him an advantage.

He straightened up, then stood a moment, mentally preparing himself. One chance. He had one chance to get this right. And not just for himself. For all of them.

Cameras . . .

He glanced up. The camera over the door was on, transmitting an image of the room. If anyone was watching, they'd have seen him get up. They would have seen him take the scalpel and the gun.

No time, he thought, knowing that if they had, they'd be on their way right now.

He walked over to the door. It was locked, but there was an override. He flicked open the panel, exposing the touchpad and punched in the first half of the code. 1.4.A.L.L. The top line went green. His fingers tapped out the second half of the code. A.L.L.4.1.

Hannah's idea. And thank the gods for it.

The corridor was empty. It curved away out of sight. The ship was on emergency lighting, so only one in three of the wall-mounted lamps was lit. It gave the corridor a mottled look with patches of brightness and shadow, spokes on a giant wheel.

He stepped out and to the left. The drugs he'd injected were doing their job, holding him together, but he felt strange, like a sleepwalker. That wasn't good. He needed to be sharper than this.

Daniel stopped and reached up to touch the back of his head, his fingers tracing the bandages. They were wet. Blood was seeping through and trickling down his back.

Shit! He should have frozen it somehow. But it was too late now.

There was a feeder corridor just ahead of him. It led straight down through the crew quarters and into the bridge itself. If they were anywhere, they'd be there, because that was where the shuttle bay was. And if DeVore had any use for them, that's where he'd want to keep them.

As he came to the branch, Daniel stopped, hearing noises. The heavy clunk of boots against a metal runged ladder. In the strange topography of the ship it was hard to know exactly where the noises were coming from. Up and down were almost arbitrary notions in space. And sound carried in strange ways inside a ship. Especially in these circumstances.

There was the faint murmur of voices, low and deep.

Cautiously he peeped around the corner, looking "down" as if into a well.

Two morphs stood at the bottom of that well, their backs to him, the helmets of their suits pressed close. They were huge, almost twice the height of a normal man, and built accordingly.

It would be easy to shoot the pair of them. Easy, yes, but stupid, because it would lose him the only advantage he had. Surprise.

Okay. So think. What are you going to do?

He moved back, then studied the walls surrounding the opening. There were various hatches, but he hadn't a clue where any of them led. There were airducts throughout the ship, but he wasn't even sure whether any of them were big enough to crawl along.

Nor did he know whether his strength would hold out. He was drawing on reserves as it was.

The voices murmured again, then, unexpectedly, he heard the sound of boots on rungs again, only this time he knew exactly where they were. The feeder corridor. One of the morphs was climbing the well, coming directly towards him.

He took out the scalpel and unwrapped it, then stood back, waiting.

As the morph's head poked through the entrance, he stepped out and, putting one hand over its mouth, dragged the scalpel across its throat, digging deep.

The creature's eyes widened with shock. It made a muffled noise, one hand whipping out to grip Daniel's shoulder, but, abandoning the scalpel, Daniel formed his free hand into a fist and jabbed at the morph's nose, putting every ounce of his strength behind the blow.

The morph's hand loosened and fell away. As it slumped forward, Daniel twisted to the side, ensuring that it didn't fall on him and trap him there.

Blood gouted from the wound at its throat. It gurgled, one hand trembling as it reached out to grasp Daniel's foot, then it lay still.

Daniel stared at it, his back pressed to the wall, the blood pounding at the back of his head once more. It didn't hurt, but he could feel the wetness dribbling down his nape and knew that he had opened up the wound again.

He gave a little shudder, then, stepping carefully over the fallen morph, looked down the well. It was empty. The other morph had gone.

He swung out onto the ladder, then climbed down, expecting at any moment to be discovered; for the morph above to start yelling, or for an alarm of some kind to go off. But nothing. Only the pounding in his head and the wetness, the slow draining of his life-force.

At the foot of the tunnel he stopped, getting his breath. He felt exhausted. Only pure will power was keeping him on his feet. From here on he would have to trust to luck. Yes, and to Emily's gun, for the scalpel was buried deep in the creature's neck.

He closed his eyes a moment, fighting the giddiness that threatened to overwhelm him, then flicked them open again. Directly ahead of him were the crew quarters, six cabins in all, arranged three to each side of the long corridor, and beyond them, through a secondary airlock, the bridge itself.

Daniel began to walk, slowly, limping he was so tired, his left hand supporting him against the wall, his right hand holding the gun.

He was sweating now. And his eyes kept blurring over.

Malfunctioning, he thought, almost amused by the realisation. *I'm fucking malfunctioning, like some broken machine.*

He stopped, leaning heavily against the wall, then lowered his head. It felt like he was going to be sick. The drugs . . .

What if I made a mistake? What if they're the wrong drugs?

Daniel looked up, his eyes slowly coming back into focus. And as they did a morph stepped from the doorway not ten feet in front of him and turned.

He shot it through the head – a single neat shot in the centre of the forehead. It dropped like a cut marionette.

But the noise of the shot reverberated on and on in that narrow space: like an alarm going off throughout the ship.

Trembling now, he staggered over to the open doorway and looked inside. Four figures lay on couches on the far side of the room, bound hand and feet, their mouths firmly gagged; Han Ch'in, Kuei Jen, Hannah and, to the far left, Emily. As he stepped into the room he saw their eyes widen with surprise.

He could hear shouting now and running feet.

The room seemed suddenly massive, more a hallway than a cabin. His head swam briefly, then cleared again.

Another shot. Give yourself another shot.

Throwing the gun down, he pulled out the injector and held it to his arm, giving himself both of the remaining shots.

For a moment he stood there, half doubled-up, then slowly, very slowly, his head cleared again.

Daniel looked across the cabin. Emily was staring at him, his eyes imploring him to do something.

He staggered across, then turned, looking about him for something to cut their bonds.

"Shit!"

They'd be here any moment. He heard the ventilation duct that led from the airlock begin to hiss, which meant they were coming through from the bridge area.

He went back and, crouching down, picked up the gun again. There was nothing for it. He would have to shoot the bonds off them.

Returning to Emily's side, he placed the mouth of the barrel tight against the bonds that secured her wrists. The explosion would burn her, certainly, but that couldn't be helped.

He twisted the gun around, so that it pointed straight out through the open doorway – the last thing he wanted was to have a bullet ricocheting about the cabin – and pulled the trigger.

This time the detonation threw him back. He fell, going down awkwardly, the back of his head smacking against the side of one of the couches as he went down.

And then blackness.

* * *

Joseph sat in Kim's chair, reading K.'s journals and notebooks at a speed that Karr, looking on, found disconcerting.

Jelka had taken the news badly. Kao Chen, concerned for her, had had Wang Ti come to Kalevala to comfort her. The two woman were upstairs even now, locked in a room together, grieving.

The gate between the worlds had been closed temporarily, but only after they had brought the bodies back from the Paradigm World. The two of them now lay in makeshift coffins on the desk in Kim's study, an honour-guard of Osu minding them. In time they would be buried, but first there was the little matter of DeVore to deal with.

"Well . . ." Joseph said, closing the last of the journals and looking up. "This *is* an eye-opener."

"So what do you suggest?" Karr said, looking to Ebert and Kao Chen who stood close by.

"Are the craft ready?"

"I believe so. Kim and K. had been working on adapting them. Jelka would know."

Joseph nodded thoughtfully. "I would rather we did not disturb Jelka right now. Where are the craft?"

Ikuro, who came into the room at that moment, answered him. "They're outside. On the surface." He stared at Joseph a moment, as if surprised to see Kim so enlarged and "normal", then, looking down, embarrassed by the way he'd stared, said. "And yes, they're ready."

"Then we have only to decide who will go through," Joseph said, his eyes studying Ikuro. "Gregor . . . you say each craft will take three, correct?"

"And sufficient weaponry."

Joseph met Karr's eyes. "You really think this is something that can be resolved by such means?"

Karr nodded. "If we kill them it's over. For good."

Ebert for once agreed. "Karr's right. DeVore's the source. Whatever's twisted emanates from him. I, for one, would welcome another crack at him."

"And I!" Karr and Kao Chen said at once, then laughed.
"And you, Ikuro?"
Ikuro nodded.
"Then that's five of us . . ."
"Six," Jelka said, stepping into the room.
Joseph stood. All turned to face her.
"But Jelka . . ." Karr began
She turned on him. "You would deny me my revenge?"
Karr stared at her, then shook his head.
"Then let us prepare what we need and go," she said, magnificent at that moment, her golden eyes burning. "Let us finish what my husbands so gallantly began."

* * *

As the glide set down on the executive parking pad Li Yuan hurried the two women ahead of him out of the irising door, carrying the two cases himself.

He had spoken to Cho Yi on the flight down, and though the markets had stabilised, there was a sense of fragility about affairs that seemed to bode ill. War had not broken out between America and China, but that was not to say that, later in the day, it wouldn't. And then the spaceports would be closed and there would be no chance at all to get away.

Which was why he was going now. Because, as a gambling man, he understood when to play a hunch. And his hunch was that the whole pack of cards was about to come tumbling down.

He had sent a message to Han Ch'in, telling him what he was doing, but making no reference to the girl and her mother. If Han came and joined him at Tongjiang, they would sort matters out between them then. But he had not wanted to have what might be their last conversation spoiled by bitter acrimony.

And so you lied to Han. For the first time in your life . . .

He did not like what he had done. In fact, his soul rebelled against it. It seemed a crime against not only brotherhood but against the mother who had died bearing him.

As they hurried across the apron towards his ship, he noted the increased activity on all sides.

So I'm not the only one playing a hunch.

Ships were rising up into the air even as they came to the foot of his own craft, the noise so loud that they drowned out his shouted instructions.

He waited a moment, until the rumble of one particularly loud craft faded, then shouted again.

"Wait here! I've got to deactivate the alarm!"

They huddled together under the port wing of the craft as Li Yuan went round and, reaching up into the panel underneath the fuselage, punched in the code.

Satisfied, he stepped out and, taking the controls from his pocket, pointed the light-pencil at the cockpit.

Lights flashed. The machine came alive.

Li Yuan smiled and looked to the two women, about to tell them to come across, then saw the expression on their faces. Fear. Sheer naked fear.

He half turned, suddenly aware of someone just behind him. A small, neat-looking man with short black hair was standing there, holding a gun up at the level of his head.

"Li Yuan," DeVore said, smiling unpleasantly. "Long time no see."

* * *

The fighting had been hard and uncompromising – to the death – but now the ship was theirs.

"We're losing air," Li Kuei Jen said, from where she sat in the co-pilot's seat. "I'll have to seal off all of the lower deck sections. It'd take us far too long to search and find out where the leaks are."

"Okay," Emily said, wondering how much time they had before DeVore hit back, "but make sure we haven't left anyone down there."

The trouble was, they were trapped up here. DeVore had the only shuttle, and that was down there, on the world below.

She turned, looking to Han Ch'in, who had just stepped onto the bridge. He seemed troubled.

"Han?"

Han Ch'in came across. "He's bad, Emily. I don't know whether he'll come through this time. The surgeon reckons there's extensive damage to the brain."

Emily grimaced. "Is Hannah with him?"

Han Ch'in nodded.

"Okay. I'll finish here, then go down and see her."

"He saved us," Han said, matter-of-factly.

"Yes," she said. "Strange, huh? DeVore's prize pupil. And look how he turns out?"

Han laughed, then gave another sigh. "I'd kill that bastard if I got my hands on him."

Emily's smile was tinged with a faint irony. She looked down at her own burned hand. "That's *if* you can get your hands on him."

"Do we know where we are yet?"

Emily nodded. "That's our home world, all right. *Geographically*. But from the transmissions we're tapping into I'd say that it has a history that's entirely different from our own."

"Meaning what?"

"Meaning that DeVore somehow shifted us into an alternate reality."

Han Ch'in gave a laugh of disbelief. But then, seeing that Emily was being serious, he narrowed his eyes. "*What?*"

"That's right. It's even possible that there are alternate versions of ourselves down there."

Han Ch'in took that in. "So what are we going to do?"

"We wait. There's nothing else we can do."

"That's not entirely true," Li Kuei Jen said, turning in her seat. "We could destroy the morph ship."

"Destroy it?" Emily frowned. "Why?"

"Because it'll send a signal back to him."

Emily smiled, then nodded. "Okay. Let's send the bastard a message!"

* * *

"Do I know you?" Li Yuan asked.

The first of them looked up from where he was busy binding the older woman's hands and grinned at Yuan. "Not in *this* world."

The other, who had arrived just after they had climbed on board, now reappeared in the cabin's doorway. "Okay. We've clearance. If you're ready, Howard."

"Ready and willing!" the first said cheerfully. Then, straightening up, he smiled at the three of them, who now sat in their chairs, trussed up tightly. "Everyone comfortable? Good. Because we're going on a little trip. A visit to an old friend. And I want you all to be on your best behaviour, because if you aren't, I might get a little angry. And when I get angry, I'm not a nice person to be with, understand?"

The two women nodded enthusiastically, but Li Yuan simply glared.

The man was little more than a common bully. A thief who used violence to get his way. Even so, the situation was dangerous and he did not want to force the man's hand.

"Okay," the man went on, "now listen carefully. When we get closer to our destination, I want you, Li Yuan, to speak to our friend – his name is Joseph Josephs, by the way – and get us permission to land on the pad at the top of the building he rents."

Li Yuan glowered. "Why should I do that?"

"Because if you don't, your young friend here," and he indicated young Fei Yen, "will have a second mouth, slightly lower than her first."

The gesture of a throat being slit was unmistakable.

Li Yuan studied the man's eyes and saw that he meant it. "Okay," he said. "But what if they say no?"

"They won't say no. And the reason they won't is because you'll tell Mister Josephs that you have information that is crucial to him. Information about myself."

"And why should that interest him?"

"Because, Mister Li, I'm behind all of this. I sent the market into free fall. I had President Newell assassinated. I pushed the world to the very brink of war."

Yes, Li Yuan thought, staring back at him and knowing in that instant that the man, though psychotic, was telling the truth; *you may have done all that, but if I'm right, our friend Josephs stopped you somehow. And now you want to get to him.*

And he could prevent that. But could he just sit by and watch the bastard cut her throat?

Li Yuan looked down. "Okay," he said. "Just tell me what I have to say."

* * *

The wheel of fire burned in the air above Kalevala; a massive, turning hoop that lit the cratered surface of the ancient moon. Close by the two craft squatted like strange insects as the six besuited figures approached them.

Watching from the window of his father's study, Sampsa shivered, wondering if he would ever see those six again.

They'll be okay, Tom said inside his head; but Sampsa could sense Tom's own uncertainty behind the words.

It seems harder to stand and watch than go oneself, he answered silently, speaking to Tom across the distance between Kalevala and their rooms in Fermi.

You think we should have gone, then?

Sampsa nodded. He turned briefly, staring across at the two figures in the room behind him, stretched out in their coffins. He had always thought his father would outlive him. Why? Because Kim had seemed so invulnerable. But time and circumstance had caught him like the rest of them, and now he lay there, those distinctive atoms that had made him what he was, slowly returning to the universal mix.

He felt Tom's unworded sympathy and smiled.

Turning back, he saw that they had arrived beside the craft and were climbing into the seats. The two machines had the look of fairground rides that have been dismantled and abandoned. They looked quite incapable of the task they would be asked to accomplish. But if his father had designed them, then they would work.

That's what I'll miss the most, he said to Tom; *the magic of it.*

Kim would have frowned to hear you call it that.

Yes, but what else was it? It didn't ever seem like normal science.

And yet it worked.

Yes, Sampsa said, and sighed aloud. Out on the surface, the six were now strapped in. There was a moment's inactivity, and then the generators at the centre of each craft began to glow, as if a luminous electric snake was endlessly climbing a pulsing silver pole.

Slowly the two craft lifted, then turned towards the massive, burning wheel.

"Good luck!" he called quietly, hearing the echo of the words inside his head as Tom, too, said them.

Good luck . . .

* * *

The explosion lit the late evening sky over Beijing. Flying back in from Tientsin, DeVore looked up, then shielded his eyes.

"Howard! Get up here quickly!"

As the light faded, DeVore stepped into the cabin. "What is it?"

"The starship. It's blown up!"

Taking a seat beside his twin, he started to tap out the code that would connect them to the starship's bridge. There was a green glow on the panel.

"No, look . . . it's still there."

"Then what?"

A face appeared on the screen above them. "Howard . . . oh, and Howard, too. How good to see you both!"

"Ascher!" DeVore said, snarling.
"Who?" his twin asked, glancing at him.
But DeVore's attention was fixed on the screen.
Emily smiled. "You let me go once before, Howard. I thought you would have learned from that mistake. Never take prisoners, you told me once. *Never*. Well, you should have killed me while you could."
"I'll kill you yet."
"You can try, arsehole."
"I'll . . ."
The screen went dead.
DeVore sat back, then slammed his fists down on the console. "Shit! Fucking shit!"
"Problems?" his twin asked, a faint amusement on his lips.
"No," DeVore said distractedly. "No . . ."
"No? Then what was that explosion?"
DeVore blinked. "The no-space ship . . ."
"So there's no way back now, eh?"
DeVore slowly shook his head.
"Ah well . . ." the other said, reaching out to pat his arm. "We'll just have to make do with fucking things up here!"

* * *

Emily sat back, chuckling to herself. "Did you see his face? Did you *see* it!"
Han Ch'in was grinning. "Looked like he'd eaten a whole orchard full of lemons!"
"Maybe," Kuei Jen said, sounding a cautionary note, "but we're still limited as to our options. And if he gets hold of a ground-to-air missile, we're done for."
"Then maybe we ought to move out of range," Emily said, sobered by that thought. "Can we manoeuvre this thing?"
"Absolutely. Only how far away is safe? And if we *do* get back out of range, how is that going to help what's going on down there? No, Emily, we need to get back into the game somehow. We need some way of getting down there."
"Could we land this thing?"
Kuei Jen shook her head. "Not a chance. It isn't designed for it. By destroying all but one of the shuttles, DeVore made sure only he could come and go."
"So we sit here?" Han Ch'in asked, disgruntled.
"Looks like it," his half-brother answered.
"Hmmm."
"What are you thinking?" Emily asked, seeing the frown of concentration on his face.
"Just that there have to be other craft that we could use as a shuttle."
"Maybe. But they're all earthside."
"Then maybe we could coax one of them up here. To help us out."
"How? We don't know anyone down there."

"Don't we? I thought Emily said just then that there are other versions of us down there."

"I said there might be."

"Well . . . why don't we appeal to some of them? Tap in to their media channels and see what happens. They certainly seemed interested enough in our appearance."

Emily looked to Kuei Jen, who shrugged.

"It's worth a try."

"Then let's do it," Emily said. "Anything's better than sitting on our hands up here!"

Kuei Jen grinned, then sat forward, meaning to make the connections, when the whole of the sky in front of the craft seemed to light up.

A great hoop of burning light was rotating in the darkness between them and the planet below.

"*Kuan Yin*!"

At the centre of that fiery circle was a darkness that blotted out that part of the planet that was directly behind it. A darkness filled with stars. For a brief moment that was all, and then, with a swiftness that made them gasp, two craft came through, looking all the world like massive flying thrones.

"What in the gods names are those?" Han Ch'in asked. But Kuei Jen simply laughed.

"It's the bloody US cavalry, that's what it is!"

* * *

DeVore stopped before the glass doors that marked the division between the company's outer offices and the inner sanctum and raised his gun, pointing it at the woman who stood behind them.

"Emily? . . . I thought it was you."

Emily Ascher narrowed her eyes, staring at the man who was holding the gun on her and gave the barest shake of her head.

"Who *are* you?"

DeVore grinned. "Me? I'm your worst nightmare. That is, if you don't open those fucking doors right now."

"And if I do?"

"Then you get to live."

Her smile had steel in it. "Why don't you just shoot your way through?"

"And have the police crawling all over the place? No. Besides, it's not you I want, it's your boss."

"Mister Josephs?"

DeVore gave a nod of acknowledgment. "He of the many-coloured coats." He raised his chin a little. "Why does he do that?"

"The coats?"

"Yes."

"A biblical allusion." No way was she going to tell the fucker the *real* reason.

"Biblical?"

There was a flicker of uncertainty in her eyes, as if she wasn't sure quite how mad he was, then she nodded. "Joseph. You know. Son of Jacob. Sold into slavery by his brothers. Interpreter of dreams. He rose to become chief minister in ancient Egypt. You *must* know the tale."

"Must I?" DeVore's gun did not waver. "Open up. Or die."

Emily hesitated a moment longer, then, shrugging, gave the command.

"Open up."

As the computer responded to her command, DeVore stepped through the slowly opening doors, tucking his gun back into his belt.

"Thank you," he said politely. "Now sit down, and don't touch anything unless I tell you to. I'd hate to have to hurt you."

"Would you?"

That iron in her – that refusal to bow to him in any way – aroused him. It was what had always appealed to him about her. So few of these mortals were like her. It made him want to have her there and then. But there was something else to do first. Something far more important.

"Call him. Tell him I want to meet him. *Here*."

"He won't come."

"Ask him. Let *him* make that decision."

She raised her eyebrows, then turned and tapped out a code on the keyboard in front of her. There was a moment's hesitation, then she turned back, frowning.

"I can't seem to raise him. It's as if . . ."

Then there was a rapid beeping. She seemed almost to sigh with relief.

"Mister Joseph?"

But DeVore pushed her out of the way. "Joseph? It's me. DeVore. We need to talk."

It was Kim. He knew it as soon as he saw that face. Kim transformed, but still Kim. That knowledge hardened his resolve.

Joseph shook his head. "We've nothing to say."

"Oh, come now . . . I think it could be one of the great conversations of all time, don't you? You could bring Master Tuan along and we could talk metaphysics."

Joseph laughed coldly. "From what I can make out, the only subject that interests you is ballistics."

Noting Joseph's background for the first time, DeVore frowned. "Where are you?"

"None of your business," Joseph answered, then, smiling, he cut the connection.

"Get him back!" DeVore snarled, turning on Emily.

But she merely pointed to the board where the flashing light had now died.

"Looks like he's incommunicado."

He reached out and grabbed her about the neck, making her flinch. "You'll fucking get him here if it's the last thing you do!"

* * *

Li Yuan looked about him at the empty lobby, then stood. He had been told to sit exactly where he was or both the women would be killed, but he could no longer sit there and do nothing – though what he *would* do was a mystery even to himself.

The first DeVore had left him to be guarded by the other, but within moments of him going into the building, the other had given his warning and disappeared, saying he would be back very shortly.

That had been ten minutes back.

Li Yuan pushed through the doors, then stopped, facing a scene of carnage. The guard behind the reception desk had been pulled right over his desk, garrotted. Two more security men had been knifed and left for dead. A cleaner, taken by surprise as he came through the far door, had been throttled. And here, at the foot of the stairs that led up to the glass doors of the company's inner sanctum, lay another guard, a look of shock in his eyes, his hands locked about the knife that was embedded deep in his throat.

Unsteady now, he walked across to the desk. The guard wore a holster. Gritting his teeth, he reached in and removed the weapon, then turned. The gun felt strange, unwieldy, in his hand. A dead man's gun.

Unused to such violence, he found himself trembling as he climbed the central steps. The gun was loaded, but he did not know whether he could use it. He had never fired a gun in anger, nor did he know if he could now.

He would be justified in shooting the bastard, but whether he could actually do it was another matter. He felt sick to the pit of his stomach. Sick and afraid.

I should have stayed in the lobby, he thought, wondering what in the gods' names had made him follow DeVore. *Or better yet made a run for it.*

Coming out onto the level he paused. There was no sign of anyone beyond the open doors. And then he saw them, on the far side of the open-plan office, the woman crouched over a communicator while DeVore held a gun to the back of her head.

He felt his nerve give. His legs wanted to buckle.

No, he told himself, closing his eyes. *Face it. Conquer it.*

Li Yuan swallowed silently, then took another step, fearing that at any moment DeVore would turn and see him.

He could barely hold the gun now, he was shaking so much.

You have to do this, he told himself, reminding himself why he'd come, *or he'll just go on. He'll kill you if you don't. And the girl.*

The thought of DeVore harming the girl, more than any thought for himself, gave him strength. He *could* do this.

He took another step, and then another. He was inside the inner sanctum now, nothing between him and DeVore but thin air. A single shot would end it.

Li Yuan raised his left hand up to steady his right, to try to keep the damn thing still, yet even as he did, DeVore yelled and stepped back, aiming a mighty backhander at the woman that sent her sprawling.

"Can't you do a single fucking thing right!"

He kicked her aside, then began to operate the keyboard himself. "Come on, you bastard! *Come on*!"

He saw the woman begin to climb up, something in her hand, and at that moment something strange happened, for DeVore's arm seemed to grow into a spike that transfixed the woman clean through the chest.

Li Yuan blinked, unable to believe what he had seen. The woman had been lifted into the air and seemed to dance on the long, steel-like pole that now extended from DeVore's expanding body. Even as Li Yuan watched, wide-eyed, the man's clothes tore apart, a dark, rotund shape emerging from within.

He dropped the gun and took a backward step. And then his legs *did* give. Before his eyes DeVore was changing . . . becoming a great, leathery black bubble that swelled grotesquely to fill that whole side of the office, pressing up into the ceiling and bursting through, eight huge, steely limbs now extending from his twin abdomen.

Li Yuan pressed his face into the carpet, not wanting to see; *afraid* to see. And then some ancient instinct overtook him and, inch by inch, he began to crawl away from there, back to the stairs and out.

Away. Anywhere but away from the nightmare that was unfolding up ahead of him.

* * *

A security guard, watching idly at his desk, was the only one to see the huge thing burst through the mesh that covered the top of the building and climb out, its long, thin legs taking it quickly, gracefully to the edge of that massive construction.

The man leaned forward, brushing at the screen. "What the . . .?"

On the screen, the giant spider paused, then seemed to throw itself up into the air, swimming against gravity, ascending as if upon an invisible thread, its long legs spinning a web of force beneath it as it went.

For a moment the man simply gaped, stupefied. Then, instinct taking over, he brought his hand down hard upon the pad, sounding the alarm.

* * *

DeVore steered the craft down onto the roof of the storage warehouse, then killed the engine, smiling as he unstrapped himself.

He had all of the necessary documentation. Now he only had to present it and the machine would be his.

There had always been a part of him that had known, but not until his twin arrived and spelled it out for him had he understood. *This* was why he was as he was. This was why he felt the black wind blowing at his back. He felt the spider shape flex inside his puny human frame and grinned.

Downstairs, on storage level nine, was the no-space ship. He had only to go and retrieve it and he could be out of here. Safe. Ready to fight another day.

Things had gone wrong. Things had gone badly wrong, and no amount of tinkering could put that right. But next time . . .

He walked through, staring at the two women a moment, seeing the fear in their eyes. For a moment he thought of finishing them. but he was beyond such pettiness right now. Turning from them, he pressed his hand against the pad on the hull and the hatch hissed open.

It was evening now and the sun was slowly setting. He stepped out, looking about him briefly at the bleak cityscape, then stepped down onto the roof.

With any luck they'd kill his twin. Deal with him for him. And maybe that would satisfy them. Whatever, it would be good for him. Because he didn't like competition. Not even from himself.

He turned, taking one last look at the world, glowering at the sun, then walked across and pulled open the door, going down into the building.

* * *

The two craft fell silently from the upper air, slowing as the great cityscape unfolded before them. Tientsin was directly beneath them now, the sea to their right. Ahead, beyond the city, the mountains lifted into the blue.

As they levelled out at ten thousand feet, Joseph gestured to Karr in the other craft.

"Gregor . . . you go after the shuttle. We'll wait at the Temple."

Karr gave a wave of acknowledgment as his craft peeled away, like a great chair gliding on the air.

Joseph turned to look at Jelka, smiling awkwardly at her. He was still not used to the way she looked at him, nor was he sure that he could even imagine what she was thinking, let alone feeling, only that he reminded her of what she had lost.

"Why the Temple?" she asked.

"Because it is the centre of all things."

"And you think DeVore will go there?"

"He will be drawn to it, if only because we are there."

She narrowed her eyes, then looked away.

"Jelka?"

She looked back. "Yes?"

"I wish I'd known them."

"Yes . . ." She paused, a small motion in her face showing how she fought briefly to control what she felt, then she smiled. "If we come through, I'll tell you of them. Or what I know, anyway. I didn't know K. long."

He nodded, then looked back at the landscape below them. The Temple of Heaven was not far now. If one looked hard one could see it, just there beyond the southern city, in the great open space between the southern sprawl and the towers of the financial district.

The centre. Where it all began, if Master Tuan is right. And where it now must end.

"Ikuro?"

"Yes, Joseph?"

"Are you ready?"

Ikuro laughed. "Let him show me the whites of his eyes and I'll drill two holes in them!"

* * *

Wisps of black smoke, drifting out of nowhere, gusted in a wind that never ceased, blowing from the dark heart of nothingness.

The great spider crouched on the mound, overlooking the ancient Temple, gnawing at the bones of its latest victim as it waited.

The darkness between the stars called to it, making it ache to leap high, away from the pull of this tiny rock, away from the irritating heat of this paltry, insignificant star, out until it could drift, free of all forces, in the silent coldness where it had first begun.

Yet something kept it here. Some dark residual thing.

It looked up, frowning, its huge eyes focusing, and then it remembered.

The game. I have not finished the game.

They were standing between the pillars of the temple. Three of them. Jelka, the one who called himself Joseph, and one other, a Han by the look of him.

He laughed, the noise issuing from his huge, beaked mouth like the raucous cry of a crow. Yet his voice, when it came, was still DeVore's voice.

"The last stone," it said, casting the bones aside then stretching on its legs, so that it towered above both them and the Temple itself. "I have come to place the last stone on the board."

The Joseph one nodded, then stepped forward. He held something in his palm. Something small and round and white.

A stone . . .

"How quaint," it said, smiling ferociously.

It took a step towards them, then stopped, seeing the man's arm go back, to heft the stone into the air.

The explosion took off two of its legs. It staggered, keeping itself upright, then, furious, twisted its abdomen round to face them, ready to pierce the barrier and release the darkness that would annihilate them. Yet, even as it turned, it froze, as the air surrounding it shimmered and went solid.

Jelka looked to Joseph, but he was staring, as if he did not understand what had happened. And then the air before them parted.

Jelka cried out; a sound both of pain and happiness.

"Kim!"

Joseph felt a ripple of pure fear run through him. It was Kim, and K. too, just behind him. But they were dead. He could see from the paleness of their skin, from the marks upon their flesh, that they were dead.

"What have you done?" he asked.

The voice that answered him was an echo that sounded from their empty mouths as if they spoke with a single voice.

"Master Tuan has given us this hour, to set things right and unify the universes."

Jelka took a step towards them, but Joseph reached out and held her arm.

"No," he said quietly.

And now she too saw the small red mark upon Kim's forehead, and groaned. And Joseph felt the sorrow that lay behind that noise, as much as if he himself had uttered it, and finally understood what she had lost.

"What has happened to it?" he asked, pointing to the frozen creature.

Kim and K. turned as one, their eyes impassive, then looked back at Joseph. "I have placed it in a temporary space."

"Will it be destroyed?"

But Kim, if he heard the question, did not answer it directly.

"The snake," he said, even as his form shimmered and disappeared from sight, "the snake must swallow its tail."

* * *

"Li Yuan?"

Li Yuan stared back at Karr, fear in his eyes, and began to back away.

"No, wait! I won't harm you. I'm on your side!"

"You know me?"

"In another universe, yes."

Li Yuan turned, looking back over his shoulder at the building, as if expecting something horrible to emerge from it at any moment. Noting that look, Karr frowned.

"What is it?"

Li Yuan looked back at him, then shook his head. "You wouldn't believe me."

"Did he change?"

"Change?"

The look of startlement told Karr that he was right. DeVore must have changed into his original form.

"Were they *both* here?"

Li Yuan hesitated, then nodded.

"So where's the other one?"

"He left, to go and do something. That's when I went inside, after his twin. But he must have come back. When I came out here again it was gone."

"Your craft?"

"Yes." Li Yuan shook his head, distraught. "He's got her."

"Her?"

"Fei Yen and her mother."

Karr looked to Chen, exchanging a look. "You're married to Fei Yen?"

Li Yuan shook his head. "No, no, I . . ."

"Look," Chen said, interrupting, "can we trace your craft somehow?"

"Yes. There's a trace-code. In case it gets stolen. I have it here."

He searched a moment, then took a small card from his pocket and handed it to Karr. Karr studied it a moment, then asked. "How do we get this to work?"

"It'll work in the computer of any glide."

"Glide?"

"The hover cars. That's what they're called."

"Ah . . ." Karr looked about him, then, spotting one nearby, went over to it. He stared at it a moment, then took out his gun and shot the lock open. Turning back to Li Yuan, he grinned. "Okay. You come with me, Yuan. Chen, you and Hans follow on in the ship. We may need it if things get too hot."

Li Yuan, however, still seemed reluctant to go with him.

Karr looked at him, concerned. "Are you afraid, Yuan?"

Yuan hesitated, then nodded.

"That's good," Karr said. "That's perfectly healthy. But now you must step beyond your fear, Li Yuan. If you want to save the girl."

Yuan looked up sharply. "Okay," he said quietly. "But I warn you, I cannot use a gun."

Karr laughed. "Oh, do not worry, Master Li, if necessary I shall do the shooting for the both of us!"

* * *

Jelka was sitting at at the bottom of the great white stone ramp, staring straight ahead, tears in her golden eyes.

Kim, standing within the no-space, watched her a moment, then turned, looking to Tuan Ti Fo, who sat cross-legged before the *wei chi* board.

"Why did we interfere, Master Tuan? I thought it was your purpose *not* to interfere. Not directly, anyway."

The ancient looked up slowly. "That is so. It feels like cheating, and I am loathe to cheat."

"Then why now?"

"To bring it to a close. To end it." He gestured towards the board. "Look . . . the board is almost filled."

Kim walked across, then made the calculation in his head. It was a draw. Or almost so. There was one single unresolved stone – one single "ko". If one could find a way to use it, one would take the whole of the western group and win the game.

Or lose it.

His hand went up to touch the hole in his forehead. It troubled him to have had to appear to Jelka in this condition, but as Master Tuan had explained, it could not be helped. Much could be planned, but in the end it all came down to improvisation. Even the greatest Master of the game understood that much. If planning were all it was, then there would be no Master of Masters. All would, at a certain level, be equal. And that was not how this universe of theirs functioned. Not until it ended, anyway.

Kim looked past the old man at the frozen form of the creature he had known in life as DeVore.

"What do you feel, Master Tuan?"

Tuan followed his gaze. "About my twin? Mainly sadness. Sadness at the waste of such immense talents." He paused, then. "When he dies, I die. You understand that, Kim?"

Kim stared at him, surprised. "But I thought . . ."

"That there could be good without evil? Darkness without light? Daylight without shadows? No, Kim. There will be no Edens. No Peng Lai. But maybe you can live in less hilly climes, neh? Without so many peaks, so many troughs." The old man smiled. "My twin was a great exaggerator of effects. He had the talent of making a weak man bad, a bad man terrible and a terrible man truly evil. When he is gone, there will still be weak men, yes, and bad men, and even terrible men. But without him, so I believe, there will be no true evil."

"And if you're wrong?"

Tuan laughed at that. "Ever the sceptic, eh, Kim? Even in death. Ever the scientist."

Kim smiled faintly, then turned, looking back at the woman who, in life, had been his wife, his soul-mate. "I wish . . ."

"That you had not died? All men die, Kim. Yes, and you were right there, too, not to seek to make immortals of your fellow men. You could have done it, Kim. You *had* the talent. But you were also given something else. The ability to chose between good and evil courses. And that – and that alone – has brought us to this final point."

"So what now, Master Tuan?"

Tuan Ti Fo smiled, then pointed to the "ko". "It is time to play the final stone."

* * *

They had tracked the craft to an isolated tower on the east side of the financial district. A storage warehouse by the look of it. Setting down beside the craft, the four men climbed down. As Chen gathered their weapons from the racks beneath the chairs, Karr turned to Li Yuan and handed him his handgun.

"Stay here, Yuan. And if he comes, blast him. Don't think, just point at him, as if you're picking him out to identify him, and pull the trigger."

Li Yuan nodded. "I'll try."

"Good. Hopefully you won't have to."

"You're going in after him, then?"

Karr nodded, then turned to take the big JPK-4 from Chen. "This time I mean to get him. Not some tank-bred copy, but him. Or one of him, anyway."

Seeing that Li Yuan didn't understand a word, Karr smiled, then laid a hand on his shoulder.

"You'll be okay. Just stay under cover and watch that doorway. Leave the rest to us."

"But what if he changes? You know . . . into one of those things?"

Chen answered him. "Then we'll let him have it anyway. Both barrels!"

Li Yuan looked from one to another, thinking what an odd trio they were. Two sixty-year-old soldiers and a blind man! Then, understanding that they were serious, he straightened up and gave each of them a bow of respect.

"Good luck, *ch'un tzu*!"

Karr smiled, then turned to the others. "Come on. Let's finish it."

* * *

They went down, level after level, checking each out in turn.

At first they found nothing. The upper floors had been deserted. Then, six levels down, they heard something. An exchange of voices. An argument, and then a single shot.

They went down another flight and out, into a corridor. Nothing. It had to be down one more floor.

Quick, Karr mouthed, looking to Chen and Ebert. Yet even as he started forward, he felt his gun tumble out of his hand, almost as if it had been knocked from his grasp.

Chen turned to stare at him.

"Go on!" he whispered. "Go on! I'll catch up with you!"

Chen nodded and turned back, beginning to run, Ebert in close pursuit.

Karr picked up the gun and made to follow, then saw that the tiny red panel beside the cartridge was flashing.

Malfunction.

"*Shit!*"

He shook the thing, as if that would rectify the fault, but all that happened was that a second line started flashing under the first.

Loading Jam.

He stared at it, unable to believe what he was looking at. Only once – *once* in all his time as a soldier! – had he had a gun jam on him. And *never* a JPK-4.

Karr looked up. Their footsteps were getting distant. If he didn't go now . . .

He began to run. As he entered the stairwell, there was a gust of warm air and then a brilliant searing light.

He turned instinctively, closing his eyes, yet he knew even as he did what it was. A light grenade. And Chen and Ebert had run straight into it. They would be crawling about down there, blind and defenceless.

There was no time to worry about a broken gun.

Karr leapt the flight of stairs and hauled himself about the turn, seeing, even as he did, the small, neat figure that stepped out from the passage to the side and raised his gun.

DeVore . . .

He saw Ebert turn, blind as he was, and face their mortal enemy, almost as if he saw him. "You shall *not* prevail . . ."

There was no time to call a warning. Throwing himself forward, Karr leapt, even as the gun went off.

Half a second too late, he cannoned into DeVore's back, slamming him down onto the floor.

For a moment he lay there, groaning, hurt himself, his leg twisted in the fall. Then, forcing himself up, he reached out and closed his fingers about the barrel of the JPK-4.

He had done this once before. In another world. In another life. Now he must do it again.

DeVore lay just beneath Karr, his head turned to the side, a small trail of blood trickling from beneath the chin.

Karr closed both hands about the barrel and raised the gun. The malfunction message was still flashing, but it did not matter now. He swung it back, then brought it sharply down, the heavy wooden butt striking DeVore's skull with a wet yet solid crack.

For a moment Karr stared at the shattered mess that had been DeVore's head, then, with a shudder, he let the gun fall from his hands.

Was that it? Was it over now?

He looked across. Chen was sitting up, knuckling his eyes and groaning. Just across from him Ebert lay still, blood pooling dark beneath him.

"*Aiya* . . ."

He tried to get up, and almost fell back, the pain from his leg was so intense.

"Chen . . ." he groaned. "Kao Chen . . ."

Chen turned his head blindly. "Gregor? Is that you?"

"Yes . . . he's dead, Chen. I got him."

Chen laughed, such relief in his voice that Karr thought for a moment he was going to cry. "You're sure?" he said. "I mean . . . it's really him?"

"Yes . . . but . . ." He swallowed, then went on, steeling himself to voice his fears. "I think Hans is dead."

Chen's groan, the grimace of pain on his face, mirrored how Karr himself felt inside.

For a moment silence. Then, quietly. "But we got him, Chen. We finally got him."

* * *

Master Tuan had felt the disturbance in the air as the first of them had died. Now there only remained the one.

"When he is gone the breach will be healed, the universe made whole."

Kim, standing beside him, looked out at the scene before the ancient temple as they brought Ebert's body from the craft and laid it in the sunlight. He watched them gather about the bier and saw the sadness in their faces, and wondered, not for the first time, what was the purpose of it all.

"One must not think in terms of purpose," Tuan said, as if he read Kim's thoughts. "One must learn to live for the day."

"Would it were that easy," Kim said. "Or do you forget I am dead."

"In this world, yes. But in the world to come . . .?"

Kim looked to him, surprised. "What do you mean?"

"Wait and see, Kim Ward. Wait and see."

* * *

Jelka turned as the three men stepped from the air. This time she was ready for it. This time she steeled herself not to show the turmoil within her.

Even so, it was a shock to see that Kim was smiling.

"Prepare yourselves," he said, K. echoing the words alongside him. "It's time."

Behind him, Tuan Ti Fo turned and, stepping within the no-space, walked over to where his twin crouched, suspended in his natural shape. For a moment he seemed to hunch, as if in prayer, and then, from within his cloak, he withdrew a long, thin blade that seemed to flicker with a strange light. Stepping forward, he plunged the blade deep into the creature's abdomen, embracing it, merging with it even as they watched. There was a cry of intense, almost unbearable pain, and then the air about the two creatures shimmered. Buildings wavered and vanished. The two gate-craft flickered and were gone. In an instant all was changed, transformed.

A ripple, and then stillness.

A bird called, high and clear.

Jelka blinked. Where Kim had been, Joseph now stood. But not just Joseph, for in his eyes she saw both Kim and K, the three in one.

And flowers! Everywhere one looked, flowers!

Jelka laughed, astonished, then turned. All about her, her friends were looking down and staring at themselves, as if they had been born anew. As indeed they had!

Even Ebert, who had died, now stood among them, his blue eyes staring about him in amazement.

Karr laughed and held up his right arm. It flared a brilliant gold in the sunlight. "Look!" he called, amazed. "I've got a metal arm!"

Jelka stared, reminded terribly of her father at that moment, then turned back, facing Joseph. Facing the stranger who was now her man, throughout all time and all realities.

"It's done," he said, coming over and embracing her. "This is all there is now. The rest . . ."

He touched his head gingerly, then laughed.

"What is it?" she asked, concerned.

His eyes met hers, sparkling eyes that seemed more alive than she had ever seen them. "It's just that I've forgotten."

"Forgotten? But you never forget."

"The equations. I know there were some, but . . ."

She put a finger to his lips. "Let them go, my love. Let them go . . ." Then, savouring the moment, finding it strange that she did not have to bend to kiss him, she put her mouth to his and closed her eyes.

EPILOGUE – WINTER 2250

LAST QUARTERS

Yellow dust and clear water beneath the Fairy Mountains
Change places once in a thousand years which pass like galloping horses.
When you peer at far-off China, nine puffs of smoke:
And the single pool of the ocean has drained into a cup.

– Li Ho, *A Dream of Heaven*, 9th Century AD

LAST QUARTERS

Eridani burned golden in the morning sky. Orbiting it, ninety-five million miles distant, its fourth planet was a green, earth-like planet; a lush, unspoiled world.

A world without predators.

It had taken them three years to catch up with the *New Hope* and another two to finish their voyage between the stars. For three years now they had lived on the surface of this new world, acclimatising, living in airtight domes as they slowly assimilated the bacteria of this agreeable yet wholly alien environment. Bacteria which, had they not taken care, would have killed them as effectively as any gun or bomb.

There was sickness and death, but things quickly improved. Thanks to Joseph and his skills, the next generation would be natives of this world and live outside beneath its pleasant, yellow sun.

In the last day of Autumn, Joseph stood in a patch of sunlight, one hand resting lightly against the curve of the dome's glass, looking out into the world they had inherited. Behind him, in the garden he had made for Jelka, his four-year old grandchild, Sampsa's daughter, ran along the maze of paths, singing to herself as she went.

For a moment longer he looked out at that overwhelming tide of green, then he turned, watching the child, a broad smile on his face. Earlier he had shown her how the spider wove its web and had told her the story of the Edderiminaru and how the universe had once been split. And she, crouched beside the glistening web, had listened awe-struck to the tale.

"Is that true, grandfather?" she had asked when he had finished. "Is it *really* true?"

He laughed and straightened up. "So they tell me," he had answered with a wink.

Now, looking across the interior of the dome, he shared something of her disbelief.

"Mileja!" he called, beckoning her to him. "Come! Let's go see Nanny Jelka!"

He scooped her up in one arm and carried her through into the next dome, smiling with pleasure when he saw that they had guests.

"Kao Chen! Gregor! Why didn't you tell me you were here?"

Gregor came across and embraced him. A moment later, Chen did the same.

"We didn't want to disturb you," Chen said, grinning up at him, then bending down to smile at Mileja, who hid shyly behind her grandfather's leg.

"And how are all your grandchildren?" Joseph asked, looking to each of them.

"Thriving," Karr answered, then shook his head. "I thought four daughters was a handful. But a dozen grandsons!"

Chen nodded sagely. "It must be the air, Gregor."

"You think so?" Then, seeing that Chen was ribbing him, he grinned.

Chen himself had eight grandsons and five granddaughters, and claimed that they would shortly have to build a bigger family dome if this went on.

"We called by," Karr said, "because Hannah asked us to."

"Ah . . ." Joseph nodded. "And how is our Hannah? It seems an age since I last saw her."

"Oh, she's been working hard, Joseph. But it seems she's finished."

"Finished?"

"Oh, not completely," Chen interceded, "but enough to give a reading."

Joseph's face lit. "A reading? When?"

"Tomorrow evening. In Fermi."

Joseph looked up through the dome at the crescent of Ganymede in the sky overhead. "Then we must be there!"

Karr smiled. "She hoped you would be."

"And Ben? Will Ben be going, too?"

Karr looked to Chen, then smiled. "He too has a new piece of work to display."

"A painting?"

Chen shook his head. "He says it's something called a symphony. He calls it Song For Eridani."

Joseph nodded thoughtfully. "I didn't know . . ."

"No," Chen said. "Nor any of us. But he has had some of the youngsters practising it these past few months, though not a word got out about it. That alone is a wonder; these youngsters talk so much!"

At that moment Jelka came out from the main house, flanked by Marie and Wang Ti. The three wives looked at their menfolk a moment, then huddled together, giggling.

"More mischief, I'll warrant," Karr said confidingly.

"Do you men want supper?" Jelka asked.

Joseph looked to the others, who shrugged. "All right," he said, "but I'll pour us drinks first. We'll be in the moon room."

He looked down to young Mileja. "You want to go and help grandma, peach?"

She nodded and ran across.

Karr watched her, then looked back at Joseph. "To think she won't remember Chung Kuo."

"And maybe that's a good thing," Joseph answered, putting out a hand and ushering them through into the small dome – the moon room – at the side of the house. "It was not a great place to live in latter years. Whereas this . . ."

Chen nodded. "Maybe so. But we should remember Master Tuan's warning. This is no paradise. Not unless we make it so. We must learn from what went before."

"I agree," Joseph said, following the two through the gate and into the dimly-lit interior, "which is why Hannah's work is so important. Why, I was telling young Mileja earlier about what happened, and even as I was telling her, I wondered how much was real and how much I had made up, it seemed so dreamlike."

Karr nodded sombrely, then gestured to their surroundings. "All those years ago, when I was a blood beneath the Net, how could I have imagined this? To stand in the light of another star, with Chung Kuo gone, abandoned to a host of plants!"

"Intelligent plants," Chen corrected him with a grin. "But come now, first things first. Joseph, have you any of that brandy left?"

* * *

The landing pad at Fermi, which normally held few more than three or four craft, was packed tonight. More than forty ships had come, from Ganymede and the planet below, which, in accordance with Joseph's wish, they had named Last Quarters.

As they gathered in the rooms about the hall where the performances would be given, there was a great sense of reunion. It was a busy life, transforming a world, and though they often saw each other on screens to discuss business, these kinds of occasion had been rare of late, so there was an air of genuine celebration.

The Osu were there, and Ikuro Ishida and his family – more than sixty in all, now that his nephews had begun to produce their own offspring. Emily, now wheelchair bound, sat amongst them, talking animatedly, while behind her, Daniel, Hannah's husband, stood silently, his intelligent eyes taking in everything.

At Joseph and Jelka's arrival, there was a great hubbub of noise. Friends flocked to greet them and shake their hands or slap their backs, for in Joseph both K. and Kim lived on, looking out through the larger man's eyes, instilling in his spirit the generosity and sympathy those other men had exhibited throughout their lives.

"Is Ben here?" Joseph asked, wanting to see his old friend.

"He is rehearsing," Chen answered him, appearing at Joseph's elbow, "Can't you hear?"

There was the sound, behind the murmur of the crowd, of strings and woodwind, starting and stopping. A faint, unfamiliar noise.

Hearing it, Joseph shivered. It had been so long since he had seen an orchestra play. So long since he had sat and listened to another read aloud. Such civilised pleasures. Nor were they to be considered simply luxuries: these were things that made life more than mere existence.

He looked about him, proud to be part of this great experiment, this great family of beings who now carried the story of humankind forward into a new age. It was not often he thought thus, for there was always too much to do day by day on a practical level, but right now it struck him powerfully.

They had been given another chance. A chance to get it right; to learn from past mistakes and create the social structures and institutions that would enhance their lives, not subjugate them.

If only Master Tuan were here to see this, he thought wistfully. But he knew that that had been the price. Old Tuan had sacrificed himself – and his race – to give them this undeserved opportunity.

He had once said as much to Jelka and she had frowned deeply, asking him just *why* he felt it "undeserved", and he had referred her to man's long history. But she, in reply, had spoken of their friends, of the good people who now shared this life with him; had argued that all they had ever needed was new air for them to become new creatures.

And so they worked towards that; to make themselves new creatures, adapting themselves to suit this Eden of a planet and not the other way about, for that had always been the mistake mankind had made – to think that all of creation could be adapted for their use.

People before machines. That had become their creed.

Machines were necessary, of course, yet they were also secondary. They took care to use machines purely as tools, utilising them in the same way that one might use a knife or a hoe, not letting the machines use them. For that path, too, mankind had erroneously followed in the past; mechanising and desensitising themselves until they were little better than automatons. As for education, their children were taught to care for the world and the creatures that surrounded them and to appreciate the balance of all things. They were taught the ancient Tao, and, through Li Yuan, learned that their natures were a balance of both the animal and the intellectual and that it was their duty to nurture both, yes and treasure them.

Joseph smiled at the thought of what they had accomplished, smiled at the thought that there was so much more to come. As for himself, he had never been so happy. He had only to look at Jelka, and at Sampsa and young Mileja, to know that he was blessed. And he knew he was not alone in feeling that. There was no discontent here, no, not even in the face of hardship and suffering – and there had been much of that these past years. And why? Because no one here was alone. Because every single person knew that they would rely on someone to help them in their need.

It would not always be so, of course. Individual men and women were often weak. Yet if one built a world in which such weakness could be channelled and not allowed to fester into resentment and bitterness, then maybe this time they would have a chance – a real chance – to build a society free of levels and hierarchies, free of greed and corruption and all the shades of human pettiness that feed upon the soul.

It was not much to ask, and at the same time, a great deal. More than anyone had ever asked before.

"Joseph?"

He turned at Jelka's gentle nudge. "Sorry. I was miles away . . ."

She gestured towards the doors at the far end of the room, which were now open. People were moving slowly into the hall beyond.

"I think it's time."

Joseph smiled and took her arm. "Then let's go."

* * *

Sitting right at the front of the hall, directly below the orchestra, Kao Chen reached into his pocket and took out his handkerchief to wipe his eyes. Beside him Wang Ti had tears streaming down her face, and, looking along the line, Chen saw that not a single one of them was unaffected.

He looked again, past Ben's back, at the sea of arms that rose and fell in time with the haunting melody, and felt something in him break, so that he let out a loud sob. But no one seemed to care.

It was beautiful. The most beautiful thing he had ever heard. And it felt . . . well, as if Ben had somehow caught the very thread, the delicate woven pattern of his feelings, and transcribed that into music somehow, so that as the music played, he too was played, like an instrument. All of his hopes and fears, all of the baggage that he had brought here from Chung Kuo – all of that was expressed in the music.

And more. Much more. For he felt at that moment that Ben's music somehow touched him and connected him with everything about him. He felt . . . *absorbed* by it.

And as it finished, he found himself on his feet, part of the great roar that went up from every throat in the hall.

It was thus a highly emotional crowd who sat once more to watch Hannah take her place behind the lectern and hear her read from the first volume of *The Book of Earth*. And when she closed the book and fell silent, there was a hush that, in its way, was as moving and as deep a response as that which had greeted Ben's symphony, before, once again, the crowd rose to its feet and applauded her, a tumultuous wave of applause that went on and on until Hannah had to raise a hand and, laughing, plead for them to stop.

And so the evening ended, with friends embracing and waving goodbye to each other on the pad.

And three days later, when the elected Council met, it was decided that they would finally change the calendar and would call that evening, when Hannah read from the History and Ben first performed the Song For Eridani, the first day of the first year of Eridani.

AUTHOR'S NOTE

The transcription of standard Mandarin into European alphabetical form was first achieved in the seventeenth century by the Italian Matteo Ricci, who founded and ran the first Jesuit Mission in China from 1583 until his death in 1610. Since then several dozen attempts have been made to reduce the original Chinese sounds, represented by some tens of thousands of separate pictograms, into readily understandable phonetics for Western use. For a long time, however, three systems dominated – those used by the three major Western powers vying for influence in the corrupt and crumbling Chinese Empire of the nineteenth century: Great Britain, France, and Germany. These systems were the Wade-Giles (Great Britain and America – sometimes known as the Wade system), the Ecole Française de L'Extrême Orient (France) and the Lessing (Germany).

Since 1958, however, the Chinese themselves have sought to create one single phonetic form, based on the German system, which they termed the *hanyu pinyin fang'an* (Scheme for a Chinese Phonetic Alphabet), known more commonly as *pinyin*, and in all foreign language books published in China since January 1st, 1979 *pinyin* has been used, as well as now being taught in schools along with the standard Chinese characters. For this work, however, I have chosen to use the older and, to my mind, far more elegant transcription system, the Wade-Giles (in modified form). For those now used to the harder forms of *pinyin*, the following (courtesy of Edgar Snow's *The Other Side of the River*, Gollancz, 1961) may serve as a rough guide to pronunciation.

Chi is pronounced as "Gee", but *Ch'i* sounds like "Chee". *Ch'in* is exactly our "chin".
Chu is roughly like "Jew", as in *Chu Teh* (Jew Duhr), but *Ch'u* equals "chew".
Tsung is "dzung"; *ts'ung* with the "ts" as in "Patsy".
Tai is our word sound "die"; *T'ai* – "tie".
Pai is "buy" and *P'ai* is "pie".
Kung is like "Gung" (a Din); *K'ung* with the "k" as in "kind".
J is the equivalent of r but slur it as rrrun.
H before an s, as in *hsi*, is the equivalent of an aspirate but is often dropped, as in Sian for Hsian.

Vowels in Chinese are generally short or medium, not long and flat. Thus *Tang* sounds like "dong", never like our "tang". *T'ang* is "tong".

a as in father
e – run
eh – hen
i – see
ih – her
o – look
ou – go
u – soon

The effect of using the Wade-Giles system is, I hope, to render the softer, more poetic side of the original Mandarin, ill-served, I feel, by modern *pinyin.*

This usage, incidentally, accords with many of the major reference sources available in the West: the (planned) sixteen volumes of Denis Twitchett and Michael Loewe's *The Cambridge History of China*; Joseph Needham's mammoth multi-volumed *Science and Civilisation in China*; John Fairbank and Edwin Reischauer's *China, Tradition and Transformation*; Charles Hucker's *China's Imperial Past*; Jacques Gernet's *A History of Chinese Civilisation*; C. P. Fitzgerald's *China: A Short Cultural History*; Laurence Sickman and Alexander Soper's *The Art and Architecture of China*; William Hinton's classic social studies, *Fanshen and Shenfan*; and Derk Bodde's *Essays on Chinese Civilisation.*

The quotation from D. H. Lawrence's "Bavarian Gentians" is from *Selected Poems*, edited by Keith Sagar and published by Penguin Books, 1972, and is used with their kind permission.

The three quotations from Dante's Divine Comedy are from the excellent Penguin Books edition, translated by Dorothy Sayers (1949) and are used with their kind permission.

The quotation from Nietzsche's *Thus Spoke Zarathustra* is from the R. J. Hollingdale translation, published by Penguin Books, 1961, and is used with their kind permission. Likewise, the quotation from *Beyond Good and Evil*, published in 1973, which is also translated by Hollingdale.

The quotation from T'ai Kung's *The Six Secret Teachings* is from *The Seven Military Classics Of Ancient China*, translated by Ralph D. Sawyer and published by Westview Press, Boulder, 1993, and is used with their kind permission.

The quotation from Li Ho's "A Dream of Heaven" is taken from my very favourite collection of Chinese poetry, *Poems of the Late T'ang*, selected and translated by A. C. Graham and published by Penguin Books, 1965.

As the number of Mandarin words used in this final volume is not excessive, I have – this once – decided not to have a separate glossary, but anyone finding any difficulty with any of these terms might refer back to previous volumes, wherein these are dealt with exhaustively.

The game of *wei chi* mentioned throughout *Chung Kuo* is, incidentally, more commonly known by its Japanese name of *Go*, and is not merely the world's oldest game but its most elegant.

Finally, might I thank the ever-growing number of fans and friends who have encouraged and supported me thoughout the researching and writing of *Chung Kuo*. Two million words on, it is at last complete, the circle closed. So here it is – my tale of "the days before the world began".

David Wingrove, December 1996